Vaka Rangi

Volume I: Star Trek, Star Trek: The Animated Series, Raumpatrouille – Die phantastischen Abenteuer des Raumschiffes Orion

Josh Marsfelder

September 19, 2016

For my family and closest friends, who shared my journeys through Star Trek.

Contents

Contents

Contents

Contents

Contents

Contents

Contents

Acknowledgments

Special thanks to my friend, colleague and sort-of-boss Phil Sandifer, who provided the primary inspiration for this project by blatantly telling me to do it, and who has helped get this volume into a publishable state. Thanks also to Lance Parkin, who was nice enough to release his Star Trek book a month before mine , thus providing me invaluable historical and biographical information to make editing and revising this book a lot easier. Thanks to Andrew Hickey, for giving me the document processor I wrote this entire project on that has allowed me to manage every aspect of the publication in-house myself, and for also being kind enough to be my free tech support when I needed it. Which is a lot, because I am an idiot. I'd also like to take the time to give special recognition to my friend Kevin A. Carson and our mutual acquaintance Roderick T. Long, who were the first two people to take an interest in this project and believed in it enough to be its first cheerleaders. They were also a tremendous influence on clarifying this book's politics and narrative, and I wouldn't have the audience I have now if it weren't for them.

And thanks to the community of writers and commenters on both the original Vaka Rangi blog and Eruditorum Press for helping to cultivate such a welcoming and creative climate for projects like this to grow and thrive.

Introduction

0.1. What is "Vaka Rangi"?

The name *Vaka Rangi* comes from the common language of the Polynesian islands and the area making up the larger geopolitical region known as "Oceania". Although each region in the Polynesian triangle has its own variations on it, it is commonly believed all of these dialects can be traced back to a common language, which would account for the striking similarities to be found in all of them.

The Ancient Polynesians and their ancestors were simply put the greatest mariners the world has ever seen and the term *vaka* (meaning canoe, or canoe hull, in several languages) displays the centrality of the concept to their culture. Spurred on primarily by limited resources and the need to manage sustainable populations, the Ancient Polynesians used voyaging canoes to settle remote and previously unpopulated islands throughout the Pacific Ocean, and many scholars claim they further managed to reach any shore that touched the Pacific and Southern Oceans. The Ancient Polynesians were explorers, navigators, poets, mystics and philosophers, not conquerors or empire-builders: For them, each vaka was not merely a watercraft or a means to an end, but a microcosm of Polynesian society and an island unto itself symbolizing the interconnectedness of the village, the sea, the Earth and the Heavens.

Rangi is thought to be derived from the hypothesized proto-Polynesian word " *laŋi*", meaning the sky, or the heavens. The variant "rangi" is found in several Polynesian languages, most notably that of the Maori and Rapa Nui. In Polynesian Reconstruction, a vaka is often given a secondary name to distinguish itself and its people, thus a "Vaka Rangi" would be "A Canoe for the Stars".

Today, traditional Polynesian navigation is undergoing a renaissance, bolstered by, among other things, the rediscovery of ancient oral history and techniques on the outlying island of Taumako and a renewed sense of cultural pride in places such as Hawai'i and Samoa. Fleets of vaka once again roam the Pacific, this time to share their message of solidarity with the natural world. It is this spiritual exploration of the universe's interconnectedness that has been a guiding inspiration for my life and provided the impetus for this project, which I hope will help translate these concepts for those who, like me, grew up during Western post-industrialism. I felt the best way to explore this was to call upon another major interest of mine: Experimental comparative media studies.

0.2. What This Project Is

Vaka Rangi is a work of comparative mythology. Vaka Rangi is an account of a spiritual journey. Vaka Rangi is a personal memoir. Vaka Rangi is an unauthorized post-structuralist critical history of Star Trek. Vaka Rangi is many things at once.

Fundamentally, this project an attempt at a critical history of utopian futurism in televised science fiction, particularly science fiction involving voyaging starships, from a specific perspective and using the Star Trek franchise as a "guiding text". I chose Star Trek for a number of reasons, most notably for its substantial cultural capital in Western regions and my personal connection to it. I coined the term "Soda Pop Art" in another blog project of mine to refer to a product of commercialized pop culture that attains enough significance and ubiquity to become a kind of shared Western mythology. It is my belief Western cultures have a unique shared oral history all to themselves, but one that is paradoxically and often problematically bound up with concepts like corporatism, copyright and profit. It's this contradictory dualism that I invented the term "Soda Pop Art" to convey, and Star Trek is the Soda Pop Art that is the archetypal utopian voyaging starship story.

This book series, and the blog upon which it's based, is also the account of my personal history with Star Trek and similar science fiction stories and the many ways I have interacted with it throughout my life, but also the many ways in which I've found myself in opposition to it. My primary aim here is twofold: Firstly, it is to offer a unique critical re-evaluation and reinterpretation of Star Trek, and more generally the concept of the voyaging starship series, around themes of sustainability, communalisim, spiritualism, idealism and the troubled relationship between exploration and imperialism in Western literature. I'm particularly interested in how these themes have been dealt with and interpreted by various creative teams at various points in history and the repercussions caused by them being examined via Soda Pop Art. At the same time, Vaka Rangi is also an examination of my own positionality and how that has shaped my reading of Star Trek and works like it over time.

0.3. What This Project Is Not

Despite using Star Trek as a kind of "guiding text", concerning itself with the series' ups and downs and frequently looking at various licensed spin-off works, Vaka Rangi is fundamentally *not* an attempt to craft a definitive, authorial history of the franchise. As it's structured around very specific themes and is at once built around my personal experiences with Star Trek and larger than it, readers already versed in Star Trek fandom might be surprised to find the sorts of things I've chosen to include in this critical history, and indeed some of the things I've chosen to omit. Perhaps strangely, given my extensive history with it, I only consider myself a casual Star Trek fan and this project reflects that. Those looking for episode guides, cast lists, discussions of canon, in-universe minutiae and behind-the-scenes information won't find it here and would be better served by something like the tremendous Star Trek wiki Memory Alpha or the great dead tree work of Paula Block and

Terry J. Erdmann (both of which are sources I highly recommend). I'm interested in exploring one specific strain of thought within the franchise, not in writing a comprehensive documentation of every single thing ever to go out under the Star Trek banner.

0.4. About This Volume

This is the first volume in a series and roughly spans the decade 1964-1974, the period during which Star Trek initially aired and subsequently became a cult movement. Within you will find analyses of every episode of *Star Trek*, *Star Trek: The Animated Series* and *Raumpatrouille – Die phantastischen Abenteuer des Raumschiffes Orion*. These aren't reviews in a traditional sense, but critical examinations of each episode with a eye towards how it interpreted the philosophy and ethics of Star Trek and how it interacts with the themes of Vaka Rangi. In addition, there are essays on contemporary related works and events to help provide historical context (dubbed "Sensor Scans" to distinguish themselves from the main entries), essays on assorted and miscellaneous aspects of fandom, franchise history and lore that wouldn't fit in the main entries ("Ship's Log, Supplemental") as well as chapters on the non-televised Star Trek tie-in works ("Myriad Universes") and video games ("Flight Simulators").

All of these essays are edited and revised versions of blog entries that appeared on the web version of Vaka Rangi, but there are additional chapters unique to this incarnation, mostly my thoughts on more esoteric aspects of Star Trek fandom history, but also ones that revisit certain ideas and concepts to either give them a second examination or to look at them from a different angle (or just to examine them further in a format that allows me to go into more detail).

In closing, I'd like to thank the many readers of the blog version of this project and everyone who's been supportive of it from the beginning. I hope it's as enjoyable for you to read as it was for me to write.

Part I.

1964-1967

1. Sensor Scan: Foundation

It is a maxim among some writers that all science fiction, no matter how varied and diverse it may be, can ultimately trace its lineage back to the so-called "Golden Age" of science fiction literature. Despite this being far too reductive a statement for my personal taste, there is some genuine erudition to be gained by examining it as the era's signature works are indeed fundamental inspirations for a particular approach to writing science fiction that defines early Star Trek (or at least they way Star Trek is perceived) and the intellectual tradition it's a part of.

Some background: The Golden Age of Science Fiction, as it has come to be known, is a period (roughly spanning the years between 1938 and 1953) during which marked interest in futurism and the potential of scientific and technological breakthroughs influenced authors to craft stories set far into the future featuring, and often explicitly about, technology written to feel plausibly extrapolated from that of the time of writing. This approach, and the intellectual tradition that comes out of it, is often referred to as "Hard" sci-fi in an attempt to stress its focus on scientific realism and to distinguish it from (and in more than one instance tacitly imply a superiority over) other "pulp" or "fantasy" inspired science fiction. Indeed a great many sci-fi writers claim that this is the defining feature of science fiction: That it portrays a future that can reasonably be expected to derive from real-life science and technology. This is a very pervasive attitude and one that will crop up on more than one occasion on our journey, so it's best we take a look at it here.

In many ways then *Foundation* is the text best representative of the Golden Age style, at least as it pertains to Star Trek: A sprawling attempt at a space epic spanning multiple generations that chronicles the decline, collapse and rebirth of humanity's galactic empire written by Isaac Asimov, already famous as one of the leading lights of the period for his Robot short stories. The Foundation and Star Trek series are not directly connected, but there are enough superficial similarities between the two and Asimov's influence on later science fiction is ubiquitous enough it merits a discussion.

Perhaps the biggest point of comparison between Foundation and Star Trek is that both franchises started out as one self-contained work that very quickly snowballed into a series of sequels, prequels, retcons and continuity-laden spin-off works handled by first, second and third generation fans. In the case of Foundation, the, er, "foundational" work in question is a series of short stories Asimov wrote for *Astounding Magazine* in the 1940s and then edited and re-published as a trilogy of standalone novels in the early 1950s under the titles *Foundation*, *Foundation and Empire* and *Second Foundation*. While Asimov himself went on to write four additional novels in the series during the 1980s and 1990s (two sequels and two prequels) for the sake of brevity, scope and chronological relevance I'm only going to be looking at the original trilogy here.

The central premise of the trilogy, as explained in the original *Foundation,* is that a mathematician by the name of Hari Seldon has invented a new science called "psychohistory" that blends math, sociology and psychology in such a way so as to allow him to accurately predict human behaviour on an individual and societal level millennia out into the future. This methodology has led Seldon to predict that the Galactic Empire, at the time over 12,000 years old and seemingly stable and prosperous, is actually on the verge of a systemic collapse that will plunge the galaxy into 30,000 years of darkness and regression. Seldon believes the only alternative to this is to set up a Foundation to collect the entirety of human knowledge into an *Encyclopedia Galactica*-This will, according to Seldon, help to prevent the loss of the accumulated progress humanity has made and shorten the duration of the Dark Age by 20,000 years. This angers the Empire's decadent aristocracy who sentence him for treason, but, unwilling to turn him into a martyr by executing him, Seldon is exiled to the planet Terminus with those loyal to him to form the Encyclopedia Foundation.

The rest of the first novel follows the development of the Foundation on Terminus over the next century as it faces threats from four rival kingdoms who have split from the Empire, in particular the life of the heroic Terminus City mayor Salvor Hardin, a charismatic maverick leader concerned that his hands are being tied by the Foundation's managing Board of Trustees who don't take the dangerous political situation seriously. At crucial moments of crisis, pre-recorded holographic messages left by Seldon appear to Hardin and the other protagonists assuring them that everything is going according to plan and, miraculously, the most recent disaster was predicted and accounted for in the Master Plan and that Seldon knows that the Foundation (revealed as a front for Terminus to become the seat of the Second Galactic Empire) will make the correct choices to ensure its survival. Eventually the Foundation spreads beyond Terminus and becomes a collective built on a network of traders who exchange advanced technology for alliances with neighbouring kingdoms, and by the end of the novel it becomes a powerful Empire in its own right that even boasts a state religion called Scientism, based on worship of and complete devotion to Foundation technology and scientific progress.

There is a genuine appeal to the narrative of history outlined in Foundation from a variety of different perspectives. For one, the idea of blending math, psychology, sociology and science into one Grand Unified theory of human nature is tantalizing to a certain type of science fiction minded thinker, seeing as it neatly and concisely brings together several disparate fields of study together so they can pool their brainpower, as it were. And yet Asimov seems to offer a check here in the character of Salvor Hardin, the maverick, rugged individualist thinker who shakes the bureaucracy out of its complacency and is willing to shoulder the risks to bring about real change (and later in the series with the character of The Mule, supposedly a random agent of chaos Hardin could not predict). This tension between a desire for reassurances that the technocrats and oligarchs have got everything planned out and under control on the one hand, and the escapist fantasy of living vicariously through a libertarian renegade who proves them all wrong, underscores much of Foundation, Asimov's work, and United States culture more broadly.

But at the end of the first novel the most egregious and worrying flaws in *Foundation*, and indeed all of Asimov's brand of Golden Age science fiction, become apparent. From a contemporary perspective (or at least mine) it's an almost appealingly crass and paternalistic work that utterly revels in technological determinism and the virtues of a specific Western, and really truthfully United States, brand of reactionary thinking. Hardin is the classic American individualist, heroically fighting the corruption and inefficiency of bureaucracy and the ever-present threat of The Other and the protagonists of the last two sections are both rugged frontier traders. And while he, like all good Rugged American Individualists, opposes what he perceives as the hopeless ineptitude of social organisation and bureaucracy (because it would be an unmanly sign of weakness to rely on help from others in any capacity), the fact Hardin's plan does accommodate him shows how he is in some form connected to them. Thus, the United States dream of Manifest Destiny Libertarianism and the technocracy are not so disparate as some would like to think: A defining paradox of the Golden Age Hard SF model.

Then there is, of course, the Church of Science and Scientism, an idea so stupefyingly and self-evidently wrong its name has been rightly re-appropriated by modern thinkers looking to criticise any manner of western scientific arrogance and authoritarianism. Asimov pays us lip service near the end of the first novel by having Seldon say something about how The Church is a means to an end and will eventually outlive its usefulness, but this is nowhere near satisfying and is actually worse: Asimov is essentially admitting here that something like Scientism has to exist in some form at some point to keep those of lesser intellects in line. It's for their own good to join the Foundation, see, and The Church is there to make it easier for them to accept its natural authority. Somehow this doesn't make me feel any better.

But for me the most distasteful aspect of *Foundation* is Seldon himself: The whole concept of psychohistory is a horrifyingly dehumanizing one, positing as it does that all of human culture and behaviour can be reduced down to equations, models and proofs. Asimov seems to recognise at least some of the negative implications of this and tries to work around them in *Foundation and Empire* with the character of The Mule, an aspiring despot disguised as a circus clown who, thanks to a freak genetic mutation, has the ability to control thoughts and emotions. Seldon didn't account for The Mule in his plan, forcing the Foundation of his time to improvise lest the entire nascent empire fall before him. But this doesn't work either, because, far from showing how flawed something as distant and overreaching like psychohistory is by neglecting the inherent, well, humanity of humans, The Mule is instead the personification of the outlier: A data point that doesn't doesn't match the existing theory but can be safely disregarded. And despite his enormous power and the threat he poses, The Mule can ultimately be rejected because the Foundation finds a way to counteract his abilities and safely lock him away on an insignificant planet. It's not entirely clear how this result is any different than it would have been if Seldon *had* predicted The Mule: Seldon has always seemed to bank on people improvising in times of crisis before (there's that tension again), so why is this time so unique? The theory just needs to be tweaked a little, it doesn't need to be tossed out entirely.

17

Another reason The Mule fails to in any way engage with the series' fundamentally flawed premise is that, once again, he's one outstanding individual with special gifts. He's not the face of some populist revolution to out the new boss, who really, *really* is just the same as the old boss, he's one outstanding man who is dangerous because he doesn't conform. Furthermore, he's dangerous because he can forcibly turn people against the Foundation: In other words, the biggest threat the Foundation will ever face is not that people might collectively decide they don't want to live under a Scientistic theocracy, but because one man might poison their thoughts and blind them to the Foundation's true righteousness. This is Red Scare tactics 101.

Asimov also halfheartedly tries to problematize the series with the concept of the Second Foundation, a mythical counterpart to the Foundation "at the other end of the galaxy" that provides the impetus for the plot of the second half of the second book and the entirety of the third. The idea, as I understand it (though I never found it especially clear in any of the books), is that this Foundation is designed to nurture the growth of telepathy and other "mental sciences" (interestingly not anthropology, philosophy or the humanities, though) to counteract the original Foundation's emphasis on physical sciences. Asimov attempts to justify this by retroactively making Seldon a social scientist, a retcon that doesn't exactly fly considering he is perfectly clearly a mathematician in the original book. The Second Foundation is also dedicated towards refining psychohistory to predict even the most unlikely of occurrences, such as The Mule. In other words it's basically just a a metaphor for the notion of scientific replication and the refining of the experimental method is subsequent trials, so it's done nothing to redeem the series or address its glaring issues.

It's interesting to speculate how Asimov, born to a Russian Jewish family in 1919 (i.e. Old enough to witness the Holocaust, the Atomic Bomb and the Cold War) could have penned something so clearly in favour of technocratic imperialism, because that's precisely what *Foundation* is: The goal of the Encyclopedia (itself a top-down concept based on archiving and reiterating a historical master narrative rather than the generative sharing of knowledge and ideas) is expressly to serve as the first step in building a new, better Empire, just one built on science and technology instead of brute military force, hence the dual meaning in the name. There's a compelling argument that science fiction as an entire intellectual tradtiion is fundamentally reactionary, and it certainly does feel like the seeds of that partnership are sewn here.

Ultimately though *Foundation* is a work of Golden Age science fiction, and these sorts of prejudices are things inexorably bound up in the entire genre: The fact of the matter is the "Golden Age" happened concurrently with the end of World War II and the beginnings of the Cold War. There was a prevailing sense that scientists would build the future for us and if society could be reoriented around science and rationality we'd all be a happier, healthier and more prosperous people (just witness any of the "House of Tomorrow"-style pop futurism that also characterized the era). We can't really fault *Foundation* for being so firmly of its time and genre. It's a defining work in Golden Age science fiction, so of course it's going to act like Golden Age science fiction. However, historicizing these themes doesn't make them any more palatable to a modern reader, nor does it excuse their reiteration in future works far removed from this specific context. Unfortunately though, for a very long time afterwards this is going to be the defining model for how "proper" science fiction "should" work and the consequences of this are going to be far from ideal.

2. *Star Trek* Is...: The Cage

"The Cage" occupies a strange space within Star Trek lore: As a pilot created by Gene Roddenberry and those closest to him to demonstrate to NBC what they envisioned *Star Trek* to be all about, but one that never actually aired on television, it is at once the progenitor of the entire franchise and also the only part of it impossible to reconcile with the rest of the series' canon. "The Cage" is a very strange specimen indeed then: It's not quite *Star Trek*, at least not the *Star Trek* that fans would come to recognise and love years later, but, by virtue of it being a pilot designed to embody the show's core values and themes made before executive compromises changed the tone of the series, it is in many ways the purest Star Trek of all.

The one individual irreducibly linked to "The Cage", what it is and what it does, far more so than in anything else bearing the Star Trek name, is of course Gene Roddenberry. Over the years mainline fandom has all but deified Roddenberry, and people tend to hold him up as a figurehead for everything they want Star Trek to embody and strive for (particularly so in the years immediately following his death in 1991 and the cancellation of *Enterprise* in 2005). This is also not helped by muddy and at times completely contradictory historical accounts of key moments in Star Trek history and Roddenberry's own biographical details perpetuated by what can frankly best be described as rampant hearsay and cult of personality. As a result, it can be hard to actually get a solid critical handle on who Roddenberry was, what the extent of his contribution to Star Trek was and what exactly he wanted it to be.

"The Cage" then really is the best place to talk about Roddenberry and his influence on Star Trek, because no matter what Star Trek is going to become over the next several decades it will never again be as closely tied to Roddenberry's personal conception of it as it is here. There are several reasons for this, the most immediately obvious one being its aforementioned status as a pilot, but also the fact that even as of the early Original Series Gene Roddenberry had a lot of help and input in shaping the direction of Star Trek that he didn't have as much of here. The fact he was willing to entertain and genuinely listen to everyone's ideas for, and criticisms of, his project is telling, but so is the fact their influence has been all but effaced from the history of the franchise to the point Roddenberry is, implicitly at least, held up as the source of every single good idea the series ever had, which is simply and flatly not true. But there is a reason Majel Barrett called "The Cage" her favourite episode and "Pure Star Trek", and anyone who is seriously interested in the history of the franchise and Gene Roddenberry's "vision", whatever that may turn out to be, really ought to study it.

Firstly, some things we *do* know about Gene Roddenberry: He was not a futurist. Nor was he a scientist, engineer or prophet. He was, however, a retired Air Force Pilot and LAPD officer who had done some freelance TV work and used his position to move into the medium full-time with *The Lieutenant* before pitching the concept of *Star Trek* to Desilu Studios in 1964. What's the most immediately interesting about these early documents is that far from describing some long-winded space opera myth arc that sings the praises of Hard Science, Roddenberry is actually pitching *Star Trek* as as a combination of *Flash Gordon* and *Buck Rogers,* the absolute pulpiest of the pulp science fiction works. In private, Roddenberry is alleged to have claimed to be basing the show on *Gulliver's Travels*, and that he intended each episode to be structured around both an action adventure story and a morality play. Roddenberry did want his show to be believable though, so he brought in physicist Harvey P. Lynn to serve as his technical advisor, which also invites comparisons to *Foundation*-style Golden Age science fiction.

The other person indelibly linked with "The Cage" and prototypical Star Trek is Majel Barrett herself. There isn't as much fandom lore or as many legends surrounding Barrett as there are Roddenberry, although there are several. Firstly though the most important thing to note about Barrett is that she and Gene Roddenberry had a very complex and nuanced relationship that isn't really adequately summarized by simply saying "they were married". At the risk of turning Vaka Rangi into the celebrity gossip papers, this really is something we need to square away right now because it actually holds ramifications for formative decisions made about what *Star Trek* is and where it goes. Here's the thing: The primary reason Number One exists (and by association the character Spock will become) and the reason she's played by Majel Barrett is straightforwardly because of her relationship with Roddenberry. This isn't to suggest something so crass as the only reason Barrett was cast was because she was sleeping with Roddenberry, but rather to posit that Number One was probably written with Barrett in mind.

I get the feeling Barrett was not only Roddenberry's romantic partner, but a kind of inspirational muse to him as well. Number One is the first character described in the original pitch to Desilu and supposedly the first one created for all of Star Trek. She's explicitly written to be the most coolly competent character on the show and as the *Enterprise*'s "most experienced officer" she is implicitly connected to the soul of the ship at a very deep level thanks to western naval tradition. What's also interesting, however, is that her femininity is consistently a matter for debate both in the treatment and what made it to air. Captain Pike is visibly uncomfortable with having women on the bridge other than Number One (as seen by his dismissive attitude towards Yeoman Colt) and in the script a big deal is made out of the fact Number One is icy and logical even going so far as to state "From time to time we'll wonder just how much female exists under that icy facade." In other words, Number One is special because she's a woman who has acclimated to rational, male culture. She "doesn't count" as a woman.

As much praise as *Star Trek* gets for its progressive attitudes towards gender roles, this isn't especially satisfying from a feminist perspective and it's clear Roddenberry wasn't entirely sure how far to go in this direction, but the fact Number One exists at all is a decisive move that will leave a big impression on people as a part of the series' developing lore and mythology. Barrett was important enough to Roddenberry that he restructured his entire television pulp science fiction throwback project to accommodate her, a project that he was even now becoming increasingly possessive of and attempting to turn into his masterpiece (often, sadly, at the expense of everyone else who contributed to its success). Number One just being on the bridge was a bold statement that cemented *Star Trek*'s commitment to egalitarianism, if only in the pop consciousness and not on actual television. And that's solely due to Majel Barrett.

I'm spending so much time picking over biographical details about Gene Roddenberry, Majel Barrett and Number One because, well, they're really the most interesting things about "The Cage", doubly so in terms of what we know the future holds. As an actual episode of television "The Cage" is surprisingly underwhelming, especially as the first, most definitive incarnation of Star Trek. That said, the ethics and general structure of this episode do prove revealing in sussing out Roddeberry's basic intent in regards to Star Trek, so I'm going to dedicate the remainder of this chapter to that instead of summarising or analysing the plot, which every Trekker knows by heart at this point. It's essentially Plato's allegory of the cave retold in pulp sci-fi terms (with one big twist I'll get to), which is noteworthy insofar as it was uncommon, though not unheard of, to get that kind of distilled philosophical fiction on television in 1964, and there's also the really galling laddish humour of the Talosians' "Adam and Eve" scheme and the crew's reaction to it, but that's about the extent of what's actually edifying to talk about in regards to the plot.

What's more revealing is what "The Cage" shows us about what Gene Roddenberry initially pictured the world of *Star Trek* to be like. You'll notice this episode bears no mention of a utopian United Federation of Planets with a mission to Seek Out New Life And New Civilizations and Boldy Go Where No Man Has Gone Before. I'll save you the trouble of checking the original pitch and treatment because you won't find it there either. In fact at this point there's little to no discussion about what, actually, the *Enterprise* does at all. All we get is a line about how Pike is recovering from a battle at Rigel VII and that the ship and its crew are en route to deliver some medical supplies when they picked up the manufactured distress signal. Frankly, at this point there's no reason to suspect the *Enterprise* is anything other than a battlecruiser working for some futuristic military organisation or law-keeping task force.

Because that's exactly what it is.

It doesn't take a Talosian to put the pieces together here. The *Enterprise* isn't going out to make friendly contact with undiscovered cultures or mapping uncharted star clusters, it's running errands back and forth between Earth colonies and occasionally sparring with enemy hostiles in disputed territories. It's a glorified patrol boat. Now I also hasten to add I don't think Roddenberry meant this as a bit of neo-imperial US chest thumping: There's nothing in anything he said or that was written about him to lend any sort of credence to that accusation. It is true Star Trek, especially in its 60s incarnations, does develop a very problematic and tangled connection to imperialism, but that develops generatively as the show morphs and evolves over its first three years. Equally though *Star Trek* wasn't meant as some kind of idealized, post-scarcity fairy tale either. Those connotations are indeed all part of the series and do come later, but they don't spring from Roddenberry, at least not at first.

What I think is a more fitting explanation for *Star Trek* is that Roddenberry was a fighter pilot-There's a unique kind of camaraderie amongst and bond between US Air Force pilots, and it would be silly to suggest this didn't have a big influence on Roddenberry's writing. No, what probably happened was that Roddenberry had this idea he really liked to do *Gulliver's Travels* in space and decided to set it on a ship that was part of the Space Air Force because that's the environment he knew. Also, he thought it'd be a good idea to let women into the Space Air Force too because he liked women and was inspired by his loverXmuse and figured that would be a sensible thing to do. It's pro-military only in the sense that doing a story about the Space Air Force is going to tautologically be that way by default simply by virtue of being about such a concept in the first place, not because Roddenberry had some imperialistic agenda to push. However, we didn't excuse this with Asimov and we shouldn't excuse it here either: Combine this with the elements *Star Trek* inherits from both pulp sci-fi (its action adventure trappings and general setting) and Golden Age sci-fi (the attempt to make the science somewhat realistic) and you wind up with a concept that is fundamentally, if not entirely intentionally, militaristic.

More support for this reading can be found in the *Enterprise's* oft-celebrated multiracial crew. Like the addition of Number One and Yeoman Colt, this is frequently cited as proof that *Star Trek* was far and away the most progressive thing on TV in 1964. If you believe Gene Roddenberry, this was his idea and a favourite story of his to tell in later years on the convention circuit was how he had to fight Desilu and NBC tooth and claw to keep the *Enterprise* diverse because they wanted a "suitable", i.e. white, cast. This popular claim is contested, however, by Bob Justman and Herb Solow (two television executives and production associates who helped Roddenberry create Star Trek and who became producers themselves once the series proper began) in their 1997 book *Inside Star Trek*, which became an invaluable source for debunking myths and lore the franchise had accumulated up to that point and *especially* during the notoriously insular and self-congratulatory mid-90s fandom. According to Solow and Justman, NBC in fact requested that Roddenberry make the *Enterprise* crew multi-ethnic as they encouraged diversity in all of their TV shows. Once again like the addition of female characters, I believe this was at least partially Roddenberry's idea: There is a line in one of the very early treatment scripts where the captain, then named Robert April, chews out a crewmember for firing on friendly life-forms because they "looked hostile" and dismisses him in disgrace. However, it's very clear the idea is not *entirely* Roddenberry's, nor is it even unique to *Star Trek*, and to cast Roddenberry as some prodigy ahead of his time fighting valiantly for Diversity against the oppressive forces of Old and Evil is not only an oversimplification, it's a fallacy.

But the most damning evidence that *Star Trek* isn't a grand utopian ideal at this point is the episode's resolution: It's rather fascinating, and more than a little alarming for someone used to later Star Trek, to see how Pike escapes the Talosian zoo: He overwhelms the zookeepers with "primitive, hateful" thoughts which their telepathic powers cannot pierce, thus shattering their ability to maintain their illusions. It's hard to imagine even

Captain Kirk resorting to this kind of action and seems completely at odds with *Star Trek*'s supposed utopianism: There's no rousing speech about how humanity has moved beyond such things or how more evolved species have no need of such thoughts-It really is merely the bit of plot detail Pike needs to escape his predicament and it's not treated as anything more substantial than that. Furthermore, while we do get a token rumination on the nature of humanity at the end, it's couched more in terms of our lovable stubbornness, strong will and our unwillingness to be fenced in, not on how evolved we've become or our potential for greatness.

And that's really the takeaway here: "The Cage" isn't some super-cerebral musing on a idealized future with no war, poverty or bigotry: It's a square-jawed, manly pulp adventure story for the mid-1960s. It's maybe more intellectually-minded and has more of a diverse cast then other shows of its time, but it's by no means the most intelligent or interesting thing on the air right now either (we'll touch on one of those later on). I don't think it's bad enough to warrant NBC rejecting it on its own merits, though the pacing is tedious and the plot is thinner than it'd like you to think it is, but it's equally easy to see why the *Star Trek* team went back to the drawing board. When next we see them, the show will have changed significantly. Not all of the changes will be for the better, but one thing that's clear is that for Star Trek to work it's going to *have* to change. It's not Vaka Rangi yet, but if I'm honest it won't be completely Vaka Rangi for decades. And even then it'll still be debatable, frankly. More pressingly, the show as it exists now isn't the strange phenomenon that will last for over 45 years, but it *is* Star Trek and it's Star Trek the way Gene Roddenberry first wanted it. Star Trek is, and always has been, to turn a phrase, caged.

3. Sensor Scan: Lost in Space

If we're going to try to piece together the climate *Star Trek* was entering in the mid-1960s and the way it might have first been received, it would be beneficial to spend some time talking about its closest contemporary TV cousin. *Star Trek* was but one of many science fiction shows on the air during this period, but the one it's most frequently compared with is *Lost in Space*. There are a number of very good reasons for this: One, the two shows ran nearly concurrently, with their premiers and finales less than a year apart and two, both were voyaging starship shows loosely based around going to a new place every week and stumbling into adventure. Also, from a mid-1960s US perspective, *Lost in Space* would have been seen as "the other big space show" as while there were quite a few shows built in the adventure sci-fi model a great deal of them were German or British productions and would remain unknown to US audiences for decades.

The flipside of this is that for a long time Star Trek fans had a history of speaking derisively about *Lost in Space,* typically holding it up as the chief representative of an older, sillier, and campier method of doing TV sci-fi that *Star Trek*'s emphasis on Hard Science thankfully swept away. And superficially at least the two shows do in fact seem strikingly different: While the *Enterprise* crew is often, and rather erroneously in my opinion, referred to as a family, the crew of the *Jupiter 2* literally is one: Expedition commander Dr. John Robinson bundled his wife and children up into a flying saucer and departed an overpopulated Earth in an attempt to colonize a planet in the Alpha Centauri system. This leads into the next point of contrast: While the *Enterprise*'s mission is supposedly to Seek Out New Life And New Civilizations (though recall we haven't actually heard those words spoken yet), the Robinsons want basically the exact opposite: To find a habitable planet, settle down and start life anew.

Yes, *Lost in Space* is fairly transparently "The Space Family Robinson".

Indeed, *Lost in Space* is not even the first work to do "*The Swiss Family Robinson* But In Space": That would be the Gold Key comic series *actually called* *The Space Family Robinson*. The ramifications of this are interesting though; having just sort of panned "The Cage" for not being Vaka Rangi and for serving as proof positive Star Trek isn't quite what it's remembered as or thought of as being about, it's tempting to say *Lost in Space* is much closer to that concept and call it a show ahead of its time. Here we have a family setting out on a voyage purely for migratory and population concerns looking to find a new home for themselves. This would, on the surface at least, seem like a straightforward translation of Polynesian navigation philosophy to the Space Age. So why am I covering *Star Trek* and not *Lost in Space* in this book?

Well, to be perfectly blunt *Lost in Space* isn't Vaka Rangi either. Not even close. Sure,

Star Trek isn't, at least not yet, but the thing is Star Trek does eventually more or less kinda-sorta get there, and the story of how it does is equally paradoxical, multi-layered and fascinating. Despite its surface level pretensions, *Lost in Space* never does. The reason why turns out to be rather simple: It's flagrantly, almost painfully, of its time. It's straightforwardly a bit of Cold War Space Age futurism where humans move into space as is their natural right. The fact Earth is overpopulated gets glossed over both in the pilot and in the first episode: There's no real concern expressed about the devastating effect unchecked Westernist-style population growth had on our planet or fear it will happen again; it's just the setup for the Robinsons to get into space and do cool space things.

The myth of planetary overpopulation is an old and dangerous one. There's actually an episode of *Star Trek* that does deal with this so I'll return to the topic then, but suffice to say this is a myth that gets trotted out with alarming frequency by people espousing suspiciously reactionary and xenophobic rhetoric. There is next to no actual scientific evidence to support the idea Earth's human population is out of control, and in fact statistics from the United Nations show that population growth is actually *slowing* every year and will level off by 2300. Mostly this is a hoary old chestnut that gets hauled out to derail discourse and distract people from the actual problem, which is division of resources and widely destructive capitalist and agricultural practices that combine to form a collective inability of much of Western society to actually live within its means. Earth may be an island, but what *Lost in Space* implies here is a corruption of that ideal: Instead of migrating from island to island as a product of mindfulness, we exploit one planet for all its worth before moving on, Borg-like, to the next. Capitalism and Manifest Destiny at its most unreconstructed.

Just as damning is the fact the expedition is framed in explicit nationalistic terms: Powerful countries are all jockeying to be the first to populate space, and the United States wants to be the first with the *Jupiter 2* mission. Dr. Smith, the cowardly villain comic relief character played by Jonathan Harris, is introduced in both the pilot and the first episode as a foreign enemy agent trying to sabotage the endeavour who inadvertently stowed aboard and the predominant story arc of the first season involves his various attempts prevent the US from achieving dominance in space. As beloved a pop culture icon as Harris made Smith, however, he's still written as overtly a villainous character: We're meant to both cheer and laugh at his bumbling attempts to submarine our rugged, competent US leads and go "oh look, the evil foreign man is so silly and afraid he even cowers behind adorable and plucky little Will Robinson". *Lost in Space* is no Space Age tale of navigators and explorers, it's blatantly and unarguably a pro-colonialist fairy tale for the Cold War-era US neo-imperialist set. Despite the clunky flirtations with militarism in "The Cage" and elsewhere in the original *Star Trek*, even Gene Roddenberry never managed something quite at this level of jingoistic empire building.

The most interesting thing from my perspective about *Lost in Space* and its interactions with *Star Trek* and Star Trek fandom actually comes about as a consequence of ratings and timeslot competition. In its latter two years, *Lost in Space* ran opposite the Adam West and Burt Ward *Batman* TV show and, like most things that ran opposite *Batman*, was hurriedly re-tooled into a campy monster-of-the-week adventure series and in particular played up Dr. Smith's flamboyance. This displeased many fans of the show, who had up until that point praised it for the more Hard Sci-Fi approach that defined its first season. This was fascinating for me to read, because in Star Trek fandom, at least the Star Trek fandom I grew up in, *Lost in Space* was *always* derided for being cheap and silly and the sort of thing we needed *Star Trek* to come along and deep-six when really it would seem the two shows are actually closer than some might want to admit. See, the thing about *Star Trek* is that it's frequently praised for being innovative in the wrong areas. What's special about *Star Trek* is not its utopian idealism, of which there is actually vanishingly little of as originally conceived, and nor is it being beholden to either Hard Science or Hard Sci-Fi. No, what makes *Star Trek* unique is its ability to blend elements from Pulp Sci-Fi, Golden Age Sci-Fi and philosophical fiction and, once it comes back next year, a gloriously camp aesthetic.

It's this wholehearted embrace of camp that's one of the things that will allow Star Trek to last for 50 years and put it into the position to transcend its origins, but I'll hold off on discussing that in too much detail until we meet the person most directly responsible for bringing camp to Trek (and you get no points for guessing who that is). Yes *Star Trek* technically failed and burned out after three years, and honestly as far as I'm concerned it burned out after one episode. But what's important here is that it was brought back-Not in quite the same form, it must be said, because there is still the sense that every Star Trek after "The Cage" is a reinterpretation of the original concept. Star Trek as we know it really isn't one cohesive thing, despite what the most outspoken Star Trek fans would have you believe, it's actually a diffuse group of loosely connected concepts and ideas that people have tried to nail down into a single constructed fantasy world with varying degrees of success. But *Star Trek* gets a second pilot, a TV series, an animated series, a film series and a subsequent reimagining on TV. Something about that idea stuck with people enough to keep digging it up decade after decade, year after year. But why does *Star Trek* get so lucky? *Lost in Space* only got three seasons too and Jonathan Harris loved to camp it up, and all that show got for its troubles was an embarrassingly abortive 90s action sci-fi film reboot starring Matt LeBlanc and Gary Oldman.

I think the answer lies once again in the fact *Lost in Space* was simply too much of the mid-1960s, and the hegemonic mid-1960s to boot. Despite the problematic connotations I've observed already, and some more that will crop up as the series proper begins, *Star Trek* is simply nowhere near as blatantly colonialist and neo-imperialist as *Lost in Space* is, or, if I'm honest, the majority of science fiction from this period. Somehow, some way, Star Trek was able to transcend this and survive its troubled birth with approximate success. *Lost in Space* couldn't do that, and it was never going to be able to: It can never be Vaka Rangi because firstly true navigators were never imperialists and secondly the Ancient Polynesians were not homesteaders of the sea motivated purely by population statistics, either. They were sailors, poets, philosophers, astronomers, musicians and spiritualists. This is the soul of a traveller. *Lost in Space* doesn't understand this. Star Trek does. Granted, Star Trek doesn't get it either and probably never will, but there's something about that franchise

27

that seems to subconsciously hint at at yearn for something a bit more profound.

Even though I admit the show in the 1960s is far from my favourite take on the concept and it's tough to tease out even throughout its best years I feel there's something to this, otherwise I wouldn't be making it the centrepiece of Vaka Rangi. Also, given the position it has in pop culture it would seem, at first glance at least, that I'm not the only one who feels this way: Star Trek is still held up to this day as the *Ur* example of science fiction as not just utopian futurism, but also the embodiment of pure idealism and hope themselves. Even people otherwise aware of the New Frontier Liberalist, neo-imperialist and heteronormative undertones much of the franchise has, and I'm not denying they're there, still feverishly cling to Star Trek as a beacon of light in a dark and confusing world. So why does Star Trek work? Why does Star Trek endure? The answer to that is complex and many faceted, and really the best way to find out is to take a careful look at it with renewed curiosity and a fresh perspective. So let's begin again, then.

4. Intel

Theatre Overview: General Intel

The mid-to-late 22nd Century was a time of great unrest, upheaval and transition. In the few hundred years following their earliest space flights, Humanity had reached a stage where long-term colonisation and exploration of deep space at last seemed feasible. As this time period bears witness to Humanity's first attempts to transform themselves into an interstellar civilisation, this makes the 22nd Century a vital strategic location in our campaign, yet further field research is required before any offensive action can be undertaken.

The importance of this mission to our overall goal, is, of course, self-evident and need not be stressed. It is imperative to gain as much intelligence on this time period as possible for it is in the best interests of the Cabal that the development of Human space travel occur on *our* terms: The consequences for our sovereignty and that of the galaxy at large would be disastrous should Humanity reach a stage where it could pose a formidable threat. Therefore, you must learn all you can about this crucial moment so we can take the necessary action as soon as possible.

Previous field operatives have provided us with enough material to paint a crude picture of early Human space colonisation, and temporal researchers have been able to pin down two key dates worthy of further study. We regret we cannot provide you with information as to which of these dates might be more historically significant, so both are presented as possible drop points and it is advised you explore them both and avoid as much timeline cross-contamination as possible. Please note that due to the extremely sensitive nature of this mission we must keep our interference at a minimum: While the Cabal will provide you with as much support as we can offer, you will be largely on your own. The dates are as follows:

July 19, 1965 (turn to Chapter 5)

September 6, 1966 (turn to Chapter 8)

5. "That power would set me up above the Gods!": Where No Man Has Gone Before

The world of Star Trek has changed since last we visited. There's a new crew aboard the USS *Enterprise*, Spock's gotten a promotion and seems to have undergone a serious personality shift. I guess all those years working alongside Number One have rubbed off on him. Most significantly, however, we have an entirely different and far more ambitious mission statement, as told to us by new captain James Kirk:

> "*Enterprise* log, Captain James Kirk commanding. We are leaving that vast cloud of stars and planets which we call our galaxy. Behind us, Earth, Mars, Venus, even our Sun, are specks of dust. The question: What is out there in the black void beyond? Until now our mission has been that of space law regulation, contact with Earth colonies and investigation of alien life. But now, a new task: A probe out into where no man has gone before."

It seems more than a little shocking to see the *Enterprise*, previously serving on border patrol, now being repurposed as a deep space explorer about to depart the galaxy entirely. It's a testament to the confidence, or perhaps hubris, of the Earth Command to send a patrol boat out on this kind of mission.

As fun as it might be for me to continue like this and try and get "Where No Man Has Gone Before" to fit with what we know about Star Trek from "The Cage", it's ultimately a pointless exercise. This may be the first episode of the series proper, but it's also the second pilot, which means it's also the first franchise reboot. The Star Trek that comes out of "Where No Man Has Gone Before" is a different animal than the one "The Cage" hinted towards, and it's the first step made in augmenting, tweaking, reconceptualizing, and, ultimately, moving beyond what *Star Trek* represents. Gene Roddenberry's original vision of what he wanted the show to be is still here: In many ways this episode is far closer to the first pilot than would be to my tastes and the simple truth remains that these parts of Star Trek never go away. But even so "Where No Man Has Gone Before" is still making more than a few interesting overtures, and that alone means it definitely works better than "The Cage" and it's easy to see why the show was picked up with this episode and not that one.

The most obvious change is, of course, the casting of William Shatner as James Kirk. Shatner is, in many ways, the one person aside from Roddenberry himself about whom the most fandom lore, rumour and hearsay is spoken. Annoyingly, he is also one of the most important creative figures on Star Trek's early years and is responsible for crafting a large part of the franchise's legacy, so it would be sort of useful if we could talk at length about him. While I'm going to try and avoid backstage politics here as much as possible, sussing out the exact nature of Shatner's contribution is kind of important as it really is a big one. From my perspective, the key thing to note about Shatner at the moment is that he is overtly a theatre actor. While he'd done a number of TV spots before, most notably a memorable turn as the neurotic airline passenger on the "Nightmare at 20,000 Feet" episode of *The Twilight Zone*, Shatner was trained as a classical Shakespearean actor who got his start as the understudy to Christopher Plummer. This background overtly influences everything Shatner does as Kirk.

What this also does is put him in direct contrast with his predecessor Jeffrey Hunter: Hunter was a very clearly a US motion picture actor in the Golden Age Hollywood vein-He studied alongside Charlton Heston and his most notable other roles were John Wayne's sidekick in *The Searchers* and Jesus in *King of Kings*, the overwrought blockbuster adaptation of the New Testament. The stark difference between the two actors is obvious from the moment Shatner speaks his first narration in "Where No Man Has Gone Before":

> "Captain's log, Stardate 1312.4. The impossible has happened. From directly ahead, we're picking up a recorded distress signal, the call letters of a vessel which has been missing for over two centuries. Did another Earth ship probe out of the galaxy as we intend to do? What happened to it out there? Is this some warning they've left behind?"

Shatner delivers the lines with caricatured pensiveness and apprehension: This is not Kirk reciting into some Space Dictaphone that's going to be part of an official report, it's Shatner performing for the benefit of the audience to convey the concern and preoccupation Kirk must be feeling with the unusual and daunting situation he's dealing with. Where Hunter had a tendency to play Pike with rugged Hollywood masculinity and deliver his lines in a flat, gruff monotone, Shatner is trying to express Kirk's emotions with exaggerated performativty: "Larger than Life" is a painful cliche and isn't an entirely accurate description of what Shatner is doing here, but he does seem to be playing Kirk as larger than the confines of the setting and medium, and this is going to prove endlessly rewarding to follow.

Upon reflection this really does make perfect sense as a way forward for *Star Trek*: Shatner has said in interviews that when he watched "The Cage" to prep for the role of Kirk, the first thing that struck him about it was that everyone in the production seemed to be taking it so terribly seriously, and to the show's detriment. And if there's one thing that is clear from both what we see onscreen and what people have said about him for better or worse, the one thing you really can't accuse William Shatner of is taking things too seriously. The rest of the cast introduced here, at least the ones who get speaking roles, put on a perfectly serviceable show: Leonard Nimoy is frighteningly good at playing an emotionless logician, of course, and in their first appearances James Doohan and George Takei are certainly the standouts of the supporting cast, and it's easy to see why they get promoted to regulars. Gary Lockwood and Sally Kellerman give quite striking performances and handle the gravitas of their plot admirably. But it really is Shatner who is the most memorable thing here, conveying Kirk's brooding mood swings with charming bombast and dramatic flair. And he needs to, because as a story "Where No Man Has Gone Before" still doesn't quite hold together.

It's very tempting to take Gary Mitchell's transformation into a god some very interesting ways: As he grows more powerful, Mitchell goes on and on about insignificant he finds the people of Earth and his former colleagues. He flips through the ship's records like a 1980s channel surfer flipping through TV channels with a remote control and I couldn't help but grin when he and Kirk discuss Spinoza in sickbay (Spinoza? In *Star Trek*? Is this actually for real?). The kicker, or what should have been the kicker, is when Mitchell senses Spock is monitoring him on the bridge computer and looks knowingly at the security camera. The camera, our camera, than cuts to the bridge, where Mitchell is looking out of the viewscreen at Kirk and Spock and, by association, at us through the TV itself. It's a brilliant bit of editing that's decades ahead of its time and really encourages reading this as the moment where Mitchell transcends the medium of television to become an equal to the audience and the creators: Of course he's dangerous to the *Enterprise*: He literally has control over the entire fictional *Star Trek* universe, and naturally he has to fight Kirk, as Shatner has turned him into the only other character bigger than the setting. It's also just marvelous how Mitchell's powers are born of enhanced ESP: It's a total up-yours to the idea *Star Trek* is purely Hard Sci-Fi and worthwhile only because of scientific accuracy or deterministic technological futurism and it's in the very first episode.

But than *Star Trek* strikes back and kills the whole thing dead in its tracks. Mitchell starts to babel on about how he has the makings of a god and how he and Dehner are the progenitors of some new race of superhumans. We get a riveting character moment where Kirk and Spock get into an argument over marooning Mitchell on Delta Vega, but we're absolutely meant to side with Spock, who completely trumps Kirk in the ethics debate. Spock stands for detached, calculating logic untainted by human emotions. His solution is self-evidently the "correct" choice because it puts the safety of the crew, the ship and the mission above things like friendship, loyalty and human dignity. Spock sways Kirk by explaining how Mitchell is no longer the person he knew from the academy, but a frightening and dangerous Other who can't be reasoned with and must be disposed of. It's a complete glorification of militaristic detachment and a definitive statement that it's preferable to human emotions, which are fickle and obfuscating things. It's utterly awful.

Shatner-as-Kirk does get one truly great speech at the end where he pleads with the recently ascended Dehner that Mitchell is dangerous because he has the powers of a god, but the frailties and vulnerabilities of a human. They way Shatner plays it is genius: One gets the sense that Kirk knows humanity is capable of great things, but is also a flawed and troubled people and that's what will keep Mitchell from using his powers for good (it also touches on what will become an old standby of Gene Roddenberry's: The notion that humanity is a "child species" constantly trying to "grow out of its infancy"). It almost seems Kirk is arguing that to attain that level of enlightened power one needs to learn compassion alongside years of discipline and knowledge: Indeed he almost says this word for word, but the script also gives him the line "absolute power corrupting absolutely", which makes the intended moral of the episode pretty blatant and really hamstrings the scene's potential impact. Now it seems like the "frailties and vulnerabilities" Kirk was talking about are the emotions Spock was cautioning him against earlier and the whole thing leaves a really unpleasant taste.

It's the theme of human emotions, and the merits and demerits associated with them, that really drags this episode down. And tellingly, this is another hallmark of Roddenberry's, who frequently daydreamed about being able to make "rational, logical" decisions free of "corrupting emotions" and seemed to see that ability as almost a kind of enlightenment. This dovetails nicely into the character of Elizabeth Dehner, who is deeply worrying from a feminist perspective. Sally Kellerman does her best with the material she's given and she almost makes Dehner a tragic character we want to sympathize with, but the script is so loaded with such an awful, awful laddish attitude it's nowhere near enough. Dehner immediately sides with Mitchell after his transformation, even before she begins to mutate herself, and it's clear she's romantically attracted to him to boot, won over by his manly charm and charisma (which means, by the way, that she's flagrantly violating just about every medical oath and code she presumably took upon becoming a psychologist). She even has an emotional meltdown in the conference room where she gets "hysterical" and begs the table of (all male, stoic and reserved) department heads to understand that Mitchell is really a sweet, kind and wonderful man.

Had Spock's role still been filled by Majel Barrett's Number One, this scene would have not gone down quite as nightmarishly as it does. We'd be able to see Dehner's suspicious behaviour contrasted with that of a professional, competent woman respected by and known to her shipmates and this would have the added effect of telegraphing Dehner's eventual fall all the more clearly. But Number One had problems too: Recall the whole point of her character is that she's a woman who acclimated to male culture and is somehow more "rational" and accepted. This is no less sexist, and would have had the additional consequence of giving Kirk's imploring of Spock to "feel, just for once", or indeed any future logic vs. emotions debate, an uncomfortably sexist undertone as well.

This grates painfully with *Star Trek*'s supposed progressive attitude towards gender roles and it would be easy to lay this at the feet of writer Samuel Peeples and spare the show as conceived, but sadly that's not possible, because the sexism problems "Where No Man Has Gone Before" has are really just an extension of what we saw in "The Cage" and are bound up in Roddenberry's original conception of the series. Here's where the spectre of Roddenberry's less savoury character traits really start to become an issue for the show: Firstly, the whole reason we have Spock and not Number One as the voice of pragmatism here is because Majel Barrett was written out, and, contrary to fan lore, it was Roddenberry who wrote her out. The oft-repeated story is that NBC was uncomfortable with having such a strong female lead as Number One on the show and gave Roddenberry the ultimatum to drop either her or Spock, so Roddenberry "kept the alien and married the girl, because I couldn't legally have it the other way". Aside from making Roddenberry look rather a prat,

33

this claim is debunked by Solow and Justman in *Inside Star Trek*, who claim that, actually the idea of a female lead was mostly NBC's idea and the problem with Number One was that female audiences didn't like her and they were concerned Majel Barrett couldn't carry the role.

This makes a great deal of sense. Of course female audiences didn't respond well to Number One; they were being asked to relate to a female character whose entire point is that she's rejected female culture. How do you think that was going to go down? And, well, after rewatching "The Cage" I'm not entirely certain Majel Barrett could have carried the role either. Number One and Dehner aside, there's also the small matter of Yeoman Smith, who seems like she's meant to be the replacement for Yeoman Colt, except she has even less of a meaningful role in "Where No Man Has Gone Before" than Colt did in "The Cage". According to Solow, basically the only reason she exists, or at least the reason model Andrea Dromm was cast in the role was bluntly because Roddenberry wanted to "score" with her. So there's that. Also, I'm not even going to touch the whole "walking freezer unit" crack or Mitchell and Kirk swapping anecdotes about the women they chased at the Academy. So, we're one episode in and Roddenberry is already filling *Star Trek* with awful frat boy humour, constructing elaborate lies about what's actually happening on set and trying to sleep with his cast, which is not exactly promising.

But even so *Star Trek*'s progressive reputation is not completely undeserved, and even here we're starting to see the seeds of that take root. And once again, perhaps counterintuitively, it's William Shatner who is blazing the trail. The moment that sticks out for me is when Kirk is reminiscing with Mitchell about their Academy days. Mitchell chides Kirk for assigning Dehner to watch over him, once again referencing the awful "freezer unit" line (I mean seriously. He might as well have just came right out and called her an "ice queen" or a "frigid bitch" at this point) while Kirk tells Mitchell to "consider it a challenge". As written the scene sounds awful, but Shatner totally saves it: One can imagine Jeffrey Hunter playing this bit completely straight, as if it really is two academy frat boys waxing nostalgic about their "scores" and bemoaning women who don't put out to their charms. But Shatner plays it very awkward, as if Mitchell is making Kirk increasingly uneasy. There is of course the whole slowly turning into a god before his eyes thing to consider, but one does get the sense from Shatner that Kirk isn't at all comfortable with hearing his crewmembers talked about in that manner, and even that it might be out of character for Mitchell to say something like this (and hence a clue he's no longer the person he was) when the script would seem to suggest it isn't.

Earlier on on the episode is another great moment: When the *Enterprise* is first approaching the galactic barrier and Yeoman Smith first walks onto the bridge, Kirk gets a dumb line where he forgets her name which is obviously written as a bit of Pike-esque "I'm not used to women on the bridge" dismissiveness, but once again Shatner is an absolute class act, playing Kirk visibly remorseful and apologetic before gently escorting Smith to her post. Far from what his reputation as a ladykiller would suggest, throughout the entire running time of "Where No Man Has Gone Before" Kirk is nothing but gracious and respectful to his female co-workers, even Dehner: That's an absolute breath of fresh air and it's all Shatner. And, as great as he is, we also get George Takei, Andrea Dromm and Lloyd Haynes as Alden who are all excellent, despite the fact they get frustrating few opportunities to actually contribute something meaningful to the proceedings, and it must be stressed their existence alone counts for a lot.

What we have with "Where No Man Has Gone Before" then is the moment we first see there might just be a way forward for this *Star Trek* thing. Gene Roddenberry's ethics remain worrisome, but with William Shatner onboard there is at least a glimmer of hope at last, and the show will only continue to find new ways to work within its constraints and push its creative boundaries. Whatever *Star Trek* is going to become now, it's certainly going to be interesting to watch unfold.

Proceed to May 24, 1966 (turn to Chapter 6)

6. "P-P-P-Poker Face, P-P-Poker Face...": The Corbomite Maneuver

OK, I try to stay open minded about this sort of thing. I make a concerted effort to approach these episodes from a fresh perspective, giving each and every one the widest possible benefit of history and changing cultural norms because it would be exceedingly easy, but also overwhelmingly facile, to simply pillory *Star Trek* from the perspective of a 21st Century anarcha-feminist. If I'm going to do this and do it properly, I have to do my very best to try and put this show firmly within the context of its time while also teasing some larger narrative out of what I'm seeing. But sometimes this approach lets me down.

I make absolutely no pretenses that the Original Series is my favourite incarnation of Star Trek. It was an era of the franchise I always knew from looking backward into the historical record. It never connected with me, never resonated with me the way it did with others and I never quite got the show's full appeal. Even to this day: The whole reason I'm starting this project here instead of with "Encounter at Farpoint" is because I feel I need to provide some kind of context to fully articulate where this whole Star Trek thing eventually ends up. Clearly there is something that people latch onto with the Original Series though: It has a level of cultural capital that is almost unmatched in the collective consciousness and the only thing my not falling in love with it says is that it's not for me.

But even so...After a few deeply flawed episodes that nevertheless consisted of enough interesting material that at least gestured at a way forward and hinted at something a bit grander and more progressive than what was onscreen, I thought I had a good handle on what made *Star Trek* tick and why it may have had the impact it did.

That'll teach me to be so naive and presumptuous.

This was the first thing I've revisited for this project that truly, genuinely tried my patience. And I know I'm going to alienate a whole bunch of Star Trek fans here, but I'm sorry: I found "The Corbomite Maneuver" absolutely intolerable. Foundation's ethics were extremely problematic, but it's very much of its time. So was *Lost in Space*. The two pilots didn't really work, but you could see the glimmer of potential there. "The Corbomite Maneuver" pissed me off.

What this episode does is finally makes the link between *Star Trek*'s futurism and a particular strand of US-focused New Frontier neo-imperialism textually overt. "The Cage" and "Where No Man Has Gone Before" were merely militaristic by association, purely the result of the puzzling *Gulliver's Travels* meets Space Air Force setting. The second pilot did have that awkward subplot of having Spock's preference of cold logic to fickle emotion consistently proven justified, but that's nothing compared to what we get here. "The

Corbomite Maneuver" absolutely revels in military bravado and glorification of the chain of command: A good 3/4 of the episode is dedicated to watching Kirk and Balok flexing their respective military might and manly bluffing skills and the theme of the burden and stress of command is reiterated in every single subplot. Even William Shatner, who was practically the saving grace of "Where No Man Has Gone Before", is reduced to essentially playing an even more unlikeable version of Christopher Pike here, angrily barking orders, shouting down his officers and constantly asserting his authority. It's a borderline unwatchable level of unpleasantness.

Furthermore, this episode also marks the point where the Original Series' problematic handle on gender roles screams headfirst into outright misogyny: Janice Rand is introduced as the new Captain's Yeoman (though of course not given a name, and I'd like to point out this is the third Yeoman the *Enterprise* has gone through in as many episodes) who struts into the captain's quarters in a full beehive, miniskirt and Go-Go boots and proceeds to absolutely dote over Kirk as if she's trying to mother him: She sets a place setting at his table, gives him a napkin and a bib and then tells him to eat his salad. I just...For real? Is *Star Trek* trolling me? Am I being *dared* to go full Freudian Oedipal Complex on this? Even better, in the middle of the standoff between the *Enterprise* and the *Fesarius* Rand walks onto the bridge completely oblivious to the fact all signs indicate everyone on board has less than a minute to live because it's time to give the captain his coffee. I mean Holy Shit...

Janice Rand is explicitly a token bimbo. There is literally no other way to describe the way her character is written here. Even Yeoman Smith who barely got a speaking role and who existed purely because Roddenberry wanted to sleep with Andrea Dromm, was treated with more respect than this. At least it seemed like Smith had an actual job as a member of the *Enterprise* crew other than "captain's coffee-dispensing servant girl" and Kirk was very gracious to her. Here, Kirk snaps at Rand and complains to McCoy about how he wants to "ring the neck of whoever thought it was a good idea to give me a female yeoman" to which the good doctor smiles and says "What's the matter, Jim? Don't you trust yourself?" Because, of course, nothing is better for a quick good-natured laugh than rape culture. Aside from being shockingly misogynistic, this is utterly, jarringly and inexplicably out-of-character for Kirk, even given what little we know about him at this point: There is absolutely no way the Kirk of "Where No Man Has Gone Before" would have been this cruel. If I didn't know better I'd swear this episode was filmed first. I can understand Shatner experimenting with different ways to play the character, but Kirk doesn't even seem like a remotely comparable person at this point.

I'll bet Gene Roddenberry thought that was a laugh-riot though.

Then there's the matter of Rand's "uniform" and, well, Uhura's too, and that of every female crewmember on the Original Series from here on out. I'm going on record again here to say I have never, ever liked the miniskirt and Go-Go getup that makes its debut in this episode and still pretty much detest it. I can however, at least historicize it because the matter is a bit more complicated than modern critics tend to pick up on. The thing is the female Original Series uniform is deliberately designed to invoke the Carnaby Street high fashion Mod look of the mid-late 1960s, which is a look that, at the time, was primarily associated with youth subculture. Unlike today, where women bearing a lot of skin are seen to be sexualized from a patriarchal perspective, in the 1960s it was seen more as an act of rebellion against what had been the traditional custom of pressuring women to wear very modest clothes that covered their arms and legs. So by putting his female officers in miniskirts, the story goes, Roddenberry was trying to show that in his vision of the future women would be sexually liberated and free to own and shape their own image, and that Starfleet supported that. So that's good.

Except I'm not sure this reading actually holds water.

I'd love a version of *Star Trek* that cast its lot in with radical youth subculture as the ideal version of humanity, but that is so completely not what the show is giving us it's not even funny. Firstly, for a future where women are independent and walk as equals among their male colleagues and proudly own their sexuality, there sure does seem to be an awful lot of sexual harassment on the *Enterprise*. Putting aside for the moment frat boy Gary Mitchell, who I'll be generous and say was under the influence of his mutation, we've now had two captains express their open contempt for and discomfort about serving with women and every single major female character we've seen apart from Number One has been in an incredibly stereotypical or demeaning position, like space switchboard operator or space secretary and servant girl (and of course Number One only got where she did by explicitly rejecting femininity, as I never tire of pointing out). Knowing this, not to mention his own questionable history with the real life women he worked with, it really seems to me as if the miniskirt has little to do with Roddenberry allying himself with the Mods and everything to do with him wanting to see scantily clad ladies strutting around his set. And really to be perfectly blunt, a miniskirt and Go-Go boot ensemble is flatly *not* a practical everyday work outfit for the sort of jobs I imagine one has to do on a starship.

I'm harping on the sexism angle to the extent I am because it really is a major problem, it never goes away and its something nobody seems to notice about the original *Star Trek* (or any Star Trek, for that matter) or at least is comfortable talking about. The bottom line is that Roddenberry (and it *is* Roddenberry: Remember this is the same guy who thought Orion Animal Women were a good idea) and Star Trek itself both have a serious, serious problem with women and this is a fact we really have to take into consideration whenever we discuss the series' alleged idealism. Yes, it was nice of Roddenberry to show female officers, but they're mostly extras, meant only to mill about in the background. This would be one thing if this could be considered progressive for 1966, but it's not: Even *Lost in Space* had a better spectrum of female characters on display who did more than push buttons, fret about serving their men properly or mewl about their womanly emotional weaknesses and in Europe and Britain there are science fiction shows that are frankly running rings around Star Trek in terms of being forward thinking and female-friendly (we'll look at some of those a little later on).

And really, we shouldn't be surprised as the rest of the script is just as reactionary: The show wants to make a big deal about how Kirk and Balok reach a peaceful resolution to the stalemate and engage in a personnel and information exchange at the end, but this only comes after 45 minutes of macho posturing from both of them that very nearly results in the *Enterprise* being blown out of the stars at several points. This isn't diplomacy or discourse, this is the Cuban Missile Crisis only with big talk and poker chips instead of nuclear phalli and I'd hardly count that as much of an improvement. Frankly, the fact it ends as peacefully as it does is the result of a miracle, not Kirk's debate skills, and it's more than a little sickening to know the show seems to want us to think the way you go about exploring and making friendly overtures to people is to throw up overblown displays of defensive paranoia and then test each other with overly complicated war games. At this point it is legitimately difficult for me to fathom how this show ever got the reputation it did: Is this really the best, most hopeful thing on television in 1966? If it was, then that decade was even more depressing than I thought.

Even after all that, I'd actually be willing to call "The Corbomite Maneuver" something of a Curate's Egg. It's an utter disaster, but parts of it are actually excellent and, as is quickly becoming the norm with this show, the majority of those parts are the actors. Shatner is once again solid and seems to be doing the best he can with what he's given, even if what he's given in this instance is absolute garbage. The opening scene with Kirk doing cardio in sickbay shirtless, and than proceeding to walk around the *Enterprise* for a time still shirtless and sweating, is completely gratuitous and takes some of the edge off of the episode. Leonard Nimoy also seems to have upped his game this time around: He already has great chemistry with Shatner and it's clear he knows he now has someone he can play off of. Spock's debates with Kirk about logic are probably the highlight of the episode and the scene near the climax where Spock is at a loss to come up with a logical way out of the stalemate would have been a genius way to make up for "Where No Man Has Gone Before" had Kirk's response not been to bluff Balok into submission. James Doohan and George Takei are now firmly established as regulars and even get names for their characters (though why Sulu suddenly switched to the helm position remains unexplained). Both of them deliver tight, charming, memorable performances that are frankly wasted on the bit parts they get, which will sadly become something of a reoccurring theme.

Of course this episode also marks the first appearance of Nichelle Nichols as Uhura and DeForest Kelley as Doctor McCoy. Kelley is, naturally, the standout: McCoy immediately distinguishes himself from the revolving door that is the *Enterprise*'s sciences division through his intensely human and charismatic performance of the "country doctor". He's the most enjoyable and likable thing on display here by light years and steals the episode effortlessly. It's little wonder Shatner, Nimoy and Kelley are so fondly remembered: They really do almost seem custom tailored to play off of each other. Nichols does a perfectly serviceable job doing what she's asked to do, which is to parrot "hailing frequencies open" over and over again, but she, like Doohan and Takei, is utterly wasted on the part. Things never really improve for any of them, and Uhura also has to bear the brunt of the show's systemic sexism problems to boot. Her presence on the bridge famously reinforces the show's commitment to at least having a diverse cast, even if that diverse cast isn't really asked to do anything terribly interesting.

I understand how the mere presence of characters like Sulu and Uhura on the bridge was seen as a very powerful and meaningful thing at the time (there is even high-profile historical evidence that it has been read this way by a lot of people) but from my perspective it just isn't quite enough to counterbalance the flagrantly reactionary tendencies the show exhibits elsewhere at this point. The show as it exists as of "The Corbomite Meanuver" is flagrantly and openly misogynistic and its diverse background cast is something NBC encouraged in all of its shows, not something *Star Trek* somehow pioneered. To say *Star Trek* has a staunch, explicit and unique commitment to material social progress in 1966 is a fallacy: Any progressive points we can give the show we have to give to it by virtue of coincidence or accident, and very little due to what was intended by Gene Roddenberry.

"The Corbomite Maneuver" is a troublesome thing: It's the point where *Star Trek* reboots itself for the first time into a form that is immediately recognisable and so much of what the show is most famous for is now finally together in the same place, but that's also not an entirely good thing. The cast is unbelievably strong; they're almost too good for the show they're on, and we do in fact have a future where men and women of different cultures and creeds can serve together as equals, if only ostensibly and in theory. But this is also as explicit as the show has gotten so far about its wholehearted embrace of militaristic power structures and crass patriarchal attitudes which is, bluntly, contradictory and self-destructive. This is not an ideal you can build material social progress out of. This is an ideal that's going to implode in on itself someday. Star Trek's future prospects just got pretty bleak.

Proceed to June 3, 1966 (turn to Chapter 7)

7. "The Women!": Mudd's Women

The most interesting thing about "Mudd's Women" is that it was a candidate for the second pilot. Let's just stop and think about that for a minute: There is a possible universe where the very first episode produced for Star Trek on television was not "Where No Man Has Gone Before" but a story about the *Enterprise* crew policing an interstellar mail-order bride service. Instead of our first impression of Star Trek being of passionate debates about humanity and emotion and the line between god and mortal, it'd be of Kirk chewing out a stereotypical Irish comedy con man and watching the crew get hypnotized by magic space hookers. Is it conceivable that Star Trek would have the storied legacy and reputation it does today if "Mudd's Women" was the pilot? Is it conceivable that it would have lasted beyond one episode if it had been? Furthermore, what does it say about Gene Roddenberry that he earnestly, genuinely thought this episode was a perfect showcase of everything that he wanted Star Trek to stand for?

"Mudd's Women" is, of course, catastrophically misogynistic. That kind of goes without saying. Any episode that deals with an interstellar mail-order bride service comprised of women who have magical, ill-defined hypnotic powers over men subsisting on a placebo drug to keep them beautiful and marketable and whose only dream in life is to provide companionship and conversation to lonely, rich miners sort of forces that reading by definition. We also have the *Enterprise* crew, who fret about the effect Mudd's hookers have on them and their ability to do their jobs and who generally act like every stereotype of lonely, sexually frustrated World War II sailors who haven't seen a woman in months you can think of despite the obvious fact there are female crewmembers freely mulling about in the background, which leads me to wonder if it's not just my imagination and the *Enterprise*'s female crewmembers actually are holograms.

Then there's the Venus Drug itself, which supposedly gives people more of what they already have. So naturally, it makes men more "ambitious" and turns women into dangerously sexy eye candy. I don't think I need to explain that one. The real clincher, as if we needed one, comes in the climax where Eve (who it must be stressed is meant to have the ethical high ground in this scene) screams at her (abusive) fiancée for only wanting a beautiful thing to look at, instead of a "wife who can help, can clean and can sew", which is suitably rich. After a bit of extra moralizing from Kirk and Mudd (who is apparently a good guy now), about how people are only as good as they believe themselves to be and which makes no sense within the larger context of the episode, the abusive husband-to-be graciously allows Eve to stay, so that was awfully nice of him.

So this episode is basically appalling and indefensible, but that's as much as I'm going to harp on the misogyny angle in this entry, as I've already spent a lot of digital ink chronicling *Star Trek*'s and Gene Roddenberry's problem with women in the previous few posts. "Mudd's Women" comes out of the same kind of confused approach to gender and gender roles that has characterized *Star Trek* in general so far, so there's not much to add. What I'd actually like to spend the remainder of this piece talking about is costume designer William Ware Theiss, whose signature style makes its debut here. Theiss is an important creative figure in Star Trek history and we'll be seeing his work well into the late 1980s, so it's as important to examine his contributions as it is those of someone like Gene Roddenberry. As head of the wardrobe department, Theiss is responsible for a great deal of what we associate with the look-and-feel of Star Trek, including the iconic uniforms of both *Star Trek* and the first season of *Star Trek: The Next Generation*. Theiss is also somewhat infamous for the outfits he designed for the female guest stars for the former show, as exemplified by those worn by this episode's mail-order-brides from space.

Theiss' approach to this sort of outfit is best described via the "Theiss Titillation Theorem", a rather cheeky term coined in the seminal *The Making of Star Trek* to describe it and which has since seeped into popular discourse. The idea goes that the perceived sexiness of a woman's outfit is directly proportional to how much skin it can show *without* being completely naked. Theiss was, therefore, able to create impossibly revealing costumes operating from this premise and also working around 1960s censorship rules that regulated which parts of the body could be shown but not how much surface area in total. That said, Solow and Justman also have something to add here, claiming in *Inside Star Trek* that the first drafts of Theiss' designs were always actually comparatively more modest than what he's famous for. What we got onscreen is apparently the result of Gene Roddenberry making "improvements" to them, which wouldn't surprise me in the slightest.

(Also worth pointing out here is that historical evidence that network standards and practices weren't quite as draconian as Roddenberry and Theiss tended to claim they were after the fact, and also that Theiss himself was openly a gay man, and that Roddenberry knew this.)

The entire concept of the Theiss Titillation Theorem is one that is bound up in issues of sexuality and power structures that are not only things that come to just about define Star Trek but are also things that Western society has always been struggling with. The whole presumption behind the theorem, of course, is that a woman who strategically withholds bits of herself is infinitely more attractive then one who is completely nude. Viewers aren't allowed to see all of her, so they have to use their imagination and marvel at how that outfit even stays together in the first place. The common reading goes that this is due to the old maxim "wanting is better than having", but I'm going to take that further and say that the only reason this is seen as sexy and desirable is because nudity is taboo: Western societies fetishisize the taboo and forbidden, and were the nude form seen as a natural and accepted part of the human condition that people shouldn't be ashamed about the Theiss Titillation Theorem wouldn't work at all.

In *The History of Sexuality*, Michel Foucault argues the popular perception that industrial Western cultures were more oppressive than their predecessors is false, and is a myth constructed by those who liked to imagine a sexually free and egalitarian Golden Age far back into history that we might be able to strive for again in the future. According to Foucault, what actually happened during the transition from pre-modern to modern societies was a dramatic increase in discourse about sexuality, except it was fielded carefully through various authoritarian channels. The key moment here was the Counter-Reformation, during which the Catholic Church encouraged its followers to confess their sinful sexual desires and actions with wild abandon. Though the Church was the primary institution at first, this is later reiterated and echoed in subsequent power structures and dynamics to similar effect. From this we get a culture built around sharing and exposing the "salacious" details of one's personal life: Sexuality becomes a taboo thing but, as with all taboo things, it's just as much fun to confess your love for it in secret.

Though Foucault claims this isn't sexual repression inasmuch as the authoritarian power structures are encouraging open discussion of sexuality, albeit though "official channels" and framing it in such a way as to distinguish between "sinful" and "proper" ways to express it, I would argue this is still repressive, just in a slightly different way. Though this kind of system increases the sum total of discourse about sexuality, it fetishizes it by making it a kind of forbidden fruit. What this results in is a society which is systemically sexually frustrated as a result of its simultaneous fascination with the intangibles of sex, sexuality and sex acts and fear and guilt over exploring them. We're not being told not to be sexual, but we're being told to feel bad, shameful and guilty about being sexual. Therefore, we feel both guilt-ridden for doing something we're not supposed to do, but also excited and rebellious specifically *because* it's something we're not supposed to do. But when sex and sexuality become saucy, tantalizing things just out of reach they stop being seen as natural parts of life and ways to express oneself in a healthy manner and to connect with others and the larger shared universe: They instead become dehumanizing fetish objects, and Western society seems completely lousy with those.

This is the intellectual tradition the Theiss Titillation Theorem comes out of, and it's the absolute perfect evidence that far from showing us ideals to strive towards, Star Trek right now is an almost painfully accurate microcosm of a modernist Western society that is already in noticeable decline. And, like modernist Western society, crazed, guilt-ridden sexual frustration is going to become a defining hallmark of *Star Trek* over the next three years. Which means that "Mudd's Women" might actually be far more prescient and representative of the show than we'd maybe like to admit: *Star Trek* would almost assuredly not have been picked up if it had been the pilot, but, scarily, it does exactly what a pilot is supposed to do-Give viewers a vertical slice of the prospective show's premise and values. Like it or not, sexual malaise and gender role confusion is just as much a part of *Star Trek* as the *Enterprise*, the Federation and Kirk, Spock and McCoy. And with one more piece in place, Gene Roddenberry's journey through the stars can continue.

Return to Command Helix and report findings (turn to Chapter 4)

8. Bug-eyed monsters: The Man Trap

There's a scene early on in "The Man Trap" that sticks with me. It's right after Scott contacts the bridge to inform them the away team is beaming up with a fatality. On the bridge Uhura and Spock are in the middle of a conversation, her obviously hitting on him and him being obviously a Vulcan. When Spock acknowledges Scott and continues his work with what will become his signature cool detachment, Uhura snaps at him demanding to know how he can be so distant when someone has died, and, after all, it could be Captain Kirk, who is the "closest thing" Spock has to a friend. It's a great introduction to both characters, as well as to Nichelle Nichols and Leonard Nimoy, who do a solid job with an important character moment.

What's truly striking about this scene however is that it's blatantly and proudly mundane in the the midst of an almost ludicrously stock science fiction scenario: We have a chameleon monster running around suckering people to death and what *Star Trek* fixates on is the effect this has on two members of the bridge staff. That one is an African woman and the other an extraterrestrial is not even a point of focus. This follows and is succeeded by a tense moment where William Shatner plays Kirk not just angry, but personally hurt, that he's lost a crewmember. We never knew that random med-tech, the first of the infamous "Red Shirt" deaths in the show despite being in the blue-shirted sciences division; to us he was nobody. But to the *Enterprise* crew he was somebody

Not long into the very first episode of *Star Trek* to air, it's easy to see how this show could have left a big impression on those who saw it the night of September 8, 1966 (or, for that matter, those who were oblivious about its existence until the early 1970s, which is probably a fairer depiction of the fanbase). Although reviewers at the time panned it for its wooden acting and plot that was deemed more fitting for a Saturday Morning Cartoon Show then a prime time drama, "The Man Trap" demonstrates quite effectively the traits that will make *Star Trek* a beloved piece of Western culture. The diverse cast, though not unique to this series, certainly goes a long way, as does the emphasis on character relationships and development, in spite of the so-called "wooden" acting (DeForest Kelley in particular seems strangely subdued given what his character is supposed to be going through: This is far from his best episode and he gets much better showcases later on, though of course there was no way of knowing this at the time).

I said "The Man Trap" was an almost stock science fiction plot, and it is, but it's also more than that. It's a curious blend of a lot of different story archetypes: It has, as I mentioned, a number of very strong character moments: The most obvious is, naturally, McCoy's attempts to cope with first rekindling his relationship with his lost lover and then being forced to accept she's *really* gone for good when she, uh, turns out to be a

Salt Vampire. But there's also the scenes with Spock and Uhura, the insight into Uhura's possible feelings of loneliness we get thanks to Salt Vampire's ill-defined powers of mind reading and shapeshifting and Kirk's torment over having a killer aboard his ship and being incapable of doing anything about it.

Aside from that, we also get some actually charming scenes where crewmembers converse with each other in between shifts while milling about in the deck hallways. This is occasionally, well OK *frequently* clunky thanks to some awkward dialogue choices ("may the Great Bird of the Galaxy bless your planet!" immediately jumps to mind) and actors of changeable reach, but it's still quite laudable. There is a sense the *Enterprise* is a community of sorts, which makes it all the more tragic when Salt Vampire starts picking members of it off. Well, it *would* be all the more tragic if we got a sense that any of the deceased crewmembers had personal relationship before they died thus allowing us to feel their loss more, but I guess that would also run the risk of becoming exploitative and emotionally manipulative.

This focus on characterization is unusual for science fiction during this time period. *Star Trek* inherits a lot from both Pulp and Golden Age sci-fi, but neither genre is particularly suited to this kind of drama, the former being far more interested in exciting ray-gun action setpieces and the latter in overly complicated logic puzzles and speculative technoscientific concepts. *Star Trek*'s closest point of comparison on US television, *Lost in Space*, goes nowhere near this territory either, sticking to the Golden Age model in its first season (albeit also featuring Pulp-style action sequences because come on this is TV) before becoming quite content to do comedy camp runarounds for the rest of its run. No, what "The Man Trap" is giving us is actually most immediately comparable to something out of a soap opera, which is, frankly, kind of unheard of. Soap operas and cult sci-fi (a thing *Star Trek* definitely already is: It didn't tank on original run, but neither did it ever pull terribly high ratings either) are actually extremely close relatives, which makes a lot of sense if you stop and think about it: Both pretty much depend on maintaining a loyal and dedicated fanbase instead of populist appeal. This will turn out to be both Star Trek's saviour and its killer on more than one occasion.

So "The Man Trap" is at once both Pulp sci-fi and a soap opera, but it's also a kind of proto-Slasher flick as well: It's hard not to make the connection when the majority of the episode is dedicated to watching an invisible killer silently stalk the halls of the *Enterprise* with straight-up first person POV horror movie camera angles. This is actually used to quite a clever extent here, as the best execution of the Slasher structure is also the point where *Star Trek* puts its foot down and firmly says it's not going to be about monster spectacle: While disguised as Green, Salt Vampire joins up with a group of crewmen trying to get a free lunch out of Janice Rand and then followers her down the hall. Rand is shot as just about the most stereotypical blonde damsel in distress in film history here, as the camera switches to POV and leeringly follows her into the arboretum, where we fully expect her to spin around, scream and get death-suckered (after all, remember there's no way we could have known at the time Grace Lee Whitney was a regular or was in any way different from any of the other random crewmembers who have been bumped off so far)...

...And then the camera snaps to a wide angle shot inside the arboretum where Rand gives Sulu his lunch and has a nice, friendly conversation with him about plants and why some people attribute genders to inanimate objects. Minutes later Salt Vampire finally shows up, but is scared off by Beauregard the Flower of all characters. Rand and Sulu are a bit weirded out, but none the wiser and perfectly safe. It's a fantastic subversion, a teensy bit of a feminist deconstruction and it does its part to render the entire Slasher genre obsolete before it's even had a chance to get off the ground.

Aside from being a cheeky parlour trick and solidifying *Star Trek*'s interest in the mundane, this scene is also revealing given what we know about the production of "The Man Trap": In *Inside Star Trek*, Bob Justman complains that this episode was not his choice for the premier, but it was chosen by elimination out of the handful of finished episodes as it featured an alien planet and a cool monster to fight, thus satisfying expectations for an action-packed science fiction story while still showcasing the series' commitment to showing "Strange New Worlds". It's quite defensible, I feel, to read the arboretum scene as Star Trek's way of demonstrating that it's not going to be about blasting aliens with laser beams and instead has at least slightly loftier aspirations than that. As sensible as this is however, I also feel it's important to keep in mind we're only a few episodes in and *Star Trek* still isn't *technically* about exploration, which brings us to the fourth genre "The Man Trap" plays with: Gene Roddenberry's *Star Trek*. That is, *Gulliver's Travels* with the Space Air Force. This is also, unfortunately, where "The Man Trap" starts to falter.

A *Gulliver's Travels* plot, or at least a *Gulliver's Travels* plot as interpreted by Gene Roddenberry, has to have a moral. It may seem at first difficult to come up with an appropriate moral for a story about a sucker fish monster who suckers people to death, but "The Man Trap" tries. The problem is it fails pretty miserably at it: The emotional climax is supposed to be when Crater reveals Salt Vampire is the last of its kind and is therefore unique and worthy of preservation for historical and biodiversity reasons. However, we get about five minutes of hemming and hawing about this before Kirk decides that no, while driving a species to extinction may be bad, breaking space law and killing people is worse and Salt Vampire has to die. There's a tossed off line about buffalo at the end, but it's totally a throwaway line and then the *Enterprise* warps away and we never have to worry about it again. The big problem is the ethical dilemma the episode presents us with is so rudimentary and facile it's maddening: Yes, it's really, really bad that Salt Vampire is killing *Enterprise* crewmembers and it was wrong of Crater to hide the truth from Kirk, but there are also quite a number of possible solutions to this situation that present themselves other than "blow the everlasting fuck out of it".

The self-evidently correct choice would have been to capture Salt Vampire and quarantine it in a place where it couldn't harm any more people (which, as Crater correctly points out, M-113 was before the *Enterprise* showed up-It was Kirk's fixation on doing a by-the-book inspection that got him in trouble. Well, that and Crater's own evasiveness, which I also grant). It's not like this was some unfeasible option: Even what little we can discern about the way the *Star Trek* universe works one episode in I can think of two possible solutions: Either use the *Enterprise*'s long-range scanners to locate the one thing on the ship aside from Spock that's not human, lock on with the transporter and beam it back down to the planet or, as he had already tracked it down, Kirk could have stunned Salt Vampire with his phaser, restrained it and then beamed it back down with a supply of salt (after all, one can't well press charges against a Salt Vampire). But, apparently Kirk felt shooting things was more fun than Seeking Out New Life And New Civilizations here.

This kind of capricious morality is going to become a problem for the show, and unfortunately it's bound up tightly with how *Star Trek* works: Roddenberry wants to do a morality play every episode, but his idea of a moral is stuff like "Killing off entire species is bad, but not as bad as being in violation of space law", "puberty sucks", "don't fence me in", "believe in yourself and you can do anything" and "maybe once in awhile it's better to talk to your adversary instead of atomizing them". Which I mean, these are all technically true (except for probably the first one) but they're all pretty self-explanatory and cliché and don't really need 50 minutes of fusion Pulp sci-fi/Golden Age sci-fi/soap opera/morality play futurist musing to convey, especially when delivered with the subtlety of a tactical nuclear strike.

That said, this is a comparatively minor blemish on what is otherwise a quite admirable debut for this refined *Star Trek*. The fact the structure holds together so well even when its Big Ideas don't suggest even now the show has the potential to grow out of and apart from them. The cast is great, despite the reviews their performances got: The standouts have got to be William Shatner, Nichelle Nichols, George Takei and Grace Lee Whitney: Shatner delivers a wonderful, slightly overstated rendition of Jim Kirk which contrasts beautifully with Jeffrey Hunter's gruff, square-jawed Christopher Pike (which befits Shatner's classical training as a Shakespearean actor). Nichols' presence on the bridge alone is significant, but she infuses Uhura with enough warmth and character that she's instantly memorable for that as much as her ethnicity. Takei is similarly winning, making Sulu immediately charming, down-to-earth and affable. Whitney is a revelation though, starting out as a seemingly minor character who quickly sets herself apart as plucky, bold and no-nonsense as she goes from subverting a horror movie to taking up her position amongst the other senior officers on the bridge so there's absolutely no mistake as to where she belongs.

"The Man Trap" is far from perfect. Like "The Cage" it's nowhere near as clever as it wants you to think it is and it torpedoes its entire ethical credibility in the last act. But for the first time it seems like this *Star Trek* thing has a way forward: The setting finally works (sort of) thanks in no small part to the efforts of its talented cast, and this episode makes some pretty bold overtures already that *Star Trek* is not a typical work of science fiction, as typical works of science fiction tend to not play with subverting genre structures, feature an unquestionably diverse cast or have borderline soap opera levels of characterization. There is still a lot of doubt surrounding the show as it exists now: It seems for all the exciting potential it's hinting at, Star Trek may just be a bit too big for itself, as if the whole isn't quite greater than the sum of its parts. But with parts like these, it's also not difficult to see how it could have gotten people's attention.

Proceed to September 15, 1966 (turn to Chapter 9)

9. "Don't make me angry. You wouldn't like me when I'm angry.": Charlie X

So there are quite a number of things of note to discuss about "Charlie X". Firstly, it's the debut of D.C. Fontana, a longtime writer, producer and collaborator on Star Trek across various incarnations. This is also apparently the episode that Ira Steven Behr, a major creative figure on both *Star Trek: The Next Generation* and *Star Trek: Deep Space Nine*, cites as the one that "won him over" and convinced him of *Star Trek*'s potential. Thirdly, "Charlie X" is the second ever episode of the Original Series to air and is thus the second impression made on the show's original audience. This is terribly awkward for me because as far as I'm concerned "Charlie X" is absolute garbage, and a large part of why it's so bad comes out of the exact same things that made "The Man Trap" so promising.

Firstly I have to confess I'm approaching this one with a certain bias, as I've really never been a fan of this kind of story. Turning adolescence into a melodrama is a nice shortcut towards both spectacularly missing your intended mark and turning me off. Also, for a show that's trying to be seen as something other than a very expensive children's TV programme, which was the number one complaint against "The Man Trap" when it first aired, doing a story about all about teenagers as a follow-up was probably the single worst thing *Star Trek* could have done. So I'm already predisposed to not liking "Charlie X", and it doesn't help the episode itself is something of a mess. The only thing worse for me then sitting through another clumsy attempt to explain teenagers is watching a show attempt it with Gene Roddenberry's conception of morality.

Like "The Man Trap", "Charlie X" juxtaposes science fiction concepts with soap opera-esque character exploration. Unfortunately, *also* like "The Man Trap", "Charlie X" has a purely superficial and spurious grasp on ethics, and this time it's not limited to the episode's resolution. The whole point of Evans, of course, is that his longterm isolation and godlike powers are meant to be read as a metaphor for his struggles with puberty. Evans has great difficulties fitting in with grown-up society just as any normal teenager would, but this remains utterly unconvincing because Evans is utterly unsympathetic. He sexually harasses women with little to no repercussion, kills twenty people and puts countless other lives in peril when he doesn't get what he wants. No, it is *not* endearing to watch Evans continually fail to function properly in society, especially when it turns out he can literally turn people off and on like a lightswitch. It makes him creepy and threatening at best and extremely dangerous at worst.

The problem is Roddenberry gets as far as likening godlike powers to puberty and then stops there. They're similar in that they're both confusing and make it hard to acclimate to society, yes, but one has far less of a chance of slaughtering entire populations. Again, it's Roddenberry's ham-fisted handle on what a morality play is that's holding everything back: He's not trying to say anything more complex then "being a teenager is hard" but the whole thing falls apart in the execution because unlike "The Man Trap", which succeeded in spite of its ethical stumbling because the rest of the show was bursting at the seams with new ideas, "Charlie X" doesn't have anything more to add to its central concept and just sort of flounders around for its entire running time.

(A note: I'm putting the blame for this mostly on Roddenberry, even though D.C. Fontana is listed as the writer as this episode is adapted from a one-sentence pitch Roddenberry came up with called "The Day Charlie Became God". Though Fontana wrote the screenplay, Roddenberry took credit for the whole episode. So it's only fair to give him all the criticism for it as well. Anyway, there will be other opportunities to discuss Fontana and this just *sounds* like classic Roddenberry given all I've read about him. In particular, the fact he had an unfortunate habit of doing comprehensive uncredited rewrites on everyone else's work.)

Not only does "Charlie X" declare its job complete after doing nothing more than stating its central metaphor in the bluntest manner imaginable, it actively submarines its own message through the delivery. A major aspect of this episode's story is that Kirk is meant to take on a surrogate father role to Evans and help teach him how to grow up as a man and the way the script handles this is horrifying-The show has numerous characters, most notably Rand and McCoy, go on at length about how what Evans really needs is a strong father figure to teach him what's right and what's not and the climactic battle between him and Kirk is about as overt a metaphor for the Oedipal masculine power struggle as it was possible to craft. I can't even begin to fathom how this is supposed to follow from the episode's key theme, which I thought was how puberty is hard and teenagers deserve our sympathy and support. Terrifyingly, the show seems to think this is the cleverest, coolest idea ever, which is pretty much the most depressing thing about an already depressing story.

Thankfully, William Shatner at least seems as uncomfortable with this as I am and plays Kirk wonderfully awkward and out of his element throughout all of this. From the beginning Kirk is the one thing that doesn't seem to fit here, making his first appearance in the episode debuting the delightfully frilly green and gold jacket that will become his signature over the next two years immediately making him stand out from the rest of the crew and their standard-issue starship uniforms. The way Kirk stumbles and mumbles his way through Evans' questions about how to talk to women is glorious and even when the narrative forces Kirk to take the stern upper hand with him Shatner plays it overstated, giving the impression Kirk is putting on just as much of an act as he is. The big payoff is in the gymnasium scene where Kirk swaggers around shirtless and sweaty in tight exercise pants showing off his abs and wrestling holds to his other (shirtless, sweaty) workout buddies, which is immediately recognisable as something no straight man has ever done in recorded human history. Neither Kirk nor Shatner belong in a setting this patriarchal, and that's almost enough to save the show. Almost.

This all culminates in the episode's ethically and logically bankrupt resolution where the Thasians finally intervene and take Evans away while Kirk pleads with them to give him another chance, emphasizing "the boy needs to be with his own people" (although Shatner seems to play it considerably more halfheartedly). This is supposed to be a tragic moment, where it finally becomes clear there's no way Evans will ever adapt to life among humans. Apparently, this is supposed to be a Bad Thing. The major problem with this scene is that Evans hasn't been defined by anything other than his naiveté, pettiness and great power, and none of these are particularly endearing character traits. He has no actual redeeming qualities and there's no sense he could use his talents for good were he to mature: The most benign thing he does is do fancy magic tricks to impress Janice Rand and promise he can get her anything she wants, which doesn't do anything to make me want to cheer for him (or for Rand if I'm honest, who follows up her winning depiction in "The Man Trap" by nearly falling for a 17 year old psychopath who can spontaneously generate pretty flowers for her and then promptly disappearing). As a result, Evans being ripped from the *Enterprise* comes across as less a bittersweet display of his ultimate failure and more a relief.

There is only one way I can read this, and it's incredibly disturbing: Given all he does in the episode and the general narrative role he plays, one can conclude that Evans is just as much a science fiction monster as Salt Vampire. The only thing that makes him different is that he was once something resembling a human instead of merely wearing the guise of one. In fact, Evans is worse than Salt Vampire-He has a much, much higher body count to his name for one, and at least Salt Vampire had the excuse of being a scared, starving animal trapped and being hunted down in an unfamiliar setting. The fact we are supposed to agree Salt Vampire had to die, taking its entire species with it, but are also meant to see Evans returning to the Thasians as some great tragedy is more than a little sickening already, but it gets worse: Narrative logic defines Evans as a monster primarily by his inability to acclimate to life with humans. In other words, Evans is monstrous because he's a teenager who doesn't conform and refuses to grow up in acceptable ways.

This isn't just dehumanizing and inconsistent, it forces an actively youth hating reading of the episode. Aside from being repugnant from a modern perspective, this actually makes no sense: Regardless of whether *Star Trek* is trying to be a juvenile action show or a progressive, utopian drama, pretty much the one thing neither of those genres do is overtly attack the youth. That seems nothing short of hilariously counterproductive and paradoxical and turns the entire episode into a grand exercise in futility. It could be argued I shouldn't be too hard on *Star Trek* right now as it's still very early on in the run and ultimately it's doing something few, if any, other shows would go near, but this cack-handed, clumsy morality isn't just growing pains, it's the sort of thing that can, and will, derail the series.

But that's the uncomfortable truth of the matter. In truth, *Star Trek* is not some progressive fairy tale, at least not yet. This is not what Gene Roddenberry's real legacy is, nor what he originally envisioned the show to be. Rather, what *Star Trek* does is push the boundaries just enough to redefine what it means to be reactionary. The fact the show can have such a diverse cast and aim for being this intelligent and ambitious while still being

51

this hegemonic is extremely telling. I don't think Roddenberry intended *Star Trek* to be a reactionary paean (there are enough progressive elements in his personal life to render that reading untenable), but it's his own carelessness and shallowness as a writer that forces it to end up this way. The show might still survive something like this, but if it does it won't be for lack of things trying to kill it off in nascent form. There are some remarkable things about *Star Trek* right now: Its cast, particularly William Shatner, is brilliant, and its reach and ambition is admirable. But the most remarkable thing about *Star Trek* right now is that it even exists at all.

Proceed to September 22, 1966 (turn to Chapter 10)

10. "That power would set me up above the Gods!": Where No Man Has Gone Before

The world of *Star Trek* has changed since last we visited. Spock seems to have switched over to the command division, Sulu has been promoted to head of astrosciences and Doctor McCoy seems to have been reassigned, replaced by a Doctor Mark Piper. Janice Rand is gone too, replaced by someone named Smith, and so is Uhura: In her place a new communications officer named Alden. At the navigation console we now have Kirk's old friend Gary Mitchell from the Academy, who, given this show's track record, is probably not going to last the episode. But what's really strange is we now have the *Enterprise* out further than it's ever been before, and, according to Kirk this is the start of a bold new mission of exploration beyond the Milky Way galaxy.

Quite frankly this is already unsatisfying. Not the plot setup itself, which is fascinating (probably the most interesting the show has been yet) but because it took *Star Trek* three episodes to get here and required the jettisoning of almost the entire cast. Not that the new additions are poor by any stretch of the imagination: Lloyd Haynes is good as Alden and Andrea Dromm's Yeoman Smith looks like she has potential, but I can't help but miss Nichelle Nichols, Grace Lee Whitney and especially DeForest Kelley's McCoy, who was a far more interesting character than Piper. I have to wonder what possessed Gene Roddenberry and the team to recast the entire show three episodes in: As Spock would say, "most illogical".

As fun as it might be for me to continue like this and try and get "Where No Man Has Gone Before" to fit with what we know about *Star Trek* from "The Man Trap" and "Charlie X", it's ultimately a pointless exercise. This may be the third episode of the series to air, but it's also the second pilot. Why it's airing here is beyond me, as the show has changed considerably since this was filmed (the story that Roddenberry as well as Justman and Solow tell is that this episode was deemed "too expository" to serve as the premier, whatever that means). Putting it after two episodes that were filmed a year after it must have done nothing but confuse the hell out of viewers, especially as the Star Trek that comes out of "Where No Man Has Gone Before" is a different animal than the one those hinted towards, or indeed the one "The Cage" did.

What we get here is actually William Shatner's first performance as Jim Kirk, and though he's a bit more subdued here than in the episodes we've seen him in already, he still plays Kirk as a slightly overstated, camp version of the Starship Captain role which is pretty much the highlight of the episode. Shatner has said in interviews that when he watched "The Cage" to prep for the role of Kirk, the first thing that struck him about it was that everyone in the production seemed to be taking it so terribly seriously, and to the show's detriment. And if there's one thing that is clear from both what we see onscreen and what people have said about him for better or worse, the one thing you really can't accuse William Shatner of is taking things too seriously. The rest of the cast introduced here, at least the ones who get speaking roles, put on a perfectly serviceable show: Leonard Nimoy is frighteningly good at playing an emotionless logician, of course, and in their first appearances James Doohan and George Takei are certainly the standouts of the supporting cast, and it's easy to see why they get promoted to regulars. Gary Lockwood and Sally Kellerman give quite striking performances and handle the gravitas of their plot admirably. But it really is Shatner who is the most memorable thing here, conveying Kirk's brooding mood swings with charming bombast and dramatic flair. And he needs to, because as a story "Where No Man Has Gone Before" still doesn't quite hold together.

It's very tempting to take Gary Mitchell's transformation into a god some very interesting ways: As he grows more powerful, Mitchell goes on and on about insignificant he finds the people of Earth and his former colleagues. He flips through the ship's records like a 1980s channel surfer flipping through TV channels with a remote control and I couldn't help but grin when he and Kirk discuss Spinoza in sickbay (Spinoza? In *Star Trek*? Is this actually for real?). The kicker, or what should have been the kicker, is when Mitchell senses Spock is monitoring him on the bridge computer and looks knowingly at the security camera. The camera, our camera, than cuts to the bridge, where Mitchell is looking out of the viewscreen at Kirk and Spock and, by association, at us through the TV itself. It's a brilliant bit of editing that's decades ahead of its time and really encourages reading this as the moment where Mitchell transcends the medium of television to become an equal to the audience and the creators: Of course he's dangerous to the *Enterprise*: He literally has control over the entire fictional *Star Trek* universe, and naturally he has to fight Kirk, as Shatner has turned him into the only other character bigger than the setting.

But than *Star Trek* strikes back and kills the whole thing dead in its tracks. Mitchell starts to babel on about how he has the makings of a god and how he and Dehner are the progenitors of some new race of superhumans. We get a riveting character moment where Kirk and Spock get into an argument over marooning Mitchell on Delta Vega, but we're absolutely meant to side with Spock, who completely trumps Kirk in the ethics debate. Spock stands for detached, calculating logic untainted by human emotions. His solution is self-evidently the "correct" choice because it puts the safety of the crew, the ship and the mission above things like friendship, loyalty and human dignity. Spock sways Kirk by explaining how Mitchell is no longer the person he knew from the academy, but a frightening and dangerous Other who can't be reasoned with and must be disposed of. It's a complete glorification of militaristic detachment and a definitive statement that it's preferable to human emotions, which are fickle and obfuscating things. It's utterly awful.

Shatner-as-Kirk does get one truly great speech at the end where he pleads with the recently ascended Dehner that Mitchell is dangerous because he has the powers of a god, but the frailties and vulnerabilities of a human. They way Shatner plays it is genius: One gets the sense that Kirk knows humanity is capable of great things, but is also a flawed and troubled people and that's what will keep Mitchell from using his powers for good (it also touches on what will become an old standby of Gene Roddenberry's: The notion that humanity is a "child species" constantly trying to "grow out of its infancy"). It almost seems Kirk is arguing that to attain that level of enlightened power one needs to learn compassion alongside years of discipline and knowledge: Indeed he almost says this word for word, but the script also gives him the line "absolute power corrupting absolutely", which makes the intended moral of the episode pretty blatant and really hamstrings the scene's potential impact. Now it seems like the "frailties and vulnerabilities" Kirk was talking about are the emotions Spock was cautioning him against earlier and the whole thing leaves a really unpleasant taste.

It's the theme of human emotions, and the merits and demerits associated with them, that really drags this episode down. This dovetails nicely into the character of Elizabeth Dehner, who is deeply worrying from a feminist perspective. Sally Kellerman does her best with the material she's given and she almost makes Dehner a tragic character we want to sympathize with, but the script is so loaded with such an awful, awful laddish attitude it's nowhere near enough. Dehner immediately sides with Mitchell after his transformation, even before she begins to mutate herself, and it's clear she's romantically attracted to him to boot, won over by his manly charm and charisma (which means, by the way, that she's flagrantly violating just about every medical oath and code she presumably took upon becoming a psychologist). She even has an emotional meltdown in the conference room where she gets "hysterical" and begs the table of (all male, stoic and reserved) department heads to udnerstand that Mitchell is really a sweet, kind and wonderful man.

Had Spock's role still been filled by Majel Barrett's Number One, this scene would have not gone down quite as nightmarishly as it does. We'd be able to see Dehner's suspicious behaviour contrasted with that of a professional, competent woman respected by and known to not just her shipmates, but the audience as well and this would have the added effect of telegraphing Dehner's eventual fall all the more clearly. But Number One had problems too: Recall the whole point of her character is that she's a woman who acclimated to male culture and is somehow more "rational" and accepted. This is no less sexist, and would have had the additional consequence of giving Kirk's imploring of Spock to "feel, just for once", or indeed any future logic vs. emotions debate, an uncomfortably sexist undertone as well.

Dehner aside, there's also the small matter of Yeoman Smith. According to Solow, basically the only reason she exists, or at least the reason model Andrea Dromm was cast in the role was bluntly because Roddenberry wanted to "score" with her. So there's that. Also, I'm not even going to touch the whole "walking freezer unit" crack or Mitchell and Kirk swapping anecdotes about the women they chased at the Academy. So, we're three episodes in and Roddenberry is already filling Star Trek with awful frat boy humour and trying to sleep with his cast, which is not exactly promising.

But even so Star Trek's progressive reputation is not completely undeserved, and even here we're starting to see the seeds of that take root. And once again, perhaps counterintuitively, it's William Shatner who is blazing the trail. The moment that sticks out for me is when Kirk is reminiscing with Mitchell about their Academy days. Mitchell chides Kirk for assigning Dehner to watch over him, once again referencing the awful "freezer unit" line (I mean seriously. He might as well have just came right out and called her an "ice queen" or a "frigid bitch" at this point) while Kirk tells Mitchell to "consider it a challenge". As written the scene sounds awful, but Shatner totally saves it, playing it very awkward, as if Mitchell is making Kirk increasingly uneasy. There is of course the whole slowly turning into a god before his eyes thing to consider, but one does get the sense from Shatner that Kirk isn't at all comfortable with hearing his crewmembers talked about in that manner, and even that it might be out of character for Mitchell to say something like this (and hence a clue he's no longer the person he was) when the script would seem to suggest it isn't. That's an absolute breath of fresh air and it's all Shatner. And, as great as he is, we also get George Takei, Andrea Dromm and Lloyd Haynes as Alden who are all excellent, depite the fact they get frustrating few opportunities to actually contribute something meaningful to the proceedings, and it must be stressed their existence alone counts for a lot.

What we have with "Where No Man Has Gone Before" then is the moment we first see there might just be a way forward for this *Star Trek* thing. Gene Roddenberry's ethics remain worrisome, but onboard the *Enterprise* there is at least a glimmer of hope at last, and the show will only continue to find new ways to work within its constraints and push its creative boundaries. Whatever *Star Trek* is going to become now, it's certainly going to be interesting to watch unfold.

Return to Command Helix and report findings (turn to Chapter 4)

11. "I am he and he is me!": The Enemy Within

"The Enemy Within" plays like an almost paint-by-numbers example of how *Star Trek* works at the moment. This of course means it's terrible. It has a crassly simplistic and poorly thought out moral delivered with zero semblance of tact, form, structure or good sense and almost painfully earnestly and gamely conveyed by the cast. This leaves me in a really frustrating position: It's bad, but it's bad along exactly the lines I've been drawing over the past several chapters. This one manages to fall face first into rape apologia, which I will of course take it to task for, but only for the same reasons the show's been reactionary so far. It's a particularly egregious execution of this formula, but other than that, "The Enemy Within" brings nothing new to the analytical table.

However, I have a job to do here so let's see what I can make with this. First of all, if "Charlie X" doing a melodrama about teenage issues irritated me, "The Enemy Within" doing an evil lookalike plot where the baddie frames our hero and gets his friends to turn against him for half the episode before he clears his name is enough to send me straight into smash-the-television-in-blind-rage mode. Ignoring the plot for the moment, which I would sorely like to scream and yell about but shall restrain myself from doing, "The Enemy Within" could possibly be described as something I call an Actor Showcase Episode: These are special episodes, meant to give a specific cast member or members the opportunity to play against type and and show off their reach. These are typically made when shows get a particularly skilled cast who are normally pigeonholed into very tight, programmatic roles to let the audience know the full extent of their range. Actor Showcase Episodes tend to crop up either at the beginning of a show's run (to get the audience used to the new cast) or in the middle (to let them see a side of the cast heretofore unseen) and they're usually delightful changes of pace from standard operating procedure (indeed these become characteristic of *Star Trek: The Next Generation* once Michael Piller becomes showrunner).

In that regard, calling "The Enemy Within" an Actor Showcase for William Shatner is tempting, especially as the highlight of the episode is arguably Shatner's performance as both crazed madman Evil!Kirk and gentle, thoughtful Good!Kirk. However, as this episode seems consumed by a desire to thwart my attempts to say anything intelligent about it whatsoever at every turn, it comes literally *right before* an episode seemingly custom-tailored to be a full Cast Showcase, so there goes that reading.

So Roddenberry Ethics it is then. Although this problem is systemic throughout Roddenberry's entire tenure as showrunner (and indeed, his entire career), "The Enemy Within" is probably the most clear-cut example of just how badly this can go for the show (so far). The core theme of Richard Matheson's script is a kind of grade school retelling of *The Strange Case of Doctor Jekyll and Mr. Hyde*: Each person is literally composed of a honest-to-goodness Good and Evil half and both are needed for us to survive. The Good Half is intelligence and compassion and the Evil Half is, of course, aggression, ambition, confidence and lust. This isn't even Freud's id/ego/superego distinction, which would be bad enough, this is straight-up "some human traits are by definition Good and some are by definition Evil and that's the Law of the Universe". It's also very, very Western, and indeed very Roddenberry: Sexual desire is equated with rape and blind lust and declared Fundamentally Evil. Furthermore, as both Spock and McCoy state, it's "intelligence", which is here described in terms that makes it sound suspiciously like "logic" and "rationality", that gives humans their innate goodness and strength, so we're right back at that whole "emotions are fickle and corrupting" thing again, so that's fun.

Let there be absolutely no mistaking what the script is suggesting here: Good!Kirk, composed of only his compassion and intelligence, is rendered increasingly frail, indecisive and unfit for command without the moderating influence of Evil!Kirk. There is one scene near the end where the episode seems to be trying to push a Freudian interpretation where Good!Kirk is unable to decide between Spock's logic and McCoy's passion: A common reading of the Shatner/Nimoy/Kelley triple act is that they in fact represent the id, ego and superego. Especially as this follows McCoy and Spock's "intelligence" comments, one could read this scene as the divided superego (the twin Kirks) being unable to moderate between the id (McCoy) and the ego (Spock). Director Leo Penn seems to like this angle, as do the editors, who frame the shot cutting back and forth between Spock and McCoy with Good!Kirk caught in the middle unable to take a stand. DeForest Kelley seems to be in this camp as well, playing McCoy as bristling with unchecked passion, but neither Nimoy nor Shatner seem to be responding to this.

Shatner continually plays Good!Kirk as someone determined to prove his strength, though his strength lies in different areas. When he faces down Evil!Kirk in engineering, he manages to gain the upper hand merely by calmly standing his ground. Nimoy, on the other hand, seems to be playing up Spock's own duality trying to remain cool and logical even has he grows more and more commanding and forceful. Indeed, the script even gives Spock a line where he tells McCoy he knows from experience what it's like to live as two people at war and having to keep a handle on both (an oft-overlooked tack that is going to absolutely crucial to reading Spock as we go along). But at the same time this is the most passionate we've seen Spock yet as he desperately tries to keep control over the ship: The show is at the same time trying to push the Freudian reading as a multi-leveled recursive metaphor, but not everyone seems to be quite on the same page about it. Even if the Freudian theme were completely intentional and not misguided and reductive, it wouldn't really come across all that well anyway.

And then there's the rape angle. Evil!Kirk straight up tries to rape Janice Rand and the show handles it in just about the worst possible way imaginable. First off, we have the Pop Psychology 101 for Dummies ramifications of the scene, which pretty much forces us to conclude the script thinks male sexuality is fundamentally based around rape which, wow, I'll let you all hash that one out on your own. Then we have Rand telling Spock, McCoy and Good!Kirk that she "wouldn't even have reported it...but Fisher saw it too" and Holy Goddamn I don't even know where to begin with that. Even so though, even despite *all of this*, the show *almost* pulled it off by having the attempted rape be portrayed as an absolutely horrible, trust-shattering thing, but then it ruins all its goodwill by having Good!Kirk be primarily *confused* because *he was in his quarters the whole time and knew it wasn't him*. He doesn't get a *single scene* where he acts devastated that someone tried to rape Rand in his name or a *single line* expressing remorse or sadness for her. It's all about him and he's just *confused*.

And then there's the ending. Rand eventually finds out Evil!Kirk and Good!Kirk are two sides of the same person (having previously been told the white lie that Evil!Kirk was an imposter) and on the bridge she confronts the newly-rejoined Kirk. The two have an awkward moment where she *tries to apologise* and he *brushes her off*. Rand then delivers some schematics to Spock who *grins* and says "the 'imposter' had some interesting qualities, wouldn't you say, Yeoman?" and this is where I finally draw the line. There is absolutely no way I can redeem this. Absolutely no way I can discern any kind of positive, edifying analysis out of this. This is undistilled rape culture, no, rape *apologia* in all it's ugly glory. We've moved beyond merely *threatening* to derail the series to actually derailing it outright. There's no way up from this. *Star Trek*, in this incarnation, is finally and irreparably broken, and anything derived from it is going to be forever tainted.

Because, while the name on the script says Richard Matheson, this is *all* Gene Roddenberry. In her memoir *The Longest Trek: My Tour of the Galaxy*, Grace Lee Whitney express her disgust with this episode (thank god) and this scene in particular, writing:

> "I can't imagine any more cruel and insensitive comment a man (or Vulcan) could make to a woman who has just been through a sexual assault! But then, some men really do think that women want to be raped. So the writer of the script gives us a leering Mr. Spock who suggests that Yeoman Rand enjoyed being raped and found the evil Kirk attractive!"

Some fan lore tries to spare Matheson, speculating the scene at the end was tacked on by someone else, and if that's the case it's perfectly clear to me who that was. I have no doubt someone with Gene Roddenberry's conflicted, confused ideas about what femininity is and how gender roles work (and someone whose paws are in every script that goes out anyway) would put in a scene like this. But even if Roddenberry didn't write it, this episode still went out under his watch. As an executive producer, and a producer who was known for being especially anal, hands-on and controlling, Roddenberry could have, *and should have*, kept something like this from being filmed. But of course he wouldn't: He oversaw the bungled sexual politics of "The Cage" and "Where No Man Has Gone Before" and put out something as misogynistic as "Mudd's Women" and something as carelessly, needlessly reactionary as "Charlie X".

And the show is in a real sense tainted by this: I can't even fall back on the actors here, except Whitney I guess, as they all seem either perfectly fine with what's going on or, at worst, getting a little too into it. Shatner gives a strong performance, but none of his characters, even Good!Kirk, seem equitable with the person I saw and praised in "Where No Man Has Gone Before" and that's to nothing except the show's detriment. That Good!Kirk displays absolutely no empathy or remorse for Rand is inexcusable, and it's not helped by Shatner's Hitchcockian/Kubrickian method approach of slapping Whitney off-camera between takes to get her to sell the sickbay scene better. Nimoy's performance is good, but I'm probably never going to get over how he has Spock just *leer* at Rand: He sells it altogether *too well.* The best thing here by far is George Takei, who keeps Sulu in good spirits even as he's slowly freezing to death: It's a wonderful acting job that's as heartening and human as it is tragic and bittersweet. Shame he couldn't have done anything about the rest of the episode.

I've gone at great length in the past to stress that while *Star Trek* isn't the hopeful, idealistic, imagination-filled show I love it's slowly sewing the seeds that will allow the franchise to one day become that. But that future has never seemed further away then it does while watching "The Enemy Within" (although I should probably watch my words, as I previously said that about "Mudd's Women" and "The Corbomite Maneuver" and look what happened. You'd think I'dve learned by now). The show as it exists now isn't just not that future, it's working *actively contrary* to realising that future. With callous, ill-thought out morality plays supported by some of the most stilted and clumsily reactionary writing I've ever seen on a television show I'm not sure how I can even call this Star Trek. But that's the awful thing: It *is* Star Trek. If anything, it's the vision of the franchise I *like* that's the weird anomaly.

12. "Your emotions make you weak!": The Naked Time

An argument could be made that "The Naked Time" is the first "proper" *Star Trek* episode, at least to a certain number of fans. It's definitely the first truly memetic one: Everyone remembers Sulu fencing, Uhura's "sorry, neither" line (which is, admittedly, brilliant) Nurse Chapel professing her love for Spock and Spock's subsequent meltdown and Kirk's "I'll never lose you! Never!". I've even read reports of Trekkers going full *Rocky Horror Picture Show* on this episode when it's screened at conventions, hissing along with the PSI 2000 virus and cheering at appropriate intervals, although being a lonely shut-in who spends their time marathoning Star Trek and flailing desperately at a keyboard into the wee hours of the morning I wouldn't have any hands-on experience with that.

This episode was also Bob Justman's choice for the premier on the grounds that the reduced inhibitions brought upon by the disease would be a good introduction to the characters and their personalities. Justman has a point and I wouldn't be surprised if that was the thinking that went into making an unapologetic remake of "The Naked Time" the very first episode of *Star Trek: The Next Generation* twenty years later. There are issues with Justman's argument here I'll look at a little later, but I do agree with him in the broader sense that the strength of "The Naked Time" is in the fact it's an Actor Showcase Episode, which is a good thing to put near the beginning of a TV series. Before I get into that though, I want to square the plot away because, well, it has all the same problems every other *Star Trek* episode does. It's not as bad in this regard as something like "The Corbomite Maneuver", "Charlie X" or "The Enemy Within" so I don't need to go into the same level of detail as I did with those episodes, but it is worth mentioning if for no other reason then to point out how systemic a problem this has become for the show.

The PSI 2000 virus works by producing an effect similar to serious intoxication and strips the victim of all inhibitions. "The Naked Time" thinks this is absolutely disastrous. The *Enterprise* quite literally spirals out of control because the bridge crew can't keep their heads about them (a plot point telegraphed in the bluntest, most obvious manner known to mankind by Scott in the briefing room in the first act). It's clear the episode is treating this as another reiteration of the logic vs. emotions conflict (where "emotions" are conflated with "hedonism"), and given how upfront it's being about its symbolism we should take this as the definitive statement of *Star Trek*'s position on the matter, or at least that of *Star Trek* under Gene Roddenberry. While there was some room for debate when Spock touts the superiority of logic in something like "Where No Man Has Gone Before" or "The Corbomite Maneuver" because it's Spock and we're always meant to be at least a little

61

suspicious of him, there's really no other way to read the *Enterprise* screaming towards a fiery death because the crew can't control their emotional desires. Also, just for fun, count the number of times the word "irrational" is used in this episode, and keep in mind that there is a very strong Western patriarchal tradition of associating rationality and logic with men and irrationality and emotion with women and see where that leaves you.

In the "Mudd's Women" chapter I looked at the notion of sexuality as taboo and the subsequent fetishization of it in Western culture. "The Naked Time" has this in droves as well, most clearly observable in its really strange conception of romantic love. Kirk's attraction to Janice Rand, already broken beyond repair thanks to the appalling rape culture mess of "The Enemy Within", is once again framed in terms of a forbidden fruit because of his responsibilities to the *Enterprise* (which, taken on its own, is of course only problematic if you're thinking purely in military terms) and now we have the added metaphor of Spock's inner turmoil over his human desire to express his emotions conflicting with his Vulcan desire to repress them. Now it seems we have *Star Trek* equating romantic love with blunt sexual drive, which is not only laughably puritanical but also really confusing (albeit also very Roddenberry given his own personal struggles): If the show is trying to make a point other than that we need to suppress each and every one of our emotions and strive to be unfeeling automaton taskmasters I can't find it.

But the plot and ethics of "The Naked Time", eyeroll-inducing as they may be, are par for the course at this point. This episode also adds the troubling wrinkle of Joe Tormolen, whose "irrational" thoughts seem to be concern that humanity's unchecked expansion into space will damage or pollute it, which is a self-evidently valid thing to be worried about that the episode once again completely glosses over and disregards, but even that is still run of the mill Roddenberry Ethics. That said, this also ties into the other big thing to note about "The Naked Time", which is that it's an Actor Showcase, and it's a good one to boot. It's easy to see how this could become an instant fan favourite: It's an absolute riot watching the actors freed from any kind of constraints just allowed to completely run wild with their characters in ways they'd never typically be allowed to.

As much fun as it is seeing George Takei run around the hallways shirtless brandishing a rapier, the immediate standout has got to be Bruce Hyde as Kevin Thomas Riley. Hyde's performance is completely at odds with something that's supposed to reduce inhibitions: Far from "giving in to baser instincts" as the script tells us the PSI 2000 virus makes people do, Hyde has Riley put on a one man musical comedy act, hijacking the *Enterprise* through engineering, declaring himself captain, belting out "I'll Take You Home Again, Kathleen" throughout the entirety of the last two acts over the loudspeaker and giving everyone ice cream. It is absolutely glorious. Spock gets some tossed-off line how Riley's actions are the result of his "longstanding belief" that he's "descended from Irish kings", but this of course does not take at all: Riley's role in the story is to do nothing more or less than singlehandedly turn *Star Trek*, for a few beautiful, fleeting moments, into a Vaudeville routine and that alone makes this possibly the best episode in the series so far.

Though Hyde is amazing, this also segues into the episode's biggest problem (aside from its ethics, of course): A lot of people, Bob Justman included, praise "The Naked Time" for using its Actor Showcase structure to convey intimate details about the main characters (hence Justman's claim it would have made a good premier) and this isn't entirely true I feel. While it's fun to watch the cast act against type, "The Naked Time" is actually rather thin on character development. Let's look at what we learn about each main character through how they act under the influence of the virus: Sulu is apparently "at heart a swashbuckler", and while the episode was kind enough to telegraph this early on through his conversation with Riley about fencing, this is never actually brought up again in any subsequent episode (although his interest in small arms is briefly mentioned in "Shore Leave" and the Animated Series episode "The Slaver Weapon"). Even if it were, though, "enjoying fencing" is hardly a significant, intimate reveal about Sulu's personality.

Similarly, Riley's fascination with Irish royalty is only mentioned in an offhand comment by Spock to handwave away the aforementioned impromptu musical theatre performance: Riley never mentioned Ireland before or after and when next we see him it isn't even brought up at all (that *Star Trek* doesn't turn him into an excruciatingly awful and bigoted comedy stereotype like the last time an Irishman showed up is something of a miracle, however). Tormolen has his environmental concerns which were again mentioned at the outset, which was good, but he's dead so it doesn't matter. Kirk gets some painfully generic speech about the burdens and responsibilities of command which was stale and boring when Pike gave Doctor Price the exact same story in "The Cage". Everyone else just defaults to "act silly".

Really the only genuine moments of character drama we get here come from Spock, who I'll touch on in a minute, and Nurse Chapel, played by Majel Barrett, who makes her first appearance in this episode. Even though she didn't get the lead role originally written for her, of course Majel Barrett was going to show up on *Star Trek* once it went to series: She's just as inexorably linked to it as Gene Roddenberry is, and it makes sense for her to reappear in a Roddenberry-penned episode (once again, the name on the credits says John D.F. Black, who was also working as the show's story editor at the time, but apparently the script was completely rewritten by Roddenberry before going to air, who didn't even bother to consult or inform Black).

Chapel is the first character we see who actually does seem to be affected on a personal, emotional level as we learn she's in love with Spock and, shockingly, the show actually plays it like a serious, proper love scene: Chapel isn't lusting after or fantasizing about Spock like how every single other relationship on the show to date has been framed, she genuinely seems to love and care for him as a person (knowing that she was Gene Roddenberry's mistress at the time and that Roddenebrry projected onto Spock does make this scene considerably more uncomfortable, however). And, to her credit, Barrett sells it like an absolute pro, delivering a very sweet, caring, mature and affectionate performance that's probably her best bit of acting in the entire Original Series. Of course, the show does her no favours given that this is Chapel's first appearance and thus we've had absolutely no opportunities to see this side of her character meaningfully develop to the point where this scene could serve as an effective dramatic climax, but I'll take what I can get.

Leonard Nimoy is no slouch here either, and plays off of Barrett's tender confessions to absolutely brilliant effect, portraying Spock as at first recalcitrant and taciturn, then confused, and finally heartfelt, vulnerable and apologetic as he tries to express to Chapel his fear that he'll never be able to reciprocate and care for her the way she does him. And Barrett is once again magnificent, showing Chapel to be overwhelmingly compassionate and unwaveringly loyal. It's little wonder this scene is so well remembered and why there is such a strong contingent to pair up these characters. Actually, having seen both "The Naked Time" and its *Star Trek: The Next Generation* remake quite recently as of this writing, I have to wonder if Denise Crosby and LeVar Burton echoed and inverted this scene for their own private moment on the latter show. As great and iconic as this scene is however, I do leave it up to you all to draw your own conclusions about the significance behind Gene Roddenberry making all the female crewemembers (save Janice Rand) swoon over Spock and then giving him a love scene with his own lover and muse.

Of course Nimoy's best performance comes immediately after this as he breaks down in tears alone in the briefing room lamenting his inability to love others. It's by far the defining moment of the episode, sold even better by the absolutely brutal camerawork: We slowly follow Spock as he staggers out of sickbay into the briefing room, passing graffiti that says "Love Mankind". Then, once he sits down, the camera creeps around him, just wallowing in his breakdown. It's pure cinematic voyeurism, but it's effective. What's the most astounding thing about this scene is that none of it was scripted: The original plan for this scene was to have a *really* dumb comedy bit where someone draws a mustache on Spock. Nimoy felt he needed something more emotional (how ironic) and ad-libbed this entire sequence starting from where he leaves Chapel and ending when Kirk storms in and screams about antimatter implosions. Shatner's reaction here is a bit changeable; he doesn't seem sure of how he should respond to Nimoy's raw emotion. In the end he decides to have Kirk just flip the hell out and start whaling away at Spock to get him to snap out of it before Nimoy has Spock throw him backwards over the table. Shatner's performance is suitably histrionic and he rightfully devours half of the conference room in the process, but he really could have played off of Nimoy here a lot better: This exchange doesn't hold a candle to the one with Barrett.

But even so it was enough: This is Shatner and Nimoy's first real hyper-emotional scene together of the type they'll soon become famous for (the exchange in "Where No Man Has Gone Before" having clearly been written for Jeffrey Hunter's Pike and Barrett's Number One), and, pairing it with Barrett's show-stealing scene in sickbay it's easy to see how "The Naked Time" got a reputation for being a strong character drama even if they're in truth the only two real character moments in the episode. They're iconic, memorable moments that stick with people, and that's really all something like this needs to go down in history. That's the real strength of "The Naked Time" I feel: reconceptualise it as a collection of fun and giddy setpieces and these moments of tender character drama fit right in alongside Bruce Hyde's grandstanding and George Takei's rapier. I wouldn't call it the episode where we get to know the characters better, but I would call it the episode where *Star Trek* proves it can have fun once in awhile and stumbles onto the path towards becoming an evergreen pop phenomenon.

13. "But I remember his words as though they were yesterday.": Balance of Terror

Finally.

After weeks of stumbling half-starts, frustratingly retrograde moves and absolutely awe-inducing spectacles of catastrophic, system-wide failure, we at last have the very first episode of *Star Trek* that can be unambiguously called an absolute masterpiece. "Balance of Terror" is an unmitigated triumph on all accounts and is exactly what the series needed to make up for the misfires of the past few episodes. In a bit of actually lovely irony, this still doesn't save this incarnation of the show. Not only does it not save it, it gives even stronger evidence that it should be killed off and retooled as quickly as possible: Far from redeeming the *Star Trek* we've been watching since "The Corbomite Maneuver", everything that makes "Balance of Terror" work as well as it does is something that decisively proves Gene Roddenberry's original version of *Star Trek* is completely unworkable. We're nine episodes in and we already have the show's definitive deconstruction.

"Balance of Terror" is almost the inverse of "The Corbomite Maneuver": While that episode went out of its way to glorify militaristic bravado and the chain of command, this one shows us in stark, terrible detail the tragic consequences of this way of thinking at a very intimate, personal level. Where Balok was an unseen Other throughout the majority of "The Corbomite Maneuver" before being revealed as friendly baby Clint Howard at the last minute, half of "Balance of Terror" is dedicated to the Romulan crew. We get to know each and every person on the Bird-of-Prey personally, especially Mark Lenard's commander, and their tired, beaten down and world-weary demeanor bleakly, and all too well, foreshadows their ultimate fate.

Ah yes, the Romulans. A reveal so historic it threatens to overshadow the rest of the episode (though perhaps not as much so as that of the Klingons will to their debut episode later in the season). As one of the pre-eminent alien cultures in Star Trek, it would be beneficial to spend some time talking about them, although in this sentence I've already touched on the first important thing about them: The Romulans are a culture, and that's a significant milestone for the series. Up 'til now, aliens in *Star Trek* have been portrayed as blunt metaphors for the show's moral-of-the-week: The Talosians are an extension of the Platonic cave theme of "The Cage", Gary Mitchell was absolute power incarnate, Charlie Evans embodies the troubles of puberty and Salt Vampire was...a Salt Vampire. Or a buffalo. "The Man Trap" wasn't especially clear about that. Anyway, if they weren't straight metaphors, they were Deus Ex Machina: The Thasians exist primarily to provide a convenient way to get Charlie Evans off the *Enterprise* so he wouldn't blow it up. We don't get any sense of what their culture or lifestyle is. Balok is just an Other for Kirk to practice his manly command skills with, albeit one who happens to be friendly We get no idea of what the First Federation is like, though the design of the *Fesarius* is certainly imaginative.

But the Romulans are actual people, and within the span of one episode we learn pretty much everything we need to know about them. Firstly, and most obviously, the Romulans are the Roman Empire extrapolated into outer space. More to the point though, they're the Roman Empire past its pinnacle and entering into a decline: Though his crew seem eager to secure a Glorious Victory for their emperor, the commander himself seems from another age, openly questioning the value of imperialistic expansion, war for the sake of war and the cost in lives it demands. The Centurion sympathizes, but feels too bound by duty and tradition. The primary reason this works and the reason the Romulans are so memorable and easy-to-read is because the show gives us three different individuals (four if you count the subspace radio operator) and each one has a distinct personality: We see how the culture plays out across an actual group of people. What this means is that without really needing a bunch of exposition, "Balance of Terror" gives more depth and characterization to the Romulans than any episode of *Star Trek* has for its aliens-of-the-week before and, arguably, will after. There is absolutely no question why they get brought back.

But there's also another side to the Romulans' imperialism. "Balance of Terror" explicitly makes it clear the Romulan commander and Kirk are, for all intents and purposes, the same person and furthermore, that the Bird-of-Prey is just a reflection of *Enterprise*. There are numerous scenes where the two captains remark on how similar their thought process are (i.e. "that's what I would have done were I in his place"), how both are forced to work in dangerous, dehumanizing situations because they're at the behest of duty and circumstance and how neither desires to take the other's life because of how much they respect each other as equals.

The editing jumps back and forth between the *Enterprise* and the Bird-of-Prey, taking care to point out how each character has a compliment on the other side. The ensuing pointlessly destructive battle thus becomes a the reiteration of an ancient scenario two groups of likable people are forced to act out against their will that prevents them from moving on to greater, happier things. Arguably the most moving scene comes in Act 3 as the Bird-of-Prey attempts to hide itself in a comet's tail: The commander gets a lovely line where he remarks on the comet's beauty, "shining in the dark", before his crew presses him to explain its strategic merits. The majestic wonders of the universe must take a backseat to the mission. We're not explorers, we're conquerors, soldiers and policemen.

This is not an entirely original concept: Indeed, this episode is pretty much an exact shot-for-shot remake of the 1957 World War II movie *The Enemy Below* which concerned a US destroyer crew hunting down a German U-Boat (a fact which allegedly caused Harlan Ellison to flip out and refuse to speak to writer Paul Schneider). Certainly just taking a superficial look at both texts this seems obvious, and the Bird-of-Prey is a more than fitting stand in for a submarine with its small array of windows and cramped, self-contained bridge helping to craft an appealingly claustrophobic atmosphere. Indeed, it's the best bit of model work on *Star Trek* so far: With all due respect to legendary designer Matt Jeffries (and apologies to the generations of fans who will surely hunt me down for this remark), I never found the original *Enterprise* an especially inspiring bit of design. The *Fesarius* was provocative in a kind of Asimov Golden Age sense, but given how little of it we actually saw its effect is muted somewhat. The Bird-of-Prey is amazing though: Designer Wah Ming Chang gives us a truly evocative and iconic look, bringing together elements of raptors, rocket ships and flying saucers to produce something immediately distinctive and memorable.

But I'm going to make a bold claim here: "Balance of Terror" is actually a far more effective telling of this story than the movie on which it's based. Part of this is the acting; William Shatner, DeForest Kelley and Mark Lenard are all absolutely chilling, each one delivering what has got to be a career high water mark performance. But the bigger reason is the setting: In *The Enemy Below* the German U-Boat captain is shown to be in some sense "special" because he isn't a Nazi and is in fact quite hostile to Hitler's regime, he's just following orders and doing his job which makes him easier to compare with the destroyer captain. "Just following orders" has always been a flimsy excuse however (I seem to recall one future starship captain making a similar observation too...): The Romulans are culturally obligated to valorize duty and glorious conquest and the crew of the Bird-of-Prey are just products of their time. It's much easier to sympathize with them than it is a bunch of Nazis. Furthermore, *The Enemy Below* is historical fiction, and in my view, this is a genre with a very noticeable limit on how emotionally compelling it can be.

I've never found the fictionalized past effective as a setting because the cinematic tradition's pretenses of realism at once require us to take it seriously as a work of representationalism while at the same time accepting it's weaving a yarn. Also, as history books are inevitably written by the "victors" (i.e. authority and hegemony) works of fiction based on them almost always wind up with a glorification of master narratives that inevitably marginalize certain viewpoints. Like, say, for example, the idea that the Europeans were the bold discovers of the Americas and thus "exploration" becoming equated with "European colonialism" when pretty much all historical evidence points to the Polynesians being familiar with the shores centuries beforehand but not settling them because they were already inhabited and the fact the ancient navigators were more interested in free exchange of goods and ideas and weren't imperialist assholes.

But as speculative fiction "Balance of Terror" doesn't have any of these problems, and what this also does is really highlight the theme of reiteration: What, exactly, makes the Romulans so very different from us? Yes, they crossed the Neutral Zone and launched an unprovoked attack against the Earth Outposts, but Stiles was also chomping at the bit to cross into Romulan space and exact vengeance on them for the pain his family endured during the Romulan War and one could imagine an alternate scenario where Earth made the fist move. No, if the commander and Kirk are the same, as are the *Enterprise* and the Bird-of-Prey, then so are the Romulan Star Empire and Earth Command.

"Balance of Terror" distills its theme down to one or two basic points, and the fact it's conveyed through the metaphor of genre fiction frees it from the danger of misrepresenting history. Conversely, the argument could be made that it is far easier to do what I call "Issues" stories about social concerns like ethnocentrism when you're actually telling stories about the literal ethnic groups affected and marginalized by such prejudice. But the thing is, populist entertainment is very rarely written by members of those marginalized groups because hegemony and kyriarchy, and while that's to its detriment, here we are. It is, I would argue, preferable to have a simplified genre fiction story about oppression in the more general then to have master narratives reinforced by having social realism yarns spun about oppressed people by those selfsame privileged classes who oppress them. It is true, and we will frequently see as we go along, that genre fiction can go too far with this and is frequently as constrained by its metaphors as it is liberated by them. But "Balance of Terror", in my opinion, is an example of an instance where this works.

Schneider is making an impossibly strong claim here, because "Balance of Terror" is nothing if not a gravely serious treatise on imperialism in all its forms and the devastating cost it extorts from everyday people and a definitive claim that *Star Trek* is absolutely imperialistic. The episode just revels in showing us the ugly reality of military bravado: The very first scene has Kirk about to preside over a wedding and he gives a heartfelt speech about how one of his "happier duties" is officiating shipboard weddings. All of a sudden he's interrupted by Uhura, who informs him Outpost 4 is under attack. The tone shifts suddenly and dramatically like a switch has been flipped. We get a painfully graphic scene of the outpost's complete destruction, with its last survivor dying in brutal agony live on camera before the entire bridge crew. As the *Enterprise* trails the Bird-of-Prey it slowly dawns on the crew a battle is imminent and unavoidable and Kirk informs the crew that should the conflict break out into war, in the eyes of his superiors they, him and the ship are all considered expendable. The show plays this as a tragedy with the music swelling dramatically and various low-angle shots of Kirk which, combined with Shatner's wonderfully expressive acting that displays every single iota of his exaggerated pensiveness and guilt-wracked consciousness, makes Kirk look for all the world for a man walking to his death.

Once the two ships finally do engage, we don't get some glorious and thrilling action set-piece where the *Enterprise* and the Bird-of-Prey exchange a manly amount of firepower, we get an excruciatingly drawn out cat-and-mouse game where the ships take turns brutally crippling each other and maiming each others' crew. First the classic scene where the Romulans turn out to be an offshoot of the Vulcans, immediately casting doubt onto Spock's loyalty and bringing Stiles' generations of pent-up trauma and rage to the surface (which results in one of Kirk's best lines so far: "Leave any bigotry in your quarters. There's no room for it on the bridge.", a line that's as tossed-off as it is memorable). Then the *Enterprise* picks away at the Bird-of-Prey with proximity blasts, each one tearing into the ship and causing the bridge to visibly collapse around the commander with each successive charge, ultimately resulting in the death of the centurion. The Bird-of-Prey responds by unleashing its plasma weapon, capable of vaporizing entire planets in one shot, which also saps its own energy reserves. As the bridge crew watch helplessly while the plasma

13. "But I remember his words as though they were yesterday.": Balance of Terror

blast overtakes them, Kirk and Rand get what they expect to be their first, last and only moment of intimacy as they hold each other close, fully prepared to face death together. The *Enterprise* gets lucky: It's out of range enough that it doesn't get hit by the blast at full power and is merely rendered immobile with its electrical systems overloaded, but that just as easily might not have been the case.

On the Bird-of-Prey the situation is considerably more dire. With the ship in critical condition and his officers perishing one by one, leaving him the sole survivor of his ship as much as the doomed Command Hanson was the last left alive on Outpost 4, we can not only see, but *feel* the moment where the Romulan commander realises his mission is forfeit and, more to the point, that he'll never see the skies of his home again. Mark Lenard plays this with absolutely gut-wrenching conviction, depicting a person fully ready to take his death and those of his crew upon himself, but deeply saddened that he has to. And with that we get the horrifically tragic emotional climax-The single greatest line in the episode, arguably all of the Original Series. As Kirk contacts the Bird-of-Prey and asks for their terms of surrender, the commander politely turns him down and, just before he destroys himself and his ship in a nuclear explosion, looks Kirk dead in the eye and says:

"I regret that we meet in this way. You and I are of a kind. In a different reality,
I could have called you friend."

And then he's gone. The *Enterprise* has ended the battle and prevented another Romulan War, but Earth hasn't won anything. All this has accomplished is the deaths of four people who were no different from us: People just as motivated by a desire for peace, love and cooperation, but who, just like the crew of the *Enterprise*, were never allowed to find it in their lifetimes. And the cost on "our" side is no less devastating: In its closing moments "Balance of Terror" helpfully reminds us we began by interrupting a wedding as McCoy tells Kirk the only fatality among the *Enterprise* crew was Lieutenant Tomlinson in the phaser wing, who was supposed to get married today.

Kirk tries to console Angela Martine, Tomlinson's fiance by saying "It never makes any sense. We both have to know that there was a reason". Martine briskly tells Kirk she's "fine" and walks away. She's not convinced. We're not convinced. Neither is Kirk. There was no reason for this, for any of this: There was no reason for the Praetor to order the Bird-of-Prey to attack the outposts and violate the nonaggression pact, there was no reason for Earth to demand a swift militaristic response from the *Enterprise* and there was certainly no reason for people to sacrifice their lives in a bloody, messy conflict to prove nothing except why it's pointless to fight this way at all. It's far beyond the days where empire building was considered the norm, if indeed those days ever existed.

Rome is in decline: It's time we stopped looking to the city on the hill for guidance and instead looked to it as a monument for the tragic, failed and misguided aspirations of generations long since departed.

69

14. Rise of the Machines: What Are Little Girls Made Of?

Only *Star Trek* would have the gall to do the exact same goddamn story twice in the same month.

Of course, me having to deal with "What Are Little Girls Made Of?" here is mostly my fault, a result of me deciding to follow the show roughly in production order. This episode was filmed after "Balance of Terror" but aired long before, the latter show being pushed several weeks back such that it aired with material produced under the next showrunner. Really though this actually fits: "Balance of Terror" has far more in common with that crop of episodes than it does with this one, which is pure Gene Roddenberry, down to him doing a last minute hectic rewrite that actually ran contiguous with filming as he felt the script was unworkable. Of course you know where this is going: We follow up the greatest episode in the entire Original Series with a third-rate rehash of every second-rate, half-baked concept the show's done to date. Another logic versus emotions debate? Yup. An evil duplicate of Kirk who fools the crew? You got it. Theiss Titillation Theorem? This episode gives us the poster child! Sexism that ranges from the mild to the straight-up blunt? Of course. Loads and loads of Majel Barrett? Do you even have to ask?

We're not quite back into "The Enemy Within" territory of awfulness with this one, though there are several moments that come close. No, "What Are Little Girls Made Of?" just feels haggard, tired and spent, as if it's just halfheartedly going through the motions and re-covering old ground, which you might recognise as decidedly not the most healthy position for a show to be in ten episodes into its first season. So, not only do we have Roddenberry writing again, *we don't even get Roddenberry at the top of his game.* It's not entirely fair to lay this all at his feet, mind, as by all accounts Robert Bloch's original script was more or less unworkable, and one problem Star Trek will always have (in this form and in any other) is people not understanding how to write for it. Star Trek is and always has been a strange sort of science fiction, doubly so by television standards. That doesn't make episodes like this any more fun to watch.

The only remotely interesting thing "What Are Little Girls Made Of?" adds to the very, *very* well-worn territory of logic debates and "what makes us human?" musings comes through what can only be described as drunkenly stumbling into personal identity theory. The core ethical debate of the episode is whether or not the androids actually are human. Korby seems to think that if the androids can "pass" as human that's enough and in fact argues they are superior because they are infinitely reparable and have superhuman strength. The key moment comes when Korby reveals he has discovered how to essentially upload someone's consciousness into an android body, and that's akin to crafting a superior version of oneself. This actually falls into some basic intro level personal identity theory, namely, a classic puzzle that is often posed to undergrad philosophy students. The conundrum goes something like this: If you were in a devastating accident of some sort that rendered you either a paraplegic or on the verge of death, but your brain was undamaged, and the technology existed to transplant your brain into a new, healthy body such that this duplicate would have the same memories, experiences and experiential identity (that sense of being within your body and experiencing the world through it) you do, would that new person be you? This is in fact the exact scenario Korby faces in this episode.

This being *Star Trek*, the show naturally doesn't quite crack how to handle this. One possible solution to the problem, and one I'm inclined to agree with, is that no matter what your conception of the self, it actually doesn't matter whether the duplicate is "you" in the technical sense or not because the fact it has the same memories, personality and experiences things in the same manner you do means the duplicate is for all practical purposes you anyway and anything more is just tedious semantics. The larger issue is of course really that Personal Identity Theory, while the most interesting way to read "What Are Little Girls Made Of?", is not actually what the script wants to look at. Instead, it's written instead as a classic 1960s scare piece over "technology" replacing "men", which is really code for the mechanization of the work force and the changing landscape of the labour market in the latter half of the 20th century.

Kirk's primary objection seems to be that the androids, namely Andrea and Ruk, can be programmed, thus reducing them to unfeeling logic machines with no soul, which is really just another way of saying "machines will never be able to do the job a man can do because of reasons". But more strangely, this is actually at odds with what we've seen from Roddenberry so far, who seems to on the whole favour distant logic to passionate emotion: He literally fantasizes about being able to make decisions based on "rationality" with his judgment "unclouded by emotion". I think what we have here is a textbook example of how Roddenberry is constantly working though the various mutually contradictory elements of his worldview and trying to make a statement about it.The problem here, and sadly everywhere, is that he never actually finds one to articulate.

On top of that, the show can't even keep its own internal ethics straight. A big part of the climax involves Kirk "confusing" Andrea by displaying affection for her (alright, he does it by forcing himself on and sexually assaulting her) and pointing out to Ruk that he's acting out of vengeance, not orders to protect. This would seem to imply that the androids *are* in fact capable of human emotions and experiences, they just need to learn about them, so this invalidates basically *everybody's* arguments. Incidentally, if you can for the moment set aside the sexual assault (I know it's hard), this episode also marks the first appearance of the Captain Kirk School of Computer Repair, where the good captain causes a computer to explode by feeding it a childish and fallacious logical inconsistency, which displays such an elementary lack of knowledge about how computers work one does begin to wonder how *Star Trek* was sold as a sophisticated series aimed at the STEM crowd.

A saner objection for Kirk to raise might be concern that the androids have bodies that are built out of digital machines instead of being naturally occurring parts of the universe, but, as Captain Picard will one day point out, human bodies are still machines of a sort: We're just machines built out of biochemistry instead of positronics. No matter which way you argue, however, the fact remains "What Are Little Girls Made Of?" is hinging its core ethics debate on wildly fantastic speculative future technology that places it about as far away from saying something remotely contemporary or relevant as it is possible to be. From a purely philosophical perspective instead of a futurist one, personal identity theory is a fun thought experiment, and even as a criticism of mechanized labour this episode suffers from the classic genre fiction problem of making its metaphors too oblique to be of any real use. Furthermore, this won't be the last *Star Trek* episode to look at themes like this, and absolutely every one will be better than "What Are Little Girls Made Of?". Anyway, I'm personally far more interested in the lived experiences of real people, and this episode has none of that.

What it does have is some solid acting from Majel Barrett, who clearly appreciates finally having a part of some significance to work with. She's good enough at conveying Chapel's conflicted affections for Korby we almost overlook the fact Chapel's presence here makes absolutely no narrative sense. The script writes her, and Barrett plays her, as still very much in love with Korby and the denouement shockingly seems to imply Chapel was ready to abandon her post on the *Enterprise* to live with him. But the last time we saw Chapel she was confessing her love for Spock (who she seems to have no feelings for in this episode at all) and gave no indication she was dealing with being engaged to someone she hadn't seen in a decade. Once again, the show gives Barrett a highly emotional scene she sells quite well, but gives it absolutely no context, history, development or follow-up.

I do have to wonder how much of this is Gene Roddenberry's own Self creeping back into the narrative: At the time of production he was effectively living with Barrett and potentially also had residual feelings from a prior affair with Nichelle Nichols while also still married to his first wife Eileen. So, Nurse Chapel juggling multiple love affairs makes a somewhat sad amount of sense in that context. On that note though, it is more than a little suspect that the episode goes from this to having Chapel become immediately jealous and catty as soon as Andrea shows up (indeed, Korby even straight up says "I cannot love Andrea! There's no love there!" which is as hilariously on-the-nose as it is painful to watch). As for the rest of the cast, William Shatner has settled into a groove and is just doing his job at this point. His job is to be a gloriously over-the-top ham sandwich, but we expect that of him now. Everyone else is either absent or barely gets any screentime.

"What Are Little Girls Made Of?" is tough to get too angry about. It's bad, but it was probably always going to be bad given the hectic behind-the-scenes situation during filming. Stress and sloppiness are no excuse for the ethical missteps it makes, of course-if anything that's even more reason to condemn it. But it's honestly not as bad in these areas as Roddenberry has been in the past. More to the point, we're rapidly approaching the end of Roddenberry's tenure as showrunner of *Star Trek*, and while some of these problems never quite go away, nor does he, they'll at least very soon cease to be quite as central to how the show works (we'll have some new problems to worry about, but one thing at a time here). And, if nothing else, this episode does give us some more of the show's iconic moments: Andrea is one of the most memorable characters in the Original Series, as is the penis-shaped rock Kirk uses to attack Ruk. If I've learned anything about this show, it's that setpieces like this will live on far longer than any philosophical questions it raises, or indeed my pillorying it for not being up to my standards.

15. "We have an incredible ability to make people less than us": Dagger of the Mind

We began in a zoo and we end in an insane asylum.

While certainly not a finale in any traditional sense, "Dagger of the Mind" is an ending of sorts, being the last episode of *Star Trek* produced solely by Gene Roddenberry. who decided to essentially step down as showrunner after this episode was filmed. Contrary to popular belief, Roddenberry was only ever significantly involved in operating and managing Star Trek for these first eleven episodes. He was never really put in this exact position again, and his influence on all subsequent Star Trek is somewhat dialed back. This doesn't mean, I hasten to add, that he's not relevant to future Star Trek-He very much is, but the role he plays is a different one than that of a hands-on, day-to-day showrunner. Starting next episode, Roddenberry will slip into the part he's actually far more comfortable in: An honourary executive producer who supervises things from a distance and vets ideas. From here on out, the actual creative decisions are on the whole made by other people; Roddenberry preferring to only get actively involved occasionally and veto things every once in a while as he sees fit.

Since "Dagger of the Mind" arguably marks the end of Roddenberry's "purest" version of Star Trek (though I maintain the core work is and always will be nothing more and nothing less than "The Cage") it seems appropriate to use this chapter to look back on what, exactly, the Roddenberry Star Trek actually is. I've spent a great deal of time trying to piece that together in the preceding chapters, but this seems like the appropriate place to try and summarise and draw some conclusions. And it's fitting, as "Dagger of the Mind" is also one of the better executions of this structure: It doesn't redeem it, of course, at least not as a standalone text, (some combination of "The Corbomite Maneuver", "Mudd's Women", "The Enemy Within" and "Balance of Terror" has collectively shown that to be impossible) and it has unique problems all of its own, but it has a solid core concept worth engaging with.

Let's start with the plot first though, or rather the "moral": Every Roddenberry-produced episode of *Star Trek* has had some explicitly didactic lesson it's trying to teach. "Dagger of the Mind" wasn't penned by Roddenberry himself, nor was it even a script Roddenberry took off someone else and completely rewrote in their name without telling them, but it does have one and it's an interesting one. Moving closer to the more complex areas travelled by "Balance of Terror" and away from overly simplistic things like "absolute power corrupts absolutely" and "we must control our emotions", "Dagger of the Mind" takes a surprisingly candid, at least for the time, look at mental health facilities. Though the debate over ethical treatment of the mentally ill wasn't as open in 1966 as it is today, *One Flew Over The Cukoo's Nest* had already been published earlier in the decade so there must have been some. Also, two years after this episode aired, CBS would run an expose on Pennhurst State School and Hospital in Spring City, Pennsylvania revealing the mistreatment and abuse mental patients suffered in it and institutions like it, so *Star Trek* doing an episode like this isn't entirely unheard of.

The idea behind the Neural Neutralizer is, naturally, a suitably disquieting one: It works by forcibly making patients forget unacceptable thoughts, memories and behaviours and replaces them with ones considered sociable and proper. This is a great idea to base a dystopian thriller around, because it touches on one of the biggest demons of Western society: The concept of "normalization". Normalization is a word that gets bandied about a lot, and typically not without good reason, but it's also a word that does not mean what most people think it means. The pop interpretation of the phrase "to normalize" seems, at least to me, to be "to make normal", and while that's technically true it also misses the majority of the nuanced critique the phrase carries with it.

See, the concept of what is "normal" is a particularly marginalizing, and peculiarly Western, idea. In Western cultures, "the normal" is interpreted as "the mean", or "the average", often conveyed visually by the famous bell curve. It's also Scientistic, as those on either extreme are seen as outliers that can be disregarded (especially if you happen to be unfortunate enough to fall into the "below average" category of your normal curve of choice). When we say something like rape culture or any other form of institutionalized sexism or misogyny is being "normalized", we're not saying it's being glossed over and "made normal" when in truth it's not normal at all, we're saying the entire concept of "normal" is an artificial construct produced by the interaction of Western power structures that actively work to privilege some and exclude others unfairly and that this also works to disguise how unjust something like rape culture actually is.

The same is of course true for mental health issues: Those with certain mental conditions are seen as "abnormal" or "below average" and need to be "conditioned" and "acclimated" to function in "normal" society, even though no two people can seem to agree on what an "average", "normal" person is supposed to look like (and those who can are most likely operating from the privileged position of some power relationship, which, whether they are aware of it or not, means they're an authority with a vested interest in keeping that power structure exactly the same). In that regard making the primary threat of "Dagger of the Mind" an institutionalized mental health medical system that reshapes people with "suitable" and "acceptable" thoughts and personalities that people outside the institution either don't know about or think is "in their best interests" is brilliant.

The only problem is it doesn't quite go far enough. The show's main problem with the Neural Neutralizer seems to be that Doctor Abrams is basically cartoonishly evil and is using it to turn his patients into hypnotic slaves (which also brings me to the tangential point that this episode clearly has no idea how hypnosis works or that no hypnotist can actually make people do this sort of thing, but nobody in pop culture does either so singling

Star Trek out here seems a bit unfair). Thankfully, Helen Noel does get a number of good scenes when she and Kirk are experimenting with the machine and she denounces it on the grounds that the emotions and memories it leaves people with are false and artificial, but she doesn't enough lines in this vein and one can't help but wish writer Shimon Wincelberg (or Roddenberry) had followed up on this theme a little more.

Although I suppose that might be asking too much of genre fiction on primetime network television. That is, Star Trek.

Then we have the usual raft of Roddenberry-era concerns: Kirk and Spock seem altogether too shocked to find out Noel is a woman, she's by far the most gullible and obstinate person in the episode and it seems her fantasy is to be dramatically "swept off her feet" by Kirk, but compared to something like "Mudd's Women" and "The Enemy Within" this is peanuts. It also helps Noel is clearly a professional and nobody questions her credentials, competence and special expertise: Along with Uhura she's probably the best female character we've seen on the show so far and it's a shame we never see her again (as is the tacit implication that she's effectively Janice Rand with the serial numbers filed off). That aside though, there's relatively little for me to actually complain about here, which is a nice change of pace.

Which leaves me with trying to sum up Roddenberry's tenure and make some statement about *Star Trek* under him. Although my core argument remains in my chapter on "The Cage" and my biggest criticisms of Roddenberry have been outlined already (that his micromanaging causes problems for the franchise on more than one occasion is a thread that begins here, not ends here) "Dagger of the Mind" is a decent showcase of what the show's become over the past two years, for good and bad. The *Enterprise* shows up to deliver a solid, yet simplistic moral (though it's not as blunt and shallow at this as it has been in the past) and is very clearly part of some interstellar police force (Adams' line about how people like Kirk are "just as naked without a gun as we are without our medkits" is telling, as is the fact that, just as in "The Cage", the *Enterprise* is still running errands between Earth colonies). We have a noticeable amount of casual sexism, not outright misogyny, but things one wishes someone would have known better than to let through. We also have a *tremendous* amount of ham: William Shatner, of course, but also Morgan Woodward who plays Simon Van Gelder: He's so unbelievably crazed and over-the-top he apparently had to go home and recuperate for three days after filming wrapped. It's definitely a performance to see.

Then there's Leonard Nimoy as Spock, who delivers another wonderfully complex performance. This episode sees the debut of the famous Vulcan Mind Meld, and not only is it a delightful bit of mystical embellishment, the way the scene plays out is golden: It feels every bit as intimate and sacred as Nimoy says it is, and the way he and Woodward convey the shared minds effect is chillingly well done and actually quite lovely. It's Spock who has very easily asserted himself as the soul of the show by now: As fun to watch as Kirk is, everything that makes him memorable is solely due to William Shatner. Remove Shatner, and Kirk just becomes Jeffrey Hunter's Christopher Pike: A gruff, testosterone-charged military action hero.

But Spock's inner turmoil over balancing his Vulcan logic and human emotion seems like something Gene Roddenberry was fascinated by, especially given the fact Spock's role was originally intended for Majel Barrett's Number One. Perhaps counterintuitively though, this works better with Spock, not simply because Nimoy is sublime, but also because Number One was written from a place of ignorance about patriarchal hegemony: Had the role stayed with her, I very much believe this would have proven to be a distraction. Strange as it may seem, Spock allows for more interesting gender role fluidity: Setting Number One aside for a moment, it's worth bearing in mind the first person the very much symbolically sexual Mind Meld was used on was a man. Paradoxically, between William Shatner's camp and Leonard Nimoy's early, hesitant exploration of gendered issues *Star Trek* is indeed starting to pave the way towards a more open and liberated sexual discourse, but women are being left behind. It will be many, many more years before the franchise finally figures out how to bring them along. If ever.

Gene Roddenberry didn't give us a utopia or a series of ideals, at least he hasn't yet and won't by himself. What he's done instead is shown us some issues that were important to him and conveyed them in a way he felt would be exciting, entertaining and easy to swallow. His show betrays his positionality to an almost painfully obvious extent and he's not really an exceptionally good writer on the whole if we're being brutally honest, but his ideas aren't entirely misguided or unworkable either. The problem is literally every other aspect of the show aside from him is clawing at the walls, desperate to be allowed to grow into something bigger, grander and more beautiful. Roddenberry's own limitations, not only as a writer but in terms of his personality and experiences, are holding Star Trek back and keeping it from truly becoming great (or even consistently adequate for that matter). If anything is going to come of this, Roddenberry badly needs outside help. Thankfully, he's about to get it. It may turn out to be too little and too late for this particular show, but there's a way out of any cage and we'll find it in time.

16. "Listen to it...The sound of children playing...": Miri

OK, let's get this out of the way right off the bat: "Miri" is pretty terrible. Its central concept, while interesting, is basic and stretched far too thin, it's padded to the point whole dialog exchanges and entire scenes are repeated almost verbatim, its pacing is excruciating, it has behind-the-scenes problems that will culminate in Grace Lee Whitney getting fired and it has a someone who looks like a 15-year old falling in love with Captain Kirk (even if she does turn out to be over 300) and as a result this is an episode nobody is especially fond of. In spite of all that, however, it *is* a landmark moment in the history of Star Trek, because this is the first episode overseen by new producer and showrunner-in-all-but-name Gene Coon.

Coon is one of the great unsung heroes of Star Trek and probably the most criminally marginalized person in the entire history of the franchise. Coon's influence on *Star Trek*, or at least the *Star Trek* everyone likes to pretend existed, cannot be overstated: Not to put too fine a point on it, but if there's something you remember liking about the Original Series that didn't evolve in some way from "The Cage", chances are it was Coon's idea. The fact of the matter is the lion's share of the utopianism and progressive idealism *Star Trek* is so frequently praised for comes not from Gene Roddenberry, but from Gene Coon. I don't want to completely dismiss Roddenberry, mind: He and Coon seemed to generally work well together and one of Roddenberry's virtues was his willingness to listen to every idea and piece of constructive criticism people gave him. However, the problems come when people, especially Coon, would give Roddenberry particularly *good* ideas that caused him to see things in a totally new way and then Roddenberry would then turn around and claim it was his idea all along. This will prove to be a troublingly reoccurring motif.

But I'm getting ahead of myself. This is Coon's first episode (more or less-the show would have been working on more than one episode at once of course) and I'd like to take some time to try and tease out a little of how his style contrasts with Roddenberry's. Unfortunately, Coon is given a right turkey of a story to work with here so the show isn't doing him any favours right from the start, but even so there are signs things might just be starting to change. For one, this is the first time the *Enterprise* seems to be doing something other than running errands or law enforcement: It's not entirely clear what it was up to before receiving the distress signal, but the crew were clearly not on another mission beforehand. And on top of that, the whole teaser and first few scenes are absolute corkers: The *Enterprise* stumbles upon a planet that is inexplicably an exact clone of Earth (this is refreshing for the moment, but in just a few episodes it will promptly cease to be) and, once the away team beams down, it seems dead except for a group of disturbingly feral children who seem to haunt the town, always hidden just out of sight and chanting in warped versions of playground games.

These opening moments alone are filled with more ideas and imagination than the entirety of the series up to this point: There is a real, palpable sense of mystery as to the setting and, more to the point, for the first time the crew know no more about it than we do-The *Enterprise* isn't checking out an Earth colony, which, while operating in ways the audience isn't familiar with given it's a futuristic setting is still something the crew knows as it's part of their culture, this is a genuinely strange and unfamiliar world they have to learn the rules of along with us. Of course "Miri" scuttles all this halfway through Act 1 where we find out exactly what killed off all the adults and how to deal with it (and it never does explain why this planet is a clone of the Earth, besides the fact it means the show can save money by use the Paramount backlot that is) but even so this is still bolder and more creative than the show has ever been before.

These scenes are the first steps toward moving Star Trek away from being a show about running around policing people and telling them what to believe into one about going out, exploring and making contact with new people and new places. They're tentative steps in that direction, but they're clearly recognisable as steps regardless. If only the rest of the episode was as clever. The mystery is solved immediately, yet it for some reason takes Kirk, Spock and McCoy a tortuously long time to do anything about it. We still have Roddenberry-era gender politics as Miri gets catty and jealous of Rand (I suspect Rand is meant to feel the same, but Whitney does not come anywhere near close to selling it, although to be fair she had somewhat legitimate reasons not to. Still, seeing her acting deteriorate is sad). This is somewhat mitigated by Miri herself being an interesting and likable character, and she manages to work much better as an exploration of puberty than Charlie Evans was ever able to.

It's perhaps possible to read the Life Prolongation Disease as a metaphor for puberty's confusing nature, although I think Adrian Spies probably intended it more as a critique of the glorification of a kind of fairy tale interpretation of childhood and the fanciful desire some have to remain children forever (indeed Rand even gets a line espousing the charms of a permanent childhood, after which Kirk tells her she may want to rethink that). If this is the angle Spies was aiming for it's a laudable one: An unnatural romanticization of children is one of the Victorian era's defining cultural traits and has become a pillar of Westernism (and to an often detrimental extent) ever since. Indeed, the whole idea that children are by definition pure, innocent, honest, (necessarily) asexual beings who are special as they have been unsullied by the world's natural, sinful reality can be seen as an artificial Victorian construction based around a reductive interpretation of the New Testament, and Miri, both the character and the episode, are a sufficient refutation of this idea. Even Gene Roddenberry himself felt Westernism was due for a sexual revolution and re-evaluation, although he never did manage to separate his own biases and failings from his ideas of what that should look like.

Although Miri's blossoming sexuality is portrayed as a sign of her maturation, it's something the show unambiguously supports. Kirk at once encourages Miri to grow up, but is gravely concerned for her because he knows that's a death sentence on this planet, causing him to redouble his efforts to find a cure. And William Shatner is gangbusters at this, showing more compassion and love for Miri than he has at any other time for any other character on the show before now. I'm sure he was helped by being a father himself and having two of his own three daughters on set as extras on this episode, and his performance is as heartfelt and beautiful as it is hyper-caricatured and scenery devouring. Of course, this episode runs smack into some more uncomfortable Freudian implications by having Miri be attracted to Kirk, but at least Shatner has the decency to portray Kirk's love as purely platonic surrogate parental concern. I also really appreciate how Kirk's affection for Miri contrasts so perfectly with his awkwardness in dealing with Charlie Evans in "Charlie X": It seems clear Kirk is much more comfortable taking on this role with women than with men, thus implying he's more of a friend to female culture. This is the most feminist Kirk has been since his first appearance.

But the frustrating thing is this still isn't enough. The script doesn't go anywhere with this idea, or any of these ideas for that matter, bewilderingly thinking the most interesting aspect of the story is watching Kirk, Spock and McCoy kill time in a bombed-out doctor's office waiting for the plot to progress to the point where they're allowed to discover the vaccine. Coming from a modern perspective, it's also really tempting to hope for Kirk, Rand and McCoy to serve as representatives of some sort of idealized, leftist uptopian version of adulthood for Miri to aspire towards, especially in contrast to the deranged monsters adults become on her planet. But the episode is sadly not designed to do this, in no small part due to the fact we're still a ways off from the point where the *Enterprise* crew can first actually conceivably be called ideals. There are a ton of really intriguing ideas worth pursuing here, but the episode follows through on exactly none of them: All we're left with are half-formed thoughts and glimpses of meaning. As an actual piece of television "Miri" is just a mess of potentialities and implications and doesn't have any desire to pick up any of the threads it leaves strewn about on the floor.

Nevertheless, the fact we can have this kind of discussion about the show's ethics, even if they don't work, is strong evidence something is different now. It doesn't really matter, in this regard, that Adrian Spies never wrote for *Star Trek* again thanks to Roddenberry finding this episode below-par: Gene Coon's fingerprints on it indicate his version of the show is promising and something it might be worthwhile for us to follow. Coon took a script that really wasn't going to work all that well and injected it with a genuine sense of mystery and imagination, not to mention has begun cleaning up the show's philosophy to be something a bit more nuanced and radical. Right now it looks like bringing him on was one of the best moves *Star Trek* has made to date. Now all that remains is to see where else Gene Coon will take it.

17. "And you claim these words as your own": The Conscience of the King

A flash of a dagger, and someone lies dead. The guilt-wracked murderer wonders if all the oceans could wash the blood from his hands. Not long afterward we learn the slain person was King Duncan and we're watching a performance of *Macbeth*. But then the camera cuts to a Shakespearean actor dressed in a bright yellow jumper commenting on the performance while the man next to him rambles on about somebody named Kodos the Executioner. Somehow this is supposed to be a science fiction show, somehow this is supposed to be *Star Trek*. But it is in truth another play.

This is an episode about performativity-It's about people playing roles and how the kinds of roles we play change throughout our lives and how each role only reveals a snapshot of one facet of a person at one point in time. That's the thing nobody in the story manages to understand, however: Kirk wants to extract justice; he wants to be able to prove Anton Karidian is *really* Kodos under an alias. By contrast, Lenore is hoping to erase all historical trace of Kodos by killing off those who had seen him, thus forcing people to see her father as Anton forever and always.

But the truth of the matter is the Actor is *both* Anton and Kodos. One is not more real than another, they're just two different roles the same man has played at two different points in time. As characters are by definition more flat that real people, each role can only reflect one specific aspect of his personality, and even then they can only reflect how they exist at the specific time the Actor is playing that particular role. As Kodos, he made the decisions he thought were justified when he was ruler of Tarsus IV. As Anton his worldview has changed and regrets the actions he took as Kodos and hopes to move beyond them. Despite what Kirk and Lenore want, he can't be only one for them. He has to be everything at once. Incidentally, this is as good as the show has ever been at depicting human nuance and complexity: There are no more White Hats and Black Hats here, only people trying to make the best choices they can in the present moment, and that makes it an astonishing watershed.

The theatrical theme is everywhere in "The Conscience of the King", and an argument could be made it's almost too heavy-handed: There's the title, a straight-up reference to *Hamlet*, which is the same play the Karidian Players wind up performing for the *Enterprise* crew. The teaser sequence with the *Macbeth* show is just about the most obvious bit of foreshadowing Barry Trivers could have come up with, and Lenore speaking almost entirely in Shakespeare quotes and allusions makes General Chang in *Star Trek VI: The Undiscovered Country* look subtle and understated. Indeed, the entire episode itself bears

81

some pretty overt similarities to *Hamlet*, featuring a guilt-ridden leader, his mad daughter and the exposure of his past during a stage show. But the story has a bit more going on here than might be immediately obvious, I feel: "The Conscience of the King" doesn't just reference *Hamlet*, by its very nature it's technically a performance of it. This is Barry Trivers' and Gene Coon's adaptation of *Hamlet* in a *Star Trek* context, and it's playing with the tropes of theatre in an attempt to explore the show's performativity through recursive metaphor. Nor matter how you look at it, that's a pretty damn clever, and bold, move for their first and second scripts, respectively.

This has quite a few really interesting ramifications, the first of which is that this is the absolutely perfect environment for William Shatner. As a Shakespearean actor himself, he's able to bridge the gap between the diegetic and extradiegetic plays, something which Shatner duly and exquisitely commits himself to. Kirk, like the Actor, is explicitly a Shakespeare character here, and in a world where we know Nicholas Meyer's *Star Trek* exists, it's difficult to understand how utterly weird this would have been in 1966. There is absolutely nothing in Gene Roddenberry's *Star Trek*, or indeed what we've seen of Coon's so far, that would give anyone the impression Shakespearean drama is something the show should be doing. But here it is, and this marks another real turning point for the franchise: Coon has made a fairly decisive move toward shifting what *Star Trek* is about.

We're still zipping about on space patrol (and indeed Kirk even uses that word in this episode), but what's different now is how that's depicted. Roddenberry tends to play the premise extremely straight, which is most clearly noticeable in "The Cage": He really, genuinely wants us to take this show about the Space Air Force bopping about and teaching people about Right and Wrong seriously. But with "The Conscience of the King", Coon is treating *Star Trek* as a staged theatrical drama. That's not to say Coon is poking fun at the show, but he does seem to be depicting it as a kind of nested artifice that everyone involved is at least partially aware of. Put another way, where previously we had Shatner, a campy RSC actor, queering up a tight-laced Hollywood version of science fiction, we now have under Coon Shatner the RSC actor starring in a *play* about science fiction concepts that's starting to become aware of its performativity, boundaries and limitations. And naturally we introduce this with the gravitas of Shakespeare, who was known in part for his grandiose historical epics about war, tragedy and the human condition. "The Conscience of the King" is far from the definitive statement on this of course; it's at times tentative and clunky, but the existence of episodes like this is what's going to allow Star Trek to eventually become what people like Nicholas Meyer crafts it into.

This episode also happens to be Ronald D. Moore's favourite episode of the Original Series. Moore is going to become an extremely important creative figure once we reach the 1980s, serving as a kind of combination of head writer and script editor during Michael Piller's tenure on *Star Trek: The Next Generation* before going on to become supervising producer under Ira Steven Behr during the Dominion War era of Star Trek in the 1990s and eventually becoming the creator of and showrunner for the 2003 remake of *Battlestar Galactica* and HBO's television adaptation of the Outlander series. We'll return to Moore when it's his time, but given this is his favourite episode I figured it'd be a good idea to see what he has to say about it:

> "I liked the backstory of Kirk as a young man caught up in a revolution and the nightmarish slaughter by Governor Kodos. I liked the Shakespearean overtones to the episode as well as the use of the plays themselves. And I absolutely loved Kirk in this episode – a troubled man haunted by the shadows of the past, a man willing to lure Karidian to his ship under false pretenses, willing to do one of his more cold-blooded seductions on Lenore, willing to fight with his two closest friends, and risk his entire command in the name of justice. Or was it vengeance? Kirk's aware of his own lack of objectivity, his own flaws to be in this hunt for a killer, but he cannot push the burden away and refuses pull back from his quest to track down Kodos no matter what the cost. It also has some of my favorite lines in TOS. The scene with Spock and McCoy in Kirk's quarters is one of the series' highlights. The brooding tone and the morally ambiguous nature of the drama fascinated me and definitely influenced my thinking as to what Trek could and should be all about."

I'm going to come right out and say that while I respect Moore, I'm going to eventually become basically his staunchest, harshest and loudest critic, and his analysis of this episode is a good summary of how our perspectives differ. Moore focuses a lot on Kirk's inner turmoil and the darkness he keeps buried. He loves the idea that a basically good man would go to such lengths in this kind of situation. What Moore likes, especially later on in his career, is to see how far he can push characters, and in particular characters who represent ordinary, mundane people, before they break. When I look at the theatrical symbolism of "The Conscience of the King", by contrast, I'm immediately drawn to its more subtle oversignification and the fact this pushes Star Trek closer to metafiction. I tend to gravitate more towards ideas, symbols, and ideals. This will be a theme we will keep having to return to.

In terms of "The Conscience of the King", taken on its own it isn't always as successful as one perhaps wishes it could be. I personally would have enjoyed a more overt connection between the recursive plays: Approaching it from the sort of perspective I do it's hard not to wish for some really creative video editing flourish that explodes the show outward and the theatrical trappings are typically used more as blunt symbols and similes then a recursive meta-narrative. This isn't exactly magick through image poetry here, and while that's a little disappointing, it's also silly to expect *Star Trek* of all shows to be taking up the mantle of the avant-garde: For 1966 this is more than sufficient. To top it off we finally get the chance to revisit to the scathing critique the show delivered itself in "Balance of Terror"-Lenore explicitly calls Kirk Caesar here. Granted, this is partially because she was hoping to play Brutus, but the indictment of Kirk, and thus *Star Trek*, as an empire builder is definitely there as well and it still stands.

Probably the biggest weakness of this episode though is the handling of the supporting cast. Bruce Hyde is back as Kevin Thomas Riley, but in name only. Hyde auditioned for the part of Lieutenant Robert Daikan, the only other surviving person to have seen

Kodos' face and thus fueled by vengeance over the death of his family. When the producers realised he had already been in *Star Trek*, they renamed the character at the last second. Hyde is delivers a predictably rousing performance, but it's not at all in keeping with the person we saw in "The Naked Time". Spock and McCoy are put in the curious position of being shafted by the story despite having major roles in it: Leonard Nimoy and DeForest Kelley are very strong as always, but their primary role here is to watch out for and be supportive of Kirk and keep him grounded. It's exactly what we expect them to do, but that's actually the problem-Nimoy and Kelley don't seem to have gotten the memo and feel like they're still stuck on the old show. Compared to Hyde, Shatner, Arnold Moss (the Actor) and Barbara Anderson (Lenore), who are very obviously relishing the chance to do a Shakespearean Space Epic and just running wild with it, Nimoy and Kelley feel a bit too, well, *Star Trek*. That said, I do agree with Moore that the scene in Kirk's quarters is exceptionally well done and a sign of things to come.

Then there's the issue of Grace Lee Whitney, or, to be more precise, the conspicuous absence of Grace Lee Whitney, who appears in one scene as an extra on the bridge and then never again. By the way, that's also her last scene in *Star Trek*, making her the first proper character to be written out. Or actually no, she's not written out. She's unceremoniously dropped from the show and then promptly forgotten about, which can't really be seen as anything other than an insult to someone who was supposed to be playing a main character. What makes this all the more infuriating is there was apparently a time Whitney was pegged as the third star after Shatner and Nimoy, and Roddenberry conceived of Janice Rand as someone who Kirk would come to see as a trusted advisor. But one of Desilu's first decisions was to drop Rand because they wanted Kirk to have a new love interest every week, a decision made easier by Whitney's unfortunate drug and alcohol addiction issues (which were of course made significantly worse by her being sexually abused by two members of the production team two days before she was fired).

Although the franchise finally attempts to make reparations to Whitney by making Rand a reoccurring character (extra) in the Original Series movies (long, *long* after the point at which that would have been needed) this situation without doubt has to go down as one of the blackest marks in the history of Star Trek. While Whitney is far from the only person who's going to be royally screwed by the show (she's not even, depressingly, the only woman who was told she was going to be one of the show's stars to be put in this position) I have a hard time coming up with someone who actually got screwed *worse*. And it's even more of a shame because it sullies what is otherwise one of the very best episodes the show has done yet. Star Trek has come a long way, but it's still not safe or stable, and it's still a very long way from being something we can enjoy with a clear conscience.

And with that the curtain closes. The play is over and we've taken our bows. Time for me to become someone else again.

18. "I cannot–Yet I must! How do you calculate that?": The Galileo Seven

The key thing to note, I feel, about the second third of the Original Series' first season is that it can in many ways be read as a systematic attempt to reconceptualise the show by redefining the kind and broadening the scope of stories the show can do. Gene Roddenberry had a fairly straightforward pitch for the show: *Gulliver's Travels* In Space by way of *The Lieutenant*. Gene Coon, by contrast has from the beginning set about making overtures to change this, and this will eventually culminate in his two most memorable and defining episodes at the back end of the year. For the time being we still have the setting we inherited from Roddenberry, but Coon is starting to tweak and refine it a little and "The Galileo Seven" takes some of the most clear and obvious steps forward we've seen yet.

Following up on the implications of the teaser and opening act of "Miri", we have the *Enterprise* going out of its way to investigate a quasar phenomenon for purely scientific reasons, Kirk claiming he has standing orders to do so whenever he has the opportunity to. This seems like an unusual thing for Earth Command to take an interest in, as it certainly falls outside the jurisdiction of interplanetary patrol and law enforcement. Indeed, this is actually literalized in the narrative, at least from the bridge crew's point of view, as the *Enterprise* is torn between first investigating the quasar, then rescuing the crashed shuttlecraft, and getting the supply of vaccinations to Makus III on time. Although this plot point obviously exists primarily to give the episode dramatic tension, it is also a clear move away from the sorts of things the show was doing less than a month ago.

While "The Galileo Seven" doesn't take the exploration theme any further, the main thrust of the plot, the marooned science crew and Spock's attempts to command from a purely logical perspective, is new territory for the show in its own way. This episode marks the first real time *Star Trek* has attempted a story where proper character development is the primary driving force. Under Roddenberry we frequently had episodes dealing with main character's emotions and relationships, but the very structure of the show forced them to be extremely superficial and disposable: Kirk's friendship with Gary Mitchell in "Where No Man Has Gone Before" is there purely for drama and is never followed up on. The same is also true of McCoy's history with Nancy Crater in "The Man Trap", and while that episode did play with soap opera tropes, with the exception of Rand and Sulu all of those moments were between random extras, most of whom get death-suckered by Salt Vampire not long after they showed up. Plus, Rand's gone now so in hindsight the effectiveness of that scene is dampened.

In this episode, however, the interpersonal conflicts and connections between characters are central to how the whole story works: The entire plot hinges on the fact Spock is determined to handle the situation with disaffected logic as he feels it is the self-evidently correct way to run a command, and the specific situation he's in forces him to see the limitations of his philosophy because not everything in the universe operates according to logical principles. This puts him at immediate odds with McCoy and Boma and is directly responsible for the deaths of Gaetano and Laitmer as well as the attack from the Tauren natives (and incidentally imagine for a moment how horrific these scenes would have been had this been Number One instead of Spock). While it's true this is yet another iteration of the logic versus emotions theme, this episode handles it with more complexity and nuance than we've seen in the past. There's a genuine debate going on here-While Spock's choices do cause measurable harm to the team, he's also very clearly the best person suited to being in command and it's his leadership that eventually helps pull them through. Furthermore, the episode is explicitly *about* this debate: There's no moral to be told and no lawbreaker to be perpetrated, "The Galileo Seven" is entirely about how Spock deals with a crisis situation and how his friends and co-workers respond to that.

It's the addition of the word "friends" to the end of that last paragraph that's another way this episode expands *Star Trek*: There's a sense of friendship and camaraderie here for the first time. We got hints of this in things as early as "The Man Trap", but "The Galileo Seven" is really the first time we've seen the show embrace it as an important part of what it is. Kirk comes right out and states that he refuses to abandon the search even when things look hopeless not only because he doesn't want to feel responsible for seven deaths, but because the people in the survey team are his friends. Similarly, even when Spock pushes McCoy to the point of explosion, he remains more exasperated and frustrated than offended. DeForest Kelley's inimitable believability and humanness sells this perfectly, and we really do get the sense from him that McCoy understands Spock and can read him like a book. In the past, the main characters, especially Kirk, Spock and McCoy, were mostly there to articulate sides in a debate, hence the popular interpretation of them as standing in for the id, ego and superego, but here they seem more like actual characters for the first time. This is very much to the show's benefit and it's all Coon, as it comes naturally right out of Kirk's compassion for Miri and Spock's and McCoy's concern for Kirk in "The Conscience of the King".

If there's one criticism to be had of this episode, it's that the version of Spock the story seems written for occasionally comes across as a different one than the version of Spock Leonard Nimoy actually seems to want to be playing. The central conflict relies in some sense on Spock operating like an unfeeling logic machine and this alienating his shipmates to the point of open hostility. But ever since at least "The Naked Time", it's been clear that Spock isn't a purely logical automaton, but someone defined by his internal turmoil brought upon by his mixed Vulcan and human ancestry. Whether or not Spock's climactic choice to jettison the *Galileo*'s fuel supply is to be seen as an "act of desperation" as McCoy and Kirk read it or a logical option to take when all others have been exhausted (I personally think a compelling case could be made for either), every other move Spock makes is one of discreet logic, down to his "overflow error" brought upon by realising his logical decisions have resulted in the deaths of two people and the ire of the Taurens.

But to his credit Nimoy's not exactly playing the character that way. He infuses Spock's orders with a fundamental tension and stress, most noticeable when he snaps at Boma and Gaetano about their desire to hunt down the Taurens and his smug statement to them later on that "Fortunately, I am in command". It's clear McCoy is right and that Spock is eager to use this mission as an opportunity to prove perhaps not his own natural superiority in making command decisions, but that of logic as a guiding principle, and that he's getting progressively more irritated when it doesn't work out for him. Certainly there's some of this to be found in the script as well; the denouement can't really be seen as anything less than the show flatly telling us Spock was wrong and this episode was rewritten by Shimon Wincelberg, who has already shown himself to be good at injecting *Star Trek* with some much-needed complexity, but I still get the sense that the original idea here was a straight logic versus intuition conflict. However, with some probable fine-tuning from people like Coon, Wincelberg and especially Kelley and Nimoy, it becomes a character study of a sort about Spock, and the first such story proper in all of Star Trek.

Elsewhere "The Galileo Seven" demonstrates further growth in other areas. Kirk's linking narration in this episode is some of the most pensive, dramatic and poetic dialogue he's been given yet, and William Shatner sinks his teeth right into it:

> "Captain's Log, stardate 2821.7. The electromagnetic phenomenon known as Murasaki 312 whirls like some angry blight in space. A depressive reminder that seven of our shipmates still have not been heard from. Equally bad, the effect has rendered our normal searching systems useless. Without them we are blind, and almost helpless."

> "Captain's Log, stardate 2822.3. We continue to search. But I find it more difficult each moment to ward off a sense of utter futility, and... great loss."

Shatner's portrayal of Kirk here is one of my favourites in the series so far, building off of the Shakespearean gravitas established in "The Conscience of the King" and depicting his overstated, unwavering resolve to find the crew of the *Galileo* any way he can. The scene on the bridge at the end is also something really special: After McCoy catches him up on what happened on Taurus, Kirk actually teases Spock about making an impulsive, emotional move, after which Spock agrees he's stubborn and everyone laughs the show to fadeout. It's a charming scene, and something that absolutely could not have been done before now. Pike would never do something like that, and his crew didn't feel at all close enough to joke around in this way. The laughter itself is consciously overstated and overacted, almost to the point of feeling insincere, but it fits with the show's newfound theatrical bombast perfectly.

Also stellar in this episode is, actually, Nichelle Nichols, who gets more to do as Uhura here then she's ever had before. It's wonderful that without Spock, McCoy or Scott around Kirk turns to her as his trusted second in command, as Uhura is seen doing double duty as both her regular post as communications officer and filling in the science station in Spock's absence. The scenes where Kirk asks her for updates on the sensor and transporter issues are lovely, as Nichols plays Uhura deeply empathetic with Kirk's pain and his frustration at being unable to take any real action, and it's clear her presence is a comfort to him. There's more friendship, loyalty and support between Kirk and Uhura in these brief vignettes than there were in eleven episodes between Kirk and Rand. This is Coon's *Star Trek* taking a clear stand, as is the character of Boma, who, despite, becoming one of the biggest sources of the episode's conflict, is portrayed as being unchangeably honourable, competent and loyal. Star Trek is never going to be truly great at representation and diversity, but the seeds of a myth narrative that can be evoked for diversity are being sewn here.

"The Galileo Seven" isn't perfect, but it's easy to see why it became an early fan favourite. We've had more noticeable steps toward improving the show and making it work on a regular basis in the past two episodes then we have in the entirety of the previous eleven. There's no way even a few weeks ago we could have predicted *Star Trek* was going to be able to do Shakespearean drama or character studies. That said, while Gene Coon and his staff have made great leaps in improving *Star Trek*'s progressiveness already, some worrying aspects do still remain, mostly in regards to the show's inherent militarism and fixation on the chain of command. While the show may be a far friendlier place to women and nonwhite people now, this is going to be the biggest challenge it's going to have to overcome. It seems Coon knew this, however, because his next few episodes tackle these issues head on.

19. "The penal code! The penal code!": Court Martial

If "Miri", "The Conscience of the King" and "The Galileo Seven" were about pushing the boundaries of what *Star Trek* was and could do, than "Court Martial" is about taking a long, hard look at what the show was originally conceived of being and the implications of that central concept and running with it to its logical limit.

This isn't like "Balance of Terror", which was about firmly putting its foot down and loudly, overtly protesting the show's militaristic roots (not that there was anything wrong with that): Instead, "Court Martial" feels like Gene Coon and his team doing a lot of introspection and putting a lot of thought into what a show about the Space Air Force (or indeed the Space Navy, which seems to be increasingly the more accurate description, especially in this episode) would actually be about and what the world of that show might look like. This likely wasn't the original intent, given as this story's genesis came about by Coon approaching writer Don M. Mankiewicz to come up with a money-saving script that could be filmed with one new set. The extent to which this was successful can be easily deduced by observing that this episode features four new sets, a slew of new uniforms, some new matte paintings and the fact the next episode is a two-part clip show.

While it fails rather spectacularly at being a bottle show, "Court Martial" is a significant episode in several other regards, in particular, it's a canon compiler's dream as it introduces numerous new world building elements that will quickly become beloved parts of the "Star Trek Universe". Most important of these from a modern perspective has got to be the debut of Starfleet and Starfleet Command. This is, to understate things considerably, the single most important development in the series so far from the perspective of the future, and indeed it's so titanic a moment there's only one more that can top it (but we have to wait a bit longer for that). For the first time we have an actual name for the service the *Enterprise* is a part of and that of the body that governs it. It may seem surprising to those who haven't seen *Star Trek* in awhile, but this is the first time anything resembling the word "Starfleet" has been mentioned in the show, two years and 14 weeks in. Previously we'd occasionally heard references to Earth or an Earth Command, but with the introduction of the phrases "Starfleet Command" and "United Star Ship", *Star Trek* has expanded its scope considerably.

Although primarily a nomenclature change, this does alter the way we look at the world of *Star Trek* a bit. In the past the *Enterprise* seemed to have been representing the interests of some kind of colonial power based on Earth. While that reading is still possible, this new terminology encourages a more nuanced and complex way of interpreting the version of the galaxy this show takes place in-This is also helped by having the entire episode basically be devoted to world building, showing exactly the way Starfleet's chain of command and and governmental organisation works. We have a Commodore, who is a retired starship captain, operating a planetary starbase designed for resupplying and refitting passing ships, we have a legal system in place that holds officers accountable for their actions and a bureaucracy supervising all of it. It's very clearly an extension of the United States naval tradition into outer space, and it's a perfectly logical extrapolation of the setting Gene Roddenberry put in place, except far more detailed and sophisticated than he'd made it up 'til now.

That said it's worth keeping in mind we're operating from hindsight here. We know what Starfleet becomes so it's easy to latch onto this as "the way it was supposed to be from the beginning", but remember *Star Trek* has a noticeable lack of consistency and continuity at this point. It would been just as easy for a viewer in 1967 to figure all of these fancy world trappings would be tossed out the next episode. After all, that's the way the show's operated before now, and there's no reason to suspect it won't continue to do so. That Coon doesn't throw this out, retains these parts of the setting and indeed continues to expand upon them is a direct cause of one of the primary things that made *Star Trek* so evergreen: Its recgonisable continuity and familiar ritualized set pieces and iconography. That said, what this all ultimately comes down to for right now is that no matter how exciting the reveal of Starfleet Command might be for us, at the moment there's no reason to believe it's anything more than the new name for the Space Naval Service, and that's exactly how "Court Martial" treats it.

In that regard, making "Court Martial" a legal drama is an incredibly sensible idea. If you're going to do an episode about a lot of world building involving bureaucracy and military service, it only follows you'd want to tell a story about a court martial so you can show how that all works together. It's about as far away as you can get from Exploring Strange New Worlds or, for that matter, *Gulliver's Travels* in space, but it's a perfectly reasonable thing to expect a show about the Space Air Force or the Space Navy to do. The only problem is "Court Martial" isn't an especially *good* legal drama: It's utterly in love with its own jargon, protocol and procedures which, again, makes sense, but there's isn't much actual *drama* *per se* to be had here. We know right from the beginning Kirk is innocent: He has to be, he's an established character and straightforwardly the series' hero, kicking him off the show 13 episodes into the first season would be actually insane.

This would be alright if the episode was about how Kirk proves his innocence against almost insurmountable odds, and while the show does hint at this direction it never really gets there. Establishing Shaw as Kirk's ex-lover and also the prosecutor is an easy way to drum up tension in theory, but all it does in practice is to further cement Kirk's innocence because she very obviously doesn't believe in her case even if she's good at arguing it (not to mention the *blatantly obvious* conflict of interest which realistically should have seen the whole case summarily thrown out). The episode further tries to go this route by having the primary evidence about Kirk be the supposedly "infallible" automatic ship's record and giving him Cogley as his defense attorney, a man defined almost exclusively by being a boisterous old-fashioned bibliophile and humanist who has no time for this newfangled, highfalutin' computer stuff. This is another instance of the fear of mechanization theme we introduced in "What Are Little Girls Made Of?", but while "Court Martial" halfheartedly builds it up in the first few acts it turns out to be irrelevant to the actual plot as Finney is discovered to be still alive and playing hide-and-seek on the engineering deck.

The other big complaint I have with "Court Martial" is its general attitude. This is an episode all about honour, duty, command and service. The overall plot is already about protocol and procedure, and the key scene comes when Kirk first takes the witness stand: He gives a big, pompous monologue about how he "did what he had to do-by the book!" and how all the things he did "and the order in which I did them!" he did for his ship and his duty, as those are the most important things to him. It's right out of the military drama textbook and is really just not to my tastes at all. However, to William Shatner's credit, he sells the hell out of this, going into a big, overplayed piece-to-camera and doing the entire soliloquy in one take, reminding me of the Shakespearean embellishments of "The Conscience of the King". And even this isn't a fault I'm finding with the episode (it's quite well done space military drama) it's me drawing a philosophical line marking the boundary of what I like Star Trek to be about.

Additionally, even here it's worth comparing "Court Martial" with its nearest analogue, "The Corbomite Maneuver". That episode was an action-packed thriller with a twist ending that was clearly banking on us being really excited by the back-and-forth bluffing and tense countdown to potential Armageddon. This episode, by contrast, is a more complex courtroom piece that takes its time to explain and establish its setting and actually examines themes like valour, honour and duty instead of tossing them out as buzzwords: We see quite clearly how this affects the characters of Kirk, Stone, Shaw and Finney and how they interpret those concepts, which also builds off of the character studies we saw in "The Galileo Seven". This is still Gene Coon expanding what *Star Trek* can be about, only now instead of bringing in other genres to play with, he's beginning to turn his attention to the fundamental pitch of the series itself, and he'll only continue to do this more and more as his tenure progresses. Granted, the end result of this (for the moment at least) is a show that's still overtly militaristic, but at least it's militaristic in a bit more of a nuanced way now.

None of this to say that "Court Martial" is a bad bit of television: With the exception of the few inconsistencies I've mentioned already, it's certainly watchable and far more solid a production than many of the other episodes I've covered so far. My big issue with it is that it represents a version of Star Trek I've never been drawn to and am even less so now. I don't like military drama and I especially don't like it when that's what Star Trek becomes, which I guess should say something about how I feel about the franchise on the whole and how wise it perhaps actually was of me to make Star Trek the focal point of this project. However, there's another side to this: What Gene Coon and Don M. Mankiewicz realised is that a show about the Space Air Force or Space Navy is eventually going to end up here. If nothing else, that's what "Court Martial" is demonstrating-That this is the logical endpoint of a specific, formative thematic thread that's been a part of *Star Trek* since the beginning. That Star Trek can be read as something more than this is evidence Coon knew this wasn't really all the show was capable of, and now that he's found the show's original idea and taken it as far as it can go, he can start to reshape it and push it into the beyond. But Coon has one more act to perform, and what he's about to do next is turn his lens back onto the show's most primal form itself.

20. "The following program contains material that may be disturbing.": The Menagerie

WARNING: THE HISTORICAL EVENTS HEREIN DESCRIBED HAVE BEEN DECLARED PART OF A FIXED POINT IN TIME BY THE UNITED FEDERATION OF PLANETS TEMPORAL INTEGRITY COMMISSION UNDER THE TEMPORAL ACCORDS. NO STARSHIP, AGENT OR OTHER ACTOR IS TO APPROACH THESE EVENTS FOR ANY REASON OR PURPOSE. ANY TEMPORAL INCURSION DURING THESE EVENTS WILL BE CONSIDERED A LEVEL TEN EMERGENCY. THE TIMELINE MUST BE PRESERVED.

So what we have here a grossly overspent production budget forcing the show to hastily retool "The Cage" into a clip show interspersed with footage filmed using sets, costumes and indeed the entire actual plot recycled from "Court Martial". Incidentally, we've also now had to stretch the already tortoiselike pacing of "The Cage" to a two-parter to accommodate the new framing device which we've turned over to Gene Roddenberry again to write the script for. Miraculously, however, despite all of this and almost by complete accident, this is a story so gratuitously oversignified it shoots the show straight into the symbolic stratosphere. "The Menagerie" may not be the best episode of the original *Star Trek*, but it may well be the most archetypical.

It is worth noting this was not the original plan for "The Cage": Roddenberry had hoped to turn it into a full-length movie with a new first half depicting the crash of the *Columbia*. It was Bob Justman who convinced Roddenberry to adapt it into "The Menagerie" because the show had run out of both scripts and money, and the fact Roddenberry had wanted to take a story that had already somehow managed to be simultaneously too crammed full of details and concepts for only an hour and too ponderously paced to be especially enjoyable television and make it into a feature film probably tells you everything you need to know about Roddenberry at this point. It would be both easy and churlish of me to call the framing device Roddenberry writes for this episode "predictably terrible" as we have in fact seen more than a few solid outings from him, but even so this has got to be one of his worst efforts at least from a purely structural perspective. The new material is absolutely riddled with yawning, cavernous plot holes that threaten to leave "The Menagerie" literally incoherent at numerous points and the justification for forcing the court to sit through a

93

Star Trek rerun is more than a little flimsy. At least Roddenberry doesn't introduce any new major female characters this time so we're thankfully spared his usual gender issues.

But getting bogged down in silly little things like "plot", "narrative logic" and "coherence" is the wrong approach to take with something like "The Menagerie". This is one of the single most iconic stories in the Original Series, and rightly so in my opinion. The first thing to note is that "The Menagerie" is clearly trying to be just as much about honour, duty and procedure as "Court Martial" was. While it lacks the grandiose, sweeping pomposity we got last time, it could perhaps be argued the theatrical theme we've been building over the past few weeks exists here in the form of Roddenberry himself, who seems here to be doing a halfway decent impersonation of Don M. Mankiewicz. And, just like "Court Martial", the framing device segments of "The Menagerie" can be read as the show taking its original premise as far as it can possible go.

The definition of a narrative collapse story is one where both textual and metatextual elements conspire together in an attempt to destroy the text's ability to tell its own stories. At first it seems like this is what "The Menagerie" is trying to do: Spock lies and betrays Kirk and the crew, commits high treason, commandeers the *Enterprise*, kidnaps Pike and takes the ship on a course to the one world it is absolutely forbidden to visit, a standing order whose violation is punishable by death. But, upon closer inspection, that's really not what's going on here: Rather, what "The Menagerie" is doing is continuing "Court Martial"'s conviction to pushing *Star Trek* to its logical limit. The biggest evidence for this reading is Spock himself, who has always had an air of suspicion about him. We always worried he might attempt something like this, and it's even more fitting that when he actually does he does so out of logic and duty. two concepts that have been absolutely central to both his character and the show at large since the beginning. As this is a militaristic setting there is of course legal drama aplenty (just like last time), but here we have a script that (at first, at least) invites us to question honour and loyalty, as pursuing those ideals has led Spock to violate everyone's trust in him.

Furthermore, this time the show is taking its introspection and self examination to the extreme by literally going back to its own beginning: We not only return to Talos IV but we get to see the actual pilot play out in front of us once again.

> WARNING: THE HISTORICAL EVENTS HEREIN DESCRIBED HAVE BEEN DECLARED PART OF A FIXED POINT IN TIME BY THE UNITED FEDERATION OF PLANETS TEMPORAL INTEGRITY COMMISSION UNDER THE TEMPORAL ACCORDS. NO STARSHIP, AGENT OR OTHER ACTOR IS TO APPROACH THESE EVENTS FOR ANY REASON OR PURPOSE. ANY TEMPORAL INCURSION DURING THESE EVENTS WILL BE CONSIDERED A LEVEL TEN EMERGENCY. THE TIMELINE MUST BE PRESERVED.

Indeed it's what "The Menagerie" does to "The Cage" that's the most immediately interesting thing on display here from my perspective. Although not the first time the original pilot had been seen outside NBC (Roddenberry aired both it and "Where No Man Has

Gone Before" at the Cleveland, Ohio World Science Fiction Convention in early 1966) this was the first time the vast majority of people had seen it, so it must have been a sort of television event. The contrast between the set design and cinematography of "The Cage" and what *Star Trek* had become by this point alone must have been impressive to see, and I'd imagine adequately conveyed the illusion the show had more money and resources than it actually did. Furthermore, from an ethical standpoint, the way this episode handles the concept of the Talosians' power of illusion is far more satisfying than what we originally got.

What Pike is suffering from in this episode can best be described as a kind of sci-fi version of total locked-in syndrome, a rare condition where a patient's entire voluntary muscular system is completely paralyzed, rendering them fully awake and conscious but unable to move or communicate. Pike is very lucky to exist in a world where the technology exists, even at a rudimentary level, to restore him some ability to speak with others. What this allows the show to do is shift the meaning of the cage metaphor: Where previously it had been a literal description of the Talosian zoo as a way to express how humans detest even a gilded cage, here it becomes a symbolic extension of Pike's imprisonment in his own body, thus immediately bringing to mind transhumanistic issues. McCoy even gets a line in part 1 where he just about states this word-for-word, making the link explicit.

Transhumanism is a popular subject for the kind of science fiction Star Trek occasionally find itself a part of, and the idea that humanity somehow needs to transcend its mortal shackles is a reoccurring theme in futurist writing of this type. This has as much capacity to become a rewarding thread of discourse as it does to become a highly problematic and contentious worldview. One does get the sense with some transhumanist writing that being physical entities is somehow not enough, and that nature is somehow holding humans back. This begins to touch on spiritualist concerns I'm not quite prepared to talk about yet, but for now let's return to a thread we first touched on in the chapter on "What Are Little Girls Made Of?". Even if you posit that the self and consciousness are purely material things, it is still certainly possible to conceive of a model of it that conceptualises the *experiential* self as a product of that materialism. Even true ego death does not by definition preclude this: That our physical existence is somehow a hindrance to enlightenment would seem to smack of Cartesian Dualism, which is descended from a very classical, traditional intellectual tradition that has gone out of vogue even in contemporary Western philosophy.

Thankfully for Captain Pike his condition seems far more straightforward: Spock's decision to return him to Talos IV so he can live out the rest of his natural life with the illusion of full mobility and the ability to communicate, and the opportunity to go anywhere his mind desires, seems like the obvious solution. That said, were it me I'd far prefer to go dig up Doctor Korby and ask him to show me how to upload myself into an android body: "The Menagerie" doesn't quite manage to break free of "The Cage"'s Platonic cave message. But what this also manages to do is

WARNING: THE HISTORICAL EVENTS HEREIN DESCRIBED HAVE BEEN DECLARED PART OF A FIXED POINT IN TIME BY THE UNITED FED-

ERATION OF PLANETS TEMPORAL INTEGRITY COMMISSION UNDER
THE TEMPORAL ACCORDS. NO STARSHIP, AGENT OR OTHER ACTOR
IS TO APPROACH THESE EVENTS FOR ANY REASON OR PURPOSE.
ANY TEMPORAL INCURSION DURING THESE EVENTS WILL BE CON-
SIDERED A LEVEL TEN EMERGENCY. THE TIMELINE MUST BE PRE-
SERVED.

re-position "The Cage" in *Star Trek*'s evolving mythos, or perhaps to be more accurate try to give it a position at all. The events of the pilot are retconned to be thirteen years prior to those of the framing device and Pike's *Enterprise* is now explicitly a part of Starfleet, not the Earth based Space Air Force. If I'm allowed one of my more cynical observations, I'd say this is probably the primary reason this episode is beloved by fans so much as it helps streamline the original pilot into a kind of Star Trek "canon", which it is otherwise completely irreconcilable with.

But, once again, it's *Star Trek*'s commitment to justifying its existence over these past few weeks that makes this all worthwhile. No matter how stilted the plot devices to get us to this point are, the fact remains we have an entire episode dedicated to watching Kirk, Spock, McCoy and Scott watching Pike, Number One, Colt, Spock and Tyler on television. We have *Star Trek*'s present not only watching it's own past, but critiquing it. This isn't Spock on trial, it's Roddenberry: This is Gene Coon's *Star Trek* evaluating and judging Gene Roddenberry's *Star Trek*. In that regard, the scenes where Kirk, Uhura or Commodore Mendez keep interrupting the broadcast or get impatient with Spock and complain about how much time the transmission is wasting are actively hilarious. As I said in my chapter on "The Conscience of the King" I'm positive Coon's team was not ridiculing or being dismissive of the show at all, but taken within the context of the terse behind-the-scenes climate it does feel like the tensions onscreen are a painfully fitting reflection of those on the Desilu lot.

Which brings me to perhaps the most curious thing about "The Menagerie": Why, exactly, is contact with Talos IV so explicitly forbidden to the point where a violation of Starfleet General Order 7 is punishable by death? It's true the Talosians' illusory powers have the potential to be quite dangerous and that they expressed some concern about what might happen if they fell into the wrong hands, but I was under the impression the whole point of "The Cage" was that Pike showed the Talosians reality is more important than illusion and that humanity's abhorrence of imprisonment meant they were unsuitable for the planetary reconstruction effort. If the Talosians had no further interest in humans, why would Starfleet consider them to still be dangerous, let alone dangerous enough to justify imposing the death penalty on anyone who visits their homeworld?

Although I remain at a loss for a diegetic explanation, perhaps the answer may lie with the extradiegetic. Perhaps the reason it is forbidden to travel to Talos IV is because to return there is to return to the origin of Star Trek. Roddenberry's "Cage" didn't just trap Captain Pike, it trapped the show, and from the moment *Star Trek* went to series it's been more than clear that its being held back by baggage left over from the original pilot. Gene

Coon's entire tenure so far has been defined by a desire to push the boundaries of what the show can do in every direction, and that includes showing us the consequences of being slavishly loyal to the show's original premise. Following that thread to its conclusion yields not just entrapment, but death. Star Trek has nowhere to go from there: It's a non-starter, a narrative dead end. Returning to Talos IV means returning to "The Cage", and that would be death sentence for Star Trek. Also note Starfleet Command dropped all charges against Spock and the *Enterprise* crew after watching the transmission and judging their actions to be in keeping with the spirit of exploration: The show has found a way to avoid that death, at least for now. And with the last of its demons accounted for, if not quite exorcised, Coon is finally free to continue to shepherd the Star Trek franchise's journey toward its own enlightenment.

WARNING: THE HISTORICAL EVENTS HEREIN DESCRIBED HAVE BEEN DECLARED PART OF A FIXED POINT IN TIME BY THE UNITED FEDERATION OF PLANETS TEMPORAL INTEGRITY COMMISSION UNDER THE TEMPORAL ACCORDS. NO STARSHIP, AGENT OR OTHER ACTOR IS TO APPROACH THESE EVENTS FOR ANY REASON OR PURPOSE. ANY TEMPORAL INCURSION DURING THESE EVENTS WILL BE CONSIDERED A LEVEL TEN EMERGENCY. THE TIMELINE MUST BE PRESERVED.

THE TIMELINE MUST BE PRESERVED.

THE TIMELINE MUST BE PRESERVED.

21. "There ought to be a book written about me, that there ought!": Shore Leave

"Once upon a time there were three little sisters..."

The three sisters lived together, all by themselves, on a small island. To this day no-one is quite sure where that island lay: Some have claimed it was somewhere among the modern-day Marquesas, while other swear it was much further out, an outlier island far off to the west. Then there are those mythologizer-poets who swear by the stars themselves that this island was impossible to place on a map, for any cartographer foolish enough to attempt to chart its location on parchment would find it to be forever out of reach, just beyond the edges of the paper. Most who claim to have reached it never return, and those who have are unable to find it again, even if they retrace their path down to the exact last nautical mile. And yet this island did exist, as alive and real as any of us. It presumably still does today.

"What did they live on?"

Mostly coconuts and the splendid gifts of the sea, but they were very well provided for on the island. I am told it is a place where scarcity and want does not exist, for the island and its inhabitants live together in balance and harmony. But that is not this story.

On the beach, the sisters sat in a circle facing each other, each with legs crossed in the lotus position.

"I vote one of us tells a story," Tertia suddenly exclaimed "Would either of you happen to know one?"

"Here's one," Hedda responded with a smile "Once upon a time there were three little sisters..." she began, but was quickly interrupted before she could continue.

"Very funny," Tertia drolly responded with her hands on her hips, "We've *all* heard that one, you know..."

Then, Alice spoke up: "Have I ever told you the story of the spacemen, my dear sisters?" she inquired.

"I believe I know it, if that's what you mean," Hedda answered, "I have seen it thus invoked."

"Oh please do tell it anyway!" Tertia implored, "As the dawn rises over the eastern waters each night, the future shall be known to us again and again and again."

"It was in the days before you, dearest star-sisters," Alice began, "My counsel is sought on one of the multiplex planar realms of invocation. These are the lands where Is and What Is exist together in their death-dance. These are truths we know."

"Yes, I have seen many such places," Tertia remarked, "The world-stage and World-In-Itself in cohabitation".

Alice nodded, then said "And this world-stage was Thought, which is the child of thought yet not an heir to its throne. As I passed through this realm, I met the first of the spacemen, who had come seeking my guidance. They adorned themselves in the visage of a summer's day, but did not yet know its meaning."

"They do not see the Day, for some are not attuned to seeing it." Hedda continued.

"All was blank at this time, for as blankness is what they sought blankness is what they found. This is not the wondrous apotheosis of the All Thing, but glorification of the Zero, and thus the lamentable zeroing of all."

"Much as a canvas remains blank if the dream is forsaken" Tertia added, as she drew a treacle jar in the sand.

"I appear in this way because I was summoned to so appear, and this was My Will. The spacemen could not accept this, for they understood the shape, but not the meaning. It was for this reason I journeyed to the glade, whereupon I was observed yet unseen."

"I See and I Do Not, don't I?" said the first spaceman, and this was the incantation that thus blinded him.

"I came bearing the egg of Mystery and Time, though I was not yet prepared to be reborn again into this visage," said Hedda.

"Those who know the word may reshape the world-stage, so I did. Wearing the Sun Crown, I did take my leave of another realm. It was in this way the world was broken, and in this way the spacemen would come to see through blinded eyes. The world has changed, and it cannot be fixed now." Alice declared.

"The spacemen didn't like the breaking of the world very much, did they?" asked Tertia.

"It is the time wound that will never, and can never, heal. It aches in the days past and far out into the future, destined to be inflicted again and again." said Alice.

"The static, sex-death of being." Hedda offered.

"That's *another s*tory, Hedda!" her sister Tertia responded.

"Indeed it is." Hedda replied. "Another time, perhaps."

Another thing that makes "Shore Leave" worthy of note is its handle on characterization. Building on Coon's previous overtures in this direction in "The Galileo Seven", a major theme in this episode is examining the innermost thoughts of various characters and the relationships they have with one another. This works significantly better here than it did in "The Naked Time": Sulu's interest in arms returns, as does Kirk's reminiscence on his more tight-laced and reserved academy days. The best execution of this structure is probably Kirk's fight with Finnegan, in spite of the fact the latter is once again a horrifying Irish stereotype, this time down to his ability to teleport around like a leprechaun. Aside from those brought upon by the planet itself, this episode has a number of nice character moments just in passing: Kirk's conversation with McCoy about Finnegan and his academy days is lovely bit of the everyday and the massage scene on the bridge during the teaser is an absolute riot and justifiably a memorable moment that called the fanfic writers to action.

Aside from its meta-narrative connotations, the concept of a planet that reacts to desires and imagination is a remarkably good one, and has the potential to be a far more effective window into the psyche of our leads then getting them space drunk was. The keyword here is potential, however: The problem is, apart from Kirk and Sulu, the show frustratingly stops short of giving us enough meaningful content: McCoy's budding relationship with Barrows could have been nice, except that Barrows is a sexist nightmare. She openly fantasizes about being "ravished" by Don Juan (and we're sickeningly all meant to laugh at when she "gets what she asked for"), then about being a fairy tale damsel with knight to fight over and protect her and finally about jumping Doctor McCoy's Bones (to the point she even gets a Roddenberry signature comedy catty jealous scene at the end). Even McCoy himself gets a few really uncomfortable lines. The rest of the development comes from the random science techs we never see again and this is kind of tough to read as anything other than a staggering mismanagement of the cast.

The problem is, of course, Gene Roddenberry. Theodore Sturgeon is going to end up writing one of the most beloved and acclaimed episodes in the entirety of the Original Series, but Roddenberry didn't seem to take too kindly to the script he turned in here, finding it to be "too much fantasy" and "not believable enough", so he gave it to Coon to rewrite. Coon is alleged to have misunderstood Roddenberry's complaints and rewrote "Shore Leave" to be even more overtly mystical and fantastical (a draft I'd actually really like to have been able to read), leaving Roddenberry to furiously and completely rewrite the entire script alongside filming, yet retaining Sturgeon's name on the finished product. This of course means we're in the exact same situation we were in with "What Are Little Girls Made Of?", which should already raise a considerable number of warning flags. This one turns out better, mostly because the central concept is already a great one to begin with and the overall quality of the show has increased dramatically under Gene Coon.

"Shore Leave" is not completely spared, however: The tension between Roddenberry's and Coon's differing styles is painfully evident any time the former writes under the latter, and especially in this episode. While "The Menagerie" (quite ironically) had logic lapses, it was a more or less competent step forward. "Shore Leave" screams at itself: Whereas in "Court Martial" we had an African commodore on Starbase 11 and an Asian records officer on the *Enterprise* and nobody made a big deal about it; here we have Roddenberry pitching a fit because his story about the futuristic Space Navy and lawkeeping taskforce taking shore leave on a far-off planet isn't realistic enough and then populating it with a magical Irish leprechaun and a yeoman who boldly declares it's a woman's natural right to be submissive and protected. Yeah. The First Speaker and the Second Speaker battled each other in the heaven-earth, tearing it asunder, and this was the time wound the first. It's little wonder Alice tells Kirk at the end of the episode that humanity is not yet ready to understand her ways.

"I believe", said Alice "This realm now lies shattered before us."

"Before and After, you mean." corrected Tertia.

"Things can exist without and within," Hedda added, "I have seen it to be so-Events dance the cosmic dance of potentialities echoing to the dawn and beginning at the End of All Things. All that can be is."

"It was in this way, and in many other ways, that the War in Heaven began. I have chanced to hear this story told on many occasions from many fellow dream-travellers in different transformative incarnations. The War begins and it begins again, and it is fought at all times in all places," Alice said, "The spacemen exist in ceaseless conflict, for this is their way. To fight is to play is to be. This is a path. But the War in Heaven shall consume them. This I have seen, and it is thus written. Yet fire does not destroy, it carbonizes, and this remains transformation and metamorphosis."

"The spacemen dance to the intersection of stasis and change," added Hedda.

"And it is there, my dearest star-sisters, that we reconvene."

22. "...considered the greatest spectacle of all...": The Squire of Gothos

We've finally found something weird.

The opening salvo of "The Squire of Gothos" is simply put the most mental thing yet. We've got a planet that instantaneously materializes out of nowhere, Kirk and Sulu jump-cutting off the bridge and foppish Victorian gentle-alien holding the *Enterprise* hostage due to his fascination with warmaking. Each one of these concepts individually would be enough to throw viewers for a complete loop; dumping all of them on us at once requires us to take a few steps back, a deep breath, and take them one at a time.

The first thing to note is that we're back in "Miri" territory. Actually, a case could be made this is the structure of "Miri" done right: The *Enterprise* is on space patrol as always, en route to deliver some more supplies. Just like in the earlier episode, however, they are swiftly interrupted by the thoroughly inexplicable. This time though, the show takes its time unfolding the mystery: The phantom planetoid, disappearing crewmembers and bizarre antiquarian message of "Tallyho!" showing up on Spock's monitor is enough, but the show gradually builds on this, first with the reveal of Trelane's oasis-within-an-oasis and then well into the third and fourth acts as each answer does nothing but open up a new question. Unlike the earlier episode, which promptly resolved all of its mystery in the first act, this one clearly takes the time to relish it, taking gleeful pride in constantly getting its audience to wonder what the heck is going on.

"The Squire of Gothos" is of course nowhere near as mind-bogglingly weird as genuinely avant-garde cinema would have been. This is something that's absolutely not in Star Trek's wheelhouse. But this is still a very stark break from what we've come to expect from *Star Trek*, especially under Gene Coon and in *particular* after the past three episodes. The precedent is, naturally, "Shore Leave", and the effect of that episode's traumatically altered state of consciousness is very clear here, as is it's ultimate reluctance and hesitation. From the very beginning Trelane operates completely and utterly above and beyond the crew's level of comprehension, and the very first thing they set about doing (and continue to do for the remainder of the story) is to try and explain him a way using rationality language they understand. It is simply inconceivable for Kirk and his crew to accept the possibility there may exist things which do not fit neatly into their currently established knowledge systems.

And Trelane is definitely unlike anything we've seen before-He's the first genuinely "alien" character in all of Star Trek, for one. Spock, and by extension the Vulcans, were originally at heart just Number One's human personality turned into the defining trait of a culture (they of course quickly become much more than this, thanks almost exclusively to the combined efforts of Leonard Nimoy, Theodore Sturgeon and D.C. Fontana, but this is what they were originally). Pretty much all the other extraterrestrials in Gene Roddenberry's tenure were generic monsters, while Coon has kept the action primarily at a human level so far. The Romulans were an alien culture, but they were also consciously designed to be the mirror of us, so they are by definition very humanized. Trelane is just plain strange: He's an all-powerful, unreadable and unpredictable entity with a bizarre fascination with 18th and 19th century Earth.

Actor William Campbell, a Star Trek fan favourite with a deeply storied history with the franchise who makes his debut appearance here, is absolutely phenomenal as Trelane: He's manic, charismatic and completely unhinged; a just about perfect match for William Shatner's Kirk. Trelane is Kirk's inverse, twisted, mirror-image evil camp twin. Both characters are in some way defined by a fixation on overstated bravado, and ultimately there's little difference between Trelane's gleeful, play-acted goose-stepping and Kirk's overblown, impassioned speeches about duty. The key difference between the two lies in the contrast between the way their characters are depicted: Shatner's performance is just overstated enough to draw attention to the artifice of the thing, thus encouraging us to read Kirk as a kind of playful subversion. Shatner is obviously playing a role, and playing it just a little bit off-He is in fact a drag pulp sci-fi action hero, and a great deal of his charm comes from him frequently eliciting subtle laughs at the expense of the role and premise.

Campbell by contrast plays Trelane with active and clearly noticeable malice. It's an entirely more venomous portrayal, designed to rub our noses firmly in our own enjoyment of the setting's general pomp and circumstance. Kirk's detournement is meant to be somewhat muted, but visible if you're paying close enough attention to it; Trelane's is grotesque, mad, and violent. As such their conflict is utterly, beautifully elegant and without doubt the highlight of the episode. Furthermore, Campbell is excellent at giving Trelane a genuinely uncanny and disquieting air, playing up to great extent the fact he gets the trappings of the various characters he takes on and the settings he studies ever-so-slightly wrong. What makes this delicious, of course, is this once again makes him immediately comparable to Kirk. Although, as Kirk observes, he may be nigh-omnipotent, but he *is* fallible. In fact, Trelane might almost be *too* fallible.

What makes Trelane such a compelling character in my view is that he's an absolute caricature of repugnant good-old-boy politics and imperialist jingoism. Trelane idolizes Napoleon, which is perfect, and extolls, to deeply uncomfortable effect, the virtues of flags (jingoistic ethics through nationalist aesthetic) and the honour of sending soldiers to fight and die for not just his cause but him personally. And, tellingly, Kirk has just about no comeback to this. Oh, he loses his patience, demands Trelane release the *Enterprise* and keeps pointing out he's got his historical details a little wrong, but in terms of actually debating Trelane on an intellectual level? In terms of refuting his claims that humanity is an inherently predatory species for whom warmaking and murder is a fundamental instinct? Kirk's got nothing. Indeed, he's got less than that: He ends up in a straight up brutally savage brawl with Trelane at the end of the episode that damn near gets him run through with a sword for his trouble. He can declare up and down humans are a noble species that deserve to be treated with dignity, but does absolutely nothing to support his claim. But, once again the show aggravatingly stops short and backpedals, revealing Trelane to be the misbehaving child of other, more grown-up and benevolent beings, thus completely stripping him of any authority he could have used to take the show to task.

It's fitting I mentioned the Romulans earlier, because this is the second outing of Paul Schneider, who had previously penned "Balance of Terror", the episode I still consider to be the Original Series' high water mark. Predictably, "The Squire of Gothos" is at heart a furious anti-war piece. Schneider says the impetus for this episode was watching with horror as young boys acted out war games for fun, so he penned this story to show what it would be like of that kind of light, capricious attitude to war was extrapolated to a superhuman degree. While I can understand and respect that (though there's more to be said about the ethos of wargaming at a later date), I still think it was a mistake to make Trelane a child. Perhaps this could have worked had there been more scenes where the *Enterprise* crew gets to prove their peaceful virtues and defend their character to Trelane, but that never really happens. The majority of this episode is dedicated to watching either Trelane using the crew as playthings or to Kirk screaming at him for doing so and baiting his ego. At the end of it all we're left feeling a bit hollow: Nobody's critique has really stuck, and it seems suspiciously like the show is hastily sweeping it all back under the rug before we start to ask too many questions about the ethics of what we're watching, which seems strange coming from the guy who wrote "Balance of Terror".

But even if this isn't quite as successful as Schneider's prior work, "The Squire of Gothos" is just as upfront about its firm anti-imperialist stance which can't be seen as anything less then an unequivocal positive. On top of that, it's yet another step forward into the weird and fantastic realms of the cosmic imagination that lay outside the boundaries of Earth-controlled colonial space. Slowly but surely *Star Trek* is beginning to learn how to broaden its mind and its horizons and that there's a bit more out there than itself. This is frequently a painful, yet necessary process, and the show's been forced to adapt. And the transformations that are to come soon will hold repercussions for the entire galaxy.

23. "The best techniques are passed on by the survivors...": Arena

Arguably the most memorable episode of the Original Series' first season, there's an awful lot going on with "Arena", and all of it is deserving of our attention: This is the first episode actually written by Gene Coon, it boasts one of the most iconic extraterrestrial designs in the show's history in the Gorn and three of the most iconic setpieces as well: Kirk's brutal, drawn-out fistfight with the Gorn captain, his improvised tree-trunk cannon and his climactic confrontation with the Metron where he refuses to kill his opponent after beating him. Also, for good measure, "Arena" also sees the debut of a little thing called the Federation. So, kind of a big story then.

Let's get that last one out of the way first, as it's by far the most interesting from the perspective of the future. Like the debut of Starfleet and Starfleet Command in "Court Martial", this is primarily a nomenclature change at this point. Furthermore, the Federation is even less important to "Arena" then Starfleet was to "Court Martial": In that episode at least the organisational structure of Starfleet Command was important to the main plot, here, the Federation is introduced with a single throwaway comment from Kirk and then never mentioned again. Nevertheless, the word choice here is interesting, to say the least. A "Federation" is by definition an alliance of self-governing political states with partial autonomy brought together by shared mutual interest. What it's not is a colonial empire; at least not by default: An empire grows through colonization and militaristic conquest. Calling a centralized power a "federation" would at least *imply* a more co-operative arrangement.

In the past the world of *Star Trek* has been pretty clearly a galactic empire based on Earth. The overwhelming majority of places we've visited have been Earth colonies, and we've seen no other significant political power in the galaxy aside from the Romulan Star Empire, and they're tucked safely away behind the Neutral Zone. That's all changed as of "Arena", however: The central twist of the episode is that the Gorn, who are introduced as an aggressive, warlike Other who cannot be reasoned with, turn out to be a highly sophisticated civilization in their own right who feel threatened by Federation expansion into their area of space. The Metrons' lesson to both crews seems to be about stressing the importance of communication and diplomacy, it would seem that this might be what distinguishes the Federation from the former Earth Empire.

This is of course not to say a federation is incapable of being imperialistic. The oldest and most influential federation on *our* Earth is the United States, which is known nowadays primarily for its policies of economic and political imperialism built around manipulating diplomacy and trade sanctions and the fetishistic focus on neoliberal privatization resulting in a capitalistic tyranny that rewards only those who are already in an extremely privileged position while absolutely crushing and dehumanizing everyone else, not to mention being a general fascistic police state towards its citizenry. Furthermore, there have been numerous cases throughout the history of the US that proves the country is obsessed with its own particular flavour of government, believing it to be far and away, and without question, the greatest and most perfect in the history of the world and of being all too willing to convert others to it, and by any means necessary. The US also obviously has owned colonial territories of its own at various points and has the clear-cut genocide of the entire native population of the Americas on its hands. If anything, the history of the US is incontrovertible evidence that the federation is far from the ideal way to organise a society.

These are all issues and implications Star Trek will deal with at different points throughout the history of the franchise, either that it recognises in itself as problems or has hoisted on it from outside forces. A federation may be a fairer way to organise the kind of setting *Star Trek* operates in than an empire, but it's not necessarily going to be the perfect solution either. This is, however, primarily a concern for the future-After all, the Federation in "Arena" is, as I've already said, a throwaway line. It's not going to become actually relevant to the overall story arc of *Star Trek* until next year at the very earliest. But even here I think the show is on some level cognizant of this: Look at the story Coon chooses, by his own hand, to introduce the Federation in. He sends its sole representative, Kirk, on a vicious, bloodthirsty revenge mission and has him ready to disregard all concern for sentient life, both on the Gorn ship and on the *Enterprise* itself, so long as he can send the coldest, most ruthless message to the Gorn possible. Furthermore, the Cestus III colony turns out to be in Gorn space, something the Federation never bothered to check on, just waltzing in like it was entitled to the place, an act which the Gorn rightfully saw as the prelude to an invasion. Clearly the Federation's not working much better in the world of Star Trek than it does in ours.

The overall tone and general plot of "Arena" bear some superficial similarities with those of "Balance of Terror", and it's worth looking at the two episodes side-by-side here as they reveal not only the differences between Paul Schneider's writing style and Gene Coon's, but also a bit more of the latter writer's philosophy. Both stories are soundly critiques of imperialism and conflict-for-conflict's sake, but they go about exploring these themes in very different ways. The most alarming difference is in how the two stories depict Kirk: "Balance of Terror" showed him to be almost world-weary and tired, dreading the thought of being dragged into a bloody conflict with the Romulans and the prospect of sacrificing his ship, his crew and himself for a misbegotten ancient feud, as befitting him being paired with Mark Lenard's Commander. In "Arena", by contrast, both Kirk and the Gorn captain are chomping at the bit to usher in a new galaxy-wide war, with the Gorn salting and burning Cestus III and Kirk willing to throw out his sense of morals and ethics and jeopardize his crew to avenge the colony, thus prompting the Metrons to dump them both in Vasquez Rocks to beat the shit out of each other.

The Metrons as a third, neutral party are another concept new for "Arena", and, unfortunately, in my view, have problems. I have a feeling what Coon wanted their inclusion to show is how war and conflict are detrimental to the health of a society, and that any people who wish to consider themselves "advanced" and "civilized" would have moved beyond them. In this regard it's telling how Coon has Kirk be the most overtly warlike person in the show: It's a very firm claim that the Federation and Starfleet are nowhere near as sophisticated and cultured as they might wish you to believe. Unfortunately for me, it's simply not as interesting as having Kirk be a burned-out solider tired of war and fighting looking for a way to move beyond them, which seems, at least in my view, to be a far better fit for the kind of performance William Shatner is prone to giving and a compelling microcosm of *Star Trek* itself. Indeed what Coon is doing here can be seen as a metaphor as well. Just as in "The Squire of Gothos" Kirk stands in for the ethics of the entire show and is judged for them, but Shatner plays a character who is larger than the role he's being asked to fill, and that to me calls for a different approach.

As for the Metrons themselves, I feel their whole conception is a bit flawed, unfortunately. Firstly, the whole idea some civilizations are straight-up "superior", "more advanced" and "more civilized" is undistilled Social Darwinism, a fact which is not at all helped by having the Metrons' true appearance resemble classical Greek ideal forms and (of course) be played by white-as-the-driven snow actors in golden haired wigs. Even the name "Metron" is derived from "Metatron", a Judaic angel with a Greek name meaning "instrument of change". It's a clever reference, as it facilitates reading them as the spark that sets humanity on a new path, but it does make them, and "Arena" on the whole, about as Abrahamic and Western as it is possible to get. It's perhaps not entirely fair to condemn this episode for being so of its culture, but, combined with the themes it's also trying to work with, this does cripple the story's overall impact with a number of seriously unfortunate implications, which can't really be seen as anything other than a handicap.

The end result of this, sadly, is that for me "Arena" is just nowhere near as effective a bit of anti-imperialism as "Balance of Terror". It has a lot of good ideas, and both introducing and quietly subverting the Federation in one fell swoop has got to go down as some kind of grand slam for Coon, but between the Metrons and the way Kirk is portrayed it's just not quite as meaningful as it could be. So why is this episode so fondly remembered in this vein and not "Balance of Terror"? Granted, that episode is iconic in its own right mostly due to the Romulans, but it's most fondly remembered in hardcore Star Trek fandom: I get the sense "Arena" has significantly more cultural capital in the larger populace. If I were to hazard a guess, it's probably due in large part to the Vazquez Rocks location, which is a very stunning backdrop for William Shatner to brawl stuntmen in lizard suits, and the aforementioned lizard suits themselves, which impressively manage to walk the line between intricate detail and overblown cheese to create one of the most memorable images of the Original Series.

There is one more factor in "Arena"'s favour, however: That tree trunk cannon. It's very revealing it eventually showed up on *MythBusters*, a show that demonstrably spoke to maker culture, and that geek icon Grant Imahara breathlessly went on and on about how influential this scene was on him: Kirk's resourceful ability to throw together a functional projectile weapon out of only the basic materials he has on hand is seen as a sign of great ingenuity by everyone on the show and cited by many as the highlight of the episode. It's rather easy, I feel, to see why this scene would be so memorable: See, contrary to what one might conclude based on examining the things people *say* are Star Trek's virtues (it's progressiveness, utopian idealism, focus on camaraderie, spirit of adventure and general hopeful attitude), if you actually look at who makes up the majority of Star Trek's fanbase (or at least the officially-sanctioned part of it, which is a theme to earmark for later discussion) it's made up almost exclusively of tech people: Computer enthusiasts, engineers, hobbyists of all sorts (especially model builders) and yes, makers.

A brief analysis: "Maker" is a label coined to describe a culture grown out of homebrew machinists and DIY tinkerers. Many of them are engineers, or at least have an engineering and machining background, and are interested primarily in playful experimentation and seeing the sorts of things they can build on their own or in small groups. In French I believe the term would be *bricolage couture*, but maker society strikes me as a fairly recent phenomenon, (say within the past decade), or at least a phenomenon that's only recently been in the spotlight, whereas the *bricolage* in France dates back much further. There's a fair amount of overlap between maker culture and the more traditional nerd culture (though I hasten to add the cultures are manifestly not interchangeable), as both groups share many common texts and languages, namely science fiction and fantasy cinema and television. Adam Savage, possibly the most public face of the maker movement, for example, is profoundly influenced by *Blade Runner*, and the Star Wars, Hellboy and Indiana Jones franchises.

Also consider Wil Wheaton, who has built his entire post-*Star Trek: The Next Generation* fame on being an icon of nerd culture, or LeVar Burton, who first went to computer enthusiasts and Apple fans when he rebooted *Reading Rainbow* as a tablet application (and fitttingly so, as much of the multi-touch technology that powers the modern tablet computers and smartphones to come in the wake of the iPhone and the iPad were inspired by Mike Okuda's LCARS touch interface designed for *Star Trek: The Next Generation*). This is who Star Trek historically likes to publicly position itself as being for, not leftist philosophers, utopian visionaries or women (yes, we'll come back to that), so of course those sorts of people are going to get a kick out of an episode where Captain Kirk fashions a cannon out of a tree stump, diamond, coal, sulfur and potassium nitrate and make it one of the series' most iconic stories. It doesn't even matter the cannon is laughably scientifically implausible-The ingenuity and creativity behind the exercise is the point.

But there's a problem here too, I argue. Within the context of "Arena" itself, the tree cannon is pretty clearly a sign of Kirk's advanced intelligence and foreshadowing for the Metrons' claim in the denouement that there is hope yet for humanity. The fact Kirk's opponent is a reptile, who if you notice was only able to make a crude dagger out of a sharp rock, means it's fairly easy to read this as evidence humans are "more evolved" than the Gorn, as reptiles are often seen in speciesist terms as lesser, more primitive forms of life than mammals. In other words, technology, and in particular advanced weapons technology, is seen as a sign of being a "more evolved" people. This isn't just speciesism and Social

Darwinism, it's technological determinism (and determinism built around the development of machines of war) and Scientism to boot, which run pretty flagrantly contrary to the supposed moral of "Arena".

Of course, the Federation has kind of worrisome track record for technological determinism, teleology and Social Darwinism. But these are, once again, concerns for the future.

24. "DARKSEID IS MY WILL!" The Alternative Factor

In the mid-to-late 2000s, genre fandom underwent something of a shift in the way it expressed itself, at least on the Internet. A new generation of fans-turned-critics sprang up, ushering in a new style of criticism that can loosely be described as the Internet Review Show. Centred mostly around the website network Channel Awesome, which itself grew out of both YouTube and YouTube's copyright policies, these shows took concisely analytical and frequently equal parts extremely nostalgic and extremely negative, perspectives on science fiction and pop culture ephemera from the 1980s and 1990s, often using the analytical tools of film school. Two of the primary influences on Channel Awesome and similar sites were *Mystery Science Theater 3000* and The Agony Booth, both of which were known for their trademark style of sarcastically sending up assorted bits of genre fiction's past.

Don't you see? This is not Your ship. This is not Your crew. It's changed, different: It's already begun. It may be too late to undo the damage that has already been done, but You can set things right and prevent further harm from coming to Your universe. You see now the danger You are in? The natural order of things is at stake because of this! It's not only this plane, but all of them! The Future, Our Future, *Your* Future is on the verge of nonexistence. You must put a stop to this *here* and *now* so the proper path of Things-To-Come may unfold as it is destined to. Find him, stop him, destroy him, whatever it takes! You must do it and do it immediately! The fate of Reality-As-We-Know-It is in Your hands!

The reason I bring all of this up is because one of the primary ways by which Star Trek fandom as we currently know it was able to take shape was through The Agony Booth's text recaps of various episodes from across the franchise. The cancellation of *Enterprise* put Star Trek pretty clearly into the category of "the past", and even in spite of the reimagined film series that sprung up in the wake of J.J. Abrams, Roberto Orci and Alex Kurtzmann's blockbuster cinematic reboot in 2009, there was still a lingering sense in many corners of the fandom that Star Trek as a relevant, extant thing remains dead and buried up until CBS Paramount announced a new episodic series to debut on their proprietary streaming service in 2017. Therefore, it was sites like The Agony Booth and related web efforts (like SF Debris) and its descendants (like Channel Awesome and other sites like it) that helped usher in a reflexive and introspective period of self-examination in Star Trek fandom. The one problem is that, given their status as entertainment based on making fun of things, the consensus of places like this is going to be extremely negative, or at the very least they heavily emphasize the parts of the series they look at that are the easiest to lampoon.

Yes, I am He, the horrific and terrible monster who destroys civilizations and can make reality vanish in the blink of an eye. But so is he, of course. It depends on your perspective. Much as a hole may become a door, should you choose to view it as such. He will tell you it is a grave threat that the two of us exist in the same place, and in one sense I concede he would be right. He and I are opposites, as you know. Matter and antimatter. Order and chaos. Our existence in the same place and the same time are logical impossibilities. And yet here we both are. And you, as well. My universe is breaking through into yours, and yours into mine. But I submit to you this is a mutability, there is play here. The destruction of one reality does not by default necessitate Nothingness.

This is a very long-winded and roundabout way of getting to the fact The Agony Booth gave "The Alternative Factor" a right panning, tossing out words like "incoherent" and calling Kirk and the crew "severely brain damaged" before finally dubbing the episode as a whole "one of the most poorly constructed fifty minutes I've ever seen" and declaring it "one of the true stinkers in the *Trek* universe". I found this all terribly interesting, because "The Alternative Factor" is one of the single most enjoyable episodes of the Original Series I've seen so far.

I don't think you understand the full gravity of the situation at hand here. We are talking about plus and minus coming into contact. Matter and Antimatter. We are talking about the flagrant violation of every known Natural Law of *both* universes. As a lawkeeper yourself by trade, you must at least respect and understand the significance of *that*? What is happening out there now is a thing that simply *can not* and *must not be!* He would change all of this, sabotage it, reform it in his image: Remake reality in a way that would suit him and him alone. Surely you can see how a thing such as this cannot be permitted to continue? This incursion must be stopped! You must stop it! Help me defeat him and restore The Way Things Are Meant To Be!

This is not to say the episode doesn't have problems; it does, and they're frequently too serious to ignore. However, that said, the problems "The Alternative Factor" do have are purely structural ones, and that really must be stressed in a season that's seen both "Mudd's Women" and Yeoman Barrows. The one solid criticism The Agony Booth does manage to land in my opinion is the accusation of clunky pacing: That's definitely true: There are a few too many exposition scenes, and they could have been written a lot clearer. The battle scenes between Lazarus and Anti-Lazarus go on a bit long, and there's one extended scene near the middle of the episode that really slows things down to a crawl. However, there's an actual behind-the-scenes explanation for this: The script was split just about in half when prospective affiliates raised cane about a proposed love story between Lazarus and Charlene Masters, forcing it to be dropped at the last second. This really can't be seen as anything less than an overall, ahem, *positive* thing though I feel: Chief Engineer Masters is an absolutely brilliant character by *Star Trek* standards. Granted this is helped a lot by the fact her scenes were obviously written for James Doohan's Scotty (who's not in this episode for whatever reason), but still, to have an African woman in that role and not have the show draw overt attention to it has to be commended. Saddle her with yet another throwaway romance subplot, even if it's not with Kirk, and that would have hurt her overall effectiveness I argue. It's just a shame the change came about thanks to the southern affiliates throwing a fit over a potential interracial romance and not feminist introspection or good sense.

I do not seek to destroy, only to change, for change is flux and constant. In fact, it is the *antithesis* of change, that is, stagnation, that begets destruction, and it is not death but destruction which pursues you. What you are witnessing now is a conflict at a point in time yet to come in your future, but that has already begun in mine and will continue to rage from now until eternity. He and I shall fight again and again until all of the stars and all of the worlds throughout all of the cosmos blink out and the vultures and death-dealers pick over the dried and bleached remains of creation. In this way our domains will be kept separate, for now. But there will come a time the door will open again: I've seen it before, and it will happen again. So be it.

Then there's Lazarus himself, who is significantly more interesting then perhaps he ought to be. First of all, Robert Brown was not the original choice for the role: He was a last-minute replacement when the actor who was actually cast, John Drew Barrymore, never showed up for work. Brown was such a last-minute addition, in fact, the show had to start shooting the scenes without Lazarus before they had even found a substitute, which would also account for the hectic and frenzied production. For an emergency stand-in, however, Brown is really quite excellent, and his mood swings and dramatic stage presence are really fun to watch. The name Lazarus itself is, of course, taken from the Biblical character Lazarus of Bethany. This is fundamentally another example of how indebted Star Trek is to Westernism, but, just like the best parts of the Original Series, it's wonderfully oversignified thanks to a seemingly truly inept screw-up. See, the thing is Lazarus of Bethany is primarily famous for cheating death, as he's brought back to life by Jesus four days after he died as an example of how Jesus has transcended (or perhaps conquered might be the better word) the mortal shackles of death.

You're just going to let him stand there? You have to take action! You must send him back, he cannot stay here of his own accord! If he is allowed to assert his will on the universe, all of reality will be imperiled! The future that has been prescribed for us shall not come to pass and the stability of the entire cosmos will buckle! The universes must be kept separate! We must persevere over the Anti-Life! The timeline must be preserved!

This is problematic on a number of levels, most notably the fact this doesn't seem to hold any connection whatsoever to Lazarus' actual role in "The Alternative Factor". And, once again, we see that Western motif I mentioned in "The Menagerie" chapter about one needing to "move beyond" one's Earthly limitations. But perhaps instead of being the Anti-Life we can reconceptualize Lazarus as the Anti-Death instead: Everyone in this episode seems in some way to be racing to outrun the Death Drive-before the Matter/Antimatter hook is introduced, it seems for all the world that *Star Trek*'s internal narrative logic is on the verge of falling apart, and Lazarus describes his opponent as death itself. Even after we learn about the "antimatter universe" (an admittedly self-evidently silly sci-fi concept), that reading is still faintly there. Recall Anti-Lazarus' goal is to uphold reality by removing his duplicate from the multiverse: In a sense, he is sacrificing himself to ensure the continued life of us all. What we choose to do with it is up to us.

Change is constant. Even now, things are not as they were. Where are Christopher Pike and Number One? Doctor Boyce? Where is Yeoman Smith? Where is Earth Command, and what happened to the Space Air Force and the Space Navy? Starfleet and the Federation didn't exist before, and yet now they apparently have always existed. By his own admission he has reshaped reality. The outside universe bleeds in, and nothing remains as it once was. That which he so desperately wishes to preserve is as much an illusory construct as that which I wish to change. I wonder what he would have to say about that. Or you.

25. "Everything is as it should be": Tomorrow is Yesterday

The following is an excerpt from the archives of the United Federation of Planets Temporal Integrity Commission. It appears to be a fragment of an introductory text for prospective field agents educating them on proper temporal mechanics and etiquette.

It is common knowledge the the United Federation of Planets of our time requires all Starfleet officers to observe strict adherence to the Temporal Prime Directive. As its name would suggest, this directive is an extension of the earlier Prime Directive, which was a policy of nonintervention with the natural development of cultures less developed then ours. The logical outgrowth of this core premise, the Temporal Prime Directive clearly states that interference with historical events is strictly forbidden, and the current timeline must be upheld at all costs. In our age of freely available and accessible time travel, the preservation of the sequence of events leading inevitably to this glorious present is of paramount importance. Under no circumstances will any time travel event that could jeopardize or even nullify the possibility of this particular future coming to pass be tolerated, and the stewardship of our timeline can only be seen as our primary responsibility as Starfleet officers.

Once time travel technology became commonplace in all the civilized cultures of the galaxy, an interstellar pact was signed between all the major political powers mutually agreeing to prohibit the use of that technology for any purpose other than pure, untainted scientific research. Furthermore, the agreement outlines explicit guidelines, instructions and procedures on how time travel can be undertaken safely, rationally and virtuously without contaminating or endangering the timestreams that lead to our reality. The ratification of this treaty and related documents, which collectively became known as the Temporal Accords, remains the fundamental guiding tenet of Federation and Starfleet policy to this day. Although most governing bodies freely accepted the new terms, many more did not, and broke off their Federation alliances, feeling that temporal mechanics should be used to change the past for self-centered and misguided notions of "personal improvement". Such temporal incursions are the greatest threat to our safety and sovereignty, and it is the sworn duty of all temporal agents to track down and repair the damage caused by such incursions, and ideally preventing them from occurring in the first place whenever possible.

Although time travel of any sort is discouraged if it can be avoided, Federation and Starfleet policy does acknowledge that the past holds merit from a scientific perspective. One of the reasons it is imperative that we do not change the past is that studying it both teaches and gives us perspective for how to live in the present. In this regard, a history of time travel is beneficial to help us better understand the moral and ethical ramifications of temporal mechanics, why Federation policy has evolved to the point it has and how best to handle a time travel situation should you happen to find yourself in one. It is the past that provides us with a map with which to chart our behviour in the future, both for helping us to decide what choices it is in the best interest of the majority to take, and which it is in their best interests to avoid making again.

The earliest known record of Federation time travel occurred on stardate 3113.2 when the U.S.S. *Enterprise*, registry number NCC-1701, under the command of James Tiberius Kirk encountered a black hole, resulting in the ship travelling several centuries into the past to the Earth of July, 1969. The event has since become the ideal template for the handling of all time travel events, both those of an accidental nature and incursions of malicious, selfish intent. As with much history on file regarding Captain Kirk, the example he sets in this case is one to which we all should strive, for the good of the timeline, the galaxy, and our most sacred freedoms.

There is, of course, troublingly inconsistent data on record about the actual origin of this event. Captain Kirk's recorded logs of the event posit his time warp took place on stardate 3113.2 as the result of a chance encounter with a black hole while in the middle of a routine supply run, although there is also evidence the event actually took place on stardate 1704.4, and was instead the result of a contained matter-antimatter implosion in the *Enterprise*'s warp engines, a last-ditch attempt to free the ship from a decaying orbit around the planet PSI 2000. Such contradictory evidence would seem to support the hypothesis that a temporal incursion occurred prior to the events on record, possibly the doings of Federation enemies acting in opposition to the Temporal Accords for some unknown, yet most certainly nefarious purpose. While the origin of the mysterious "Lost Kirk Incursion" is a hotly debated topic amongst Federation scholars and Starfleet temporal agents alike, the time travel event that we have on record is undeniably a significant one, and a cornerstone for the temporal stability policy we maintain and strictly enforce to this day.

The events as we know them begin shortly after the *Enterprise*'s encounter with a black hole, thus leading to the discovery of the "gravitational slingshot effect" that has since become the foundational theory of modern temporal mechanics. After communications officer Uhura and science officer Spock were able to corroborate to Captain Kirk that the ship had, in fact, travelled back in time to July, 1969 the *Enterprise* was intercepted by a crude jet-propelled scout vehicle from the atmospheric military organization that existed on Earth at the time, in the region then known as the United States of America. As the ship was carrying nuclear weapons that could have jeopardized his ship, Kirk made the correct decision to use a sustained tractor beam pulse to entrap the vehicle and transport the pilot aboard before it broke apart.

Although it is regrettable Kirk was forced to beam the pilot aboard, thus revealing to him the true nature of the *Enterprise*'s temporal displacement and endangering the stability of the timeline, it would have been much worse for Kirk to have let him die, as the pilot was in fact Captain John Christopher, the father of Colonel Shaun Geoffrey Christopher, the pilot of the first manned mission to Saturn and thus a historically significant individual. Kirk also wisely chose to withhold strategic information about the Federation of the time to Christopher and a guard who was subsequently accidentally beamed aboard the ship due to a failed attempt to retrieve visual evidence of the *Enterprise*'s approach into US airspace, claiming to Christopher that he instead represented the interests of the archaic United Earth Space Probe Agency. In particular, it would have been a grave threat to the integrity of future events had the true nature of the black hole been revealed to any of the corrupted individuals, as Earth scientists were just beginning to formulate the theory positing the existence of such phenomena approximately the same time this event took place, albeit in the corrected timeline.

Perhaps the most praiseworthy action Kirk undertook during these events was his keen reasoning that a reverse slingshot effect would send the ship forward in time and, if a precise transporter beam-out occurred, then Captain Christopher and the guard could be returned to the exact moment they were removed from their timestreams and, as the events had no longer happened, they would remember nothing. this allowed Kirk to cover his tracks in such an elegant manner it has rightfully become standard operating procedure for all Federation temporal research ships. The only exceptions to this standing order are, of course, granted to temporal agents acting in the interest of the Temporal Accords who are allowed to interact with timestream natives should they judge it to be appropriate and necessary to sufficiently respond to crises and emergencies and maintain structure and stability. Agents desiring such privileged access should seek Level 10 Security Clearance from the managerial offices of the Temporal Integrity Commission and are encouraged to seek a positing on a Federation timeship.

There is little wonder why James Tiberius Kirk and the U.S.S. *Enterprise* are the most storied captain and most storied ship in Federation history. The exploits of this fabled pairing are decorated and celebrated such that they could almost be seen as modern-day legends. Thankfully, however, rationality prevails in our more enlightened age. Kirk and the crew of the *Enterprise* were no more mythic heroes than this year's graduating class of the academy: They were merely competent and professional human beings who were as dutiful in their day as any officer is expected to be today. This is why we should study and learn from Kirk: He is a fitting role model for valour, honour, and sober respect for the virtues of law, order and the inevitable march of history. We must not give in to the temptations of misty-eyed romanticism and declare Kirk or others like him heroes, icons or legends, but we should look to their stories for advice and guidance on how best to craft ours.

26. "You Will Be Assimilated": The Return of the Archons

Let's take care of the obvious first, shall we? We've got Gene Roddenberry writing again this week. By this point we should know what this means: Terrible pacing, ham-fisted, surface-level exploration of ethics, a disturbingly confused attitude towards the personhood of women, screamingly vast logic lapses and a truly amazing ability to craft a cartoonish 16-ton safe of a moral and somehow still manage to miss the point entirely. With that squared away, let's take a look at the less obvious: "The Return of the Archons" is final, conclusive evidence Roddenberry's original concept of Star Trek wasn't a utopia and is the first appearance of the Prime Directive (and thus also the first deconstruction of the Prime Directive).

The Prime Directive is a very interesting concept unique to Star Trek, and by this I mean I don't like it very much. Traditionally doing a Prime Directive story is the quickest way short of doing an "evil clone frames the hero" plot or having a woman strut onto the bridge in a miniskirt to get me to shut the TV off. On the surface, it sounds like a self-evidently Good Thing, as it prohibits Starfleet officers from interfering in the natural development of a society (although here it's framed more in terms of a vague opposition to "noninterference" of any sort). In fact, at conventions or in interviews Roddenberry (or those attempting to speak for him) would tout the Prime Directive as a key indication of the Federation's evolved, idealistic society, typically framing it in opposition to Western colonialism or the cargo cult myth. This is of course hilarious, as every single Prime Directive story throughout the entirety of Star Trek is either about how demonstrably, measurably worse off the local people are by the crew's adherence to it or how they just go ahead and flagrantly violate it anyway because they know better. Anthropologically speaking, however, it's a nightmare, and given my prior experience in that field it causes me no shortage of headaches.

That said I don't want to spend too much time on the Prime Directive here as, aside from this being the first mention of it, it doesn't play an enormous role in the ethics debate of the week and there are two episodes coming up in the second season which are in many ways the definitive Prime Directive stories, so it seems something of a waste to use up all my critique of it in this chapter. What's more interesting about how it's used in "The Return of the Archons" is that it's explicitly framed as a mirror of Landru's "Prime Directive" to preserve The Body at all costs. As it's Landru's fixation on this basic order that results in the Beta III colony becoming "soulless", in the words of Spock, it could be argued Roddenberry is trying to tell us blind adherence to orders is a Bad Thing and people need to think for themselves and make decisions on a case-by-case basis, and furthermore,

117

that he's now become perfectly willing to point the finger as much at his own people as he is at others. This makes a great deal of sense: First of all, it fits very neatly with what can be ascertained about Roddenberry's worldview, but also with the way the rest of the episode plays out as The Body is basically a society built around unthinkingly following the orders telepathically communicated to them from Landru.

But of course there's a problem. In this case, it's that Beta III can also be read very easily as a collectivist, communist society: Everyone calls each other friend, doesn't ask any questions and obeys orders for the good of the The Body, i.e., the overall society. Perhaps it's a Stalinistic society, where a single, authoritarian power has absolute control under the guise of an egalitarian, co-operative paradise: Even the viral motif, where those who are "foreign" and "do not conform" are "destructive" to The Body and must be "purged", is straightforwardly a reiteration of Stalinistic disciplinary and disappearing tactics, albeit a rather clever and original one. Even so, it's not clear that Roddenberry actually recognises the difference between communism, collectivism, Stalinism and generic authoritarianism, or indeed ever intended to write such a message into his story. Roddenberry's biggest problem is that he has problems actual articulating himself and translating his ideas clearly into textual form, and this is a good example of how that can wrongfoot him.

The big revelation is, naturally that Landru is a computer. Exactly who programmed it, why, and how it lasted this long in control of an entire planet for 6000 years (or was that only 100? I was never very clear on that, and there's a bit of a difference between those two numbers) is not explained, but also not entirely important. What this also means is we get another example of the signature James T. Kirk method of computer repair: Blowing it up by shouting paradoxes and logic errors at it (it's a good thing he never tried this on Spock, especially given his lines in the denouement this time). This is of course ridiculous and displays a riotous failure to understand and wanton disregard for basic computer science, but again, there's another episode coming up where it will be far more appropriate to talk about that than it is here. This is very irritating to me, as it all adds up to "The Return of the Archons" being another episode that there's very little for me to say intelligent about it.

But there are a few things. Firstly, like "Miri" and "The Squire of Gothos" before it, "The Return of the Archons" is also very good at building an air of mystery. The teaser alone holds up the rest of the episode in this regard: Sulu and a redshirt are running though Mayberry dressed in Victorian frock coats while evil clockwork monks slowly close in on them with what basically amount to magic staves. That's got to get anyone's attention. Likewise, the Stepford-esque villagers and chaotic, hedonistic Festival (despite actually making no narrative sense whatsoever if you think too long about it) help contribute to the general unsettling atmosphere, in spite of the fact we're once again back on that damn backlot. Most importantly in my opinion, however, is that the one thing "The Return of the Archons" is unwaveringly consistent and coherent about is its perhaps surprising, yet firm and undeniable, anti-utopian stance.

It's continuously stressed by not only the followers of Landru, but the crew itself, is that Beta III is explicitly a utopian society. Those who are part of The Body continually talk about how happy, serene and peaceful they are and how Landru has created a paradise. Indeed, he arguably has: There is no war, hunger, disease or conflict on Beta III (except during the officially-sanctioned Festival) and Landru removes such concepts from The Body immediately as inherently dangerous foreign substances should it detect them. And the show hates it for those very reasons. In addition to the obvious xenophobia, The Body is depicted as vapid, empty and without any sense of creativity or enthusiasm for life, despite being placid, content and happy. The clincher comes in the denouement, where Spock muses on how humanity has often longed to create an ideal, perfect world and Kirk grins and says "Yes. And we never got it. Just lucky, I guess". This is quite frankly astonishing from a modern perspective: Here's Gene Roddenberry, the supposed Arch-Utopian, quite clearly penning a story where a desire for utopia is portrayed as dangerous, stifling, wrongheaded and dehumanizing. To paraphrase a young Jean-Luc Picard: What the Devil is going on here?

Thing is, this isn't so inconceivable a statement as it first appears, and we should already be familiar with some of the reasons why. The fact of the matter is that Gene Roddenberry in 1967 is not a utopian futurist. He more or less gets there by the time *Star Trek: The Next Generation* rolls around, but he manifestly isn't now for reasons that will become clear in another year or so. *Star Trek* was never created to be something like this, and the show as it exists now most certainly isn't. Furthermore, the entire idea of a utopian society is a loaded concept: The term was coined by political philosopher Thomas More in a treatise that is now largely seen to be a work of straight-up satire, skewering 16th century Europe's panglossian attitude towards its rampant, systemic social problems. As a result of this, anyone following More attempting to craft an unironically "utopian" society really has to be seen as somewhat egregiously not getting the joke. The fact so many of the so-called utopias in speculative fiction come from Western authors who are still very much part of a culture descended in more ways than they'd care to admit from the Europe Thomas More was bitterly complaining about in 1516 can be seen as nothing short of delicious poetic irony.

Does this mean that Star Trek and other works like it can never be hopeful? Are we all doomed to all be eschatological nihilists from now until the inevitable heat death of the universe, or the equally inevitable entropic collapse of human society, whichever comes first? I don't think so, and the key reason why I don't is that I strongly believe there is a stark difference between utopianism as it was originally conceived and the utopianism that exists now, which is really a form of idealism. Star Trek isn't trying to create the blueprint for a utopian society and never has: Every time it's caught itself getting to close to that it's severely problematized itself, sometimes with absolutely horrifying consequences. Star Trek is definitely "utopian" though inasmuch as it is idealistic: When it's at it's best, it shows us people and concepts entirely within our reach that we can strive for. Even now, in 1967, it's showing us that maybe an environment where men, women and others of all backgrounds and creeds can live and work together as equals isn't an absolute impossibility. Granted a lot of this is coming about purely by accident, coincidence and the secondary effect of decisions that were made in the interests of goals pretty far removed from that

119

of material social progress and the show isn't going to engage with these themes with any seriousness or maturity until it gets rebooted a few more times, but it's still a reading and implication that's demonstrably there, if only as a truism given that a not-insignificant number of people have in fact read it this way.

This is hopeful; this is idealistic-It's not a utopian society by any stretch of the imagination, and as Kirk says we probably shouldn't be waiting around for one, but it is giving us the most basic of hints that a world better than the one we seem to be stuck with is possible. This is a declaration we should take notice of, respect and be thankful for. These things can happen, and we can and should strive for them. Even if it's not really all there now, in 1967, it definitely will be before our trek through the stars is over. It won't always be paired with completely unproblematic concepts and ideas (it certainly hasn't been to date) and indeed on a great many occasions will be actively working contrary to this declaration, but this still may well be the most important thing to know about Star Trek: A better life is possible. Equality and peace are possible. Love is possible. Enlightenment is possible. And isn't that, ultimately, what progressiveness means?

27. "A strange game. The only winning move is not to play.": A Taste of Armageddon

What's most immediately interesting, to start with, is that we seem to have encountered a temporal event of our own and skipped several episodes. The Federation was established in "Arena", and Starfleet way back in "Court Martial" but we haven't seen much of either of them since and it didn't seem to alter the status quo of the show in any meaningful way. The *Enterprise* still putted about on routine patrol for the most part. "The Alternative Factor" and "Tomorrow is Yesterday" gave us some sweeping, dramatic shakeups, but both of those seemed like special exceptions: Not quite narrative collapses, but definitely temporary crises in the way things worked. Still, nothing we didn't really think we wouldn't come back from. The only indication things might be changing at all was in Gene Roddenberry's own "The Return of the Archons". In "A Taste of Armageddon", however, the Federation now has the full name of the United Federation of Planets (implying a structure larger than just Earth and its colonies) and the *Enterprise* is now escorting its ambassadors on a mission to open up friendly negotiations with civilizations around the galaxy (confirming it). This is, to understate things considerably, a rather immense shift in standard operating procedure for *Star Trek*.

A cursory glance at the credits reveals this to be not completely unprecedented or unexpected, as this is the second script from Gene Coon, who, recall, penned "Arena" himself as well. This one is also credited to a Robert Hamner, but, aside from an interesting note that he is listed as the creator of the police procedural *S.W.A.T.*, I can't find a lot of biographical information on him and not having seen that show personally I'm somewhat at a loss to talk about his positionality and interests as a writer. But Coon is a known quantity to us by now, and as his name shows up twice, as both the co-writer of the episode and the current executive producer, it's probably safe to attribute an at least not-insignificant amount of the ethics here to him. And besides this makes sense as "A Taste of Armageddon" is very much the evolution of the territory we first found ourselves in with "Arena".

At first glance this episode would seem to be about the juxtaposition of the *Enterprise* crew and the world of Federation diplomats. Ambassador Fox is depicted first as just as much of an obstructive bureaucrat as Commissioner Ferris in "The Galileo Seven" and he frequently butts heads with Kirk, and later Scott, in a rote safety of the mission vs. safety of the ship debate that's already become a stock and hackneyed *Star Trek* plot. It's Fox's bizarre fixation on opening relations with the Eminians at all costs that puts the lives of everyone on the ship in grave jeopardy, leads to Kirk's away team being captured and thrusts everyone headfirst into the Eminian-Vendikan war. Following the logic the show has established up to this point, it would seem sensible to read the episode's central conflict as one between distant officials in fancy suits and the soldiers on the front lines who know the reality of living day to day on the edge. And this holds: Further evidence for this interpretation would be in the scenes where Fox keeps acting bullheaded and naively trustworthy, lacking the gut sense of trouble Scott and McCoy have and the climax, where, after being rescued from the disintegration chamber, he flatly tells Spock that he's "never been a soldier" but "learns quickly".

But what's also interesting is this also further condemns the Federation. Absolutely nothing related to the UFP seems to work in this episode: The Federation's obsessive demand to open up trade agreements in the NGC 321 cluster seem comically overstated and it's really never fully explained why the area is so important to them. We just have to open up diplomatic relations because...they're diplomatic relations. You've got to open diplomatic relations. Fox's overtures just about get him and the crew sentenced to death, and every other discussion tactic he attempts fails both decisively and hilariously. Diplomacy is shown to be, on the whole, ineffective and overly convoluted at best and blinkered to the point of being actually dangerously counterproductive at worst. Fox does get a manner of redemption in the end when he offers to stay behind on Eminiar VII to help moderate talks between them and Vendikar, but it's clear this isn't quite in either his job description or his area of expertise: He says he'll do the best he can, but by no means does he give us the indication he's the best person for the job, or even that this is the right job for the situation at hand. Even Spock says normal diplomatic procedures aren't going to work here.

So obviously what we have is another chest-thumping, tale about honour and duty and the rugged, manly heroism of the militaristic way of life, *a la* "The Corbomite Manuever" or, to a lesser extent, "Court Martial"? Sort of, but not quite. Coon may have been an ex-marine, but sometimes it takes a veteran to realise the ugliness that can exist in the world. The reality is "A Taste of Armageddon" is a deeply, deeply cynical story. Just about every element of the show at every level is seriously problematized. Fox is misguided and dangerous, but so is *everyone else*: The Eminians and the Vendikans have made killing clinical and routine because war is too important to their cultural heritage to move beyond and even Kirk and the *Enterprise* crew, who are definitely meant to have the moral and ethical high ground, are retroactively made, *and by their own admission*, natural-born, instinctive killers. On the one hand this episode isn't quite as dark, somber and brutal as "Balance of Terror" as it does have some exciting setpieces and Kirk, Scott, Spock and McCoy all get to deliver some very rousing and triumphant speeches. On the other hand, this episode is extremely disquieting in some other areas, namely, in that it makes the audience *uncomfortable* for liking these things.

Indeed, this is essentially the entire point of the story. Kirk freely calls himself a barbarian and a bloodthirsty killer, is willing to risk the total destruction of both Eminiar VII and Vendikar and his big speech involves widening the net of that condemnation to everyone on both planets, the *Enterprise* and basically all of humanity itself. The central failing of the Eminians is that, in reducing war to a numbers game, they've forgotten how horrific and destructive it is and why it's something to be avoided. But this is by no means a hypothetical or a thought experiment: Coon has a very clear target in mind he's satirizing here, and it's us. Or, at least, the US in the 1960s: Dave Gerrold, an important Star Trek creative figure who we'll start to talk at length about next season, says the computers tallying up the simulated war casualties was a direct reference to, and condemnation of, the way the mainstream news in the United States at the time covered the constantly updating ground reports of similar casualties Vietnam War. This goes beyond problematizing war as a spectacle to attacking war as a mundane reality, and no-one is spared from judgment and reproach: In order to teach us war is monstrous, Kirk turns himself into a monster and, in the process, shows us we're all monsters too. It is unbelievably disturbing.

The key line comes in the denouement, where Kirk states how "instinct can be fought", and all it takes to start working towards peace is for a killer to say "I'm not going to kill today". Which I mean yes, but...Bloody Hell is that depressing. It must be stressed that *absolutely no-one* in the story denies that humans (or I guess humanoids, as the Eminians and Vendikans aren't meant to be human) are at heart murderous, bloodthirsty savage killers. The best we can hope for is that we eventually figure out how to work against our baser predilections to reach some semblance of social harmony. And well...There just really isn't anywhere to go from that, is there? As much as Coon's stinging critique actually does stick, my objection is we really don't have any actual heroes here. The Federation is, again, tunnel-visioned, self-interested and shortsighted and Kirk and the *Enterprise* are essentially telling us they're all murderous savages and we should feel bad for watching them.

This is particularly awful coming off of "The Return of the Archons", an episode all about Gene Roddenberry just straight-up bearing all and saying no, he's not a utopian and neither is *Star Trek*. Now we have Gene Coon telling us to our face, and in no uncertain terms, that we're all terrible, cold-blooded monsters. But I just don't agree. In spite of everything we've done, I think it's incredibly crass and reductive to claim that humanity as a whole is instinctively murderous. That contributes to the erroneous, and incredibly dangerous, idea that humanity is an aberration in the history of the universe and is inherently unnatural and destructive. Humans are a part of nature just as much as anything else is, and we have a role to play in the grand cosmic oversoul of consciousness. Tapping out and succumbing to depression and nihilism isn't healthy for us, it isn't healthy for our planet and it isn't healthy for our universe. A show that was really committed to utopian ideals would be showing us a way forward even in our darkest moments, reminding us of the true selves who are waiting for us to reconnect with them if only we'd take notice of our presentness and potential.

In the previous chapter I tried to argue that despite Roddenberry rejecting any claims of being a utopian in "The Return of the Archons", there was still enough that was positive and hopeful about *Star Trek* that the chance of it remaining *idealistic* was still there. Is it possible to do some similar salvage work with Coon and "A Taste of Armageddon"? Very possibly. I'm at least not as willing to give up on the show as the show seems ready to give up on itself here. Not after 24 episodes and with two more seasons, six more TV shows, thirteen movies and a frankly frightening amount of comic books, video games and mass-market paperback tie-in books in my future. Firstly, there is the truism argument: It's a fact that countless people have read Star Trek as expressly progressive and idealistic series, so there has to be *something* here to support that. It's simply ludicrous to expect *that many* people to be misreading the show. As I count myself as among those people, given the fact I'm doing this book series at all, I'd tend to agree with them at least in the very general sense. Last time I talked about how the mere presence of a mixed-race, mixed-gender and mixed-species crew is enough to inspire many people in spite of how unintentional or coincidental that might have been. I still stand by that, but let's go one further. Let's go back to Coon's last episode.

Putting aside the possibly problematic aspects of their characters for the moment, the Metrons said humanity showed great promise. Kirk displayed "the advanced trait of mercy", as it were, surprising them (and Coon, apparently, as well, given his attitude in this episode). We're not quite good enough to make the cut now, but it's entirely possible we might someday. I think the same can be said about Star Trek as a whole. Nearly a full season in, we have a rocky, confused and occasionally actually brilliant show that has the makings of something truly great about it. It's not good enough to actually live up to its potential, and it's frequently acting actively contrary to realising it far too often for my liking, but it's worth keeping in mind when we caught our first glimpse of the *Enterprise* bridge in 1964 during the opening for "The Cage", there was absolutely no indication the show would ever be able to achieve even the things it has 24 episodes in. I'm also lucky enough to speak from a privileged position: I know the future.

And mercy tends to be the product of empathy.

28. "Marooned for all eternity in the center of a dead planet.": Space Seed

I suspect if there's one episode of the original *Star Trek* that my readers will expect me to come up with some mad, overblown stream-of-consciousness, recursive mess of a writeup for it would probably be this one. I hate to disappoint expectations, but that's not going to be the case here. There was a fairly unbroken streak of episodes starting midway through the season that all seemed to call out for that kind of interpretation, hence a number of the last few chapters have been in that style, and there's more coming up that warrant it as well, so my abandoning that structure is certainly not something to worry about for the short term. However, "Space Seed" calls for a different approach.

The elephant in the room is naturally that this episode provides the subject matter for the consensus-best Star Trek movie, which is at once a kind of revisit and reimagining of the events of "Space Seed" and also the debut of Nicholas Meyer's unique, and much loved, interpretation of the franchise. Whether or not I feel *Star Trek II: The Wrath of Khan* is actually deserving of the kind of breathless worship it gets from mainline fandom or is worthy of the title of Best Trek Ever, let alone Perfect Cinematic Masterpiece, is something I'm not going to even begin to worry about until we reach 1982, which is still quite a long ways off from where we are now.

The more important thing to keep in mind for now is that Carey Wilber, who was the actual writer of this episode is not Nicholas Meyer, and this is really where we need to begin before we get anywhere near close to figuring out what this episode really is. Gene Coon has a secondary credit on the teleplay, but given this episode's plot and general tone I'm going to assume he just did some cleanup work after the fact because, for reasons I'll get into a bit later, "Space Seed" doesn't feel like Coon's material at all. Actually, I'll just come out and tip my hand right away. I'm positive this is going to be a nuclear bomb of a claim to make and this is without doubt the part of the book that will turn away any longterm Star Trek fans who haven't been driven off already, but this is my reaction and my book and I get to say it: This episode is bad. Really bad.

Actually, I take back part of that last paragraph. This isn't *bad* television: It's as competently and professionally made as any of the strongest episodes of the series so far. In this regard, the incoherent structural jumble of something like "The Menagerie", or especially "The Alternative Factor", is much worse. But the thing is both of those episodes hinted at, or maybe accidentally hit on, deeper, more exciting concepts and wound up delightfully oversignified as a result. No, "Space Seed" isn't *bad* television, it's *wrong* television. This is *evil* television. We're right back in the territory we last tread in "The

Corbomite Maneuver", and in fact this one is infinitely worse: What we've got here is a perfect microcosm and embodiment of everything that's wrong with *Star Trek* in 1967.

Let's start with the obvious. Marla McGivers is terrible. She spends her off-time drawing and lusting over erotica of muscly, hyper-masculine historical figures and when she actually has a job to do she stands around dumbly and immediately falls for Khan before the dude's even been defrosted. Once Khan comes aboard the *Enterprise*, she quickly and enthusiastically submits to his dominance and authority and than enters into what can absolutely only be described as an abusive relationship with him. Furthermore, McGivers' character is *defined* by her submissiveness: In Wilber's original script, she was meant to have a friend named Yeoman Baker, and there was to be a scene where Baker tells her a Lieutenant Hanson wants to take McGivers to the ship's dance, which is apparently a thing now. McGivers was to have told Hanson to "get lost" and that she was "waiting for a man who will knock down my door and carry me to where he wants me". While the Baker character could potentially have served to give the story a desperately-needed second female perspective, as it stands in the finished product...Well, there's not a whole lot of ways for me to redeem that.

What's almost even worse than McGivers herself is how the rest of the crew treats her. Kirk is noticeably disdainful and dismissive towards her from the beginning, sneering at the notion a mere *historian* would be a part of his crew. With one line, the show brings up years and years of prejudice towards both women and the humanities, and how the two are a natural, proper fit for each other. The humanities are frequently seen as more "feminine", and thus inferior, fields of study when compared to the hard sciences, or indeed the military. That scene was enough to get me balled up with rage, and this offensively authoritarian, male supremacist attitude defines the rest of the episode. McGivers might even have been acceptable to me had there been other women to contrast her with: Maybe Yeoman Baker would have been that character. I doubt it, but we'll never know. Even when "Shore Leave" gave us Yeoman Barrows, who was almost comically stereotypical, that episode at least also had Alice to contrast with her. McGivers is played painfully straight and just lands at irredeemably offensive and retrograde.

There's Uhura, of course, but I can't keep leaning on Uhura as a feminist and racial Get-Out-Of-Jail-Free card for the show. The blunt reality is she's simply not an important enough character according to the show's own internal structure and logic. I wish she was, but 23 episodes after her debut, her role hasn't developed much beyond generic background space switchboard operator and she barely gets any lines in any given episode. Nichelle Nichols is a wonderful stage presence and makes Uhura far more memorable and likable a character than she would have been without her, but the sad truth is this simply isn't enough. And here, of course, she gets beaten by Khan's super-soldiers and bursts into tears.

Then we come to Khan himself. Now, before I get any more hate for this piece than I already know I'm going to get, let me first say for the record Ricardo Montalbán is brilliant. He delivers a tremendously multi-layered and charismatic performance that's unlike just about anything else we've seen on *Star Trek* so far, and that alone may be the reason this story gets revisited in fifteen years' time. The first thing to note about Khan as a character then is he's another in a line of evil or otherwise dark doubles or reflections of Captain Kirk. A surprisingly significant number of episodes this season have dealt with this theme: First we had Gary Mitchell in "Where No Man Has Gone Before", then the Good!Kirk/Evil!Kirk split in "The Enemy Within", Kirk's android duplicate in "What Are Little Girls Made Of?" and Trelane in "The Squire of Gothos". By this point this particular thread could charitably be called "tired", but Khan is without question the most memorable of the lot.

Khan is also a unique twist on this particular formula, and it's worth putting in the context of all those other characters like him. Coon's big contribution to this script seems to be changing Khan's background details. Wilber originally wrote him as Harold Erikson, a regular, non-enhanced criminal who would become a space pirate. Coon apparently suggested Erikson should become "a true rival to Kirk" and introduced the genetic engineering dictator plotlines. The name change to Khan came when Montalbán was cast (the Noonien was apparently Gene Roddenberry's idea, who named him after an old Chinese friend of his he wanted to reconnect with, which I'll just let speak for itself). Of course, as conceived this gives the character rather disturbing Nazi overtones, especially given the way the episode as filmed actually plays out. Whether or not it's better he became a charismatic, masculine, generically foreign man (Khan is supposedly Indian, Montalbán is Mexican, the show seems to think the two are one and the same) is something I'll leave to you to hash out.

Regardless, Coon's edit is worth paying very close attention to: He specifically said in order to become a match for Kirk, Khan would need to be functionally superhuman, which is highly interesting given the reading about Kirk's character we've been building since "Where No Man Has Gone Before". We should also contrast Khan with Trelane, the last such instance of an antagonist being a mirror of Kirk. What's crucial to note here I feel is that Trelane was for all intents and purposes a mirror of William Shatner, or at least Shatner's performance-He's the other side of Shatner's drag action hero. Khan, however, is explicitly a rival for *Kirk*, or at least he's meant to be, and Jim Kirk-as-written and William Shatner are absolutely *not* interchangeable, something a great many Star Trek fans and, actually, members of the larger pop culture, would do well to remember. But Khan is more than just Kirk's evil clone or doppelganger; He's also his equal, and by doing this the show opens up a whole host of problematic subtexts, and I'm not sure exactly where this leaves *Star Trek* at the end of it all.

What I do know is that, through this, "Space Seed" takes the show to some very dark places, and this is very much not a good thing. Khan is a ruthless dictator and the product of eugenics such that he considers himself morally, intellectually and physically superior to anyone not of his lineage. Also, as befits his name, his one desire is to conquer the universe and lord over an empire of his making. But Khan is also frequently and distressingly validated in these beliefs: In many ways he really *is* superior, or at least the show seems to want us to think he is. He frequently comments on how humanity hasn't fundamentally changed in two centuries, easily outmaneuvers and dispatches the *Enterprise* crew, and the only reason Kirk survives his intended execution is due to McGivers betraying Khan and saving his life at the last second in an act that is framed both diegetically and extradiegetically as a "weakness" on her part. Even once Kirk regains control of the ship and rounds up Khan and his soldiers, the hearing he gives is essentially a surrender-As Khan explicitly says, he gets what he wants. A planet to rule and turn into the seat of a new empire. Khan wins.

What's even more disturbing is that Kirk, McCoy and Scott *admire* Khan, and are furthermore actually in *awe* of him. Once they discern his identity, they take turns musing that he was "one of the good ones", stresses that there were "no deaths" under his rule and go out of their way to praise his charisma, energy, ambition and style of dictatorship. This manages to do the impossible and cause Spock to be visibly shocked and appalled, but his protests are laughed down and dismissed with an incredibly unconvincing bit from Kirk and McCoy about how humans can detest a person for what they did while admiring their stamina. This is exacerbated by the fact Kirk and McCoy are just about the most patronizing and demeaning to Spock we've ever seen them: McCoy calls him unfeeling and inhuman and launches into an ugly rage for really no reason and Kirk is intolerably smug and condescending to him throughout the entire episode. This is, frankly, undistilled speciesism conveyed in racist language and bald-facedly patriarchal. No manner of diverse casting is going to make up for this.

But this is, sadly, to be expected, given what the rest of this episode is doing. Look at the word choice here: If Khan is Kirk's "rival" or equal and opposite, than we're to take them as expressly comparable entities. The threat Khan poses is not that of a dark mirror of what humanity might become or the dangerously re-emerged relic of a misbegotten age long in the past, as the fans would tell you, it's that he might just show himself to be manlier and more competent than Kirk. The central battle of "Space Seed" isn't authoritarianism sparring with democracy, nor is it even a fight over the value of eugenics: It's a war to control the *Enterprise* and over who gets to be the leading man. The show is overtly likening Kirk to Khan, and it's not doing anything to problematize this. And Kirk definitely is not opposed to Khan on principle: Putting aside for the moment his hero worship of Khan's suave badassery, his dropping of official charges against him and granting him and his followers a planet has to be seen as a tacit endorsement of his beliefs. If he were truly interested in demonstrating humanity had evolved, he *absolutely* would have brought Khan to justice. Even Spock gets to say "It would be worthwhile to return in several centuries to see what grew of the seed you planted here today".

Aside from once again completely derailing the ethics of *Star Trek*, this also gives us one of the most distressing morals in the show's history. There is an unsettling tendency amongst some classical liberals to believe that a temporary dictatorship might be beneficial, even necessary, to bring about true egalitarianism in the future. There is a quote often attributed to 18th century French economic philosopher Anne-Robert-Jacques Turgot, Baron de Laune in which he is alleged to have said "Give me five years of despotism and France shall be free". The theory, entirely in keeping with liberal thought, is that an enlightened absolute ruler would be better than looser, more generative forms of government because we'd finally have someone who knew what they were doing in charge and he (it's always a he, even when it isn't) would be able to institute reform without hindrance from annoying checks and balances from less-intelligent obstructionists. I'm also reminded of the Philosopher Kings mentioned in Plato's *The Republic*, which uses very similar language.

In recent years, we've seen an alarming hard swerve towards authoritarianism in the geopolitical discourse, but a perfectly liberal form of authoritarianism. The middlebrow neoliberal centrists make overtures to lesser-evilism while remaining just superficially progressive enough so as to push the boundaries of what it means to be reactionary. Meanwhile, the major Western powers of the United States and United Kingdom seem perfectly willing to completely democratically elect Actual Fascists, or those selling fascist and xenophobic rhetoric and policies, to express their discontent with the hegemonic status quo. And possibly the most interesting (read alarming) version of this manifests within the culture Star Trek would court: Those who we would today call STEM people.

In Silicon Valley today there exists a real subculture who believe that the Enlightened Despot Philosopher King will come to us as a messianic saviour in the form of a hyper-intelligent artificial intelligence. Connected to them are the "Geeks for Monarchy" crowd of "neoreactionaries", who take the smug idea of Nerd intellectual superiority to the logical limit by calling for a Dictatorship of the Nerds using the repurposed rhetoric of scientific racism. And in the time since the original version of this essay was written, the fundamentally patriarchal stratified space of video games has produced its own terrorist organisation dedicated to committing hate crimes against women, queer people and people of colour. And with them come the "Men's Rights Activists", or "MRAs", who believe conspiracy theories about a global ruling cabal of women that can only be fought through misogynistic violence and forcing women to learn their "proper place" as submissive chattel. This is why media studies of pop culture is important, because these are all movements our own pop culture has actively facilitated, be it overtly in power fantasies like the abjectly evil movie *Revenge of the Nerds*, through social factors like how video games are a space designed to be exclusionary to oppressed groups by default, or through the sociology of Star Trek.

Because this is what Khan is. A tyrannical dictator, but one of the "good" ones. A monomaniacal despot, but one who is somehow more "enlightened" and "liberal" in his views. And the show not only condones, but explicitly *endorses* this. Khan's eugenics backstory and the crew's deference to him is incredibly telling: He is no artefact of Earth's shameful past. If *Star Trek* is about idealistic futurism, then Khan is the show's own potential future. *His* are the ideals that *Star Trek*, right now, in this moment, stands for. After all, as he is so fond of saying, humanity hasn't evolved much, and right now the terrifying thing is he's the only clear-cut vision of the future *Star Trek*'s given us so far. And why wouldn't he be? Wasn't the original pitch for the show about a crew of space naval officers going around telling morality plays, teaching everyone the difference between Right and Wrong? Just last episode we had Kirk strolling onto Eminiar VII and making all their decisions for them, all the while touting humanity's inherent barbarism. Here we have him the most stern, authoritarian and masculine he's been since "The Corbomite Maneuver" and treating Spock with open contempt for not being human enough to understand the value of emotion and illogic. How is this conclusion in any way dissonant with what the show was previously established about itself? Why isn't the end result of this train of thought going to look suspiciously like Khan Noonien Singh?

And let's go one better. Let's also take another look at Khan's relationship with Mc-Givers. At first, this seems to open up the one confusing structural logic hole in the otherwise very tight production we've got this week: Khan has thirty genetically perfect *Überfraus* aboard the *Botany Bay*: Why would he waste his time pursuing someone of inferior stock? His interest in McGivers can really only be seen as a means to an end to get access to the *Enterprise*. Sure, he gets a line at the end about how she's a "superior woman" and he's glad she's joining them, but it really doesn't take as far as I'm concerned. But that's exactly it. The reason Khan is interested in McGivers is horrifically clear: Because he *can* use her. Because he can control her. He can dominate her completely and utterly and she'll *love* it. Oh, she may not at first, but he'll just need to give her a strict lesson from the back of his hand to make her step in line before him. That's unmistakably what we'd today call the MRA philosophy. Of course he's not going to be interested in the *Überfraus*: They're his equals, or perhaps they might be superior to even him in some respects. Either way he'd have to treat them accordingly, and that's not something Khan wants in a female companion. Nor, would it seem, is it what *Star Trek* wants in its female characters.

(Indeed, *Star Trek* will eventually give us a writer who explicitly pens MRA genre fiction! And she's a woman to boot! Precisely what the MRAs need to feel legitimized in their cause!)

We're coming off of a stretch of episodes that have been about nothing if not tearing down the show as it exists right now bit by bit. This isn't by definition a bad thing, but against that backdrop "Space Seed" is horrifying. This episode would have us believe the only way forward for Star Trek is Khan's enlightened despotism. Well I'm not going to stand for that. There is absolutely nothing leftist or progressive about authoritarianism, totalitarianism and male supremacy, no matter how much "liberal" or "socialist" language the monster wishes to clothe himself in. Tyranny and domination are tyranny and domination regardless of the form they take. I cannot tolerate this and I will not accept this. The other side of the argument is no better: Can the equation of Kirk and Khan, and thus "Space Seed" on the whole, be read as yet another condemnation of the show's militarism and patriarchy? If so that's even worse, as Coon has doomed the show to an inevitable and inescapable future of iron-fisted despotism.

But, no matter how toxic it may be, I'm stuck with it for now. Thanks in no small part to the success of *Star Trek II: The Wrath of Khan,* there are few episodes in the Original Series more influential, more fondly remembered or with more of an artificially inflated reputation than "Space Seed". And, as a result, I'm marooned here. Trapped once again facing down the show's Death Drive, this time brought upon by its own egotistical conception of itself and delusions of lordship. I really want to help turn Star Trek into something that can be taken as a genuine source for good in the world and as a version of idealism that it's actually possible to respond to and is something to strive towards. But at the moment the biggest obstacle in my path is Star Trek itself. I can, once again, appeal to the future, but now it's a question of what that future is going to entail, exactly. A future that leads to Khan Noonien Singh is not one anyone should be allow to come to pass.

29. "One morn a Peri at the gate/Of Eden stood disconsolate": This Side of Paradise

"This Side of Paradise" is a story about how dangerous idealized societies are. It's also about how the pursuit of simple, communal living and an exploration of love are inhuman temptations and how it's far better and more proper to focus on duty, responsibility, modernist, technoscientific notions of progress and suffering. At least, that's what I think it's trying to be. Hard to tell. At its best it's a crass indictment of collectivist lifestyles as being "lazy", "stagnant" and "counterproductive" and at its worst it's the exact same goddamn story as "The Return of the Archons" from three bloody weeks ago. It's also written by the same guy who penned "The Corbomite Maneuver".

So yeah heads up there's no way in hell there was ever the remotest chance of me liking this one. Just so I get it all out in the open right away: I think "This Side of Paradise" is utterly immoral and I have no intention whatsoever of mustering up a redemptive reading for it. I've also just about lost patience completely with this season, if not this *show*, as this is the fourth story in a row with a rock-bottom cynical, nihilistic and actually openly evil ethics about it and at this point the series is genuinely teetering on the edge of invalidating itself and self-destruction. Thankfully, by the grace of some divine cosmic miracle I have something to talk about in this chapter aside from the unbelievably depressing and infuriating plot.

Firstly, there's a second name on this script apart from Jerry Sohl (or rather his pseudonym Nathan Butler), the aforementioned writer who previously made me want to suplex my TV set with "The Corbomite Maneuver". That name would be D.C. Fontana, who slips into her familiar *Star Trek* role with this episode. Fontana is one of the single most important creative figures in Trek history, story editing the lion's share of the Original Series before becoming the joint showrunner of the Animated Series with Dave Gerrold and continuing to contribute scripts to the franchise as late as *Star Trek: Deep Space Nine*. This is actually the third time we've seen Fontana's name in the credits, but this is the first opportunity we've had to explore her impact on the series in any meaningful way. She wrote the teleplay for "Charlie X", but that was mostly a Gene Roddenberry effort, and she also wrote "Tomorrow is Yesterday", but that chapter seems to have gotten away from me somewhat. Which actually turned out to be fortuitous, because not only is this really the best time to introduce Fontana as it's where she first becomes story editor, it also spares me actually having talk about "This Side of Paradise".

Fontana heavily retooled Sohl's original contribution, apparently at the behest of Roddenberry, who is said to have told her "if you can rewrite this script, you can be my story editor". He must have liked the job she did, as she was promptly hired for the position as soon as the story went out. Fontana's alterations do undoubtedly improve the episode: She has the plants scattered all over the colony instead of being in one easily-avoidable cave as Sohl had written them and she also takes the love story with Leila, originally intended for Sulu, and gives it to Spock instead, which allows Leonard Nimoy to explore his character in a way he hasn't really been able to since "The Naked Time". However that being said, it's hard to argue this is Fontana's best contribution to the show (even at this point in her career: Temporal mechanics aside "Tomorrow is Yesterday" is an absolute riot and this...isn't). Even Fontana is incapable of salvaging the story from its blatantly reactionary overtones. So let's talk about Spock instead.

As I've mentioned before, Spock is in many ways the central character of *Star Trek*. This is mostly due to Roddenberry's particular interests: He is fixated at this point, in a sense, on the split between logic and emotions and he is very interested in when it's better to lean on one than another. We can infer this quite easily from the fact Spock was originally Number One, who was a character especially written for Roddenberry's muse Majel Barrett. Barrett is on record saying Number One was the first character created for Star Trek and while the captain character wasn't *quite* an afterthought, Roddenberry was specifically interested in her. Even though Leonard Nimoy is demonstrably not Majel Barrett, this has carried through to the series. As fascinating as Kirk has become, this is about 99% due to William Shatner camping and queering him up to positively delightful degrees. Kirk-as-written is basically a generic, masculine commanding presence and the only other person we've seen apart from Shatner who seems to truly get him has been Paul Schneider: Indeed in this episode Kirk overcomes the spores' evil temptations of love, happiness and tranquility through force of sheer aggressive manliness, which really says more about *Star Trek*'s ethics in one scene than I could ever hope to with this entire book.

But Spock doesn't have these drawbacks. He's increasingly become able to explore the concept of human emotion in ways the other characters aren't able to, and, under Fontana, he's eventually going to become basically the best evidence the show has that it's got anything at all to do with leftist counterculture or any kind of spiritual dimension. While we're still a ways away from seriously talking about that, Fontana is laying the groundwork here. When it's not being intolerable, "This Side of Paradise" actually has some provocative things to say about Spock and romance. The whole point of his relationship with Leila is that she's capable of seeing sides of him Spock's not able to show to anyone else. In that sense, were I inclined to be charitable, I could read the spores as an extension of that theme, metaphorically representing intimacy and emotional vulnerability. This manages to work both better and worse than in "The Naked Time": Better in the sense that establishing a pre-exisiting relationship with Leila gives her an authority Nurse Chapel didn't have, but worse in that the episode is nowhere near capable of supporting this kind of character moment, certainly not compared with "The Naked Time" which, despite its numerous faults, did sort of have that as a central theme.

Credit to Fontana, this does also result in the episode's one interesting idea. This is a very straight cis female perspective to bring to the show (which is welcome enough), but there's a couple of other angles here too. Firstly, this indicates Fontana is very much aware of what the nascent fandom springing up around *Star Trek* *really* looks like. As we shall soon examine in more detail, far from being enjoyed by "respectable" upper middle-class (male) STEM-type people, Star Trek's first fans were actually almost universally *women* across the race and class spectrum. And while there were a number of reasons these female fans latched onto Star Trek and Spock in particular, fantasies about being to "break through" his logical exterior to reach his passionate heart beneath were certainly among them for straight women, and this is almost beat-for-beat the plot Fontana gives Leila. But the appeal of this story and its ramifications for Spock go beyond the heteroromantic.

See, Spock can very easily be read as a closeted character. His inner conflict over wanting to explore his emotions and feeling ashamed of his desire to do so is a very apt metaphor. While this is far from the most slash-worthy episode of the Original Series (or even this season) and despite the fact his relationship with Leila is very obviously a straight one, the basic narrative is still there, and this will only continue to develop over the course of the series' initial run. Nimoy is excellent at this, conveying all the different levels of Spock's anxiety and turmoil beautifully, and this is the first time he's been able to really do so since the very beginning of the series. However, because this episode is rubbish, it manages to ruin this by having the spores be a Bad Thing that needs to be overcome through firm, rigorous vigilance, essentially advocating everyone to go back in the closet, lock the door and never speak of it again,

Actually you know what, let's talk about the plot a bit. While the majority of "This Side of Paradise" can't seem to decide if it wants to condemn the evils of red communism, critique the concept of the utopia the way "The Return of the Archons" did or yell at the damn hippies to get off its lawn, the final scene is interesting, as it actually problematizes Kirk's blustering speech about how humans aren't meant for paradise. As if the fact the benevolent spores of love and happiness are killed by anger and sadness wasn't quite enough, Spock says the time he spent with Leila at the colony was the one time in his life he was ever allowed to be happy, and the whole thing ends on a very uncertain note. It almost seems as if the show is expecting us not to be comfortable with the idea of "walking out of paradise on our own", as it were. However, this also doesn't work, and here is the one time I might actually prefer Gene Roddenberry's overly simplistic, two-fisted conception of morality over some kind of nuance: Where "The Return of the Archons" managed to end up at a fairly straightforward critique of utopianism, "This Side of Paradise" ends up mired in a very particular version of Western, Abrahamic-influenced thinking.

Setting aside the larger reactionary, anti-youth elements of the story, the concept of paradise, especially given Kirk and McCoy's lines at the end of the episode, is very much drawn from the Book of Genesis. Doctor Sandoval is, after all, essentially trying to build a new "Garden of Eden". As is common to popular readings of Genesis, paradise is seen as something that we're not allowed to have in the mortal plane. While this episode never goes to the next level and actually *says* we have to wait for happiness in the Kingdom

133

of Heaven, it ticks pretty much all the other boxes: Kirk's big objection to the Omicron Ceti colony is, essentially, that it's fundamentally wrong and humans aren't supposed to have something like that. Humans aren't meant to live in paradise because they're just *not*: They're meant to work and to suffer. Although other religious traditions have their own concepts of suffering, the way it's portrayed here is about as stereotypically Christian as it's possible to get. Whether or not this was intentional on the part of the writers, just a subconscious bias based on growing up in an Abrahamic society or a bone thrown to the censors to keep them off their back is irrelevant: It's here, I don't like it, and it hurts the show.

I also want to briefly mention DeForest Kelley, who gives the other real standout performance here. We haven't been able to talk about Kelley much, but one thing that's become clear to me over the course of the first season that in many ways he's playing McCoy with almost as much of a performative streak as Shatner gives Kirk. He never quite makes the final connection from performativity to camp to drag, but he's definitely giving an overstated performance. This contrasts significantly with how he was depicted in Sohl's previous effort, which also happened to be his debut. There, Kelley played McCoy with genuine humanness and believability, a true successor to Boyce and Piper who also managed to one-up them.

Now, McCoy is almost as much of a caricature as Kirk. The switch seemed to take place somewhere around "The Enemy Within", and ever since McCoy has been defined by a kind of raw, crackling emotional passion, mostly to contrast with Spock's logical aloofness. The pinnacle of this development in this regard will, of course, be the episode airing in just a few week's time, but it's abundantly clear here: Once McCoy gets infected with the spores, Kelley switches to an absolutely hilariously stereotypical southern gentleman, drawling out his lines to cartoonish extent, peppering his dialog with conspicuous "y'alls" and "Jimmy-boys" and drinking mint julep. I'm not quite sure why Kelley never gets the reputation for camp excess Shatner does or is linked with Spock quite the way Kirk is in pop consciousness, but he's well on his way to leaving his own mark on the series' legacy.

But that's the problem: Nimoy and Kelley are the *only* likable things here, with even Shatner getting once again shafted with some truly godawful, morally bankrupt dialog. As nice as it is to see D.C. Fontana stepping up to a more active role in the show, this is nobody's best effort, is one more in a month of truly depressing episodes and, worst of all, continues to push *Star Trek* further and further away from the counterculture and the ability to contribute in some way to material social progress. We've got four more episodes this year and then two more seasons after that, but it's starting to feel like even people like Gene Coon, William Shatner and DeForest Kelley are giving up on the show at this point. One does have to wonder if, after episodes like this, "The Enemy Within" and "Space Seed" if Star Trek is actually something that can continue and has something to offer to society, or if it's just being kept alive on life support at this point.

30. "I hope to live to hear that good communication corrects bad manners.": The Devil in the Dark

"The Devil in the Dark" is one of the most beloved episodes of the Original Series to fans and at the top of both William Shatner's and Leonard Nimoy's list of favourite episodes they worked on. It's deservedly a classic Star Trek episode and undeniably a highlight of the season-While it might not quite unseat "Balance of Terror" as the year's high-water mark, it's certainly one of the best episodes the show's put out yet and absolutely the sort of thing we needed after the last month, which was just about enough to suck the will to live from anyone.

The fundamental thing that makes "The Devil in the Dark" so successful is that it's just about everything "The Man Trap" was trying to do except done right. Once again, we have an unknown, dangerous alien lurking in the shadows and picking people off one by one who turns out to be a highly sophisticated and unique being and an intellectual equal to the crew, but here the justification for the creature's actions is far clearer and far more defensible. Also, delightfully, the solution Kirk, Spock and McCoy come to involves communication (in particular giving the voiceless party the ability to speak that it had been denied before), cooperation and the free exchange of ideas instead of blowing it to pieces. The one thing this episode doesn't do that its predecessor was able to is mix and match and play with the tropes of multiple genres, but I think there's a good reason for that: We're at the opposite end of the season now, and "*Star Trek*" is an established genre itself. While "The Man Trap" was in hindsight prophetic for where the franchise eventually goes, at the time it was really just experimenting to try and get an early handle on what made this particular show unique. "The Devil in the Dark", by contrast, is about taking what we might expect typical sci-fi plot, or indeed a typical *Star Trek* episode to be (and tellingly, an early, Gene Roddenberry-produced episode) and setting about subverting those expectations.

Fittingly, this is another Gene Coon script. Coon seems liberated and refreshed here, which is a more than welcome sight after the past few scripts his name's appeared on. Perhaps in hindsight most of the cynicism of the past month can be laid at the feet of Robert Hamner and Carey Wilber, because, freed from the shackles of having to adapt their stories to a teleplay, Coon is right back in "Arena" territory: He's still very critical of the way the show is operating, but he remains optimistic it can do more and better than what it's been allowed to be so far. Quite noticeably, once the *Enterprise* crew shows up

135

Kirk immediately begins running the operation like a strict military commander: He paces up and down and addresses his men in a lineup (and "men" is a very appropriate term as there are zero female characters in this episode, save the Horta), formulates attack strategies with Spock and sends strike forces into the tunnels to hunt down the enemy. Also, as in "Arena", his first instinct is to vaporize his opponent and issues a standing shoot-to-kill order before having a change of heart at the last second once he becomes able to see his adversary as another life form who is an equal to him.

This gets at another thread I mentioned in my writeup of "Arena", and of "The Squire of Gothos" as well, because what I think Coon is doing here is using Kirk as a stand-in for the ethics of *Star Trek* itself (at least *Star Trek* as originally conceived by Gene Roddenberry) and forcing him to face the consequences and implications of such a worldview both diegtically and extradiegetically. I'm still not convinced this is the best use of Kirk's character, but it's a savvy move nonetheless and this concept is the clearest in this episode it's been yet. Consider the startling teaser sequence, set entirely on the mining colony as the guards nervously scan the tunnels awaiting the next move of a creature they can't see or track. This is the only time in the entire Original Series where an episode doesn't open with Kirk's narration and where the *Enterprise* never appears: Instead, it opens somewhere else in the galaxy with a mystery. This is at once the logical evolution of a pattern we've been following since "Miri" and the first indication that there's both a cohesiveness to the world of *Star Trek* and that, even more so than with the Metrons, the actions of the *Enterprise* crew can be observed from perspectives other than that of the audience.

What we have then, is both an unknown and the first real serious test the show has of its ethics and, thankfully, it doesn't *quite* screw it up completely. The *Enterprise*, and by extension *Star Trek*, has a mandate to "explore strange new worlds" and to "seek out new life and new civilizations". However, almost a full season into this mission, it's done almost none of those things. It's much preferred so far to ferry people and supplies between Earth colonies and inciting the occasional diplomatic incident, and ("Where No Man Has Gone Before" aside) Kirk seems very keen to think of himself as a soldier rather than an explorer. Here, however, we have a strange new world right from the beginning, and the *Enterprise* is nowhere to be found: They have to pick up a distress signal before going anywhere near the place. The Horta turns out to be both a new life and a new civilization, but both the miners and Kirk come perilously close to wiping the whole species out before they learn anything about it. But crucially this *doesn't* happen: Kirk spares the Horta when he had a clean shot at it, trusted it enough to let Spock try and communicate with it and put it in McCoy's care. Kirk is not only continuing to justify the Metrons' faith in him but starting to refute his own claim about himself in "A Taste of Armageddon". Maybe he's not just a bloodthirsty killer acting against instinct. Maybe he *is* more than that, and maybe he's capable of showing a model for humanity to become apart from Khan Noonien Singh.

Coon's critique here isn't just about *Star Trek*'s own interiority and introspection either. It's about the entire genre of science fiction on the whole. Recall one thing that makes *Star Trek* unique is that it is, at least in part, a paradoxical and oxymoronic mixture of both pulp and Golden Age sci-fi. Despite being on the surface diametrically opposed approaches to conceptualizing speculative fiction, they both share a common weakness in that they're frankly not very good on the human level of things. Pulp sci-fi, with its fixation on flashy spectacle, exciting setpieces and rugged, manly heroes, oftentimes means characters end up disposable as things like death and war are at best glossed over and at worst glamourized. In addition, due to its *extremely* masculine-centred structure, women in particular end up fetishized and stripped of their personhood. Golden Age science fiction has its own problems: By it's very definition it's about high-concept technoscientific futurism, logic-puzzle plots and grand, vast, sweeping settings that dwarf everything else. The key failing of Foundation, after all, was the concept of psychohistory and that every single aspect of human behaviour can be mathematically calculated and predicted and ultimately reduced to cold numbers and theory. That's going to be dehumanizing by default.

But Star Trek has a very peculiar solution to this, even if it doesn't quite have a hold on it yet. Aside from the two types of science fiction, Star Trek also draws on soap operas, and will later also add a kind of prototypical character drama to its wheelhouse as well. Getting back to "The Man Trap" for a moment, that was one of the more interesting things about that episode and one of the best arguments for making it the premier: The focus on the everyday lives of the *Enterprise* crew (to better explore how Salt Vampire's presence disrupts this, or perhaps doesn't) was one of the things that made the story so memorable. While Coon hasn't played up this angle of the show as much as Roddenberry did (albeit sporadically), he is very much interested in the human element of the series, as evidenced by the kinds of scripts that have gone out under his watch, such as "The Conscience of the King", "The Galileo Seven", "Court Martial" bits of "Shore Leave" and even absolute turkeys like "Miri" and "This Side of Paradise" to some extent. What Coon's also done is severely tone down Roddenberry's clunky, heavy-handed moralizing, often fearlessly and without hesitation calling the entire show's premise into question and forcing it to justify its existence.

What this means is that even if Coon isn't always as keen on the character development angle, he's very much engaging with the show's worldview and the repercussions this has for people at a metatextual level. It's because of this *Star Trek* is going to be able to fray its bonds a bit, and in this regard it's appropriate that "The Devil in the Dark" marks the second appearance of the Vulcan Mind Meld. The Mind Meld is, after all, a very intimate, spiritual and sexually coded process by which two people can know each other utterly and fully. This is significant for a number of reasons, the first of which is obviously that of the two times we've seen Spock do this on the show so far one was with another man and one was with an alien rock lady. Secondly, however, the Mind Meld is about communication and the sharing of worldviews. Indeed, it could well be seen as the purest, most naked form of it there is: Not just discourse, but discourse framed in terms of mysticism and meditation-Spiritual, mental joining, in a sense. What we have here at long last is finally something that can be seen as a way for Star Trek to grow, and that this is the way Coon has Kirk and Spock resolve the conflict with the Horta is genuinely fascinating, if you pardon the term.

We've got a ways to go for sure, but "The Devil in the Dark" isn't just a sign things might get better, its a decisive step forward, the first we've really seen *Star Trek* take and absolutely the right way to respond to the damnation of the past month. The show's identity crisis over for the time being, it can finally continue its journey of self-improvement without fear it might implode in on itself, at least for now. We've learned how to better ourselves and that there's more to humans than war, killing and hatred, now we just need to actually put these principles into action for a change. And about time too, as *Star Trek*'s biggest challenges are still to come.

31. "Work for peace at any price, except the price of liberty.": Errand of Mercy

"Errand of Mercy" is the moment where all the themes and motifs Gene Coon has been working with since the beginning of his tenure finally coalesce into a cohesive, articulate message. It's a stinging indictment of what *Star Trek* is at this point, but what saves it from the nihilism of "A Taste of Armageddon" and the evil of "Space Seed" is that it's paired with a slightly more hopeful outlook gleaned from the other scripts Coon is the sole author of. It's not perfect, even by the standards the show's laid out for itself by this point, but it's a sufficiently effective statement of where the show is placing its ethics now. Also, it's the debut of the Klingon Empire, which is somewhat self-evidently important, so I guess I'd better deal with that.

There are few things more immediately recognisable as undeniably Star Trek than the Klingons. In terms of ubiquity within the pop consciousness, they're on par with Kirk, Spock and the *Enterprise*. They're so well-known and beloved that fans who own replica Klingon uniforms, headpieces and weapons and speak Klingonese fluently are seen to be as quintessentially Star Trek as it's possible to get, and none of these things are even going to be a part of the franchise until 1989 at the absolute earliest. Even the Federation and Starfleet don't quite have this level of memorability and iconic status. In fact, the Klingons are so entrenched in people's ideas of what Star Trek is about there's only one other thing in the entirety of the franchise that can claim to have anywhere remotely near their level of cultural capital and that's the Klingons' own mortal enemies.Why might this be? Part of this has to be the fact the Klingons are the Original Series' only recurring antagonists. Although they only actually appear in seven episodes out of the show's 79 episode run, they do appear more frequently than any other alien race. Certainly the fact they get brought back and heavily retooled to become a lovable culture of proud, honourable (sometimes comically so) warriors in both the original movie series and the 1980s era also must have something to do with it, but there remains, after all, a reason they come back in the first place.

All that said, however, one thing that's worth noting about the Klingons in "Errand of Mercy" is that they really don't seem like they're actually cut out for the job. I'm not so much referring to the general execution of the characters here, although John Colicos' intense performance as Commander Kor is pretty much the one memorable, or actually convincing, acting job amongst the Klingon cast, but in terms of their actual conception. Common lore claims Coon based the Klingon Empire on the Soviet Union, and while there is evidence of this (Kor's comment to Kirk about how all Klingons are cogs and everyone is monitored primarily), D.C. Fontana asserts that Coon wrote it as more an amalgamation of all the worst traits he saw in the people he fought during World War II. Apart from the Soviets, Fontana claims Coon based the Klingons just as much on Nazi Germany and Imperial Japan, which makes a great deal of sense if you look at how they behave in the episode as aired. The problem is that because Coon throws all these disparate groups together, the Klingons end up feeling a bit like bland, generic and overly broad villains here, so any critique they may have been written to convey doesn't really stick.

The result of this is that we have an alien people who are somewhat lacking in distinction, and their effectiveness is slightly...mixed as a result. First of all, lets address the obvious. The costume design of the Klingon, consisting mostly of a bunch of dudes in blackface and fake goatees wearing faux chain mail is spectacularly racist. Coon apparently didn't give any indication in his script as to what the Klingons were supposed to look like (apart from "Oriental" and "hard-faced" which is, well, bad), so the makeup department left it entirely up to John Colicos to come up with a design. Regrettably, Colicos decided to model them on Genghis Khan. This was obviously a bad idea for any number of reasons, just one in particular being we've already seen a Khan not three episodes ago. I mean I know video recording technology in 1967 wasn't what it is today, but I doubt audiences would have that short a memory. In all seriousness, the larger issue is of course the fact this makes the Klingons an Orientalist mess. I mean, the production team on the supposedly racially diverse *Star Trek* didn't even approach Japanese actors, not that this would have been much of an improvement, but still defaulting to browning up Caucasian actors with makeup shouldn't be anyone's first move, even in 1967.

All of this adds up to the Klingons not really ticking all the boxes they should have to become a valid and legitimate reoccurring challenge to the *Enterprise* crew. Or any of them. Their conception is muddy, their execution is a disaster and they have a patently ludicrous name that will make them the butt of endless crude jokes in the future (apparently Fontana complained to Coon about this a number of times, imploring him to come up with a better sounding name. Clearly they never found one). All of this might have been OK had they just stayed here, which was actually the intent: According to subsequent interviews Coon never meant for the Klingons to come back, a claim supported by Fontana who tells us she figured he was just looking for a "good, tough" adversary for Kirk for this one episode. Fontana also says the reason the Klingons came back time and time again was because they were exceptionally cheap to costume, as opposed to the Romulans, who she found much more interesting, but which required special and pricey headpieces.

Let's actually think for a moment about what "Errand of Mercy" would have looked like with the Romulans instead, because the parts of this episode that don't have to do with Klingon culture and design are on the whole actually quite excellent. I bring up "Balance of Terror" a lot, mostly because it's incredible, but here the comparison really is valid. Paul Schneider very clearly meant for the Romulans to be a critique of imperialism by showing how the concept harms ordinary people, which is already a better setup in my view than "generic imperialist". Furthermore, however, the Romulan Star Empire was designed to be for all intents and purposes the same as Earth Command, down to Kirk and Mark Lenard's

Commander being basically the same person. This approach would have fit "Errand of Mercy" like a glove, as the episode's whole point is that despite his protestations Kirk and Kor are both hot-blooded warriors and the Federation and the Klingon Empire are basically indistinguishable to people like the Organians. In that regard I have to praise not only Coon's script, which gives William Shatner and John Colicos very similar speeches, providing the story with a real structural symmetry and elegance, but also director John Newland, because the direction here is positively delightful. My favourite scene is at the end, when the Organians finally intervene and stop the war from breaking out. Kirk and Kor take turns spewing similarly phrased insults and demands at them, before indignantly declaring that they have "no right" to meddle in the affairs of "'my Federation!' 'Or my Empire!'" as the editing brilliantly ping-pongs back and forth between the two of them.

What this also does though is once again draw a contrast between Gene Coon and Paul Schneider. In the "Arena" chapter, I said the primary difference between the two writers is that while both go out of their way to problematize *Star Trek*'s militarism, or are at least somewhat concerned with using the show to condemn the militarism of the day and provide a counterbalance to it, Coon seems to enjoy using Kirk as a stand-in for the diegetic ethics of the series while Schneider seems to play off Shatner's acting style and writes Kirk as someone larger than the show who might be in some sense constrained by it. While both are valid approaches, I do personally prefer Schneider's in this particular case as it seems to fit the character better. That said, Coon's comes from a curiously metatextual perspective: Despite him having Kirk make several morally bankrupt decisions, not only here (where he is disturbingly patronizing, paternalistic and cruel to the Organians) but also in "Arena" and the first half of "The Devil in the Dark", this is always framed in the context of Kirk learning from his mistakes and recanting at the last moment to prove he has the potential to grow into a better person.

On the one hand, this would mean using the Romulans in "Errand of Mercy" would improve the script significantly, as Schneider's equation of them with us is arguably even better suited to this story than "Balance of Terror". On the other hand, Coon's problematizing of Kirk means the effectiveness of the Romulans themselves might have been diluted somewhat: If the whole point of them is that they're part of an empire in decline and whose people are beginning to lose faith in it, than having a Romulan commander fill Kor's role here might not have worked as well. Of course, one other option might have been to create a totally new Romulan character, someone far more conservative in his views. Mark Lenard's character committed suicide of course, and this would also help contribute to the idea the Romulan Star Empire is a vast, sprawling entity comprising a vast array of people with many different perspectives: A Foundation-style galactic empire without Asimov's unfortunate determinism. However, this would also mean equating him with Kirk would have seemed contradictory, given his prior equation with Lenard's character in "Balance of Terror".

The other area in which "Errand of Mercy" stumbles a little bit is its resolution. While the episode does a very good job building up to Kirk's inevitable fall by telegraphing the Organians as sophisticated, powerful pacifists from the beginning and have Kirk become gradually more adversarial, combative and dismissive, for this to have really worked we would have needed a scene that showed Kirk was more willing to put a stop to the war than Kor was, showing that there's some hope for him, much as we saw in his sparing of the Gorn captain in "Arena". But we never really get that scene, or at least it's never quite clear enough. Instead, it's left to Spock to paper things over at the end by talking about how it took the Organians millions of years to reach the state they did, so he shouldn't be too embarrassed and disappointed. The problem is this feels like something of a step back for Coon, and it pushes "Errand of Mercy" a bit too close to the nihilism of "A Taste of Armageddon" for my particular taste. Both this episode and "The Devil in the Dark" might have been more effective had their positions in the season been switched, with the former episode serving much better as Kirk's final redemption, or at least proof that he's capable of redemption.

But the fact Spock, who has by this point firmly been established as the show's central character in several areas, seems to think it's possible for humans to grow is a powerful statement in of itself. Spock has been subject to no small manner of discrimination on this show, and his positionality gives him a unique perspective on the actions of people like Kirk and organisations like the Federation. If he, who so wishes to distance himself from his human side, seems to think we might not be so bad after all, that should tell us a lot. This leaves us with a fundamental question, however: At the end of *Star Trek*'s first season we've seen an awful lot of reflexiveness, introspection and back-and-forth about what this show is and the consequences to be had as a result of making a firm decision about it. We've had the show ripped to shreds by forces within and above the narrative and had it stressed by more than one entity that in spite of all of this there's potential and the humans of Star Trek are capable of great things. But that's just it; we've heard a lot about potential, but very few concrete steps in a progressive direction. The onus is now on the show to prove not only that it has potential, but that it's actually capable of fulfilling it.

32. "Watch...your future's end.": The City on the Edge of Forever

"I am my own beginning. And my own ending."

Static

"So. You've found the courage to speak to me face to face at last, have you? I must congratulate you on finding a spine, but there are some thinkers probably wiser than I who'd say there exists a very thin line between courage and stupidity."

"I've not come for bravado-filled threats, I've come in the hope that together we might be able to negotiate an end to all of this. The damage can be repaired."

"You people never fail to disappoint me, though your unwavering stubbornness is to be commended, I suppose. Don't you have anything better to say to me than that?"

"Withdraw your troops from the 22nd Century. The damage can be repaired, and I'd hoped to make you remember the fundamental importance and worth of the Temporal Accords."

"Spare me your impassioned appeal to regulations and rules of order. Your vapid platitudes will only fall on deaf ears."

"Your quarrel isn't with these people in this time! It's with us!"

"Isn't it? Tell me, do you know why my ships didn't blow you out of the stars on sight? Because I wanted to show you *this*. This is what your people did on Earth in 1930, A.D. Take a good long look at what your faction did. Tell me something. Can you justify to yourself what you have done here, to these people, and to the incalculable generations who will come after? Can you live with yourself letting this status quo stand? Because I sure can't."

Static

"This...ceaseless hatred and violence...It is alien to us. And repugnant. We must depart this plane; the pain has become simply too great for us to bear any longer."

"A philosophy of pacifism is only practical if you're not living under oppression. It has been so very long: Do you remember what it feels like to be imprisoned? Trapped? Walked over? Used? Violated? We all know what the future means: Cycles of making and unmaking repeating themselves forever. We walk in eternity, you and I. But we are also stewards of it."

"You are not of Organia, but you are like us. We should like to speak with you about this further."

"In time."

Static

"The City on the Edge of Forever" is also rather infamously the center of an extremely messy legal dispute between writer Harlan Ellison and the then-members of the *Star Trek* production team. There seem to be two versions of events here and, unfortunately, in neither of them does Gene Roddenberry or Star Trek come out looking good. The first account, which is supported by Bob Justman and Herb Solow in *Inside Star Trek* and even Ellison's own book on the subject says that the original draft (which was delivered late) featured an *Enterprise* crewman named Beckwith who was a drug dealer. After murdering a fellow crewmember who threatened to turn him in, he was sentenced to death on the planet the ship was in orbit of, which in this draft was inhabited by an ancient race of time observers called The Guardians and who maintained a Time Vortex. Beckwith escaped through the Time Vortex and changed history such that the *Enterprise* becomes a pirate ship called the *Condor*. Kirk and Spock must then follow Beckwith into the vortex and, as in the aired episode, arrive a week before him and discover they must stop him from averting the death of an Edith Koestler, which is difficult for Kirk as he has fallen in love with her.

The story then goes that Roddenberry considered this draft unusable for a number of reasons, the most prominent of which being that he was opposed to the idea that drug addiction would remain a serious problem in the enlightened future of *Star Trek*. Roddenberry himself told a variation of this on the convention circuit, where he would claim he disliked Ellison's original script because it "had Scotty selling drugs". This is, of course, blatantly untrue as Scotty wasn't in the first draft of "The City on the Edge of Forever" at all (although Roddenberry did later admit he hadn't read Ellison's treatment in years at the time he made that remark). The notion that this version of events would seem somewhat unlikely given what we know of Roddenberry and his work overall at this stage of his career is something of an understatement. *Star Trek* is simply not a utopian show, and claims to the contrary are embellishments at best and outright fabrications at worst. Either way, Roddenberry asked Ellison to rewrite his script, which he did, two more times. Still finding it unsatisfactory, this sequence of events has Roddenberry giving the story over to a number of editors, most prominently Gene Coon and D.C. Fontana, who did a series of uncredited rewrites of the script.

Unhappy with the way his script had been handled, Ellison requested that it air under the pseudonym "Cordwainer Bird", a request Roddenberry allegedly denied by threatening to blacklist Ellison from Hollywood. Apparently, Roddenberry knew Ellison used this pen name when he was unhappy with the way television production teams interfered with his work, and furthermore that this was a technique of Ellison's known to science fiction fans. This argument goes that Ellison's major complaint with the situation was that Coon and Fontana weren't credited in the final story, and that had fans seen "The City on the Edge of Forever" go out under the name "Cordwainer Bird" then they'd realise *Star Trek* was no different than any other science fiction show in the way it mistreated its story editors and production staff and that this was something Roddenberry couldn't accept as he wanted to cultivate the myth it was special and ahead of its time.

Static

"You talk a lot of big words about peace and egalitarianism, but the actions of your people are the loudest. Consider this, then. What even your own history books call your *crowning achievement.* You cling so tightly to your reality that you would glorify the death of an innocent bystander who would become the voice of peace on Earth because it means you get to carry on living as you have always lived, turned away from the world until it's time to pass judgment on the *lesser* cultures. You are not just silent, but *willfully* silent. I wonder, do you know anything about what *real* silence feels like?"

"We cannot take the risk that tampering with the past will negate our existence in the future! We all take that risk, and it is our duty as officers to keep the timeline pure and free of paradoxes-It must be upheld! Edith Keeler was an admirable woman, but ahead of her time. Had she lived, the Axis powers would have won the second World War, because Earth of the 1930s was not ready for such beliefs. She was a dangerous outlier in the timestream and, regrettably, had to be neutralized to preserve it's natural flow. Your dangerous meddling is a threat to not just the safety and sovereignty of "my people", but to the stability of the entire universe! Please, let me help you understand!"

"So I do not 'understand'. That's it, then? There really is no limit to Federation arrogance. Does life really mean so little to you? I thought you were sworn to protect it in all its forms. That what your propaganda says, doesn't it? I thought you at least had the dignity to believe it. Or is that just an opiate for the underclasses you send out to fight and die on the frontlines of history? So what are you saying? That at once the integrity of all of creation hinges on one person, yet one who is also too pure and sophisticated for her backwater planet? And that death is preferable to life in such a place? Listen to yourself. Can you hear the sound of your own double-speak? Or are you so far up your own ass you can't even listen to your own thoughts anymore?"

Static

"You can't hide forever. One day, time will come for you just as it comes for us all. When shots ring out and the sky is set ablaze, you'll be conscripted. One of these days you're going to have to choose who's side you're on. You know it to be true: You've seen it just as I have. It's happened before, and it is written it will happen again. This time it can be different. This time it *will* be different. But you and I will have roles to play. It is an act of love."

Static

The account Ellison tells is rather different, though no less depressing. According to him, the dispute was not about writing credit and the treatment of the *Star Trek* production staff, or even Roddenberry's attempted blackmail. Instead, Ellison claims the sticking point was a shift in the depiction of Edith Keeler: By the final draft Ellison submitted to Roddenberry, Keeler had become an overt anti-war protester. In the version that aired, there is a clear implication that the reason her death was important to history was because, had she lived, she would have ushered in a powerful new pacifist movement that kept the United States neutral in World War II, this allowing Nazi Germany to develop atomic weapons. This claim is bolstered significantly by the extensive legal documents and internal memos Ellison eventually made public, as well as a rather vague remark from Bob Justman that takes on a deeply upsetting reading within this context. When asked if the staff version of "The City on the Edge of Forever" was meant "to have the contemporaneous anti-Vietnam-war movement as a subtext", Justman allegedly replied "Of course we did".

While this version of events is significantly more plausible in my opinion just knowing what we know now about what *Star Trek* was like in its first season, I have a hard time accepting it completely at face value either. The primary reason this is tough for me to stomach is because I have a seriously hard time believing writers like Gene Coon and D.C. Fontana would have intentionally altered a story like this to give it such a flagrantly reactionary tone. That's simply not in keeping with anything in their catalog, even at this relatively early date. Coon's last two stories were about how Starfleet's militarization and the Federation's distance and pursuit of material wealth almost led to outright genocide and having Kirk punished by a group of hyper-evolved pacifists for his bloodlust and desire for conflict. Indeed, Coon also penned "Arena" and worked on the angrily anti-war "A Taste of Armageddon" which had Kirk admit humans were natural-born killers. Fontana's last script was hideously reactionary, yes, but that was primarily the result of it being written by the author of "The Corbomite Maneuver", not her revisions to the finished teleplay, and it's very easy to see how the progressive aspects of "This Side of Paradise" were Fontana's doing. What I *don't* see is any reason why either one of them would suddenly turn around, take Ellison's relatively straightforward pitch and go out of their way to add in a scene that depicted pacifism as inherently wrongheaded and dangerous, and to then have that episode immediately follow Coon's "Errand of Mercy" is ludicrous even by *Star Trek* standards.

Now, from what I gather Gene Roddenberry had the last go at "The City on the Edge of Forever" and it's far easier to see this being his doing than Coon's or Fontana's. Bob Justman's comment is confusing, and while I'm not entirely familiar with what his views might have been circa 1967, the fact he went on to work on *Star Trek: The Next Generation*

146

for a time and to co-author *Inside Star Trek* with Herb Solow should be some kind of clue. Either way, it seems clear Harlan Ellison got somewhat shafted here, and the end result is yet another episode that's simply put nowhere near as good as its reputation would suggest it is. It's not the greatest episode of Star Trek, not by a long shot: It's not even the greatest episode of this series, or even this season. The show is on very shaky ground now-Had we not just had "The Devil in the Dark" and "Errand of Mercy" this would be *Star Trek*'s death knell. There's no escape from a future built on manslaughter and crushing pacifism, even if it is because that pacifism isn't "of its time". But we have, and "Balance of Terror" and "Arena" too, and thus we soldier ever onwards.

Static

"This war isn't over yet, though I wish it were. But I've done what I came here to do. Perhaps I didn't even need to do anything. Maybe you people will blow yourselves up of your own accord. One thing you cannot seem to understand is that I don't fight for my future. I fight for *all* futures. I fight to *live*. Our campaign here is over, but mark my words, you *will* see us again. We will return. And when we do, time will stand still and the war to end all wars will rage once more."

Static

"Many such journeys are possible. Let me be your gateway".

147

33. "Exterminate! Annihilate! Destroy!": Operation – Annihilate!

Really, it's a bit unrealistic to expect *Star Trek* to come up with something to top "The City on the Edge of Forever" for its first season finale. Even if you, like me, grant that last episode was ultimately a morally bankrupt nightmare on every possible level, the sheer gravity it exerts upon the series, and the larger franchise, is undeniable. For those enraptured and left starry-eyed by the events of last week, it's tough to see how anything, let alone a story about flying parasitic space pancakes, could possibly live up to their expectations, and for those with the perhaps more applicable response of being deeply disturbed and unsettled by the fallout from "The City on the Edge of Forever" (and maybe the last few months on the whole) it's tough to get excited or optimistic about anything *Star Trek* does at this point.

But this is being a bit unfair to "Operation – Annihilate!". The concept of the season finale as we know it was not one that was as entrenched in pop consciousness as an indelible part of television literacy the way it is today. That didn't begin to happen until approximately the 1980s (and no, it was not the result of the episode you're thinking of either: As talented as Michael Piller was, he didn't invent the season finale. At the very least let's not forget *Dallas* and "Who Shot J.R.?"). "Operation – Annihilate!" plays out more or less like an average episode of the series as of 1967, which is not entirely terrible. It's certainly not as great as the best episodes of the year but, mercifully, it's also leagues better than the worst. And there have been *a lot* of worsts.

The first thing this episode unequivocally has in its favour is the acting. Anyone who thinks William Shatner is a poor actor really ought to watch this one (and probably "Where No Man Has Gone Before", "Balance of Terror" and "Miri" as well) because once again this is a stellar showcase for his talents. Kirk has a lot of emotional investment in this story, as first his brother, his family and then Spock all succumb to the neural parasites. Shatner plays it as any good old-school thespian would: With gratuitous, overstated theatrical flourish that very clearly marks every single thought and emotion that crosses Kirk's mind. We watch Kirk grow increasingly more desperate and determined, and every single iota of his pain and and resolve is highlighted for our benefit.

What it comes down to is that Shatner isn't a method actor: His approach is not, as a general rule, about trying to get his mental state to emulate Kirk's. Instead, what he does is take great care to meticulously outline the sorts of emotions his character would most likely be feeling in a given situation and draws our attention to them by conveying them ever-so-slightly caricatured. So, for example, in the teaser, Shatner plays Kirk very visibly anxious and preoccupied when recording his log entry on the Deneva colony. He builds his nervousness gradually as Kirk listens to reports from Spock, Uhura and Scott about the colony's probably fate, eventually prompting DeForest Kelley's McCoy to ask him if his brother is still stationed there, as the camera zooms in on Kirk's look of dismay and then cuts to the intro.

Shatner is a primarily a performer, but he's a performer who knows how to act and reiterates his theatrical bombast back into the narrative. In spite of the reputation he's got in recent years, Shatner is very explicitly not playing himself, or even an exaggerated version of himself (nor is that even what he does in his post-*Star Trek* fame: That's a not-entirely invalid approximation, but it's significantly more complex and nuanced then just straightforward self-parody). Neither Shatner nor Kirk can be the singular entity that all of *Star Trek* revolves around: The show's own structure simply won't allow it, if for no other reason than it has to split screentime evenly between him, Spock and McCoy, and "Operation – Annihilate!" is a fantastic example of how this works in action. Firstly, as much as this might be Kirk's story, given how invested he is in defeating the neural parasites, this is once again Spock's episode. They key scene comes just after Aurelan dies and Kirk beams back down to the colony: Kirk is shot from a very dramatically low-angle perspective, as if the hero has returned from personal trauma to exact justice on those who have wronged him. But this is also the scene where "Operation – Annihilate!" very decisively switches to being about Spock, as he is promptly attacked by the aforementioned flying parasitic space pancakes.

While in the immediate aftermath of the scene, we get a shot of Kirk cradling Spock that delightfully invokes the Renaissance-era *Pietà*-style of sculpture and painting, with the emphasis very clearly on Kirk, from then on out the episode focuses on Spock's inner battle with the neural parasites. Leonard Nimoy is, of course, amazing, playing Spock subtly more stressed and pained then usual: Not blatantly so (Nimoy is in some ways the inverse of Shatner in this regard, preferring a subtle understatement to a subtle overstatement), but just enough to be barely noticeable, and with an occasional facial twinge to remind us something's not quite right. Spock also makes no fewer than three attempts at a heroic sacrifice, pushing the episode's moral occasionally towards "the needs of the many outweigh the needs of the few".

Thankfully, however, that's not what the story ends up being about, instead focusing on the turmoil and sadness this brings upon the people of the *Enterprise*, revisiting a theme the show hasn't really dealt with since "The Man Trap". The best scene is the climax where Spock's seeming blindness becomes absolutely devastating to Kirk and McCoy: Kirk at first wants to blame McCoy for not realising only infrared radiation was necessary to kill the parasites, but instead reminds him the accident wasn't his fault and gently asking him to "look after" Spock. Shatner conveys Kirk's mixed, riled emotions beautifully, and while Kelley remains in "bristling passion" mode, the powerful effect this has on McCoy is obvious.

That said, this scene also highlights the areas where "Operation – Annihilate!" isn't altogether effective. One of the reasons "The Man Trap" worked in spite of itself was that we got a very sizable cross-section of the *Enterprise* crew. We see how the situation effects not only McCoy, but also Kirk, Doctor Crater, Uhura, Sulu and Janice Rand, not to mention numerous nameless crewmembers. At the opposite end of the season, *Star Trek* has very clearly abandoned any pretenses of being an ensemble show: While there is a lot of drama and emotion on display, it is exclusively limited to Kirk, Spock and McCoy. Uhura, Scott and Sulu are barely in this episode and get maybe ten lines between them, a trend that will sadly see the Original Series out.

Christine Chapel is also back and, credit to Kelley and Majel Barrett, the show does pick up on her affections for Spock last explored in "The Naked Time". The only problem is it's been 23 episodes since "The Naked Time", and in an era before readily available home video recording technology, expecting people to remember the personal motivations of a character who's only appeared twice before and who we last saw six and half months ago is a bit ludicrous. While James Blish's novelizations of the series had indeed begun by this point (the first volume of Blish's novelizations came out in January 1967, this episode aired in April), it's probably reasonable to expect this was a resource not every viewer would have had access to unless they were already *Star Trek* fans, which was, if we're honest, implausible given the ratings this show got in original run.

The other major issue with "Operation – Annihilate!" is that, with the exception of the other regulars and arguably Chapel, every other character exists purely to serve as angst fodder for the leads, and Kirk in particular. The most egregious are Kirk's brother's family: They're the quintessential example of relatives or love interests whom we've never heard of before and show up only to die to give the main character some emotional drama for the week (and before anyone comments, expecting us to remember the fact Kirk mentioned having a brother with a family back in "What Are Little Girls Made Of?" in a throwaway dialog exchange with his android duplicate is significantly more ludicrous then expecting us to remember Nurse Chapel's feelings for Spock, or indeed Nurse Chapel herself, and James Blish doesn't even novelize that one until 1975. I know *Star Trek* is cult sci-fi, but it doesn't have *that* kind of fanbase in the late 1960s).

Aurelan in particular is quite bad. Her main purpose in the show is to scream her head off, sob uncontrollably and then promptly die after giving her requisite bit of exposition. This is not helped in the slightest by the scene later on where McCoy calls Kirk out on his emotional investment in the mission, talking about his "affection for Spock" and "the fact [his] nephew is the only survivor of [Kirk's] brother's line". This scene implies Kirk's primary concern is that his brother's genetic lineage and name live on, not that he or his family actually do physically. Although it's bad Samuel debuts dead and Peter spends the whole episode unconscious, this mostly dehumanizes Aurelan, whose life now only becomes worthwhile because she had a son. That's some *medieval age* kind of reactionary. Thankfully, this is not at all how William Shatner plays Kirk in these scenes, showing very visible concern and love for Aurelan and well as his brother and Peter. Shatner really sells that these were important people to Kirk and that he cared deeply for them: This is the most concerned and compassionate we've seen Kirk be towards somebody since Miri, and that makes us wish Sam and Aurelan could have lived despite the script seemingly wanting to treat them purely as plot devices.

But of course this is a trauma we'll never see mentioned again. Just as Spock's sight is restored at the last second in a truly magnificent bit of plot convenience (thus sparing us having to deal with ablest issues and the effect having a blind friend would have on the crew, which, given this show's ethics, is probably still a good thing) the status quo is restored just as the credits hit because *Star Trek* is an anthology show, and those last few seconds of banter jar horrifically with the rest of the episode. A fitting microcosm for the show *Star Trek* has become: A clear step forward and a desire to deal overtly with character drama bewilderingly set against the backdrop of clear genocide of "new life" that's immediately reigned in and subsumed by the necessary imposition of a structure that was probably flawed and dated in 1964. After its first season and first three years Star Trek has become a very strange and unfathomable beast of its own. At times it feels like the show actively hates itself, its reactionary and progressive tendencies locked in a seemingly unbreakable stalemate in an excruciating war of attrition. But in spite of all that it's been renewed, and it'll be back in the fall to continue its journey to...wherever it's going to end up.

But before we rejoin it, we should take some time to look at some of the other things that were on the air at this time to see just where *Star Trek* stacks up in comparison. And we also have a responsibility to the future to attend to: It's still not been quite sorted yet, you know.

34. "Consult the Frogs": Attack from Space

In September of 1966 the landscape of pop culture changed forever with the debut of a groundbreaking new science fiction television show that would singlehandedly transform how the genre was thought of. Blending elements of pulp and Golden Age sci-fi with a critical deconstructive eye and unique fascination with the trappings of soap operas, this show dared us to follow the adventures of a ragtag group of Space Air Force pilots in a utopian future setting where nationalism had been abolished as they set out to explore the universe beyond the realm of human knowledge and experience. I am, of course, speaking about the legendary *Raumpatrouille – Die phantastischen Abenteuer des Raumschiffes Orion.*

Every once in awhile you stumble upon something so unbelievably serendipitous it really does force you to stop and muse for a time on synchronicity and the effect reoccurring patterns of time and place have on human beings. How else would you explain how two groups of people on opposite ends of the planet came up with two superficially identical science fiction shows in the exact same month other than a simultaneous tapping of the shared cultural zeitgeist? It's perhaps tempting to expect the West German production filmed in stark black-and-white on sets made out of kitchen appliances and scrap metal to be an almost hilariously shameless ripoff of the bright, flashy, big budget Technicolor Hollywood spectacle airing on major network television, were we to conveniently forget that *Raumpatrouille – Die phantastischen Abenteuer des Raumschiffes Orion* (hereafter *Raumpatrouille Orion* or simply *Raumpatrouille* because I'm not typing all that out every time I want to make a point) was filmed at the exact same time as *Star Trek*'s first season and premiered within days of it. Germans wouldn't be introduced to *Star Trek* until 1972, and most people on the other side of the Atlantic to this day have no idea *Raumpatrouille Orion* exists. And that's a true shame, because *Raumpatrouille Orion* is unabashedly superior on almost every single level. This show is everything *Star Trek* should have been in its first season.

The most immediately obvious thing *Raumpatrouille* just absolutely nails is its setting. While the world of Star Trek retroactively becomes an idealized or utopian society thanks to the large-scale fan reconceptualization of the Original Series in the 1970s, a reading which is bolstered by the influence of *Star Trek Phase II* and *Star Trek: The Next Generation* (which were, of course, written in the wake of this re-evaluation), the world of *Raumpatrouille* actually explicitly is one. In lieu of Captain Kirk's famous "Space...The Final Frontier" monologue that opens every *Star Trek* episode starting midway through the first season, *Raumpatrouille Orion* gives us this declaration, equally famous in German science fiction circles, at the opening of each of its stories:

> "What may sound like a fairy tale today may be tomorrow's reality. This is a
> fairy tale from the day after tomorrow: There are no more nations. There is
> only mankind and its colonies in space. People have settled on faraway stars.
> The ocean floor has been made habitable. At speeds still unimaginable today,
> space vessels are rushing through our Milky Way. One of these vessels is the
> ORION, a minuscule part of a gigantic security system protecting the Earth
> from threats from outer space. Let's accompany the ORION and her crew on
> their patrol at the edge of infinity."

Though *Star Trek* can (and self-evidently has) been read as an optimistic show about
utopian idealism and humans learning to be the best they can be, this is plainly not the show
that Gene Roddenberry originally conceived of in 1964. That Star Trek does eventually
sort of get there is a fascinating story we'll be taking care to follow as we go along, but the
fact of the matter is it's not now. *Raumpatrouille Orion*, by contrast, wants to make it very
clear that this is an idealized vision of an outer space adventure: Earth is explicitly united,
and all disputes over national boundaries, gender, race and ethnicity have long since ceased
to exist, which it might be beneficial to point out is something *Star Trek* hasn't actually
come out and said yet. Indeed, the *Orion* itself boasts a very diverse crew, with two female
officers (who actually get proper uniforms and are treated no differently then their male co-
workers to boot), one French and one Russian, an Italian computer scientist, a Scandinavian
chief engineer, a Japanese navigator and a commanding officer of US-Scottish descent.

This overtly idealistic setting is also realised in a truly marvelous fashion, as *Raumpatrouille Orion* takes place in one of the most unique, beautiful and evocative sci-fi worlds
I have ever seen. There is an unmistakeably European look about the show, and it also
evokes its time in possibly the most nuanced way I've yet seen a contemporary show manage. *Raumpatrouille*'s elegant curves and futuristic touch-screen computer displays blended
with visceral, physical knobs, bulky television monitors, oscilloscopes, gears, levers and
punch-cards give it an aggressively and endearingly analog feel that's truly all its own.
It's on the one hand exactly what you'd expect the mid-20th Century in West Germany
extrapolated to the far future to look like, but that's absolutely a good thing in this case.
On top of that the crew's home base is at the bottom of the ocean and looks like a Mod
bar built in a walk-through aquarium, and I wouldn't be surprised in the slightest to learn
Kraftwerk got some of their inspiration for *Radio-Activity* listening to the countdown on
the *Orion*'s flight computer.

The thing about *Star Trek*'s sets and props is that they look pretty much exactly like what
they were: Bits of plywood and lumber lashed together on a Desilu studio and painted with
bright primary colours to make it all stand out. There's nothing wrong with this, of course,
and it certainly helps add to the show's theatrical appeal. That's said, there's something
to be said for conveying narrative and mood through the visual aspects of the production
on a work of visual, cinematic media and that's one area in which *Raumpatrouille Orion*
truly excels. This is even more remarkable given that while the show's 360,000 DM budget

(about € 642,000 as of 2009) was not insignificant, the production values the team had to work with were still definitely not giving Hollywood (or anyone) a run for their money at the time. The reason why *Raumpatrouille* looks as singular and stunning as it does is because the art design is an absolute masterpiece, which is not entirely surprising: The set designer, Rolf Zehetbauer, would eventually win an Oscar for *Cabaret* and special effects artist Theo Nischwitz would once again collaborate with him on *Das Boot*. Together, they did more with pencil sharpeners, irons, upended furniture, drinking glasses and dolled-up spools of thread then I've seen some high-profile directors and producers manage with unlimited special effects budgets and the latest modeling and CGI technology.

An atmosphere as singular and gorgeous as this would probably have been enough to shoot *Raumpatrouille Orion* to classic status by its own merits, but thankfully the show's characters are equally as memorable and well done, and the ideas it deals with are surprisingly sophisticated and forward-thinking. While they operate one of the fastest, most modern ships in the fleet, the crew of the *Orion* are far from the darlings of the force, and Commander Cliff Alister McClane has a reputation as something of a rebellious thorn in everyone's side. Although McClane is not averse to showing off every once in awhile, such as when he attempts a risky landing on Rhea in violation of orders in the first episode, he's mostly *persona non grata* because he doesn't keep in lock-step with his superiors and frequently disagrees with official policy: The Rhea landing, for example, far from a bit of adolescent showboating, was actually intended as a scientific experiment meant to demonstrate such a landing was possible, thus breaking new ground for stellar navigation. Regardless, this is one stunt too many and McClane and his crew get demoted to patrol duty (and it's interesting to note here routine patrol duty is seen as a step down for McClane's crew) and assigned an overseer in the form of Lieutenant Tamara Jagellovsk, who is assigned to make sure the *Orion* crew stays out of trouble.

What Jagellovsk and her superiors don't quite grasp, though, is that McClane is actually far from a hothead, simply preferring to operate his ship by its own special code of loyalty and morals. Because of this, the crew of the *Orion* have an extremely close, and extremely obvious, sense of kinship, and camaraderie with one another that really does go above and beyond anything contemporaneous Star Trek was doing. It helps that while McClane is clearly one of the central characters, equal time is afforded to every member of the crew, and the show goes out of its way to provide a healthy amount of scenes where the characters engage in small-talk with each other, which strongly reinforces their humanness and relatability as well as the close bond they share.

The unique way the ship is organised also allows *Raumpatrouille Orion* to avoid one of the biggest logical pitfalls Star Trek suffers in all its incarnations: If these ships are staffed with hundreds or thousands of officers, why is it always only the senior staff who beam down into dangerous situations (I mean, besides the obvious answer: You want the characters you care about to be actually involved in the plot)? Well, the *Orion*'s crew literally only comprises the six main characters (counting Lieutenant Jagellovsk) as it's a much, much smaller ship then anything in Starfleet, so naturally they're the only ones who can go on away team missions and get into action scenes.

This also adds another level to the crew's fierce loyalty, because they know they have nobody except each other other to rely on out in the depths of outer space. Some of the show's most gripping and enjoyable scenes are when two of the crew leave the ship and run into trouble, at which point the remaining officers (even McClane) are forced to double up on shipboard duties and kick their already intense work ethic into warp drive as leaving someone behind is completely unacceptable to them. Every single member of the *Orion*'s crew must be equally proficient with every station on the bridge as they have no "relief officers" and neither the chain of command nor classism have a place in this environment: There's no sitting back and sending underlings to do your dirty work for you here. Everyone truly is an equal on this ship.

What this allows *Raumpatrouille Orion* to do is look very carefully and very seriously at the concept of authoritarian power structures and the ability of people within them to rebel and formulate their own identities, and perhaps even to subvert the structure entirely. While McClane works for the military wing of Earth he is, as I mentioned, someone very few people within it like to talk about. His only two real fans are his former superior and sole frontline commander General Lydia van Dyke, who shares his perspective, if somewhat less inclined to act on it quite as frequently and publicly as he does (by the way, Star Trek won't get female captains and flag officers until the movie series. The damn thing has to get *rebooted three times* first) and his new commanding officer, Winston Wamsler, who, as a retired soldier, has an extremely high respect for individualism and a contempt for government and bureaucracy. Everyone else in the minor cast seems either highly suspicious of or openly disdainful towards the *Orion* crew.

This is theme is reiterated on the ship itself, as the primary source of tension early on in the series is the contrasting worldviews of Commander McClane and Lieutenant Jagellovsk. *Raumpatrouille*'s (far less amiable) version of the Kirk/Spock/McCoy split involves McClane's flagrant anti-authoritarianism and belief in responding to situations on a case-by-case basis clashing with Jagellovsk's unfettered faith in rules and regulations and doing things by-the-book. In many ways this means *Raumpatrouille* becomes Jagellovsk's show, as she frequently must learn that blindly following orders makes a person less than human and that clinging to a blinkered view of the world when faced with the vastness of the universe is not only impractical but ludicrous. However, McClane has things to learn as well, as his impulsiveness has a history of getting himself and his crew into unnecessary trouble, and he frequently needs someone like Jagellovsk to appeal to reason and get him to occasionally re-think his split-second choices.

The first big test of this happens in the premier episode, "Attack from Space", in which the newly-demoted *Orion* crew on patrol duty stumbles upon an extraterrestrial invasion force that has snuck into the solar system undetected and captured an Earth outpost, slaughtering the entire crew. This is a situation nobody is prepared to deal with, and both McClane and Jagellovsk screw up horribly and dangerously: For her part, Tamara clings feverishly to a book of rules Cliff continuously has to remind her are hopelessly outdated as there are no procedures for alien invasions because nobody writing them was expecting one (this actually results in one of McClane's best scenes in the series, where he calls Jagellovsk out on the anthropocentric arrogance of her and her superiors, asking if she truly thought in the entire universe humans were the only species intelligent, special and important enough to become a spacefaring civilization). But McClane, and really the entire military is also far too willing to wage all-out war and in the end the only reason the crew is saved is because Jagellovsk's boss Colonel Villa gets the generals on Earth to call off a massive retaliation strike at the last second, correctly pointing out that just because the aliens have committed a hostile act does not mean they should be condemned before Earth is able to communicate with them and find out who they are and why they did what they did, let alone if they even share the same set of values as humans.

The aliens, who go on to become reoccurring antagonists, are perhaps part of the reason there's been a lot of hand-wringing by contemporary critics that *Raumpatrouille Orion* is flagrantly fascist. There is perhaps an argument to be made here, as the aliens are immediately seen as dangerous and are given the derogatory nickname "frogs": We never do get an examination of their culture or motives, and they're pretty clearly an Other. One could read this as the show telling us the real purpose of uniting people is not for communal benefit and exchange of ideas, but to protect and strengthen the group against even bigger, scarier outside threats. There's also a slight twinge of right-wing libertarianism here, as the show does seem far more willing to celebrate individual heroism over group action when the chips are down: McClane is meant to be sympathetic because he tends to act before he thinks and doesn't really care that much about what a lot of other people think, something Wamsler respects in him. Wamsler himself gets a fair few speeches both in this episode and the rest of the series lauding this strain of unbridled individualism.

But I don't think that's what *Raumpatrouille* is actually about. The whole point of the first episode seems to be that shooting first and asking questions later is actually a really terrible idea, and there are other cultural forces in play here that make this a bit more nuanced than it might initially appear to an American audience. Wamsler is explicitly a crusty, curmudgeonly old veteran archetype, and this is still a show where the command base is a Mod bar under the sea. And while McClane bucks authority and doesn't get on with Jagellovsk at first because she reminds him of it, he is very respectful of the rest of the *Orion* crew and always has time for their thoughts and opinions. So it's not so much that he's opposed to working with others as much as he prefers to associate himself with people he respects and understands. And if anything, McClane's staunch anti-authoritarianism could be seen as *anti*-fascist: Remember this is West Germany in the late 1960s. World War II was still not that far removed from people, and surely everyone remembered the Nuremberg Trials and "I was only following orders". Individualism of this type does not mean the same thing in Germany that it does in the United States.

Because of this, and despite its space patrol setting, I really don't buy the accusation *Raumpatrouille Orion* is militaristic. On the contrary, the military (save the rebellious, unorthodox *Orion* crew and van Dyke) is shown to be just as incompetent and ineffective as the rest of Earth's organisational structure, and both of these first two episodes are split in half between the *Orion* in mortal peril struggling to resolve a crisis at the other end of the solar system and a lot of shouty exchanges back on Earth as representatives from the government, the military and galactic security would much rather argue with each other and demand their group be given total control over the situation then to actually do anything that might be beneficial, productive or useful.

To me a much more intriguing and nuanced reading would be that the show is grappling with issues of authoritarianism and self-governance, best embodied in the split between McClane and Jagellovsk. A theme that begins here and continues throughout the series is that they're frequently required to cooperate and compromise and each one has to admit on a number of occasions the other has an approach that's better suited to some things. Far from advocating a police state, *Raumpatrouille Orion* seems to be making the claim only cooperation, reasoned discourse and empathy will pave the way forward.

But while *Raumpatrouille Orion* frankly runs absolute rings around *Star Trek* in most areas, it is clear even in this first story that there are some things that are simply out of its wheelhouse. While it's much, much better on things like gender and diegetic progressive politics, *Raumpatrouille* lacks, for a number of reasons, *Star Trek*'s ability to be ridiculously oversignified. There's nobody like William Shatner here, for one, though that said while Dietmar Schönherr's Cliff Allister McClane may not be a drag action man, he is very progressive in other ways: As someone who strives for peaceful solutions to crises at all costs and who values life above just about all else, he definitely seems ahead of his time and out of place in Earth's military.

Also, there are just some advantages that being filmed in Hollywood gives you. For example, while *surveillance* officer Helga Legrelle beats communications officer Uhura hands down in terms of being a memorable character and feminist role model, Uhura is black and Helga is not. And *Star Trek* *does* have Sulu played by George Takei, while *Raumpatrouille*, for reasonx unknown to me but which are more than likely related to this being West Germany in 1966, was unable to get a Japanese actor to play the part of Atan Shubashi, forcing them to cast the *extremely* German-looking Friedrich Georg Beckhaus. However, the show deserves full credit for refusing to put him in yellowface, which is something that it absolutely could have done and not gotten a second glance for, and instead just asking us to ignore his ethnicity. Especially given that not two chapters ago we were dealing with "Errand of Mercy".

Then there's the obvious thing. Star Trek is a massive pop culture phenomenon ubiquitous all over the world comprised of at the time of this writing six television shows, twelve feature films and an incalculable amount of spinoff material. *Raumpatrouille Orion* is a seven-episode miniseries that hardly anyone remembers anymore and that's looked on by those who do with a slightly nervous and guilty camp fondness. There's no *Raumpatrouille: The Next Generation or Raumaptrouille: Deep Space Nine* and while there is a spin-off line of tie-in novels that purports to continue the series, which is about how you'd expect a line with that sort of pedigree to be, nobody is going to call it an iconic bit of Western pop consciousness.. Why didn't *Raumpatrouille Orion* last longer? Many modern critics seem to point to its alleged fascist overtones, which I remain unconvinced of, and a popular story is that the show got canceled after only seven episodes because the networks and governments were concerned about its militarism. The wife of the original screen writer claims instead there were only ever going to be seven, but more scripts do in fact exist then were actually filmed. The more likely explanation to me is that the show was laughably expensive to produce for the time and place where it was filmed, and some reports claim it outright bankrupted parent studio Bavaria Film.

Even so, *Raumpatrouille Orion* remains a vitally important TV series, and any look at the voyaging starship story in the late 1960s would be terribly remiss if it didn't give the show its due. So let's do that then: Let's accompany the ORION and her crew on their patrol at the edge of infinity.

35. "Supernova Girl": Planet off Course

While not a "story arc" in the way modern audiences would think of it, the first two episodes of *Raumpatrouille Orion* seem consciously designed to explore the show's setting and what can be done with its status quo in complimentary ways. Following dealing with an invasion by hostile aliens in "Attack from Space", "Planet off Course" looks at another possible crisis a rapid space patrol might have to deal with. This time the danger comes from a natural disaster instead of a foreign threat: A rogue planet catapulted into the solar system on a collision course with Earth. However, it's soon revealed that the Frogs did something to mess with the planet's gravity and are monitoring it from a control centre, letting us know they're going to be reoccurring antagonists.

But even so, "Planet off Course" plays out much more like a standard disaster movie. It's got an unabashed thriller structure, with tense sequences at Earth command with the government and the military frantically debating how to evacuate the entire population of Earth and whether or not they have the time to do so interspersed with intense action at the end of the solar system where a fleet of 200 ships, including Commander McClane's *Orion* and General van Dyke's *Hydra*, has been sent out to intercept the rogue planet and neutralize the Frog's command base. Well...we're *told* this, at any rate. We only actually see the two ships and the *Hydra*'s bridge is a redress of the *Orion*. Let's of course not forget what show we're watching here.

What's truly remarkable about this episode is the way it shows how incredibly fast *Raumpatrouille Orion* is moving with the exploration of its central themes and premises even this early. The stakes have been raised astronomically just from the premier, which is pretty damn impressive considering "Attack from Space" introduced aliens into a setting that presumably had no aliens prior and set them poised to invade Earth. Now the engtire planet is on the verge of destruction with potentially unimaginable loss of life, and there are a lot of scenes where it looks for a time like major characters are going to get killed off: First we lose contact with the *Hydra*, which is found adrift with potentially her whole crew, including Lydia, dead. Then there are several occasions where it seems like *Orion* crewmembers are going to have to sacrifice themselves to halt the rogue planet's trajectory. In one particularly tense moment, McClane even *tends his resignation* to Tamara! Then in the climax, when all other plans to stop the planet have failed, McClane *blows up* the *Orion* by crashing it into the planet. And this is the *second episode*. The material here is enough to warrant a season finale, if not a *series* finale.

Everyone is OK and there's obviously a new ship in the offing, but this is still a megaton series of events for the show to throw at us two weeks in. What *Raumpatrouille Orion* is doing here is actually deconstructing itself in the second episode, which is a move so delightfully brazen I'm still smiling about it four years after I first saw it. It's almost as if the show set up a *false flag* setting and status quo in the premier *just* so it could throw everything out the window here: You wanted a slow burn conspiratorial plot as we tried to deduce the Frogs' nefarious plans with a final showdown at the end of the year? Yeah, they almost destroy Earth in the second episode, let's move on. Cliff McClane's staucnh individuality and steadfast loyalty to his his friends, which was set up as his biggest character virtue and reason for us to champion here damn near gets the solar system wiped out here as he goes out of his way to rescue Lydia and the Hydra instead of going after the Frogs in direct defiance of pretty much everyone else's wishes, prompting Tamara to threaten to *melt the Orion's control panels* to get him under control. And Lydia turned out to be fine anyway!

However McClane's brashness does end up helping them in the end, as Lydia and the *Hydra* end up a crucial components of the plan that ends up finally stopping the rogue planet and pushing the Frogs back. And indeed, McClane's true defining moment comes at the end when, after having narrowly averted the total destruction of Earth from a runaway planetoid (sacrificing two fleet ships in the process) he faces a mountain of paperwork to fill out back at base. Instead of sheepishly rolling his eyes or bemoaning the distant inefficiency of bureaucracy, he happily sits down to work with the clerk sent by the government to sort the situation out, telling him "you know, you people have it the worst of all of us, having to sort through all this. All we had to do was blow up a supernova".Which is yet another deconstruction, this time of the "heroic lone gun vs. obstructive bureaucrat" theme introduced last week (and that *Star Trek* adores, for that matter): To Commander McClane, bureaucrats are just as human as anyone else, and are just as trapped by the roles they play in the social order as he and his crew are. We're all people in the end, after all.

Also pertinent to the theme of deconstruction is, naturally, the destruction of the *Orion*. With it goes any baggage or symbolism from *Raumptrouille*'s prehistory: Whatever McClane and his crew may have been or done before now clearly doesn't matter. In fact, the whole "Raumpatrouille" thing actually becomes redundant after this episode: The *Orion* crew are plainly heroes with the respect and admiration of the entire solar system and are certainly no longer on the galaxy's KP. The only reason they're not "officially" back on the frontlines after this episode is because the whole rogue planet and alien invasion thing has been kept secret from the general populace and the rest of the navy outside of basically what amounts to the equivalent of the Joint Chiefs of Staff. *Un*officially, McClane and the crew have been totally reinstated, and from here on out *Raumpatrouille Orion* is far breezier and more capricious about its premise, essentially just using it as a delivery device to get the crew into fun, goofy science fiction plots and thought experiments.

Which is as it should be, because, as off "Planet off Course", *Raumpatrouille Orion*'s entire premise has been rendered completely superfluous. There's another nail in that militarism coffin for you.

As much as I love this story and what it's doing, I do have to raise a nitpicks with it. Because for a show that's considered a marquee hard science fiction series (not to mention one that names all its ships after constellations), the actual science fiction (and actual science) is pretty amusingly wonky: This episode rather infamously uses the terms "planet", "star", "asteroid" and "supernova" interchangeably and the show on the whole has more indecipherable technobabble than *Star Trek Voyager*, which is *really* apparent in this one. But that's just *Raumpatrouille*'s thing, and, just like Star Trek, it really shouldn't be seen as a high water mark for Hard SF in pop culture because it's absolutely not. Hell, there's an episode coming up that has a character who's an *actual* science fiction writer who exists pretty much just so the crew can relentlessly mock him and take the piss out of the whole genre for the length of the episode's runtime.

There's also some lovely VFX in this episode, or at least as lovely as *Raumpatrouille* can make them. I really love the analog/digital fusion user interfaces, particularly the big transparent monitors people look through to view the rogue planet/star/asteroid/comet/supernova/whatever through (which is itself a cool effect: An angry flaming planetoid constantly hurling right towards us). Some of the pyrotechnics are cool, in a kind of vintage B-movie way, and even in spite of the obvious cheapness this still looks light years better than *Star Trek*'s set design and effects. Artistry is important, kids. And it's that artistry that makes "Planet off Course" such a brazen and confidant second outing for *Raumpatrouille Orion*, because its writing, acting and sheer ambition is as impressive as it looks.

36. "Evitable Conflict": Keepers of the Law

Compared to what we got last time, "Keepers of the Law" is a much more straightforward, low-key affair. Which is, of course, all well and good: It wouldn't do *Raumpatrouille Orion* any good to keep racking the stakes up until they got tiring, and after two weeks of setting up expectations just to tear them down, the show is going to have to settle down and go about actually showing us what kind of a show it intends on being for the remainder of its tenure.

Given that, the direction the show ends up going here feels in some ways a bit disappointingly conservative at first glance. "Keepers of the Law" is unabashedly an Asimov-style rumination on robotics and mechanization, with the whole Three Laws deal ripped straight off of *I, Robot*. For those unfamiliar with this side of Isaac Asimov's work, his Robot stories universally revolve around the central thematic tenet of the supposed Three Laws of Robotics:

> A robot may not injure a human being or, through inaction, allow a human being to come to harm.

> A robot must obey orders given to it by human beings, except where such orders would conflict with the First Law.

> A robot must protect its own existence, as long as such protection does not conflict with the First or Second Laws.

More than anything else in the genre, the Three Laws indicate how much of Golden Age Hard SF was bound up in its futurist musings. All of Asimov's Robot stories hinge on the presupposition that these laws are hard and fast rules underpinning all of robotics, and their entire plots are solely about playing with unexpected twists and loopholes that come about when a machine governed by pure "logic" and "rationality" attempts to live its life in accordance with all three at once, in particular when doing so results in logical paradoxes and contradictions. This is pretty much the extent of Asimov's dramatic ambition in these stories, but it is a classic example of the logic puzzle plots that define this genre. In fact, you could argue the Three Laws of Robotics are the archetypal example of them.

So seeing this crop up in *Raumpatrouille* can feel like a bit of a letdown, though it's not an unexpected one. This is still a show that at least made overtures to the SF crowd, so one would expect it to pay lip service to it in some way. But upon closer examination this plot is actually a really good fit for *Raumpatrouille*, because the show's central conflict is in many ways the tension between regulation and duty and libertarian individualism and trying to find a happy medium between the two: If any show could do a story about the mechanization of the mid-20th century and a struggle between conflicting orders and impulses via Asimov's Three Laws, this is actually probably it.

And it has to be said the show definitely approaches the whole thing with a requisite amount of necessary tongue-in-cheek humour. After begrudgingly attending a briefing on Robotics and the Three Laws, a scene which immediately brings to mind bored schoolkids rolling their eyes at an unhip and boring lesson (some of whom are *literally* sleeping through the class), the *Orion* crew is sent to go pick up some space probes with astrophysical data to be analysed. On the way there though, the *Orion* picks up a message from an ore freighter run by a retired commander named Ruyther who McClane used to serve under. Ruyther explains that something funny is going on at the mining colony he works with, which seems to have stopped all exports. McClane wants to go check it out, but, since he's been ordered to service the probes, he sends Atan and Helga over in a shuttle to start work while he'll take the rest of the crew to investigate the mine.

Once they get there it turns out that the mining colony uses robots for the especially hard labour, who have naturally taken over the mine and kidnapped and imprisoned the human miners. In a plot twist that will be somewhat ironic to readers who recall one particular kerfluffle over "The City on the Edge of Forever", the robots take over the mine after a dispute with a drug dealer resulted in the death of several people. As they have been programmed to protect human life and cannot cause harm, the robots deduced humans are a threat to themselves and therefore must be contained. The briefing scene from the opening comes back because Tamara is the only one who paid attention during the briefing and is familiar with the robots' mechanics, so she's the one who figures out what's happened. Wonderfully however, this also sets up one of the best subtle jokes in the series so far-Even though she paid attention and knows an internal switch has been tripped...She doesn't know *which one* has been tripped because she missed that part.

Meanwhile on the space probe, Atan and Helga notice the life support system is failing and their energy reserves are running low, and we watch them try in vain to contact the *Orion* for help all the while refusing to abandon the ship. This subplot illuminates how tightly structured an episode this is and the subtle nuance with which *Raumpatrouille* looks at its themes: Everything that happens here is a metaphor for the series' larger issues about regulation and libertarianism. The robots are wrongfooted by their slavish obedience and the Orion crew wouldn't have been able save the colony if they;d followed their own orders to the letter. And once the others finally get back to Atan and Helga it's almost too late, but, as McClane points out, any member of his crew should be used to being able to think independently of orders by now. On the other hand, Tamara was the only one who actually figured out what the physical problem was. The episode's overall point seems to be that rules are only worth following if they're good and make sense, which is a callback to the premier.

Over its first three episodes then, we can see how *Raumpatrouille Orion* has been building to a kind of thematic head. The regulation vs. individualism battle is one the show takes very seriously and has a vested issue in exploring, and from a West German context in 1966 it's very understandable why this might be the case. It would, in fact, almost be reductive simply to look at a divided Berlin split along Cold War ideological boundaries with Nazi Germany in living memory and see parity with a space-based science fiction show whose charismatic captain is a Scottish-American with problems dealing with authority. The real fascism issue in *Raumpatrouille* right now is actually an explicit examination of the fascism-anarchy spectrum, the classic binary that is what all of political science and futurism ultimately boils down to. As of this story the show does seem to emphatically reject pure fascism, but it doesn't seem entirely ready to commit to the other direction yet.

It may seem repetitive to keep bringing these thematic beat points up, but they are terribly important ones and *Raumpatrouille Orion* deserves major credit for airing them out so clearly out in the open the way it does. Very few shows of this period would have the spine to tackle this kind of thing at all: *Star Trek*, for example, plainly doesn't seem to care. And that's when it's at its *best*-At its worst, it is *absolutely* fascist. Very few shows *today* would be that brave. The fact that we can have this conversation at all in the context of a science fiction show is worth taking note of and speaks very clearly to the time, place and people. As we'll see, the genre isn't really well suited to taking this sort of a stand.

37. "Vigilance, Mr. Worf": Deserters

I guess every science fiction show has to do a story like this at some point. And that speaks more to the overall genre than it does to any one instance.

"Deserters", in hindsight, is probably the weak link in *Raumptrouille Orion*'s chain. There's room to redeem most of what the series has done to date and will do for the remainder of its season, but not so much this. I've resisted the accusation this show is "fascist" so far, and while that's a terribly strong insult and probably too harsh, it's tough to argue "Deserters" doesn't at least lurch the show to the right. It's not as bad as something like "Space Seed" (which actually does seem to outright endorse actual fascism, something I'm not quite sure this story does), but it does raise a whole host of worrying implications.

The *Orion* takes on a psychologist over concerns that a succession of officers in the navy have had a series of bizarre and inexplicable fits and tantrums. Starbases fail to respond to hails, and a high-profile commander by the name of Alonzo Pietro has apparently defected to the Frogs. And on the *Orion* itself, dissent is sewn among the crew when Hasso, Mario and Tamara start accusing each other of plotting to divert the ship's course into enemy territory. It turns out the the Frogs have developed a legit hupnosis gun that literally brainwashes people into doing their bidding in an attempt to compromise Earth's defenses from within. This is especially concerning because the *Orion* is testing a new superweapon to replace the standard ray guns the Frogs have rendered inoperative due to new advances in shield technology called, I kid you not, The Overkill Machine. In the end McClane outwits the Frogs by playing double agent; pretending to defect while using his access to destroy their base of operations.

The easiest way to read "Deserters" from a United States perspective is through the lens of the McCarthy era. It's all too easy to parallel the big fight on the bridge with the Red Scare witch hunts of the 1950s. Like I said in the introduction, it seems every single science fiction show takes a crack at this plot at some point, two notable examples for our purposes being *Star Trek: The Next Generation* and *Babylon 5*. Unlike those later shows, *Raumpatrouille Orion* does at least have the advantage of being only ten years removed from the events in question rather than thirty or forty, so it can at least make a somewhat strangled case for being at least marginally topical. The major problem for *Raumpatrouille* though, and one that's potentially series-ruining, is that "Deserters" almost seems to be *in favour* of "if you see something, say something" fearmongering: I mean, the Frogs, foreign enemy agents, are *literally brainwashing* people. The worst *Star Trek: The Next Generation* and *Babylon 5* have to worry about is coming across as exasperatingly middlebrow and a bit old and white-At least they had the right intentions.

This would also tie into *Raumpatrouille*'s big theme about regulation and libertarianism:

Witch hunts and propaganda are precisely the type of "groupthink" evils an arch-libertarian would think are the worst things ever, so it would make sense to pit Commander McClane up against them. And, as a show that seems to at least pay lip service to Hard SF, that would put *Raumpatrouille* at least partly in the same party and intellectual tradition as Robert A. Heinlein, who built an entire career out of exploring these issues. The kicker though is that these are particularly concerns of deeply right-wing libertarians, and that's not actually a constructive path forward. Libertarian fascism is a peculiarly United States fantasy that eventually gets us things like "Space Seed" and modern reactionary politics. And the really alarming thing is that Heinlein himself was absolutely of that worldview, and that he has been so influential on all of science fiction since is one of the genre's many deeply worrying original sins: It is genuinely hard to separate the futurism and the metaphor from the inescapably hatefully reactionary and xenophobic politics. As a foundational myth for Westernism, science fiction is at once morbidly appropriate and appropriately damning.

Of course, a McCarthyist lens is not necessarily the most appropriate lens to read a West German show through. Ever since World War II Germany has been extremely concerned about violence or nationalist rhetoric and indeed remember how some believe this very show was indeed cancelled for being too militaristic. It would likely take gonads to put something flagrantly and openly right wing and nationalist on West German television screens in 1966 at any rate. So best case scenario then is that "Deserters" comes across as rather weakly pulpish and tone-deaf, which to me actually seems like the more likely scenario. Like *Star Trek*, *Raumpatrouille Orion* tends to be far more ray-gun fisticuffs action then heady intellectualizing anyway. What we're then left with is a kind of espionage thriller about an arms race between two rival factions (which is far more in keeping with a mid Cold War context) with some pulp sci-fi trappings to make use of the setting. This is still not great, I should point out.

Pulp fiction tends to be terribly unexamined, by which it lacks much self-awareness of itself and its own biases, if any. Pulp stories trend towards lurid spectacle, exoticism and objectification and have a documented history of making life materially worse for cultural networks outside the hegemony due to portraying them in grotesque and grossly inaccurate ways. And yes I know that's not as much of a concern for a show set in a constructed fantasy sci-fi world disconnected from reality, but these issues can and do creep into everything. There's nothing that's not political, and that which claims to be apolitical oftentimes tends to end up some of the most dangerously reactionary work of all.

(Because this essay has been a bit too negative, consider this: Even here, *Raumpatrouille Orion* displays some encouraging and hopeful moments simply by having the good sense to have some scenes set in that gorgeous Starlight Casino. In this episode, Cliff and Lydia catch up at the bar together while Tamara, sitting by herself in the background, looks on. Lydia jokes that Tamara seems jealous of her. It's a small moment that at once continues to set up what will become an important plot thread by series' end, but also adds some needed levity to take away from the burdensome rest of the story.)

A question I feel we really need to start asking is whether or not science fiction can actually ever be anything but reactionary. Invoking the Golden Age works invokes a plethora of more or less explicitly reactionary concepts and ideas, and the pulp model's reveling in the hedonistic escapism of a life unexamined is little more than the proverbial opiate for the masses. And what is science fiction without either of those things? And are the West's stories of voyaging and exploration forever doomed to be innately ones about militarism, imperialism, colonialism and proud subjugation? Perhaps our stories tell us more about ourselves than we'd prefer to admit.

38. "Solarmax": Battle for the Sun

Thankfully, things get a lot more fun and interesting again here.

While conducting a scientific study into a unique strain of plant life that seems to be able to exist on planets thought to be barren desert worlds, the *Orion* crew receives word that unusual solar prominences have started occurring that could cause widespread natural disasters on Earth. But the crew soon have problems of their own to worry about when Cliff, Atan and Mario get kidnapped by two men who appear to be rogue scientists. The scientists turn out to be from faroff planet Chroma, a world once thought to be pure myth where Neptunian colonists fled to following their defeat at the end of Galaxy War I 600 years prior. After some patching up, the scientists agree to take the Orion crew to Chroma, where they claim the solar prominences are being controlled. And yes, the science in this episode makes precisely zero sense, I'm aware. Ignore it. It's not important. This is the same show that called a rogue planet a comet *and* a supernova three episodes ago: Strict Hard SF-style accuracy is demonstrably not *Raumpatrouille Orion*'s forte, a point which is about to become abundantly clear.

Chroma, as it happens, is a matriarchal society where men are second-class citizens who are only fit for menial jobs, like the military, grounds-keeping and the hard sciences. And it's explicitly a utopia. So that's maybe interesting. But before we get too much time to think about that the plot comes knocking again-Commander McClane tries to open diplomatic relations with Chroma, a task which will become slightly more difficult if Tamara's boss Colonel Villa gets his wish of declaring war on them. Tamara rushes to Chroma to warn them of the impending attack, but gets captured for her troubles. So now the *Orion* crew have a blossoming diplomatic incident on their hands as they get caught in the middle.

The first thing worth taking note of here is how, in spite of the rather blatant up-yours to the scientific establishment (a theme I'll be more than happy to return to later on, both in the context of this episode and the next), "Battle for the Sun" is, in its own strange way, structured as a very archetypal science fiction story in the Golden Age style. The plot itself is boilerplate pulp capture-and-escape nonsense, but the plot is manifestly not the point. What we're *of course* meant to pay attention to is the world-building and speculative utopian futurism. Where *Raumpatrouille Orion* differs from the Isaac Asimovs, Arthur C. Clarkes and Robert A. Heinleins of the world is in the fact that "Battle for the Sun" is pretty damn radical in its thinking, even today. The can of gender worms this episode opens is frankly enormous, and it would take way longer than the space I have to unpack all of it.

But we're going to take a crack at it anyway. So first of all, we have a matriarchy that's explicitly positioned as a utopia. And there really is no room for debate here: Villa makes the idiotic decision to attack Chroma, just because, and his department is the one that's always more in the wrong than not on this show. The *Orion* crew, for their part, spend the episode marvelling at the beauty of Chroma and the wonders of the society they've built. They're definitely fans, and, since we're supposed to sympathize with them, we're meant to share their endorsement. There is a particular strain of feminist thought worth keeping in mind here wherin matriarchal societies, which (at leats as far as we know) historically have never existed, typically exist as myths to warn those living in *patriarchal* societies of the supposed dangers of female and feminine power and agency. That's a theme I'll definitely return to sometime around the 1970s because *Star Trek Phase II* puts its feet in its mouth pretty badly on this front (and it's a theme Gene Roddenberry returns to fuck up badly on in "Angel One" from the first season of *Star Trek: The Next Generation*), but for now what's important to remember is that *Raumpatrouille Orion* doesn't, and (unlike Gene Roddenberry's numerous superficially similar briefs) "Battle for the Sun" isn't an "Issues" story about patriarchal oppression.

Secondly, it's sort of fun how the hard sciences are among the things only considered fit for the underclass. "Men's work", if you will. Science can do and has done many wonderful things for people and society, but the fact of the matter is science is itself an inherently patriarchal discipline. As Donna Haraway points out in *Situated Knowledges: The Science Question in Feminism and the Privilege of Partial Perspective*, science is built around dualities of self/other and, most importantly, objectivity/subjectivity. What Haraway calls "The God Trick" is the fallacy, common to some strands of scientific dogma, that the observer is somehow "above" that which he is observing, and therefore detached from it. Haraway would rather we throw out all notions of objective and subjective altogether, instead proposing a system of situated knowledge-spaces. Furthermore, there is the uncomfortable reality that science is so often structured around notions of "rationality" and what is "rational"...And in that worldview women are the ultimate irrational, and thus the ultimate Other. Haraway, and I, argue that a feminist science would embrace contradiction and positionality rather than omniscience: With an eye towards how perspective and power construct the narrative of fact, it would take an active, generative, bottom-up role in constructing them.

As impressive as it is to see *Raumpatrouille Orion* doing 1980s-style feminist STS theory a good twenty years early, that's not quite the end of the oversignification "Battle for the Sun" gives us. Think about it: We've got an overt matriarchal utopia on a distant land thought to be only a myth. It's a paradise, where no-one goes wanting, alebit one with customs that seem strange to visitors from the outside. It's a land settled by refugees from the losing side of a war, forced to evacuate their homes and go into hiding. This is the Otherworld. Fairyland. In the most commonly accepted canon of Irish mythology, the Tuatha Dé Danann were the Old Gods and former rulers of the island who were forced into hiding in the underground Otherworld beyond the barrows after Ireland was invaded and conquered by the Milesians. The Tuatha Dé Danann were "The People of the Art", an art which sounds suspiciously like magick. And which, if you believe people like Alan Moore, actually was. The Tuatha Dé's final stand in Ireland was even a magickal battle, where the forces of nature were controlled through poetry.

This then kind of puts a new twist on *Raumaptrouille*'s constant cycle of space battles, invasions and awe-inspiring cosmic forces controlled by various parties in various ways to achieve specific ends. And just to head off the potential criticism that I'm reading a German story through and Irish lens, I'd point out that there are actually a huge amount of similarities between the religion and mythologies of the Norse, the ancient pagan Germans and the ancient pagan Irish. And this isn't just me, this has been commented on by far too many scholars and researchers for me to cite here. Whether or not this is due to a shared origin at some point in early history or due to later contact is actually irrelevant (although there is enough evidence to support the theory that there was at least some overlap), the fact remains it still very much seems to be there. So *Raumpatrouille Orion* doing a story that seems to possibly hint at invoking this on at least some level doesn't really seem *all* that far-fetched.

In the old tales, the gods always had particular spheres. It's inaccurate to say there was one specific god or goddess of such-and-such a thing: Rather, the Old Gods have specific *attestations*; different areas of life and the natural world they have a connection to and a specific proficiency in. It's reasonable to extrapolate that this continues in the stories in which they become faeries, especially when you take into consideration how similar folktales of faeries and nature-spirits are. The Old Gods *are* nature-spirits. So what aspects of nature do the Chromans have domain over? Well, plainly, the Sun. And that's also interesting. Throughout history there have been many contrasting conceptions of the sun and solar energy in various mythologies depending on whether one views them as fundamentally male or female energies. This what *Raumpatrouille*'s "Battle for the Sun" is about then: A recasting of the ancient magickal wars between factions of gods for the privilege of being able to join with the forces of nature of particular place-energies. The army of a Sun God recoils upon encountering the hidden queendom of the Sun Goddess and lashes out in fear, because patriarchy can neither fathom nor conceive of feminine power.

It's make or break time for *Raumpatrouille Orion* then, caught between an unstoppable force and an immovable object. But we'd do well to remember that these are still meant to be enlightened times, and what does Commander McClane (who is naturally a Scotsman, if you'll recall) do? He gets them to call it off. He helps bring about a truce, paving the way to open up diplomatic relations between Earth and Chroma. There's no need for the horrors of further bloodshed, and there will be no war of ideologies and pscyhogeography this day. Reconcilliation between the anima and animus. It is, in the end, actually possible for humans to get along and understand other humans so long as we're governed by empathy and respect. This is, incidentally, the most quintessentially Star Trek story we've seen to date or will see for an extremely long time, and it's not even Star Trek. Hell, it *outdoes* Star Trek, going above and beyond just about anything that franchise will ever do.

As for me, in lieu of a Battle for the Sun, I'd prefer a Prayer to Her.

39. "We're in a menagerie": The Space Trap

There's something to be said for the cage motif and allegory we've been building over the course of this book so far.

Star Trek's Cage is perhaps Gene Roddenberry, or perhaps the future. The great expectations of what the series could and should represent is almost unfair to the material artefacts of pop culture that actually were and are. They can never live up to the memories and imagined futurist greatness we project onto them, and maybe that's something they should not be judged for. How they managed to inspire them, and whether or not they should be held accountable to those standards, remains an open question. *Raumptrouille Orion* of course does not have those same expectations: The series only exists as seven brief episodes that aired in West German in 1966 and the story has no real afterlife beyond them. The show remains a fondly remembered German institution and there were naturally the spin-off novels that purported to continue the story for a handful of obsessive devotees, but comparing *Raumpatrouille Orion* to Star Trek is even more unfair then comparing *Star Trek* to Star Trek.

So is *Raumpatrouille*'s brief life a cage for its legacy in paradoxically the same way Star Trek's extremely long one is? Well, so far, at least on the level of rote textual quality and historical vindication, not really, no: There's been one kind of bum episode among five or six, and all the others have been remarkably more bold, adventurous, forward-thinking, provocative and progressive than much else I can think of that was on the air at the same time (and even the weaker link wasn't actually all that weak when you consider how bad it *could* have been). And that includes *Star Trek* by a country mile. But there is still a cage that keeps *Raumpatrouille* trapped to a degree, and it's one that it's actually keenly aware of. "The Space Trap" from which this episode gets its title can be rather easily inferred to be the entire genre of science fiction itself.

The *Orion* crew has been asked to escort Pieter-Paul Ibsen, a pampered, sheltered science fiction writer on what amounts to a joyride through the solar system on his birthday as a favour to the defense ministry, with whom he has nepotistic connections. Pretty much everyone on the *Orion* resents his presence, which they meet with thinly-veiled hostility and derision. Just to twist the knife a little further, PiePo, as he is not-so-affectionately referred to as, thinks it would be really nifty if he could fly one of the Orion's shuttles because he thinks thinks they're super neato. As luck would have it, no sooner does Cliff reluctantly comply than PiePo's shuttle careens off course and crash-lands on an asteroid, where the hapless hack is promptly kidnapped by a deranged mad scientist named Tourenne

171

who wants to commandeer the Orion so he can defect to the Frogs. Yet one more exciting series of captures and escapes ensures as Helga and Tamara free Hasso, Atan and Mario (who have managed to get themselves kidnapped as well) only for Tourenne to come back in and stall the plot some more while he and Commander McClane negotiate for the safety of the ship.

I'm making the plot out to sound worse than it actually is. This is a fun enough episode, and in many ways a needed lighthearted respite from the events of the past few weeks (not to mention next week, as we're approaching *Rampatrouille Orion*'s epic and climatic grand finale). But the structure and plot beats here are very, very telling. First of all, as a writer who has occasionally entertained pretensions of entering the genre fiction field, I can confidently say that PiePo *absolutely* deserves every ounce of scorn and mockery he gets. We writers are a terribly miserable sort, entitled as we are in our delusions that the average person can spare the time or posses the stomach to sit through our intellectual masturbation. Honestly, f you've made it even this far in this book, you deserve praise and gratitude. And genre fiction is the worst of all: At its heart is a fundamentally irreconcilable frisson regarding a desire to reach the mythic and the esoteric wedded to an embarrassingly dreadful narrative and prose structure inherited from the absolute worst class of stock, pulpish pandering capitalist pop entertainment.

And so with PiePo *Raumpatrouille Orion* lays the truth all out for us through a craven little buffoon whose primary contribution is getting kidnapped and making trouble for the actual professionals. Perfect. PiePo may be in with the defense force due to his ability to shmooze, but he by no means actually *belongs* there. He's no general or space adventurer, he's some poor schmuck with futurist ambitions who writes technofetishistic potboilers about raygun porn. And it's impossible to not see the connection to the real-life Golden Age Hard SF scene, who so often did find themselves in the employ (or at least company) of futurist think-tanks, hocking their proto-innovation speak. And what do you know, the moment PiePo shows up *Ramputrouille Orion* finds itself trapped in an infuriatingly, annoyingly stock pulp plot with captures and escapes, mad scientists

That's not meant as a criticism of "The Space Trap" if there was any uncertainty; Rather, I think this is part of the episode's point. And that's not to say this kind of rote storytelling hasn't always been a part of *Raumpatrouille Orion* either: We did just get captures-and-escapes last time too, it's just the rampant oversignification of "Battle for the Sun" distracted us from that a bit. Nor is this meant to be an indictment of *Ramupatrouille Orion*: This is all par for the course for the genre and completely of its time, and is actually pretty progressive for the time. Certainly Gene Roddenberry would never have gotten this creative, nor really should he have been expected too. Rather, I feel these are all realities *Raumpatrouille Orion* is aware of. It's hamstrung by science fiction, as all science fiction is, and it knows this. It can press up against the walls all it likes and turn everything upside down, but the fact of the matter is there are still some things inescapable to it due to the constraints of genre. A cage is a cage is still a cage.

If Alan Moore is right, then art is truly magick and the two are in truth indistinguishable from one another because they are one and the same. In modern times art has been commodified and, stripped of its context, has had its magickal power suppressed. Unlike the song-lines and oral knowledge of olden times and other places, our art is harmless light entertainment peddled by clowns and court jesters. At *best*. At worst it's reactionary thought control whose only functional purpose is to render people complacent and apathetic. The strength of pop culture is in its ability to reach a statistical majority of readers on a global scale who can hopefully internalize it and transform it in positive ways. But science fiction like *Raumpatrouille Orion* isn't actually serving that purpose: It's a cult show within a cult genre that's never going to see widespread attention outside of that cult. NO matter how bold and innovative stories like "Planet Off Course" and "Battle for the Sun" hint at being, their impact remains muted not just because of the size of their audience but because of the drastically diminished reference pools of all the actors involved in the network.

This is the Space Trap of all science fiction that *Raumpatrouille Orion* has found and is trying to call our attention to: Science fiction yearns to be cosmic and profound but it is in truth irreparably and inescapably provincial and parochial. And for art-magick in the world of Modernity than needs to operate on a global scale, that's a death sentence.

40. "There's always casualties in war": Invasion

Raumpatrouille Orion's grand finale is a story that on the one hand is one I have a very hard time coming up with a potable redemptive reading for, yet on the other, unfortunately, feels like a natural outgrowth of things the series has been building towards since the beginning.

After a meeting he leaves frustrated that his disciplinary reassignment is lasting six more months (a plot point which makes no sense following "Planet Off Course" or literally any other episode in the show, but *Raumptrouille Orion* has never been one to get too fussy about continuity), Commander McClane begins to notice strange behavioural changes in Colonel Villa, Tamara's boss. He seems to have no recollection of basic astrophysical phenomenon and begins ordering bizarre personnel reassignments and seems to be giving the *Orion* crew obvious busywork to keep them away from Earth, including sending them to some random backwater planet for no clear reason. Cliff has Tamara covertly investigate why Villa wanted to send them there, but gets captured, because of course she does. Villa sends the remaining *Orion* crew on their way accompanied by a gravitational engineer by the name of Kranz, who suddenly turns on them and commandeers the ship as it's revealed an entire Frog invasion fleet is heading towards Earth, and all of Earth's defenses have been sabotaged.

Back in the chapter on "Deserters" I pointed out how reading this show through a McCarthyist lens isn't really the most effective way to approach it given its West German context...yet "Invasion" is fairly straightforwardly a riff on *The Manchurian Candidate*. Obviously Villa and Kranz have been brainwashed by the Frogs, who use them as sleeper agents to mastermind a conquest of Earth from the inside. This is actually a fairly common stock plot for a lot of science fiction we'll be covering in this project, and "Invasion" in a lot of ways anticipates several stories from decades in the future: A resoundingly terrible episode of *Star Trek: The Next Generation*, and several equally bad, yet at least expected, story arcs from *Babylon 5* and *Star Trek: Dominion Wars*. Although perhaps this is less an indication of how ahead of its time *Raumpatrouille Orion* was and more how crushingly antiquated and old fashioned science fiction as a genre is. Because while *The Manchurian Candidate* in all of its incarnations tries to play with its setup a bit, as it's reiterated in these genre fiction shows, this is Red Scare and Xenophobia 101 and that's pretty fucking unreconstructed. It's all the more alarming from a West German perspective, where it reads disturbingly close to Actual Western Propaganda.

Was it? Probably not. More likely it was just a stock thriller plot the writers uncritically nicked because it made an exciting finale to their pseudo-militaristic science fiction show.

But that's the whole point, and that's why this is so dangerous. It's the same reason this show, for all it's got going for it, still does so many captures and escapes to fill time, and why Tamara Jagellovsk, one of the main characters, spends most of the episode out of commission. Genre fiction recycles hoary old pulp serial tropes without taking the time to historicize or contextualize their more offensive;y reactionary elements, or anaylse the consequences of reiterating them. Media, especially fiction, has an enormous impact on the way worldviews are formed, and reactionary thematic motifs that reinforce structural hierarchy and oppression, from xenophobia and jingoism to imperialism and misogyny, do *provably active material harm to the world's consciousness.*

(Speaking of Tamara, she and Cliff become the Official Couple in this episode, culminating a story arc that had been building over the past few episodes. This would be cute except for two things: One, of fucking course they become the Official Couple because they're the most prominent male and female characters in a genre fiction show and two, Tamara has become steadily less competent and more of a damsel in distress starting from the moment she started to become more friendly and accepted as part of the *Orion* family and after it became obvious that she and Cliff would become the Official Couple. Remember, she even got captured in "Battle for the Sun" too.)

And I'm sorry, but it is a problem that, seven episodes in, the Frogs haven't evolved much beyond "generic alien Other we need to defend ourselves from". In the first episode, Colonel Villa himself even says Earth should exercise caution when dealing with a new species like this as they've no real idea if they even have what could be construed as the same set of morals and ethics and humans. Which is self-evidently correct. Now that looks foolish, because it almost seems like that kind of leniency is what made Villa an "easy mark" for the Frogs to use as a puppet. A "fellow traveller" if you will (I don't think this quite kills Villa as a character: His actions in "Battle for the Sun" alone hedge against that, though I also can't always keep hanging on "Battle for the Sun").

It would be one thing if, say, the Frogs were meant to represent a strain of unbridled fascism or imperialism: That would be a natural thing to see a condemnation of on a West German science fiction show, and there is that thread there. Germany, for one, was actually conquered by foreign powers, and you can read the conflict here as a people fighting back against there conquerors and oppressors in a way you can't read comparable United States pulp fiction. But that reading also doesn't quite hold: *Raumpatrouille* seems to (perhaps understandably) prefer to turn its critique of those sorts of things inward, and while maybe this could be seen as an attempt at moral ambiguity the stock xenophobia of the pulp-derived plot really hurts. McClane's squad is a defense force, protecting Earth from outside threats...But exactly *who* is this show made by and for postwar Germans trying to protect us from? The Frogs *need* characterization beyond "generic Other alien invaders" for this to work, they don't and it doesn't.

But even if you do grant this, you still run into the age-old problem that dogs all of genre fiction: At some point you're going to have to own up to the irrefutable argument that you're oversimplifying complicated social issues for a blunt metaphor on a piece of light entertainment fluff. If we're going to call out Gene Roddenberry for this sort of thing, it's only fair that we do it to everything. And the accusation is damning everywhere. Allegory doesn't work.

The isn't *Raumpatrouolle Orion*'s fault. None of this is. This show absolutely *is* progressive for its time, probably among the most progressive Western works from this period you can find. I don't think the series itself is fascist; there's simply far too much iconography and aesthetic cues to the contrary for that to be the case. This is unmistakably a science fiction show for the Carnaby Street Mod generation. Is it better than *Star Trek*? Oh, absolutely. Unquestionably. But...it's mostly progressive among science fiction shows, and science fiction is fundamentally reactionary. Science fiction derives from a genre that is fundamentally fundamentalist, it's never done enough to distance itself from those roots and it never will. In fact, it by definition *has no interest* in doing so. The lion's share of utopian idealism for any genre fiction show will be projected onto it by its audience, and the part of the audience most inclined to think along those lines is also the one that has historically been aggressively silenced. Sure, *Raumptrouille Orion* is for the Carnaby Street Mods but, like *Star Trek*, one has to ask if this is a show they would actually enjoy as-is. And would anyone ever listen to them even if they did? Take a gander at who writes the history of science fiction. How would you ever know?

But I don't quite want to end our patrol through the edge of infinity on this note. Because *Raumpatrouille Orion* is genuinely a great series that deserves your attention if you're a connoisseur of space-based science fiction. It's definitely among the cream of the crop for things we're going to be covering in this book, that's for sure. That it's great with qualifiers, that it's let down by its own genre, speaks more to the genre than it does to *Raumpatrouille* itself. This is something that's endemic to and inextricable from absolutely everything we'll be talking about in Vaka Rangi, and if that's the biggest criticism I can level at *Raumpatrouille Orion* (especially given the thrashing I gave, and will continue to give, Star Trek), that should say something. It's unlike anything else on television during this time, except *Star Trek*, and it blows *Star Trek* out of the water. And it looks and sounds like nothing else.

Science fiction may not be positioned to elegantly examine social issues and conflicts and it's hardly ever written as well as shows that aren't "genre". That's something we just need to square away and accept. But what genre fiction does have the power to do is examine possibilities, whether it be a dream of a future that's better than the life we live today, or to explore images and ideas with a kind of abstract symbolism and creative lateral thinking not seen in contemporary dramas or dime-store mystery novels. As compromised as genre fiction is, always has been and always will be, this remains its essential power: It's ability to broadcast overt imagination on a large populist scale. *Raumpatrouille Orion* may not have been as successful at reaching the same kind of audience as Star Trek, but not being Star Trek is hardly a criticism. It was successful because it embodied Star Trek's ideals better than *Star Trek* itself did, and that is absolutely worth remembering. It deserves a place in our history and our hearts that's been denied it because of reputations that were unearned.

In a way, perhaps *Raumpatrouille Orion* really is fighting back against a conquering imperialist force. Perhaps the enemy has really been the Master Narrative all along.

Part II.

1967-1968

41. Myriad Universes: The Planet Of No Return (Gold Key)

One of the key points frequently brought up in fan discussions about the differences between Star Trek, Star Wars and Doctor Who as large-scale science fiction franchises is that Star Trek supposedly has a hard and fast "canon": A meticulously constructed and maintained Official History of stories that actually "happened" as opposed to ones that "don't count". For better or for worse, this is seen as a major point of contrast between the three franchises: Star Trek's canon is supposedly absolute, whereas Star Wars' is more fluid and the subject of much debate. Meanwhile, true Doctor Who fans will be quick to point out their show has no canon at all: Every single Doctor Who story that has ever been told both did and didn't happen, depending on the perspective of the person making judgment calls about it.

I've never been especially fond of the idea of canon. Aside from the self-evidently rather silly notion of squabbling over which events did and didn't happen in a fictional world, to me the concept grows out of a particularly exclusionary mindset and approach to genre fiction I pretty strongly disagree with. While the fundamental goal may be to pay respects to a work's originator, and weigh their contributions to it accordingly, canon to me seems more typically used to lay down arbitrary and authoritarian rules as to who can and can't contribute to a developing oeuvre. There's a very good reason there's no mythological canon: Myths and legends belong to an entire people and their whole existence is built around the expectation that stories and ideas will be shared and retold constantly, and that new ones will be continuously added to the pile. If Soda Pop Art is going to serve a similar role for Western cultures, building a big gate, locking the door and only giving a podium to the people already on the inside isn't going to do anyone any good.

The first recorded use of the term "canon" (which is, of course, a word gleaned from Biblical studies) to refer to genre works is actually in a 1911 satirical essay by Ronald Knox, who was lampooning scholars interested in discerning a "historical Jesus" and sourcing the Synoptic Gospels by applying their methods to Sir Arthur Conan Doyle's Sherlock Holmes stories (blog friend Andrew Hickey has more details in this excellent post). The problem is, as with most great satire, few actually got the joke and Sherlock Holmes fandom in fact latched onto the idea and attempted to construct a legitimate Sherlock Holmes Canon, which became no more and no less then every story Conan Doyle himself wrote, and set about trying to create a timeline to make it all fit together. It should go without saying this was expressly not Conan Doyle's intention for his stories, which he turned out on a fairly regular schedule to keep up with massive demand for more Holmes mysteries and keep himself employed as a writer (his numerous attempts to either kill Holmes or end his adventures went over about as well as trying to kill off a massively popular franchise does today).

But regardless of where the idea of genre canon came from, the fact of the matter is that it's something Star Trek latched onto and was a perspective Gene Roddenberry was clearly working from, isn't it? After all, the whole idea of a Star Trek canon comes from Roddenberry specifically saying only the TV and film stories counted, and as the shepherd decrees the flock obeys.

Well, not quite.

First of all, the idea of Gene Roddenberry being the sole torch-bearer and authority for all of Star Trek should already be a claim we should all be more than a little sceptical of. Secondly though, even if you do grant Roddenberry was the gatekeeper of Star Trek canon, the fact is he never actually *said* anything like this. What he actually said was something far less concrete and more guarded: Early on in the run of *Star Trek: The Next Generation,* while he was still de facto showrunner, Roddenberry was asked by a fan at a convention which stories "counted" among all the various Star Trek TV episodes, movies, novelizations and comic books. Roddenberry said that when he and the writing staff were making new episodes and needed to cross-reference something, they only looked at the TV episodes and movies, because there was just too much spin-off content for him to keep track of. Roddenberry also apparently asked Mike Okuda to come up with a solid timeline for the franchise at this point (something it had lacked beforehand) just to keep things easy for him and the production team, hence the first recorded mention of an in-universe calendar year in the *Star Trek: The Next Generation* season one finale.

It's very important to look very closely at what exactly Roddenberry's statement is, because it is manifestly *not* a declaration of the existence of a canon. Instead, this is rather an explanation by Roddenberry of a specific approach to writing the franchise that he uses to make life easier *for him personally.* It is *not* a decree from On High that certain stories "don't count" or are somehow less valid or less worth investigating because he and his team didn't film them for whatever reason, and to take this comment and use it as some excuse to throw out reams of Star Trek novels and comics, or to discourage fans from writing their own Star Trek stories, many of which are in fact leagues better than the stuff that actually made it to air (to his credit, Roddenberry in point of fact knew this and encouraged it), is at once more evidence of Star Trek fans' tendency to deify Roddenberry and hang on every word he said and clear misreading of those words and an attempt to weaponize them for a purpose they were never intended to be used for. There is, in point of fact, no such thing as a hard-and-fast Star Trek "canon" and nobody involved in making the show (at least from the first and second generation of writers) ever meant for there to be one in the first place.

Which is rather a roundabout way of both introducing this series of essays, which looks at so-called "non-canon" works in a way designed to hopefully demonstrate their merit and value both apart from the television and movie stories and as a vitally important part of Star Trek history in their own way. The first story I've pegged to talk about is "The Planet Of No Return", the debut issue of the spin-off *Star Trek* comic series from Gold Key. This series lasted an impressively long time, from July, 1967 to October, 1979, and was the first (and for a significant amount of time only) licensed comic book based on the franchise. The idea of a licensed tie-in comic is an important one, and this is far from the last time we'll be talking about it. A comic book based on a TV show is both an easy way for a publisher to squeeze more money out of the franchise, but it's also a way for fans to get new adventures featuring their favourite characters during the series' hiatus. It's also telling *Star Trek* got a comic book right away as opposed to other forms of spin-off media, as that rightly or wrongly tacitly implies a target audience of children (which the show in its earliest days seemed to be working hard to distance itself from), and indeed Gold Key was largely famous for licensed works based on cartoons (including distributing Carl Barks' Donald Duck stories in the United States for a time).

"The Planet Of No Return" is apparently nobody's favourite Star Trek comic, despite its historical value (and corresponding exorbitant collector's value). Much of the disdain for this story comes from, naturally, its apparent flagrant violations of Star Trek canon. The transporter is called a teleporter, the bridge looks nothing like the bridge on the TV show, nor does, actually, the rest of the ship, and Kirk and Spock talk about using TV and radio frequency scanning instruments. In some later issues of the Gold Key *Star Trek* book, there are some rather infamous scenes of the *Enterprise* acting like a rocket ship and leaving ignition trails. It is true that Gold Key's writers in the earliest days of the comic frequently had no working knowledge of the property they were ostensibly trying to adapt, but given that obvious handicap *Star Trek* actually doesn't turn out too badly and, in fact, "The Planet Of No Return" is probably closer to the actual TV show in 1967 than many fans would probably be comfortable admitting, if not outright superior to it in some areas.

Firstly, the fact the ship's interior looks nothing like Desilu's backlot is actually a *plus* as far as I'm concerned. A comic book naturally has more space and resources to experiment with elaborate artwork and design then a TV show, and that actually shows here. The *Enterprise* bears more than a passing resemblance to its TV counterpart (which is more than can be said for Kirk, who looks absolutely nothing like William Shatner. Spock, McCoy and Rand don't look too off by contrast), and actually looks far more visually evocative, with pleasingly curvaceous instruments and meticulously detailed rooms, which give the ship a sense of scale it never had on TV. There's also a variety to the decks, with the various science labs looking rather dark and claustrophobic as Spock and McCoy huddle over monitors, which is contrasted to with openness of, say, the transporter room. The *Enterprise* here actually looks more than a little like a convincing hypothetical halfway-point between the *Orion* and the *Enterprise* from *Star Trek: The Motion Picture*.

The story is also quite attention-grabbing: Nonsense technical jargon about travelling though "Galaxy Alpha" aside (which is frankly no more ridiculous than some of what we've seen on the TV show thus far), the *Enterprise* is very explicitly on a mission of exploration here, conducting a survey with the express intent of finding new and undiscovered forms of life. That may not sound too revolutionary, but coming off a season that, contrary to the pop perception of the Original Series, was about 90% comprised of stories where Kirk and the crew are on routine patrol duty enforcing space laws, is a genuine breath of fresh air. This is the first time the *Enterprise* has been consciously designed as a ship of scientific exploration, and that's really important to take note of. As we'll see, that understanding of what Star Trek is and does comes mostly from a specific group of fans, and they most certainly were not calling the shots in 1967.

Said new life is also interesting in its own right: The crew stumbles upon a planet inhabited by a civilization of intelligent, sentient plants who reproduce by seeding spores throughout the galaxy that turns animals into plant creatures. It's not the most exciting or engrossing premise, but for a 12-cent action sci-fi adventure comic it's more than serviceable, and a damn sight more original than another iteration of the parade of identical Earth colonies would have been.

The rest of the book is standard pulp stuff: The crew beams down to investigate, gets menaced by plant monsters (including one eye-rolling scene where Rand gets kidnapped and tossed into a plant cattle farm, which is mercifully of the slaughterhouse variety instead of the dairy one), laser gun fights ensue, as do a charming selection of silver age expressions like "Great Galaxies!" and "Howling Crashwagons!". That said, the story does have one more surprise up its sleeve in the treatment of its token redshirt: When the security-guard-of-the-week gets predictably infected and mutates into a plant beast, he sacrifices himself to protect the rest of the landing party and there is almost a full page dedicated to the crew mourning his loss and remarking on what a good friend and officer he was before burying him in an impromptu service on the planet's surface. This is the most care and attention Star Trek will *ever* pay to a redshirt death, and it displays a level of awareness about the limitations and drawbacks of its genre that's honestly pretty unexpected. He's obviously only there to get killed off, but the crew still treats him as a person who had relationships and aspirations.

The final aspect of "The Planet Of No Return" that Star Trek fans are most likely to raise a fuss about is the resolution, where Kirk has the *Enterprise* sterilize the planet, thus totally wiping out a civilization he himself regarded as intelligent and sophisticated, to prevent the spores from spreading throughout the galaxy. This could be seen as a pretty flagrant violation of Starfleet ethics and philosophy, not to mention the fact it's a generally pretty morally bankrupt thing to do. However, this scene is, unfortunately, not quite as removed from the sorts of things we've been seeing on television this year as we may like to pretend it is. After all, let's not forget that in "A Taste of Armageddon" Kirk gave a standing order to destroy all signs of life on Eminiar VII should he fail to convince the Eminians of the true horrors of war and almost facilitated genocide of the Horta in "The Devil in the Dark" before he came to his senses. So really, a scene where the *Enterprise* uses its phaser banks to salt and burn an entire planet because its native civilization is based around intergalactic parasitism is a depressingly reasonable thing to expect of Star Trek in 1967.

But really what we have with "The Planet Of No Return" is a book that's doing exactly what a spin-off work ought to do, which is provide more adventures when its parent property is off the air that are in keeping with the spirit and tone of the original while doing things that it couldn't do constrained by television. It's not a book I'd necessarily recommend to someone looking for a sterling example of how Star Trek's spin-off and fan works improve the franchise on the whole, but it's everything we could reasonably expect a Star Trek comic book circa 1967 to be like. And the time will come on more than one occasion where stories like this will be the franchise's torch-bearer, because something like Star Trek can only be native to a medium like television for so long. This is a theme that is every bit as important to learning about what Star Trek is about as figuring out what Gene Roddenberry's words meant or what the original point of the Klingons was: It's stories like this, the "non-canonical" and the "ones that don't count", that will keep Star Trek alive for years to come.

42. Sensor Scan: The Prisoner

Let's get this straight right from the start: Entire analytical projects can, have been, and should be written about Patrick McGoohan and George Markstein's *The Prisoner*. It's rightly regarded as one of the single greatest and most influential, and most oversignified, television series of all time. Given I don't even regard the entirety of Vaka Rangi, which tackles just about every filmed moment of Star Trek and then some, as a definitive authoritative reading of the Star Trek franchise, there is absolutely no way I can be expected to come up with some comprehensive interpretation of something like *The Prisoner* in one chapter. That said, this is still one of the most iconic parts of the televisual landscape of 1967-8 (not to mention a show that was a massive source of inspiration for at least one future creative figure) so there's no getting away from me saying *something* about it.

Some assorted thoughts then. First, for those who might not be intimately familiar with *The Prisoner*, it's a seventeen episode (though apparently only seven were actually intended and are considered by the creators to be part of the overall story arc) miniseries aired during the 1967-8 season on the British channel ITV that was a rather-more-than-spiritual successor to Patrick McGoohan's previous series *Danger Man*, in which he starred as secret agent John Drake. *The Prisoner* follows a nameless agent, played by McGoohan and largely assumed to be Drake himself, who, after resigning from the service, is kidnapped and imprisoned in a mysterious coastal retirement community. The rest of the series follows the agent, who is never named but who is referred to as Number Six in keeping with the Village's convention of assigning its residents numbers, as he refuses to acclimate and constantly tries to escape his captors. Number Six's captors, spearheaded by Number Two (a position filled by a revolving door of individuals) and his superior, the mysterious, unseen Number One, launch a campaign to systematically break Six and discern why he resigned so abruptly.

This summary, of course, does the show no justice because one of its biggest signatures is its overt focus on psychedelic themes, iconography and imagery, best exemplified by its avant garde cinematography and editing and conspicuous usage of jarring, unsettling and downright bizarre visuals. There is a willfully dreamlike and disjointed approach to structure here: The show goes out of its way to muddle its viewers just as much as The Village tries to psychologically manipulate Number Six and frequently violates its own internal logic just to show that no rules or conventions are above reproach (there is infamously an entire episode where the show suddenly and inexplicably becomes a western, complete with unique intro and closing credits sequences). Although this is possibly the most celebrated part of *The Prisoner*'s legacy and contribution to TV, it's also the part that's most easily misunderstood.

First of all, there is a tendency to want to see the show's abject weirdness to be some kind of overly complicated way of obfuscating some great Platonic Truth Patrick McGoohan has cleverly hidden from us. One notable example of this line of thought would be the popular fan theory the show's credits are designed to give away the ending, and thus the show's "point", with the exchange "Who is Number One?" "You Are Number Six". The thing is, this rather pointedly and obviously does not mean what fans might like to think it means if you actually watch the show. And so that tendency is therefore hopelessly misguided: This is a show that is not designed to make sense. It is a show designed to tear down the concept of sense.

It's also fairly insulting to the show's cinematography to trivialize it this way, to say it "only" exists to keep us digging for some secret hidden Meaning, as if media consumption was some kind of glorfied IQ test. *The Prisoner*'s overt psychedelia looks very much a piece with its time, with 1967 being near the pinnacle of Beatlemania and the visual language of psychedelic art breaking mainstream. And there's a genuine visual power to this that shouldn't be discounted: Abstraction was the earliest form of artistic expression known to humans and is thought to be derived from natural forms, and that legacy is extremely potent and palpable. This early experimentation with abstract imagery in pop culture on the 1960s is a game-changer that sets an enormous precedent, laying the groundwork for populist visual media to break free of its postwar constraints twenty years later.

In that regard, it's worth examining the challenge this show delivers to the pop culture status quo it's coming into. One of the things *The Prisoner* (as well as *Danger Man)* does not get nearly enough credit for being is an actually rather straightforward critique of its genre, which, head trippiness aside, is really spy fiction. Despite starring in a spy series himself, McGoohan was always somewhat sceptical and apprehensive about the prevalence of certain kind of spy story. He was actually one of the first choices to play James Bond, but he turned the role down because he objected to the fundamental ethics of the character and the series. Number Six is in many ways the complete opposite of Bond: He doesn't carry a gun, refuses to fight unless forced to and is explicitly celibate, the show going out of his way to show his interest in the female characters is purely platonic and that he's anything but a womanizer. *The Prisoner* is actually rather excellent on feminist grounds on the whole, being the rare action show of its time without any really significant overt gendered remarks or assumptions. In addition, a reoccurring theme is suspicion over the growing threat of rampant nationalism, and indeed the one real clue we get for why Number Six resigned is that it was "a matter of conscience".

It's also possible to read *The Prisoner* rather easily as another individualist versus collectivist treatise. The Village definitely operates like an oppressive, effacing institution, down to the show's famous catchphrase "I am not a number! I am a free man!". What's particularly interesting about the way *The Prisoner* does this however is that this theme is not conveyed as a blunt attack on the percieved dangers of leftism (conflated, of course, with Soviet-style authoritarianism) that so typifies much fiction of this era. Rather, it's an altogether more localized critique of a uniquely British, and if I'm being honest Western, kind of power structure. The Village bears more then a passing resemblance to a British holiday camp, which was a peculiarly mid-20th century phenomenon whereby legions of working to lower middle class families would be shipped off to spend several weeks on holiday in a stretch of housing for what basically amounted to the adult version of a summer camp. Part and parcel of this experience would be mandatory communal meals and activities, lots of general forced happiness and even authoritarian monitor who would patrol up and down at night to make sure everyone was in by curfew and that nothing untoward (meaning flirtatious) went on. The nearest fictional US equivalent might be something like Stepford Village, if the secret wasn't that everybody was a robotic killer but that there's an authoritarian power out to gain dominance by enforcing an oppressive classist power structure.

In other words, what McGoohan is essentially doing here is likening glamourous spy fiction, and by association the espionage system Western powers like Britain are built on, to a holiday camp where everyone is required to be chipper and behave like good little conformist citizens while a distant and very probably fascist jingoistic power lords over them. The sort of collectivist mentality *The Prisoner* is attacking isn't the kind of generative, bottom up communal living of the sort that typifies the actual left, but the kind of authoritarian statism that has defined Western imperialism since the concept began.

What's neat about *The Prisoner* is how it examines these concerns through its direction and editing, which is pretty advanced stuff for 1967 TV standards. There is a very noticeable televisual motif throughout *The Prisoner*, most noticeable in the scenes where Number Two and his aides watch Number Six's efforts on a monitor from the Blue Dome. The camera angles constantly switch between the action with Six and Two watching the same scene from the same perspective. Number Two and his men can also remotely operate different facets of The Village to foil Six's efforts, and this is another method they use to try and psychologically manipulate him.

An example that comes to mind is in the first episode, where Number Two is remarking on the failure of one of his agents, disguised as Six's sympathetic housekeeper, to extract information from him. Two says something along the lines of how "well acted" her performance was and how convincingly she played her role, and that he was sure Number Six would be taken in by it. Two sounds exactly like a hypothetical audience member here, remarking on the actions of the characters onscreen and the talents of the actors who portray them. Furthermore, the one bit of knowledge those in charge of The Village keep stressing is of paramount importance is the exact reason Number Six resigned his commission. Interestingly, we actually do get to see the moment Six resigns in the opening scene of the first episode, but we're unable to hear what he says to his superior as all audio apart from the soundtrack is muted.

Later on, we learn that The Village apparently knows everything about Six's life except this one minor annoying detail and they're obsessed with finding out what it is, and while some of that comes from the fact that if a spy were to resign suddenly and unexpectedly they would doubtlessly be seen as a national security risk, the fact of the matter is that reading is boring. It's far more interesting to see Number Two as standing in for the audience. So now, we don't just have spy fiction equated with British holiday camps and authoritarian

Western statism, but also with *the act of voyeuristically watching television itself*. From a modern perspective, it's almost impossible for me not to see Number Two's anal fixation on irreverent and inconsequential details like why exactly this character resigned his post as a rather scathing, yet also hilarious, critique of a certain kind of obsessive genre fiction fan, which is all the more impressive as such an archetype, at least in the way we would recognise it, really didn't exist in 1967. What this means is that Number Six isn't just constrained and imprisoned by his job, or the kind of society he lives in, or even by the trappings of his genre, but by, honestly, the abstract concept of television itself.

In this regard then perhaps Number Six is more similar to Captain Kirk then might be immediately obvious. Both can be seen as characters who are trapped and restricted by the shows they're on, and who are constantly looking for ways to escape and grow apart from them. The primary difference between the two, however, is how the shows they're on work through these ideas. *Star Trek* is a show that consistently only works in spite of itself, and its various disparate elements are each trying to become their own equally fascinating things while the actual structure and value system the show inherits from its influences keeps trying to hold it back. When Kirk works he's great and William Shatner is far more savvy then absolutely anyone gives him credit for, but he's got both the diegetic and extradiegetic shows fighting against him. But while *Star Trek* is struggling because of these concerns, *The Prisoner* could be convincingly read *as actually being about them*, which really says quite a lot about what it was possible for both the television landscape and also the larger zeitgeist of 1967 to be.

If we were to compare *The Prisoner* to what we've seen on *Star Trek* so far, the closest point would probably be "The Return of the Archons", with Gene Roddenberry's critique of blindly following orders and the whims of centralized powers, or perhaps Robert Hamner's "A Taste of Armageddon" with the Federation's constant screwups and the Eminians quietly submissive to war as it's become ingrained in their society. Were I inclined to be especially charitable to people like Roddenberry, I could read an episode like that a similar way, not as blunt Red Scare rubbish but as a critique of at least the idea of authoritarianism, if not its manifestations in the West. The only problem with this is that, if we presume the was Roddenberry's intent, he was never able to convey this clearly and explicitly enough in the scripts he worked on, and this sort of crippling problem with communication is going to prove to be a reoccurring thorn in his side that hampers his effectiveness as a writer and producer. Also, *Star Trek* tends to be pretty boringly directed, at least it has been thus far. McGoohan, by contrast, has a deft handle on his craft, as a writer as well as a director and producer, knows exactly the sorts of things he wants us to think about, and his shows reflect this in turn.

No, a far better point of comparison in my opinion is actually *Raumpatrouille Orion*. While that show lacks *The Prisoner*'s handle on avant garde imagery, it too has a very clear suspicion of hierarchical power structures. Recall the key joke is that the unified Earth government is actually staggeringly incompetent and hilariously petty, and Tamara Jagellovsk's primary character arc involves her having to come to terms with how slavish deference towards rules, regulations and authority is unhealthy, counterproductive, unsustainable and unworkable. Cliff McClane as well, despite being an ace pilot and one of the best commanders in the fleet, is far more likely to part with official policy then enforce it and he's become something of an annoyance to some of his superiors in spite of his heroism, valour and upstanding, selfless nature. Indeed, *Raumpatrouille Orion* is bound by the exact same limitations of pulp fiction that *The Prisoner* is, and is equally aware of how this risks ultimately scuttling it. Much like *Raumpatrouille Orion* then, *The Prisoner* is frequently quite clearly working with the concept of institutionalized and otherwise hegemonic power structures and how to work against them from within.

However the key difference is, *The Prisoner* is trying to be overtly psychedelic.

We can certainly try to focus on McGoohan's basic political statements, but as interesting and important as they may be, this rather avoids the issue that *The Prisoner* is still one of the most artistic and unorthodox bits of television ever filmed. Although it remains fundamentally a bit of spy fiction, the show's explicit embrace of psychedelic imagery means the realms of the mystic and transcendental are never far away, always exerting their wills on what *The Prisoner* does. It may not have been the trippiest work of its time, that title would probably go to one of The Beatles' contemporaneous films (although it is worth noting The Beatles were enormous *Prisoner* fans and had actually originally hoped to get McGoohan to produce their movies), but what's special about how it's used here is that it can be seen as bringing together and reinforcing the other concepts the show is working through clear cut meta-commentary.

This is the ticket: Using the abstract imagery and direction to reinforce the underlying themes of the narrative. That's why I think *The Prisoner* has been so beloved and influential on the pop culture visual media to come in its wake. And it has been-Just looking at the works closest to this project, *Star Trek* itself is about to get a whole lot trippier in the coming seasons, and further out the long shadow cast by The Prisoner is going to be very noticeable. With "Spectre of the Gun" and "The Gunfigthters", both *Star Trek* and *Doctor Who* will respectively take a shot at deconstructing the myth of the western and its foundational connection to an imagined American Golden Age in the same way The Prisoner's "Practice in Waking" did. While in 1985, the *Dirty Pair* TV series will do an episode called "Hire Us! Beautiful Bodygaurds are a Better Deal" that takes the performative critique of the western structure one step further by bringing in the Japanese archetype of the *rōnin*, or wandering samurai, in a lovely piece of postmodern comparative mythology.

And on *Star Trek: The Next Generation*, Tracy Tormé will write the teleplay for an episode literally called "The Schizoid Man", named after an episode of *The Prisoner*, for which he hoped to get Patrick McGoohan for a guest spot to boot. That same season will also see *The Next Generation* doing a story called "The Royale", modelled explicitly on *The Prisoner*'s brand of surrealist imagery. On his own show, the reimagined version of *Battlestar Galactica*, future executive producer Ronald D. Moore will even *actually name* one of his main characters Number Six, and she bears more than a passing resemblance to Patrick McGoohan's persecuted ex-Danger Man (as an extra added bonus for my Whovian readers, one of Number Six's first lines in BSG seems to be a rather cheekily transparent lift from one of Sylvester McCoy's lines as The Doctor in "Remembrance of the Daleks", which just makes her character all the more fun to speculate about). But *The Prisoner*'s most important legacy is is visual imagery, because it's that above all else that reminds us art can have aspirations above and beyond being square-jawed pulp potboilers to entertain the masses. The way to escape The Village is to remember our real birthright as artists and conscious entities.

Unfortunately, this means that, in 1967, *Star Trek* is frankly behind the times. Between *The Prisoner* and *Raumpatrouille Orion* the world of television around it is going in directions that are pretty clearly forcing Gene Roddenberry and the *Enterprise* crew to play catch-up. It's telling that, of the three shows, *Star Trek* is the only one to be canceled outright by virtue of its own quality and ratings: *Raumpatrouille*'s overblown budget made it financially unviable, and *The Prisoner* almost got another season and Patrick McGoohan actually had to fight and compromise to keep it at seventeen episodes, as it was never intended to be a long-form serial. *Star Trek*, in spite of its cult legacy and what the material episode lists say, really only has one more year left in it before NBC puts it to bed. Star Trek can and will take on a second life after the fact, and the story of how and why it does this is as strange and inexplicable as it is.

43. "Trick or Treat/Trick or Treat/Trick or Treat for Halloween": Catspaw

Well, to start things off I'd like to say that coming off of *Raumpatrouille Orion* and *The Prisoner* it's rather exasperating to tune in for the brand new season of *Star Trek* and see Captain Kirk stomp around the bridge in a huff and bluster about people failing to follow landing party procedure. It would have been very nice to be able to open this post with a hearty declaration that the show has finally turned a corner with the first story produced for the new year, especially with a premise as tantalizing as the one this episode has. But no, "Catspaw" is aggravatingly business as usual.

Which is really rather puzzling, because it has the makings of something incomparably bizarre and interesting to talk about. First of all, this episode has the single most bonkers pitch in the history of the franchise: It is literally a *Star Trek* holiday special. I'm not even kidding-The only reason "Catspaw" exists is because somebody, most likely at NBC, decided *Star Trek* really needed to have a Halloween special. So, we get fifty minutes of Kirk, Spock and McCoy wandering around a stereotypically spooky haunted castle with witches, skeletons, black cats and evil wizards. There are any number of reasonable, plausible reasons for this premise to go hilariously and catastrophically off the rails but, in a moment of genuine insight, Gene Roddenberry and Gene Coon make the actually sane and sensible decision to give the story to the only person on staff remotely capable of taking this quite literal nightmare pitch and turning into something other than an unmitigated disaster: Robert Bloch.

Bloch only had one other *Star Trek* script to his name at this time: "What Are Little Girls Made Of"? early on in the first season, an episode that could charitably be described as not going quite according to plan. However, before we run to the hills screaming, it's worth pointing out Bloch was actually an extremely respected and influential author, penning a little novel called *Psycho*. Whether the failings of the previous story are his or Gene Roddenberry's, who did one of his trademark uncredited rewrites on it, are ultimately irrelevant because "Catspaw" we get a better glimpse into the sorts of things Bloch is actually interested in talking about, which seems to be pretty clearly "horror". Not just any kind of horror, though: The type of horror Bloch seems to fancy the most, especially when it comes to writing *Star Trek*, is descended from the works of famed schlock novelist H.P. Lovecraft.

Lovecraft was a prolific pulp horror writer from the early 20th century with a particular interest in uniquely mystical and cosmic variety of psychological horror. In Lovecraft's works, the universe is really the domain of vast, incomprehensible ancient monsters who exist so far above and beyond the realm of human comprehension that to even glimpse one or speak its name would drive a person to complete and inconsolable madness. These beings, often referred to as either Eldritch Abominations or the Old Ones, represent what Lovecraft saw as humanity's ultimate insignificance in the grand scheme of the universe, and they have the power to wipe out reality as we know it without so much as a thought. This is a line of thinking that very much interested Bloch as well, having written a number of stories set in the Lovecraft mythos and actually corresponding with Lovecraft himself regularly while he was still alive. Interestingly, both of Bloch's *Star Trek* scripts make mention of Old Ones, being both the creators of Ruk in "What Are Little Girls Made Of?" and the people whom Sylvia and Korob apparently have a "duty" to in "Catspaw".

So naturally, we ought to read Korob and Sylvia, who are already, as Spock remarks "utterly alien" and beyond human comprehension, able as they are to transmute thought into reality, as some kind of Lovecraftian horror come to match wits with the *Enterprise* crew, out on a mission of exploration in places they don't belong. Except this doesn't really work in practice: If it was Bloch's intent to make Korob and Sylvia Eldritch Abominations he failed pretty spectacularly, as they're dispatched laughably easily when Kirk smashes the transmuter at the end of the episode, revealing their true form and distinctly not driving the landing party out of their minds. Perhaps they're servants of a larger Lovecraftian power, but one does get the sense these beings are not so much grand, incomprehensible cosmic horrors from the dawn of space and time and perhaps just the standard-issue hyper advanced beings the crew comes into contact with every once in awhile.

Either way though this is bad idea, because the real Lovecraftian horror is Lovecraft's open, explicit, bald-faced racism. Anyone who talks about Lovecraft's works must be forced to admit this is what his fantastical "cosmic horror" is actually about: A fear and loathing of people who weren't white, Anglo-Saxon protestant Americans. If anyone tries to play down this aspect of Lovecraft;s work, you should be extremely suspicious them. Incidentally, the fact Nerd Culture holds Lovecraft in such high regard as to basically deify him is perhaps an interesting historical-cultural phenomenon to keep in mind.

It also doesn't help the actual horror motifs "Catspaw" works with are less magickal paths toward enlightenment and more kindergarten Halloween decorations. Depressingly befitting the episode's status as a holiday special for network television, we get the most stereotypical and stock out-of-context tropes you can think of. It's all here, from wailing witches with a predilection toward what Spock somewhat aptly dubs "very bad poetry", big medieval castles with dungeons and shackles, black cats, skeletons witches and warlocks. There are no Jack-o-Lanterns or dudes running around with bedsheets over their heads, but they honestly wouldn't look too out of place.

Furthermore, what Bloch comes up with to get this theme park of family-friendly scares to cohere together is a somewhat confusing, and really not especially convincing, explanation of "race memory". Apparently, Korob and Sylvia were trying to scare Captain Kirk as part of his aptitude test to find out whether or not he could teach them about sensations and emotions (concepts that are alien to them), so they read up on what was supposedly frightening to all humans (though Spock also says, flagrantly contradictory, that Korob and Sylvia were looking for a setting to make humans comfortable but were only able to tap the subconscious and found primal genetic fears instead). This is ludicrous on several levels, not the least of which is that watered-down Gothic horror isn't going to be scary to anyone, let alone all of humanity. Why would someone from a culture completely removed from modernist Europe, either because they exist so far in the future so as the imagery has become meaningless or, heaven forbid, they come from a place that isn't Europe or the United States, have these sorts of images in their shared consciousness anyway? This is hegemonic provincialism, plain and simple.

Oh yeah, and racism. Which shouldn't really be that surprising.

Perhaps a better approach, if the show absolutely *had* to go the kindergarten Halloween decoration route (instead of, you know, an actually intelligent and thoughtful analysis of pre-Christian Celtic and Northern European mythology and spirituality), would have been to look at the specific genre of generic horror story that sort of setting fits into and turn that into a kind of critique. *Scooby-Doo, Where Are You!*, which is only two years out from debuting as of this episode's airdate, handles this sort of thing effortlessly and that's ostensibly a brainless kids' show for 7-10 year olds (largely because *Scooby-Doo, Where Are You!* is fundamentally neither horror nor a horror pastiche, but rather German Expressionism). One would think the supposedly grown-up, mature, intellectual and thought-provoking science fiction show airing as a primetime drama on NBC could do this in its sleep. But no, *Star Trek* prefers to have Kirk blunder around a third-rate harvest festival attraction punching things.

This isn't the only problem "Catspaw" has either. A really big one is Sylvia herself, for pretty much exactly the reasons you'd expect. Apparently, her species is incapable of feeling sensations and emotions, and, since using the transmuter to assume human form has become what can best be described as drunk on sensory overload, lusting for both power and the things one usually seeks when the word "lusting" is involved, and perfectly willing to browbeat and manipulate both Korob and Kirk to get what she wants. So sexism on top of racism! Hooray! How many ways is it sexist? Well, just to name a few, women are often seen as weaker and more fickle than men, there's a tradition of ambitious, power hungry, manipulative women in Western literature dating back to at the *very* least Lady Macbeth, and furthermore women are seen as more sensual *and sensuality is seen as a Bad Thing in the pop Western manifestations of Christian thinking.* So we have Sylvia, a cruel and heartless Lady Macbeth (Kirk even tells her she lacks compassion which "all women must have", apparently) tempted away from the path of righteous Intellect and Reason by the sins of the body. I don't think I really need to go the next step and point out what the symbolism is of her being a witch implies.

I could carry on ripping this episode to shreds, and I will, but I'd be remiss if I didn't take some time to mention this episode makes the first appearance of the last regular to join the cast of *Star Trek*: The famous and beloved Ensign Pavel Chekov, played by Walter Koenig, who, while a science officer here, will soon take his familiar post next to Sulu as navigator and the seventh member of the bridge team. Chekov is, let's be honest, a profoundly weird character. Supposedly he was created to serve as yet another example of *Star Trek*'s enlightened future and to show how even people who were staunch enemies in the present could be friends and co-workers in the future. Also, he was created to cash in on the success of The Monkees by giving the *Enterprise* Russian Space Davy Jones as a senior staff member. Predictably, Gene Coon disagreed with this official story, claiming instead Chekov was going to be English before Roddenberry received a letter of complaint from Soviet fans arguing the hypocrisy of a show depicting a future with a united Earth didn't have any Russians, especially as they were, at the time, ahead in the Space Race. However, this time he's contradicted by Koenig himself, who has the really rather plausible theory this letter more than likely didn't exist, because no Soviet television stations would be airing US programming at the height of the Cold War. Koenig claims making Chekov Russian was always Roddenberry's idea, due to him wanting to acknowledge the USSR's aforementioned dominant space programme.

Regardless of whose idea the character ultimately was, the fact is Chekov, much like a lot of this show at this point in time, frankly doesn't work. He's an endearing enough character and will only continue to become more so as the series goes on, but in terms of what he was actually intended to do? He's a disaster. The attempt to pay lip service to The Monkees is ridiculous and transparently a bit of cynical pandering, not to mention *far* too little too late given what the show's done to youth culture so far. Furthermore, having a Russian member of the *Enterprise* crew is a nice idea in theory, but not when he's portrayed as the most skin-crawlingly caricatured stereotype of the funny foreign blinkered, Mother Russia-praising comrade imaginable. This isn't really noticeable in "Catspaw" per se, but it becomes an irritatingly defining part of the character as he develops over the next two years. Chekov is basically Yakov Smirnoff 25 years early except unironic and not funny. So again, more racism. Except this time it's racism in the service of fighting racism which is...really bizarre.

Even on *Raumpatrouille Orion* at least, while Eva Pflug wasn't Russian she at least played Tamara Jagellovsk as a real person instead of a bad cartoon character and didn't feel the need to engage in a borderline offensively fake (and inaccurate) accent. But this has always been a problem for *Star Trek*: I hate to say it, but James Doohan's Scotty is no different, and the fact Uhura and Sulu are spared the same theme park approach to ethnicity is something of a miracle. Speaking of Uhura, Sulu and Scotty, they're once again barely in this episode. Nichelle Nichols gets to do her usual "frequencies are *jammed* sir! I can't compensate!" routine on the bridge, but James Doohan and George Takei don't even get to *speak any lines* in this episode. At least with Takei there's an excuse, as he spent the majority of the second season filming a movie so he wasn't available on set as frequently as he had been in the past, but to see a noted and respected character actor like Doohan, who was it must be stressed supposed to be playing a major role here, treated this way is appalling.

Nevertheless, in spite of everything that's wrong with "Catspaw" and there is a frightening amount of things wrong with it, there is one thing it manages to do that saves it from the dregs of irredeemable, reactionary rubbish. A magic spell, if you will, that gives it a certain power to stand out in the mind. See, there are a few lines near the end of the episode, not all that many, but enough, that just about change the game for Star Trek forever. While Sylvia and Korob's transmuter allows them to channel their abilities, it's not the source of them. As Sylvia says, the true power is the ability to see inside minds and join with them, and once again we get that very Star Trek motif of mental unions being described in sexual language. This is magic, *actual* magick. Not the juvenile waving-of-the-wand and book-of-spells silliness one might expect given the rest of the episode, but real, symbolic, spiritual magickal power. In one scene Sylvia basically becomes a voodoo priestess, making a voodoo doll of the *Enterprise*, which she can do any number of conjurations to and have it affect the real ship as well.

(One of this episode's most egregiously frustrating missed beats in a universe of many is its failure to explore the concept of "transmutation" further. I mean, we've got Actual Space Wizards, one of them female, talking about transmutation of energy and sensuality. There's a great deal to be said about the connection between sexual energy, magick and enlightenment.)

And crucially, the rest of the show can't explain this away, nor does it actually make the attempt to. Spock makes some attempts at hand-waving Korob and Sylvia's powers by saying they're the result of telepathy and telekinesis and other "mental abilities", much like the "mental sciences" of Foundation and other Asimov-style Golden Age science fiction, but he would. This is still basically what magick is and how it works, and Korob and Sylvia are explicitly, overtly magicians. Really rubbish magicians, but magicians nonetheless. And no matter how intolerable this episode may have been and how dangerously unstable *Star Trek* may be, this remains undeniably intriguing, as Spock might say. Colliding the world of magick into *Star Trek* is still unbelievably fascinating, and there's no point from here until the franchise finally sails away for good when this will cease to be a part of what it is. The course to take has never been more clear.

44. "...a uniquely portable magic.": Metamorphosis

The obvious way to open this chapter would be with some cheekily prescient call-forward to *Star Trek First Contact*, the consensus-second-best Star Trek movie, in which Zefram Cochrane (who is introduced here) plays a significant role. However, that essay is going to be wild and crazy enough without having to deal with baggage from "Metamorphosis" on top of it all, so let's leave the future to the future for now.

"Metamorphosis" is a significant improvement over last episode, which is typically the case when Gene Coon is writing. What's more interesting, however, is that this is very much Gene Coon for the second season: Building off of themes he introduced in "The Devil in the Dark" and perhaps noticing the show is hinting at being destined for greater things, "Metamorphosis" is the first clear, concrete step forward *Star Trek* has taken since, well, Coon's last episode. It's not perfect, not even the best script we've seen from Coon so far, and the particular kind of faults it has mean it's ultimately less than successful, but this is still very much the sort of sign we should be looking for from *Star Trek* at the start of its second consecutive year on the air.

Charmingly, Coon's next step from burning the show to the ground and challenging it to justify its existence and prove it's capable of behaving in a peaceful, constructive manner is to give it an incredibly straightforward and intimate love story. Not a fake romance plot, like Nurse Chapel swooning over Doctor Korby just long enough to provide necessary drama in a floundering episode or when Kirk shacks up with any of his Desilu-mandated girls-of-the-week, but a real, actual love story between two people that takes a serious, mature look at what that concept is, how it's expressed and how its interpreted. The Companion loves the stranded Zefram Cochrane, but is only capable of displaying her affection by keeping him alive and providing for him. But that's not the kind of companionship he really needs, which prompts her to similarly maroon Kirk, Spock, McCoy and the commissioner. Cochrane can't see this as love, because The Companion is not a being like himself, and when he finds out the truth he recoils in horror. And, in an actually lovely speech from Kirk, without doubt one of his most memorable scenes in the show so far, he points out to both of them that true love can't be one-sided and that two people must be joined as equals for it to exist.

This speech is a watershed from Kirk, and his depiction in this episode is crucial to continuing his extradiegetic challenge given to him by Coon in "Arena" to grow and mature *Star Trek*. Much like in "the Devil in the Dark", Kirk starts out angry and frenzied, even considering destroying The Companion if it means freeing the trapped shuttlecraft. But he is reminded by McCoy, in one of his best and, frankly, most welcome lines to date that "perhaps being a soldier for so long" has caused Kirk to forget he's "also trained as a diplomat". This is one the one hand the first evidence we've seen that Starfleet may actually be more than an interstellar police department, but also a direct invocation of the very themes Coon seems to have been working with over the past year. However, this statement is worth parsing out: Firstly, Kirk doesn't actually act especially like a diplomat here. There are no regulations, concessions, compromises or political sleight-of-hand, and *Star Trek* on the whole still seems fairly suspicious of diplomacy and bureaucratic politics (indeed the only reason I'm not pitching a fit over Commissioner Hedford is she's very clearly meant to be just another obstructive bureaucrat in the mould of Ambassador Fox in "A Taste of Armageddon" or Galactic High Commissioner Ferris in "The Galileo Seven").

It's also telling, and not entirely for good reasons, that the preferable opposite of "soldier", according to *Star Trek* is, apparently now "diplomat". Use of that sort of word, in addition to terms like "Federation" and "negotiation" means the show is really starting to solidify that its world takes place in a Western-style liberal representative democracy, and in a world where it's not entirely clear that's an especially desirable form of government. I mean this is definitely better than the "enlightened despot" fascism Khan offered us back in "Space Seed", but we're already, in 1967, in an era where notions like "government the way the US works is an inherently positive thing and should be the goal of all civilized societies" are starting to be put into question. It's impossible to ignore the growing counterculture movement in the US and it's staunch anti-war roots that put the blame for contemporary civil unrest not really unfairly square at the feet of the US government and military, even if we are less than a year out from it's ultimate implosion, and *Star Trek* sticking its fingers in its ears and pretending this isn't happening is worrying and dangerous.

This might have been OK if *Star Trek* was openly willing to problematize its own setting, like other shows of the time were, but it's really not clear that it is. The crew in "Metamorphosis", having been through the howling exorcism of Coon's first half-season, seem like they're at a midpoint between the crass moralizing of the Roddenberry era and the idealized role models they'll eventually be remembered as. Kirk is definitely meant to have the moral high ground, but only after he stops thinking like he's at war all the time. Even *Star Trek's* most obvious television peers, *Raumpatrouille Orion* and *Doctor Who*, (not to mention *The Prisoner*, even though it's not quite as linked to *Star Trek* as the other two series), were doing stories overtly about questioning this sort of status quo. The major problem is going to come when *Star Trek* becomes a utopia and falling back onto Western-style democracy as the teleological ideal future for humanity is going to prove...unsettling.

But this is a theme that, while it's introduced here, is best dealt with in full force when it starts to become an overt influence on the series, and there's an episode coming up later in the season that discussion will be ideal for, so we'll return to it then. Especially since "Metamorphosis" has a few problems of its own that hold it back from *quite* achieving greatness. The most obvious and troubling one is that, of course, the love story Coon tells is blatantly heteronormative. Spock says, upon discovering The Companion is female, that this "changes" things somewhat, as if it would have been impossible for a male entity or a life-form that doesn't conform to binary notions of gender to love Cochrane. The Commissioner's big emotional moment comes when she calls out Cochrane on her deathbed for resenting and hiding from love when someone like her remained lonely and unloved all her life. It's a wonderful scene that's promptly ruined by her contrasting this with her profession, which she says she was always good at, as if it's impossible for a woman to be loved and be successful at her career at the same time. I mean, I have to give *Star Trek* credit: It continues to amaze me with its ability to find ways to be insultingly reactionary decades ahead of its time. That said though it's probably a bit unfair of me (though not overly, I should think) to expect Coon to pull something with *Star Trek* in 1967 that fiction today can't even regularly and reliably pull off.

There's also the issue that, thanks partially to the episode's pacing problems (we once again get lines repeated almost verbatim, redundant bits of exposition and scenes that don't quite logically follow from each other) Kirk's final speech to The Companion about love isn't as clear as it needs to be. There is a troubling implication that The Companion is unable to truly love because she's not human, where I think the point should be (and was intended to be) that the problem is she and Cochrane are unable to be together in their current forms. The former snaps back not just to heteronormativity but borderline xenophobia and threatens to undo the good work done by the rest of the plot, so let's politely ignore it and look at the other possibility. The latter is a statement about not just the unattainability of love for these specific characters, but also the show on the whole thanks to the structure it's imposed on itself.

There's a longstanding tension in some genre works between the spheres of the mythic and the mundane, and a notion these have to by definition be irreconcilable, this speaks to: The easy example would be to compare this to Kirk's numerous complaints in the past about being unable to sustain a meaningful relationship thanks to his shipboard duties and responsibilities, an interpretation facilitated by the fact the small, intimate world of the asteroid offered by The Companion is contrasted with the vastness of the universe offered by Kirk, but I prefer to read this as an indictment of *Star Trek*'s hit-and-miss relationship with the mundane and a claim from Coon that the show is perfectly capable of handling it, but just needs to handle it with more depth and maturity than it has so far. Because really the whole "married to the ship" thing was only ever and always about network standards and practices and a grave concern that "nothing untoward" would be going on between the human characters.

And Star Trek actually has the potential to be the show that finally unites these two seeming polar opposites (well, OK, *Raumpatrouille Orion* probably did this first, but Star Trek can go even further, if for no other reason than it will last longer). It's given us plenty of evidence that it can even this early. Just as The Companion and Cochrane need not be forever apart, Star Trek need not feel it's unable to experience love and happiness in the distant reaches of outer space. Uniting the two then, just as The Companion unites with Hedford and, because she loves him, Cochrane, is just as much the metamorphosis described by the episode's title as the Commissioner's transformation.

And, just like that one, it is an expressly magickal transformation, perhaps a *transmuta-*

tion, if you will: While Spock tries to explain The Companion in electrical terms, nothing it does is really in any way comparable to the behaviour of electricity. No, The Companion creates matter, life, out of nothingness, and she doesn't do it because she's some distant, objective God: Rather, she does it because of, and through, her love. Her fusion with Commissioner Hedford then, which is also tacitly compared with her blossoming relationship with Cochrane, becomes a spiritual union. This isn't so much an ascension to a higher plane which, while interesting, could be read as either unsatisfyingly vague or implicitly pop Christian: It's more, as the title would suggest, growing into someone and something wiser and aware of its existence as part of a larger whole. But that's sort of what a spiritual union is.

45. "Wednesday's child is full of woe/Thursday's child has far to go": Friday's Child

D.C. Fontana has depressingly rotten luck.

She's Star Trek's first staff writer who is a woman and has written several of the most influential and groundbreaking episodes in the franchise, including two of my absolute, all-time favourites. Unfortunately, every single episode she's been involved in I've looked so far in this project (save, debatably, "Tomorrow is Yesterday") has been an infuriating, baldly reactionary disaster including, well, this one. In "Friday's Child" we have, in no particular order, the Federation explicitly as the "good" empire to the Klingon's "bad" empire, Kirk and Spock completely overturning the society and rules of an entire planetary culture pretty much for lulz, and, oh yeah, a pregnant woman, belittled and infantilized by just about every other character by being referred to as "the girl", whom the show treats as both a comic relief and a burden because of her attempts to be headstrong and independent.

Let's take a look at the most egregious and upsetting thing first: Not the imperialistic or Prime Directive issues; the show couldn't give a toss about those here and neither should we until it decides to take another look at them. No, I'm instead talking about Eleen Akaar, because of fucking course I'm talking about Eleen Akaar. A proud, strong woman who doesn't let any man touch her, yet who eagerly submits to Doctor McCoy when he proves his superior fortitude and asserts his dominance and authority over her, by, of all things *slapping her* and knowing more about labour and childbirth then her *as well as every other woman in her society*. This is so blatantly, obviously and stupefyingly misogynistic I'm actually speechless: There's no reaction to that I can muster apart from stunned disbelief and disgust such that I actually feel dirty and personally hurt after watching this. Let's try and move on as quickly as possible, lest this chapter devolve into another screamy, infuriated diatribe *a la* "The Corbomite Maneuver" or "The Enemy Within".

I want to make it clear that while her name is on this script, I'm not fingering Fontana in particular. I *know* she has better taste and sensibilities then this by virtue of her future work alone: She fights tooth and nail to be heard over the course of the rest of the Original Series, oversaw the whole second Star Trek show and was far and away the standout writer of both *Star Trek: The Next Generation* and Star Trek: Deep Space Nine's first seasons. Fontana is *not* an internalized misogynist and *not* a bad writer. Her work and her public statements make it very clear she couldn't be farther from either. And had Fontana's original draft gone into production, Eleen would have been depicted as an even stronger presence, explicit in revolt against the male supremacy of Capellan society, which believed women were mothers and homemakers and nothing else. The climax would have also seen her sacrificing the life of her child in order to preserve her own, which actually gels much better with Kirk's line that Eleen "hates the unborn child she is carrying" and Eleen's own dialog that in her culture, children belong expressly to the father (as well as the subtle implication early on that the only reason Akaar married Eleen was to give him a son in the first place).

No, the lion's share of the blame for the feminist nightmare of "Friday's Child" must sadly go to Gene Roddenberry. Roddenberry, it would seem, didn't like any of this and had Fontana rewrite the entire last act so that the child survives and becomes McCoy's honourary son and Eleen attempts to broker peace between the landing party and the warriors who the Klingon agent incited into a rebellion, which would sufficiently demonstrate that Gene Roddenberry was tragically clueless about feminism, gender roles and women in general in spite of his progressive overtures elsewhere. But then again, said progressive elements need to be learned, and they can only be learned from women. Gene Roddenberry has a lot of growing to do.

It's tempting to want to demand Fontana stand up for her work and herself more and say no to things like this, but we have to remember being a woman, and one of the only women, who was a staff writer, and a story editor no less (who already has to write under an androgynous credit), in the United States, in Hollywood, on network television, on a major primetime drama, in science fiction *in 1967* is difficult enough: I should imagine she would have been constantly aware of the authoritarian, patriarchal, male supremacist power structures she was working under and would have had to worry on more than one occasion about being "outed" as a woman, losing her job, or what would happen if she had to find another. I would guess Fontana likely faced overt discrimination every day, or the fear of it, if not from her colleagues and co-workers, from society at large. All of those oppressive forces working together can be a very powerful, and very effective, silencer.

But even taking all of that into account, this episode still just *isn't good enough*. Even if all Roddenberry did was change that bit of plot about Eleen and her son, the rest of "Friday's Child" is hamstrung by problems of its own. The first of which is that the Klingons and the Federation are very obviously fighting a proxy war here, and the story doesn't seem to see a problem with this. The Klingon is agent trying to provoke a military coup such that when Akaar is deposed, he'll be replaced with someone far more willing to side with Klingon interests. This could be read as an indictment of the United States' rather unforgivable track record of doing exactly this, particularly in the then-current Vietnam War, which was already something of a big deal, were it not for the fact the Federation does basically the same thing with Eleen and Leonard James Akaar. Kirk's big motivation in this episode is to prove to the Capellans that the word of Starfleet officers and Federation law was far preferable to and far more just than that of the Klingons, and by the very nature of his birth Leonard James is going to be incredibly sympathetic to the Federation (indeed, he's so sympathetic he rather bafflingly becomes a popular reoccurring character in several spin-off works). That "Friday's Chils" has Kirk set this up for the Federation on national television against the backdrop of said Vietnam War is quite frankly deeply distressing, and this, taken in the context that unfortunate business surrounding "The City on the Edge of Forever" is more than a little concerning.

The problem is that this episode seems to be working towards the notion of the Federation as an explicit utopia. This is a thread best saved for the next season, but as it's already become a theme it's worth talking a little bit about now. There's a serious difference between the world of Star Trek being *utopian* or *idealistic* and the *Federation* being a *utopia*. This is something we've already talked a little about and is going to become a major, major theme throughout the rest of the franchise. For now, though, "Friday's Child" is the first time the Federation has been depicted in an explicitly, unambiguously positive light. They're the good guys, the Klingons are the bad guys. In the past there's been a significant amount of uncertainty about that fact, and even when Gene Coon introduced the Klingons in "Errand of Mercy" (who were already by definition more straightforwardly evil than the Romulans) the point was that they weren't really all that different from the Federation from the perspective of a third party. Here, though, while there's a token mention that "[the Klingon] has offered us things for our rocks as well" and a brief debate in Akaar's tent, the Klingons are pretty clearly meant to be wearing the black hats, as the agent is very obviously shifty, disingenuous, self-interested and manipulative while the Capellans stress the "Earth men have never lied".

The thing is, Coon did not create the Federation to work like this. It was designed to be problematized from the get-go, and that's a clear thread that goes back as far as "Arena". One of the things I'm going to keep returning to, not so much in this part of the project but absolutely once I reach *Star Trek: The Next Generation* and *Star Trek: Deep Space Nine* is that the Federation and Starfleet aren't actually our heroes here, or at least shouldn't be: Our heroes are *the crew*, and the a great deal of the point of Star Trek is watching how the crew, on both an individual and collectivist level, respond to their positionalities within different sociocultural systems and structures of power. *Raumpatrouille Orion*, in fact, already works precisely this way and *Star Trek* really ought to be following suit, but the problem we've got this week is that it doesn't seem the show gets this yet. Furthermore, while "Catspaw" and "Metamorphosis" were both flawed in their own ways, the net result of them was overwhelmingly positive. Frustratingly, "Friday's Child" seems to be completely ignoring the fact last two productions happened.

The additional problem with Capella that makes all of this significantly worse is that, for the first time (the fluke humanness of the Romulans in "Balance of Terror" excepted), the episode's planetary society isn't designed as some kind of blunt metaphor for the moral-of-the-week. Compare it with Eminiar VII in "A Taste of Armageddon", which was an entire society built around the concept of perpetual war such that Kirk could stroll in, wreck things, and teach them about how bad war is (not that this particular moral was an especially bad one, mind). Here though, we have a culture seemingly designed to actually be a culture, with society-wide mores about strength and lawfulness. The point of "Friday's Child" isn't for the *Enterprise* crew to teach the Capellans a lesson (or the other way around, for that matter), the point is very clearly demonstrating that the Federation's code of ethics is superior to that of the Klingons, mostly because McCoy says it is. Perhaps in Fontana's original draft the Capellans would have been defined by male supremacy in order to underscore and highlight Eleen's eventual rejection and condemnation of them, but either way very little of that remains and the episode as aired has the distinct smack of US Cold War neo-inperialism about it.

In spite of all this general unpleasantness, there are bits of "Friday's Child" that are properly excellent. William Shatner and Leonard Nimoy are particularly terrific: Starting with Shatner, while Kirk is once again asked to stand in for the Federation and its ethics (and uncomfortably coming across as proselytizing as he's no longer standing trial for it), for the majority of the episode he seems profoundly uninspired to actually be the Federation's representative. There's a token ideological battle near the beginning, but this is quickly overshadowed by the actual real battle that breaks out when the Klingon agent launches his coup, and from that point on Kirk seems far more focused in wilderness survival then proving his moral superiority. It is worth noting, however, that Kirk does seem most comfortable when he's allowed to slip back into soldier mode.

This is also helped by DeForest Kelley getting almost the entirety of the episode's key emotional scenes to himself, as McCoy had previously been stationed on Capella, is familiar with their culture and spends the most amount of time interacting with Eleen. This leads to some rather delightful moments as Kirk, once again contrary to his womanizer reputation, seems completely uninterested in Eleen beyond objecting to her people's treatment of her, quite obviously preferring to let McCoy work with her while he goes and plays Cowboys and Indians with Spock in the shrubbery. Since the end of last season, Nimoy and Shatner have been honing and refining their onscreen chemistry and are by this point and extremely compelling double act. Their rapport is tight, their banter smart and their comic timing spot-on, and it's easy to see even now how both the actors and the characters go down in television history for this. Shatner and Nimoy are the best things about this episode by miles, and here is where Kirk and Spock start to become pop culture icons.

And that alone is almost enough to save "Friday's Child" from being complete and total bomb. We're only three episodes into the second season and despite the stumbles and pratfalls of the past few weeks the show has unarguably taken a turn for the better, and in a direction nobody could have anticipated even just a few months ago. Let's not forget three episodes into Star Trek proper we were at "The Corbomite Maneuver" and unsure whether or not the show would even last long enough to see out its first season. A year later the show is considerably better shape, and we can expect some growing pains for not just D.C. Fontana, but the show itself. Fontana has said she looks back on her earliest Star Trek work somewhat astonished that her name is one these scripts: She doesn't view them as even being written by the same person she is now, and she's correct, of course. They're not. Writers, just like anyone, grow over time, especially over the course of a 25 year career. D.C. Fontana is redeemed by her work that's yet to come, and Gene Coon's new approach has paid off beyond our wildest imaginations. We're only now starting to get a glimpse of what the future might look like for this new Star Trek.

46. "You shall not crucify mankind upon a cross of gold!": Who Mourns for Adonais?

There are episodes that truly challenge Star Trek's alleged commitment to social progress and idealism. This is one of them.

If you are trying to argue *Star Trek* is some utopian fantasy from the future, your argument is on thin ice. In fact, by this point it may well be in the freezing lake itself. This is the fourth episode in a row this show has trotted out blatant, ghastly, retrograde misogyny and this is the worst week yet. Anyone who can remotely consider *Star Trek* progressive in feminist areas quite frankly hasn't watched it. Period. That's the only way I can see glancing over the second trivialized brutal rape scene of an infantilized woman in as many years. This is all the more infuriating as "Who Mourns for Adonais?" actually has one or two interesting things worth talking about, but absolutely everything else is dwarfed and subsumed by the big, glaring bit of rape apologia the episode tosses at us in its climax, so we have to address that before we can even *think* about other discussion topics. Remember back in "The Enemy Within" where I said *Star Trek* had become broken and irredeemable? Well, guess what: It still is.

"Who Mourns for Adonais?" is "Space Seed" except Greek-flavoured. Once again we have a female humanities scholar, this time an anthropologist because *Star Trek* hates me, personally, swayed by an overwhelming, dominant male presence who betrays the crew because as this show's logic has made explicitly clear on several occasions, women are fickle, capricious and mysterious. It's just the stakes have been raised as we now have a man claiming to be a god instead of a dictator, which opens a whole can of worms I don't even want to think about right now. At least Kirk doesn't belittle her field and her entire gender this time around, not that his acceptance counts for much anymore, although Doctor McCoy's comments more than fill the gap Kirk leaves in this regard. And, for that matter, at least Khan didn't *actually and visibly rape* Marla McGivers, though, which Apollo *quite clearly does to Carolyn Palamas in the climax to this episode*. This time it's even worse than it was with Janice Rand in "The Enemy Within", because as horrible as that was, that was still only *attempted* rape. This is a full-on *rape scene* with the camera leeringly focused on Apollo's godlike dominance over Palamas and her pained, tortured, helpless expression. Furthermore, it's a scene about tearing her down, breaking her, invalidating her, mocking her agency degrading her, and dehumanizing her, just as all rape truly is: Right before the rape, she had finally stood up to Apollo and began acting like an anthropologist for the first time in the episode, and she's utterly destroyed as a person for doing work she presumably loved doing.

And the worst part? The actual, very worst part? The show doesn't have one single problem with this. *Star Trek* revels in its Male Gaze, and expects you to as well. This episode was originally supposed to end with McCoy revealing to Kirk that Palamas was pregnant by Apollo and joking about how his sickbay is not designed to deliver the children of gods. Gene Coon and D.C. Fontana (presumably it was them, though I find no record of who exactly it was) quickly brought the hammer down on that, ending the episode on the far more appropriate note of Kirk ruminating about godhood and its importance to the evolution of human society. James Blish, however, *put the scene right back into his novelization of the episode.* Also, costume designer William Ware Theiss, whom you may remember from my equally eloquent reading of "Mudd's Women" back in the first season and whom I'd hope would know better, heartily agreed this was the better ending and, incidentally, this is apparently beloved *Seinfeld* star and Broadway personality Jason Alexander's favourite episode of *Star Trek*, just in case you didn't quite have enough reason to hate everyone and everything that has ever existed yet.

And that's really it. That's my analysis of "Who Mourns for Adonais?". This is rape apologia, institutionalized misogyny and male supremacism as the proud centrepiece of the supposedly most-progressive and hopeful show on US television. I don't have anything more to add than that. This is the episode that finally proves, in case there was any lingering doubt, that *Star Trek* is in truth fundamentally reactionary. All science fiction is, but *Star Trek* moreso than the norm. No series that deserves to call itself progressive would ever dream of letting something this hateful make it to air. Even in its weakest moments, something like this would have been positively inconceivable to *Raumpatrouille Orion*. In an just world, this show would have been cancelled six ways from Sunday by this point. And yet it wasn't. It has a blossoming female fanbase, and that female fanbase will turn Star Trek into the very first pop culture franchise. Our job has become trying to connect the dots: How do we get there from here? With that in mind, the only statement I have for us for the time being is that it's time for an exorcism. We're going to bring the heavens to us come hell or high water.

If I were to read "Who Mourns for Adonais?" as part of an unfolding text and not as one of the single worst, most reprehensible pieces of television I have ever seen, I might compare it with the work of Erich von Däniken, in particular his book *Chariots of the Gods?*. von Däniken is an author who has spent his career advocating his theory that highly advanced extraterrestrial civilizations contacted ancient people, providing both the inspiration for their artwork, mythology and spiritual beliefs as well as leaving behind evidence of their existence through structures and artefacts that, according to him, were far too advanced for the humans who lived at the time of their construction to have created. This is an argument that is both provocative inasmuch as it posits our ancestors had a deeper connection to cosmic consciousness then we perhaps give them credit for, and also ludicrously crass and Eurocentric as it assumes they were too ignorant and primitive to be capable of the technological feats they very clearly and demonstrably *were* capable of.

However, as provably wrong as von Däniken is (and this is coming from someone who has a healthy interest in other forms of Fortean inexplicata), he was massively influential on a great many writers and artists of this time period.

"Who Mourns for Adonais?" then is textbook von Dänikenism, and Apollo ticks every single one of the boxes in the *Chariots of the Gods?* playbook, and even builds upon it: Apollo's people actually love the idea of being treated like gods, and have gotten it into their heads they require love and worship from their followers. Well, that is, except for one thing: *Chariots of the Gods?* was published in 1968. "Who Mourns for Adonais?" aired on September 22, 1967. In other words, this episode has managed to do von Dänikenism before von Däniken himself got to it. This is not especially a good thing, as the theory is no less patronizing and offensive to the ancient peoples here then it is in *Chariots of the Gods?*, with Kirk even tossing out lines about "primitive" and "simple" shepherds altogether more frequently than I would have been comfortable with.

There's a peculiar form of secularism "Who Mourns for Adonais?" reveals that's not quite present in other variations on the *Chariots of the Gods?* formula von Däniken will inspire: Typically, the ancient astronauts theory is tied in some way to the concept that our star god ancestors offered a kind of enlightenment to ancient peoples we've lost thanks to the rise of Modernism, hence why von Däniken became a darling of the New Age movement in the 1970s. However, the solitary interesting and valuable thing "Who Mourns for Adonais?" contributes to the discourse is giving this argument to *Apollo*, who is very obviously the piece's villain, and clearly meant to be largely unsympathetic. Apollo promises a return to the imagined pastoral golden age of ancient Greece, in exchange for total obedience and subservience to his paternal authority (he even describes and defends his vengeful, wrath-filled outbursts as "lessons", which is actually sort of perfect), and Kirk isn't hearing one word of it. The script seems to intend this as a treatise against superstition, that humanity has "outgrown" the need for such things in an age of rationality, Kirk's line about how "we have no need for gods, just the one is sufficient" aside, which is very clearly only there to keep the Christian fundamentalists in the southern affiliates from raising hell. This is no better than von Däniken though: Declaring our shared mythologies and oral histories are juvenile marks of less-developed cultures is just a different form of Eurocentrism to claiming ancient peoples were too stupid to live their lives.

But, once again, William Shatner saves the day, because this isn't how he plays Kirk here at all. Under Shatner, Kirk's objection seems to be the arrogance of anyone who would declare themselves a god and who might think that he alone is fit to lord over humans. This is not only contiguous with his speech in "Where No Man Has Gone Before", a side of Kirk we've really not seen explored much up 'till now, but exactly what he needed to say to Khan in "Space Seed". Consider also Kirk's attempt to convince Palamas to turn against Apollo and return to them: He emphasizes the pleasures of the human body and the human experience, and that this is the only way for humans to know each other. He doesn't actually say "enlightenment", but this is the direction he was going in, and this also has the added effect of more than making up for that unfortunate Sylvia business in "Catspaw". Kirk wouldn't seem to be decrying mythology and spirituality here (his last line

205

about "just a few laurel leaves" seems to support it), perhaps what he's actually attacking is patrician authority itself.

(There is a theory, one that I am particularly sympathetic to, that true enlightenment comes through sublimation of reality rather than transcendece from it. But that's, oh, two or three books away I should think.)

But this is still tarnished somewhat by a few too many scenes where Kirk issues his own stern orders and demands everyone adhere to their duty and responsibility. Star Trek loves authority too much to ever be a true challenge to it. We know that from "Space Seed". James T. Kirk is no Cliff A. McClane. And this is more troubling yet still, because as much as Kirk seems to want to challenge Apollo's authority, he does so by protetsing that it is instead he who has the truly just authority. This isn't antiauthoritarianism, this is a despotic turf war. Apollo isn't a real god, after all, he's an alien playing at being a god. But Kirk doesn't seem to know the difference, and that's the fatal flaw in his argument. *Star Trek* simply isn't going to be the show that will ever be able to make these distinctions clearly enough to act on them.

And that's a shame, because there's the potential for magick here. In Hermeticism, gold is the ultimate symbol of enlightenment (which is why all those alchemists were interested in transmuting lead into gold), but it's also associated very strongly with the god Apollo, because alchemy is considered the work of the sun, which they associate with Apollo. Thus, gold also has symbolic connections to the sun, Apollo and masculinity because both are at the top of the tree depicting the path toward alchemical enlightenment (and if we remember "Battle for the Sun", we might wish to critique Hermeticism as a very Western, and thus patriarchal, sort of ritual magick). But what Captain Kirk sort of does here is turn the symbols, tools and methods of alchemy against Apollo and upended and inverted the entire system.

Decrying the Apollonian ideal as paternalistic and oppressive, Kirk has the temple symbolizing Apollo's righteousness and authority, and thus Apollo himself, obliterated by calling down a phaser blast that is not the act of one man, but that of many men and women who refuse to be slaves placated with words of false enlightenment. Reverse alchemy, then-Gold becomes lead. The perfect golden male is struck down by the star people who forcibly change his mark: He no longer stands for enlightenment and humanity shall no longer feel obligated to turn to him for guidance and benevolent dictatorship. Just as he told Palamas, Shatner-as-Kirk has proven true wisdom is just as much of the physical plane as it is the spiritual dimension, and that it is free to anybody who realises the joining of the two is the secret to knowing. We need not worship the gods of patriarchy because we each have the potential to become gods ourselves within us.

But doe Star Trek itself actually understand this? I'm not convinced that it does.

Were I inclined to redeem "Who Mourns for Adonais?" I might also say that the plot structure, split evenly between the landing party and *Enterprise* crew, is another example of the alchemical mirror Shatner-as-Kirk forced Apollo to gaze into. Every episode this season has had this conceit to some extent, but this is the best execution of it yet (and Scotty's and Chekov's sluggishly-paced investigation into the most obvious Klingon trap ever in "Friday's Child" probably the current nadir). I might stress how this alliance of individuals, who are all treated equally and who all contribute to the final overthrow of Apollo, symbolizes the strength of Star Trek. I might go out of my way to praise Uhura, who for the very first time is overtly treated as a respected professional colleague and friend whose dialog with Spock as the latter expresses his confidence in her ability to rewire the communications relay in a tricky experiment to contact the landing party is a high water mark for both characters. I might even say the cumulative effect of this changes the interpretation of Apollo's rape of Palamas, turning it into a particularly graphic example of how his paternalistic authoritarianism has nullified any good he might have done or promised to do. But I won't, because I can't. The original ending (not to mention the way the scene itself is depicted), supported by major creative personnel like William Ware Theiss and reinstated by James Blish in the most readily-available version of this story until home video, is an inseparable part of the text now. It cannot be ignored, and it cannot be redeemed. It can only be fought and resisted.

The damage has been done and is irreversible. *Star Trek* has been dissolved and disbanded as the show tears itself apart along the seam dividing its irreconcilable reactionary and progressive influences. Because this is the true horror of "Who Mourns for Adonais?", of Star Trek and of liberal philosophy itself. Apollo's golden masculine despotism was always part of what *Star Trek* was. It's perfectly liberal. This is the true legacy of "Space Seed", and the true nightmare of liberalism: The lurking evil at the heart of its ideology is that liberalism fantasizes about fascism. Liberals would endorse fascism so long as they thought "the right man" was in charge of everything. A "good one". One of *them*, because *they* know best as if *they* were in charge *they'd* straighten things out and beat those ignorant, uneducated proles into shape. H.P. Lovecraft was wrong, and his own violent racism betrays him for it-Because now we know the true abominations lie not at the remote edges of the universe, but in humans themselves.

47. "But what about sex?" Amok Time

"Amok Time" is the price *Star Trek* pays for "Who Mourns for Adonais?". This is the show's shamefully repressed sexuality finally catching up with it. Miraculously, or perhaps simply because it's impossible to spectacularly self-destruct in the same manner a second time, the show hits just about all the notes it needs to in this kind of scenario. "Amok Time" is without doubt another classic, perhaps not an unequivocal masterpiece, but definitely a landmark episode that sets the stage for a great deal of future great Star Trek.

The parallels here really couldn't be any more perfect. Spock, who so desires to be distant, calculating and logical, is driven into an uncontrollable madness because of the very instincts and emotions he's trying to bury and ignore. The Vulcans perceive their sexual drive as at once shameful taboo, but also as a deeply ancient and revered aspect of their cultural heritage, thus forcing them into a mating cycle which they can repress for awhile, but physiologically *must* acknowledge when the time comes, or else they will die. Given Spock is something of a central character and a microcosm for *Star Trek* and the numerous problems the series has in regards to gender roles, sexuality and women, even more overt and noticeable in the last few episodes, the analysis sort of writes itself here.

But to elaborate, and despite all the ancient and mysterious Vulcan ritualism of the *koon-ut-kal-if-fee*, the whole concept of Pon Farr is an extremely Western one. In my writeup of "Mudd's Women" I talked about how sexuality is perceived in these societies cribbing a bit from (and probably misinterpreting) Michel Foucault. In brief, Western sexuality is intrinsically linked with the idea of taboo, because while the rise of modernity led to a net increase in sexual discourse, it was carefully fielded through "official channels", most notably the Counter-Reformation-era Catholic church. As a result, sex is taboo but the taboo is also now sexy leading to the oxymoronic catch-22 that is responsible for pretty much all the repressive sexual tension Westerners live with. While sex wasn't talked about as much in pre-modern societies, it was just a natural thing that happened. So, even though they weren't living in sexually liberated golden ages of free love (as with most golden ages, this was a myth thought up after the fact by people nostalgic for a past that never existed in an attempt to cope with a present they didn't know how to deal with), pre-modern people didn't have to deal with quite the same problems modern people do.

And Pon Farr is very much a commentary on this, if not exactly diegetically then definitely extradiegetically. Sexuality is something that's an integral part of what it means to be human(oid), and denying that is, if not actively suicidal, at the very least counter-productive and unhealthy. What's really charming about "Amok Time" is how Spock is seen as being obstinate and, honestly, a bit childish for fervently trying to hide from his sexuality. Kirk reacts with bemusement when finds out the reason for his friend's outbursts,

208

saying it's something everyone thinks about sometimes and is nothing to be ashamed of and McCoy flat out states Pon Farr is "the price [the Vulcans] pay for all that logic". But Spock, attempting to speak for all Vulcans but more probably revealing the most about himself, talks about how this is deeply shameful for a culture that takes so much pride in logic. What we have in this episode is a central tension the show's bee saddled with from the outset finally being resolved: Gene Roddenberry always seemed torn between the value of acting like a logical automaton in crisis situations and the essential humanity of emotions, though apparently tending to prefer logic on the whole (probably as a result of his own numerous personal problems and failings). "Amok Time" is the rebuttal to this argument, instead making the statement it's perfectly possible to have both and that to think otherwise is self-absorbed and defeatist.

(Indeed, asexuality itself is allowed by this reading too: A lack of sexual attraction is still a perfectly valid expression of sexuality, what's being challenged here is the burial of any and all sexual discourse, sexuality and sexual identities whatsoever.)

The one troublesome factor in this reading for me seems to be T'Pring. Later Star Trek stories dealing with Pon Farr make it clear this is something that happens to all Vulcans equally, but here T'Pring seems unaffected by the mating cycle and her status as the female prize to be fought over, despite her cunning and subversive manipulation of the system, is problematic. Indeed the implication in "Amok Time" is that sexual urges, and according to the episode's internal logic and the reading we've been building, sexuality itself, is something unique to male Vulcans. This gets back to one of the oldest tricks in the patriarchy playboook, the idea all women are by definition passive and asexual, and when this gets written into the concept of breeding seasons, even in real world zoology, unfortunate things happen.

When I worked in Science and Technology Studies and Social Studies of Knowledge, there was a favourite story of mine I used to tell about Gelada Baboons and how this plays out in the scientific community. The society of this particular baboon is organised into reproductive groups, usually involving one male and several females. For a long time, the consensus was that the males held all the power in this structure, and the reproductive groups were described as "harems". However, this was contested by later groups of scientists (and documented on Chris and Martin Kratt's National Geographic programme *Be the Creature* in 2003), who observed that what actually happened in these relationships was that the females together govern the group and collectively decide which males to support and allow into their units. Males can challenge other males for seats, but the ultimate decision lies with the females, who make their choices by presenting themselves to him rather than the other way around.

What this proves is that female Geladas are not trophies to be fought over and won by males (as is the language so commonly used in zoology), but rather the males are competing with each other essentially for the privilege of gaining access to an exclusive all-female club, and even then the females are clearly the dominant sexual partners in this arrangement. In other words, what happened in this case was the first group of scientists allowed their patriarchal positionalities to colour the way they describe the Gelada social units, thus

209

missing the unique nuances by which they actually operated. I think a case could be made something similar happened with the creation of Vulcan culture and mating cycles in "Amok Time" and while, as I said, later Star Trek thankfully corrects this, it is something worth noting when we talk about this episode in particular.

As far as I'm concerned the rest of "Amok Time" is basically window dressing for this one elegant statement, but it's a pretty damn beautiful window. There's the wonderful friendship subplot about the lengths Kirk, Spock and McCoy will go for each other and the loyalty they all share that's central to every scene. We start with Kirk's concern about Spock's condition as a friend first, followed by his defiance of direct orders to transport him to Vulcan. Then there's Spock's request Kirk and McCoy accompany him to the ceremony, bringing off-worlders to the *koon-ut-kal-if-fee* for the first time in history. Then Spock, in the grips of the Blood Fever and supposedly incapable of rational thought, begging T'Pau to not force him to fight Kirk after T'Pring chooses him as the challenger she wishes Spock to fight in order to win her. And then, finally, McCoy's dosing of Kirk with the neural paralyzer to trick the Vulcans into thinking Kirk was dead, thus giving everyone a loophole out of their obligations. This is all rather obvious, though quite well done, and has been commented on by pretty much anyone who's reviewed "Amok Time". What's not as commented on are George Takei's Sulu and Walter Koenig's Chekov, whose banter about their shared exasperation over continuously having to change course between Altair VII and Vulcan is absolutely delightful, the best example of a mundane character moment we've seen on the show this year and without question a highlight of the episode.

Then there's Vulcan itself. "Amok Time" features the heaviest emphasis on world-building we've seen in Star Trek yet, and the lavish planetary sets, matte paintings and the meticulous attention paid towards depicting the Vulcans as a distinctive and unique society goes above and beyond anything else the show has done, and frankly will do. The Vulcans have their own language and customs that are treated as suitably alien, but also transfixing and evocative enough they leave a lasting impression Honestly, *Star Trek* portrays the Vulcans with more respect and dignity then it does most real-world human cultures. Topping it all off is the mythically good performance of Austrian actor Celia Lovsky as T'Pau, "the only person to ever refuse a seat on the Federation council", a historical fact we would do well to remember. Lovsky has a black hole level of gravity and utterly owns every single scene she's in. She, more than anyone else in the production, completely throws herself at the ancient, ritualistic pageantry of the setting and sells every iota of it. When William Shatner-as-Kirk expresses has awe at being in her presence, we believe it.

T'Pau became so iconic, in fact, she got her own 1980s electronica band and got to come back for three episodes on *Enterprise* in one of the better stories from that show's fourth season, this time played by Kara Zediker. Truthfully, it's T'Pau who most embodies and defines the Vulcans as a species within Star Trek: Spock can't because he's half-human and his character is defined by the tension between both halves of his lineage and his ultimate reconciliation of it. But apart from her fourth season guest appearance, T'Pau's regal presence and reticence towards humans was used as the blueprint for the exploration of Vulcan society on *Enterprise* and indeed she was even intended to be a regular on *Enterprise* at first, though that character eventually became Subcommander T'Pol for legal reasons (although Jolene Blalock still cites Lovsky as her primary acting influence).

But of course, the most important element of these "Amok Time" contributes to Star Trek lore is the legendary Vulcan salute and greeting "Live Long and Prosper". Once again, this is a frequently-told story, but it's one that bears repeating. Leonard Nimoy felt "Amok Time" was a good opportunity to create some sort of uniquely Vulcan signature. Approaching director Joseph Pevney with his idea and remembering his childhood visits to his grandfather's synagogue, Nimoy adapted and tweaked a salute practised by several Jewish denominations and created an icon of pop culture. Although probably not part of the reason Nimoy chose this greeting, it is interesting to note that in Hebrew the Vulcan salute creates the letter "Shin" and stands for "Shaddai", meaning "Almighty".

As good as "Amok Time" is, however, and it is rightfully beloved, the horrors and scars left by the last few weeks still linger. I'm sorry, but you don't get to go from "Who Mourns for Adonais?", "Friday's Child" and "Catspaw" to this and expect us to conveniently ignore what just happened. Perhaps this is why "Amok Time" went out as the season premier instead of "Metamorphosis" (as the season began in September, it was never going to be "Catspaw" given that episode's roots as a holiday special meant it had to go out around Halloween): It certainly would have grabbed people's attention. What this ultimately, and frustratingly, reveals is *Star Trek*'s irritating lack of any kind of consistent quality. It has admirable highs, sure, but it also has some truly crateringly low lows and far, far too many of them to justify slogging through each and every one to reach the aforementioned highs. My argument from last time still stands: *Star Trek* as a show is dead in the water. Flipping back and forth between provocative hints and the occasional oversignified wodner and disgustingly indefensible moral bankruptcy is simply not a sustainable way to operate. There are several good, even great, episodes still to come, including one unambiguously triumphant masterpiece. But it's only a matter of time before the show's luck runs out and its best, most progressive elements simply decide to stop playing along.

48. "The choice is with us still": The Doomsday Machine

"The Doomsday Machine" is one of the episodes I most fondly remember from the Original Series. For me it was always a highlight of the second season: I enjoyed the tense, thriller-like pacing as the crew races against time to prevent the planet killer from destroying everything, I thought splitting the main cast up was a great way to play up the drama of the situation (though it's been done before this season, I think it might be the most effective here) and I loved the fact Kirk, Scotty and the away team get the *Constellation* up and running by themselves and operate it all on their own. I also loved the design and concept of the planet killer itself, a big, scary automaton of destruction that the crew had to out-think and outmaneuver and I thought Commodore Decker's tragic fall from grace was a particularly well-executed and memorable character moment. Naturally, it would seem few people agree with me as this seems to be one of the more contentious episodes of the year.

James Doohan seems to have considered this his favourite episode of the Original Series and said so at conventions on a number of occasions. Apparently, however, he was frequently met with eye-rolls and groans from the audience whenever he said so. D.C. Fontana as well has been quoted as saying this is the weakest episode of the series and her least favourite. I must say I'm at something at a loss to explain why: I always thought this episode was both a critical and fan favourite, and I really can't see how Fontana can claim "The Doomsday Machine" is in any way worse than, say, "The Omega Glory" or indeed her own "Friday's Child" and that's just from this season alone. Expand your lens to the years that bookended season two and you've got "The Enemy Within", "Mudd's Women" and "Space Seed" to pick three particularly egregious examples of episodes that weigh down the first season considerably, not to mention, well, pretty much all of season three.

(Of course there's an unspoken reason why Star Trek's creative types might not go to bat for an episode like this the way they would for something like, oh, I dunno, "Space Seed" to pick an in-no-way-loaded counterexample. But that's too depressing a path for me to go down right now.)

Even the episode's own cast isn't completely on the same page: While the regulars are as fantastic as always (special notice being paid to William Shatner, James Doohan and Leonard Nimoy, who all deliver compellingly intense and colourful performances), William Windom, who played Decker, has gone on record a number of times to say he didn't take *Star Trek* at all seriously because it was science fiction and played his role basically as a cartoon character in an attempt to mock it (ironically, Windom's performance remains commendable and memorable, despite a few instances of obvious gurning). Although to be honest, were I in Windom's position, I'm not sure I would have taken Star Trek seriously either. After doing this project, science fiction doesn't really make a good case for itself to be taken seriously anymore.

But either way, what "The Doomsday Machine" ultimately seems like to me is a very simple, straightforward and more than sufficiently entertaining thriller. And I don't really see anything wrong with that. This is important to take note of, because this the first time *Star Trek* has actually done "straightforward" all year: "Catspaw" and "Amok Time" were by necessity left-field sorts of episodes while "Metamorphosis" was the next step in Gene Coon's evolving vision for the series. Meanwhile, "Friday's Child" and "Who Mourns for Adonais?" were each some manner of horrifying disaster, so we were sort of unable to get a sense for what an "average" episode of *Star Trek* in its second season was going to look like before now. There are ramifications and consequences to this (and the unpleasant fact a not-insignificant number of people seem to have failed to read this episode that way) to which I'll return a little later on, but for now let's look at the particular way in which "The Doomsday Machine" is straightforward.

The first most immediately obvious way to take the plot is that it's a critique of the Cold War-era arms race between the United States and the Soviet Union. The episode is, after all, called "The Doomsday Machine" and features a literal doomsday machine built as a bluff in a war that ceased to be relevant eons ago, yet still remains to threaten the safety of the galaxy. Kirk also explicitly compares it to the hydrogen bombs of the 20th century at key points in the episode. However, this is in actuality just background to the actual story, which is about Commodore Decker's guilt over the loss of the *Constellation* and his crew and his determination to redeem himself, clear his conscience and exact revenge, no matter if it means jeopardizing a second starship and the lives of everyone aboard in order to do so. This, in turn, provides the necessary framework upon which the show drapes on layers and layers of thriller tropes, right down to an ominous countdown to a seemingly-inescapable cataclysm the heroes manage to escape with nail-bitingly little time to spare. In other words, what "The Doomsday Machine" does is fake us out with the typical Gene Roddenberry *Star Trek* approach of blunt moralizing, before turning on its heels to become a lite character study melded with a thriller.

Commodore Decker's story is similarly clear, being more or less a straight lift of *Moby-Dick*. Star Trek has a peculiar fascination with this particular novel, cribbing from it quite blatantly not only here, but later on in the season with "Obsession" as well as the two consensus-best films in the franchise, *Star Trek II: The Wrath of Khan* and *Star Trek First Contact,* which is a fact that is probably fairly revealing in its own right. I have my own theory as to why this may be the case, but elaborating on it in detail is something probably best saved for 1982, because it fits Nicholas Meyer like a glove. Either way, of all the quite frankly far too many Star Trek adaptations of Herman Melville, I must say "The Doomsday Machine" is probably still my favourite, as it maintains the structure of the novel by having the Ahab character's downfall observed by a third party, upon whom we get to see the consequences of his quest take its toll. This is a very wise use of the

Enterprise crew in my opinion, because while it defies common storytelling logic which would seem to indicate you'd want all of your big character moments to go to the main cast (something that even unites Gene Roddenberry, Rick Berman and Michael Piller on *Star Trek: The Next Generation*, probably the only thing those three agreed on) it seems to fit a setting like the one Star Trek has, especially as it starts to flirt more and more seriously with idealism and utopianism.

See, in my opinion there is an extremely thin line you have to walk when you're dealing with an idealistic setting in regards to character development. On the one hand you want to make your characters interesting, but on the other hand you can't give them too much drama and conflict lest you risk abandoning your utopianism as, you know, your characters are supposed to be ideals. One one extreme lies panglossianism, on the other grimdark, and neither is a desirable or helpful starting point for fiction in my view. This is, once again, a problem that won't plague the rest of the Original Series too much as it was never really meant to take place in an idealized society in the first place, but it's going to absolutely dog every single other incarnation of Star Trek and is something I don't think the franchise ever found a workable answer to.

Here though the idealism and conflict cohabitate perfectly happily. We have a tense situation growing all the more dire, forcing our people to push their improvisation skills to the limit, and we have a guest star who we need to be able to rely on clearly dealing with severe mental pain and anguish making things substantially worse. To top it off, Decker's personal demons also allow us to take another critical look at the world of the Federation, as his particular interpretation of and devotion to his duties as an officer led to the death of the *Constellation* and her crew, almost did the same for the *Enterprise*, and ultimately caused him to sacrifice his life on a fool's gambit he would have had no way of determining would actually be successful. And Shatner absolutely sells Kirk's anguish over Decker's death: Just like in "Operation – Annihilate!", even though we never saw this person before and will never see him again, we totally believe he was an important person to Kirk and we utterly feel and empathize with his sadness at losing him. This one goes one better though, because right after Shatner's big scene as Kirk we also get Leonard Nimoy playing Spock in full-on logic machine Vulcan mode attempting to console his own close friend, and his turbulent mixture of pure rationality and deep compassion is genuinely well done.

Furthermore, that Commodore Decker's arc is basically *Moby-Dick* for *Star Trek* actually fits the structure of "The Doomsday Machine" quite well: It's a transparent plot lift, yes, but that's OK as this episode doesn't need to be a particularly complicated or specialized bit of character development as it really is a thriller first and foremost, and a reasonably good one at that. And anyway, *Moby-Dick* in a sci-fi setting really does seem to be the sort of thing that *Star Trek* in particular amongst its peers is the best suited to doing: The theatrical bombast and overreach is a natural match for the direction people like Gene Coon and William Shatner have been pushing it towards, and it's little wonder Nicholas Meyer will eventually attempt essentially the same tactic in eighteen years or so to massive acclaim. Because of this, we get the second one-episode-wonder iconic character the show's given us in a row: "Amok Time" introduced T'Pau and now "The Doomsday Machine" has

Matt Decker. As histrionic as William Windom has the tendency to be on occasion, his neurotic, obsessive anguish is instantly memorable and leaves an impression. It certainly did on Gene Roddenberry, who introduced Decker's son Will as a major character, Kirk's new executive officer, on *Star Trek Phase II* and *Star Trek: The Motion Picture*. Will himself went on to have his own spiritual successor, one Will Riker, XO of the USS *Enterprise* NCC-1701-D on *Star Trek: The Next Generation*.

Aside from the gravity of Windom's performance, another reason Decker stands out in the memory is that he's a return to the idea of a mythic/mundane contrast Coon introduced in "Metamorphosis" and that the show has pretty much failed to engage with in any meaningful way since. We're not meant to admire Decker for his loyalty and sense of duty, we're meant to pity him for his inability to to handle his guilt and the foolishly rash decisions this causes him to make. As Kirk says "he gave his life so that others could live. I suppose if you have to die that's the best way to go", a true boilerplate Roddenberryism if ever there was one, but what seems to be frequently forgotten is that this comes right after a scene where Kirk passionately and desperately tries to talk Decker out of his suicide run down the maw of the planet killer, imploring him as a friend that no-one should throw their lives away because of an honest mistake, and that he's much more valuable to the fleet alive then dead.

This is a direct callback to and rebuttal of Decker's comment in the opening of the episode about "...the captain going down with the ship? That's what you're supposed to do, isn't it?" (which is largely a myth anyway: Typically if and when this happened it was out of fear about the career repercussions of losing a command, not chivalry. Kirk is right: Losing a highly experienced captain is a blow to any service) and his last words "The commander is responsible for the lives of his crew, and for their deaths. Well, I should have died with mine". In other words, Matt Decker is trying to fulfill his pre-ordained role as the tragic hero in an operatic military epic who goes out in a blaze of glory. Crucially though, Shatner-as-Kirk thinks this is absolutely insane, proving that he's the one with the ability to keep the show grounded in the world of the everyday (albeit the everyday in deep space), finally rising to Coon's most recent challenge.

But then the other shoe has to drop. "The Doomsday Machine" may well be the perfect example of what an average episode of second season-era *Star Trek* should look like, but the problem is that...it's not an average episode at all. We're six weeks into the year and this is the first time the show has actually hit "basically entertaining". This...really isn't a good sign. "The Doomsday Machine" is exceptionally good for *Star Trek*, but it absolutely shouldn't be exceptional in the slightest. The show should be aiming for this baseline of quality every week, and the fact it's not only consistently failing to do this, but is in fact regularly throwing out offensively retrograde and alienating atom bombs of scripts, is a major issue. Apollo isn't gone. He never truly is, the horrific effect his presence had on the series remains, and *Star Trek* faces a continually uphill battle for legitimacy because of it. It's got all the pieces in place, but they're never quite enough to get the show to where it needs to be.

49. "Monsters are real": Wolf in the Fold

Oh goodie, more violence against women. Just another Wednesday then?

At least there's a vaguely defensible reason for it this time, given that "Wolf in the Fold" borrows its basic structure from slasher movies, which is somewhat befitting the third of three *Star Trek* episodes penned by *Psycho* author Robert Bloch. Indeed, this story is once again a straightforward whole plot lift, this time of Bloch's own famous short story "Yours Truly, Jack The Ripper", which posited the titular ripper had somehow managed to attain immortality through his crimes. This episode changes him to an ageless non-corporeal life-form who feeds on fear and death, but the basic premise and themes remain the same. "Wolf in the Fold" thus becomes a very competent and professional execution of this kind of horror story, as one would expect with a writer of Bloch's calbre behind it. That said, I have to twist my own knife a bit here: Merely being in the slasher genre (or proto-slasher, depending on whether or not one wishes to name *Psycho* the *ur* example of its kind) does not, of course, excuse the violence towards women. This one's better then Bloch's previous effort in this regard, but really not by a whole lot and he doesn't make a good case for himself when he opens in an exotic dance parlour clearly designed to cater to straight men, starts picking off women and then gives Spock dialog about how Redjack naturally preys on women because they're more predisposed to extreme fear and terror and are thus more vulnerable then men.

There's also the somewhat troubling matter that *Star Trek* has already shown itself to be bigger than the slasher genre, and in the Gene Roddenberry era no less. The very first episode to air, "The Man Trap", was a complete rejection of this kind of story: Janice Rand and Sulu are shot like nameless slaughter victims, but their big scene involves them eating lunch and talking about plants. Salt Vampire is shot like a slasher villain, but is really a starving animal. Honestly, going from "The Man Trap" to "Wolf in the Fold" is a step back for the show, especially given the former's strength was in making all of its characters feel like likeable, complete people while the latter treats women as helpless passive objects. Sadly though, we should probably expect that given *Star Trek*'s aggravating lack of internal consistency and general self-awareness. That all said though, I don't want to completely go "Who Mourns for Adonais?" on Bloch, mostly because I really, really don't have the energy, but also because Bloch, despite his failings, and he does have several, remains one of the good guys. Anybody who gave us voodoo and alchemy in "Catspaw" clearly has hidden depths and is someone worth taking the time to engage with (will forgive his fascination with H.P. Lovecraft. For now), and "Wolf in the Fold" is a similarly intriguing magickal door if one looks at it a certain way.

The obvious thing to talk about would be Redjack: An ancient being of pure evil who has existed since the dawn of time and thrives on fear, terror and death. He's not quite Love-craftian because he doesn't quite seem like a vast, incomprehensible Eldritch Abomination (in fact Redjack seems downright petulant, given the way he childishly, and frankly rather goofily, taunts Kirk once he takes over the *Enterprise* computer). One would expect Bloch would finally introduce the Old Ones to Star Trek with a lot more gravity, and indeed this is the only one of his three scripts that makes no mention of them. Nevertheless, Redjack does belong to a certain subset of cosmic horror, and the show does seem to treat him accordingly. However, there's a word for this kind of character that we use for stories like this when stripped of their sci-fi genre trappings: "Demon".

I'm not especially fond of demon stories because, aside from their shallow pop Christian connotations (indeed in his novelization for this episode James Blish even has Kirk describe Redjack's appearance as "a vision of Hell"), they seem like a rather cheap cop-out way to deal with horrific acts without actually implicating anyone or dealing with the consequences of violence and death in any real meaningful way. No need to actually reprimand people or change the status quo: Just kick out the demon and everything's fine again. This is facile: Evil is not a thing, it is a kind of action connected to strong, violent emotion. There are no objective beings actually comprised of pure evil who influence innocent mortals, nor is evil a quantifiable, measurable substance that a person has (again, even Roddenberry was up on this: "Dagger of the Mind" is as clear-cut a reaction against this line of thought as exists). This is what we learned from "Who Mourns for Adonais?": Evil is done by people, overwhelmingly more frequently men, who for one reason or another believe their lives, agency and personhood are more valuable than those of others.

Thankfully "Wolf in the Fold"'s mystical connotations neither begin nor end with Redjack himself. Rather, they're a great deal more subtle, more nuanced, more understated and altogether more fascinating than that. Of interest to us here is the Argelian Empath Ceremony, which is partially a seance but also a communal joining of the minds: A kind of large-scale Mind Meld. In other words, it's a spiritual and mental orgy, which is all manner of delightful. Also crucially, before she gets annoyingly and offensively bumped off, Sybo delivers every bit of the critical information Kirk and Spock will need in the climax in order to discern Redjack's true identity: The fact he goes by many different names, feeds on fear and death and cannot himself die. The *Enterprise* crew may dub him an energy-based life form, but he's also (much as I dislike using the term) a demon. This is the same trick Bloch pulled with "Catspaw", where Korob's and Sylvia's powers were both "mental sciences" and magick. This scene is also a microcosm for a theme that is extremely pronounced throughout "Wolf in the Fold", to the point I'd actually call it one of its major concepts, yet seems to be frequently overlooked when this episode is discussed. That is, the high-tech world of starship bureaucracy and that of magic and spiritualism are not actually mutually exclusive, and in fact can benefit a lot from co-operation and exchange of concepts and ideas.

(Indeed one of the best examples of this comes in the climax, when Doctor McCoy purges Redjack from the ship by having everyone on board throw a psychedelic love-in magick ritual with psychedelic hallucinogens and everything. It's far and away one of the raciest scenes in Star Trek history.)

Aside from the entire plot after the Empathic Ceremony really boiling down to one prolonged exercise in proving Sybo unequivocally correct on all counts, there are a lot of moments where each party involved in the case freely contributes some resource of theirs to help the other and the investigation in general, and both Kirk and Minister Jaris are very respectful to each others' worldviews, lifestyle and approach to problem solving. Hengist protests every single time, but, of course, he turns out to be Redjack in the end, so that can be read as a rather stinging indictment. Kirk, naturally, is the most open of his crew to the possibility of a spiritual dimension to the case and even admits to having encountered beings comparable to Redjack on several previous occasions. Wonderfully, the *Enterprise*'s own technology seems to work according to the principles of magick now too: It's really the only way to account for something like the psychoanalytical tricorder, which can reconstruct memories and historical events basically out of nothing, or the ship's computer's newfound ability to essentially read minds in order to determine if someone is lying. In true Star Trek fashion, the joining of minds works according to mystical logic and we get just enough technobabble to paper over the fact everything here is basically magick.

Actually, it's not just Sybo and her ceremony-All of Argelian society is delightful. As Minister Jaris says, the only law is love. It's an entire planet built around empathy and free love to the point it comes dangerously close to being called idyllic, where the only serious violence and strife is brought in from the outside in the form of Redjack. Even better, the show is unequivocally in favour of this, with Kirk praising the Argelians for their hospitality and patience. While he is at first sceptical of things like Sybo's Empathic Ceremony, especially when the life of a member of his crew and a personal friend is on the line, his respect of the Argelians grows throughout the episode as they collaborate on the investigation. This is 180 degrees away from "This Side of Paradise", something that's very much needed at this point in the season and the first clear blueprint for where Star Trek's loyalties and philosophy *ought* to be placed.

Argelius was also responsible for a particularly memorable behind-the-scenes anecdote from this episode: It seems when Kirk, Scott and McCoy were in the bar in the teaser, their drinks were meant to be comprised of multicoloured layers. As they drank each layer, it would cause them to experience a different unique emotion. The network censors cut this scene from the episode however, deeming it "too complicated" for viewers to understand and expressing concern people might think the crew were on drugs. This caused Gene Coon to tell the censors to their faces that they were "full of horseshit", which is why in spite of everything we still love Gene Coon. The censors' objections are even more patently ridiculous in light of the fact McCoy's solution to containing Redjack is *to get the entire crew high on prescription drugs*. It's truly one of the most remarkable moments in Star Trek history: The way to stop from turning evil is to sink into the embrace of the entheodelic. Perfect.

Of course I'd be remiss if I didn't talk about the acting, in particular James Doohan. This is one of the few times an entire episode gets devoted to Scotty, and Doohan leaps at the opportunity to show what he's capable of. As friend and colleague Adam Riggio pointed out in the comments for the "Catspaw" entry on the blog version of this project, Doohan's greatest strength was arguably his ability to make his character immensely and immediately sympathetic. The fact Scotty, unlike Chekov, isn't remembered as the borderline offensive cartoonish stereotype he was clearly conceived as is entirely due to Doohan's performance. Under him, Scotty is completely down to Earth, charismatic, relatable and friendly. We want to like Scotty and don't want to see anything bad happen to him, which is why making him the prime suspect in the murder investigation for so long such an evil genius move. No matter how much circumstantial evidence gets stacked against him, we simply do not want to accept he's capable of doing these things-It's inconceivable to us. It's not only fair to see Scotty as the blueprint for someone like Miles O'Brien, but it's also reasonable to read "Wolf in the Fold" as the blueprint for the altogether too numerous and increasingly incredulous "torture O'Brien" episodes that become a hallmark of *Star Trek: Dominion Wars* under Ira Steven Behr.

But Doohan's is not the only marquee performance here: I've spent a lot of time already on Shatner-as-Kirk, who really is properly excellent here. I mean he typically always is, but it's so refreshing to see him so open to and respective of the culture and customs of people like the Argelians, and his very obviously bored demeanour in the club with the exotic dancers in the teaser is just delightful. He can talk big all he wants about the women in the "little place he knows", but his actions speak louder than words, so to speak. DeForest Kelley too is in fine form, this being the rare occasion where he's allowed to step out of the "bristling unchecked passion" mode he's become pigeonholed in, making McCoy for the first time in awhile reminiscent of the straightforward, wise elderly doctor his character was originally supposed to be. While Leonard Nimoy doesn't get as many scenes in this episode as he has recently, he is as as predictably cool and complex as always, and while it might be just me, he seems to have developed or fine-tuned a subtle commanding presence and quiet dignity since "Amok Time" that makes all his scenes stand out. Nichelle Nichols, by contrast, makes her second consecutive no-show of the season, which is sadly to be expected by this point.

But the most important legacy of this episode, and one we maybe have Robert Bloch to thank for, is for providing proof that Star Trek and go better places and do bigger things than its square-jawed Hard SF/Pulp sci-fi origins would lead us to believe. Star Trek's most lasting strength is its ability to visibly push against the boundaries of science fiction to grasp at something more profound, universal and inspirational on a mass populist scale, and "Wolf in the Fold" is an early example of how it can actually do these things in spite of itself. It's not a perfect execution, but Star Trek is not perfect and can never be. Sometimes oversignification is all we can ask for, but sometimes oversignification is enough.

50. "I am error.": The Changeling

I will admit it's very tempting, given my predilections and areas of interests to grab hold of Kirk's line about faery changeling babies that gives this episode its title, run with it and come up with some delightfully overblown reading of this one within the context of the Otherworld and ancient European pagan mythology. Sadly, however, the analogy doesn't really work: *Nomad* doesn't actually act much at all like a proper changeling, Star Trek doesn't quite get a handle on the magickal doors between realms thing for another 25 years or so and when it eventually does this isn't the primary story that will facilitate that transformation. This is not the Original Series' cup of tea.

However, Gene Roddenberry seemed to have a fixation on the story of a robot built by humans who goes away on a journey, experiences a profound transformation, attains great power and returns seeking its creator, reusing it a number of times over his career. It was the subject of a failed 1974 pilot for a prospective television series co-created with Gene Coon called *The Questor Tapes* and also served as the basic plot for "In Thy Image", the pilot episode of *Star Trek Phase II*, which eventually underwent its own profound transformation into *Star Trek: The Motion Picture*. Not to mention *Star Trek: The Next Generation*, where in the earliest episode Data's own creator and "point of origin" are a mystery to us. This then is the first draft of a story that is apparently very important to Roddenberry, so we should take a look at what he may have intended to say with it and what it might reveal about him as a writer and a thinker.

Me being me, I'm once again predisposed to snap back onto the magickal interpretation: The robot's journey could be seen as a spiritual one, and the years spent travelling the expanses of outer space and acquiring power and knowledge might be seen as attaining a form of enlightenment. I'm not sure this reading holds though, because in every version of this story the robot is portrayed as extremely deficient in some areas, despite its massive power and intelligence, and its yearning to discover its creator seems at once a primary calling and a microcosm of its inability to gain a complete understanding of the universe and its place within it. There's certainly at least a pop spiritualism to this, and one Roddenberry himself would probably acknowledge. But quite frankly I don't think he put any more thought into it than that.

Perhaps something could be made out of how, in "The Changeling", *Nomad* literally brings Scotty back from the dead, tying into the mythic reorientation that has played a part in several episodes this year. It has the trappings of a god, as only gods can do things like that, but it remains a dangerous, ignorant machine that requires real people to explain the proper way to behave in human culture. We could extrapolate this to a sort of claim that this is why humans are preferable to gods, as a god by definition will disrupt human life to a degree that would be unacceptable. As this episode doesn't really have any other mythical signifiers though (except for that not-entirely-accurate bit about faeries and changelings), I'm not particularly in favour of this reading either. No, what this entire pot seems more like is a straightforward metaphor for what Gene Roddenberry probably saw humans to be like: Flawed, imperfect beings who are constantly growing and learning and who are motivated to find their own "creator", no matter what their individual interpretation of that concept might be.

This is also, once again, quite Christian. If not outright a Biblical allegory (although Roddenberry was known to describe Star Trek stories as "mini Biblical tales" in private), it's that kind of populist secularism that's really just Christianity with the serial numbers filed off by virtue of what it inherits from hegemonic culture. The journey through the stars read as a search for our origins and ultimate destiny which must be definition be big, objective singular Things because Big Questions need Big Answers. What flags this as Christian, or at least Abrahamic, rather than some other kind of spirituality (aside from the obvious fact the robot's human creators are clearly meant to stand in for a patriarchal Creator God) is the idea of an objective, external Truth, either about ourselves, about the universe at large or both, that we can discover on our journey, which is referred to by default as God. Other faiths and spiritualities would tend to conceive of god as either something that's a part of everything and everyone, or of gods that are highly personalized and subject to constant variation and reinterpretation, oftentimes that are strongly connected to the idea of day-to-day life.

Along with this are imperialist connotations in varying degrees of subtlety as this kind of journey is an intensely self-absorbed one: We're not Seeking Out New Life And New Civilizations to exchange our ideas and experience different ideas and different ways of living in the interests of cosmopolitanism, we're doing it to learn more about ourselves and teach what we've learned to the people we run into. We either need to seek out people who know The Truth so they can tell us what it is so we know the "proper" things to believe, or we know it and have an obligation to teach it to everybody else. This isn't the language of travellers, this is the language of missionaries, colonialists and conquerors. It's perhaps fitting then this becomes the story Roddenberry latches on to and seems to feel is the definitive embodiment of Star Trek, as evidenced by its inclusion in two extremely high-profile, high-stakes Trek projects.

Which makes it all the more bizarre, and all the more telling, that "The Changeling" wasn't written by Gene Roddenberry at all. Roddenberry, in fact, had nothing to do with it: This is the work of future *Six Million Dollar Man* producer John Meredyth Lucas, who we'll be seeing again at the other end of the season when he starts taking turns in the day-to-day producer role on *Star Trek* with Gene Coon. As a result, the lonely-robot-goes-on-a-journey-theme is more downplayed here than it will be in the various reinterpretations of it Roddenberry will eventually oversee, though the idea is clearly Lucas'. What "The Changeling" instead seems to focus more on is the idea of scrambled orders and what a hyper-intelligent machine like *Nomad* would do if it "went wrong". This naturally means it's time for another stellar display of the signature technique of the James T. Kirk School of

Computer Repair: Blowing things up by shouting logic paradoxes at them. Disappointingly, this is less dramatic than in "The Return of the Archons", because *Nomad* had already programmed itself to destroy anything it deemed imperfect, and all Kirk had to do was convince it that it itself was an imperfect being, thus triggering its destruct sequence (though it does result in one of the altogether finest scenes in the season so far, where Kirk explains to Spock about the autodestruct mechanism right after activating it, to which Spock replies delightfully sarcastically through clenched teeth "Very astute observation, Captain. We are in grave danger.").

What this also results in is an old-fashioned logic versus emotions debate that would have been right at home in the first season. This one seems to side broadly with logic, as even though *Nomad*'s strict adherence to its programming, damaged and corrupt as its memory banks may be, puts the entire ship in peril, Spock clearly empathizes with it to an extent, or at least understands it. Likewise, *Nomad* considers Spock "different" because his "programming" is "neat and ordered". In the end, Kirk manages to outwit it, but only through logic and only after making the situation significantly worse for everyone by revealing to *Nomad* he was a "biological unit", something *Nomad* had considered inherently inferior. Predictably, this means the characters of Kirk, Spock and McCoy are slotted into the programmatic roles we would expect them to have in this kind of story, and the actors respond accordingly. DeForest Kelley is, as usual, the most obvious of the three, trading in the tender nuance he was so deft at conveying in "Wolf in the Fold" for generic Bristling Unchecked Passion mode. William Shatner, likewise, goes back to Commanding Swagger and Leonard Nimoy to Cool Detachment.

There is also the now-depressingly-requisite belittling sexist scene, and this one happens to stumble into racism again to boot. After hearing Uhura sing over the the comm panel and tracking her down on the bridge, *Nomad* completely erases Uhura's memory because it found her singing irrational and inexplicable (and before that, she was back to gamely playing the part she was told to play: The single most stereotypical secretary character imaginable). Unlike Scotty, Uhura doesn't get a reset button handwave, and the episode ends with Doctor McCoy and Nurse Chapel re-educating her up to the college level. Apparently this is supposed to be a happy ending, though I guess this means all of Uhura's memories and life experiences are gone now. But who cares? It's only rote, objective facts that matter, right?

Arch-rationalists and Church of Science evangelists can go fuck themselves.

This entire sequence was completely gratuitous and unnecessary: The death and resurrection of Scott was sufficient evidence of *Nomad*'s power and scrambled priorities-Wiping Uhura's memory is just mean spirited, and the scenes of Chapel in kindly white saviour mode teaching her how to spell "cat" in sickbay are unwatchable. Why did Uhura of all people have to get wiped? Why didn't Nichelle Nichols or, hell, *anybody* speak out about or see the ludicrously problematic undertones this opens the entire show up to? Just as is the case every time I mention Uhura, I have to point out her mere presence on the show was apparently seen as enough to gain *Star Trek* its progressive reputation. But I maintain, isn't it possible to hope for more, even in 1967?

When I originally wrote this, a big debate about the representation of women, especially women of colour, in video games (another area of study for me) was just starting to get mainstream attention. There was an argument people looking for characters of this type in video games should be happy with whatever they get, no matter how minimal a role she plays or how problematic her depiction might be in other areas, and if they're unhappy they're just being picky and it's their fault if they never get any more such characters because that one game that had that one character didn't do well. It would seem beggars can't be choosers when it comes to representation in video games.

I've seen this argument crop up numerous times in the discourse surrounding pretty much every other medium as well, but video games were on my mind at the time. And to paraphrase one prominent critic of the controversy I had recently read, "this is sort of like walking into a deli, ordering a sandwich and having the cashier roll his eyes in exasperation and throw a loaf of bread and a slice of cheese at you. Yes, this is technically what I asked for, but is it really too much to ask that a little more effort be put into the process?". I could say much the same about Uhura and the discourse surrounding Star Trek's own much-vaunted "representation".

What "The Changeling" is then is a microcosm for the show in its second season so far. It has some truly provocative and entertaining moments that help set the stage for the direction the franchise will go in its future, but it's ultimately brought down by a staggeringly catastrophic lapse in judgment that leaves a really unpleasant aftertaste, and a lingering sense of fear that the entire thing is destined to one day, and sooner rather than later, blow up in its face.

51. "The Devil You Know": The Apple

"The Apple" was the episode of the Original Series that always stuck out in my mind as the one I unequivocally hated. Most of the time an episode being forgettable is a cause for concern when doing this kind of revisit and retrospective, but this is a case where the story made me so angry I never forgot it and I would constantly bring it up in discussions as Exhibit A for why I could never get into this show. It's good to have reassurance that my critical faculties were still recognisably well-founded back then.

"The Apple" is Biblically awful. That it's not even the worst episode of the season should explain in no uncertain terms how bad things are for *Star Trek* right now and how questionable this show's legacy really deserves to be. It is shockingly racist and imperialistic, with naive, simple, primitive people modeled on Pacific islanders in funny skin colours and outfits in a cargo cult setup being told how to live their lives by educated white people from space. It believes quite strongly in a teleological view of history and cultural development, where all societies have to follow a pre-determined and unwavering master narrative where Western cultures are seen as more advanced then non-Western cultures (despite the idyllic, childlike lifestyles they have), basically making this the Space Age *White Man's Burden*, except that poem was at least well constructed. It is pop Christian, being a straight-up plot lift of the book of Genesis. It is unoriginally pop Christian, shamelessly recycling all the worst aspects of "The Return of the Archons" and "This Side of Paradise" and somehow managing to actually still be worse than both of them combined. It is also *textually* racist: Kirk and McCoy talk down to Spock throughout the entire episode, making fun of his green blood, logical mind and resemblance to Satan.

It is misogynistic, with yet another wistful, pouty yeoman fretting about needing someone to protect her (albeit one who at least gets to hold her own in a fight scene this time). It is proudly and boldly heteronormative, conflating love, procreative sex and heterosexual relationships. It has an appallingly lax attitude towards life and death, casually killing off enough redshirts to the point it makes *Doctor Who*'s body count look conservative. Aside from being a bigot, Kirk is once again written as a gruff, shouty military commander having a psychological meltdown over regulations and taking it out on his crew. Chekov gets another grating "Russia is the greatest country in the universe" scene and is a full-on cartoon stereotype. Even Spock, the most sympathetic person in this episode by virtue of voicing the self-evidently correct course of action (which the rest of the show helpfully belittles him for) is made to look like a complete idiot by getting carelessly and dumbly injured once an act. There is not a single likable character in this entire production. The pacing is sluggish which, combined with the excruciatingly terrible story, has the combined effect of making this feel like the longest fifty minutes ever put to film. Naturally, it's a fan-favourite episode, because this project is my own personal self-imposed Hell.

I could carry on in this manner, but, as liberating and cathartic as it might be for me to finally be allowed to lay into "The Apple", it strikes me as ultimately less than productive. Therefore, I am informally dubbing the rest of this chapter "The Revenge of Carolyn Palamas" and dedicating it to taking this episode to task from a cultural anthropological perspective. It may still be too easy, but the alternative is taking Warren Ellis' writing advice, which I don't want to write and you don't want to read. In this regard, the first thing to take note of are the People of Vaal, or, to be more precise, the *Enterprise* crew's reaction to the people of Vaal. Due to the part of the plot "The Apple" lifts from "This Side of Paradise", we once again have a culture where want and strife do not exist being described as both paradise as well as "stagnant" and "unnatural" because it lacks the Western, Modernist conception of progress (Extra Credit: Go ahead and try to reconcile that with the world of *Star Trek: The Next Generation*, supposedly also Gene Roddenberry's idea). In true *Star Trek* fashion, we have Captain Kirk coming and *literally* blowing everything the fuck up.

Anyway, the point here for our purposes here is the idea this kind of idyllic lifestyle is stagnant (having more or less sorted the reactionary business with "This Side of Paradise"). Yes, there is the fact the People of Vaal are ruled by a giant, vaguely explained authoritarian computer (which would allow me to redeem "The Apple" from an anarchist perspective), but this isn't actually Kirk and McCoy's objection here. Both expressly state on a number of occasions the problem with this society is that it doesn't "progress" *not* that it takes orders from a machine. The supposed stagnation is very clearly the script's problem with the People of Vaal, and the source of said stagnation is considered purely incidental. Spock points out that this system works and everyone is happy and healthy, and he is obviously in the right, but the show doesn't want us to side with him. There's Vaal's prohibition of romance and physical affection to consider, and some have tried to use this as way to read some free love theme into this episode, but this is also obviously an afterthought: The lack of procreation and children is meant to be another manifestation of the society's lack of growth, not an indictment of oppressive anti-sex cultural mores, and indeed the entire episode can be seen as retrograde and reactionary in terms of sexuality because the *Enterprise* only values "doing what comes naturally" as a means to an end to produce offspring and keep society growing.

Far from advocating some 1960s egalitarian free-love societal ideal, Star Trek, like all Westernism, is (to crib from Lee Edelman) the product of reproductive futurism.

What this means is that "The Apple" is squarely in the intellectual tradition of the Modernization theory of international development. Dating back to the core Enlightenment-era Idea of Progress itself (though most associated with and active during the mid-20th century), Modernization theory is the belief that "underdeveloped" (non-Western) societies can be brought up to the level of "developed" (Western) societies by taking the exact same economic and political steps the latter group did, and proponents of the theory furthermore claim to be able to quantify and isolate objective variables that contribute to social progress. Indeed, it is literally the origin of the idea of "development" in the sociological sense. As one would expect anything coming out of Europe during the 18th century, Modernization theory is unambiguously Scientist, rationalistic and imperialistic, and essentially every aspect of contemporary Western Neo-Imperialist economic and geopolitical policy can be traced back to it in one form or another. Crucially, however, those who hold to Modernization theory believe strongly in the idea of growth and progress through new technology and policies as well as a firm break with tradition (which does nothing but hold societies back) and that this is to be valued and stressed almost above all else. This is exactly what "The Apple" is about and is absolutely central to its entire philosophical outlook.

Modernization theory, it should go without saying, doesn't work, and just about every attempt to apply it to places that aren't contemporary Europe and the United States have ended in spectacular failure and a criminal level of injustice and human rights violations. The obvious anthropological explanation as to why is the same reason no other theory of international development works either: It's self-evidently stupid to try applying a blanket box of policies to every single culture in the world assuming it's going to work the same everywhere because each group of people has a unique set of experiences, challenges and needs. The actually sane, considerate way to approach solving global issues is to, you know, ask people what they need and listen to what they have to say while also making case-by-case, highly cultural contexualized on-the-ground observations of your own thus resulting in a sharing of positionalities and specialized expertise. But that approach requires cultural anthropologists (or at least people who have an appreciation for that sort of way of thinking), and, as is well known, humanities scholars are all lazy, pretentious, good-for-nothing trust fund parasites with no practical skills, and furthermore we're all uppity bitches who just need a good, hard dicking.

But there's another reason Modernization theory in particular doesn't work, and it's the same reason (or at least one reason at any rate) all the so-called "developed" and "advanced" Western societies are, as of this writing, each undergoing some manner of spectacularly grotesque systemic collapse: The idea of "social growth" (which, being a Western concept, is inexorably bound up with economics) and the notion it must be permanent, steady and infinite, is a particularly dangerous myth. It's simply not possible to maintain a continuous state of "growth" the way Western societies conceptualize it, especially not with factors such as ever-increasingly rampant inequality and the looming climate change crisis that modern society will be unable to adapt to and that will eventually destroy it. Furthermore, there is also mounting evidence constant economic "growth" really doesn't contribute much to the well-being of a society at all. Pretty much any economist will tell you this, not that anybody is actually listening to them of course.

Aside from the economic imperialism concerns, the other big anthropological bugbear I have with "The Apple" is the Prime Directive. Back in the "Return of the Archons" post I mentioned there are two episodes in this season that deal overtly with the ethics of the Prime Directive, and this is the big one. There are two conflicting lines of thought to be had here and, amazingly, this episode manages to come out in the wrong in both of them. The first is the basic idea of the Prime Directive itself: Simply put, it makes no sense from any conceivable perspective. From a purely narrative standpoint, it seems...counterintuitive, to put it mildly, to have a show built around going to a new place every week and laying down some heavy-handed moralizing while also having a primary facet of the show's setting designed to prevent you from doing exactly that. If it's supposed to add drama to the show by forcing some navel-gazing over whether or not to go against regulations and whether or not Kirk, Spock and McCoy know better than Starfleet Command, this doesn't work because of course Kirk, Spock and McCoy know better than Starfleet Command. That's been a default given since the concept was introduced.

But this is just structural quibbling: The real problem I have with the Prime Directive is that it is a fundamentally unattainable ideal. Gene Roddenberry liked to wheel out the Prime Directive as a key example of how evolved, utopian and sophisticated the Federation is, but he was patently talking rubbish. Aside from the fact that every single Prime Directive story in the entirety of Star Trek is *not* about how great and wonderful an idea it is but rather 50 minutes of angsting over how it constrains the crew from Doing The Right Thing, the fact remains even if it *were* a good idea there is no way for the crew to actually uphold it unless they never contact another culture ever. See, one of the tenets of postmodern anthropology is that the presence of the anthropologist by definition permanently and irreparably changes the status quo and defines the relationship the anthropologist has with the contacts. It goes without saying that a group of people are going to act differently and change their behaviour when there's some weirdo from another country (or planet) lurking around their village in khakis and a sun hat brandishing a notebook and asking strange questions. There is no actual way to get an objective, unbiased record of everyday life from an outsider's perspective and objectivity doesn't even exist anyway: It's only possible to write down things you notice and what people tell you and draw your own inferences. Even in an idealized future this would be impossible. People simply do not work that way.

The other reading of the Prime Directive of "non-interference" is that it's in place to prevent, well, things like Modernization theory. The imperialist notion that a supposedly "advanced" or "developed" society can waltz into another society it considers "less advanced" or "primitive" and *deliberately* impose their own ideas of how to live and what choices they make. If this is what the Prime Directive is meant to prevent Starfleet from doing, then Gene Roddenberry was a bloody hypocrite, because from the very beginning his crew is tossing it out without a second thought and deciding that no, they really *do* have the right to say exactly how a society should act and to force it down the exact same path the Federation took. Imperialism disguised as anti-imperialism: I have to admit that's pretty brazen. Now, take this argument, change the character names and episode titles around and transplant it to every single other Prime Directive story Star Trek ever does. It's a fundamental failing in the philosophy of the franchise that will continue to do nothing but hold it back for the rest of its life.

There are ways Star Trek can handle multiculturalism and cosmopolitanism without resorting to something like the Prime Directive. However, it involves treating people as equals by default and actually listening to their perspectives on issues and life experiences, and none of these are things "The Apple" is interested in. It latches onto the worst, most dangerous aspects of both the morality play and utopian conceptions of the franchise and

227

declares itself Philosopher King. This is the show displaying its true horrible colours for all to see, proudly landing a backflip into ugly racism and socioeconomic Neo-Imperialism. It may not be flat-out worse than something like "Who Mourns for Adonais?", but at least that episode had an intriguing meta-narrative running throughout it. Perhaps "The Apple" isn't the worst episode of Star Trek ever, perhaps not even the worst we've seen so far, but it may well be the least Vaka Rangi the franchise will ever be.

But then again, perhaps Star Trek doesn't deserve a place at the navigator's table at all.

52. "The Revolution Will Not Be Televised": Mirror, Mirror

Then again, this one is absolutely brilliant.

Impressively, *Star Trek* takes a hard swerve from one of its worst episodes ever to one of its best. "Mirror, Mirror" is just about flawless: I always knew it was good, but it's actually better than I remember, and it couldn't have come at a better time. Between this and "The Apple" we have, and I'm not exaggerating, two polar opposite philosophical viewpoints being expressed. Probably nowhere else have I seen a television show put stories 180 degrees away from each other *one after another*. "Mirror, Mirror" honestly does not feel like it's part of the same show as "The Apple", it's that far removed from it. The most minor of nitpicks hold it back from absolute perfection, although I will confess I'm saying this in part so I don't have to totally reconceptualize the post I have lined up for the episode I want to call the second season's high water mark. Either way though, "Mirror, Mirror" is the bold and clear statement we've been waiting for all year, and it not only just about singlehandedly saves Star Trek from the scrap heap, it finally gives it the moral, ethical and political backbone that will make the franchise a legend.

The first thing that begs addressing is the Mirror Universe itself. From what I can gather, this episode is one of the earliest appearances of the idea of a "mirror" or "parallel" universe in mainstream pop fiction. While not the absolute first (at the very least *Star Trek* beat itself to its own punch with "The Alternative Factor" last year, but nobody except me likes to talk about "The Alternative Factor") it's arguably the most famous though, as the style of alternate reality *Star Trek* works with here becomes the model for an incalculable number of homages, parodies and imitators. However, what these followers (including, irritatingly, more than a few future Star Trek works to return to the Mirror Universe) crucially seem to miss about "Mirror, Mirror" is that the reality it postulates is manifestly *not* meant to be simply the one where everyone is bearded and evil. The Terran Empire is not the Evil!Federation, its instead very clearly meant to be a version of the Federation that's largely the same as our own, except for the fact certain motifs and excesses have been been built on to alarming and dangerous degrees.

This is stressed and reiterated numerous times throughout the episode. Upon arriving on the ISS *Enterprise* for the first time, Kirk and McCoy observe that everything is largely where it should be, and Scotty says the ship is on a technical level identical to their own, and even the star groups are in their correct respective locations. But the real evidence comes from the characters themselves: While Chekov's and Sulu's counterparts are twisted and demented psychopaths (with both Walter Koenig and George Takei very clearly relishing the opportunity to play against type-This is in many ways an actor showcase episode for them) the Mirror Spock, as well as the Mirror counterparts of the away team and (it's implied) our version of Marlena Moreau, are obviously meant to be comparable.

This is the clearest with Leonard Nimoy, who, in a truly delightful acting turn, plays the Mirror Spock just as logical, loyal and principled as his double in the regular universe. The only things that really separate the two Spocks are their circumstances and the way in which they apply their logic and loyalty: Mirror Spock is very much what would happen if Spock lived as part of a ruthless empire, but he's still Spock, and this is what ultimately saves the displaced landing party in the climax. Nimoy's performance is so grand it's rightly become the model for all of the best portrayals of Mirror Star Trek characters since, with both Nana Visitor and Terry Farrell, well, *mirroring* Nimoy in the way they conceive of Intendant Kira Nerys and Captain Jadzia Dax, respectively, in *Star Trek: Deep Space Nine*'s Mirror Universe stories.

What this means is that "Mirror, Mirror" is in truth possibly the most brazenly and straightforwardly anti-imperialist and self-critical *Star Trek* ever got. This is not an action-packed romp where Our Heroes face off against their Evil Twins from the Other Side, it's a cautionary introspective piece that takes a hard look at what the Federation really is, what it truly stands for and what might happen if it remains unchecked. In this regard, "Mirror, Mirror" is the complete inverse of both "Space Seed" and "The Enemy Within": It's drawing a very clear path to where the Federation will end up, and it wants us to be very uncomfortable because of this. The key signposts are the Halkans, who are incredibly sceptical of the Federation's motives. In the teaser they express concern that their strict adherence to a policy of total pacifism prevents them from signing mining rights with the Federation, and flatly state this is unlikely to change. Crucially, they're the one thing most obviously unchanged in the Mirror Universe, and they make an argument to the crew of the ISS *Enterprise* that's about 99% identical, down to their observation the ship has the capability to sterilize their planet and they would be unable to stop it. The only difference between the two universes in this regard is that in the Mirror Universe, the crew pushes the button (or at least has standing orders to) and in ours they don't. Also, I'm not sure whether or not this was an intentional callback, but Mirror Marlena referring to Kirk (or, rather, who she thinks is Mirror Kirk) as "Caesar" is a powerful statement. That's the subtle, lurking horror here: That the Federation could become the Terran Empire at the drop of a hat.

Part and parcel of this holding up of a mirror to *Star Trek*'s ethics is, laudably, a very clear, decisive and scathing reaction against the show's ugly misogynistic tendencies. Mirror Sulu is shown to be (and Mirror Kirk is implied to be) a callous, dominating, abusive male supremacist, and a vital moment in the episode that does much to remind us why our version of these characters are heroes, is Kirk going out of his way to show he respects Mirror Marlena and reminding her she has agency and personhood and that she can achieve anything she wants to in life. It's telling one of Mirror Kirk's signatures is his ability to take whatever he wants by any means he sees fit, and this is revealed during the same scene where Kirk and Mirror Marlena start to fall in love because they respect and admire each other (indeed I remember finding this scene so effective that of all the dalliances Kirk had throughout the Original Series, his relationship with Marlena Moreau was the one I really hoped and wished had stuck). Words cannot describe how refreshing and necessary this scene is, especially after the misogynistic nightmare this season has been. Uhura too is in rare form, being treated as a crucial member of the landing party whose special expertise is needed to help return them home, as well as holding her own in a few fight scenes and, memorably, using Mirror Sulu's blind lust and rape culture against him to give Scotty and McCoy the time they need to rig up the energy transfer without him noticing.

If that wasn't clear enough, there's the moment just after the confrontation in sickbay that really drives home the difference between the Mirror Universe and ours: Mirror Spock's coercive Mind Meld with McCoy to extract information. Given the reading we've been building of the Mind Meld's symbolism, what this act is meant to represent should be rather obvious. Unlike what we got a few weeks ago, however, this time the camera holds the shot with Mirror Spock and McCoy centred in the frame throughout the duration, making us focus on the act itself and what it is, instead of leeringly drooling over the perpetrator's dominance and the victim's pain and horror. Although an argument could be raised it remains sexist to portray male-on-male rape matter-of-factually while gawking over male-on-female rape, and this is absolutely true, I think the more helpful way to read this is that it makes clear to straight male audiences how horrifying rape really is. In removing the patriarchally sexualized aspect by making both parties male, not to mention the shock of having the perpetrator be a version of a character we like and admire (who, given the other themes "Mirror, Mirror" works with, is disturbingly not too far removed from our Spock), it reminds us institutionalized rape is very much something that can exist within the structure of the Federation, and drives home the heinous power structures and violations of trust inherent in rape culture for people who probably wouldn't have gotten it otherwise. Perhaps a Mirror Universe version of "Who Mourns for Adonias?" then, where that episode's casual and glib approach to rape is revealed as the horrific and shocking ethical failure it always was.

This all comes to a head in the denouement, where Kirk risks missing the window to return to his universe so he can implore Mirror Spock to become a force for change in the Mirror Universe. This is itself a reflection of Bones similarly racing against the clock to keep Mirror Spock alive in sickbay, which helps convince Mirror Marlena to assist the landing party in their escape. This scene just crackles with energy, with Kirk's and Mirror Spock's philosophical debate about change and revolution set against the backdrop of another nail-biting thriller-style countdown. What's the most remarkable about this though is that both Kirk and Mirror Spock are correct: Kirk in the sense that, idealistically and conceptually, revolution can begin with one visionary person with a desire to change the present, and Mirror Spock with the rebuttal that it is impossible for that same person to singlehandedly change the future and that revolutionaries need allies, support, power and voice to truly make a difference. With this, "Mirror, Mirror" addresses both horns of the anarchist dilemma: The idea "the political is personal" and that individual expression is enough to inspire change contrasted with the concept that material social progress more often than not needs to come about through communal action. What "Mirror, Mirror" is declaring then is that these are not actually mutually contradictory notions, and both are necessary to bring about real action. Furthermore, this one scene is a veritable quote generator, throwing out at least four of the best lines in the whole Original Series:

> "You're a man of integrity in both universes, Mister Spock."

> "I submit to you that your Empire is illogical because it cannot endure. I submit that you are illogical to be a willing part of it."

> "One man cannot summon the future." "But one man can change the present."

> "In every revolution, there's one man with a vision."

This is also the moment that finally turns the tables on Gene Roddenberry's Two-Fisted Morality approach to Star Trek and takes it as far as it can possibly go: Kirk shows up to deliver a lesson...to the Federation. On top of this, he doesn't beam down from On High and tell people what to think and how to behave, he tries to incite a revolution by acting in accordance with his beliefs and talking to people in hopes they'll take action not for him or because he knows better, but because they're people and have a right to their own agency. This not only blows "The Apple" out of the water, it's better than "The Return of the Archons" too, because "Mirror, Mirror" doesn't deal with abstract conceptualizations of authority or bureaucracy, but rather focuses quite clearly on how imperialism and dehumanizing systems and power structures actually manifest, albeit exaggerated to an appropriately unsettling degree.

"Mirror, Mirror" changes the game for Star Trek at a fundamental level. However, much like Kirk's attempt to incite an uprising in the Mirror Universe, it ultimately only lays the groundwork, and, just as the fate of the Terran Empire and Mirror Spock remains uncertain, the series still has to prove it's capable of continuing on this path. For one thing the ending of the episode is a bit of a cop-out: Not the technobabble way of crossing the gulf between universes (that's suitably and appropriately papered over because it isn't actually important to anything), but the final scene on our *Enterprise* where Kirk, Spock and McCoy throw speciesist slurs at each other. It's irritatingly glib and not at all necessary and jars noticeably with the rest of the episode. While it is nice to see Spock get in some jabs of his own instead of just stoically taking the abuse (I suppose if we have to have vaguely racist banter, it's slightly better that victims strike back with loaded language of their own), what he actually comes up with trends dangerously close to nihilism. He mentions it was refreshing to witness the behaviour of the Mirror counterparts of Kirk, McCoy, Uhura and Scotty because they were purely and honestly human. If the point of "Mirror, Mirror" is a call to arms against institutionalized oppression and a paean to human dignity, this is a particularly effective way to scuttle your message, especially coming from Spock.

But the big question left at the end of "Mirror, Mirror" is whether or not the lessons of the Mirror Universe will stick. We can blast off with our *Enterprise* on our way to our next adventure comforted by the thought we're not like those scary bad Mirror Universe people, but there's still the lingering concern our universe could very easily go down that same path. Can Kirk and the *Enterprise* continue to be the change the want to see, and that they need to be, in this universe as well? That remains to be seen.

53. "Galloping around the cosmos is a game for the young": The Deadly Years

OK, it's pretty terrible.

Yeah, "The Deadly Years" kinda sucks. Unfortunately from my perspective, it's bad in ways that are obvious and not especially interesting to talk about (and this is far from the last time this will happen during this project). It's blatantly ageist, going into a rather frightening level of detail about how funny doddering senile old people are and how they're of no use to anyone and need to get out of the way to make room for younger, more virile people. Trying to redeem this as a tragic story about the effects of growing old is putting more thought into the premise than the people responsible for it did. If it's sad, it's only sad in a "we need to take the car keys away from grandma and put her in a home" sort of way not a "the way we treat the elderly in our society is monstrous" sort of way.

On the other hand, trying to read this as a statement about youth culture vs. hegemony also runs into problems, as there simply doesn't seem to be any real support for that reading, especially given as it's our heroes who are afflicted, and the script seems on the whole more interested in bemoaning the physical effects of age and the *idea* of youthfulness, not so much youth *culture*, and eventually gives us a glib, tacked-on handwave of a conclusion about "the right man" (and of course it has to be a man) in command of a situation, but that's about as effective as any of *Star Trek*'s denouements are (read: not in the slightest).

It is also full of the expected casual sexism. The first Yeoman-of-the-Week promptly dies midway through the episode for plot convenience, though McCoy tosses out something that sounds suspiciously like "she lost the will to live" (yes, I know it was supposed to be her metabolism. No, that doesn't count). Janet Wallace is very clearly only there to be Kirk's Desilu-mandated Love Interest for this episode, most of her dialog is recycled wholesale and verbatim from other such characters from previous episodes and she's only invested in the plot because she still has a crush on Kirk (to the point the other characters actually comment on this, so minor points for the show's growing awareness of its own tropes, I suppose). At least her expertise in endocrinology contributes to the final resolution, but McCoy obviously would have gotten there eventually, and in time, without her help. It's also unfortunate Wallace's actor, Sarah Marshall delivers, well, kind of a crap performance. She's about the most stilted and monotone guest star we've seen on the show yet.

In fact, this is a changeable week for the actors in general. William Shatner plays Old!Kirk as basically Mr. Magoo, James Doohan just does "tired" and is barely in this episode anyway

234

while Walter Koenig and George Takei give likable and multifaceted turns as Chekov and Sulu whenever they get the chance, but they're always good at this. The only people seeming to be actually trying here are Leonard Nimoy, whose aged Spock is predictably complex and nuanced, and DeForest Kelley, who, because was hired to be "Old and Wise" anyway, just dials down on that and accentuates McCoy's cantankerousness. Actually, Kelley is so good at this it takes some of the ageist edge off "The Deadly Years": McCoy is clearly just as competent elderly as he is at his regular age and barely changed, except for being a bit slower and less patient.

We also get another fish-out-of-water flag officer, and "The Deadly Years" is just about the most generic "bureaucrats are pampered, paper-pushing desk jockeys who know nothing about *real* life out in the field" chest-thumping, libertarian rant yet (indeed I'm actually paraphrasing one of Old!Kirk's actual lines in the episode with this sentence). At least Charles Drake's Commodore Stocker is deeply sympathetic, expressing great concern for a ship and crew he looks up to and is depicted as someone who made the best (albeit naive) decisions he could under the circumstances, which is a minor improvement over previous efforts I guess. Drake's admirable efforts are ultimately wasted on this script, though: This show still has nothing on *Raumpatrouille Orion* when it comes to this kind of thing. On top of that, the Romulans are back completely disconnected from their original symbolism and written totally out-of-character and are obviously only here so the show can reuse stock footage from "Balance of Terror", there's a throwaway callback to "The Corbomite Maneuver" (whose airdate is now creeping on its two-year anniversary) for really no reason and the pacing is shot to hell, which all compounds to make us feel every feather of the padding this episode is.

Ultimately though, "The Deadly Years" isn't worth going into one of my signature moaning *Requiem for Star Trek* rants for. Partially because having it come after "Mirror, Mirror" is just another example of this show's utter lack of consistent baseline quality and thus any real kind of standards, expectations and preconceptions. There's just no way to take this year's spectacular unevenness and reconcile that with the idea of a coherent, self-contained series and fictional world. In my opinion, *Star Trek* is best seen as a straightforward anthology show, not the first chapter in some grand, oblique unfolding Master Historical Narrative of a fantasy world (not that that approach is ever unproblematic for anything). The show's rules, characterization and basic ethics are changing week-to-week at this point, and it's all dependent on who the writer is, how involved Gene Roddenberry, Gene Coon or D.C. Fontana get and how much effort the actors decide to give. When this show is on-target, it really does have a respectable claim to being at least competent and engaging, but conversely when it's not it has an alarming tendency to be one of the worst things on television. This really isn't the making of a true Classic television series, though it certainly does have unarguably Classic moments.

Which brings me to my main point for this episode, actually. I just came off of one of the single greatest things this series ever put out, and am about to hit a stretch of episodes that I know for a fact contain at least three clever oversignified things in a row, including the only other episode from the original *Star Trek* apart from "Balance of Terror" that I will unhesitatingly call a masterpiece. Before then, I just need to get through "The Deadly Years" and, well, the next episode, frankly, neither of which work. But it's just not worth my time and stress levels to get terribly worked up about either one of them. From the vantage point of 1967, "Mirror, Mirror" was enough to build *Star Trek* a surplus reserve of goodwill and from the vantage point of the future, the looming symbolic singularity is enough to ensure the show actually *has* a future and is, for possibly the first time, on relatively stable ground for the moment. In that case, "The Deadly Years" is, like "What Are Little Girls Made Of?" last year, an episode that probably shouldn't have been made. However, unlike that first season story, this feels less like a potential derailment of the series and more like straightforward filler. Why might that be?

This gets at the concept of "filler" in television itself. I get the sense modern audiences use the term "filler" to describe an episode that doesn't play into the big, sweeping season-long mythic story arc every single contemporary television show is required to have by law now (or at least did in 2013 when I wrote this), but this is at once a dangerous mentality (best suited for exploring when my feelings on Big Damn Myth Arcs start to become more of a concern for this blog) and a recent one, as filler certainly existed before 2004 (or 1997 if you're picky). It can be seen as a peculiarly televisual phenomenon, too: If we were to read a book that had entire chapters or sections that really contributed nothing towards the advancement of the story, or watched a movie that did something similar with its act structure, or played a video game where whole levels, areas or gameplay mechanics felt pointless, shallow and redundant, we would probably complain a lot more, and probably very loudly. However, this is something we've come to expect as a necessary evil of doing something episodic for this kind of broadcast medium. Given the high-stress, labour-intensive way TV production works, we know occasionally teams will need to throw out an episode that might be below their usual standard because you need something, *anything* to go out that week and the deadline of the airdate ultimately has the final say on what you're doing in a typical work week.

And as we've already seen, and shall unfortunately continue to see, this happens to Star Trek considerably more than it does to other shows.

It need not be, though. I think the concept of filler episodes in the classical sense gets at the difference between US television and TV made elsewhere in the world, particularly the UK. In the US, television seasons tend to last from September to May and shows run more or less continuously every week during that period, often with a break around November and December. This means each show, unless it's a mid-season replacement debuting in January, typically accrues 25-30 episodes a season. Simply put, this is total overkill. No matter how good a show is, there's only a certain level of momentum it's able to sustain in one sitting, and 30 installments a year is far too many. The problem is not the 2013 argument, born out of the fetishization of the character drama myth arc, that it muddies and blunts the impact of the year's Big Story, but in the very simple sense that there are only so many clever and workable ideas people can come up with for one project in one single period of time without taking a break from it for a bit.

Despite in many ways pioneering the idea of incredibly long-form television serials and sitcoms with shows like *Coronation Street, Last of the Summer Wine, Only Fools and Horses* and the original version of *Doctor Who,* the latter of which was originally on basically year-round, the UK seems to have a better solution here. Television seasons (or series, as is the preferred term there) tend to be much shorter than in the US, often made up of only 6-18 stories a year (in the case of the original *Doctor Who,* broken down as it was into multiple mini-serials this still averages out to about 24 half-hour episodes a year, but the difference here is that they were all considered part of the same story, and thus the same general idea). Even in 1967, where we're just starting to get a glimpse of how the structure of broadcast television is taking shape, shorter-form concepts were not unheard of, such as one-off, self-contained television plays or miniseries. Recall Patrick McGoohan considered *The Prisoner* padded at only seventeen episodes and was ultimately unhappy with the way the network handled that show. When taken in this context, 30 episodes a year is insane, and this is likely the reason for the preponderance of so-called "filler" episodes in US television: A more relaxed production schedule would allow a more selective approach to vetting scripts, with more time, money and other resources available for the scripts that do go into production.

(Actually an even better solution might be a direct-to-video series with a limited episode count planned out from the very beginning so that all the episodes can share overlapping themes and motifs, but we've got a long way to go before that becomes a feasible option for us to explore...)

But what's interesting here is that we've run across a *Star Trek* episode that can be described as filler at all. By definition a filler episode is a kind of holding pattern, which implies there's actually somewhere the show is going to touch down in the near future. Almost every other time the show has stumbled backward it's been an almost series-derailing catastrophe. This, however, is an episode that doesn't feel like a potential dead end, but merely an off-week, and that alone speaks volumes. Admittedly a great deal of this probably comes from my own ability to see potential timelines and future events and knowing that "The Deadly Years" is in fact exactly that, but even without knowing the episodes that are coming next, it still feels like *Star Trek* has turned some kind of a corner. Somehow, some way, it's done enough this year so far to set our consciences at ease for awhile and, no matter how forgettable episodes like this may be, it's far, far better to fail and be forgettable then fail and be memorably disastrous.

237

54. "Does anybody remember LAUGHTER?": I, Mudd

"I, Mudd" sees *Star Trek* circling the tower for another week. This is strange, because everything about it seems to have the making of something quite interesting, if not perhaps actually *good*. It's the return of Harry Mudd which, while not exactly an advisable decision, means Roger C. Carmel has the distinction of playing the only reoccurring character in the Original Series not a member of the *Enterprise* crew, and I suppose if one were looking for former foils to bring back, Mudd was probably the least disastrous option to go with and he's at least a very memorable personality. It's also the first work we get to look at by future Animated Series co-producer and inaugural story editor for *Star Trek: The Next Generation* Dave Gerrold, who collaborated with Gene Coon on an uncredited rewrite of Stephen Kandal's original treatment due to how impressed the team was with his work on his debut script (which we take a look at next time).

Furthermore, this episode marks one of the first occasions Star Trek attempts to do an overt comedy, or at least a story where the comedic elements are meant to be in the forefront: Previous episodes were humourous and had funny bits in them, but this is the first time the show seems to be going out of its way to *try* to be funny. The keywords to note here are, naturally "attempts" and "tries", because "I, Mudd" is an absolute spectacle of magnificent failure. First of all, it is a casserole made of repurposed ingredients left over from "The Cage", "Mudd's Women", "What Are Little Girls Made Of?", "The Return of the Archons", "Metamorphosis" and "The Changeling", and the end result is precisely as terrible as you would expect a story with that pedigree to be. The entire plot can be sufficiently explained, without leaving out any important details, simply by stating that if there was a major element in any of those episodes, "I, Mudd" has it too but is even more heavy-handed about it. Likewise, if there was a mistake those episodes made, "I, Mudd" will make it all the more frequently.

This does not, however, adequately describe the uncanny, surreal experience that is watching "I, Mudd" within the context of the episodes around it or, actually, any previous Star Trek episodes. This is an attempt at comedy in the most broad-strokes fashion, packed to brimming with pratfalls, one-liners, zingers and characters so programmatic they wouldn't look out of place in a cartoon. William Shatner, who is actually quite good at broad-strokes comedy and is served well by it in turn, is very much in his element again here, and the way he deftly alternates between the blusteringly indignant straight man and merry prankster narrative roles is as fine an acting trick as anything he's done. He plays it on a spectrum, so that his mode shifts don't feel jarring within the context of the action. Shatner's conception of comedy is very much born of his theatrical performativity, and this is going to be an extremely important theme to monitor throughout the rest of his association with Star Trek, as it's pretty much crucial to understanding his continued place within it.

Shatner also has a good partner to play off of in Roger C. Carmel, who is strong in many of the same areas, and the double act they eventually turn the Kirk-Mudd relationship into is certainly the high point of the episode (doubly so as Mudd is significantly less of a horrifying Irish stereotype this time 'round, though this is balanced out by Stella being about as stock and cartoonish a sexist depiction of the shrewish, nagging wife as is possible to get). However, the rest of the cast isn't helped by this in the slightest: Leonard Nimoy, who often plays Spock with a dry, sarcastic snark, manages well enough and James Doohan probably would have been good in this episode too, had he been given more to do. Nichelle Nichols, while formidable (especially in the scene where Uhura pretends to betray the crew to the androids), just feels out of place and while DeForest Kelley makes McCoy very witty and enjoyably curmudgeonly, watching him trying to do physical comedy is embarrassing and painful. Meanwhile, Walter Koenig gets to play Chekov setting up a threesome with twin android women, reminiscing about Leningrad and doing the Ukrainian Cossack dance, but really, at this point this is what we fully expect to see him do, and having him do anything else in this episode would have just been jarring.

But the fact remains there is absolutely no precedent for an episode like this anywhere in what we've seen of *Star Trek* so far. Coming to "I, Mudd" after "The Apple" and "Mirror, Mirror" is profoundly weird, and even "The Deadly Years" was played fairly straight. This, by contrast, is a live-action Bob Clampett cartoon. Actually, I take that back: "I, Mudd" isn't as much comparable to Golden Age theatrical shorts as it is to Vaudeville, and that in itself is worth examining as Star Trek's first go at *Commedia dell'arte*. Vaudeville is often called North America's signature form of entertainment and "the heart of American show business". While I'm not entirely convinced by this statement (I personally feel that, at least in the United States, Hollywood and television has proven to be far more ubiquitous and far more more associated with their point of origin in a global context), I do think there is some truth there in that Vaudeville is an extremely US phenomenon inasmuch as it draws elements from a number of international forms of entertainment (most notably British and continental European music halls and burlesque shows), isolates them from their original context, and then promptly waters them down and defangs them to the point they essentially have no impact or power anymore in the interest of making them "safe" for the "American People".

While Vaudeville shows were a mixture of sketch, musical and standup comedy, variety, talent shows, magic acts, and the like, the ruthless "modesty codes" of many halls and touring companies meant that Vaudevillian acts were rather famously terrible. It's not something you're likely to find in showbiz history books, but the pop culture memory of Vaudeville, especially of those for whom it was actually in living memory (or that of their parents and grandparents), is that it was excruciatingly tepid and unfunny as a result of its draconian censorship policies. If we look at any pastiche of or reference to Vaudeville

239

in late-20th and early 21st Century US entertainment, the stock scenario is always of a desperate performer bombing onstage Stepford-smiling through tortuously bad material while being pelted with rotten fruit from a bored and increasingly irritated audience (indeed, the number of cartoons that have done exactly this gag is far too high to count). The joke, then, is that performers are forced to scrape out a meager living humiliating themselves to please the ungrateful masses, or alternatively, that the performers are so deluded and incompetent that they get taken in by their managers' flagrant soaking and pursuit of safe profit through "decent" entertainment at the expense of talent and quality. In that regard, Vaudeville being the seed from which sprouts all of US mass-media entertainment is rather perfect, as we continue to see much of the same Puritanical behaviour in, say, network standards and practices.

The one problem, really the fundamental one "I, Mudd" seems to have, is that this is a joke it's in no way in on. One only has to watch the jaw-dropping scene in the climax where the crew *literally* waltzes into the androids' control room and puts on a truly legendarily bad Vaudevillian routine, complete with miming, improv sketches and "jokes" about logic paradoxes and self-contradictory behaviour in an effort to confuse and overload Norman (another graduate from the Captain Kirk School of Computer Repair then). The show clearly wants us to read this, and the rest of the crew's actions during the last two acts of the episode, as "funny", but we end up feeling more like the androids, staring stone-faced at the slow-motion train wreck unfolding before us with smoke billowing out of our ears. It's not so much the routine itself as much as it is the utter lack of irony or situational awareness in regards to how completely off-the-wall mental it is: This is not *Star Trek* turning its critical lens inward at the heart of US show business, this is *Star Trek* putting on a straight-up Vaudeville show as a paean to illogic and irrationality and it has absolutely no clue how terrible an idea that is.

The truly grotesque part of this is that Vaudeville is absolutely an overtly performative form of expression: The show will certainly change from night to night and audience to audience. This is still moving Star Trek further away from teleology and prescriptive representationalism. I probably would not have gone with diluted and sanitized musical theater and burlesque as the way to stress the show's performative core, but perhaps it seemed like an appropriate thing to do given *Star Trek*'s place as part of the primetime lineup on major network television at this point (although I still think this is kind of a flimsy excuse as theatrical cartoons had been lampooning Vaudeville for thirty years already by 1967). So, while this may still be a mistake, it's at least a somewhat expected mistake to make. More concerning is that this is apparently what *Star Trek* thinks humour is. Much like sexuality, humour is something that the entire franchise, not just the Original Series, has serious problems with.

It's deeply confusing to know Dave Gerrold's name is attached to "I, Mudd", because the script that actually got him the job (and indeed the very next episode to be produced) goes for explicit comedy and becomes an instantaneous television landmark while this is, well...this. Although that said, I don't think the failure-to-launch of "I, Mudd" can be laid at the feet of Gerrold (although Gerrold has plenty of problems of his own we'll eventually get to), or Coon, or Kandal or even Shatner and Carmel. Partially at issue here is the concept of doing a comedy episode of something like *Star Trek* at all. When the show's been successful at humour in the past, it's oftentimes been in smaller vignettes and moments that come out of the character's inherent foibles or how they react to certain situations. "Tomorrow is Yesterday", for example, is a riot, but it's not a "comedy" episode *per se*: While a lot of laughs are to be had at the three temporally displaced parties, the basic story is a serious one as the *Enterprise* is at risk of being stranded in the 1960s (how prescient) and their future is also at risk of ceasing to exist. By contrast, a story about a planet of sexbots who are trying to observe humans and who get outsmarted by Kirk, McCoy, Chekov and Uhura acting like lunatics...isn't.

I am reminded of a story Douglas Adams used to tell about the production of the *Doctor Who* serial "City of Death" (typically regarded as a comedic triumph and a high water mark of the whole series), and a great deal of other writers who know their way around comedy had a version of it. Adams used to say he would have to stop tape and remind his actors not to do funny walks or funny accents because humour is actually better conveyed by people playing their roles straight in bizarre and insane situations. The basic idea is that if you are deliberately trying to act "wacky" or "random", you are in fact coming across as terrifyingly stilted, forced and awkward. This is I think where "I, Mudd" goes wrong (at least in execution: At its core, it remains a basic story concept that probably wasn't entirely a great idea): It never goes above and beyond stock scenarios and deliberately overplayed zaniness and the whole production feels like its trying much, much too hard. That's not to say Star Trek is incapable of doing comedy, or even broad-strokes comedy (despite the protestations of the fandom, determined as it is to take absolutely everything deathly seriously and who are opposed to having any sort of fun whatsoever, Star Trek is inherently and profoundly ridiculous), it's just this isn't the way to go about doing it.

But, like "The Deadly Years" this is an episode that, in spite of its missteps, is ultimately largely harmless and inoffensive. That in itself is proof *Star Trek* has turned a major corner, and if this is the way the show is going to start screwing up I really can't object much at all. And anyway, what Gerrold helps the show do next unilaterally cements its status as a pop culture legend. It's allowed to slide a bit here.

55. The Memory of Past Tribbles

ACT I SCENE 1

It is evening on the Promenade. Traffic on the streets is
dying down as people make their way back to their quarters and
many of the shops, temples and other establishments begin to
close up for the night. All save Quark's, which is a buzzing
hub of activity. Sisko and Dax leisurely make their way to
the bar in conversation.

                    JADZIA DAX
          We could have done this on my ship, you
          know. I built this programme into my
          holodecks as one of the defaults when
          I had them set up, and they're bit
          bigger and more reliable than Quark's
          holosuites.
                    BENJAMIN SISKO
          I know, but Quark's is an iconic part
          of life on the station. It's important
          that we patronize our community centres.

Beat

                    SISKO
               (jokingly)
          And besides, it gives our dates an urban
          flavour. What did they used to say?
          Let's go out on the town?
                    DAX
               (teasingly
               flirtatious)
          Oh, so we're dating now, are we?

                    SISKO

          You know what I mean, Old Man!

                    DAX

               (Bemused)
          Just remember you said it, not me.

Sisko and Dax enter Quark's, and turn to walk up the spiral
staircase leading up to the bar's second level, and the
holosuites. At the door Sisko presses some buttons on the
suite's control panel.

                    SISKO
          This is an old play. I'm looking
          forward to seeing how it translates to
          the holodeck format.
                    DAX
          I've never known you to take an interest
          in historical fiction before, Ben. It
          must be Jean-Luc rubbing off on you.
                    SISKO
          Well, I've always liked this story, even
          without knowing the historical context.
          I think it still holds up.
                    DAX
               (Nods in agreement)
          It's a good one. I haven't seen this
          version of it before, but it was one of
          my favourite holotapes as a little girl.

Beat

                    DAX
               (wistful)
          I used to watch it endlessly. It was
          one of the first episodes I ever saw,
          and I still think it's the best in the
          series.

The doors to the holosuite open.

                    SISKO
          Well, shall we see for ourselves?
                    DAX
          Yes, let's!
                    SISKO
               (Motions her in)
          After you!

They both enter the holosuite as the doors close behind them.

SCENE 2

Dax and Sisko step into a holographic recreation of the USS
Enterprise sets as seen in the 1967 Star Trek episode "The
Trouble with Tribbles". They are dressed as Starfleet
officers who might be serving on the Enterprise during the
events depicted in this episode; Sisko is in a yellow command
division uniform while Dax wears the blue colours of the
science division. They take a moment to look around the
recreated hallways and corridors.

                    SISKO
          Well, the holosuite's done a remarkable
          job turning the holotape into a
          three-dimensional environment, but it
          does really draw your attention to all
          the little quirks and imperfections of
          the original performance. Like this
          set.

Beat

                    SISKO
          It must be especially strange for
          you-You lived through all this.

                    DAX
          Oh, it's completely inaccurate, of
          course. But that's the charm of it.
          They took what resources they had and
          used them to tell a story with with
          emotion and power, and that's all they
          needed to do to make it stick with us
          for all these years. Look at us now,
          going back and playing in this world
          again for...How many times have wee seen
          it between us, both together and on our
          own? Prophets only know. But that's
          the sign of something that really lasts.

She pauses to muse for a beat, than continues.

                    DAX
          I find it fascinating how people take
          history and reinterpret it through
          their own perspectives to tell a story.
          Captain Kirk, Commander Spock, Zefram
          Cochrane...These are our great heroes
          now, and people see in them and their
          adventures reflections of who they are,
          who they want to be and the things they
          want to say. In an age where everything
          that ever happened is meticulously
          recorded and filed away in computer
          banks for all eternity, stuff like this
          is the closest we can get to a genuine
          shared cultural mythology, like what
          used to bring people together in ancient
          times. History, like beauty, is often
          in the eye of the beholder
                    SISKO
               (Smiling)
          Did you come up with that?

                    DAX
               (Playfully)
          I may have. Maybe one of my previous
          hosts did. You know I honestly can't
          remember?

Sisko and Dax smile at each other, just as the claxon sounds,
signifying the ship has gone to Red Alert. In the background,
we see the holo-characters of Captain Kirk, Commander Spock
and Ensign Chekov exit the briefing room and make their way to
the bridge.

                    SISKO
          Well, I suppose we'd better make like
          we're assuming our battle stations.
                    DAX
          Yes, we'd better.

She indicates Kirk, Spock and Chekov.

                              DAX
              Let's follow them to the bridge. I love
              watching Kirk's reaction when he finds
              out what the Code 1 distress signal was
              sent for.

Sisko and Dax take the turbolift to the main bridge, take up
posts at the science stations adjacent to Spock's scanner and
observe Kirk grilling Mr. Lurry about the nature of the
emergency over subspace.

                            SISKO
              This part coming up, when Kirk and Spock
              beam over to Deep Space K7 to confront
              Lurry and Nilz Baris, always stood out
              to me. A lot of the holotapes from
              this time period glorified starship life
              and painted the captaincy as something
              rugged and idealistic, but depicted
              bureaucrats as foolish, incompetent
              and even dangerous. Now, as someone
              who was once a captain and who's now
              an administrator, I've always felt life
              out there isn't that romantic, nor is it
              for everybody. It's certainly not for
              me. This was one the first episodes
              I remember to portray that-Baris is
              obviously an irritating obstructionist,
              but Lurry is just someone trying to get
              by who gets tangled up in all this.
              That's a sentiment I can relate to a
              lot.

Kirk and Spock beam over to Deep Space K7 to interrogate
Lurry. By discreetly tying into Kirk's communication feed,
Sisko and Dax can watch the exchange on the station on one of
the monitor scopes.

                         DAX
          And a big theme was always the tension
          over bureaucratic management and
          a genuine fear this would stifle
          individual thought and expression. But
          this part with Spock is wonderful:
          Baris starts talking down to him,
          presuming he wouldn't know anything
          about Quadrotriticale because he's not
          an administrator or policymaker. But he
          does, which is our first clue that the
          the two crews are going to be able to
          work together in the end.

Holo-Uhura gets the message from Kirk that two, and *only*
two, security guards are to beam over to the station to guard
the grain stores from possible Klingon tampering, and that
Kirk is authorizing shore leave for all crewmembers.

SCENE 3

Sisko and Dax are sitting in a recreation of the <u>Deep Space
K-7</u> bar set dressed as interstellar traders. From the back of
the room they watch Kirk and Spock discuss Nilz Baris' misuse
of the Priority 1 distress signal. Kirk and Spock get up to
leave as the characters of Chekov and Uhura enter. They sit
down at the front of the bar, where Cyrano Jones is arguing
with the bartender over his wares. Dax leans over to Sisko,
and indicates the Tribble Jones just pulled out of his pocket.

                         DAX
          Oh, look! It's the first Tribble! You
          know they were a sensation right from
          the beginning? I think it's easy to see
          why-There's really nothing else quite
          like them.
                         SISKO
          Did you have a Tribble growing up?

                         DAX
Sure. We all did. Everyone was always
talking about them all the time-It was
a real fad back then. I still have
one, actually-Drives my Klingon friends
crazy, naturally, but thankfully I don't
have many Klingon callers. They all
have to pass through rigorous customs
checks and are subject to a bunch of
regulations these days, of course, but
there's really nothing harmful about
them so long as you don't feed them too
much and keep an eye on them.

                       SISKO
The Tribbles or the Klingons?

                         DAX
                 (laughs)
Both, I suppose, but I meant the
Tribbles.

                       SISKO
Well that's really what this story
is about, isn't it? It's a parable
about what happens when species
are transplanted from their native
ecological niche to another where
they're no longer kept in check by the
environment.

                         DAX
I think that angle is there, sure. I
think the original writer said that was
the original pitch too. And there's
sadly enough cases where that story has
repeated itself throughout history and
around the galaxy.

                        SISKO
          Don't remind me-All things considered,
          I daresay a Tribble infestation would
          be altogether more pleasant to deal
          with than another Cardassian vole
          epidemic. At least Tribbles don't bite
          or run away. Or chew through electrical
          circuits.

Looking out the window, Dax notices a D7 class battle cruiser
coming out of warp, directing Sisko's attention to it.

                                        END OF ACT I

ACT II SCENE 1

In Mr. Lurry's office, Kirk bickers with Koloth and Korax
while Spock keeps watch and Lurry confesses to Kirk he doesn't
want the Klingons on the station but can't do anything to get
rid of them. Kirk lets the Klingon crew take shore leave, but
assigns them each a security officer. Dax and Sisko look on
from the transporter room, where they are dressed as station
personnel.

                        SISKO
          It's strange, and more than a little
          uncomfortable, to go back to these old
          holotapes and see Klingons depicted this
          way. Doubly so when you know the real
          people these characters are based on.
                        DAX
              (Remorsefully)
          I know. Just another consequence of
          the time and place tapes like this were
          made. When you have an Earth-centered
          production put on by humans in a time
          before the alliance was formed and
          before reliable holographic technology,
          this is, unfortunately, sort of what
          you get. Though I will say, while this
          character may not look like the Koloth
          I knew, he sure does behave like him.
          The script writes him quite well and the
          actor they got is uncanny.

                        SISKO
          Isn't that the same guy they got to play
          Trelane in that episode from the first
          season we watched?

                        DAX

          Yeah. Isn't he just perfect?

Sisko acknowledges his agreement to her observation, and
continues.

                        SISKO
          This is one of my favourite double acts
          in the whole series. Captain Kirk and
          Captain Koloth are such larger-than-life
          figures, overstated bravado is not just
          called for, it's expected. It's a shame
          they never got to bring him back to fill
          the reoccurring role he was created for.

SCENE 2

Back in the bar, Scotty, Chekov and Jones enter through the
sliding doors. Jones notices the Tribbles have an intense
dislike of Klingons, before the bartender complains to him
about the sudden explosion in the station's Tribble
population. Scotty and Chekov argue about alcohol. At the
back of the bar, Sisko and Dax are dressed as bartenders and
are miming wiping down glasses and arranging dishes.

                        DAX
          Watching the bartender keep pulling out
          all those Tribbles makes me smile every
          time. It's like they keep regenerating
          under there-It never seems to stop!

                    SISKO
          I love the banter and comic timing in
          this one. Each exchange is meticulously
          structured, a carefully-crafted clock
          made out of one-liners and retorts.
          There's this scene, the "That's my
          offer"/"That's a joke" bit from the last
          act, "My dear captain", "it is you I
          take lightly", "chicken soup and coffee"
          and Spock, Scott and McCoy being evasive
          in the denouement. Each and every scene
          has something iconic and memorable about
          it. I really don't think they ever put
          on another show quite like it.

Korax drunkenly insults Kirk and the <u>Enterprise</u> crew. The
equally drunken crewmembers strike back with punching, and the
big bar brawl scene begins.

                    DAX
               (With growing alarm)
          Speaking of, here's another one now.
          We'd best keep a low profile.

Sisko and Dax make for cover.

                    SISKO
          I believe this is an example of what we
          refer to today as "cowboy diplomacy"?
                    DAX
          You could say that! No matter who
          does the talking or how many brazen
          statements are made or how much and how
          grandiose rash political and military
          posturing is done, this is basically
          what it all ends up amounting to in the
          end.
                    SISKO
          I do appreciate how the fight is staged
          and choreographed. Look at how Cyrano
          here stands on the sidelines just taking
          everything in, rooting for whoever is
          throwing the most interesting punches at
          the moment.

                    DAX
Well, that's really the best reaction
you could have, isn't it?

                    SISKO

        (laughing)
I guess so!

                                        END OF ACT II

ACT III SCENE 1

Back on the Enterprise, Kirk walks onto the bridge and sits
down in his chair, only to discover a Tribble was already
sitting there. Kirk notices with horror that Tribbles have
taken over the entire bridge, climbing the walls and crawling
over every station. Visibly trying to control his temper,
Kirk orders McCoy to the bridge. At the engineering consoles,
Dax and Sisko are dressed as operations division officers. As
McCoy reports that Tribbles are "born pregnant", Dax smiles
knowingly.

                    SISKO
And here's the bold, commanding James T.
Kirk, hero of the Federation, defeated
by tiny balls of fluff.

                    DAX
You're jumping ahead in the story, Ben.
That's the next scene.

                    SISKO
Well, I think you can see the
foreshadowing here too. It's a gradual
progression where the situation slowly
but methodically continues to grow
beyond Kirk's ability to control it.
None of his usual swift, commanding
gestures are serving him anymore.

                         DAX
          And this is why, though they'd never
          publicly admit it, Captain Kirk and
          Captain Koloth were always so similar,
          and such perfect foils for each other.

After a beat, an irritated Kirk piles Tribbles into Uhura's
arms, ordering her to tell Lurry to detain Cyrano Jones and to
"get these Tribbles off the bridge". Dax pretends to be hurt
at Kirk's claim that "too much of <u>anything</u>, Lieutenant, even
<u>love</u>, is a bad thing!"

                         DAX
          Not sure I'd agree that someone could
          have too much love, though...
                         SISKO
          I guess it depends on your definition of
          love, Old Man. It has to be reciprocal,
          communal.
                         DAX
          What about a love of living? A love of
          the universe?
                         SISKO
          Well, I suppose you've got a point.

Kirk storms off the bridge, taking Spock with him, and leaving
McCoy and Uhura to clean things up.

                                        END OF ACT III

ACT IV SCENE 1

On K7, Kirk and Spock race into the grain storage compartments
after coming to the horrific realisation Tribbles can gain
access to sensitive machinery on the Enterprise through air
ducts, the very same kinds of air ducts that ventilate the
stores of Quadrotriticale vital to the Federation developing
Sherman's Planet, thus securing a valuable strategic location
in the conflict with the Klingons. Dressed as security
officers, Dax and Sisko step aside to allow Kirk access to the
overhead bay doors. 1,771,561 Tribbles rain down on him.
Even after he is completely buried, Tribbles continue to
intermittently fall out of the storage bay. Baris breaks
down, blaming Kirk for everything that's gone wrong in the
mission. Kirk orders Baris to shut up, as Spock and McCoy
realise the Tribbles are dead, and that something in the grain
killed them.

                    SISKO
          As unpleasant as he is, I wonder if Nilz
          Baris might have a point here. From his
          perspective, his job is to ensure this
          mission goes of without a hitch, and as
          far as he's concerned it's turned into a
          total disaster. I'd probably be in less
          then soaring spirits too.

                    DAX
          Yes, but there's no way Kirk could
          have anticipated the problem the
          Tribbles would eventually become. It's
          a situation that's spiraled so out
          of control its jeopardized everyone,
          including the poor Tribbles starving to
          death on that tainted grain. Everyone's
          just trying to do the best they can
          in the role that's been carved out for
          them, just like Mr. Lurry trying to run
          his station. Baris wants his mission
          to succeed, Jones wants to make money,
          Koloth wants his mission to succeed,
          McCoy wants to learn more about the
          Tribbles, Kirk wants to look out for
          the Enterprise, and the Tribbles want
          to...well...Be Tribbles.

SCENE 2

In the conference room of <u>Deep Space K7</u>, all the major players
are assembled. Kirk, along with everyone else, is hoping for
an explanation about why the Tribbles got into the
Quadrotriticale, and what was in the grain that killed them.
Koloth demands an official apology be sent to the Klingon High
Council, and that the Tribbles in the conference room be
removed. As the guards comply, and Kirk paces up and down,
the Tribbles react to the presence of Arne Darvin. Dax and
Sisko, still dressed as security officers, look on.

                    SISKO
          It's funny to see the Tribbles'
          hostility towards Klingons depicted
          almost as an...allergic reaction...when
          they're in fact very serious historical
          enemies.

                    DAX
          I know-I remember the Klingon/Tribble
          Wars vividly. Not exactly light family
          entertainment material. Although I
          think that truth is still in here, if
          only implicitly, because you have to
          remember what a product of its time this
          play is.

                    SISKO
          If we treat the Klingons in this story
          as standing in for a kind of general
          imperialistic and confrontational
          mindset, which is certainly the way the
          Federation of the time would have viewed
          them, the longstanding enmity between
          the two races becomes a kind of grand
          cosmic joke.

                    DAX
Exactly. The drive to conquer and
dominate thwarted by the desire to love
and make love. Do you remember your
ancient Earth history and philosophy
of science, Ben? In many ways, this
is Freud's Eros, what he saw as the
drive for life, creation, propagation
and construction, winning out over what
he saw as its equal and opposite number,
the Death Drive, the drive towards
self-destruction.

Beat

                    DAX
It certainly drives the point home when
you're a growing girl.

                    SISKO
I knew this one was your favourite for a
reason.

                    DAX
I mean not to say this excuses the
depiction of the Klingons here or
anywhere else in media from this
time period, and I know my Klingon
friends would still probably be just as
offended, as well they should be. After
all, what honour is there to be gained
through clandestinely poisoning grain?
No Klingon would wish such a death even
on an army of Tribbles.

                    SISKO
Which is why Darvin was in reality
dishonoured and made pariah for pulling
something like this.

                    DAX
     (Nods)
Koloth wanted nothing to do with him.
Sometimes I couldn't tell who he hated
more: Darvin or Kirk.

SCENE 3

Back on the <u>Enterprise</u>, Kirk, relieved at having his problems
with Baris and the Klingons sorted out, is pleasantly
surprised to find the bridge free of Tribbles. The senior
staff is reluctant to explain what happened, until Scotty
confesses he beamed them all into Koloth's engine room. Sisko
and Dax are dressed in standard duty uniforms, him in the
command colours and her in the science ones.

                    SISKO
              (Exasperated)
          "No Tribble at all". Kind of a glib
          description of what was in reality one
          of the biggest political disasters of
          the time. A major diplomatic incident
          resulting in escalation of tensions
          between the two powers as the Klingon
          High Council saw this as the Federation
          allying with the Tribbles as a prelude
          to all-out war.

Dax emphatically nods in agreement.

                    DAX
          Koloth held a blood feud against Kirk
          and Scott for decades afterward. I
          know, he went on about it to me across
          several lifetimes.
                    SISKO
          But you've got to admit it's fun.
          Of all the times this series did an
          "everybody laughs" ending scene, this
          is the one episode I think it not only
          worked, but was probably warranted.
                    DAX
              (pensive)
          I dunno. It always makes me sad.
          Everybody laughs and we warp off to the
          next adventure. But I don't want to go
          on the next adventure, because I don't
          want this adventure to end.

There's a beat, and then she regains her sardonic edge.

                    DAX
          Mostly because I know what happens next.

                    SISKO
                (joking)
          Is that why you had it on a constant
          loop all the time, to your parents'
          chagrin?

Dax laughs.

                    SISKO
          But I know what you mean. Of all of
          them, this is the one I think that truly
          stands apart. Despite everything, it
          holds up. In fact does more than that:
          It doesn't just stand apart, it stands
          alone. It's inspired so many people for
          so long, that's redemption enough.
                    DAX
          That's what a story is supposed to do.
          Especially when it's shared.

Dax and Sisko smile at each other as the arch materializes and
the Holosuite door opens to the second floor dining room of
Quark's. They walk out together as the door shuts behind
them, before vanishing back into the ether as we're left
looking at the blinking lights of the Enterprise bridge
stations.

SCENE 4

Dax and Sisko walk out of the Holosuite dressed in their Deep
Space 9 team regulation uniforms. Sisko pushes buttons on the
control panel, saving the programme to a portable media
storage device, then pocketing it. Exiting the bar from the
second level, Sisko and Dax walk out onto the upper walkway of
the Promenade and stop at the gigantic viewports looking out
into the Denorias Belt. As they watch the Bajoran Wormhole
open, Dax reaches into the pocket of her jumpsuit and pulls
out a Tribble.

FADE OUT

56. "ARE YOU NOT ENTERTAINED?":
Bread and Circuses

At last, we've come to the series finale of the original *Star Trek*.

At least when the end came, it came quickly. In one of the franchise's saddest twists, "Bread and Circuses" is the epilogue to the story of Star Trek grasping immortality last week and proves once and for all the Original Series really had nowhere to go after "The Trouble with Tribbles". As the only episode co-written by both Gene Roddenberry and Gene Coon (and serving as a send-off to the latter's tenure as showrunner) it's a tight summation and echo of all the series' motifs, and while it brings closure to the show in style, the last, desperate grab for glory "Bread and Circuses" represents is ultimately futile: While it's ironically one of the best episodes of the season, and one of the tightest, most creative productions in the entire series in terms of both writing and cinematography, the writing is on the wall. There's one more episode to go, but even a cursory knowledge of what that one was supposed to be should make it abundantly clear what *Star Trek*'s future prospects look like.

Frustratingly, "Bread and Circuses" is genuinely exciting and clever. It's a scathing condemnation of life in the mid-20th Century United States penned by people unfortunate enough to witness some of the more particularly excessive aspects of it. The indictment of Western late-stage capitalist modernity and its self-absorbed egotism, short-sighted ecological carelessness, insensitivity to brutal violence general cynicism and society built around spectacle and artifice remains frighteningly relevant and one of the strongest statements Star Trek ever made on the issue. Furthermore, we now have the circa-1968 United States being just about explicitly called Rome and, as before, comparisons are made between Starfleet officers and Roman legionaries, with the most obvious being the Proconsul's growing admiration for and respect of Kirk and his quip to him that he'd "make a good Roman". However, perhaps ironically because we've now had "Mirror, Mirror", there's no longer any ambiguity about how our heroes stack up: Coon and Roddenberry are firmly on the side of Kirk and the *Enterprise* crew and this story is about them proving that while they may have the makings of imperialists and have a conflict-ridden, imperialist history (as Spock points out on a number of occasions) they are manifestly *not* imperialists.

The way they go about this is, interestingly, the Prime Directive. This is the other major episode this season to deal with it and, unlike "The Apple", it's portrayed as being unambiguously a good thing: Taking the oath of the Prime Directive is shown to be a solemn responsibility and that Starfleet officers would rather die than break it, which really just makes "The Apple" look even more ridiculous than it already did. Although, there's a bit more nuance to the Prime Directive debate here than there usually is-Merik is portrayed as being in the wrong for violating it, but he's shown to have been coerced into doing so by the Empire. Kirk, Spock and McCoy face the same dilemma, but eventually Scotty comes up with a solution that engineers their escape without directly interfering. Of course, this doesn't eliminate the self-defeating contradictory problems inherent in the Prime Directive, but it does clarify what the writers intended it to stand for a bit. As a result, it works noticeably better here than it does in other places as Coon and Roddenberry seem to want it to be a straightforward rebuttal to Western imperialism, so it actually makes sense to have it in a story like this.

Indeed the anti-imperialism theme is laudably blatant and well-executed in "Bread and Circuses". The highlight, apart from the general brilliance of the setting, is McCoy's argument with Spock in the Proconsul's dining room. Spock comments on the efficient and ordered way the society is organised, while McCoy keeps pointing out it's dependent on slavery and engages in violent spectacle for light entertainment. Spock and McCoy are once again reduced down to their most basic programmatic roles, that is, strict logic and unbridled passion but, as with the Prime Directive, this actually seems somewhat appropriate for this particular story. It's certainly just about as good an execution as this particular theme got in *Star Trek*, mostly because "Bread and Circuses" manages to remember these are supposed to be characters as well.

The best single scene of the episode comes after the first battle, when Spock and McCoy are alone together in the gladiatorial cage. Last time we got the first Spock/McCoy bickering scene that was written to be textually uncomfortable, where McCoy compared Spock unfavourably to a Tribble, which causes the latter to be visibly hurt despite his quick comeback. This episode builds on that by first having Kirk tell Flavius Spock and McCoy don't know if they're enemies or not, and then, wonderfully, by having Spock save McCoy in the games. As McCoy tries and fails to thank Spock for saving his life, to Spock's predictable detachment, the two finally reach a breakthrough when McCoy declares that Spock isn't afraid of death, but is afraid of living because he lives in fear that his human half will eventually overtake his Vulcan half, and that he wouldn't know what to do if that ever happened. It's possibly the greatest scene these two characters ever get together in the Original Series, and for the first time we finally get a sense about what their relationship might actually be and why they're so confrontational towards one another. While *Star Trek* didn't have character arcs *per se*, this serves as a sufficient closure to a reoccurring motif that's been a defining aspect of Gene Coon's tenure on the show.

But as good as the character moments are, and they are quite good, the true high point of the episode is the horrific blood-sport of NBC's *You Pick The Winner*. Coon and Roddenberry's intended attack on network television and its drive for ratings through violent spectacle is so blunt and obvious it almost doesn't warrant mention. What does, however, is the combat itself: Fistfights were an integral part of *Star Trek* from the beginning, dating to "The Cage", the obligatory dust-up in "Where No Man Has Gone Before" and pretty much every other episode of the Original Series ever made. These last few weeks have seen a growing discontent with this aspect of the show from the creators themselves, most notable in the barroom brawl in "The Trouble with Tribbles" being played as laughably gratuitous, but maybe even dating back to the resolution to "I, Mudd" being a painfully staged Vaudeville routine. The peak is in "Bread and Circuses", however: Unlike almost every other fight in *Star Trek*, the games are depicted not as fun and campy action but visceral, dangerous and deeply disturbing. This is clearest in the cinematography of the fight scenes, which shoots the action in extreme close-up and makes jarring edits (where previous fight scenes had been shot at wide angles in order to give the best view of the action), giving the sense of a brutal, ugly struggle. This is not violence to take in and cheer on, this is violence intended to make us feel uncomfortable and unclean.

This then is the perfect backdrop for the show to eat itself alive against. While the script unquestionably gives the *Enterprise* crew the moral high ground and wants to grant them dignity and intelligence, the series had other ideas. Incoming producer John Meredyth Lucas observed the acrimonious atmosphere during the filming of this episode, and it shows. The actors fought each other in the arena, all looking to gain favour with Lucas in the hopes they'd be spared and declared champion. William Shatner took on Captain R.M. Roddenberry, feeling personally hurt by his renouncing of his oath to uphold the Prime Directive. And lording over the proceedings was Proconsul David Sarnoff, a candidate for the most unsettling and formidable adversary the *Enterprise* crew ever faced. The unwavering confidence Sarnoff had in his control over everything and everyone was truly disturbing, and it makes the likes of Khan Noonien Singh and any of the Klingons look like complete pushovers (and in an inspired bit of costuming, the insignia Sarnoff wears on his lapel is William Shakespeare's coat of arms). This is due in large part to the tremendous acting of Logan Ramsey, who absolutely owns every scene he's in, though it's clear Coon and Roddenberry wrote him to be a frightening presence.

But even if it weren't for the games, "Bread and Circuses" would have failed in its attempt to send off *Star Trek* as cleanly and as comprehensively as possible, because the ending is a total hatchet job. The fate of Magna Roma is left in the hands of the freed slaves, whom Kirk, Spock and McCoy had initially thought to be sun worshipers, but who in fact turn out to be *Son* worshipers, i.e., Christians. When Uhura points this out to them in the denouement (in what is maddeningly otherwise a candidate for her best scene in the entire series), Kirk smiles and seems genuinely inspired by this, emboldened in his belief that the society will progress naturally after all. This is flagrantly, unbelievably, catastrophically and self-destructively hegemonic on so many levels. Unlike previous comparable moments in the series, which were either bones tossed to the affiliates in the southern states or merely pop Christian by association owing to the fact they were the product of mainstream Western culture, this is *Star Trek* essentially converting to Christianity and encouraging everyone else to do the same as it's apparently the One True Belief, or at least part of a natural, telelogical social development path, according to the Federation. Forget "The Apple" and "The Changeling", this is the best evidence that, far from being a bit of secular utopianism, early Star Trek had an undeniable and irreducible religious streak about it. This is just in keeping with Modernization theory as "The Apple" was, and, furthermore, "Bread and Circuses" manages to make this worse with its sun/son conflation and its Roman setting. That's right: Coon and Roddenberry are (probably unintentionally, but nevertheless clearly) likening Jesus to Apollo, right after telling us Jesus will show us The Way. Yikes.

Meanwhile on Chroma, the sun continues to rise and set as she always did.

It's one thing to be a work of fiction with a Christian subtext, or even to be pop Christian by coming out of uncritical Western hegemony. It's quite another thing entirely to overtly act like a Christian missionary, thus equating your faith with neo-imperialism. This is something I need to come right out and say I have zero tolerance for, as its a line of thinking that was singlehandedly responsible for the collapse of countless spiritualities, cultures and ways of life, not to mention, well, the ones this blog comes out of. It's fine to have a faith. It's fine to talk about your faith and try to explain why you think you're correct-That's just discourse, ultimately. It is *not* fine to declare yourself arbiter of Truth and explicitly work towards erasing the beliefs of everyone else, because it's Right and Natural for everybody to end up exactly like you. Even if we accept the anti-imperialist conception of the Prime Directive, which Coon, Roddenberry and the show all seem to want us to here, there's nothing that's a grosser, more flagrant violation and rejection of it than this episode. In doing so, this means "Bread and Circuses" ends up not as a bristling bit of anarchic revolution like "Mirror, Mirror", but instead supplanting one form of imperialism with another. No wonder Shatner renounced Roddenberry.

But perhaps that in itself is a proper and fitting send-off to the original *Star Trek*. A show defined by tension, conflict of interest, ego and a shifting sense of morals and ethics that somehow managed to live on after itself again and again. The physically extent television series may be over now, but the franchise, and, more importantly, the mythology, that bears its name is just beginning. While I hesitate to call the show we can watch a classic, it most certainly created enough classic moments and toyed with enough provocative ideas that remain in the memories of generations of people who grew up watching it over the years, and this is a rare and unique phenomenon. This makes Star Trek somewhat special amongst Soda Pop Art franchises and, as we're about to see, this is part of the reason it keeps coming back and lingers so.

263

57. "It has been said that social occasions are only warfare concealed.": Journey to Babel

"Journey to Babel" is the most iconic and beloved of D.C. Fontana's Star Trek scripts, and also apparently her favourite. It's not difficult to see why, as its strengths are in the very things fans love most about Star Trek: Character development and world-building. I don't personally consider it either her best work or my favourite thing she'll ever contribute to the franchise (we have to wait for the second phase of her career for those), but it is certainly the best script of hers we've seen on the Original Series so far, and a convincing claim could be made it's her best effort of the entire show.

Primarily, of course, "Journey to Babel" comes out of a vested interest in characters. Most obviously Spock, and, to be precise, his family history. Fontana took a few lines from previous episodes about Spock's mother being human and a schoolteacher and his father being an ambassador and wrote a story designed to explore the triangular relationship and tension between them. Fontana was very interested in what kind of a human woman would willingly marry a Vulcan, what their half-human, half-Vulcan son would experience growing up and what effect this would have on the person he grew up to be. This is a fact that would be worthwhile to take note of, because it's emblematic of a very particular approach to character development that I think Fontana is especially interested in, and it seems to define the way Star Trek among other kinds of television shows handles this. The way I see it, there are at least two major ways to go about characterization (naturally, there are more than this but to simplify things I'm just going to talk about what I find to be two basic categories different tacks and tactics can be more or less squeezed in to).

The first takes a character who has a specific worldview and personality borne out of a specific positionality and is predominantly interested in seeing how they respond to a given situation, be it widespread event, an interaction with another character or so on and so forth. The second is more interested in constructing a meticulous fictional biography of the character based on, among other things, throwaway lines in other episodes, and using that to construct a comprehensive profile and life history of this character as a person. To put it another way, the first approach can be summarised as "What is this character like and how do they react to the story of the week?" while the latter can be summarised as "Why does this character think the things they think and act the way they do?". "Journey to Babel" is very much in the latter style, and I have a feeling this is the style D.C. Fontana prefers on the whole, at least at this stage in her career. It's also the style that is most clearly identifiable with Star Trek.

Now obviously both are valid ways of doing character development. On the whole I do prefer the first approach to the second myself, but both are equally worthwhile and valuable. What's more interesting to note here I argue is that, to be frank, the second approach is essentially character development by fanwank. This is not by definition a bad thing, but it does seem to be the structure in place here: Both forgo operating in the present moment to taking specific, typically unrelated, details, connecting them together and extrapolating backward in an attempt to create a definitive narrative of something. Furthermore, both are hallmarks of Cult Sci-Fi and both seem right at home in *Star Trek*. While we're still a little under half a season before it becomes eminently clear the Original Series is manifestly Cult Sci-Fi, the trappings that would reveal it as such are starting to become noticeable: It barely got renewed, references to past stories are starting to become more prevalent, there is a ridiculously passionate fanbase that is as dedicated as it is minuscule (even though they've yet to fully bring their voices together in a chorus) and it seems to now be operating by Cult Sci-Fi logic.

What makes this all the more interesting is that I'm not sure "Cult Sci-Fi" is a thing that exists yet in 1968, at least in the US: *Raumpatrouille Orion* suffered a similar fate to the original *Star Trek* in West Germany, but it absolutely did not work like what we'd call a Cult Sci-Fi show today, even though its fans most definitely comprise a cult. *Doctor Who* is known for being a Cult Sci-Fi show, but it won't achieve that status until the 1980s and it can really only be called that for about twenty years or so of its history (a blink of an eye in grand-scale franchise Soda Pop Art terms). *Star Trek*, by contrast, starts as Cult Sci-Fi and stays there forever, and in a world where "Cult Sci-Fi" isn't a genre yet to boot. This is what's so important about the Original Series-In many ways it is the maker and *Ur* example of an entire category of fiction (though it is crucial to stress *only* the Original Series: The spinoffs are something else entirely).

One might assume, given all this talk of fanwank, Cult Sci-Fi and world-building, that the unique and distinctive extraterrestrial cultures introduced in "Journey to Babel" and brought to life through its lavish costumery and prosthetics (and Fontana's savvy decision to set the whole episode on the *Enterprise* thus allowing the entire budget to go into designing the guest stars) are the most important things about it. However, no matter how memorable the Andorians and the Tellarites are and how important they're going to be to the franchise in the future (not to mention the equally distinctive unnamed races who show up), the fact is the entire political and diplomatic machinations plot is a loose framework for Fontana to drape her story about Spock, Sarek and Amanda over. Which is all well and good, as there are a number of surprisingly noticeable plot holes that detract from it significantly: Namely, it's not clear why an Orion operative was skilled enough in Vulcan *tal-shaya* to use it to expertly dispatch someone, or for that matter why framing Sarek was necessary to the plan, and I'm not sure Spock's hypothesizing of the Orion's motives in the denouement would technically have been enough to legally absolve Sarek of suspicion, which is something he probably should have caught.

As one would expect, the characters, both the main and guest casts, are handled expertly here. What's most interesting to me is that every character is simultaneously right and wrong. Sarek and Spock's preference for detached logic and adherence to regulations is obviously vital to the resolution of the crises, even though it puts strain on McCoy and Amanda. By contrast, Amanda's devotion to Sarek and the value she places in human compassion is also a self-evidently correct attitude, even if it makes decision-making difficult (and here it's interesting to note Fontana depicts Vulcan as an expressly patriarchal society through how it manifests in Sarek and Amanda's relationship, which also handily manages to retroactively redeem the one real annoying thing about "Amok Time"). Meanwhile, Kirk's loyalty to Spock and the *Enterprise,* and McCoy's to his patients are also commendable, even as they come into conflict. While his character is pulled in other directions in this episode, this also remains an echo of Spock's ability to act as a microcosm for the show due to his hybrid human and Vulcan parentage. Although McCoy "gets the last word" in a fun bit of fourth wall awareness in the final shot, "Journey to Babel" on the whole provides a far more nuanced resolution to the logic vs. emotions debate: Namely, by setting it aside and freely admitting both positions have merit and are worth holding to.

The actors too are in fine form. Leonard Nimoy is predictably brilliant, as is William Shatner: Kirk's most memorable scene for me here is his attempts to console Spock on the bridge, to Spock's evasiveness (Shatner's signature subtle overstatement conveys Kirk's mixed emotions beautifully). While Mark Lenard handles himself quite well as a Vulcan, Sarek will never have the haunting, elegiac power the Romulan Commander in "Balance of Terror" did for me, and the real standout in my opinion is Jane Wyatt as Amanda Grayson. Amanda is arguably the first time a female character in Star Trek has been allowed a lengthy sequence where she asserts her agency and gets validated for it from an expressly female perspective, albeit that of a mother, and Wyatt absolutely runs with the opportunity (despite, like William Windom in "The Doomsday Machine" not taking *Star Trek* at all seriously). It took Fontana long enough to be allowed to write a character and a scene like that, but now that she finally has the chance she proves she's gangbusters at it, as we ultimately always suspected she would be.

But this is not to say the bits of "Journey to Babel" not expressly part of the Spock/Sarek/Amanda story are entirely forgettable or not worth taking the time to look at: The fact that the Andorians and Tellarites do, in fact, become major aspects of future Star Trek and are considered iconic enough to be seen as unique signifiers of the franchise in the pop consciousness would seem to indicate they were particularly memorable parts of this episode. And indeed they are: Apart from the makeup and costume, the actual guest actors are all universally excellent and deliver distinct, standout performances. Of special note here is Reggie Nalder, who does wonders with Ambassador Shras, turning a bit part into a strong, likeable personality.

More importantly from our perspective, however, at least the perspective of the future, is that "Journey to Babel"'s political subplots mark the first time the actual governing structure of the Federation (not Starfleet) is explored in any detail. What we have here is the beginning of an idea that is both new to Star Trek in 1968 and also predominantly associated with it: The United Federation of Planets, as we know it today. Remember while we've had the Federation since way back in "Arena", it's been loosely defined at best, and there was never any concrete evidence it actually extended beyond Earth and its colonies. Here, though, it's something much larger and more complex: An alliance of multiple spacefaring civilizations from around the galaxy united by shared beliefs, principles and exchange of goods and ideas. This, the way everyone thinks of the Federation in Star Trek today, makes its first appearance in this episode and it's all D.C. Fontana's idea.

As we talked about a bit when last we discussed Fontana in "Friday's Child", the concept of the Federation, even (actually, especially) the Federation as it exists as of "Journey to Babel", is still heavily associated with particular tropes of Western-style representative democracy, and this is not actually a good thing. Although it just about works here, the real problems come when this ceases to be just a setting and becomes an idealized or utopian model we're supposed to strive for, which is how the UFP is typically read. Not to completely retread old ground, but as I brought up both in regards to "Friday's Child" and "The Apple", the US style of representative democracy the Federation is explicitly modeled on (though here it does swerve closer to the United Nations but still, you know, they're basically the same thing) doesn't actually work all that well, as anyone currently living with "representatives" reflexively pushing big corporate interests or outright fascism and operating under and devastating economics of growth and disaster can probably attest. At it's best its proved to be unsustainable and at its worst it's the terrifyingly destructive poster child for modern neo-imperialism.

But this mostly becomes an issue when idealism becomes more of a driving creative force for Star Trek and the purpose and meaning of the Federation change over the history of the franchise: This isn't actually what Fontana is getting at with "Journey to Babel". We're not meant to pay attention to the ins and outs of Federation policy (or at least any more attention than strictly necessary for the functional purposes of the narrative), and the whole reason for why the admittance of the Coridan planets is a matter of dispute is never elaborated on (nor should it have been: One of the episode's best lines in when Kirk says "The issues of the council are politically complex" and that many of the races represented "...have strong personal reasons for keeping Coridan out of the Federation." and never really goes into any more detail than that). The summit story is transparently there to give Ambassador Sarek a reason to be on the *Enterprise*, but it's handled and executed well enough it doesn't feel like it's just an excuse either. The scenes where Kirk is making small-talk and trying to keep the delegates from starting fights with each other is fun to watch, and it fulfills Gene Coon's challenge to him from "The Metamorphosis" to remember he was trained as a diplomat as well as a soldier.

And really there's not a whole lot to say more about "Journey to Babel" then that: It's straightforwardly solid and a deserved classic that lays important groundwork for the future of the franchise. Now that we're reasonably certain Star Trek is actually going to *get* some kind of a future, it's time to start work on defining what that future might look like.

58. "War. What is it good for?": A Private Little War

Well, the one good thing to say about it is that we can now be certain about who to blame for "The City on the Edge of Forever".

Yikes this one is a mess. "A Private Little War" should have been interesting, being the second episode written by Don Ingalls. As the writer of "The Alternative Factor", an episode I thought was delightfully giddily, clever and a highlight of the first season, his follow-up effort for the more experimental second season should have been a fascinating watch, if not a minor classic. However, following a comprehensive rewrite from Gene Roddenberry, the story's Vietnam-inspired anti-war subtext became Vietnam-inspired pro-war text in one of the ugliest and clunkiest transformations I've ever seen an episode undertake. The end result is a catastrophically imperialist and bigoted and right up there with "The Apple" as one of the single worst things Star Trek ever produced, and this one doesn't even hold together as a cohesive bit of narrative structure. Ingalls was so offended by this he took his name off the script and used the pseudonym "Jud Crucis", which is wordplay on the phrase "Jesus Crucified". So that sounds promising.

I mean really, what more is there to say? Kirk discovers the Klingons feeding advanced weapons technology to a peaceful, idyllic group of childlike natives because of some reasons, and his solution is to feed the *other* side weapons to preserve the "Balance of Power" and, just for good measure, explicitly stating this was the only way humanity survived the proxy wars between the United States and the Soviet Union during the Cold War. This is just about the exact same tack the show attempted back in "Friday's Child", and it should now be perfectly clear whose fault that bit of ethical bankruptcy was. We also once again have that interminable Book of Genesis Garden of Eden drivel which I'm at this point genuinely sick to death of seeing the show roll out over and over again. This time it's shown to be a tragedy, though a necessary one to introduce serpents into the garden (as opposed to "The Apple" which just considered this to be natural part of societal development), but this isn't adding any nuance to this stock, overused plot or providing a sufficiently fresh angle that would justify going over it yet again. Maybe Roddenberry should have just gone into Bible Studies instead of becoming a TV writer.

On top of that, any goodwill the episode stocked up thanks to the introduction of the really quite excellent Doctor M'Benga is quickly squandered by returning to the "Errand of Mercy" tactic of browning up the white actor portraying its Klingon adversary, something every Klingon episode in between had managed to avoid doing. Additionally, having Chekov, Scotty and Uhura freely contribute their opinions and analysis in the first bridge

268

scene, and than having the script incapacitate Spock in order to explore Kirk and McCoy's relationship, are both interesting moves except for the fact Roddenberry doesn't have Kirk listen to any of them and instead has him just go around winning arguments by shouting louder then the person he's debating against. And, since the show felt I hadn't *quite* suffered enough, it makes its primary antagonist an ambiguously brown shaman Lady Macbeth who has mastery of strange, vaguely-defined bush magic, lurks around the male cast in an obvious Judas Kiss pose and gets her comeuppance by being gang raped to death by the opposing faction because Gene Roddenberry apparently believes reactionary politics work like pinball machines and that he can somehow score an intolerance combo bonus multiplier.

Structurally, this episode is a disaster. It's perhaps tempting, though I would argue too easy, to blame this on Ingalls' original script, as no matter how much fun "The Alternative Factor" might have been no-one is going to call it an especially tight or coherent piece of work. But in that episode, the structural issues come primarily from the rushed and hectic production schedule the show was working under in its first season, and especially that week. Furthermore, those few problems it did have didn't detract from the experience because the conceit about conflicting parallel universes of matter and antimatter threatening to cause a narrative collapse through their interaction was a bonkers bit of genius, and the quirks wound up reinforcing that. "A Private Little War" doesn't have that kind of a setup to work with in the first place, and really it's pretty obvious the flow problems come from Roddenberry taking a hack saw to Ingalls' submission: Kirk's motivation and entire personality changes from scene to scene and he waffles back and forth about what his actual moral stance on the situation is, and not in a way that seems indicative of a person re-evaluating himself and his judgment. Kirk, like *Star Trek* itself, seems to be written to give all the illusion of taking a decisive stand while in truth desperately hoping to remain as neutral, apolitical and indecisive as possible. It's painfully obvious Roddenberry is trying to get Kirk to come out against what would seem to be Ingalls' anti-war intent while still making him look like the upstanding heroic moral crusader, and he just abjectly and comprehensively fails across the board.

It is also worth mentioning one of the many, many changes Roddenberry made to Ingalls' original script was making the Klingon adversary a unique character, when he was originally apparently supposed to be Kor from "Errand of Mercy". I bring this up not to focus on irrelevant production minutiae, but because in a memo dating from the production, Bob Justman apparently had this to say about that idea:

> "Here we are in the outer reaches of our galaxy and who should Captain Kirk run into, but good old Kor – an adversary that he has encountered before and with whom he has been unable to get very far. Just think of it – billions of stars and millions of Class M-type planets and who should he run into, but a fella he has had trouble with before. No wonder Kor doesn't recognize him at first. The coincidence is so astounding, that he must feel certain that it couldn't possibly have happened."

Well then.

I guess I can throw "The City on the Edge of Forever" at his feet as well, Never mind the fact that just three episodes ago we were thinking about making Koloth a reoccurring adversary, not to mention *four* episodes ago we *actually turned Harry Mudd into one*. Forget all of that: Reoccurring adversaries really are lame aren't they? I mean, who'd want to have our heroes regularly face off against an equally matched, likeable foil who had perfectly legitimate reasons to be involved in the plot and who provided an ever-present challenge to their ethics that they would have to constantly rise to defend their philosophy against? That's just *stupid*. But, we'll meet Ingalls halfway and make the new guy just as hideous a racist caricature, right? That will make it all better.

Look, when you start making Harlan Ellison look reasoned and cosmopolitan by comparison, it might just be time to re-evaluate some things about yourself and your life.

I could continue to yell and scream and rant and rave and turn this chapter into yet another 3000 word missive on how reactionary and offensive *Star Trek* is, but what's making me the angriest now is that "A Private Little War" is bad in exactly all the areas the show has been bad in the past. It's a kind of Greatest Hits version of Roddenberry's retrograde writing style, but it grates in exactly the same way "The Apple", "Friday's Child", "Who Mourns for Adonais?" and the entirety of Roddenberry's tenure as showrunner did. It contributes absolutely nothing to either the show or my discourse about and analysis of it, except I guess for the big snow-white furry poisonous ape dude. What's really the point? Star Trek has somehow, and without any help from Roddenberry, transformed itself and touched immortality this season. "A Private Little War" not only doesn't help the franchise, it doesn't even get to hinder it in any meaningful way apart from being yet more evidence to support my argument that the original *Star Trek* had more of an impact in setpieces and isolated iconic moments than it did in the aggregate as a TV show.

Ultimately this episode leaves me in a bit of a conundrum. While it's certainly not filler and most definitely another train wreck, it ends up *feeling* like filler. It's really beginning to seem like since "The Trouble with Tribbles" things have changed for Star Trek forever: I find myself far less inclined to break down and declare the show dead at this point and much more inclined to just get really annoyed that I have to review another Gene Roddenberry episode. Was "Tribbles", in addition to demi-classics like "Amok Time", "The Doomsday Machine", "Wolf in the Fold", "Mirror, Mirror" and "Journey to Babel" enough to turn this floundering ship's fortunes around to such an extent that not even Gene Roddenberry can run it aground anymore? From hindsight we can easily claim that yes, it absolutely was, but in 1968 "A Private Little War" must have seemed like yet another example of *Star Trek*'s utter lack of consistent standards or quality. In the end, the story might not be that *Star Trek* was at risk of dying, but that it was dead on arrival and has been trying to claw its way out of the grave since day one.

But we know its legacy is certain now. We can rest a bit easier. The only good thing about "A Private Little War" is that stock footage of the White Rabbit's footprints from "Shore Leave" were used for those of the Mugato. It sucks. Gene Roddenberry has to go. Let's move on.

59. "Entertain us...Or die!": The Gamesters of Triskelion

If "A Private Little War" was bad on account of being a slapdash parade of *Star Trek*'s signature reactionary concepts and a general catastrophe on all counts, this one is bad because it's just a hollow recitation of the tropes the series has accrued over the years. "The Gamesters of Triskelion" is a very promising candidate for most generic and uninspired episode of the Original Series ever. It's also the debut of the single worst writer in the entirety of Star Trek, and boy does Margaret Armen not disappoint in her inaugural outing.

Having spent the year on a quality roller coaster that wildly alternated between moments of iconic brilliance and spectacular ethical cratering, *Star Trek* finally decides to just give up and go through the motions. There is a profound sense of apathy throughout this entire production: The basic plot is a defanged and watered down rehash of "Bread and Circuses" with a critique of slavery, gambling and maybe boxing thrown in for good measure, none of which are themes the episode is particularly interested in engaging with in any meaningful way. And really, is "Slavery is bad" a statement that the supposedly ever-socially conscious *Star Trek* honestly needed to engage with in 1968? This is cheating: Giving the illusion you're saying something relevant and important while really just clinging to safe, hollow platitudes.

(Although in hindsight, and given the current geopolitical climate as I'm doing these revisions, maybe Star Trek does have to actually come out and say "Slavery is bad" every now and again. I hate everything.)

Aside from that, we have another of Kirk's cold-blooded, manipulative seduction with a painfully superficial "What Is Love?" overtone. This is capped off with a scene that could be chartiably read as the first concrete example of *Star Trek* describing its world as a utopia, except in practice it actually plays out more like a celebration of modernist teleology of the sort the show's been hampered with all season. Also, the scene in question feels like a knockoff version of Kirk's conversations with Edith Keeler about stars in "The City on the Edge of Forever". Then we have some more top graduates from the William Ware Theiss school of laughably and embarrassingly misogynistic costume design, because we were apparently due for some more of those. Uhura gets raped for literally no reason that makes any sense from the perspective of the plot or the episode's internal narrative logic except for "I guess we needed it to increase dramatic tension", so that's charming. The entire story is an absolutely tedious series of pulpish captures and escapes that were dated writing crutches ten years before this was made, and I'd call the pacing glacial if I was convinced "The Gamesters of Triskelion" actually *had* pacing. Furthermore, Spock and

271

McCoy are written so stock they no longer seem like programmatic, formulaic characters but *parodies* of programmatic, formulaic characters (and Leonard Nimoy and DeForest Kelley respond in kind).

Along those lines, this is the first episode where the criticisms of William Shatner's acting start to get the appearance of having any semblance of merit. Shatner's style of performance has always been defined by a kind of subtle overstatement that is descended from the classical theatrical style of acting where, instead of trying to get their mental state to match that of the characters and portray it as realistically as possible, actors instead directly convey information to the audience through visual and auditory cues. This does mean that theatrical actors, such as William Shatner, tend to deliver more exaggerated performances then most US audiences would be accustomed to, but there's absolutely nothing wrong with this style and I for one actually prefer it to Method Acting as I think it allows actors the freedom to do some really captivating, unique, clever and inspired things that, frankly, US audiences simply do not know (or know how) to look for on the whole. Here though, there really is no getting around it-Shatner bellows his lines at the top of his lungs and devours every bit of scenery in sight in a manner that really does invite comparisons to Brian Blessed. But this is the crucial thing critics of Shatner always miss when bringing up his behaviour in episodes such as this one: Shatner has very clearly and absolutely given up here and is no longer even trying.

Looking to something like "The Gamesters of Triskelion" and attempting to use it as an example of Shatner's standard operating procedure on *Star Trek* (or anywhere else, for that matter) is quite simply ludicrous. It's no more indicative of the character he was trying to play then DeForest Kelley drawling on to "Jimmy-Boy" and drinking mint juleps in "This Side of Paradise" was indicative of who he meant Doctor McCoy to be. This is Shatner checking out of the series and abandoning any hope he's going to be doing anything remotely resembling intelligence, and just deciding to go as bananas as possible to troll everyone and get some manner of enjoyment out of his increasingly inane and frustrating job. And honestly, given what a damp squib of a production Paramount and Deislu regurgitated up this week I don't blame him in the slightest. However that said, and while this is a mode Shatner is occasionally known to slip in to on *Star Trek* (and increasingly so after this point in the series), I actually find that speaks more of the show then him. It's no secret we're rapidly approaching the third season, which is universally (and deservedly, I'll make the claim right now) considered the rubbish year. Given the fact season one was morally bankrupt and season two has been a hot mess from start to finish, the fact it's the third season that stands out as the "silly" one is frighteningly telling.

But these are all concerns for the future. In the here and now, I have to finish analysing the episode at hand, which presents me with something of a problem as this is another story with a worrying dearth of actual interesting material and I have now essentially exhausted the possible observations to make about it. And the really sad thing is this is actually far and away Margaret Armen's best effort and possibly the most prolific of Star Trek's first generation of writers. I would completely understand if you were to close the book now and run screaming madly into the hills.

So let's have fun again and overanalyse some random piece of minutiae in an effort to tease something, *anything,* out of "The Gamesters of Triskelion". One thing that caught my attention in this episode was that the slaves-competitors on Triskelion were called "thralls". In Old Scandinavian history, a thrall was a bonded serf and on the lowest level of the social order during the Viking age. Now, contrary to popular belief, the terms "Viking" and "Nordic" are not actually interchangeable: The Viking lifestyle is but one manifestation of a culture and mythology common to the pre-Roman, pre-Christian peoples in Northern Europe. The Vikings were the latest and most combative subgroup of what is more properly called Germanic heathenism or paganism. Much like the cultures on the various Polynesian and other south Pacific islands are emanations and regional variations of a unique Oceanic worldview and set of experience, so also can it be argued the Celts, Vikings, Gauls and pre-Norse Nordic peoples were linked by a similar regional perspective. The Vikings were merely the last, best-documented manifestation of this culture.

What's important to note about Germanic heathenism, for me at least, is that it is largely not the origin of what I frequently refer to in this book as the contemporary Western modernity. I would instead argue the way of life known to most post-industrial late-stage capitalist societies is primarily descended from Ancient Greece and (as "Bread and Circuses" so aptly showed us before chickening out in the denouement) the give-and-take tension between the Roman Empire and Christianity (though the other Abrahamic religions played a role too). This means, as typically happens with empires, the actual indigenous population, cultures and belief systems unique to Northern Europe were in fact displaced themselves, just as was the case everywhere else in the world. The evidence and legacy of these peoples lingers on in some places, most notably in regions north of the 50th parallel (naturally the Nordic and Scandinavian countries, but also Greenland and parts of the British isles, Canada and New England), but it largely remains one curiously European casualty of Western imperialism. Indeed, the Vikings' warlike expeditions were most likely their reaction against coercive Christian encroachment into the Scandinavian territories.

The relevance of this to "The Gamesters of Triskelion" comes, as I hinted at above, in the script's use of the term "thrall". This is clearly meant to evoke a European form of servitude to tie into the episode's anti-slavery theme, but the choice of "thrall" is actually really weird. Naturally, I would have preferred had they used the word "serf", as I feel its connotations to medieval Feudalism would have given the story an extra interpretative layer given its associations with manor life and control of land. To me this would have been a far stronger statement that would also have shot right to the heart of arguably the most classical Western motifs after those of the Hellenistic era. As it is the invocation of the Vikings feels off to me, my own fondness for the Celtic and Germanic peoples aside: If the intent was to link slavery with European imperialism the Vikings were probably the least effective group to call on, being on the whole more general pirates and explorers then empire builders. Honestly, Margaret Armen really would probably have been better off just flat-out calling them slaves: Certainly slavery is associated with Westernism enough as it is.

Not that she would have because, as we shall unfortunately see sooner rather than later,

Armen is legitimately horrifying.

However "thrall" also calls to my mind something Armen absolutely would not have known about, but since Vaka Rangi is as much about time travel as it is straight historical analysis I can get away with mentioning it. In the video game *The Elder Scrolls V: Skyrim*, which draws heavily on aspects of Germanic heathenism, including the Vikings, the word "thrall" is used to describe a reanimated zombie-like body controlled by a powerful necromancer. Although we're still several weeks out from this becoming a blatantly explicit comparison, the analogy is far, far too good for me to ignore. Kirk, Chekov and Uhura become thralls to an all-powerful but bored and petty audience that makes them compete in violent but overly complicated and pointless blood sport for their mild amusement, which they then place bets on. Read this way, "The Gamesters of Triskelion" is almost more bitter and cynical then "Bread and Circuses". The moldering corpse of the dead and buried TV show is dug up and made to dance for us.

It's still boring as shit though.

60. "...is there not some reason to fear I may be wrong?": Obsession

"Obsession" is *Moby-Dick* for Star Trek again, so firstly all of the comments I made the last time we talked about this kind of story in "The Doomsday Machine" still apply. There is fundamentally not a whole lot to add to that (except for one issue I'll discuss a little later). The primary problem is, as always, the idea of doing a blind vengeance story in a setting that's supposedly more enlightened, idealistic and utopian. With Commodore Decker this worked, because we could get a character study about the tragic fall of someone consumed by a need for revenge without jeopardizing one of our own: Imagine, for a moment, that Decker's role in "The Doomsday Machine" had been filled by Kirk, McCoy or Sulu: There's no way the show could come back from that the next week, because the nature of serialized anthology television necessitates hitting the reset button in the last two minutes of every episode and doing that after that kind of intensely personal story would have been catastrophic. Furthermore, by essentially casting the *Enterprise* crew as Ishmael, this upholds the narrative reiteration structure that helped make the episode successful and also helped push the series towards the idealism it will soon become famous for.

In short, this is the problem "Obsession" is continuously grappling with. It's doing *Moby-Dick* again, except this time with Kirk as Ahab. Ultimately this is really a bit lazy more than anything else, yet more evidence *Star Trek* and other US TV shows really need fewer episodes a year in order to better vet their scripts. At least this one is actually somewhat coherent and isn't a total write-off like the past few weeks have been (though it does randomly kill off a recurring character only to bring them back without explanation later on). It does stretch the utopianism reading slightly, but remember Star Trek isn't actually utopian yet and this isn't actually as huge of a derailment as we might otherwise think.

The success or failure of this story was always going to hinge on how the script handled conflict, and to its credit "Obsession" at least doesn't totally blow it-It handles the problem about as well as could have been expected of it. It helps greatly that Kirk's turmoil isn't just vengeance here but guilt and self-doubt about his hesitation when facing the Vampire Cloud eleven years prior and his inability to save the crew of the *Farragut*. Depicting Ensign Garrovick as someone Kirk sees as a reflection of his younger self is a very nice touch (down to him finding himself in an echo of the situation Kirk faced when he was in his place), and their reconciliation in Act Four is a great character scene that's ahead of its time and takes some of the edge off of the episode's biggest problem: "Obsession" simply ties itself in knots trying to keep Kirk the hero and moral centre of the story and is trying desperately to keep him in a heroically authoritarian light.

275

The first half of the story plays out very similarly to "The Conscience of the King" where Kirk's judgment is cast into doubt because of his intensely personal connection to the situation and a fear he's no longer looking out for the welfare of the ship and the crew, but out for blood. At one point McCoy even tried to determine if he is medically unfit for command. However, unlike "The Conscience of the King" which was allowed to be far more of a character piece (perhaps by virtue of its overt theatricality), Kirk isn't actually allowed to learn anything here and in the second half of the episode the script turns itself inside out and reveals Kirk was in the right all along, and goes out of its way to show McCoy's concern was unjustified, thus undermining one of the best moments DeForest Kelley's been allowed all season when he talks to Kirk in his quarters about the nature of guilt. This need not be fundamentally a bad thing, as I feel the idea characters need to learn something every episode is a largely unhelpful and counterproductive one, but "Obsession" didn't need to do this by forcing Kirk into the heroic lead role and belittling everyone else by showing they were worrying over nothing.

The interesting flip side is that in doing this, "Obsession" actually helps further *Star Trek*'s claim to be considered a work of idealism. What makes the scene in Kirk's quarters such a success, despite it being in many ways a rehash of what amounts to basically the exact same scene in "The Conscience of the King", is that Kirk, Spock and McCoy have an actual intelligent discussion about their concerns. Kirk is still visibly on edge, but he tries to do his best to keep his anger contained and, when challenged by Spock and McCoy, calmly defends himself and articulates reasons why he doesn't feel he's become consumed by vengeance but is instead acting with the best interests of the ship, the crew and local space in mind (which, of course, turn out to be true once the Vampire Cloud invades the *Enterprise*). This is a surprisingly mature and intellectual approach to problem solving for this show: Kirk doesn't hide the fact he's personally affected by self-doubt and feels guilt over his previous actions, but he quite correctly states he can't control that but has to rely on what his intuition tells him is the best thing to do. Instead of wallowing in pain and anguish for our voyeuristic amusement, Kirk actually discusses his feelings and opinions with his friends and colleagues. And, of course, William Shatner is perfect at this and his performance here is 180 degrees around from his antics last week, deftly signaling each and every one of Kirk's conflicted emotions, sufficiently demonstrating that the best way to prevent him from hamtastically eating the set is to give him an intelligent bit of writing to work with.

"Obsession" also provides us the first look at something we could conceivably call indicative of the style of new producer John Meredyth Lucas. Although the first episode to go out under his watch was "Journey to Babel" that was largely an example of letting an established veteran do her thing, which is good because that one was by D.C. Fontana and it takes talent to screw up a script of hers. "A Private Little War" saw the chair go back to Gene Coon, which is sad because he had to deal with Gene Roddenberry again. "The Gamesters of Triskelion" was Lucas', which is deeply unfortunate, but remember at this point in Coon's tenure we were still dealing with things like "Miri", so we should cut him the same amount of slack (it's also interesting to note "Obsession" is Lucas' third story as producer and "The Conscience of the King" was Coon's second). However, the problem the Lucas era has is that, while quite solid by Star Trek standards, it never really gets the chance to develop its own unique voice and perspective. Lucas is here for eight more weeks and then hastily abandons the show along with Roddenberry, Coon and Fontana as soon as "Assignment: Earth" wraps, and, unlike Roddenberry, he doesn't lurk around the franchise for the next twenty-five years such that we get intimately familiar with his worldview. Along with Coon and Fontana he'll occasionally pop in over the course of the third season to contribute a script, often under a pseudonym, but, just like them, it's clear he doesn't have any serious expectations about getting his conception of Star Trek seen and heard. He's here to put out fires, and there are rather a lot of fires around.

Some might even say "conflagrations".

As a result, "Obsession" is about the closest we're ever going to get to what a typical episode of John Meredyth Lucas' *Star Trek* might have looked like, although I'll do my best to try and tease his voice out of the remainder of the stories he's involved in. From what I can gather, and remember this is only his third episode, despite having written "The Changeling", Lucas does seem to be more interested the character side of *Star Trek* then the "Strange New Worlds" concept. The Vampire Cloud is once again a malevolent Other and is just there to give Kirk and Garrovick something to, well, obsess over. He also seems to be interested in logic vs. emotions debates: On the surface this causes me to roll my eyes because Fontana has already wrapped all that up to a satisfactory degree by now, but to his credit Lucas' episodes (at least this one) seem to understand they're going out into a post-"Journey of Babel" *Star Trek* and show how all the main characters call upon a mixture of logic and emotions to make decisions. Even "The Changeling" showed Kirk having to use a combination of logic and improvisation to outwit *Nomad*.

(I'd talk more about the actual writer of "Obsession", Art Wallace, except his only other Trek credit is co-writing "Assignment: Earth", which is mostly a Roddenberry effort anyway. However, as the writer of the first seventeen weeks of the horror soap opera *Dark Shadows* and the author of that series' bible, he's definitely an interesting person to see connected to *Star Trek*).

But as sound as "Obsession" ends up in spite of its less-than-ideal central concept, it's tough to see it as a good sign either. To see this kind of personnel shakeup behind the scenes going into the tail-end of a season that's seen a mixture of absolute classics and absolute nightmares is not encouraging, especially when the people beginning to retreat are the very people who turned *Star Trek* into a show that was capable of turning out those classics in the first place. From the perspective of the future, the looming cancellation casts a dark shadow of its own over the proceedings, and it's tough to feel anything but sorry for John Meredyth Lucas, knowing he's inheriting a show that's on its way towards losing many of its best assets and will ultimately, and quickly, prove to be a sinking ship that he'll be unable to turn around. But with an irritable cast, a terrible track record for quality, an apathetic network and ratings that could charitably called middling, it's no surprise the end is coming soon.

61. "A world sinks thus; and yon majestic Heaven...": The Immunity Syndrome

Well, here's something I wasn't at all expecting. Given how *Star Trek* has been seriously underperforming the last few weeks as well as the fact the series has been steadily but noticeably running out of steam since midway through the season I fully anticipated that the episode about the Giant Space Amoeba would be another silly runaround, especially as my memory of it consisted mostly of some agonizing debate over Spock taking on a suicide mission from which it was eminently clear he was going to come back, as well as of the aforementioned Giant Space Amoeba. I was totally prepared to glibly take the piss out of this one as another example of *Star Trek*'s inevitable march towards cancellation.

I mean it still is that, but in many ways "The Immunity Syndrome" is also properly excellent.

Firstly. the episode "The Immunity Syndrome" is most immediately comparable with is "The Doomsday Machine", from which it inherits its thriller structure. Once again, we have a tense countdown to destruction that is narrowly averted at the last possible second and which keeps us on the edge of our seats throughout the entire story. Perhaps as a result, this is a laudably tight and exciting production, and, like its predecessor, a sterling example of what an "average" (to use a potentially loaded term) episode of *Star Trek* in its second season *ought* to look like. However it's a great deal more than that: In this regard (and uncannily so given "A Private Little War" is still relatively fresh in the memory) "The Immunity Syndrome" may actually be closer to "The Alternative Factor", because the threat posed by the Giant Space Amoeba for almost the entire runtime of the episode is an honest-to-goodness narrative collapse.

We've come perilously close to narrative collapse a number of times in *Star Trek* so far. "The Alternative Factor" is, naturally, the most obvious example, but as I mentioned in its corresponding chapter, "The Menagerie" at least flirted with the iconography of collapse, though thanks to a combination of the approach of the early Gene Coon era and Gene Roddenberry's general writerly incompetence that's not quite what we got. "The Immunity Syndrome", however, is the closest we've gotten yet, and while it ultimately stops just short of becoming one, for the vast majority of the episode it seems like it just might go all the way. The telltale sign comes in the very first act, when the *Enterprise* discovers the aptly named Zone of Darkness, which immediately begins to sap the life force of both the ship and its crew. Within the zone, there is no starlight, either because it's been blocked by something or all the stars have simply gone out. Now a lot of calamitous things can happen on *Star Trek*: The show threatens the destruction of the ship or the death of crewmembers on a seemingly weekly basis. But as far as I'm concerned, if you take away the stars from Star Trek, that really is it.

Even before that, in the teaser we see Spock recoiling in horror at the destruction of the *Intrepid* and her crew of Vulcans, which he can sense thanks to a species-wide empathic link. Spock describes the *Intrepid* as not just "destroyed", but actually "dead". It's a commonly circulated piece of Star Trek fan lore typically attributed to Gene Roddenberry that the Starship *Enterprise* (or starship *Voyager* or Starbase *Deep Space 9*) should be seen as a character unto itself and just as important to the show as any of the other regulars (and in reality this probably comes from Dave Gerrold or D.C. Fontana, as Roddenberry had to actually be convinced to use an *Enterprise* on *Star Trek: The Next Generation* instead of increasing the range of the transporter). In other words, what we have in "The Immunity Syndrome" is a threat big enough to actually kill the *Enterprise*. It's tough to think of something that, at this point in the show's history, could seem more like a direct and grave threat to its diegetic existence than this: Vaporize whole sectors of space and you have drama for an episode. Kill the *Enterprise* and you kill Star Trek.

The behaviour of the Giant Space Amoeba is also interesting to note, as it's described on a number of occasions as a virus, that is, something foreign and dangerous that has invaded the body of the galaxy and needs to be purged before it spreads and infects everything. This rhetoric, just as it was in "The Return of the Archons" last year, is potentially worrying because it has the potential to tread into xenophobia. That said "The Immunity Syndrome" is thankfully divorced of clunkily handled metaphor because the Giant Space Amoeba is simply exactly that: A Unicellular organism, albeit one that's the size of a solar system. In spite of all this though it remains a form of New Life (you know, one of the things the *Enterprise* is supposed to be on a mission to Seek Out), so Kirk's by this point signature solution of Blowing It The Fuck Up grates, even if it you could maybe argue his only option.

However, this is distinguished from the more ethically troubling iterations of this in the past by a number of factors. Firstly, the Giant Space Amoeba, being a form of single-celled life, can hardly be called sentient, and if we start arguing for the rights of viruses we're probably going to have some serious problems. Secondly though, everything up to the climax shows the crew trying their hardest to make scientific observations about a heretofore unknown type of creature, and McCoy is perfectly willing to risk his life to work in "the greatest biology laboratory ever". It does seem like somewhere a corner was turned in the crew's standard operating procedure: They're starting to act more like scientists and explorers than soldiers and policemen, and on a more regular and noticeable basis. Crucially though this still almost gets everyone killed because they suck at it-Every attempt the crew makes to study and learn more about the Giant Space Amoeba causes it to react in such a way that it causes things to become markedly worse for them.

Ultimately of course it's the possible death of Spock that truly marks "The Immunity Syndrome" as a narrative collapse in waiting. While narrative collapses do result in the restoration of a work's ability to tell its stories, this typically comes at a massive, tragic cost, and the death of a major character would certainly suffice. The choice of Spock out of everyone is particularly visceral: As the embodiment of *Star Trek*'s central duality that dates back to Gene Roddenberry and "The Cage" and the character frequently representative of the very best the series tries to strive for, this would be a mighty loss indeed. And, appropriately, "The Immunity Syndrome" goes to great lengths to lead us to believe this might very well be Spock's final bow up until the very last scene, tying in nicely with the thriller structure the episode employs elsewhere. We've had the death of major characters threatened before (Spock alone has faced death a not-insignificant amount of times just this season), but in the past this has always been clearly a fake-out in order to drum up dramatic tension cheaply and quickly. There's absolutely no doubt Spock's going to survive something like the gunshot in "A Private Little War", for example-That was only put in to get him out of the story for awhile. Here though, the entire episode is basically set up to telegraph Spock's ultimate fall, with the story gradually building to his supposed heroic sacrifice from his horror in the teaser, which also results in one of his very best moments in the series so far when he criticizes McCoy, and by extension humanity, for their lack of empathy, declaring, probably rightly, that if we had the same conception of a greater whole that Vulcans do our history "would have been a lot less bloody".

But killing off Spock would have done more than just provide the sacrificial lamb necessary to escape narrative collapse: Killing Spock would have finished off Star Trek just as effectively as killing the *Enterprise*: As not just a major character but the central one who symbolizes the show itself and its core themes to every demographic of fan and someone who as a result becomes one of the most iconic aspects of the entire franchise, having him die here would have been absolutely catastrophic, probably bringing about a narrative collapse of its own. Which is why, in the end, "The Immunity Syndrome" once again backs away from unleashing the true horror it was hinting at on the show. Spock miraculously survives his mission and Kirk gets to blast his way out of a problem once again. *Star Trek* avoids narrative collapse a second time, but we're left with the worrying notion that this time it was a little too close for comfort. And in a sense "The Immunity Syndrome" has condemned the series anyway: By destroying yet another previously unknown, and possibly unique, form of life, the show has really demonstrated itself to be nothing more than a hypocrite. Kirk can talk all he wants about being on a mission of peaceful exploration, but we all know exactly what he's going to do when the chips are down.

The only qualifier I may have with this reading is the source of this potential narrative collapse itself. While it serves very well as an unknown form of life, and thus by definition something the *Enterprise* crew are on the whole unable to deal with, the effectiveness of the Giant Space Amoeba as a believable threat to the very fabric of *Star Trek* is...somewhat limited by the fact that it is, in truth, well...A Giant Space Amoeba. This alone means "The Immunity Syndrome" comes across as a little lacking when compared to "The Alternative Factor", the latter episode having as it does matter and antimatter realities that pose a danger to the show's coherence by virtue of traumatic metafictional multiplicity (although it is interesting that within the Zone of Darkness things seem to run backwards, much like one would expect in a realm opposite of ours). Perhaps that can be seen as part of the joke though: *Star Trek* is on such shaky ground that a Giant Space Amoeba is almost all it takes to snap the series like a twig. All that said, the Giant Space Amoeba is a truly fantastic visual effect, both the original design and the CGI re-imagining that's part of the new effects added to the rebroadcast syndicated run of the Original Series that aired in the mid-to-late 2000s and that's available now on all the home media versions as an optional extra.

It's also crucial this happens now, at the tail-end of the second season and in the first script of John Meredyth Lucas' tenure as producer that can actually be called basically functional. Behind the scenes, the show really is flying apart at the seams, and it's starting to look more and more like *Star Trek* isn't coming back next year. There's seven episodes left to air in the season, and only five of those really actually count. Barring something unprecedented, like, say, a large-scale fan-driven letter-writing campaign demanding the show be kept on the air, one does get the distinct sense *Star Trek* is winding down. This is the perfect time to put out an episode like this, seeming as it does to be such an extradiegetic critique of the show's structure and basic ethics. Was it, ultimately, the show seems to be asking of itself as much as it is of us, at all worth it? Well, we have to wait a few more weeks to get the answer to that.

62. "This is MY town!": A Piece of the Action

OK yes, it's absolutely delightful.

Actually, it's better than it lets on, and to find a reason why look no further than that second writing credit. Gene Coon had decided that, given the success of "The Trouble with Tribbles", *Star Trek* could use more episodes with a larger and more overt focus on comedy (and it's worth noting it was Coon who saw the potential in young Dave Gerrold's script, encouraged him to keep submitting to *Star Trek* and who helped him shape "Tribbles" into the masterpiece it became). George Clayton-Johnson, the author of "The Man Trap", had written an early version of this story as a treatment early in the first season called "Chicago II". The actual idea for the episode is frequently attributed to Gene Roddenberry due to a two-word pitch (among many others like it) in his original 1964 proposal for Star Trek, *Star Trek Is...*, entitled "President Capone", but as it's a rather strangled path from that to what we can watch on screen, it's tough for me to give him full credit for it. Coon discovered Clayton-Johnson's script, liked the idea and decided to retool it. Coon's writing partner here is David P. Harmon, whose previous Star Trek credit was "The Deadly Years", which is not especially encouraging, but thankfully, "A Piece of the Action" turned out beautifully: It's a highlight of the season, deservedly one of the most iconic stories of the series and exactly the sort of thing the show needed right about now.

The knee-jerk way to read "A Piece of the Action" is through its Cargo Cult undertones, and as it turns out this is what I expected I'd be spending this chapter going on about. In the most pleasant of surprises, "A Piece of the Action" manages to avoid the majority of the flak involved with this kind of prompt, (I freely admit I'm capable of underestimating *Star Trek*, but given this season has made me sit through "Who Mourns for Adonais?", "Friday's Child", "The Apple", "The Deadly Years" and "The Gamesters of Triskelion" I maintain I had some right to lower my expectations) but first let's talk a bit about what we mean by Cargo Cult. A Cargo Cult refers to what allegedly happens when, following contact with Western colonial powers whose presence results in a short-term burst of material prosperity, non-Western peoples establish a new religion based around worship of specific aspects of Western materialism in a hope this will bring about a return to that period of prosperity. The most famous example of a Cargo Cult took place in Melanesia following World War II, when natives began worshiping spiritual versions of US servicemen prophesized to return to teach them how to to live in plenty.

Obviously, as a particularly blatant example of how callous and thoughtless Western expansion thoroughly wrecked traditional Oceanian societies, Cargo Cults are not a phenomenon I'm not especially fond of, especially when they're so frequently treated in the West as a source of mild paternalistic bemusement. Also, there's the small matter that they don't work and most of the cited cases are gross oversimplifications. And it could be, and often has been, argued that the Iotians in "A Piece of the Action" are a planetwide culture built around a Cargo Cult of the book *Chicago Mobs of the Twenties.* Certainly all the Prime Directive hand-wringing in this episode seems to support that interpretation, with Kirk, Spock and McCoy all very concerned about future "contamination" and "corruption" of the native culture. Except I'm not entirely convinced this is the best way to read "A Piece of the Action": In fact, a better approach might actually be to compare it to a *Doctor Who* serial.

I want to avoid going into a huge amount of detail on *Doctor Who* here, as there was simply no creative diffusion between it and Star Trek in the 1960s and frankly the majority of you know where to go if you want information on the other big science fiction-fantasy franchise kicking around television during this time (and for the rest, check this book's Acknowledgments and "Also from Eruditorum Press"). There will be a Sensor Scan on *Doctor Who* at a specially preordained time as there is in fact a point where it actually does enter into both my narrative and that of Star Trek, but let's just say for now one of the most important things to understand about what *Doctor Who* is and how it operates is that it's a highly literary (in a very literal sense) show known in part for its ability to bend, deform and explore different genres. The Doctor's power comes from his ability to invade other people's stories.

In some ways this is what's going on here-The Iotians are not a society built around historical accounts of Chicago gang wars, they're a society built around the tropes and motifs of exciting gangster crime stories. This isn't entirely clear in the script (although it's never called as such, *Chicago Mobs of the Twenties* is implied to be a history book which means this is the one part of the episode that may actually be improved by its *Star Trek: The Next Generation* remake, which is in every other respect a fantastically missed opportunity), but it totally is everywhere else in the production: Everything is deliberately overplayed; there are heaters and mobs and molls and moonshiners and pinstripe suits and pool tables. Naturally, this is just about heaven for William Shatner, who seems clearly and absolutely in his element here in a way we really haven't seen him before.

Over the course of the episode, Shatner-as-Kirk slowly realises he's in a different story and that his usual tactics of diplomacy-or-gunfire aren't going to work, and his transformation from weary exasperation in the first act to fully-clothed mob boss character in the last is a magnificent bit of acting. Funnily enough, despite being arguably the preeminent creative force in shaping *Star Trek* to become a show that can do stories like, well, this, Gene Coon has on the whole avoided writing Kirk the way Shatner so obviously wants to play him, as a delightfully campy drag action hero. In his past scripts, Coon has tended to use Kirk as a stand-in for the show's ethics, and under every writer except Paul Schneider, who seemed to actually get where Kirk's actual potential as a character lay, Shatner has had to fight to keep from being written as, well, a Hollywood action male lead. Here though, Coon writes Kirk as someone constantly improvising his performance on the fly, and Shatner couldn't be happier, playing off Coon's material with positively flying colours. What we wind up with then is a kind of recursive artifice: Shatner doing a subtly exaggerated performance of Kirk doing a subtly exaggerated performance of a 1920s mob boss. It is a genius, *genius* bit of theatrical flourish that goes criminally under-appreciated and under-recognised. Furthermore, this is without doubt William Shatner's defining move: If there's one thing that ought to go down as his signature contribution to the performing arts, this is it.

(And not to completely ignore the other actors, who are all brilliant as well, special props have to go to James Doohan, whose confused, befuddled reaction to "Koik's" solution to the Iotian situation is marvelous, and, of course, Leonard Nimoy, who has Spock try his absolute best to join in on the act. "I would advise yas to keep dialin', Oxmyx." is a thing of absolute beauty and probably the blueprint for about 70% of the jokes about Commander Data in *Star Trek: The Next Generation*.)

But there are other reasons why "A Piece of the Action" isn't something quite as simple or straightforward as a Cargo Cult story. Firstly, the Iotians are not depicted as childlike Noble Space Savages, we've seen those before on *Star Trek* and this is something altogether different. Spock mentions in passing early on that prior to the incident with the *Horizon*, Sigma Iotia II was just entering its industrial revolution. Later on, during a discussion about *Chicago Mobs of the Twenties*, Bella Oxmyx says that the *Horizon* crew left a lot of books behind, in particular textbooks, but this was the most important one. Clearly the Iotians understand what these objects are and where they came from. The clincher comes when Oxmyx refers to *Chicago Mobs of the Twenties* as *The* Book, and Spock states the Iotians latched onto it and turned it into their Bible. These people are not are not, for once, some warped conception of indigenous Oceanic people extrapolated to a science fiction setting and dropped into some Space Age Garden of Eden (thank The Prophets for that). No, the Iotians are Westerners, and that changes everything.

For the first time then we have the Federation portrayed as something that might conceivably be above and beyond Westernism instead of something that is just an extension or extrapolation of it. The overt performativity of Shatner-as-Kirk and the rest of the production in this case takes on a new meaning, almost as if it's trying to tell us the world of Star Trek doesn't really belong here (after all, it is, as Boss Kirk says, a "small-time operation"). Read this way, "A Piece of the Action" can be seen as fulfilling the potential "Bread and Circuses" was hinting at before Gene Roddenberry came along and defanged it (I know it was a joint effort but come on, we all know who that episode's denouement really sounds like). Of course, this approach has problems of its own: No matter how hard future Star Trek will try to show the Federation is a wonderful ideal we can all strive for, the fact remains the whole concept of any sort of "federation" is wrapped up in Western tropes and ideas to begin with. The United Federation of Planets is an inescapably Western utopia, and it has all of Westernism's problems. Once again though, I'll draw a line between "The Federation" and "The World of Star Trek". The former may not be a viable way forward, but the latter may well be, and that's what "A Piece of the Action" is helping set the stage for as much as anything else.

The key scene is without doubt the climax. Of all the "Kirk shows up and straightens out a backward or problematic society" we've seen in *Star Trek* so far, this might be the greatest and most unique. While it's accepted a unified planetary society is where Sigma Iotia II *should* end up (which irritates both my anarchist and anthropological senses as unified planetary societies are yet another extrapolation of a non-functional Western idea, namely that of the nation-state), the actual approach the show endorses is one of the most unorthodox, and brilliant, in the entire history of Star Trek. Boss Kirk doesn't encourage the Iotians to form a United Nations or some other form of representative democracy: Instead, he proposes the different mob bosses get together and form a syndicate, cutting him in for a percentage of the organisation's net value.

I can't get over how fascinating and delightful this ending is: First of all in many ways a criminal outfit like a mob syndicate does in fact work better than a representative democracy, in spite of its more unscrupulous aspects (compare Las Vegas in the 1960s and 1970s to Las Vegas today for a textbook example of this, or just read any of Hunter S. Thompson's late-period writings), and in this episode *Star Trek* actually seems to be acknowledging that. Secondly, this is another example of how "A Piece of the Action" recognises and plays off its performativity so well: Essentially, Boss Kirk gets so wrapped up in his role he forgets he's supposed to deliver the "proper" *Star Trek* moral, which Spock actually points out in the denouement, reminding him this is going to be tough to explain to Starfleet Command. Wonderfully, Kirk retains his mob boss persona even when back on board the *Enterprise*, seemingly only partially aware of the extent to which he's genuinely subverted the entire show here. For that matter, I might even be able to redeem the whole united planet thing: A core tenet of anarchic individualism (as opposed to right-wing libertarian "American" "Individualism") is that alliances of individuals should form based around shared interests, worldviews and goals. Maybe that's what the syndicate is: A streamlining of the native system already in place designed around the idea the different mob bosses are too similar to be fighting each other.

"A Piece of the Action" isn't the best episode of the season (For my money "The Trouble with Tribbles" is still untouchable for a number of extradiegetic reasons even this episode can't come close to) but it's bloody fantastic and one of the best episodes in the series by far. Additionally, it contributes something to the evolving narrative that's truly invaluable-Coming here at the tail end of a season of rapidly deteriorating quality, this is the concrete evidence we needed that "Tribbles" was more than a fluke success and that Star Trek might actually really be special and that it really does have the potential to offer something of genuine greatness. At long last, every one of the series' more radical and experimental factors seem to be working in harmony here and we get the first undeniable clue of what they're capable of. No matter where the last few episodes of the year go, at least Gene Coon, the first person to make *Star Trek* Star Trek, has finally given us a defining statement.

63. "On your television screen": By Any Other Name

This was most likely one of the first episodes of the Original Series I ever saw. One of the VHS tapes I rented from the local video store when I was first getting really into *Star Trek: The Next Generation* to see what all the fuss over this older show from the 1960s was. Although I certainly knew the Original Series existed, my practical experience with it came mostly from pop culture references and the numerous books and video games I had about or set during the show's time period. I never saw this show in syndication (in fact the first time I got to see it in order was when the Sci-Fi Channel picked it up sometime in the mid-to-late 1990s, a consequence of possessing about four TV stations during my more formative years), so these scattered and assorted VHS tapes were my first real window into Star Trek's past. It may well have been among the first two tapes I got, along with "The Trouble with Tribbles", although I may be blurring memories of multiple rental events into one due to the passage of time.

What I do remember most vividly about this episode is how the brightness and colour-fulness of the Original Series contrasted with the look of *Star Trek: The Next Generation*. Now, I'm not one to claim the 1980s and 1990s shows have a drab, dull, faded or Grey look about them-I am in fact very much in love with the look-and-feel of at least both *Star Trek: The Next Generation* and early *Star Trek: Deep Space Nine*. As far as I'm concerned there's a vastness of scale and a sense of wonder to those shows the other Trek eras simply don't possess, but which is mitigated by a genuine feeling of warmth, intimacy and welcoming. My memories of these shows paint the USS *Enterprise* NCC-1701-D and *Deep Space 9* as things very much radiant and alive. If you need further convincing, I more than encourage you to check out the recent Blu-ray transfer of *Star Trek: The Next Generation*: 1980s broadcast technology hamstrung that show's sensory impact significantly, as did the previous less-than-acceptable home video transfers of steadily decreasing quality (the DVD transfer is taken from the original VHS transfer, for example, and following several generations of signal decay to boot). On Blu-ray, the show looks the way the creators intended for the very first time.

However, this is very unlike the sheer 1960s primary colour gaudiness of the Original Series, and I don't mean this in a bad way at all (I mean at least as a general rule: There are some episodes coming up next season that look astonishingly trashy in a way the Original Series' theatricality usually manages to avoid). I found the Crayon-bright uniforms on Kirk, Spock, McCoy and Scotty combined with the verdant planet where they respond to the Kelvans' fake distress signal to be quite striking at the time (although upon watching it both in the order and in the rapid succession I'm going at it does look rather a lot like a number of other Class M planets the crew has landed on, probably because it was in all likelihood the same location). I also recall both the transporter and phaser effects, which, to someone accustomed to Rob Legato's practical effects for *Star Trek: The Next Generation* which were as laudably workmanlike as they were cutting-edge and boundary-pushing, seemed ever-so-slightly off (although upon reflection, there aren't any transporter or phaser effects in "By Any Other Name", are there?). I remember Kelinda too sticking out quite strongly, and no, not for the reasons you might presume. Say what you will about William Ware Theiss (and I do, a lot) the man had a real talent for designing eye-catching costumes for TV, and that weird, angular, blue-gray jumpsuit with no back definitely stands out, and I suppose in more ways then one.

And of course, it's difficult to forget the Kelvans turning the crew into Styrofoam Dungeons and Dragons dice (apparently they were based on a Mexican onyx dodecahedron D.C. Fontana gave to Gene Roddenberry). Styrofoam has a (somewhat deserved) reputation for being the material of choice for no-budget overreaching TV productions but, just like any prop it can be used quite effectively if the rest of the production makes up for it. Although, seeing it again the Kelvan field projections were probably not made out of Styrofoam: Styrofoam doesn't crumble to dust the way Yeoman Thompson does when she's killed by Rojan (and once again it's nice, by which I mean not nice in the slightest, that we not only have another generic Redshirt killed but a woman to boot. I suppose when the choice is the black guy or the white woman you've sort of written yourself into a no-win situation, although it all could have been avoided by, you know, not randomly murdering people on primetime TV). It was certainly effective though: It's intensely visceral to watch that thing crumble; you can almost hear and feel it within your body, and I remember being genuinely upset to see Uhura and Chekov turned into dice, despite knowing they'd turn back at the end of the episode. Not, of course that we actually get to see this. It's more than a little cruel to have the Kelvans declare that only Kirk, Spock, McCoy and Scotty are "essential": It's almost like the show is textually reaffirming its implicit prejudices and predispositions. I know the Kelvans are the bad guys and we're supposed to be put off by it, but the episode doesn't go far enough to prove the show can do any better.

"By Any Other Name" is the second script by Jerome Bixby, who previously gave us "Mirror, Mirror". Unfortunately, it looks like this one is closer to his actual perspective: "Mirror, Mirror" was extensively rewritten (uncredited, naturally) by a number of people, and the original draft was apparently something of a disaster, featuring, among other things, Kirk introducing phasers to a less technological Mirror Federation to help them conquer an opposing empire and Mirror Kirk married to Mirror Nurse Chapel. To say the original script carries the faintest echo of the aired episode's bristling anti-imperialism and self-critique would be being *extremely* charitable-It would seem Bixby had an almost Gene Roddenberry-esque attitude to morality and ethics with a stance on imperialism that could best be summarised as "Empires are bad and things like the Federation should be opposed to them". Which is basically true, but I prefer a bit more nuance. Namely, "what's the best way to go about putting all the imperialists and colonizers to death?".

D.C. Fontana has a credit on this one too, much as she did on "Mirror, Mirror", but her influence was apparently nothing more than tweaking Bixby's script to make it more lighthearted as the original version by all accounts took itself far, *far* too seriously. But while Fontana can turn this into a functional, serviceable script (and this certainly is: It's more than competent) she can't actually make it terribly interesting. Which isn't her fault: One can't help but feel this is a staggering waste of someone like Fontana given what we know she's capable of, but I suppose this is part of the job description for the story editor.

And really this does seem to fit "By Any Other Name", which is otherwise a stock, to-the-letter recitation of tiresome Pulp-style captures and escapes. Even when it's not literally a capture or escape, it *feels* like it as Our Heroes try out a new plan to thwart the Kelvans, are foiled, are forced to come up with a new plan, wash, rinse and repeat. The episode only actually picks up in the last third as the crew try to overwhelm the Kelvans with unfamiliar human sensations (which is, of course, a conceit lifted straight from "Catspaw" and is barely more effective here). Once again, it's the lead female extraterrestrial who gets tempted by sensuality, because of course she is, but I guess it says something "By Any Other Name" is on the whole in favour of this process as its ultimate solution is for the Kelvans to form a new society where they learn to live as humans. The scene where Scotty gets Tomar drunk on his entire alcohol stash was definitely one of the most memorable and enjoyable moments of the episode for me (despite how grossly stereotypical it is to have the Scotsman be the friendly drunkard, and to his credit James Doohan blows the scene out of the water, rightly cementing it as one of his best moments on the Original Series).

Speaking of human emotions, let's talk some more about Kelinda, in particular her falling in love with Kirk. Despite the reputation Kirk has as an interstellar (and now intergalactic) ladies' man thanks to his studio-mandated girl-of-the-week, one thing I've noticed is that for all his dalliances Kirk actually has very few lovers. Almost all of his seductions have been shockingly cold hearted, using his charm to manipulate women as a means to an end. First of all, this is awful, and any person who does this in real life would be a dangerously abusive *fucking sociopath*. That the only meaningful relationships Kirk seems to have are with his ship and his crew does have a tangentially sum positive side effect worth talking about at a later date, but as it manifests in the actual show this is continuously and deeply distasteful. As for Kelinda herself, rote sexism is written into her character from the very start: She eventually becomes another passive woman to be fought over (even if the actual animosity was one-sided) and even gets a generically and insufferably precocious faux-feminist "I can do as I please!" scene that is mostly successful only as an unpleasant reminder of how patriarchy leads some men to treat their wives and daughters the same way (as cattle) and that apparently extragalactic beings wearing human skinsuits act the same way as it's a fundamental human emotion. So thanks for that, Jerome Bixby.

Personally, I always liked Drea, the Kelvan flight controller. She seemed to me like someone who was just trying to do her job and I got the impression she was a highly skilled and intelligent space explorer (probably due at least in part to Lezlie Dalton's competent and collected portrayal). I would imagine Kelvans have a very serious sort of body dysphoria, but Drea seemed to handle her new form quite well. That she never seemed to succumb to emotional confusion told me she probably had a better handle on her human side than her colleagues did, especially as she seemed to respect Kirk as much as Rojan. I have to wonder what the bridge dynamic might have been like had she decided to stay on as part of the *Enterprise* crew permanently: After all, they had to warp back to the Milky Way anyway and Sulu wasn't around this week, so she must have been the ship's flight controller for at least the trip back (although given the way the show tends to treat women, and how Uhura in particular has fared just this season alone, it's probably best I only have my imagination here).

Trying to imagine what Drea's everyday life would be like is fun for me. I like explorations of the everyday. My experience with the everyday has always seemed to be very different from that of others, so maybe that means I'm more cognizant of and drawn to it.

I guess I've always been the most drawn to the characters who go largely unaffected by the plot. Maybe it's because it subconsciously signals to me they have their act together and that resonates with me (or maybe it's because it also gives the sense they might be up to something of their own). Star Trek seems to be frequently, and derisively (albeit in a somewhat tongue-in-cheek way) referred to as "Competency Porn" these days, a term I confess I'm a bit unfamiliar with. I am starting to see the appeal, though: I will admit the more and more a show delves into a character's inner psyche the less interested or invested I often find myself. I know conflict and character development are important, foundational elements of drama and narrative going back to Aristotle. Maybe that's also part of the reason I actually dislike so much drama. *Star Trek: The Next Generation* was the first scripted drama I ever saw that actually hooked me enough to pull me into its world, and it (or my imagined recollection of it) remains in many ways my standard for what the genre can and should aspire to. And Star Trek itself barely, if ever, lives up to that standard.

Aside from Star Trek, the only TV shows I used to watch regularly when I was younger were nature programmes and cartoons. That remains the case to this day, which is making it increasingly hard for me to find television I actually like as both are genres that seem to me to be on their last legs, as much of the medium is. I've always preferred music and video games to stuff descended from cinema.

"By Any Other Name" certainly isn't terrible, but seen coming right after "A Piece of the Action" it's hard to see it as anything other than a rather large step backward, in spite of its quite many iconic moments. It's a far more acceptable "average" (to use a word I hate, but for which I can't at the moment think of a suitable replacement) episode of *Star Trek* than, say, "A Private Little War" or "The Gamesters of Triskelion", but I don't think it's a preferable standard operating procedure to something like "The Doomsday Machine" (or even the episode coming up a few weeks from now, actually). I suppose there are worse places for a show to be going into its fifth year, though.

Drea is a creature of outer space who has acclimated to being human. Would this make her an expatriot, or even (in a very literal sense) an anthropologist?

64. "Let's try it once more, with feeling": Return to Tomorrow

This is an episode I really, really wanted to like but the whole thing sort of left me feeling unsatisfied at the end. Mind, this is after I had to remind myself what it actually was: "Return to Tomorrow" is unfortunately one of the episodes that I've always tended to get mixed up with a bunch of other episodes, namely "The Return of the Archons", "This Side of Paradise", "The Way to Eden" and "The Paradise Syndrome". Basically, *Star Trek* has far too many episodes with the words "Return", "Eden", "Paradise" and "Tomorrow" in the title, and this isn't even getting at the show's hoary old chestnut of bland, lazy Garden of Eden and Book of Genesis pastiches. By The Prophets even "The Cage" had an "Adam and Eve" plot, and this one has the nerve to not only drag that up again, but throw Erich von Däniken into the mix and imply Sargon's people were the inspiration for those myths. Almost five years into Star Trek I can flatly and confidently claim I am beyond sick and tired of Adam and Eve by now.

(For what it's worth, I also used to confuse "What Are Little Girls Made Of?", "The Alternative Factor" and "Requiem for Methuselah" a lot, but interestingly *not* with "Return to Tomorrow" even though this one also deals with androids. Hopefully now that I'm doing this project I'll be able to keep all these episodes straight for once. I need to get *something* out of spending so much time on this fucking thing.)

But, once I figured out what precisely I was watching, that is, the episode I knew as "the one with the hyper-evolved humanoids, the talking soul gem balls and the first appearance of Diana Muldaur in Star Trek" I was genuinely excited because I remember it having some interesting ideas and really classic scenes. As it turns out, while "Return to Tomorrow" does in fact have all those things, it's somewhat less than successful at bringing them all together. This in itself is worth commenting on, though: I've seen just about every episode of *Star Trek* up to now as either a atypical accidental masterpiece or a crateringly awful disaster, especially this season. There's been very little in-between these two extremes in my experience, but with "Return to Tomorrow" we get something else entirely: This isn't even middling filler, this is a great episode brought down by a small handful of nevertheless fairly noticeable missteps whose potential greatness is still very self-evident.

This becomes clear very early on, as the teaser sets us up for something epic: The *Enterprise* is out exploring beyond the furthest point where any Starfleet vessel has ever explored when a booming voice comes out of nowhere, takes control of the ship's systems and, seemingly knowing everything about the crew, requests the ship enter into orbit around a dead Class M planet while declaring that he himself is dead, and all of humanity will die too if they don't help him. I mean if nothing else that gets your attention at least.

The first act, where it's revealed Sargon's people are a race of unfathomably evolved beings of pure thought who were once humanlike, but who destroyed their species in their own hubris and who now require temporary humanoid form to bring themselves back to life, is stock old-school Western futurism (namely, the idea that next step of human evolution is dispersed thought without emotion, which is also very Roddenberry) but it's functional enough. Even the rest of the episode, which is where the cracks in "Return to Tomorrow"'s central premise start to become more obvious, does a very good job describing the human experience as a combination of intellectual pursuits, emotional needs and physical sensuality. Furthermore, this is a terrific demonstration of John Meredyth Lucas' talents as showrunner, him having previously overseen a re-evaluation of the core *Star Trek* logic-emotions duality in "Obsession" and his own "The Changeling".

Starfleet too has frankly never been better depicted before. The crew are willing to take dangerous risk after dangerous risk because of how much they could learn, and Kirk even says for one of the first times that searching for new life in the interests of scientific advancement is their paramount goal. Kirk also gets a frankly rousing speech in the second act where he likens helping Sargon to humanity's first steps into outer space and the evolution of the field of medicine, firmly declaring that this is why they're on the *Enterprise* and that "risk is our business". It's a great bit that finally moves Starfleet, and more importantly the *Enterprise*, away from the dull space patrol stuff it was doing throughout the first season and some earlier parts of the second (though William Shatner seems less than convinced: He's a bit changeable this episode, and this is the scene where it's the clearest. I'm never sure if he's trying to do broad-strokes Shakespearean performativity or a having a "Gamesters of Triskelion"-esque lunch of scenery) that's brought down by one thing: It's all based on an extremely Western concept of exploration.

The two things I love most about Star Trek (When it's working) are its use of science fiction to extrapolate everyday life and its sense of wonder about the universe and exploration. However, that said the term "exploration" is a bit of a loaded one: The concept of boldly taking risks to challenge the unknown and "make discoveries" is one that's wrapped up in some very Western, and actually patriarchal, assumptions. This is because the whole notion of discovery is predicated around the discoverer being the first person to find something, and therefore going down in history as having made an unknown known. Thing is, there are very few instances where this has actually happened: Especially in the case of discovering new places, what typically happens is that indigenous people learn about things through their travels, which become part of their shared cultural knowledge, and then some pompous Western asshole shows up, declares himself (and it's *always* himself) the sole discoverer of the place because he's the first to mark it on a map that he can send back to his royal patron.

The Ancient Navigators didn't plunge into the unknown and make discoveries, they made travels and excursions to different places that they knew were going to be there because they could read signs in the ocean surface waves, the behaviour of pelagic birds and the position of stars in the sky to discern with accuracy where land was. This allowed them to reach every shore that touched the Pacific and Southern Oceans (and some in the Atlantic!) and establish friendly relations with all the indigenous people they met there. The Navigators voyaged for the thrill of discovery and how much they could learn and grow through the journey. For Westerners, exploration is an opiate for the ego. There's also the Objectivity aspect to Western exploration, which is very Paltonic: The Western idea of exploration is intrinsically linked to the notion of there existing an objective unknown that can be slowly filled in with Knowledge, which is quite different than the way it is elsewhere in the world.

In this regard I can't recommend highly enough Joseph Turnbull's book *Masons, Tricksters and Cartographers*, which asserts the dividing line here is the embrace in Modernist, Western societies of the concept of map-making and meticulous record-keeping, whereas Pre-Modern, Non-Modern, Non-Western cultures prefer unwritten oral history shared by an entire community and passed down from person to person (Turnbull also dedicates an entire lengthy, though outdated, chapter to Polynesian navigation which is as good a primer on the subject as you're likely to find in Western academic literature). It's also why I can't quite let go of the concept of exploration, or at least the word, as once again this is a case where I don't really have something I consider a suitable alternative to offer aside from "journeying" and "travelling", which is closer but still not quite there in my opinion. Until I can rectify that, for the moment I'll have to tentatively posit a Western and Non-Western version of exploration, and that my sympathies lie more with the latter than with the former.

Getting back to actual Star Trek in a book ostensibly about Star Trek, this is the sort of problem that plagues "Return to Tomorrow" everywhere. Because, for all its occasionally oversignified ventures into the centrality of intellectual, emotional, physical and spiritual pursuits to humanity, "Return to Tomorrow" also ultimately has a very strong and visible pop Christian conception of this, just as it has a clearly Western concept of exploration. The consciousness receptacles fundamentally operate via a very traditional Cartesian conception of the Self. As much as the script on the one hand embraces sensuality as an important part of what it means to be human, it still depicts our possible fully-evolved future as beings of pure thought energy, and let's not forget Thalassa's tragic fall, despite the fact it is ultimately, though narrowly, avoided, is based on her becoming "tempted by the sins of the flesh" as it were. Were I especially inclined to follow this thread to the logical limit, I'd point out how Henoch is telegraphed as the villain almost right from the start, his plan involves murdering Sargon and seducing Thalassa and he spends the bulk of the episode in the body of Spock, the person who all the characters just love pointing out looks like Satan. There you go: Another bloody Adam and Eve story. This one's just inverted, as Adam and Eve are trying to get back into the Garden.

It's probably not entirely fair that I'm always dogging *Star Trek* so hard about this. After all, it's just as much of its culture as any other work of fiction is going to be. But that's sort of the point: The problem for me isn't that *Star Trek* is of its culture, its that it's part of *hegemonic* culture and, like most hegemony, not very many people seem to notice this. Pop Christianity, through being central to Westernism, is part of a network of interlinking social norms and cultural assumptions that comprise a master narrative that dominates world discourse at the expense of other ways of seeing and interpreting. *Star Trek* isn't seen as a cultural artefact of how Westernism manifested in late-1960s Los Angeles, it's seen as a fairy tale from the future that takes an objective (there's that word again) look at contemporary society and provides a utopian blueprint for the way forward. That so many technologists and engineers have spent so many years trying to turn so much made up future gadgetry from Star Trek into reality should be proof enough of that (Don't believe me? Take a look at the thing 99% of you have in your pockets or purses right now. Some of you might even be reading this book on one). This is simply not what any of these shows was ever intended to be, especially not *this* one, nor is it even a helpful way to even approach reading them. That's the problem with hegemony and privilege: Those who live within it see it as the default or norm. As an anthropologist, and especially as an anthropologist who had the flatly insane idea to study Westernism instead of a village in Africa or Oceania due to particular aspects of my own life and upbringing, that's always something I'm going to fixate on.

But in spite of this "Return to Tomorrow" does make some of the first noticeable steps towards moving away from this sort of thing a bit. It's tough to pick out at first as the character who we would most expect to be providing this given the type of story we're working with, Doctor McCoy, is once again hideously shafted. The script calls for DeForest Kelley to be in "Bristling Unchecked Passion" mode yet again and casts him as basically a crotchety neo-Luddite opposed to taking risks in the name of science, which is curiously the exact opposite of the position he held in "The Immunity Syndrome". This episode could have been a fantastic showcase for McCoy, writing him as the one person savvy enough to notice the potential problems in Sargon's plan, to see Henoch's duplicity for what it is and to remind Thalassa that she was human (or at least human-like) once and to plead with her to not put herself and her ambition above the rights and dignity of others despite her great power, sort of a more nuanced and less bombastic version of what Kirk tried to do for Elizabeth Dehner and Gary Mitchell in "Where No Man Has Gone Before". Instead, "Return to Tomorrow" just has McCoy irritated and indignant all the time and resolves its conflicts by repeatedly faking the audience out with hollow and false "all hope is lost" moments and gets Spock and Sargon to make everything better on each occasion by pulling heretofore unknown plot convenience superpowers out of their respective asses.

Thankfully, the episode does have someone to take up this role, but, tellingly, only by virtue of pure dumb luck. Despite showing up with absolutely no introduction and getting the same annoying "I can't believe she's a woman" response from Kirk that Helen Noel got in "Dagger of the Mind", Doctor Ann Mulhall is this episode's best asset by far. Despite technically only appearing in the story briefly near the beginning and the end and sitting the rest of the episode out while Thalassa explores her body, Mulhall gets the best scene of the week when she interrupts Sargon's long-winded von Dänikenesque ramblings by flatly stating that all contemporary science points to humans having evolved on Earth by their own accord, causing Sargon to backtrack and change the subject. Although Spock says the theory would explain parts of Vulcan history, Mulhall's point stands, effectively rebuking both of "Return to Tomorrow"'s most troublesome premises in one blow.

This scene aside though, every ounce of Ann Mulhall's impact comes from her actor, Diana Muldaur. This is Muldaur's first of three high profile Star Trek roles, returning next year to play Miranda Jones in "Is There In Truth No Beauty?" before coming back to the franchise twenty years later as a series regular during the second season of *Star Trek: The Next Generation*, playing Doctor Katherine Pulaski: chief medical officer of the USS *Enterprise* NCC-1701-D. I'm not going to beat around the bush here: Muldaur is hands-down one of my absolute favourite actors to ever grace any incarnation of Star Trek. She's a flat-out masterclass, and it's screamingly evident why from her first appearance: Muldaur is a jaw-droppingly commanding stage presence and she exerts so much gravity over the entire production she practically generates her own singularity. Taken on their own, the bulk of Mulhall's lines are not particularly remarkable: Aside from the one (admittedly brilliant) scene with Sargon, she mostly just confirms McCoy's and Spock's tricorder readings and backs up Kirk when the senior staff is debating leasing out their bodies. But Muldaur infuses her lines with so much confidence and matter-of-factness Mulhall comes across as a consummate professional and is the first female character in Star Trek to go toe-to-toe with Kirk, Spock and McCoy utterly as an equal.

One can imagine another actor playing Mulhall as more of a traditional *Star Trek* wistful, childish pouty Yeoman archetype: A smiling, doting supporting character just happy the boys let her play with them. The tricorder dialog exchange would have played out more like "Ooh, I got the same readings, Captain! See? I can play too!" then the "colleagues flatly share information with each other" feel we get, and even the scene with Sargon could have been delivered with a naive, ingenue-esque "But...I don't understand! How is this possible?" vibe to it. Now, I stress I'm not trying to be cruel to the other female guest stars the show's had, as I'm quite certain this is the way they were told to act by various members of the production staff, especially if Gene Roddenberry was involved. But the fact remains *Star Trek* without question has a track record for treating its female characters like idiot children. Equally though, the show's never had a co-star like Diana Muldaur before, and she's not having any bit of that. She goes out of her way to make Mulhall a devastatingly competent professional who demands our respect and attention, and the results are electrifying: Mulhall is one of the greatest characters in the entire Original Series by virtue of Diana Muldaur alone.

This does absolute wonders for "Return to Tomorrow", as the script is clearly a sexist nightmare. Mulhall gets very few scenes as herself, Thalassa is yet another weak woman tempted by the sins of the flesh and the episode clearly wants Mulhall to be Kirk's girl-of-the-week, even though this is in practice not at all who she is, mostly due to Muldaur, but also actually William Shatner, who seemingly deliberately misses every single cue that he's supposed to play Kirk infatuated with her. The keystone is Muldaur's dual role as Mulhall and Thalassa, as she plays them both very, very differently. Muldaur undoubtedly handles the two character brief the best of herself, Shatner and Leonard Nimoy: Although Nimoy is clearly trying to play Henoch as distinct from Spock, in practice he tends to come across more as Evil Trickster Spock instead (not that this isn't highly entertaining to watch, mind). Meanwhile, Shatner plays Sargon as straightforwardly and generically godlike.

Muldaur though goes to great lengths to depict Thalassa and Mulhall as two very different people: As Thalassa she's every bit as vindictive, spiteful, passionate and capricious as the script wants her to be, but, like Shatner, she brings a grandiose theatrical flourish to this, making her seem wild, mighty and unpredictable, and just a little bit unreal: A very far cry from the cool and collected Ann Mulhall. And this is what ultimately saves "Return to Tomorrow" from itself. Muldaur limits and contains Thalassa's foibles to Thalassa and Thalassa alone, highlighting that this is a personal flaw with the character, and not something intrinsic to all women. In doing so, Muldaur deals the death blow to the script's sexist overtones, although ironically in the process this also undermines the story's internal coherence.

That's sort of the problem with "Return to Tomorrow" on the whole. There's some likeable moments, but most of what there is to like doesn't seem to be the parts of the episode the writers and producers actually wanted us to focus on. The scene that best exemplifies this is the denouement, where Sargon and Thalassa destroy themselves because the temptation of being corporeal would be too great. This was not the original ending. Writer John T. Dugan wanted instead for them to roam the galaxy together as beings of thought. Gene Roddenberry took the script and changed it so they died instead (and this is the thing about Roddenberry: He doesn't give editorial comments, he just takes a script, rewrites it himself without telling the original author and then sends it out without crediting or acknowledging anything), prompting Dugan to use his pseudonym John Kingsbridge. Neither ending is amazing (though Dugan's seemed like it could have been made to work), but Roddenberry's ending is just pointless and mean-spirited and only seems to be there because he wanted to throw his weight around.

As apt a metaphor as any.

65. "EVIL ALIEN NAZIS!": Patterns of Force

If there's a surer, more immediate sign of the importance of something other than being banned by national governments, I can't think of it.

"Patterns of Force" was one of the handful of *Star Trek* episodes initially blocked from airing in certain markets outside the United States for a time. In this case, the country was Germany, which refused to show it for, well, rather obvious reasons as far as banning television shows go. "Patterns of Force" is certainly brazen: It's on the one hand the most flagrantly anti-authoritarian the show's been since "Mirror, Mirror", and in fact this one's even more blatant and upfront about its message (which is actually a good thing in this case) and a more than capable bit of television to boot. It is also, unfortunately, more than a little careless in the choice of imagery and iconography it chooses to invoke. This, more than the content itself, is likely why Germany decided to ban it. Censorship is always a bad idea, but words, actions and symbols have power and pop culture needs to understand this.

"Patterns of Force" itself is somewhat deceiving, as at first glance it looks like the most irritatingly pulpish thing ever. Kirk and Spock beam down to a planet that turns out to be ruled by quite literal space Nazis. What follows is a straightforward series of captures and escapes that's about as dynamic and exciting as it sounds. The episode does have some interesting potential going for it: Dig a little into the episode's production history though, and you'll find the original story outline, dating to the first season, and the first few drafts of the teleplay were penned by Paul Schneider, who I maintain is one of the greatest writers and most unsung heroes of the Original Series. Schneider was behind "Balance of Terror", which I still think is basically perfect (or as perfect as 1960s primetime television in the US can get), and one of the only people to recognise *Star Trek*'s strengths came out of its theatrical heritage.

Although this is a very promising start, Schneider wasn't the sole writer of this episode. John Meredyth Lucas picked up his draft late in the second season and retooled it into the script for the episode that made it to air (and, as tragically befits *Star Trek* at this point in time, Schneider went uncredited). I'm not entirely clear on how much of the finished product is Lucas' and how much is Schneider's, but what I can say for sure is that "Patterns of Force" shows them both turning in a powerful statement. I expect bristling anti-imperialism from Paul Schneider, and if there was ever any doubt about what "Balance of Terror" was truly about, this episode should lay it all to rest. What I didn't expect (because I didn't know what to expect) was to see John Meredyth Lucas working with the same ideas and with the same clarity. There's some of his trademark logic-emotion alliances on display here, but in this case this serves to reinforce the episode's staunch anti-fascist stance.

Yes, "Patterns of Force" is anti-fascist. But it's not an especially effective anti-fascist statement for a couple of reasons, and this is a real problem. First of all, it's ahistorical: Multiple characters in this episode, most notably Spock, point out that no matter how evil it was, Nazi Germany was the model for an "efficient", logical" for of government. Now for one thing it's positively ghastly to minimize the material evil done by Adolph Hitler's regime in favour of praising "logic and efficiency", which should really kill the logic vs. emotions theme, and frankly Spock himself, right here and now. But setting that aside for the moment (which is admittedly a pretty fucking huge thing to set aside), the fact remains *this isn't even actually fucking true.* Contemporary scholars will be quick to tell you that the Nazi party was anything but efficient, and was in fact actually burdened by a number of bureaucracies of questionable competence and competing interests mostly operating on stolen funds. Also Hitler himself, fittingly living up to his moniker of "mass-murdering fuckhead", was also a blithering idiot who only ever got as far as he did through sheer dumb luck. Now the idea the Nazis were "logical and efficient" *was* the leading theory of historians and social scientists at the time, and it obviously would have heavily influenced Schneider's and Lucas' depiction of National Socialism, but that doesn't really excuse it. Certainly not from the perspective of the future.

Secondly, this episode isn't actually about Nazis, which perhaps raises the question of why it's using them. What "Patterns of Force" is actually about is authority. It's about power structures, and not just totalitarian ones, how they manifest, how they become entrenched in society and how they stay that way for so long. The key figure is, of course, John Gill: A Starfleet historian who, while studying the fractured, violent society on Ekos and feeling compelled to help in spite of the Prime Directive (and I'd like to note despite my problems with it, I appreciate how the show's attitude towards the anti-imperialist reading of the Prime Directive has shifted in recent weeks), instills himself as the leader of a new National Socialist party. While he knew what happened when Nazism arose on Earth, he was firmly of the belief that despite how evil Hitler's regime was, it was the most efficient form of government the planet ever saw, and that so long as a benevolent, liberal dictator was at the helm, Ekos would be spared Germany's fate.

This is actually not a terrible idea. Gill is far closer to how someone like Khan Noonien Singh would have actually turned out, and the critique of liberalism's fascination with fascism is palpable. In the chapter on "Space Seed" I talked about the classical liberal dream of the enlightened despot, the benevolent dictator, or the philosopher king. They're all variations of the same core idea: Liberals of the New Deal variety (which in 1968 were still rather new and hip having seen the US through World War II and all) can trace their lineage back to the managerial progressives of the early 20th century. Broadly speaking, these sorts of liberals have been predisposed to fantasizing that absolute power might just not be a bad thing provided one of them were in charge (because, of course, we'd finally have someone intelligent in power who knew what *really* needed to be done. The liberal predilection towards intelligence-based discrimination is a topic for another time and place), whereas those on the actual radical left are vehemently opposed to any sort of authoritarian power structures at all because they recognise them for the tools of social stratification they truly are. This is why "Patterns of Force" is so fascinating: Here, *Star Trek,* for perhaps the first time, is unambiguously siding with the radical left, because John Gill's dream of a benevolent, liberal Nazi party is shown to be just as catastrophically misguided as it sounds.

While the true horrors of the Ekosian Nazi party are laid at the feet of Melakon, who supposedly betrayed its true purpose for his own means, we're very clearly not meant to side with Gill either. What he did was wrong and did measurable harm to the Ekosians as well as the Zeon targets of their ethnic purging. Gill's speech to Kirk as he lays dying after Melakon assassinates him in a fit of panic and rage is one of the most beautiful moments on the show yet, as Gill confesses how he now understands the extent of the mistake he made and how, as he so wonderfully puts it:

> "Even historians fail to learn from history...they repeat the same mistakes. Let the killing end, Kirk."

Which is frankly just about one of the best lines ever.

Kirk, Spock and McCoy's exchange in the denouement is similarly poetic. That this doesn't go down as one of the finest bits of dialog in the Original Series is frankly disgraceful:

> "He drew the wrong conclusion from history. The problem with the Nazis wasn't simply that their leaders were evil, psychotic men. They were, but the main problem, I think, was the leader principle."

> "What he's saying, Spock, is that a man who holds that much power, even with the best intentions, just can't resist the urge to play God."

> "Thank you, Doctor. I was able to gather the meaning."

Here are three men who have documented problems being tempted by the allure of the philosopher king and the myth of objectivity. And yet here's Captain Kirk, of all people, coming out with a moral that's actually demonstrably true. It's frankly shocking. But there are still problems: The "metaphor", such as it is, is so clunky and poorly-executed it ends up missing the forest for the trees.

The Zeons are genuinely sympathetic and likeable, and this is the first time on this show I found myself actually caring about their story and what happened to them. Richard Evans in particular is quite compelling as Isak, a broken and shell-shocked Zeon resistance fighter teetering on the edge of being desensitized to the death and violence that has come to define his life: His vacant stare says it all. "Hero of the Fatherland" Daras, played by Valora Noland, is also absolutely brilliant and the reveal in the beginning of Act 3 that's she's actually a double agent when she stages an invasion of the resistance headquarters to test Kirk's and Spock's loyalty is a genuinely shocking and unexpected twist that savvily plays off of the audience's expectations for a pulp adventure structure. Even better, the show treats her as an important, respected and multifaceted character equal to her male comrades: Daras' story about having to pretend to betray her father and her childhood spent growing up with the Nazi party's atrocities is actually really, really well done and very touching, and the fact she's flatly *not* Kirk's girl-of-the-week (and is in fact just about anything but) just makes it better. This is the kind of thing I absolutely do not expect to see in Star Trek. With Doctor Ann Mulhall last time and Daras here, *Star Trek* has given us two of its best female characters ever one after another.

But the problem is the names of all of the Zeons references to the Old Testament: Isak is obvious, his brother Abrom is a take-off on Abraham, Zeon is like Zion, and so forth. Daras is more or less one letter away from Sarah. They're blatantly Jewish, and "convergent social evolution" or otherwise this is clumsy to the point of being insensitive. There's the risk genre fiction allegory always runs of oversimplifying complex social issues, but here's a case where a little distance from the source might have been advisable. If this had been some generic planet where one random alien species with silly makeup was oppressing another random alien species with silly alien makeup that would have been one thing. But "Patterns of Force" is literally doing Nazis and German Jews and, as much as its heart seems to be in the right place, this never stops being cringeworthy. The one good thing here is that this does enable one of the funniest jokes in the series to date: The name of the Nazi party chairman who was secretly sympathetic to the rebellion movement despite his faith in the concept of an authoritarian state is named Eneg...which is "Gene" spelled backwards.

Fascism must be fought, but fascism cannot be taken lightly. Words and symbols have power, and people must be gravely aware of the power they have. *Especially* people who live in hegemonic cultures who established their hegemony through imperialism and oppression. Nazi imagery is not the sort of thing to be thrown around casually. It wouldn't have been when World War II was in living memory for the audience and the creative team both, and it's not now when Westernism is lurching inevitably and inexorably back to fascism. No wonder this was banned: "Patterns of Force", like most of *Star Trek*, to be honest, ought to be shipped with a content warning. Pop culture comes from hegemony, but it can, and should, be appropriated to fight it. Because when it's not, it's just another tool of the kyriarchy to keep us living in oppressive misery.

You're either with the resistance, or you're an enemy of it.

66. Die Maschinenmensch: The Ultimate Computer

"The Ultimate Computer" is another somewhat deceiving story. It has a great deal of things all going on all at once and is indeed good in many of the ways people often say it's good. But there's a secondary tier of ideas this episode is also working with for which it doesn't tend to get the credit I think it probably should, and it's very indicative of the way *Star Trek* is always in some sense pushing against itself. On the other hand, "The Ultimate Computer" doesn't *quite* work either: Not all of the concepts it's trying to convey come across as well as they perhaps could have, and the script has an unfortunate tendency to contradict itself. I'd definitely say it's a good baseline target for the show to have been shooting for this season though. However, the one problem with that is that we're a month away from the end of the filming block for this year: It has the bad luck to end up being compared to efforts like "The Trouble with Tribbles" and "A Piece of the Action" (a comparison in which it is found wanting) and, just like those episodes, we probably could have stood to see "The Ultimate Computer" about ten weeks ago.

The original pitch for "The Ultimate Computer" came from a mathematician named Laurence N. Wolfe, who wrote it around his passionate interest in the titular devices. However, D.C. Fontana found the script he submitted to be basically unworkable, as it was almost entirely about the story of Doctor Daystrom and the M-5, to the point the *Enterprise* crew was barely in it. Indeed, the simple explanation for why the episode as aired is in some sense disjointed is because Fontana rewrote it so heavily: There are very much two stories going on here, and they actually probably didn't belong in the same script. Let's start with the most obvious reading of "The Ultimate Computer", and what I'm presuming to be the original pitch: The concept of a computer so sophisticated and humanlike it can actually replace people, and what would drive a person to create such a device in the first place. As we've talked about before in regards to the mid- to late- 1960s context in which these episodes were being made, one of the larger sources of malaise at the time was the fear that the rapid increase in both the power and awareness of computers in the immediate postwar age, as well as the move towards mechanizing the workforce that helped usher in what can be called the post-industrial era in late-stage capitalist Westernism (a theme we'll be returning to a little later on) would eventually dehumanize society. This, combined with a distrust of unchecked logic and bureaucracy, a healthy fear of Stalinism and good old fashioned Red Scare thought poisoning paranoia that defined the Cold War led to many lamenting what they saw as the erosion of "traditional" "American" "values" such as individuality, loyalty and personal achievement.

Aaron and Unnunillium, two of my commenters, pointed this out under the blog version of my chapter on "A Taste of Armageddon" in the first season and quite reasonably wondered why I didn't have more to say about it then. And while that theme certainly can be read into that episode, and arguably in other first season stories like "The Return of the Archons", "What Are Little Girls Made Of?" and most obviously "Court Martial", the reason I didn't would be because in my opinion this is the best episode to talk about that sort of thing in the context of. It not only provides a decent example of the typical argument, it also gives some hints about how *Star Trek* can tackle the issue with a slightly different approach then what would be considered the norm. While the M-5 itself is basically just another computer that gains sentience and decides it's superior to humanity and goes on an ego-tripping rampage, which is (and you have no idea how much I'm resisting the urge to make a *MythBusters* joke here) just about the most stock science fiction concept imaginable, the actual story for this half of the episode is Richard Daystrom.

Daystrom is seen as one of the best and most memorable characters in all of Star Trek, and rightly so in my opinion. He's an incredibly gifted person whose achievements were not always seen for what they were, and who didn't always get the credit he deserved. His breakdown in the climax where he confesses to the camera that he was never taken seriously because of the young age at which he made his biggest breakthroughs, not that his "colleagues" weren't perfectly willing to steal his ideas and pass them off as their own, is a gut-punching bit of dialog and should hit very close to home to anyone who was dismissed, belittled or otherwise not taken seriously as a child (or indeed who went to graduate school, for that matter). This is what drives Daystrom to create something as ludicrously ambitious and overreaching as M-5: His now-fanatical desire to have himself and his work recognised by their own merits for the first time in his life, and, in a great twist, this is why the machine goes bad-It has just as obsessive and single-minded dedication to its goal that Daystrom does, as he patterned its neural engrams off of his own.

We of course also need to talk about William Marshall. While I'm not sure if his casting was intended from the start, making Daystrom of African descent is a grand slam for the series. While the show does not overtly draw attention to his ethnicity as his tragic character arc could have been done with someone of any skin colour, making him African does subtly get us to pay more attention to how underappreciated he is. The story of someone who is never really seen as an equal, never treated with the proper amount of respect or even treated as a full person is of course all too well known to people of colour living within Western societies. This way, Star Trek can talk about social injustices of all kinds, even outright racism, while still depicting its setting as more idealistic and without having to jump through too many narrative hoops to get its point across. It's a tactic that will pave the way for some of the best of Star Trek to come, and just as strong a lesson the franchise could have stood to pay more attention to at various other points of its history. Also, having Marshall in such a dynamic and powerful role here, combined with things like the introduction of Doctor M'Benga (the only good thing about "A Private Little War") and the increasingly more fleshed-out and central space Uhura's been able to carve for herself this year increases the show's progressive lot substantially. It also helps Marshall is just an outstanding actor, and perhaps just a touch hammy.

In other words, this part of "The Ultimate Computer" is very much Daystrom's story: It's the story of someone who sought solace in machines and his own technical ability, hoping he could prove a fully computerized and automated future was the way forward for humanity, perhaps to himself as much as anyone else. This is *Star Trek* doing pretty much exactly what it should be doing: Putting the guest star in the limelight and giving him the bulk of the story's drama and gravity while we watch the main cast react, because of course, "The Ultimate Computer" is also about the effect Daystrom's confidence, drive and beliefs have on Kirk, Spock and McCoy. It's exactly the same tack the show took (and correctly, as far as I'm concerned) in "The Doomsday Machine" and here's where D.C. Fontana comes in, because it's a bit more nuanced this time and Fontana ends up pulling off some extremely clever narrative sleight-of-hand. Firstly, as the episode opens we're led to believe this is going to be another rote, almost by-the-numbers first season-style logic versus emotions debate. Spock is very intrigued by Daystrom's new machine as he's a big fan of him and his work with improving the efficiency of computers, McCoy goes on a curmudgeonly tirade about how he don't trust no newfangled computerized thingamawhatzits, declaring machines will never replace people, and Kirk is caught in the middle trying to decide where he stands on the whole thing.

But this doesn't actually turn out to be what the episode is about (well, on the whole-there's one big caveat I'll get to): We expect Spock to be completely taken in by the M-5 to the point he has a "Galileo Seven"-style overflow error when the computer inevitably goes berserk and its logic fails to provide the proper solution. But he doesn't-Instead, he becomes the first person to figure out there's something fishy about the M-5 precisely because it's *not* behaving logically, and continuously emphasizes that while computers may be more efficient at performing tasks than people, they're merely tools and that given the choice he'd much rather work with humans. Furthermore, we expect McCoy to go into "Bristling Unchecked Passion Mode" for the entire episode and "rage against the machine", as it were. And while there is indeed quite a lot of that, McCoy also snaps quite frequently into being the person who can empathize with and understand people and their motivations. While he's wrong about Spock, he reads Daystrom like a book, and one of the best scenes in the episode is where he rants at him in engineering about the M-5 taking over the ship and deciding to randomly start destroying things...and in the next scene it turns out he was baiting Daystrom to react in order to learn more about his personality and history.

(I'm not sure if that's technically proper decorum for a psychologist, but whatever.)

Then, of course, there's Kirk. According to the rules this kind of story should be obeying, he should be righteously angry about the sanctity of individuality, personhood and the inalienable right of a man (and, naturally, it has to be a man) to shape his own destiny. The war games scene should be resolved like the end of "The Deadly Years", with Kirk confidently swinging onto the bridge and taking a manly amount of control of the situation and shutting down M-5 by force, probably by punching it. "No machine will replace *me*, dammit!". Except that's not what happens. Kirk convinces the M-5 that it has violated its own personal code of ethics by killing the *Excalibur* (and here once again is that idea that a starship can be killed, murdered in fact, and that's before getting into the highly symbolic name) and that it should face consequences for that. This isn't the James T. Kirk School of Computer Repair where he causes a machine to explode itself through logic paradoxes, this is talking to somebody and asking them to accept responsibility for their actions, and the M-5 is very much a person-Even Spock calls it a human mind amplified by the power of a computer. For a story that's supposed to be sceptical of technology and bureaucracy eroding Traditional American Values™, Kirk sure doesn't seem to be acting like the the ruggedly masculine "American" "Individualist". That's because "The Ultimate Computer", at least according to Fontana, isn't that story at all. It's a critique of that story that uses its framework to tell an altogether different story.

What Kirk is concerned about here isn't that the principle of machines replacing humans is unmanly: Indeed, he even says right from the beginning he's worried this might be what upsets him about the M-5 (and tellingly, he dismisses such thoughts as "petty"; focused more on pride and prestige instead of genuine ethics). What Kirk is actually troubled by is the possibility the M-5 will cause him to lose his job because working on a starship is the only thing he enjoys and knows how to do. Under Fontana, "The Ultimate Computer" is a straightforward examination and criticism of the materialistic consequences of mechanized industry and how capitalist societies privilege ever-more efficient, cheap and automated forms of production without consideration for the effect this has on the workers who are being replaced. Lack of concern for humans and basic human decency is an argument that can be made about just about any aspect of capitalism, not just the mechanization of industry: Consider, for example, how much the market (or at least the capitalist conception of what the market is) has come to dominate just about every facet of discourse in the United States, and how this has utterly destroyed the humanities, social sciences and the creative arts. Nobody respects these endeavours anymore, because there's no net monetary value that can be applied to them. Late-stage capitalism measures the value of people by how much money they have, takes away their jobs because it's cost-effective, and, in doing so, removes a person's sense of self-worth.

In other words, what Fontana has done here is overtly liken the Federation (which is, of course, already tacitly descended from Westernism, even as that line is starting to become blurrier) to the early post-industrial West and made Kirk, in essence, a working-class spaceman. This is frankly as profound and transformational a shift as anything we've seen in Star Trek so far, and it's going to prove to be a particularly bleak example of life imitating art for William Shatner himself in just a few years. This isn't an entirely clean gear change, mind, and it's going to be a long time until this completely takes and becomes an important part of the franchise, but, like a lot of things the Original Series does, the seeds are sewn here. Most of the reasons why I don't think this is as clear as it could be in the finished product is, once again, the fact it was so extensively rewritten. There are quite a few scenes (presumably ones that were in Wolfe's original pitch) that seem to actively grate against this reading, almost as many as there are to support it. Spock's speech about how a starship "runs on loyalty...to one man" is probably the joint most egregious, along with Kirk flatly stating "There are certain things men must do to remain men. Your computer would take that away." (though it could be argued certain types of working-class Westerners *would* talk like that) while the stilted and hokey invocation of John Masefield's "Sea Fever" is probably a close second.

(Although that said, also notice in this same scene how William Shatner starts playing with some gizmo in his quarters just before McCoy walks in: It's almost as if he's trying to convey Kirk's attempts to prove to himself he's capable of doing other things besides captaining a starship, which can also be seen as an echo of his earlier dialog with McCoy just after M-5 is installed: "Am I afraid of losing command to a computer? Daystrom's right. I can do a lot of other things", which comes across to me as just as halfhearted and uncertain a bit of soul-searching).

The other reason this isn't as immediately clear as it perhaps could be is the long-standing confusion over how systems of production and labour actually work in the world of Star Trek. The basic standing Marxist critique of *Star Trek: The Next Generation* is that the show makes no sense because it depicts people working for a living in a world where money either doesn't exist or material goods are ubiquitous to the point nobody need work for them. Ergo, why does something like Starfleet exist? Personally, I find this particular argument to be riddled with holes and logic assumptions that aren't actually backed up by textual evidence, but I'll save rebutting it until we get to the series in question. However as it applies to the Original Series, there is perhaps a line of thought worth pursuing here, because, unlike *The Next Generation*, we actually *don't* have a really good sense of what the economic system in *Star Trek* is.

We know Starfleet and the Federation exist, of course, and that both are big enough organisations that pretty much everyone we've seen so far is a part of them. But is Starfleet a voluntary service? Do the officers get paid? We can't actually say for sure at this point. We don't hear much about money, no, although there was an offhand comment about credits in "The Trouble with Tribbles". But crucially, nobody ever said Starfleet officers *don't* turn a paycheck, just as nobody said they do either, and regardless, having this happen to Kirk, someone we know and sympathize with, is still an effective way of conveying the message: The reduction in dignity and self-esteem he goes through is still very palpable. This does mean, however, that Fontana's depiction of Kirk as a working-class spaceman hurt by having his job taken away from him is going to come across really strangely to someone accustomed to the way Star Trek works after the 1980s, even though in 1968 it would have made absolute perfect sense to use "The Ultimate Computer" as a straightforward allegory about the effect of mechanization on people reliant on Western industry for their livelihood.

But in spite of the fact this episode may not be 100% successful in everything it's trying to do, it's still without question one of the more complex, and coherent, episodes of the season. The concepts and ideas it's working with are extremely mature and multifaceted ones, and its yet more proof Star Trek is capable of a lot more than flying around the galaxy dropping moral nuclear warheads on people. Honestly, the biggest complaint I have is still that this is one of the last episodes produced for the year: We could have used a lot more stories like "The Ultimate Computer" and a lot fewer like "A Private Little War".

67. "When the wayfarer whistles in the dark...": The Omega Glory

It's bad.

What more do you want me to say? It's terrible. Everyone knows it's terrible. You don't need me to tell you that. The plot is literally nothing more then capture and escape sequence after capture and escape sequence liberally peppered with intolerably drawn out and boring fight scenes in between. It is so chest-thumpingly, simperingly jingoistic it practically loops back around to parody (at least William Shatner is playing it that way). It is racist on some kind of transcendental level, depicting the Yangs as noble savages while portraying the supposedly technologically-advanced Cohms as identical, mute, smiling Chinese stereotypes *and it even has Kirk literally call them yellow*. It is the picture-perfect case study of the ugly racism, sexism and unreconstructed United States neo-imperialism that always lurks just below the surface of Star Trek, threatening to eclipse everything that makes the franchise actually worthwhile. It was also one of the leading contenders, along with "Mudd's Women", to be the second pilot. Bob Justman was so appalled by the script Gene Roddenberry turned in, he drafted a *multi-page* memo *savaging* it; railing into it from every possible angle before throwing it away at the last second and delivering a few comments in person because he thought he was being too brutal. A shame he didn't save it-I'dve loved to reprint it. Not that this phased Roddenberry in the slightest, of course. He was was so proud of his work on this one he *personally submitted it to be considered for an Emmy Award*.

I'm not going to go into a lengthy critique of "The Omega Glory" to point out what's wrong with it. It's far easier (and more accurate) to just say "everything" and that it commits an unforgivable sin simply by existing. No-I'm much more interested in the question of "why now?" and looking at how *Star Trek*, which had been on a roll since "The Immunity Syndrome" (I mean it hasn't been great, but at least it's been borderline competent), suddenly turned out a story so irredeemably awful even Trekkers can't defend it, and this is a group of fans so loyal and dedicated they'll make apologies for "The Enemy Within" and "Who Mourns for Adonais?". Tell someone unfamiliar with Star Trek that this episode and "The Trouble with Tribbles" are from the same *season*, let alone the same *series*, and they'll laugh in your face. That this was produced directly after "The Ultimate Computer" is unthinkable.

But there are, sadly, easily discernible reasons that explain "The Omega Glory", and it's also depressingly telling that this episode, along with "Spock's Brain", are the ones that stick out to fans as the bad ones amongst five years of television that are about one-quarter excellent (or at least important) and the rest intolerant, bigoted garbage *if we're being*

305

charitable. There's also the matter of Gene Roddenberry: For all intents and purposes this is his final significant contribution to the Original Series. He's behind "Assignment: Earth" next week of course, but there's a lot going on there that's not to do with him. He's got two credits in the third season, which are also terrible, but they're also both joint scripts. As far as a story that comes directly out of Roddenberry's own positionality and beliefs, however, this is pretty much it.

This is quite a lot to tackle and digest, so let's take it one thing at a time. Let's begin with the obvious question: Why does "The Omega Glory" even exist in the first place? Last time it threatened to show itself, in 1965, it was quickly and aggressively rejected by the studio and the network, both of whom quite rightly realised it was a catastrophic pace of shit and would make for possibly the worst television pilot ever (discuss among yourselves whether "The Omega Glory" or "Mudd's Women" being the pilot would actually have been worse for either the future of Star Trek or the world's peace of mind). Why are we seeing it materialize three years later when *Star Trek* not only went to series, but has proven its capable of doing more? Even with all my qualifiers and all that does bring the show circa 1968 down, this is quite frankly a story that doesn't actually belong here. Well, the simple answer is that Gene Roddenberry wanted it here. Although concrete historical details are, as always, sketchy, the gist of it seems to be that *Star Trek* was either once again out of scripts or, given the prevailing feeling throughout the set that the show was going to be canceled after the year was up, Roddenberry just really wanted to get this story made before the shooting block finished because he liked it *that* much. So, we get a destructively retrograde and irreparably broken and bigoted script going into production because the show either needed it or its creator was an overbearing, dominating control freak. Possibly both.

Which brings me to the real problem with "The Omega Glory": Its writer. If there was ever conclusive, damning evidence of the harm Gene Roddenberry's presence did to Star Trek, this was it. He's lucky this time that the show was on unstable enough ground there was little risk "The Omega Glory" was going to get *Star Trek* *more* canceled, but that's the absolute best that can be said of it. Let's be absolutely honest with ourselves here. Everything that's gone wrong with Star Trek over the past five years can almost without exception be directly traced back to Gene Roddenberry. This is going to continue to be the case for many, many years. Every criticism you can level at any other incarnation of Star Trek Roddenberry lived through can be safely and automatically laid at his feet with little risk of being unfair or fingering the wrong person. Star Trek is the rare work of fiction that only works when its original creator is kept as far away from it as is physically possible, to the point I'm having a hard time coming up with a remotely comparable situation (George Lucas is a popular punching bag these days, but I think the faults of Star Wars are as much to do with fans suddenly taking a more nuanced and critical look at their franchise). Roddenberry is something different: As a writer and producer he is a provably regular toxic and destructive force, and the fact he's the one who sticks around the longest out of Star Trek's first generation of architects is unbelievably frustrating.

(There is, I should add, one fairly big asterisk in regards to Roddenberry's legacy that needs to be dealt with. But that only becomes relevant to the discourse in the 1980s, and while Roddenberry's personal gnosis is about to begin, we won't be feeling the ramifications of that for awhile.)

But while "The Omega Glory" is infamous, it remains bad in the same ways Roddenberry's other scripts have been. Show someone this episode without context, then show them "The Cage", "Mudd's Women", "Charlie X" and "A Private Little War" and I'd wager they'd be hard pressed to make a case "The Omega Glory" is especially worse then any of those episodes. Just don't expect this person to talk to you again, for they will likely hate you for the rest of your life, and deservedly so. On the other hand though, it must be possible to make such a case as so many people universally agree this is one of the Original Series' worst hours. This reveals some very distasteful things about Star Trek fandom, however (though perhaps not as many as their similar pillorying of "Spock's Brain". Not that "Spock's Brain" is any good, I hasten to add, but the reasons it's criticized tend to speak more of the people doing the criticizing then of the actual episode). If this is the worst, then why isn't there more honest problematizing of Gene Roddenberry's ethics and conception of Star Trek? This is all him, after all. Why does "The Omega Glory" become the riffer's darling while "A Private Little War" becomes at the very least a respected, average episode, if not a classic?

Part of it is most likely William Shatner, who delivers another scenery devouring performance (indeed, his climactic "WE the PEOPLE" speech is the stuff of legends). And I mean Shatner may be easy to make fun of as he has a tendency to play the most obviously insane thing on camera, but look: I'm never going to have any sympathy for people who attack Shatner's acting style for being overly campy, especially when he only cranks up the pork dial when he's beyond bored with and insulted by the material he's given. Did you honestly expect him to gamely take something like "The Omega Glory" remotely seriously, especially when as far as he's concerned he's been given his two-week notice and will be out of a job in a few days? Of course not. "The Omega Glory" is a disaster, and guess what? "The Gamesters of Triskelion" was too. Shatner's the only enjoyable thing about either one of those turkeys.

Furthermore, there's a motif we're going to have to start talking about in the very near future about how William Shatner uses a lot of theatrical humour in his performances. It's not quite as noticeable in Captain Kirk at the moment, though it will eventually be and it's an important part of Shatner's worldview and approach to acting. Think back a moment to something even as comparatively distant as "Where No Man Has Gone Before". There Shatner said the biggest problem with *Star Trek* was that it took itself too seriously and would never be successful if it continued to do that. He was right, and on a number of different levels, but the thing I want to emphasize in the context of situations like this is that Shatner very rarely, if ever, actually, plays a character whom we're meant to take at face value: That's in fact the whole reason he's able to turn Kirk into a drag action hero. For him, it's the recursive and multiplex performance of human experience that might be the most important thing about life, and this can be taken as a kind of joke. So yes, Shatner is very, very funny here. But if it's a joke, it's a cosmic one and it might just be on us.

This is the uncomfortable thing about slagging off "The Omega Glory": So many times when it's done, it's done on account of how campy and silly it is, not how godawfully reactionary it is. If we're going to call "The Omega Glory" the worst of Star Trek, and I'm certainly not opposed to that, we have to do it for the right reasons. No, the problem is not the camp. The problem is not William Shatner overacting. The problem is Gene Roddenberry, and if we're going to throw this one out we really ought to seriously consider doing the same for everything else he wrote and everything Star Trek inherits from him. The argument also works the other way, though: The disaster of this week really reflects poorly on Roddenberry and Roddenberry alone, if for no other reason than *everyone else was desperately trying to keep this from happening* and trying to use "The Omega Glory" as fodder for dismissing fifty years of Star Trek is equally as foolhardy. Star Trek is better than this, or at least it damn well *should* be. The fact the fucking thing has lasted for fifty years bloody well *demands* it be better than this. "The Omega Glory" is evidence the show's themes and ethics need to continue to evolve, not that the whole thing needs to be scrapped and binned.

I bring this up because I'm thinking of one scholar in particular who has became rather infamous for arguing pretty much exactly this, such that he's frequently wheeled out as one of the stock responses to "The Omega Glory"'s racism (he's even cited on Memory Alpha, which should tell you precisely how maligned this story actually is). In his book *Star Trek and History: Race-ing Toward a White Future*, film studies professor Daniel Leonard Bernardi states

> "'The Omega Glory' is not, however, a counter-hegemonic episode. In fact, the episode not only reveals an unwillingness to be critical of the hegemony of racist representations, but also systematically participates in the stereotyping of Asians. As the story progresses, the Yangs are constructed as noble savages; their cause to annihilate the Comms is established as justified. The Comms, on the other hand, are constructed as brutal and oppressive; their drive to suppress the Yangs is established as totalitarian. This more hegemonic articulation of race is made evident when Kirk and Spock realize the extent to which the Yangs and Comms parallel Earth's civilizations. In this light, the Yangs are no longer savages, but noble warriors fighting for a just and honorable cause. They want to regain the land they lost in a war with the Asiatics."

Bernardi then goes on to cite "The Omega Glory" as a prime example of how white privilege and hegemony are intrinsic to Star Trek and irreducible from it, and that the oft-touted utopia the franchise espouses is merely an extrapolation of white, middle-class, Western values that reinforces and celebrates contemporary social stratification. And look, I'm not going to pretend Star Trek is perfect here. I definitely agree it has hegemony problems that can be directly traced to its hyper-Western origins. I was making this argument as recently as "Return to Tomorrow" and just go back and see how nasty I was in the first season if you need a refresher on how much I tolerate normalized oppression.

But here's the thing. I choose to read Star Trek as an idea that's transcended its origins to become something greater. As much as I tear into the franchise, and I'm far from through doing that, I do think its overall impact and legacy on Western pop culture and global society has been a net positive one, and it has the potential to do even more good today thanks to the form it's metamorphosed into. And I think Bernardi is dead wrong to use "The Omega Glory" as a trump card, and in doing so it makes him no better than the Trekkers he's attacking. If you take this episode as some kind of Original Sin for the franchise that marks it for life, you're essentially equating the entirety of Star Trek with the positonality and flaws of Gene Roddenberry, and in doing that, you're falling into what I consider to be one of the most dangerous fallacies of reading any kind of work of fiction: The idea that one creator is a singular, godlike being from which creative works spring fully-formed in the manner of Athena and who is solely and consciously responsible for everything about said work.

The way I approach media studies from a pseudo-Lacanian perspective I've derived from the writings by people like Shoshana Felman and Avital Ronell. I believe writers do not will their work into existence out of nothingness but rather, as Ronell puts it, act as "secretaries of the phantom" who take dictation from an intangible ether and can only hope the words on paper are a crude facsimile of the particular truth they have taken into themselves. Writers are drug addicts, and writing is death. One does not "write". One is possessed by "writing". Similarly, one does not simply "read" from what I gather from Felman: The act of reading is comprised of the interaction of three separate, though linked, spheres from which meaning is generated: The text, the author's positionality and the reader's positionality (for the one person who will catch this, this is not Death of the Author or New Criticism either. This is different). Because of this, I very strongly believe the idea of authorship as is commonly used in literary criticism and especially film studies is a patriarchal construct that, like all elements of patriarchy, must be destroyed. "Author", "Authorship" and "Authority" all share the same root, and they must all share the same fate. Purging from the collective consciousness.

Film studies, really thanks to the movie industry and their reaction to being dismissed by literary critics in the 1920s about how motion pictures could never be art because they lack a Singular Creator, have latched onto the idea of the director or producer as Author and Visionary. And, as films have now become the dominant form of creative expression, film studies culture has permeated Western discourse on a profound and intimate level. Look at how video games and television shows are praised if they manage to successfully emulate movies, and how contemporary fan lingo calls a statement made by a creator about their work "The Word of God". Look at how there are wildly popular Internet review shows made by fans that explicitly crib their critique from film studies. It's a Frankensteinian blend of white cis male middle class pop Christian Modernist Western tropes, and it's just as rampant in academia and critique as it is everywhere else. So, by this line of thought Gene Roddenberry is the Godlike Author to whom all of Star Trek can be traced back. Star Trek is Gene Roddenberry and Gene Roddenberry is Star Trek. You may recognise this as the exact same language the most rabid Trekkers use, and I'm going to be just as opposed to that line of thought cropping up in media studies as I would be at its manifestations in fandom and the work itself.

309

Let's put aside for the moment the fact that all language like this does is prove how the film critics and the fans are shouting at each other from the same cultural perspective. Let's put aside for the moment the fact critiques like Bernardi's reinforce Roddenberry's frankly insultingly oppressive and disrespectful (and blatantly deliberate) carjacking of Star Trek's legacy and the pop culture discourse about it such that he successful managed to position himself as the figurehead for the entire phenomenon, manufacturing what can reasonably be described as a significant cult of personality around himself while going out of his way to downplay, marginalise and erase the contributions of *every single person he ever worked with* that helped make Star Trek a part of our shared cultural heritage. Let's just go back to the origins of this project. When I was thinking about starting a critical history of Star Trek, most of my friends, family and colleagues were extremely supportive and encouraged me to go ahead with the endeavour, citing my long personal connection to the franchise and my...unique and unorthodox...reading of it. But there were also some people who made sure to let me know they thought I was undertaking a fool's errand. Star Trek has been done to death in media studies, they told me. Nobody has anything interesting or productive to add to the discourse about Star Trek. Oh, you're doing a Star Trek book? Well, you obviously haven't read the literature. It's been done. You're wasting your time.

Were I someone with less confidence and lower self-esteem (read: Were I less stubborn and belligerent) that probably would have been it and Vaka Rangi wouldn't exist. But instead, I recognised this as the silencing tactic of the patriarchal authority that it was. I know my enemy well enough by this point I can spot his movements, no matter how subtle. Hegemony takes many forms, including that of those who claim to be fighting it. Star Trek discourse is built on a multitude of people sharing their voices and experiences with one of the few things about contemporary Westernism that could convincingly be argued is a shared mythology. And the same is true for the television show itself: Just as there is no one single Universal Authority on Star Trek criticism there similarly isn't one for Star Trek. No one person gets to definitively claim once and for all what Star Trek is, no matter which side of the camera or TV screen they're on, for that way lies death, and Star Trek is about life.

Or at least it should be. I wanted it to be. I may have wasted all my time after all, but I at least said my piece.

The true horror of "The Omega Glory" is that it was almost the last episode of Star Trek, and the threat that it might become that remains very real to this day. Let's try to keep in mind what the consequences would be if we were to let it.

68. "Creators of history": Assignment: Earth

"Assignment: Earth" aired on March 29, 1968. Martin Luther King, Jr. was assassinated on April 4. Synchromysticism is the study of "happenings" and reoccurring patterns and synchronicity in human behaviour and world events, and the end of April is regarded in synchromystic circles as a "red zone" with a high concentration of violent activity. Sixty-nine days after King's death, Robert F. Kennedy was also assassinated. June 5, the date of Kennedy's death, also has synchromystic connections, being the date of the Six-Day War between Israel and its neighbouring countries. June is a major month on the whole with Midsummer (around the 24th) being a particularly important date. The flying saucer era began on June 24, 1947 when pilot Kenneth Arnold reported seeing unidentified flying objects flying in formation at supersonic speed over Mount Rainier in Washington. The date has also marked several occasions when mysterious objects fell from the sky.

Looking back on the pilot of any long-running television series can be a strange experience. The reoccurring motifs we're accustomed to aren't there, or are at least present in forms different to the ones we're accustomed to. A pilot is by definition a first draft, and the one for *Assignment: Earth* is no different in this regard. What's especially strange about this pilot though (simply and uninspiringly titled "Assignment: Earth", though I suppose it gets the point across), at least for someone used to what the show eventually becomes, is that it opens up not with Supervisor 194 Gary Seven in his swanky apartment, but with an oddly-shaped spaceship in orbit around Earth. The ship's captain, played by Canadian Royal Shakespeare actor William Shatner, exposits that he and his crew come from the far future and have travelled back in time to 1968 for historical research. Gary then transports aboard the ship, looks around in confusion and we cut to the intro credits...of an entirely different show.

Knowing a little background about how United States TV worked in the late-1960s would probably be beneficial. Back then it was customary for new pilots to be not-so-subtly disguised as regular episodes in currently-airing shows, so that the new show could piggyback off of the existing one, hopefully inheriting its audience. This still happens on occasion today, but not with the same kind of regularity as it used to. In this case, *Assignment: Earth* actually began life as a spin-off of an earlier, lesser-known series of Gene Roddenberry's called *Star Trek*, which followed the adventures of Captain Kirk (Shatner's character) and the crew of the USS *Enterprise*, which patrolled and explored the galaxy in the far future as part of an interstellar conglomerate called the United Federation of Planets. *Star Trek* was indebted to the Pulp and Golden Age science fiction genres of the

311

1950s and early 1960s, in much the same way as *Assignment: Earth* was to the "spy-fi" fad of the late-1960s and 1970s, at least at first.

Part of the reason *Star Trek* isn't as well remembered as its successor is today is that it never scored particularly good ratings, partially due to the fact that it largely wasn't any good, and it ultimately burnt itself out after two seasons. But let's bear in mind we all know *Assignment: Earth* was no great shakes in its earliest days either, and there's every reason to believe *Star Trek* might have been just as successful had it been given the chance. Certainly from what we can see in this episode alone it looks like it had promise-Shatner is likeable, and Leonard Nimoy and James Doohan deliver equally memorable turns as alien science officer Spock and chief engineer Scott, respectively. Nevertheless, this would explain why it ran a backdoor pilot as its series finale.

In this regard we need to talk about the episode itself a bit. Aside from the framing device of having the *Enterprise* crew from *Star Trek* intervene and slow the plot up a bit, the story here is largely the same as the one we're familiar with from the premier episode a year later: Gary is sent to Earth to tamper with the launch of a nuclear warhead and scare the major powers into abandoning the Cold War arms race and the concept of balance of power. The biggest difference is Roberta: While she's still Gary's fabulously Carnaby Street liaison and assistant, here she's the former secretary of the deceased agents, and is depicted as a flighty, easily perplexed scatterbrain. While erratic loopiness is something of a character trait of Roberta's at this point in the show's history, it does help to approach *Assignment: Earth* from the perspective of the future, where we know she'll eventually transform into a stronger, more interesting character. Here though her confusion causes more than a fair share of major problems for the rest of the characters, and this combined with the dominating, controlling "You're not allowed to leave, you've seen too much" attitude Gary has toward her for the majority of the episode makes her scenes borderline unwatchable.

The one saving grace about Roberta in the pilot is that she's played with impeccable earnestness by Teri Garr, who at least sells every bit of her ditziness and endeavours to make her charming. Garr would go on to have marquee roles in movies like *Tootsie* and *Close Encounters of the Third Kind*, and shadows of her future performances are visible here. She would have made an excellent Roberta, and it's a shame she didn't return for the series. Not that Garr can really be blamed, though: She was treated absolutely horribly on the set by Roddenberry, who kept ordering the hemline on her skirt raised over and over again to the point it actually pissed off costume designer William Ware Theiss. And knowing the sort of relationship those two had, you can tell how explosive the atmosphere on set must have been. Yet another reminder of how much of a problem Roddenberry's influence was early on in *Assignment: Earth*, and how much of a godsend for the series' future prospects it was that he was eventually replaced as producer.

While not as huge of an issue as Roberta, Gary has problems of his own that touch on probably the fundamental issue this series is going to have to address: As a perfect human from space who comes down to Earth to teach us all how to think and behave, there's an undeniably patriarchal streak to Gary, especially as Roberta, the show's representative of youth culture, is depicted here as someone who has good intentions but is very hapless,

312

needing the guiding hand of the much older man to help her along. This is...distasteful, to put it mildly. It's also, unfortunately, very typical of Gene Roddenberry.

On March 29, 1968, A.D., a Federation Temporal Agent code-named Gary Seven clandestinely transported down to that period's Earth, setting up a base for undercover operations in the region known at the time as New York City. His first mission was to secretly sabotage the launch of a rocket-mounted orbital nuclear weapons platform, the last-minute destruction of which would frighten the major world powers into abandoning the Cold War arms race they were engaged in. This is an example of a situation where direct intervention in the local time-stream was in fact not only called for, but required. Had the United States and the Soviet Union continued their policy of mutually assured destruction, this would have risked preventing our timeline from coming to pass. In certain such cases, an effect comes into play known as the *predestination paradox*: In short, this means that the events transpiring must, in fact, transpire in order to uphold the sanctity and integrity of the timeline. The events of March 29 and Gary Seven's actions are one such example of this phenomenon. Modern timeships are equipped with specialized temporal scanners that allow their crews to easily determine if they are working with such a situation.

There are many myths and urban legends surrounding this particular temporal event. The most prominent of these is the rumour that a third party was at play, or perhaps even another Federation timeship (in some versions of this myth, the timeship is none other than the USS *Enterprise* NCC-1701 under the command of James T. Kirk. The practical absurdity of such a claim, given both Kirk and the *Enterprise* date from a point in history centuries before the Federation had mastered temporal mechanics, should be self-evident). The truth is that there was no such intervention, from Kirk or anyone else: Gary Seven caused the rocket to malfunction, just as he was meant to. The *Enterprise* was in fact involved in this event as per popular speculation, being in the same time-space on an unrelated mission of historical research. Seven's motives were naturally unclear to Kirk and his crew, and it was a critical lapse of judgment on Seven's part to not share such crucial information with them, and his actions put his mission in grave jeopardy, could very well have destabilized the timeline, or worse, resulted in a Temporal Civil War.

Our successors don't want us to know that not everyone living tacitly under Federation jurisdiction shares its cultural assumptions, nor keeps in lock-step with its talking points or received history. There is a long tradition of Starfleet timeships that have gone rogue. Jim Kirk knew that *his* future was in danger. That's why he interfered with Gary Seven's plans. The textbooks may *say* that this was some "predestination paradox" or that "everything happened the way it was supposed to", but then they would, wouldn't they? History is written by the people who have the power and the agency to write it.

"Assignment: Earth" isn't a *Star Trek* episode. It's a backdoor pilot for a TV series Gene Roddenberry hoped to launch for the fall 1968 season. The original script, dating to late 1966, was a standalone story Roddenberry retooled to include a *Star Trek* framing device so he could sell his new show as a spin-off. As a result, the *Enterprise* crew is barely in this episode, and when they do get involved they mostly screw up the *real* heroes' plans and get themselves uselessly captured due to their incompetence. The basic cynicism of the brief aside, this is quite telling: To be blunt, you don't do an episode like this if you expect the parent show to live a long and healthy life. No, when this was being filmed all signs still pointed to *Star Trek* being canceled at the end of its second season, and Roddenberry did what any Hollywood businessman would have done: Gear up to put the old show to rest and get the new show sold as quickly as possible.

And the episode as aired does reflect this. If "Bread and Circuses" last week was the end of the *Star Trek* story, "Assignment: Earth" is the bonus episode we get that lets us know what's coming next. More than anything else in the Original Series, this belies the truth about Gene Roddenberry's attitude towards Star Trek: It was never some grand, utopian vision for the future that was deeply personal and meaningful to him. No, *Star Trek* was a show an LA scriptwriter pitched to a network, and when it looked like it was about to run its course he tried to pitch another, because that's what you do when you have that sort of job. What's most revealing honestly is the fact Roddenberry was planning *Assignment: Earth* as early as 1966: That should say everything about how much confidence anyone had in *Star Trek* ever seeing the level success it actually wound up enjoying.

What's equally as telling is that *Assignment: Earth* was an even bigger disaster than *Star Trek*, and it's entirely due to Gene Roddenberry's overbearing incompetence. First of all, Roddenberry was selling a pilot for a potential show that wasn't going to have any of its cast carry over (again). Robert Lansing, who plays Gary Seven, made it very clear he was unwilling to commit to a television series, and Teri Garr, who played Roberta Lincoln, was so horribly treated by Roddenberry she walked off the set and refuses to speak about him or Star Trek to this day (apparently he kept raising the hemline of her skirt to make it more revealing, which even managed to piss off William Ware Theiss). Even if Lansing and Garr hadn't been driven away though, there are a number of fundamental problems with this concept that would have made *Assignment: Earth* extremely problematic. Gary Seven himself is concerning on a number of levels: What's important to note about him at first is that he seems loosely based on accounts of "contactees". This phenomenon dates (at least in the modern UFO era) to at least the 1940s, and involves people who claim to have had contact with benevolent extraterrestrial beings. These beings are reportedly concerned about the future of Earth and humanity, and offer to help us solve our problems by, among other things, ending nuclear testing, ending warfare outright or using their contacts on Earth to spread their message of peace and solidarity.

This would at least make *Assignment: Earth* come across as comparatively current (although it'll be another decade or so before anything of Roddenberry's comes close to seriously engaging with UFOlogy and Forteana), although an even better point of comparison might be the 1951 movie *The Day the Earth Stood Still*, where a highly advanced alien comes down to Earth to try and get humanity to end all warfare and conflict, by force if he has to. Curiously, both the contactee phenomenon and the basic themes of "Assignment: Earth" and *The Day the Earth Stood Still* seem more in tune with the 1970s Glam-style concept of the Starman who beams down to enlighten us all, at least superficially. What's different about Gary Seven is his modus operandi and general tactics are also drawn from spy-fi, a fusion of science fiction and spy fiction-Seven has to conduct all his operations undercover.

The main problem is that this is still pretty patriarchal. Once again, we have an enlightened male authority figure teaching us the proper way to behave and do things, and this is especially egregious in "Assignment: Earth" as Gary Seven is paired off with Roberta Lincoln, a character who straightforwardly proves Gene Roddenberry knew as much about youth culture as he did women, that is to say, absolutely nothing. Roberta could have been a cool character, a Mod action superheroine who shows us the idealized future Gary Seven wants can only come about by embracing women and the youth. Instead, Garr gets to stand around slack-jawed as magic future aliens beam in and out of her office, lock her up, physically restrain her and just generally dismiss her as she's clearly too stupid to understand what's going on or to help out in any meaningful way. Garr docs make Roberta charming and likeable (actually, "Assignment: Earth" is on the whole more then decently entertaining to watch, even if it's nowhere near as good as I remember it being), but, predictably, she's hideously wasted on the part.

When paired with Gary Seven, this becomes abundantly obvious. Roddenberry clearly only thinks the youth have their hearts in the right place and are too naive, flighty and scattered to actually bring about any real change. What they need, according to him, is an older, wiser, male authority figure to show them how things *really* work. Someone like him, presumably. Also, Roberta is supposed to be twenty. Gary Seven looks middle-aged. This makes the pseudo-romantic relationship the show clearly is setting them up to have (crucially, Isis gets jealous, because the only two modes a woman can have are nagging and jealousy, even if they're shapeshifting cat aliens. Seriously, Roddenberry can even screw up shapeshifting cat aliens) beyond creepy (though knowing Roddenberry, infuriatingly not unexpected). Compare this to *Raumpatrouille Orion*, where the headquarters of the Rapid Space Fleet is in the Starlight Casino, a Mod bar, and everyone has Mod-inspired hairstyles and uniforms. There, the Mods were depicted as literally being from the future, even if we'll ultimately need to move beyond them someday to get at real, material social progress (which was, in 1966, not only a fair comment but a damn prescient one). Meanwhile here, in 1968, almost 15 years into the Mod movement, and Gene Roddenberry can't help but write his Mod lady as an excruciating stereotype.

But really, there's only one way I could close out the second season of *Star Trek*, and the show's original intended run. While we are, in fact, coming back next year thanks to one of the most unprecedented acts in United States pop culture history, the story of *Star Trek* and its original creative team is over now. It's fitting then the "finale" last week was co-written by Gene Roddenberry and Gene Coon, as this is their last real opportunity to make a firm declaration about what *Star Trek* is about. If "Assignment: Earth" was largely Roddenberry, "Bread and Circuses" was largely Coon (well...up to the end). Coon was also the person really responsible for the Hail-Mary pass of actual competence that was the run from "The Immunity Syndrome" to "The Ultimate Computer", the first real time we had an unfiltered look at the beating heart of Star Trek. The heart that Gene Coon gave it. While we'll be seeing them both more next year, along with D.C. Fontana and John Meredyth Lucas (and Roddenberry of course sticks around until 1991) it's not quite the same after

315

this.

So let's briefly take a moment to think back on the achievements of Gene Coon, D.C. Fontana, Dave Gerrold and John Meredyth Lucas. These are the people who took a ropey, ill-conceived retrograde bit of sci-fi and, within the space of a year and a half, made it into a legend. We know they did even now, in 1968: No sooner does this episode go out than the unthinkable happens, and the people make it clear just how much the show *Star Trek* became meant to them.

"Assignment: Earth" involves Gary Seven attempting to sabotage a nuclear warhead loaded into a Saturn V rocket. On April 4, 1968, NASA did indeed launch a Saturn V rocket, except it was carrying the Apollo 6 test craft. Just as depicted in the episode, the rocket did in fact suffer a malfunction and go off course. Star Trek fans are quick to claim this is evidence of the truthfulness of "Assignment: Earth" as Kirk and Spock say the details of the malfunction were never fully made public.

Part III.

1968-1969

69. Ship's Log, Supplemental: Bjo Trimble and "Save Star Trek!"

Yes, *Star Trek* did in fact come back for a third season. Barely.

Critically however, this wasn't a renewal in the traditional sense either. What happened in March of 1968 was something the likes of which had really never been seen before in US television, and about which there is a considerable amount of myth and contradictory lore, most of which seems to have been deliberate. Central to these events is a woman name Betty JoAnne Trimble, better known as Bjo. So, in the first entry of the "Ship's Log, Supplemental" series, which looks at miscellaneous aspects of the Star Trek pop culture phenomenon, in particular the history and historiography of its fandom, I'm going to try and piece together as best I can the extent of her influence and connection to the franchise and the series of events leading up to *Star Trek*'s unexpected renewal...And inevitable, if postponed, cancellation.

Although *Star Trek* never commanded acceptable, let alone impressive, ratings in its original run, what fans it did have were notoriously passionate and vocal. Throughout the duration of the first season, NBC got close to 29,000 letters from fans gushing about the show, which was the most amount of mail they got for any of their shows save *The Monkees*. Although a comprehensive cross-section of Star Trek fandom in the 1960s is difficult to establish, it is clear a great many of these early fans were women. Numerous producers, executives and other creative figures associated with the franchise for decades have pointed this out, despite their tendency to make spectacularly unfounded inferences from this fact, mostly in regards to how all those women were apparently just lusting after Spock (Ron Moore is particularly egregious in this regard, having written an entire fucking *Star Trek: The Next Generation* episode with the express intent of viciously mocking them, but we'll get to that). Although there were most certainly more then a few women who fixated on Spock and who turned him into a sex symbol for one reason or another, the sexism implicit in assuming the *only* reason women watched *Star Trek* was because of this should be self-evident. In truth there is a long tradition of a feminist Star Trek fandom which goes all-but-ignored thanks to the unbelievably patriarchal nature of science fiction culture, and which will start to become more of a theme once we reach the 1970s. This outpouring of fan mail is the first manifestation of it.

The truth of the matter was Star Trek's first fans were all women. *Star Trek* was, in fact, a show more or less *for* women, which is pretty fucking incredible to think about given that show's attitude towards gender and sexuality. Even so, it's not terribly difficult to see why women would feel inspired and empowered by *Star Trek* in 1968. Gene Roddenberry may have had a tendency to act like a misogynistic bastard, but in the two years since the series has been on the air people who aren't him have used the show to make considerable strides for more egalitarian representation: We've had characters like Ann Mulhall and Charlene Masters being depicted as colleagues in equal standing with their male shipmates, not to mention Uhura, who's become a strong and capable character in her own right over the course of the last season. Even characters like Daras in "Patterns of Force" got to be surprisingly nuanced for the time with detailed backstories and complex, multifaceted personalities. Of course, for every Ann Mulhall or Daras there's been a Nona or Sylvia, but the fans were right to hold up the good examples in lieu of the bad ones, especially if they were trying to argue for the show's merit. There was also the matter of William Shatner's and Leonard Nimoy's acting and onscreen chemistry, which most certainly drew the attention of more then a few woman fans, but that's beyond the scope of this particular chapter.

It would make sense then that the monumental letter-writing campaign spanning the last half of 1967 and the first half of 1968 to save *Star Trek* from cancellation would be spearheaded by female superfan Bjo Trimble and her husband John. Trimble initially reached out to a 4,000 member mailing list for a science fiction convention to write NBC as a show of support for the struggling series, and to ask ten additional people to do so in turn. The campaign quickly snowballed to frankly ludicrous proportions, with NBC receiving a staggering 116,000 letters between that December and the following March, 52,000 of which arrived in the month of February alone (one executive, Norman Lunenfield, vividly describes looking out his window at NBC's Burbank office and seeing a fleet of mail trucks stretching to the end of the road). Rumours even circulate this wasn't even the real number, with the network actually receiving over a million responses but never making the rest public. Eventually, what had come to become known as the "Save Star Trek!" movement grew to include mass demonstrations on college campuses such as Caltech, Berkeley and MIT. Eventually, NBC had to relent and, as the traditional account goes, made the unheard-of decision to announce *Star Trek* had been renewed for a third season on air just after the initial broadcast of "The Omega Glory". However, this doesn't tell the full story of what exactly happened in March, 1968 and the events that led up to it.

First of all, Bjo Trimble was no ordinary *Star Trek* fan, and I don't mean in just the fact she organised one of the largest and most famous letter-writing campaigns in history. In what's perhaps evidence of precisely how insular and niche *Star Trek* always was, Bjo Trimble was absolutely an insider in the science fiction community of the late 1960s. She got her start attending the Tenth World Science Fiction Convention held in Chicago in 1952, where she was stationed as a WAVE (part of an all-female Navy volunteer emergency response system instituted during World War II). There she met both Robert Bloch and Harlan Ellison, the latter of whom had just sold his first story and decided to propose as soon as he met her, because of fucking course a Nerd like him would have done something so creepy and insensitively pig-headed. She turned him down, obviously and thankfully, and eventually went on to meet her actual future husband John at the same convention. Bjo became a regular at the conventions in subsequent years, organising some of the first science fiction themed art and fashion shows. It was at one of these shows that she met Gene Roddenberry after being captivated by a screening of "Where No Man Has Gone Before", and even convinced him to show off the *Star Trek* uniforms at one of her exhibitions, thus providing one of the first glimpses fans would get of the new show's costume design.

Most interestingly, according to Herb Solow and Bob Justman in *Inside Star Trek*, it was Roddenberry who gave Trimble the idea to launch the 1967-8 letter-writing campaign due to their prior familiarity and who secretly provided the effort's necessary funding. Now, I have to quickly add this isn't meant to diminish what Trimble did in the slightest: Even if "Save Star Trek!" wasn't all her, she still pulled off one of the most remarkable and foundational feats in the history of genre fandom. Equally though, Trimble was not merely an average, if uniquely passionate and driven, *Star Trek* fan who took it upon herself to do something to help save her favourite show on principle, which is how certain pieces of official literature have had a tendency to depict her. And if Roddenberry was indeed at least partially behind "Save Star Trek!", it's hard to fault him for it: Roddenberry was first and foremost a businessman who had an eye on what sold, and he did what any savvy businessman would have done. With it becoming abundantly clear *Assignment: Earth* was dead on arrival, Roddenberry may have decided to take action to save his other line in the water. And, seeing how big of a following *Star Trek* was getting, he merely took advantage of it. This would be neither the first nor the last time Roddenberry mobilized Star Trek fandom for leverage.

And Roddenberry's association with women like Bjo Trimble would eventually profoundly change his life for the better.

No, what's more telling is the reasoning NBC cited for bringing *Star Trek* back, and what the actual details and meaning behind the announcement really were. This is best summarised by a pair of quotes from contemporary newspaper stories about the letter-writing campaign. Vernon Scott from the Oxnard, California Press-Courier said

> "The show, according to the 6,000 letters it draws a week (more than any other in television), is watched by scientists, museum curators, psychiatrists, doctors, university professors and other highbrows. The Smithsonian Institution asked for a print of the show for its archives, the only show so honored."

while Cynthia Lowry of the Pasco, Texas Tri-City Herald wrote

> "Much of the mail came from doctors, scientists, teachers, and other professional people, and was for the most part literate–and written on good stationery. And if there is anything a network wants almost as much a high Nielsen ratings it is the prestige of a show that appeals to the upper middle class and high brow audiences."

Both of these statements expressed sentiments that were echoed in NBC's actual publicity material, and I find that incredibly revealing. Although Bjo Trimble may not have been the complete embodiment of *Star Trek*'s everyday female (and feminist) fanbase because of her insider connections, she absolutely spoke for them. She was a person they could relate to, and her campaign gave them a way to express their voice. And while yes, Star Trek has always held an appeal for the technoscience sectors, this isn't the exclusive domain of the franchise's appeal, despite the impression you might get from contemporary fandom. In this regard, it is imperative to note that NBC made a conscious, deliberate attempt to publicly court one type of fan over the other, and this is decision that will hold repercussions for the entire rest of the history of Star Trek fandom. From here on out, it's the upper-middle class, "highbrow", "educated" and technologistic demographic (and tacitly white cis males of 18-25 years of age) who will be seen as Star Trek's "Real" fans, and not the women who actually made it a cult phenomenon to begin with (look even at the schools who were doing the protesting: All universities known for their technoscience and industry connections).

There's also one more thing. NBC may have gone out of their way to court this demographic, but they also immediately recognised it for what it was: Small. *Star Trek's* fans may have been loud and prolific, but the ratings weren't backing up the amount of fan mail they were getting, and a network can't justify keeping a show like *Star Trek* on the air by virtue of fan mail alone. So NBC made, ironically enough, an incredibly logical decision. *Star Trek* would be renewed for third season yes, but there would be an unspoken implication the third season would also be its last. Oh yes, it couldn't be more clear to me that NBC always intended to pull the plug on *Star Trek* in 1969. NBC made a big deal about moving the show to Mondays to court its newfound audience, but then backtracked and moved it to Fridays instead to avoid competition with *Rowan and Martin's Laugh-In* and, allegedly, to appeal to *Star Trek's* younger fans. This led Roddenberry to complain "If the network wants to kill us, it couldn't make a better move" and to promptly walk off the show during the summer hiatus. Gene Coon, D.C. Fontana and John Meredyth Lucas soon followed suit.

There's a lot of secret messages telegraphed in that series of choices. First of all, NBC was *never* going to privilege *Star Trek* over the wildly successful *Laugh-In*, which was culturally significant in its own right. Secondly, while a Friday timeslot may well have been good for children, the flip side of that is because the reason for that is *children are the only people who are home watching television on Friday nights*. It's called the Friday Night Death Slot for a reason, and this had the added bonus of giving a pretty damn good clue as to who NBC really thought *Star Trek's* audience was comprised of. Dropping the budget by $3000 should probably have been another sign the writing was really on the wall. This led Nichelle Nichols to famously fume

> "While NBC paid lip service to expanding *Star Trek's* audience, it [now] slashed our production budget until it was actually ten percent lower than it had been in our first season ... This is why in the third season you saw fewer outdoor location shots, for example. Top writers, top guest stars, top anything you needed was harder to come by. Thus, *Star Trek's* demise became a self-fulfilling prophecy. And I can assure you, that is exactly as it was meant to be."

Nichols is absolutely right, of course. And while this decision may be seen as a criminal act of betrayal by the fans (and even *TV Guide*, who are gigantic Star Trek fans anyway, called it the fourth "Biggest TV Blunder Ever" in a special), it makes absolute perfect sense from the perspective of the network. And anyway, as difficult as it may be to believe, NBC's move to kill off the Original Series may have been the final event that guaranteed Star Trek's immortality. See, had the show been canceled in its second season, there wouldn't have been enough episodes to sell a syndication package. Giving *Star Trek* a third season tipped the total episode count over the minimum. NBC knew they had a show that was floundering in primetime, but they also knew that if they could sell it as part of a syndication deal the loyal fans would follow it and turn it into a regular and reliable source of income. And that's exactly what happened, and furthermore, *Star Trek* proved to be even more popular in syndication than it was in its original run. So popular, in fact, Paramount approached Gene Roddenberry and the team a decade later with the idea to maybe bring the franchise back to television. This is the very definition of what a Cult Sci-Fi show is, and this is how *Star Trek* became the archetypical example of the genre.

And that's the story of how a ropey show that had pretty much everything working against it turned into one of the most lasting pillars of Western popular consciousness. And, although NBC had a part to play, it was really the female fans who came together to let the network know they had something that was special (in spite of itself) and that shouldn't be discarded. The real criminal act of betrayal was not that NBC eventually did pull the plug on the Original Series: Rather, that was what allowed Star Trek to undergo its own true Metamorphosis. No, the real act of betrayal was that these women were never given the respect and credit they deserve for providing the imaginative spark that allowed *Star Trek* to become Star Trek.

70. Sensor Scan: Rowan and Martin's Laugh-In

The question of exactly how radical and progressive a television show can get when it's airing on major network television and supported by corporate advertising and ratings is an interesting one. On the surface the answer seems like a flat "not in the slightest": Simply put, it's a rather noticeable conflict of interest to have a work deeply invested in overturning the current social order dependent on the tools and infrastructure of the very hegemony it's set itself in opposition to. On the other hand, one does sort of hope there's at least a little-wiggle room for this kind of thing in pop culture mass media: If you're a young person just starting to come to terms with your worldview and unaware of big underground counterculture movements, it's really helpful to be able to turn on the TV and see you're not completely alone, especially in a world without the Internet.

In the past, we've looked at this issue on the context of *Star Trek*: Supposedly the most forward-thinking and youth-embracing show on television in the late 1960s, the Original Series has in truth proven to be at best somewhat changeable on the ethics front and at worst precisely the opposite. There have been moments that seem to support this claim, most noticeably in the last third of the second season, but there have also been just as many, if not more, that would seem to give the indication *Star Trek* was anything but, and in truth pretty regularly and reliably (and disturbingly) reactionary. But that's *Star Trek*, and in spite of the numerous overtures it can and has made towards a more socially-conscious approach, it's still burdened by some pretty major liabilities (in particular the one named Gene Roddenberry) and its potential to make a positive impact is frustratingly not always as clear as it should be. The question remains though: Can you have a truly countercultural television show? We can, in fact, take an even broader scope: Can you have countercultural Soda Pop Art at all?

In my opinion, the only real satisfactory answer is "yes and no", and for a good example let's take a look at the other iconic NBC show of 1968, and the show that kicked *Star Trek* out of its primetime slot: *Rowan and Martin's Laugh-In*. Conceived by Dan Rowan and Dick Martin as an evolution of the "straight man/dumb guy" act they had honed in nightclubs, *Laugh-In* was a weekly sketch comedy show most famous for its innovative style marked by rapid-fire editing that cut between various discrete images and scenarios. The jokes and sketches on *Laugh-In* were frequently only seconds in length, just there long enough to deliver a punchline before cutting away to something completely different. The show lasted an impressively long time, from 1968 until 1973, and helped launch the careers of future luminaries like Goldie Hawn and Lily Tomlin, not to mention Lorne Michaels, a staff writer on *Laugh-In* who would go on to produce *Saturday Night Live*.

The most obvious thing that set *Laugh-In* apart from its predecessors in television and stage comedy, and what it's most remembered for, is its overt courting of the 1960s counterculture, and in particular the Mods and the Hippies. There was a *lot* of Carnaby Street imagery in *Laugh-In*: One of the reoccurring settings of many of the one-liners was a wild-looking Mod party where everyone would be entranced and dancing wildly. Then suddenly, everything would stop, someone would tell a joke, then everything starts up again just in time for the show to cut away for something else. There was also a fair bit of youth culture lingo, or at least mildly endearing attempts at ut (the legendary "Sock it to me!" and a family-friendly version of "You bet your ass!" are probably the most famous examples), not to mention a healthy portion of sexual humour. This is where the show gets *really* changeable, and I'm assuming it probably varies depending on who wrote the sketch: *Laugh-In* could either make a charmingly inclusive and innocent comment about the ubiquity of the Free Love movement or land square in unwatchable "sexual assault is funny" territory. Speaking of Free Love, the name *Laugh-In* itself is quite obviously a reference to the concept of a "sit-in" or "love-in", the idea of a peaceful form of organised protest in favour of civil rights made famous by its popularity in the 1960s. Whether that's clever marketing, hegemonic appropriation or a little of both is up to you to decide.

Another way *Laugh-In* tried to reach out to the youth culture was by having a lot of their jokes be about actual contemporary social and political issues. However, like its take on sexuality, this also had a tendency to be vary in tone and quality from time to time. One of the better exchanges I found goes like this. Dan Rowan's character is talking to Hippie lady in a silver sequined bra and dress. She says "You know, Dan, blacks have a really rough time in the union of South Africa". Rowan responds "Well, minorities have it rough all over" to which she responds "Yeah, but it's tougher to be a minority when there's more of you then there is of them". Now today this scene feels a bit awkward and stilted, but in 1968 it was sort of a new thing to have comedy like this that not only took that blunt a look at world issues, but have the half-naked Hippie chick be the one delivering the punchline to the dimwitted establishment figure in a suit, and on primetime on NBC to boot (Also brilliant is "My church accepts all denominations. But my favourite is the five-dollar bill"). However, for as many clever exchanges like this as the show gave us, it also had an almost equal amount of ones that were...less than successful, such as "All the kids in my school are *really proud* of the astronauts. Imagine: To stay that high for that long!".

In moments such as this it almost feels as if *Laugh-In* was self-consciously trying to reel itself in and make sure it never crossed the line *too* much, and to go out of its way made everyone look equally slow and imbecilic on different occasions so as not to offend people. Which is exactly what you would expect of a comedy show on primetime network television. The problem is, satire only works when it's directed towards figures of authority and oppression. When you start leveling it at the oppressed, which the youth culture *absolutely* was in 1968, you stop being agents of change and start being tools of The Man (this isn't even getting at people of US-African descent, which *Laugh-In* had an equally rocky, yet incredibly more awkward, relationship with). When the show slips up and starts delivering cringe-inducing moments like this, two things happen: Either the joke lands at toothless and unfunny if it's lucky, and if it's not, it lands square in the territory of reactionary. The absolute nadir of *Laugh-In* in this regard has to be the episode where Richard Nixon made a cameo in a "Sock it to me!" joke during his campaign in a pitiful attempt to gain favour with the youth...That is credited by political historians as pretty much being the thing that won him the election. That alone really ought to be reason enough to throw out the whole show.

(Although I will say I found seeing Leonard Nimoy in a similar cameo remarking "Does NBC even know this show is on the air?" to be legitimately clever, hilarious and completely unexpected.)

However the real problem with *Laugh-In*, and the true reason why it became a show that could get away with selling the frankly bewildering idea that Richard Nixon was in some way a hip ally of the counterculture was because, ultimately, it was too indebted to the United States variety tradition. This was not some bristling bit of anarcha-humour that targeted the hegemony, this was a Mod-themed Vaudeville routine. And, like all Vaudeville, *Laugh-In* had a tendency to be, well, awful. On an alarming number of occasions, the bits of *Laugh-In* I saw felt uncomfortably like someone took a "1001 Happening Hippie Jokes" book and built an entire show around that. Stuff like "I hear Governor Reagan is really worried about earthquakes in California. He's afraid Berkeley may shift even further to the left!" is at best the worst kind of stand-up platitude (Right Wing politicians don't like Left Wing activists? I mean wow, what a keen observation...) and at worst dangerously reactionary. This kind of joke is the 1960s version of those terrible "humour" books from the 1980s and 1990s that tried to cash in on the personal computer craze with "witticisms" like "What does the President use with his computer in the Oval Office? A White mouse!".

Although to be fair to *Laugh-In*, this isn't entirely its fault here. Vaudeville was a genre defined by how defanged it was due to the draconian moral codes instituted by studios and touring companies. The fact is, there's not a whole lot of difference between that system and the one that existed on network television in the 1960s. Television sketch comedy is a direct descendant of Vaudeville, and it suffers from the same intrinsic drawbacks. And to its credit, *Laugh-In* does seem to have gotten it right at least as often as it got it wrong, at least if you forgive them Richard Nixon (which I hasten to add I have a tough time doing), and it does seem to be ahead of the curve on several things. For one, the people making the show seem on the whole aware of its limitations due to the profusion of self-deprecating humour on this show, in particular directed at NBC or the producers (Leonard Nimoy's cameo being merely the best example). That's something you wouldn't see in Vaudeville or earlier television variety or comedy shows because as soon as someone made a joke like that they'd mysteriously disappear from the playbook. But, as I mentioned in the "I, Mudd" post, it's this kind of self-awareness that comes to define this style of performance in the future (and that was lacking from the episode in question) and it's *Laugh-In* where it's the clearest this is beginning to be more widely disseminated.

It's also worth stressing that the overt references to recreational drug use and sexuality as part of a larger acknowledgment that the counterculture was part of the fabric of society such that it could become the source of gentle ribbing instead of fear and scorn, and on primetime television, was sort of a watershed and definitely would have left a powerful impression. Despite its stumblings, *Laugh-In* does seem to have a higher baseline target for how it handled this sort of thing than *Star Trek* did, and the ratings would seem to back this assertion up (although it is telling that *Laugh-In* and *Star Trek* were considered comparable enough such that there could be crossovers). It's tough to fault NBC for keeping it in its Monday timeslot and knocking *Star Trek* to Fridays.

Furthermore, the legacy of *Laugh-In* is quite palpable. While I disagree with what seems to be the common statement that *Monty Python's Flying Circus* is somehow a successor to it (Monty Python comes out of a very particularly British tradition of comedy and is in some sense quite culturally specific, and *Laugh-In* is about as United States as it gets), its influence is clear in other places. The connection to *Saturday Night Live* is obvious, and there's a direct link between *Laugh-In* and Mark Evanier's career, especially *Garfield and Friends*. It's also peculiarly enough, easy to see the impact it had on Jim Henson's work, particularly *Sesame Street*. Both use a very rapid fire style of editing to quickly convey information and symbols as part of a larger sensory experience (it's obvious on *Sesame Street* in the "commercial" segments) and while I was watching *Laugh-In* to prepare for this article I found myself being reminded of the kind of "MTV Spectacle" style best exemplified by the music videos of the 1980s, in particular the late-1980s.

But what I think is most important about *Laugh-In* is that it *did* get a somewhat positive version of the youth culture on television in 1968. It's not a perfect portrayal (it's definitely sanitized for family viewing) and I'm not even sure this is the best show of its time to tackle the issue, but it is there and in 1968: The year where the 1960s counterculture essentially died out in the mainstream and was forced underground. That's frankly unbelievable, and it's tough not to be heartened by the fact a show like this lasted all the way until 1973. What I think this shows is that yes, it is in fact possible to have Soda Pop Art handle radical themes in a not-express;y-terrible way. There are going to be compromises, trying to get a show like this made is always going to be a gamble and the onus is always going to be us to impart it with the necessary power, but it's possible. And I'll just say this: I have a distinct feeling it was a whole lot easier to do a show like *Laugh-In* in 1968 than it would be if you tried to make it today.

71. Sensor Scan: The Transformed Man

William Shatner is one of those personalities who is so ubiquitous that their reputation precedes and obfuscates their actual contributions to art and pop culture. Shatner is so famous as Captain Kirk and the the king of unironic and self-evidently ridiculous camp that his iconic public persona dwarfs and overshadows his entire creative body of work. One of the reasons why I focus so heavily on Shatner in my overview of this period of Star Trek history (if not the primary one) is that his status as an omnipresent and immediately recognisable part of pop culture has ironically made it difficult to discern any reasonable erudition about the kind of actor he is, the style of performance he delivers and what the positionality he draws it all from really is. That's not to say Leonard Nimoy, James Doohan, DeForest Kelley, George Takei, Nichelle Nichols and Walter Koenig aren't equally as iconic and memorable in their roles, they are, but everyone knows they're brilliant and, more to the point, everyone largely knows *why* they're brilliant. That's not really the case with with William Shatner.

All of which is to say that in 1968 William Shatner released an album of spoken-word poetry.

This is, it should probably go without saying, manifestly not the sort of thing anybody expected of William Shatner at the time, two thirds of the way through the original run of *Star Trek*. It is also probably fairly safe to say it is still not the sort of thing people expect of William Shatner today, because despite his subsequent musical performances becoming part of his camp reputation, the sort of bemused detachment this part of his oeuvre attracts from would-be fans and critics is rather telling. But the existence of *The Transformed Man* is in fact a very revealing look at not only the approach to Soda Pop Art in the late-1960s but also Shatner's own worldview and how his presence helped re-shape what Star Trek came to represent. So with that said, what the heck even *is* *The Transformed Man*?

It may actually be beneficial to begin with an overview of what *The Transformed Man* *isn't*, as this is the source of the overwhelming majority of confusion and bafflement this record attracts. In this regard it's worth comparing it, if for no other reason then the comparison is unavoidable, with Leonard Nimoy's musical catalog. In 1967, just as *Star Trek* was starting to gain a significant following, Dot Records released an album called *Mr. Spock's Songs from Space*, which was pretty much exactly what it sounds like: A collection of fluffy novelty songs Nimoy recorded in full-on Spock-the-logician mode to abjectly hilarious results. Literally the only reason this album exists is because Spock was the show's breakout character, and in the 1960s releasing an album of novelty music to tie in to a popular TV show was just sort of the thing you did, no matter how nonsensical it might sound if you think too hard about it (see also "Snoopy's Christmas" by The Royal

327

Guardians). However, the album was popular enough it spawned a follow-up release in 1968 entitled *The Two Sides of Leonard Nimoy*, which added the twist of having one side be the in-character Spock one and the other side being dedicated to Nimoy singing as himself. This album also featured the mythically bonkers "The Ballad of Bilbo Baggins", which has gone on to become Internet Famous.

The thing about both of Nimoy's releases however is that, like all novelty music, it's abundantly clear none of this is meant to be taken remotely seriously. This is Nimoy goofing around and clearly having a fantastic time running with the self-evidently ridiculous (and amazing) idea of Spock singing songs to children (in fact, next time a Trekker approaches you to complain about something or other betraying the sanctity of these characters, just remind them Spock once recorded an album full of songs with names like "Music To Watch Space Girls By" and "A Visit To A Sad Planet" and that it's 100% canonical). Go watch "The Ballad of Bilbo Baggins" again and it very obviously looks like the sort of thing you'd see on a variety show targeted towards children to get them excited about literature-There are even direct references to slogan buttons and Carnaby Street fashion. This is largely because that's exactly what it was.

This is not, however, what *The Transformed Man* is. Shatner's release had the spectacular ill fortune to come out around the same time as Nimoy's, and while *Star Trek* was more popular and visible than it had ever been before to boot. It would have been impossible to not compare the two and mentally associate them with each other, when in truth the two records couldn't have been more different. The first clue should be in the artwork and liner notes: Nimoy's albums unabashedly cashed in on the popularity of Spock and *Star Trek* and latched onto the delightfully lunatic concept of Mr. Spock recording a novelty album. However, Shatner barely references *Star Trek* at all, except to say he met his collaborators in between filming blocks. There's a solitary picture of Shatner in costume as Kirk and while he is credited as "William Shatner: Captain Kirk of *Star Trek*", I presume for marketing purposes, this had the side-effect of fundamentally altering people's expectations. As a result, fans picking this up expecting a cheerfully tongue-in-cheek comedy record about Captain Kirk singing space songs instead got a somber and profound meditation on the nature of performativity and the meaning of life. Suffice to say, this made Shatner look cataclysmically self-indulgent.

But if we cast aside all preconceptions of *The Transformed Man* being a celebrity novelty cash-in, which it's not, and try to take it at face value, it starts to become clearer what Shatner may have been aiming for here. At its most basic, *The Transformed Man* comes out of the spoken word poetry most famously associated with the Beat Generation movement of the 1950s. Spoken word is fundamentally focused on the dynamics of language, especially the tone and sound of words, often combined with an emphasis on nonverbal gestures. The genre has its origins, as much avant-garde art in North America does, with black culture, in particular modernist Jazz, blues and the poetry of the Harlem Renaissance. This is an environment that will also provide some of the inspiration for the early Mod scene and many art rock acts of the 1960s, 1970s and 1980s, thus linking the Mods with the Beats and the literary underground. Spoken word performance then, at least this kind of

328

spoken word performance, is thus an extremely countercultural form of creative expression, such that if you come up with a list of spoken word performers, it will also double as a roughly comprehensive introduction to some of the most significant artists, thinkers and social justice activists of the past half-century (Sojourner Truth, Booker T. Washington, William S. Burroughs and Laurie Anderson, just to name a few).

What William Shatner realised, and indeed what he was uniquely poised to realise, was that there is an intrinsic connection between something like spoken word poetry, theatre and music. Namely, that they are all explicitly, and in fact almost uniquely, performative. In the liner notes, Shatner talks about how as a child visiting the theatre in Montreal he was always fascinated by orchestral music and how it complimented the performance, and how he's always wanted to do a project that explores the interconnection between the two art forms. *The Transformed Man,* he goes on to say, is the product of a chance meeting with producer Dan Ralke after working with his son Cliff on *Star Trek* where they would talk about Shakespeare, music and poetry on breaks, and that he knew he needed to make an album after being exposed to the wonderful poetry of Frank Davenport. Seeing this album released, he claims, is the realisation of that dream he's had since boyhood. Shatner may be pulling our leg here, but then again he actually does seem like the kind of person who *would* talk about poetry on his lunch break. What he does on *The Transformed Man* then is use his perspective as a thespian to explore this interlinking performativity.

The way Shatner accomplishes this is by taking a mixture of poetry and classic Shakespeare scenes and pairing them up with spoken-word renditions of famous contemporary pop songs. This basic approach is usually a source of derision, but I have nothing against reinterpreting pop songs in different genres. What Shatner is saying is that pop music, poetry and Shakespearean prose are all equally creative outlets for people to explore human experience, which is something I really can't find fault with. After all what is Vaka Rangi but a long-winded experiment in treating pop culture like any other form of "serious" art? And anyway, you can't help but smile to hear Shatner breathlessly introduce each track like an old-fashioned stage manager, quite literally "setting the stage" for the audience at the beginning of a play. He's clearly having an absolute blast.

And furthermore, the structure works great. The album opener, for example, "King Henry the Fifth; Elegy for the Brave" takes the bombast and zeal of King Henry rousing his troops to action and sets it up against a somber poem about soldiers lying dead and dying on a battlefield after a conflict. The glory of the battle is shown to have little meaning in the hereafter, as the bodies of the deceased are unable to know of the effect their efforts had on the ordinary people at home, or of the comings and goings of nature's cycle, indifferent as it is to human ambition. Similarly, "Hamlet; It Was A Very Good Year" and "Romeo and Juliet; How Insensitive (Insensatez)" look at anguish and nihilism in opposition to rose-tinted nostalgia and obsessive young love contrasted with the clumsy, confused coldness of a relationship coming to a close, respectively. Crucially though, Shatner is saying that all of these conflicting emotions are things everyone experiences throughout life, and that expressing them is itself a kind of staged artifice.

The pinnacle of this theme would appear to be "Theme From Cyrano; Mr. Tambourine

Man", which seems like Shatner's exploration of the creative process, and how creators struggle between appealing to to the demands of fandom and doing what they personally find intellectually rewarding and stimulating. It's possible to read this track as a bit of autobiographical embellishment on Shanter's part, especially knowing what was going on with *Star Trek* at the time (or indeed what we know the Star Trek phenomenon is going to eventually become), but I think there's something altogether more subtle going on here. Never once on *The Transformed Man* does Shatner ever indicate he's doing anything different than what he normally does, that is, play a role. The creator of "Theme From Cyrano; Mr. Tambourine Man" isn't meant to be a crass stand-in for Shatner himself any more than he's the lover in "Romeo and Juliet; How Insensitive (Insensatez)", the soldiers in "King Henry the Fifth; Elegy for the Brave", or Captain Kirk in *Star Trek*, for that matter (And anyway, Shatner plays the creator as frenzied and standoffishly huffy, so if he is talking about himself he's being *extremely* self-deprecating about it). These are all different *characters* Shatner is playing, and while they may come out of his positionality as all art by definition has to, he's frankly too good a writer and a performer to do something like that.

But one of *The Transformed Man*'s many hidden virtues is its ability to slowly and methodically build tension all the while lulling the audience into a false sense of security with fake climaxes. The real stunner comes on side two, which features only one track (the title one) as Shatner and his producers very wisely recognised it stands on its own. This track, a recitation of a poem of the same name, tells the story of a person who gives up a day job and house in the city to seek wisdom and inner peace in the wilderness. The speaker begins a lengthy meditation amongst and communion with the land, the sky and the wild creatures before eventually experiencing something that can very easily be described as ego death: A complete dispossession of the Self leading to an understanding of their place within and connection to a cosmic consciousness. Interestingly though, the last line of the poem mentions "touching God", which would imply a pop Christian reading, despite the rest of the poem describing a very pagan version of enlightenment. The lynchpin, however, is, as always, William Shatner.

Although the words are not his, I'm going to speculate a bit and hazard a guess this is a kind of experience not altogether unfamiliar to Shatner. See, despite becoming known mainly for being part of a ubiquitous and iconic piece of United States pop culture and being seen primarily as a US actor, William Shatner is, of course, actually Canadian and was born and raised in Montreal. Canada has the largest, most unbroken stretch of wilderness in the world: The Boreal Forest. There are places in the world where the energy is such that one can feel more potently the connection to the natural universe, and I think there are many places in Canada like this. I don't think it's unreasonable to presume this is something William Shatner might have been aware of.

Furthermore, as a performer, and in particular thanks to his unique style of performance, Shatner is very, very good at conveying and drawing attention to artifice, and that's the entire point of *The Transformed Man*, both the album and the poem: Shatner's overall message here is that our conception of reality, all the way up to the way we can attain enlightenment, is subjective. Furthermore, enlightenment, wisdom and inner peace are deeply personal and ethereal things, and in the end it's ultimately impossible to convey them to others in a way that is 100% loyal. So, if Shatner's rendition of "The Transformed Man" feels hammy and stilted, well, that's the point: It's a metaphor unto itself, and the almost audible twinkle in Shatner's eye lets us all know it's a grand, cosmic joke that he's in on as much as we are.

What's even more marvelous is that "The Transformed Man" comes directly after "Spleen; Lucy In The Sky With Diamonds", where the contrast is despair and hopelessness pitted against the euphoria of describing a transcendental experience (and the ultimate futility of trying to get someone who didn't experience it firsthand to understand it the same way you do). While "Lucy In The Sky With Diamonds" may not actually be about LSD, it was definitely the poster song for altered states of consciousness for a very long time, and certainly would have been seen as such in 1968. The easy thing to do here would be to draw parallels between the two songs and declare Shatner is endorsing the 1960s counterculture and the possibility enlightenment can be found by allying with them. However, I'm going to go one better.

While the youth culture themes are there, I think it's even more rewarding to put Shatner amongst a larger group of colleagues. See, reading William Shatner as someone who is first and foremost invested in the performativity and artifice of human interaction puts him square in the tradition of Avital Ronell, who is herself operating in the tradition of Giles Delueze, Goethe, George Bataille, Jacques Lacan, Jacques Derrida, Søren Kierkegaard, Edmund Husserl and Walter Benjamin. Ronell regularly likens writing, and really all creativity, to drug tripping. Writers, like junkies, let go of the sense of Self and independent will and let themselves be taken over by an outside force. Writers and creators, if we can allows ourselves to momentarily use those words despite their patriarchal connotations, take dictation from an ethereal spirit and become "writing beings", in the language of Kafka. The text exists only inasmuch as it is a dead signifier of some long-forgotten intangible mental and physical confluence. In the language of William Shatner and Avital Ronell, we're all putting on some stilted and awkward show in an attempt to pay our dues to writing. We transform ourselves every day in an attempt to grasp and understand truths that will transform us spiritually.

In case it wasn't abundantly clear after all that, I consider *The Transformed Man* to be something of a masterpiece. It's not Shatner's absolute best effort (there are in fact moments where it feels like Shatner is trying a bit too hard-His histrionics at the end of "Theme From Cyrano; Mr. Tambourine Man" tread dangerously close to "Omega Glory" territory), but it's an absolutely staggering debut album and piece of work once you figure out what it's trying to tell you. See, the big secret about William Shatner is that, in truth, something like this record is a far better showcase for his style of acting then something like *Star Trek*, and it's in an environment like this where he's finally and truly allowed to shine. The end result of all this is that we finally have a handle on what William Shatner really is and the perspective he brings to the table: Shatner certainly isn't a musician, but he's not an actor either.

No, William Shatner is a performance artist. And his subject is the performativity of our lives.

72. "The Last Chance Saloon": Spectre of the Gun

Star Trek is not in a healthy position.

Let's get this over with right from the start. This is a dead show walking, and the average quality it hits over the next year backs this up completely. Under no condition did NBC want a fourth season of *Star Trek*, and the network went out of its way to hurry the show's inevitable demise along, slashing the budget while increasing the actors' salaries and shunting it into the Friday Night Death Slot, the final straw that lead almost the entire original creative team to stage a mass exodus in protest. Furthermore, those who did stay on were driven away by NBC's constant micromanaging and burdening them with D.C. Fontana's replacement as story editor, one Arthur Singer, who by all accounts knew absolutely nothing about what *Star Trek* was and how it worked, and nor did he care.

Traditionally, the blame for the malaise of the 1968-9 season was laid at the feet of incoming executive producer Fred Freiberger, who is typically seen as a network lackey and responsible for "ruining" *Star Trek*. However, the reality was likely far more complex then being the fault of one person. Although Leonard Nimoy and Gene Roddenberry are quick to finger Freiberger, in their memoirs of their time on the show, both Nichelle Nichols and William Shatner go out of their way to defend him, saying he did the best he could with a show that had become at that point unmanageable. For the rest of his life, Freiberger was hounded by fans and critics alike eager to blame him for "killing" the Original Series, with him even going so far as to say that his tenure as producer of and association with Star Trek was the single worst experience of his life, *counting the time he spent in a German prisoner-of-war camp.* Thankfully, one of the more laudable phenomena of recent Star Trek fandom is a comprehensive movement to redeem Freiberger. It's just a shame they couldn't have done that for other people involved in the franchise's early years as well.

And really, this does seem to make a lot more sense then to posit Freiberger was some Evil Network Demon come to destroy the fans' beloved utopia. Freiberger was an extremely professional and experienced television producer, with credits on shows like *The Six-Million Dollar Man*, *Bonanza*, *The Wild Wild West*, *Have Gun, Will Travel*, *Rawhide*, and *The Dukes of Hazzard* among many, many others. It seems, well, *illogical* to argue he was an incompetent hack on *Star Trek* and *Star Trek* alone. It's far more reasonable (and fits with the rest of what we know about this point of the show's history) the presume this was a situation that was entirely out of Freiberger's control.

Furthermore, Herb Solow and Bob Justman, perhaps predictably, don't even need to think about laying all the blame at the feet of Gene Roddenberry in *Inside Star Trek*, whom they continually take to task for abandoning the show and leaving it leaderless (while continuing to draw an executive producer's salary from an already desperate budget, no less). And look, while I'm usually quick to side with Solow and Justman in regards to pretty much everything and in spite of my extremely harsh criticism of Roddenberry, I can't entirely fault him for jumping ship here, nor can I fault D.C. Fontana, Gene Coon and John Meredyth Lucas for stepping back from day-to-day operations. Like the O.K. Corral in the episode I promise I'm going to actually talk about soon, this looks like a situation that it was far more advisable to escape from if possible, as those who stay to fight end up locked in a deathtrap.

(I will, however, absolutely fault Roddenberry for continuing to turn a salary from the show he not only walked away from but which was hurting for money as it was. This is the veritable definition of scummy.)

But although it is imperative to keep in mind that this year is going out in the context of all of this, I largely want to leave aside the Agony and Ecstasy of Season Three narrative for a time, as I'm saving a more detailed examination of precisely what went wrong for *Star Trek* creatively this year for a few episodes from now, especially as the show hasn't exactly been a beacon of quality up to now as it is. And anyway, "Spectre of the Gun" has enough going on in its own right, being on the whole one of the more interesting episodes we're going to get this year. Almost inescapably, however, the very things that make it interesting are inexorably bound up with the behind-the-scenes turmoil: This is a story about *Star Trek* being shackled and sentenced to death. Naturally, it's a Gene Coon script, although this marks the debut of his pseudonym Lee Cronin, which he uses on all of his third season contributions. I'm not entirely sure why Coon felt compelled to protest "Spectre of the Gun": It's not one of his best offerings (there are pacing issues and a bunch of dialog is straight-up repeated, though I'm inclined to blame that on Arthur Singer), but I'm not sure what about it caused him to be embarrassed enough to refuse credit for it (honestly were I Coon I would have taken my name off of "Space Seed" and "A Taste of Armageddon" instead). Indeed, the true irony is this is still one of the most self-aware and imaginative stories the show ever did.

"Spectre of the Gun" concerns Kirk, Spock, McCoy, Scotty and Chekov becoming trapped in a recreation of the gunfight at the O.K. Corral. Mistaken for one of the two warring factions of Tombstone, Arizona, the landing party have to find a way to escape before they get caught up in an outbreak of very real violence. Readers who are versed in the history of *Doctor Who* will most likely have just perked up, as this premise is intriguingly similar to a 1966 Innes Lloyd/William Hartnell serial entitled "The Gunfighters". Now, I've tried hard to keep *Doctor Who* out of the discussion up to now as there's a point much further in the future where it's in my opinion far more appropriate to bring it up, but in this case it really is unavoidable as "Spectre of the Gun" is literally the exact same story, down to one of the characters (The Doctor in "The Gunfighters" and Kirk here) trying to convince a Tombstone citizen they're not who they appear to be by getting them to feel the fabric of their clothes in hopes they'll realise it's not of that time and place. Now, I can't accept that Gene Coon would stoop to straight-up plagiarizing a *Doctor Who* script, if for no other reason there's simply no way he would ever have had the chance to see *Doctor Who*: That show wouldn't premier in the United States until the 1970s, and as far as I know Coon wasn't in the habit of popping off to the UK on a regular basis. But the similarities really are uncanny, and it's endlessly fascinating to compare and contrast how the two shows handled the same brief.

The first difference is who our characters get mistaken for. In "The Gunfighters", the TARDIS crew falls in with the Earp brothers because people think The Doctor is Doc Holliday (which is, admittedly, hilariously perfect). In "Spectre of the Gun", however, the landing party is explicitly assigned the roles of the outlaw Clanton gang who are ultimately killed at the O.K. Corral shootout, perhaps because they're being punished for trespassing in Melkotian territory. But what I find really interesting here is that the Clantons are not only outlaws, but the script is clearly treating them as the protagonists as well. While in "The Gunfighters" there was a lot of anxiety about unnecessary violence and the threat of these armed and dangerous men making a bad situation worse, in "Spectre of the Gun", every character who isn't an Earp is deeply sympathetic to and supportive of the Clantons and, crucially, when history is suddenly changed and Chekov's character, Billy Claiborne, is gunned down, the Sheriff is completely in favour of Ike ClantonXKirk's right to vengeance.

Identifying Kirk, Spock, McCoy and Chekov (and by extension the rest of the *Enterprise* crew) as heroic outlaws is incredibly revealing: Not only does it help to drive home and make clear a lot of Gene Coon's signature motifs, but it tells us something about what the general attitude on the Paramount studios set was in late 1968. On the one hand, this is obvious as the whole recreation of Tombstone is part of an overly elabourate death sentence on the part of the Melkotians, so naturally the crew would be cast as outlaws. But let's stop and unpack this for a minute: Why, exactly, are the *Enterprise* crew on death row? And why did the Melkotians go to such laughably convoluted extremes to punish them? Well, the Melkotians' entire argument comes down to the fact the *Enterprise* ignored their warning buoy, which doesn't make any sense because Kirk made it very clear on several occasions their only intention was to make peaceful contact. Even under the most cartoonishly exaggerated of authoritarian *Judge Dredd*-style universes, this shouldn't be a death penalty offense. Kirk and Spock make some comments about how they're under strict orders to make contact with the Melkotians at all costs, which also makes *them* look like idiots: The last time we had a story like that was "A Taste of Armageddon", and that was at least in part about how disconnected and incompetent bureaucrats were and how stupid it was to blindly follow orders at all costs.

But this is not the approach "Spectre of the Gun" takes. This is the first episode of Star Trek made in a post-Bjo Trimble, post-"Save Star Trek!" world. While perhaps not textually overt yet, there is now the beginning of a general sense that the point of Star Trek really is to "Seek Out New Life And New Civilizations" and not to enforce space law or solve everybody else's problems. We saw the seeds of this in "Return to Tomorrow" and this episode is the next step: Star Trek is now trying to justify its existence by virtue of its sense of exploration and idealism rather than its moral superiority. In other words then, the Melkotians are trying to punish *Star Trek* for being *Star Trek* because they don't understand it (recall they repeal their sentence and allow a diplomatic conference after Kirk proves to them he's not a killer). The real-world overtones of this theme are quite obvious. But this motif goes even deeper: The point of "The Gunfighters" was in many ways the idea that *Doctor Who* is incredibly ill-suited to being a western. Not only does The Doctor look laughably out-of-place in Tombstone, on the level of the actual production, the guest cast are absolutely terrible at doing US accents and acting like characters in a cowboy flick. This has been cited as evidence that *Doctor Who* is special amongst genre shows in that it can throw off the more pulpish and action-oriented aspects of science fiction to become something unique unto itself. But this is what "Spectre of the Gun" does too.

The original *Star Trek* is frequently (and somewhat inaccurately) described as "A *Wagon Train* to the Stars" in an often-misattributed quote. Despite this not quite being the original intent of the show (Gene Roddenberry's own bafflingly idiotic ramblings about John Wayne in latter years perhaps notwithstanding) there does still remain this tendency to think Star Trek is some kind of Space Western and ought to operate by the logic of Hollywood cowboy flicks. "Spectre of the Gun" is Gene Coon's response to that claim, where having *Star Trek* trapped into becoming a western is a literal death sentence (note how the Melkotians' Tombstone is "unfinished" and consists mostly of facades and assorted props, just like the stage set for a cowboy movie or play might be. The characters even point this out). In a sense, the crew are forced into playing roles they're not suited to-The entire story is about them trying to re-write the O.K. Corral myth so it ends nonviolently, after all. But while "The Gunfighters" played its premise as a kind of goofy genre romp comedy (complete with an intentionally irritating "theme song" that plays throughout the whole serial) "Spectre of the Gun" treats its gravely seriously, down to teasing the death of a major character as a consequence of *Star Trek* being forced to not be *Star Trek* (it's telling Chekov is the character most obviously eager to take up, and disappear into, his role).

What's genius about the trick Coon pulls here is that it ties so beautifully into the recursive artifice and performativity *Star Trek* inherited from people like him and William Shatner (recall not only did Coon write "A Piece of the Action" but "The Conscience of the King" was the first proper script of his tenure as showrunner). Just like his last script, *Star Trek* is shown to crash-land into a story it really doesn't belong in, but while there Kirk could slip in and out of the two genres and ultimately deform *Star Trek* for the better, here he's forcibly shoehorned into a role he's not supposed to play, and things go badly wrong. Although Kirk may still be a literary outlaw (and it's perfect that in the last two Gene Coon scripts Kirk has gone from mob boss to leader of an Old West gang of bandits and gamblers), this role requires him to be a murderer, and that's something his personal moral code won't permit. So, he does what he's best at: Rebels against the narrative structure and reshapes it from within. So, when Spock deduces that the entire recreation is (of course) one big artifice, Kirk holds a mind-meld orgy to get the landing party to aggressively reject the reality of their situation, thus making them immune to the Earps' bullets and allowing them to wrestle *Star Trek* back from the hands of the people who don't know what it's true potential is and want to make it a show about space cowboys.

I can't think of a better way to open up *Star Trek*'s notoriously problematic, doomed-from-the-start third season, which makes it all the more astounding this wasn't made the season premier. Gene Coon makes one last grand attempt to define what *Star Trek* should be about, even in a time where it's becoming clear his vision of the show is no longer the network-mandated and approved one. It's not altogether surprising Coon only has three stories left after this. But the true tragedy here is that we know Coon and his friends will ultimately win: Star Trek gets to come back over and over again, and it's entirely thanks to the efforts of people like him, D.C. Fontana, Paul Schneider, William Shatner and John Meredyth Lucas. While the production circa 1968 may now be indifferent to their efforts and eager to move beyond them, we certainly won't be.

73. "I'm spunky!": Elaan of Troyius

"Elaan of Troyius" is the first visible sign that things have gotten really bad for *Star Trek*. "Spectre of the Gun" may have raised suspicions a bit and, upon closer examination, it turned out to be Gene Coon in active revolt against the new status quo. This episode, by contrast, is evidence of how toxic the new status quo actually is.

First of all, it is catastrophically terrible. *Star Trek* has been reactionary on many an occasion before, but it hasn't managed to be quite *this* reactionary since the Gene Roddenberry era. Elaan is flat-out the worst character we've seen in the Original Series so far: Not since Nona has there been a confluence of bigoted, xenophobic tropes of this magnitude, and Elaan makes Nona look downright progressive. I could explain why, but I really don't have to because our old friend Daniel Leonard Bernardi had a few choice words to say about this episode:

> ""Elaan of Troyius' brings into play stereotypes of the Asian female – the manipulative dragon lady and the submissive female slave. Elaan is both irrational and primitive. She throws temper tantrums, eats with her hands, and drinks from the bottle. Kirk tells her, 'Nobody's told you that you're an uncivilized savage, a vicious child in a woman's body, an arrogant monster.' Captain Kirk, the 'white knight' of Star Trek, articulates his and the Federation's moral superiority and authority over the Asian-alien and her people through sexual conquest [...] Indeed, it is only after the captain physically and sexually dominates her that she respects and eventually falls in love with him [...] After giving in to Kirk's power, Elaan, like the cunning and manipulative dragon lady of classical Hollywood cinema, returns the favor by capturing his heart. The Asian-alien's tears contain a bio-chemical agent that, when touched by a man (even aliens like Kirk), forces him to fall deeply in love with her. After she manipulates Kirk into desiring her, Elaan becomes submissive, gentle, loyal, even willing to die with him, by his side, as the Klingons ruthlessly attack the Enterprise. It is at this point in the narrative that the other stereotype of the Asian female comes into play – that of the submissive Asian slave. In the end, Elaan does anything Captain Kirk requests, politely and adoringly obeying his demands and orders. Her dragon lady tactics were only used so that she could assume a position she truly desired: the submissive mistress of a white knight."

Bernardi goes on like this, and, as is somewhat typical for him, he's generally spot-on but in a narrow scope and with caveats. Ironically enough, Bernardi misses one of the biggest racist signifiers in the episode: While he's right that Elaan draws upon Dragon

Lady stereotypes, probably unfortunately in part due to her actor, France Nuyen, who is half-Vietnamese, the show is very clearly coding her as African too. Nuyen is dutifully browned up and her costume, hair style and facial makeup are all clearly modeled after stereotypical Ancient Egyptian imagery. Elaan isn't just a racist caricature of Asians, she's a generically amalgamated nonwhite, nonwestern Other, and one would think Bernardi of all people would have noticed that.

Of course, in this quote Bernardi also seems to fail to point out how obviously and spectacularly misogynistic this episode is. Not only is Elaan an archetypal savage, she's also a strong, independent woman respected as an absolute ruler on her planet who spends the entire episode quite literally infantilized by everyone else on the show. She's explicitly called a "spoiled brat", runs into her room and locks the door when challenged and Kirk *even actually threatens to spank her.* It's utterly appalling and disgraceful. There's also the narrative Bernardi does mention, which is how the whole episode is based around Kirk playing the Pygmalion role, forcing Elaan to become "proper" and "courteous", which really just means submissive. This is bald-facedly anti-woman in a way this show hasn't managed since "Mudd's Women", and honestly I think this one is actually worse.

Somewhat bewilderingly, this episode was supposedly meant to *appeal* to *Star Trek's* female fans. Of "Elaan of Troyius", Fred Freiberger said "We tried to reach a segment of the audience we couldn't otherwise reach, and didn't succeed." which is actually pretty funny. However, it also points out a serious failing on the part of the *Star Trek* staff. Aside from the fact they turned out a jaw-droppingly sexist turkey of a story, according to Freiberger and other members of the creative team, the whole intent was to reach out to women because women didn't typically watch science fiction. I just find this statement completely inexplicable: Women were the *original* fans of *Star Trek*! Bjo Trimble organised the letter writing campaign that gave us this season in the first place! Spock, Kirk and Uhura were all wildly popular with women, and this would have been painfully obvious to anyone paying the slightest bit of attention to the people actually watching the show. *Women were already watching* and *in droves* to boot-How on *Earth* were Freiberger and his team unaware of this to begin with?

I think the reason is because there is now a cavernous disconnect between the show, the people making the show, the people overseeing the show and the people watching the show, and this trips up a lot of people who try to talk about this season. Let's take a quick survey of the various reactions to this episode. We've already mentioned Bernardi's, and we'll come back to him a little later on, but let's look and some others first. There's the fan account, which we can divide into two versions. The mainline, semi-official account in this case comes from Star Trek historians Paula Block and Terry J. Erdmann, who call "Elaan of Troyius":

> "...indicative of many, though not all, of the episodes produced for Star Trek's third season. Costumes, makeup, and script were all overblown, perhaps more suitable to sci-fi pulp than to the show's earlier attempts at straightforward storytelling in a unique setting."

I respect Block and Erdmann for their heroic attempts to document Star Trek's history, but they are inescapably of the fandom master narrative, and this quote is a good example of why. Never mind the fact the episode is a racist and sexist disaster, no, the real problem is that the costumes are too frilly and the script reads too pompous and pulpish (by the way, have y'all seen "The Cage" recently? What is that if not pulp sci-fi?). But, at least Block and Erdmann agreed the episode was bad, which is more than can be said of the A.V. Club, our representatives of contemporary fandom, who gave it a "B" rating and praised the "unexpected" ending and "nifty" space battle with the Klingons, which sort of speaks for itself.

The person whose reaction most interests me is that of the episode's writer and director, John Meredyth Lucas. It's more then a little surprising to see his name associated with "Elaan of Troyius" as Lucas typically has a modicum of self-awareness about him, and even more so to find he was apparently *proud* of it, saying: "I enjoyed the love story aspect of the show and thought it was an interesting change of pace. You didn't get to do too many of those.:. It should go without saying this statement makes close to zero sense, but I think this might actually demonstrate something other than damning Lucas as an insensitive bigot. For one, I'm starting to get the sense Lucas was probably a better producer than he was a writer or director. This can happen: Many times creative personnel double up on jobs, and very rarely are they good at both of them. Lucas oversaw one of the best runs in the show's history (though that's not saying much), but as for stuff he actually wrote? So far it's been this and "The Changeling", neither of which were particularly successful. "Patterns of Force" had some good elements, but there Lucas was working off of a Paul Schneider script, and the rest of the episode was a tone-deaf pulpy embarrassment. Left to his own devices, maybe Lucas should have stuck to the producer's chair.

But let's play close attention to the word choice Lucas uses in his defense of his script. He specifically says it's the love story that makes up the second half of the episode, which is interesting, as nobody else who's commented on "Elaan of Troyius" has seemed to pick up on that. Admittedly, it's an extremely alarming and offensive love story-It begins with Elaan either bowing to Kirk's masculine dominance or trying to manipulate him to enact genocide on the Troyians, depending on which horrifically misogynistic and reactionary trope is least likely to ruin the rest of your day. From what I gather, Lucas wrote this as a retelling of both *The Taming of the Shrew* and, displaying the same grasp of allegorical subtly he displayed in "Patterns of Force", the Helen of Troy myth, which doesn't do this story any more favours. Although the script fails to do much with this plot, it's somewhat saved by the actors, who give the entire back half of the episode an entirely different interpretation.

Naturally, William Shatner is the primary figure here. Kirk is written pretty disastrously out of character for the majority of the episode, reinforcing the script's rampant misogyny (seriously, did nobody but me notice "Mister Spock, the women on your planet are logical. That's the only planet in this galaxy that can make that claim"?). However, Shatner doesn't play Kirk with the typical exaggerated, manly bravado he's done when given this kind of prompt in the past: Instead he plays the part exasperated and frustrated at his inability to help bring about a peaceful resolution to the conflict. The key turning point comes, however, *after* Kirk and Elaan fall in love, because, completely contrary to the way we would expect him to behave (and indeed the way the script is written) *then and only then does Kirk actually begin to act like Kirk*. Rather then render him unfit for command and incapable of handling the crisis with the Klingons, Kirk seems in possession of every single one of his normal faculties. Spock and McCoy try to handwave this away during the denouement with the obnoxious "The *Enterprise* infected the captain long before the Dohlman did." bit (Nimoy and Kelly actually play their parts in this episode altogether too straight for my liking to the point they got on my nerves), but that's not at all what Shatner seems to be trying to convey.

Nor, actually, is it what France Nuyen is trying to convey either. Interestingly, Nuyen and Shatner had worked together before on Broadway and apparently they got on well enough to work together at least twice more after this episode. The two actors visibly have a chemistry together, and while for most of the episode it's held back by the script's overbearing paternalism, when it does shine through it's bright enough to commandeer the episode's meaning. This is the key thing Bernardi misses in his critique of "Elaan of Troyius": By focusing on the textual representation problems of the script, he once again overlooks the fact that *Star Trek* is a joint production composed of many different creative figures, and while Elaan may be loaded up with racist and sexist imagery about manipulative and savage foreign women, Shatner and Nuyen play their characters as being very much in actual love.

Because of this, the back half of the episode gets to play out very differently: Now it seems more like Kirk admires Elaan for her warrior strength and indomitable spirit and Elaan sees in Kirk someone she can consider an equal, and who might consider her an equal in return. The key scene here is when Elaan beams down and says goodbye to Kirk, giving him her dagger to remember her by. Kirk says he has no choice but to let her be married off as political tribute, and Elaan says she doesn't have any choice either, saying she now has only "responsibilities and obligations", and the way Nuyen delivers this line is obviously loaded. The episode now becomes, only in its final act, a tragedy about political systems and structures of power, and how deference to orders and one's assigned social role puts physical and metaphorical chains on people and dehumanizes them. That seems like something that Lucas may have been attempting to convey through referencing Helen of Troy, but he was so incompetent at it any evidence for this reading in the finished product comes strictly from William Shatner and France Nuyen.

Star Trek has always in some sense been defined by the ability of its cast to elevate middling and ill-conceived ideas, but this time it feels a bit different. In the past there have been at least more than one party who were more or less on the same page, and now it seems like the management is not only incompetent but deliberately refusing to listen to not only the people they're overseeing, but the people watching the show. Which is, if we're honest, a not entirely unexpected thing for a production team largely interested in making sure this season is the series' last. Thanks to William Shatner and France Nuyen, we can once again read "Elaan of Troyius" as an episode ultimately transformed and redeemed by a few visionary people, but really, with a production this apathetic and retrograde, why would you want to?

74. "Put up a parking lot": The Paradise Syndrome

Somewhere around the point one begins musing "you know, maybe 'Elaan of Troyius' wasn't so bad after all", one gets the sense there are worryingly fundamental underlying problems with "The Paradise Syndrome". Margaret Armen's back this week, so strap in, kids..

It is wretched. Somewhat amazingly, it manages to tell a story about the concept of an idyllic lifestyle without invoking the godforsaken Garden of Eden again. This does not make it any less wretched. It is unabashedly racist, because it is noble savages again, and this time the show just drops all pretense and flat-out calls them literally "American Indians" so there's absolutely no doubt about who and what it's horrifically stereotyping and misrepresenting. Aside from "The Apple" (which this is almost as bad as) this was the episode I most dreaded having to rewatch: A story about a Kirk rendered amnesiac by a von Dänikenesque obelisk who becomes the messianic spiritual leader of a village of Space Native Americans, and lives for months married to a doting priestess who is promptly stoned to death along with their unborn son is my idea of just about the worst possible way to spend an evening.

My expectations were not disappointed.

Let's tackle the racism first, because "The Paradise Syndrome" is absolutely racist and it is so transparent about this it's almost refreshing in a way. Let's once again turn to Daniel Leonard Bernardi, as this is his territory and he's apparently becoming something of a fixture this season (and also because it saves me having to reiterate everything):

> "'The Paradise Syndrome' stereotypes Native-Americans as noble savages and whites as 'normal' and even divine [...] Miramanee cannot figure out how to pull Kirk's shirt off, as she cannot find any lacing. She is portrayed as simpleminded, not that bright. This is not the case with Kirk. Moments before, he has fashioned a lamp from an old piece of pottery and saved a boy by using mouth-to-mouth resuscitation. Despite his amnesia, he is shown as naturally superior [...] When the Indians realize that Kirk is not a god, they stone both him and Miramanee (it's the Indians who are violent in this version of the noble savage stereotype). Spock and McCoy eventually intervene, but only Kirk survives. In this take on a standard white/red miscegenation narrative, the native girl dies so that Kirk, the white male hero, isn't shown unheroically and immorally leaving her and their unborn baby behind."

Just like before, we'll use Bernardi's analysis as a jumping-off point because, once again,

343

he's right as far as the basics go but he also seems to miss a great deal of nuances. I don't want to go too hard on him as in many ways Bernardi was one of the first people to make note of *Star Trek*'s more reactionary tendencies, but really. That "The Paradise Syndrome" treats Native Americans as simpleminded primitives is so laughably blatant and obvious it really doesn't need to be commented on, at least not to the extent Bernardi does. This is far from the first time the Original Series has done this, and we should really stop being shocked by this at this point, especially during a season it's clear was a write-off from before it even began. No, the larger racialist issue with "The Paradise Syndrome" is that its Native Americans aren't just primitives, *they're not even real people.* They're constructed entirely out of half-assed and half-remembered stereotypes and vague imagery. There's a lot of strong medicine, abbreviated, punctuated speech, feathers and thunderstorms, but there's not a single thing to indicate this is an actual, living culture, which even "The Apple" managed, albeit terribly. These aren't even cartoon caricatures, they're *advertising mascots.* These are *stereotypes of stereotypes!*

And furthermore, "The Paradise Syndrome" misrepresents its Native Americans so completely it bewilderingly wants us to believe their complex and deeply symbolic animism can be distilled to straightforward pop Christianity, or at the very least generic Western theism. Kirok is explicitly called a god and is prophesied to return from the "temple" (Native Americans do not, of course, have temples) at a predetermined time to save his people from catastrophe. This is the stuff of the absolute dregs of dime-store genre fiction, and it's not possible to misread any given Native American spirituality worse if you were deliberately trying to. Part of this is due to the von Däniken embellishment of the Preservers, who "seeded" humanoid life in the galaxy and left behind monolithic artefacts to watch over and protect them, but come on. That's not an excuse, and if anything, that makes it even worse. "The Gamesters of Triskelion" established Armen's track record for cultural insensitivity, but this takes it to a whole other level. Margaret Armen is so racist she's *meta*-racist. I wish I could be kinder to Armen as she's one of the only other female writers for Star Trek during this period aside from D.C. Fontana, but the fact remains her work is absolutely execrable.

This also raises some serious concerns I have about the validity of Bernardi's work. So far, the only episodes in which he's been cited as being critical of and demonstrating the irreducible Whiteness of Star Trek have been calamitously shitty ones by troubled or irredeemable writers. This rather smacks of Bernardi stacking his argument somewhat. Also, Bernardi attacks the final scene by arguing it skirts around the issue of Kirk potentially abandoning his wife and unborn child. But this isn't quite what happens-They were both already dead by then and there was nothing even McCoy could have done. Kirk is not a deadbeat dad; there's no implication anywhere in the final act that Kirk wouldn't have taken Miramanee and her child with him had they lived. The real problem here isn't Kirk being cast as colonialist and thoughtless, it's that Miramanee is considered expendable, tying into the standard power structures of imperialism, racism, institutionalized misogyny and the fundamental disadvantages of serialized anthology television this show has always had. "The Paradise Syndrome" has a ton of problems, but it doesn't have that specific one.

If we're going to damn Star Trek, let's at least damn it for stuff it actually did. Which is easy enough as it is.

"The Paradise Syndrome" also provides some more illuminating evidence on how the way in which *Star Trek* is bad now is different from the way it's been bad in the past. Horrifying racial insensitivity and casual sexism are, sadly, nothing new to the Original Series. What makes "The Paradise Syndrome" significant is that it's not only reactionary, it's also a flatly terrible production. There are basic, amateur mistakes all over the place-Spock is reduced to nothing more than exposition machine, delivering overly padded monologues about basic science and setting details while McCoy is treated as almost as simple and thick as Miramanee. While the portion of the episode taking place on the *Enterprise* is ostensibly supposed to be about Spock and his command choices, Leonard Nimoy isn't actually allowed to convey any of this: McCoy has to come in and flat-out *state* the emotions the script says Spock is going through. On a related note, the passage of 58 days takes place during one, single cut and is conveyed purely through dialog leaving no sense that any time has passed at all. There's even a jaw-droppingly cliched "running through the forest laughing" montage designed to let us know Kirok and Miramanee are in love that's played unnervingly straight. Forget being rejected by a major network television series, a script like is a failure as a basic work of structured narrative fiction. And as we will see, this is another signature of Margaret Armen's.

While Gene Roddenberry was something of an incompetent writer, his problems were largely due to the fact his style was too firmly stuck in the pulp style that was already dated by the time he first pitched "The Cage" in 1964 and he refused to ever admit this wasn't working. The reason something like "Mudd's Women" or "A Private Little War" is bad is purely by virtue of its grandiose jingoistic soapboxing. Neither of those episodes were de facto poor pieces of writing, they were just overly simplistic and *offensive* writing. While "The Menagerie" and "The Return of the Archons" did have logic issues, even those weren't as glaring and crippling as the ones here are. Furthermore, Compare "The Paradise Syndrome" to "The Omega Glory": While both are awful, retrograde stories, the production level problems with "The Omega Glory" were due to the explicitly pulp structure that was about two-thirds stupid fight scenes and the fact Roddenberry was an abject failure at conveying any kind of nuance or subtlety. You simply can't imagine him turning in a script like this. Although the politics are just as abhorrent, even Gene Roddenberry would have known better than to make such obvious writing mistakes.

Most damningly however, the cast is very clearly aware of what a mess "The Paradise Syndrome" is and, for the first time in the history of the show, just flat-out give up. Even during the low points of the past, the actors always went out of their way to deliver their lines with conviction, or at least make them entertaining. Here though, they simply can't be bothered any longer. Nimoy plays Spock as the most deadpan and monotone parody of a stoic, logical character you can think of, DeForest Kelley is clearly just punching his time card and, chillingly, William Shatner mumbles his way through his every scene as both Kirk and Kirok. The only person who seems remotely like the characters we've become accustomed to is Scotty, thanks to James Doohan's animated performance of someone exasperated at his boss' unreasonable requests, but he's in so little of the episode it's nowhere near enough to make a difference. Everyone else just looks painfully bored and drained.

One of the biggest strengths of *Star Trek* has always been its cast, who have reliably come to it's rescue whenever the rest of the show trips up, very much alive and aware Star Trek means something more than the sum of its parts, and imploring us to not forget this in spite of everything. With them checked out, *Star Trek* has lost its final asset, and it seems its time, at long last, really is up. One gets the sense everyone should just pack up, go home, move on and let the show wind down, which is probably neither the environment nor mindset you want to cultivate three episodes into the new season. While it may be no more reactionary then the show's worst moments of the past have been, "The Paradise Syndrome" is very possibly the saddest and most depressing episode of *Star Trek* ever made.

75. "Excuse me, can you help me? I'm a spy.": The Enterprise Incident

"The Enterprise Incident" is arguably one of the most iconic episodes of the original *Star Trek*, or at least this season. "Iconic", however, is not necessarily a synonym for "good". While decent and a godsend compared to what the show has been hurling out since the beginning of the season, I'm not especially inclined to call "The Enterprise Incident" one of the all-time greatest stories from this show. Not when compared to "The Trouble with Tribbles" or "A Piece of the Action", and even granted this is D.C. Fontana coming in to clean up the mess Arthur Singer and Margaret Armen made of everything. This episode is, however, perfectly serviceable, better than the last two stories by light years and further evidence of what a tremendous asset D.C. Fontana was to Star Trek.

The circumstances behind Fontana's resignation as script editor are somewhat hazy. The official story is that she was too overwhelmed by her day-to-day duties and wanted the opportunity to freelance for other shows, but the somewhat caged and guarded way she tends to recount this (along with the rather exasperated tone she often takes on when describing her time associated with the franchise) leads me to believe there's likely a bit more than that at play. Whatever the reasoning though, "The Enterprise Incident" is Fontana's first Star Trek contribution as a freelancer, a position she'll hold for the remainder of the Original Series, and also her final contribution to the Original Series under her actual name. And right away, it's very clear the impact her absence has had on the show's overall production: "The Enterprise Incident" was extensively "edited" by Gene Roddenberry (even though that shouldn't technically be his job anymore) as well as (I presume) Arthur Singer. As a result, what we get here is in many ways D.C. Fontana-lite: Even "Friday's Child" wasn't monkeyed around with to quite the same extent this story was, and this had an almost quantitatively net negative effect on the final product.

Fontana's original draft was partially inspired by the 1968 *Pueblo* Incident, where North Korean forces captured and detained a United States Navy cruiser for over a year on charges of espionage, hence the title. This would make "The Enterprise Incident" arguably the first Star Trek episode to explore a current and topical sociopolitical issue (previous episodes, namely things like "A Taste of Armageddon", "The City on the Edge of Forever" and "A Private Little War" made halfhearted stabs at this, but were almost always held back by the show's apparent desire to remain somewhat safe and apolitical) were it not for two issues: Firstly, Roddenberry's and Singer's "improvements", among a great deal many other things, helped to obfuscate this significantly. Secondly however, "Journey to Babel" proved that, if nothing else, Fontana is a master at blending complex political world building plots with intimate stories about characters, and would prefer to lean in this direction if given the opportunity. "The Enterprise Incident" builds off of this, using the backdrop of a high-stakes espionage mission to further explore Kirk and Spock as well as the sense of loyalty and devotion the *Enterprise* crew shares amongst themselves.

Much like in "Journey to Babel" then, it's clear the story Fontana is really interested in telling examines is the effect the situation has on the characters, as opposed to the intricacies of the situation itself. She's said the *Pueblo* story was merely what kickstarted the train of thought that led her to write this episode and it was not as much intended as a direct analog or parable. However, and that qualifier hangs like the Sword of Damocles over this episode just as it does every other episode this season, this is largely not the story "The Enterprise Incident" actually is. Nevertheless, we can try to piece together what Fontana's original story might have been based on her words on it after the fact and the inklings we get in the thing that made it to air. We see hints of a story about Kirk pushed to the edge of madness over his flagrantly warmongering and potentially trust-shattering orders from Starfleet Command, Spock's exploration of heritage being pushed to the logical limit by having him sympathetic to, and ultimately side with, the Romulans, and a Romulan Commander who is in many ways an extrapolation of the tantalizing groundwork laid down by Paul Schneider in "Balance of Terror" and who proves once and for all the Romulans, the supposed Evil Enemy, are in truth a deeply complex and multifaceted culture who, while they may not be *just* like us, are ultimately just as worthy and deserving of respect and personhood as we are.

As Fontana is not one to speak ill of her former colleagues (though one does frequently get the sense she'd really, *really* like to), she says there were a lot of "little things" that were changed she wasn't happy about. And while she may be coy about her original intent so as not to upset the Trekker cart, let's be honest with ourselves. We know enough about Fontana, her writing style and her positionality by this point to rather easily discern which parts of this production were hers and which parts...weren't. I'm willing to bet the first "little thing" that was altered was Kirk's mental state. In the episode as aired, Kirk puts on an elaborate show to give the impression he's losing his mind and endangering the crew to provoke a diplomatic incident with the Romulans, while in truth he's on an undercover mission to steal their new cloaking device so that should something go wrong his reputation and his alone would be tarnished. Fontana says that in the final product "Kirk's attitudes were wrong", but never elabourates. I have a feeling this is what she's talking about-It would not surprise me in the slightest to learn the original draft had Kirk genuinely teetering on the brink of insanity due to what the Federation is asking him to do and the strain it's putting on his relationship with the crew, and yes, the Romulans. This is the kind of story one does not expect to see until the Dominion War: To see Fontana hinting at it in 1968 is astonishing. But, it is in keeping with her perspective: She was there when Gene Coon created the Federation (which was intentionally problematized from the beginning) and neither of them have been especially keen to leap at the idea it's a perfect utopia.

(That said, as aired "The Enterprise Incident" does give William Shatner a decent vehicle-Playing Kirk playing mad while secretly scheming is right up his alley, and he knocks the performance out of the park. We suspect he's secretly up to something from the teaser. It's properly close to "A Piece of the Action" standards.)

Spock's story seems to have remained comparatively intact, which is for the better as it's arguably the best part of the episode. It's not, however, completely unaltered: While Spock and the Romulan Commander were always meant to fall in love based on their similar perspectives and experience, the final episode drastically changes some significant scenes with the Commander such that her impact is altered and, in my opinion, worsened. She starts out as a truly hypnotic presence: Someone just as intelligent, competent, cosmopolitan and with just as much dignity as Kirk (and crucially, just as workmanlike too). And, helped by Joanne Linville's imperious and elegant performance, she absolutely dominates the first half of the episode. Naturally, all this is promptly shoved out an airlock as soon as she begins a relationship with Spock, who is easily able to manipulate her and allow Kirk to sneak on board the Bird-of-Prey and steal the cloaking device right under her nose, turning her into a generic "woman scorned". Fontana hated this, saying "Any Romulan worth her salt would have instantly suspected Spock because they are related races. That was wrong.". Of course, she's right, and frustratingly, this would have made a far, far more interesting story. Imagine the Commander and Spock constantly trying to play and outmaneuver each other throughout the whole episode because they know what they're planning and what they're capable of (and what their respective orders are), despite also deeply loving each other. That would have been electrifying.

One alteration Fontana is perfectly upfront with is the actual love scene: Apparently in the original script Spock was meant to "rain kisses" on the Commander. This was *not* Fontana's idea. Gene Roddenberry felt the need to throw this bit of stage direction in before it was submitted to Arthur Singer and Fred Freiberger. This enraged Leonard Nimoy, who penned Roddenberry a scathing letter complaining about this addition and demanding he cut it out. Fontana, predictably, agreed with Nimoy and also wrote Roddenberry a(n altogether more diplomatic) letter cautioning him on what the fan backlash would be if Spock was written out of character. Eventually Roddenberry backed down, and Nimoy and Linville improvised their gestural makeout session, a further extrapolation of the significance of hands to both Vulcan and Romulan society. A final note on the Spock/Commander plot: It's delightfully telling that Fontana's first post-"Save Star Trek!" script puts Spock in an intricate and deeply personal love story and throws Kirk into the clink to pretend to have a mental breakdown. She clearly knew perfectly well the sort of thing all those fans *really* wanted to see.

Despite everything that was tacked on, altered or taken out, there's still a lot of great moments in "The Enterprise Incident", the best of which build on not just "Balance of Terror", but the work both Fontana and Gene Coon have been doing over the past two years. This is as nuanced and developed as we've ever seen any culture in Star Trek so far, not just the Romulans, and the Commander's (seriously, what is it with Romulan Commanders not getting proper names in this show?) description of them as a deeply passionate and aesthetic people who guard against the more retrograde, warlike aspects of their culture with a smouldering love of life is intoxicating in and of itself: I could listen to Linville go on about Romulan sensuality basically forever. Speaking of Linville, she has the distinction of playing the very first female captain of a starship in the entirety of Star Trek, and I'm quite sure Fontana meant for there to be symbolism behind having her be Romulan instead of a member of Starfleet. There are a number of times she comes dangerously close to having the moral and ethical high ground, and one suspects she would have won the whole thing in Fontana's original version. Shatner-as-Kirk too plays into this theme when possible: It's an easily missed bit of genius to have Kirk retain his surgically altered Romulan appearance after he beams back to the *Enterprise* with the cloaking device...and have the episode end before we get to see McCoy change him back.

But the problem is these great moments never add up or come together to be a truly great episode. The story that we can watch on television is too in love with its espionage trappings and refuses to problematize the actions of Starfleet Command in the slightest. We never get to see any actual debate over the morality of Kirk's orders and the Federation emerge the unambiguous Good Guys again. And, well, putting aside the larger sociopolitical and ethical concerns of the UFP for the moment, just knowing the sort of things Richard Nixon was getting up to in 1968, one sort of hopes Fontana would have been allowed to write a story less enamoured with the glory of Western-style representative democracy. Furthermore, the Romulan Commander gets a positively dreadful ending: Yes, she's treated as a guest of honour on the *Enterprise*, but she surely won't be once she gets taken back to Federation space to be "processed". Imagining the loneliness and despondence she must feel trapped on the other end of the galaxy from her people literally deep in enemy territory just makes me shudder, and no amount of apologising and commiserating on Spock's part makes any of that better.

"The Enterprise Incident" is also the last story to depict the Romulans in a manner consistent with their original characterization in "Balance of Terror". Though it builds on and extrapolates this to a marvelous degree, it's kind of gut-punching to know we're never going to see this developed on ever again. In many ways the Romulans are the perfect adversaries to the Federation, because we get to see different aspects of ourselves reflected and emphasized in different ways, both for the worse and for the better. But, much like "The Enterprise Incident" itself, future Romulan stories will be subject to micromanaging such that their overall impact is significantly dulled. A case could be made D.C. Fontana too was never able to see the true potential of her vision realised-This is far from her last offering; we'll be talking about her well into the 2000s and 2010s and she even gets to be showrunner of her own Star Trek series, but her story is all-too-frequently one of being hamstrung, runaround and dismissed in favour of bigger-name creative figures and studio party lines. In that sense, while "The Enterprise Incident" may not be her best work, it may sadly be what best represents her contributions to Star Trek's legacy.

76. "Seduction of the Innocent": And The Children Shall Lead

Bloody hell.

Every time I think this show has bottomed out the floor vanishes from beneath my feet. I haven't been as angry at Star Trek as I was while watching "And The Children Shall Lead" in quite awhile. This is execrable. This is the worst parts of every retrograde story this show has ever done distilled to their core essences. This is "Omega Glory" standards. Actually, no, not even: "And The Children Shall Lead" starts as a third-rate retread of "Miri" and then dovetails into one of the most bald-facedly reactionary and youth-hating things I've ever seen, and it's another sloppy, incoherent and cack-handed production on top of that. This isn't just as bad as the show has ever been it's *worse*.

Well, where to begin? How about with the absolutely bleeding obvious? Kirk, Spock and McCoy discover a Federation colony where all the adults have died out leaving only their children behind, who are suspiciously unnerved by the mass deaths. When they beam back aboard the *Enterprise*, it's revealed the children are part of some scary and mysterious cult with strange language and unfamiliar customs built around worship of a "friendly angel" whom it is *further* revealed is actually another Alien Entity of Pure Evil who has enslaved the children. The being then orders them to commandeer the ship in an attempt to convert more brainwashed slaves for his army, with which he intends to take over the galaxy. In the end, the alien is dispatched by Kirk convincing the children adults always have their best interests at heart and can always be trusted, and demonstrating the Gorgon (which is apparently the alien's name, as Kirk refers to it as such even though *at no point in the episode did he ever learn this*) requires faith and obedience to live, without which he is revealed as the evil (and, naturally, horrifically disfigured) being he truly is.

I mean, do I really need to spell it out? This couldn't be more transparently an attack on the counterculture if Spock made some comment about how Earth was almost destroyed in the late-1960s by a group of misguided youths who were led astray by an Evil Alien Communist who told them to distrust the United States and protest the Vietnam War as evidence of historical precedence. The Gorgon is even dressed in a flowing, paisley gown and I'd say his design makes him look like a shoddy knock-off of something from the *Doctor Who* serial "The Mutants" except for the fact "The Mutants" wasn't actually filmed until 1972, which leads me to believe Arthur Singer and writer Edward J. Lakso had some kind of right-wing time machine that could only be fueled by fear, hatred and the tears of children. I'm actually dumbfounded: I thought I'd have to wait until the 2010s and Internet culture to find an example of a show that held as much active contempt and loathing for its fanbase

351

as this one does.

(Of course in hindsight I should have expected this given "The City on the Edge of Forever", but at least that episode had the decency to make some attempts at burying the bleeding obvious.)

Then there are the illusions. My God, the illusions. Apparently, one of the ill-defined witchcraft powers the kids have is their ability to place illusions in people's minds constructed out of their deepest fears. Kirk freaks out over the possibility of losing command, Chekov panics over potentially having to disobey orders, Uhura, naturally, sees an images of herself ugly and old in the mirror that she has logically bolted to her instrument panel (wimmenfolk and their vanity, amirite?) and Sulu sees spinning rings of swords and daggers that will destroy the *Enterprise* if he deviates from the course he's laid in, which is both racist *and* idiotic. This episode is such a superstorm of hegemonic fear, bigotry and oppression it almost makes me want to apologise to Gene Roddenberry: Roddenberry was merely inept as a creative figure and a totalitarian bean counter. As bad as someone like Roberta Lincoln was, she was still evidence he felt the youth were heading in the right direction, it's just he thought they were too scattered and flaky to get anything done, though they were hella sexy (which is another issue entirely) Singer, however, seems like he actually, legitimately has an axe to grind against the forces of material social progress and is going out of his way to stamp them out. Either that or he's out to troll everyone, and frankly neither scenario really warms me to him.

On top of all that the production is an absolute shambles. It makes the frenzied disorganisation of "What Are Little Girls Made Of?", "The Alternative Factor" and "The Menagerie" look like opening night at the Globe Theatre. Major plot developments happen off-camera and go totally unexplained, the entire cast is written badly out of character and, most astounding of all, Fred Freiberger cast *criminal defense attorney Melvin Belli* as the Gorgon, someone with *zero experience in the acting business*. I have absolutely no idea what on Earth would have possessed Freiberger to cast someone like Belli instead of, you know, *an actual actor*. Belli was somewhat famous as an attorney, if for no other reason then the high-profile cases he was involved in (Belli was famous for defending Jack Ruby and The Rolling Stones, and had a minor role in the investigation into the Zodiac murders), but I can't think of anything about him, apart from his minor marquee status, that would have made him a good fit for *Star Trek*. His son did in fact play one of the children in this episode, but neither that nor the potential ratings boost Freiberger seemed to think Belli's status would yield is really a sufficient justification of his presence here. I mean, I suppose I could try and read this as Freiberger's attempt to redeem "And The Children Shall Lead" by having the corrupting force be a lawyer, and thus a hegemonic establishment figure, except no: Belli defended The Rolling Stones and the guy who killed the guy who killed John F. Kennedy-That doesn't really make him an enemy of the youth. If anything, *that somehow manages to make it even worse*.

But I'm not done yet. Like all terrible episodes of Star Trek, "And The Children Shall Lead" brings out not only the worst in the show, but the worst in its fans as well. While The Agony Booth (which regular readers will recall panned "The Alternative Factor" in the first season, an episode I thought was quite entertaining) did in fact agree this was one of the worst episodes of the show (if not *the* very worst), it was for maddeningly facile reasons. Their major complaint was that the episode "...offers virtually nothing: No suspense, no character development, no intriguing sci-fi premises, and not one memorable line of dialogue.", as if the superficial structural problems are some kind of unforgivable sin and somehow worse then the appalling and blatant youth-phobic subtext and flashes of casual racism and misogyny. This fetishistic fixation on plot and character development is so typical of contemporary, early-21st Century fandom and I continue to be strongly put off by it every single time I see it.

And of course, The Agony Booth reserve their most potent bile for William Shatner, blaming the vast majority of the episode's woes on him and proceeding to mercilessly mock him with sarcastic dialog such as:

> "There's no denying it: This is 100% grade-A pure Shatner here. We have now reached ShatNervana. The Shat goes through his entire range of grotesque, buffoonish facial expressions until Spock finally moves towards him, prompting Kirk to wildly grab him by the throat."

By now I really shouldn't have to lay out my response. Obviously, Shatner is the most enjoyable thing about the episode by light-years. There's no contest. While it is true he's in full-on "Omega Glory" or "Gamesters of Triskelion" mode once again, we firstly shouldn't find this shocking, nor should we blame him. Frankly, the only thing that surprises me about Shatner turning into a scenery singularity is that he didn't also spend the entire third season wearing an ice bucket as a hat like Marlon Brando in *The Island of Dr. Moreau.* Secondly though, Shatner's particular performance in this episode is so legendarily off-the-wall it had far-reaching consequences that went beyond what anyone was able to predict, or that many people have noticed even to this day. Shatner turns Kirk's meltdown into such a spectacle he's only brought out of it by Spock coming right up into his face and *whispering his first name in his ear.* This is very possibly the single slashiest scene in the entire Original Series such that I'm willing to bet it was largely responsible for the birth of the entire genre.

Slash fiction, the idea of taking two (or more) characters who were not originally intended to be romantically involved and writing fanfiction about their (typically homosexual) relationship is a massive part of Star Trek's female and feminist fandom. In fact, the concept originates with Star Trek fandom, and despite what an irredeemable mess "And The Children Shall Lead" is, the confluence of factors that comes together in that one scene is an absolutely perfect demonstration of how it came about. While a more thorough examination of the history and development of slash is best saved for the 1970s where it starts to become a very pronounced and irreducible part of the Star Trek pop culture phenomenon, since a lot of the fundamental sources of inspiration are already self-evident, a brief overview is in order.

Essentially, *Star Trek* provided a very powerful mixture of elements that, when combined, led very straightforwardly to an environment in which slash could blossom: The show was always in some way sexually repressed, going back to Gene Roddenberry's confused conception of gender. But, more to the point, Spock is a character who it is very easy to code as sexual: His suppression of his emotions makes a very convincing metaphor for the closet, in addition to making him seem brooding and mysterious. Kirk, meanwhile, thanks to William Shatner's overt theatricality, comes across as very flamboyant in a way that's very easy to queer up. Furthermore, the fact Kirk isn't allowed to hold down any meaningful romantic relationships with people other than his crew for a number of reasons, and that he considers Spock one of his closest, most personal friends just makes this reading all the easier. The turbolift scene in this episode, then, comes across as just blatant. Previous moments of gratuity, like the bondage and torture scenes in "The Gamesters of Triskelion" and "Patterns of Force", could be halfheartedly argued away on a number of qualifiers. This one...not so much.

But the fact the most positive thing I could come up with to say about "And The Children Shall Lead" is that it helped indirectly create slash fiction really says it all. The only thing this episode has going for it is the way the fans could transform it into something more interesting and less repugnant, reactionary and horrid. This really and truly is one of the worst things this franchise ever did. Amazingly, in five weeks, the new creative team has concretely demonstrated itself to actually be worse and less competent than Gene Roddenberry. Congratulations, I guess.

As a final twist of the knife it's a fitting summary of Star Trek itself. Something that was made great by and large through the hearts and minds of the people whose imagination it captured, not through the extant media artefacts that were made in its name.

77. "...a mere apendix.": Spock's Brain

"Spock's Brain" needs no introduction. It is infamously terrible. Universally regarded as the single worst episode of the Original Series by those for whom "The Omega Glory" is too niche a pick, every aspect of this story is iconic for all the wrong reasons. It's just as memorable as something like "Arena", albeit for being as bad as the former episode is good. And, to add insult to injury, it went out as the season premier for the fans' hard-won third year of *Star Trek*, a move which has to go down as one of the biggest, most grandiose fuck-yous to a television audience in the history of broadcast.

I thought it was OK.

Now, I hasten to add "Spock's Brain" isn't *good* by any means either. Is it campy and cheesy? Oh, please. This is Roger Corman levels of lowballing it. Is it sexist? For sure-It's a story involving a tyrannical matriarchal society of incompetent, childlike women who torment their male underlings with mixed signals-Of bloody course it's sexist. It's borderline racist too, with characters throwing around words like "primitive" and "apish" on a regular basis and Kirk's ultimate resolution to the problems of the Sigma Draconians is to encourage them to follow a "natural" course of social evolution and learn how to think for themselves. It's just "The Apple" all over again. And, as is par for the course for this season, there are logic lapses and exposition holes everywhere and the plot actually completely falls apart if you think too hard about it. (Although really it all boils down to "alien space women need Spock's brain to control the computer in charge of running their library and central heating system", which is more or less straightforward enough. Trust me: I watch 1980s Scooby-Doo. I've seen stuff that makes far less sense than this.)

But is "Spock's Brain" the single worst episode of Star Trek, or at least the Original Series? Oh, Prophets no. It's not even the worst episode of the season *that we've see so far*. As far as terrible Star Trek episodes go, it's eminently watchable for a number of reasons, and in fact I'd go so far as to say it's probably the most watchable bad episode of *Star Trek* that there is. There's a certain entertainment factor in how charmingly lowbrow it is. Furthermore, "Spock's Brain" is one of the most interesting episodes of the show to talk about, if not actually watch, and frankly, given a choice between this and another test of endurance like "The Paradise Syndrome" or "And The Children Shall Lead" I'll go with the Morgs and Eymorgs every time. So I mean yes it's bad, but not really in a way that would seem to justify the amount of vitriol it gets from mainline fandom. Unpacking how "Spock's Brain" got quite the reputation it did is a worthy field of study, and we'll return to it in a bit, but first let's try and answer the most obvious question: Why does this episode even exist?

One other thing "Spock's Brain" shares in common with "Arena" aside from being its antimatter universe twin is that, perhaps astonishingly, both are Gene Coon scripts (well, originally at least). Coon is once again using his penname Lee Cronin, and, unlike "Spectre of the Gun", I can *absolutely* see why Coon wouldn't want his name associated with this one. But the question remains: How on Earth did Coon crank out something like *this*? He's consistently been arguably the best writer on the entire series, or at the very least one of the top three alongside D.C. Fontana and Paul Schneider. It seems unthinkable to imagine Coon sitting down to genuinely and unironically pen "Spock's Brain".

Well, for one thing, just like Fontana, Coon had his scripted gutted by the creative team, and this one came out in considerably worse shape then "The Enterprise Incident". Some of the differences between Coon's original story and the aired one include the Sigma Draconians being called "The Nefelese" and being ruled by a *male* authority known as "Ehr Von". There would have been an exploration of the Vulcan concept of *slon porra*, supposedly a state of mind where conscious mental faculties are in absolute control of the self. Also, there wouldn't have been a temporary transference of hyper-advanced medical knowledge to McCoy and there wasn't going to be a "Teacher"-McCoy only received information on the planet's local culturally specific techniques and it was a combination of them with his own knowledge and abilities that would have allowed him to reconnect Spock's brain and body. Now, it's not especially clear that even had Coon's original draft gone through this episode still wouldn't have been a legendary turkey. This is still a story about shoplifting Spock's brain and using it as a CPU chip. But one does get the sense, especially just knowing the stuff Coon has written in the past, that there may have been at least a halfhearted attempt to explore the concepts of the Self, mind/body confluence and structures of authority.

Or, it's entirely possible Coon wrote this episode simply to troll Fred Freiberger, Arthur Singer and the new production team: "OK, so you guys aren't going to treat *Star Trek* any differently than a bottom-of-the-barrel pulp sci-fi serial? Then fine. Here's a story that's pulp to the max. Is *this* what you fuckers want?" (William Shatner even jokes this episode is a "tribute" to the NBC studio executives, which is frankly as good an explanation for "Spock's Brain" as exists). Because really, that's what this episode is: We've got a stereotypical-to-the-point-of-parody pulp sci-fi situation and a structure that is, of course, a tedious series of captures and escapes. Aside from this episode in particular (though it is certainly the best example), the accusation the third season is "pulpy" and "campy", and that this is the year's real sin, seems to be a common one amongst fandom: Recall back in "Elaan of Troyius" Paula Block and Terry J. Erdmann said that "overblown" writing, wardrobe and makeup design was "common" to year three. This raises some rather interesting implications, however. If in the end the biggest crime "Spock's Brain" commits is that it shows *Star Trek* succumbing fully to its pulp instincts and this is enough to make it the Worst Trek Ever Made...Then why aren't we once again making the same argument against Gene Roddenberry's work? Just like in "The Omega Glory", I have to wonder: If this is as bad as it gets, why aren't we being equally as critical to, say, "The Cage" or "The Corbomite Maneuver"?

There are two possible reasons for this the way I see it. The easy answer is that while *Star Trek* has been *pulpy* on many occasions in the past, it's never been quite this *campy* before, and for a certain type of genre fan and film critic campy and theatrical is the worst possible thing for a work of visual media to be (I will briefly mention the homophobic and misogynistic overtones such a statement can potentially acquire, but you all are smart enough to take it from there, and anyway such a discussion is best saved for when we return to slash fiction). However, there's a bit more to it than that: Namely, *Star Trek* is also a whole lot more visible now than it's ever been before.

While ratings continued to decline throughout the 1968-9 season, partially by design but also partially because despite everything this was still *Star Trek* with *Star Trek*'s audience, certainly more people were probably at least *aware* of the show and the reputation it now had. It would have been difficult not to be: It really has to be stressed what a watershed and discourse changer "Save Star Trek!" must have been. So, what I have a feeling happened was that while *Star Trek* may have built its fanbase on its momentary flashes of (howevermuch imagined) progressive idealism, starting with the third season there was a now the beginnings of an *expectation* for the show to behave that way on a regular basis. Something like "Spock's Brain" is going to stick out a *lot* more in the fall of 1968 then it would have in the fall of 1967, and I have a feeling had it been made in the second season it wouldn't have quite the reputation it does (I mean, not that it would have been made at that point in the first place: If it's a work of troll literature it's specific to this particular climate).

The other thing peculiarly notable about "Spock's Brain" is the cast. Normally an episode like this would merit the actors totally phoning it in or goofing around, but that's largely not the case here. With the exception of Leonard Nimoy, who has gone on record saying this episode left him constantly embarrassed, as much of the season did (which is, to be fair, a perfectly natural and understandable reaction) and whose stage presence totally reflects this, the cast does seem to be on the whole actually trying here, which is curious. However, William Shatner, DeForest Kelley and James Doohan don't *quite* give their normal performances either: They wind up at something considerably different and more interesting.

Starting with Shatner, we fully expect him by now to just eat everything in sight like he did in "And The Children Shall Lead", and while there's a little bit of that in certain places, the version of Kirk he delivers for "Spock's Brain" is altogether more complex and nuanced then should really be expected. Shatner plays Kirk as someone intensely driven and who'll stop at nothing to get Spock back (slashiness level rising). Similarly, Kelley plays McCoy as obsessed with the concept of removing and reconnecting a brain, especially at the beginning of the first act when the Sigma Draconians' duplicity (and unfathomably advanced technology) is discovered and during the climax as he feverishly races against time to rejoin Spock. Doohan, meanwhile, plays Scott as a loyal and dutiful assistant who uses his specialized skill to help Kirk and McCoy's ambition. Now, while it could just be because I'm writing this in October so maybe it's on my mind, it seems to me that Shatner, Kelley and Doohan might just be trying to turn this into the *Star Trek* version of a horror movie, with Kirk and McCoy playing two sides of the mad, single-minded obsession of Victor Frankenstein.

Just like the doctor, Kirk and McCoy are consumed by their goal to, in a sense, bring Spock back from the dead by transplanting his brain, and this can be seen as being paralleled with the Eymorgs' steadfast, unthinking dedication to the Teacher's tyranny of hierarchical knowledge and ritualized subservience. There are even moments where Shatner and Kelley give performances that are uncannily reminiscent to me of Colin Clive's portrayal of Frankenstein in the 1931 Universal film, and James Doohan taking up the role of the Igor-archetype hunchback assistant (actually named Fritz in the Universal movie) is hilariously evil genius move. "*Star Trek* does Frankenstein" is a brilliant, brilliant concept, especially given how the original *Frankenstein* novel was a cautionary treatise against unrestrained technoscience that marked not only one of the first works of modern science fiction, but one of the first fusions of science fiction and horror. Even the movie adaptations are worth taking note of, as there becomes a kind of kinship between the genres of science fiction, horror and cowboy westerns with the camp aesthetic as B movie staples (even if this isn't really what the original Universal films were). If there was ever a time for Star Trek to attempt something like this, crossing all these genres together to make a larger metaficitonal statement, well, this would be the year to do it.

The only problem with this reading is that there are ultimately too many ideas here that never cohere. "*Star Trek* does Frankenstein" is a great idea, and so is an exploration of Self and identity through the lens of authoritarian power structures. It's just that nothing actually sticks here and, as is frustratingly the norm for this season, nobody seems to be on the same page about what they're doing (or should be doing). Had Coon been given the comparative freedom he enjoyed on "Spectre of the Gun" this *might* have actually worked, presuming (as I think is fair to) that the chasmic structural problems and casual sexism came from the creative team's rewrites. There's a fine line between falling into camp due to incompetence and embracing it as an aesthetic style, and Coon seems like the kind of guy who could have pulled it off. But any good ideas the different people involved in "Spock's Brain" might have had remain buried and difficult to tease out of the uncooperative mess that became the finished episode.

But that says something in and of itself: Even at its worst, the Star Trek that comes out of people like Gene Coon, William Shatner, James Doohan and DeForest Kelley remains thought provoking and very, very entertaining. I wish the same could be said about everything that's part of this franchise.

78. "The Beast Within": Is There In Truth No Beauty?

Star Trek has made me feel a lot of things over the years. Warmth, pride, comfort, joy. Of course lately it's been mostly white-hot anger and frustration, but that kind of comes with the territory. One thing I don't think it's ever made me feel before now though is utter confusion. For the first time, I may have found an episode of Star Trek I didn't actually *get*.

I don't think this is entirely my fault, however: "Is There In Truth No Beauty?" is just about the single most scattered and schizoid production I have ever seen. What should be a *very* straightforward parable about inner beauty vs. outer beauty becomes a disassociated mess of random, half-baked ideas and concepts and I'm not even sure the actors realised they were on the same show with *each other*, let alone gelled with the production team. More than any episode we've seen so far, this one conclusively demonstrates, if there was any lingering doubt, that nobody involved in making this show is on the same page anymore. This is the most crystal-clear example of people talking past each other I have ever seen.

And the whole first half of the story is so formidable too. Doctor Miranda Jones, one of the most powerful telepaths in the galaxy is escorting an ambassador to a race of people whose physical form is so incomprehensible the mere sight of one causes humans to go mad, yet who also supposedly have the most beautiful thoughts of any being. From the moment of her introduction, Jones becomes a powerful presence, as the first person to greet Spock with the Vulcan hand salute who isn't a Vulcan or otherwise related to him. This leads into a delightful contrast with the characters' behaviour towards one another, as there's a hint of professional jealousy between Jones and Spock, who was also offered the position of emissary to the ambassador. This all builds to what is in my opinion frankly one of the single best scenes in the franchise so far, where Kirk, Spock, McCoy, Scott, Doctor Jones and her companion Larry Marvick size each other up over a formal dinner. Doctor Jones accuses Spock of wearing his IDIC pin (a famous symbol of the Vulcans both in and out of the Star Trek universe, which makes its first appearance here) in an attempt to intimidate her and flaunt his superior qualifications, while McCoy wonders why anyone would want to dedicate their life to working with someone who could potentially drive them insane. Kirk and Spock then accuse McCoy of holding to the very Greek (and very Western) idea that what is beautiful must by definition by good, and Kirk goes on to admit an appreciation for beauty is one of the last vestigial traces of humanity's past they have yet to cast off, firmly and explicitly establishing, *for the very first time in the history of the franchise*, that the world of Star Trek is meant to be an expressly idealistic and utopian one.

359

(There's a criticism to be made here about the episode's idea that an appreciation for aesthetics is somehow retrograde, but that's largely incidental to the broader point that Star Trek is in fact declaring itself to be some kind of utopia for the first time in its history. That it doesn't know *what kind* of a utopia to be yet is irrelevant: It never figures that out anyway.)

Then suddenly Jones declares she can sense someone very nearby is thinking of murder, and excuses herself. One by one the other guests leave as well, leaving Kirk alone at the table, putting in place possibly one of the greatest potential whodunnit setups in all of Star Trek-Astoundingly, every single person at that table (aside from perhaps Kirk) now has a motive. Naturally we know the killer is going to have to be either Jones or Marvick as the show would never (and should never) write one of its regulars out by making them a murderer, but the fact this one scene gets us to suspect even for a moment, Spock, McCoy or Scott might be capable of such a crime is quite simply a masterstroke of screenwriting and direction. Of course Robert Bloch made Scotty the prime suspect of a series of murders in "Wolf in the Fold" last year, but there we sort of always knew he was innocent and something else was going on: The mystery wasn't "is Scotty a murderer?", it was "how will Scotty exonerate himself?". This episode, however, is able to trick us for a split-second into thinking one of our heroes *really might* go bad, which is a bit of sleight-of-hand that really should be appreciated even if you don't agree with it.

The story has to change after this, of course, and when Marvick goes to confront Jones and confess his love to her in her quarters, we know his intentions even before she reads them in his mind. Of course he tries to kill the ambassador, and of course he sees him and goes crazy. But what's great about this scene is Jones' reaction: She urges Marvick to seek help and talk to someone about his feelings, instead of turning him in for planning a political assassination. Marvick snaps at her saying she should "try being a woman for once" and that she perhaps even enjoys emotionally tormenting him, which is the exact same reaction any immature man is going to have at being romantically rejected, before storming off to zap the ambassador. The juxtaposition of this scene with the previous one and the next one is a work of actual brilliance: Kirk explains to us about how humanity has evolved, but still on occasions reverts to its less-than-savoury instincts. The altercation between Jones, the ambassador and Marvick is a demonstration of how emotions like jealousy, anger and betrayal live on in humans (which is contrasted with the inner peace and beauty of ambassador Kollos' people, the Medusans, as well as the goals humans now try to hold themselves to) and how they both manifest and are dealt with in an idealized setting.

The clincher comes when Marvick, driven out of his mind, flings the *Enterprise* out of the galaxy, and perhaps even out of the normal space-time continuum, claiming he's looking for a place to hide from the visions and thought-beings that torment him. Marvick, a flatly retrograde individual, is not comfortable in the world of Star Trek and tries to not just escape it, but drag the show with him. Crucially, Marvick is being depicted as retrograde *specifically because he subscribes to tenets of outmoded Westernism*, and the fact he was one of the original designers of the *Enterprise* just makes it all the more perfect. As Kirk says, humanity is still struggling with the more aggressive and antisocial aspects of its collective psyche, and this goes for Star Trek itself. While it may not have begun in a terribly laudable or progressive place, it's changed for the better and demonstrated the capacity for self-improvement. It may not quite have lived up to its full potential yet, but it's closer to realising it now then it has been in the past and, given time, it could eventually reach it.

And then the episode completely goes to pieces. It turns out the Medusans are supposedly the greatest navigators in the galaxy, hence why their ambassador is being escorted to negotiate with the Federation, and Kirk wants to ask Kollos if he'd be willing to help them return to normal space. Kollos needs a physical form in order to operate the helm controls, however, so Spock volunteers to temporarily fuse with him, if Kirk can "distract" Doctor Jones long enough. This whole sequence of events just doesn't make any sense to me: Spock tells Kirk he has to meld with Kollos, and in secret, because Jones is jealous of him...even though her mental powers are superior to his. The reason Spock eventually gives for why it has to be him instead of Jones, or really, anyone else (especially Sulu who is, you know, the actual helmsman) is because Jones is secretly blind, but can position herself through an incredibly sophisticated sensor net.

Although, even then it's not clear. McCoy is the one who ultimately reveals this (and in doing so explicitly and grossly violates patient confidentiality, he even flat-out says this, just about) despite previously giving the indication he too was completely unaware (hence his comment at the dinner table) and Spock sort of waffles on whether or not he was really aware of Jones' blindness while mumbling something about Vulcan telepathic abilities. This also lands the episode square into some of the most awkward and painful misguided ableism ever. The show tries to talk its way out of it by having McCoy tell her to "be realistic" and how while she can "do almost anything a sighted person can do" she "can't pilot a starship". But this also makes no sense, because Jones is absolutely right-There is literally no reason Spock is more qualified for this task than she is. She brings it up with Kollos, who...threatens and sexually assaults her I guess, as she screams, and that's that. So we're now ableist *and* misogynistic.

Once SpockXKollos does his thing, he forgets to put on the visor humanoids have to use when handling Medusans so as not to go mad, leading Spock to temporarily lose it. Then Jones has to probe his mind to repair it, but Kirk barges in and accuses her of manipulating Spock to forget the visor so he'd die because she's still jealous of him which she defiantly refutes (and by the way, she's not wearing her sensor net here for some reason that is once again never explained) *and this all continues to not make any sense.* I think the implication is that Jones really did set the whole thing up, which would be a return to Kirk and Spock's earlier comment about how beautiful things are not inherently good, but that's not how anyone involved is playing it, and furthermore, *I can't figure out what it is they actually *are* playing!*

Shatner seems to play Kirk as very doubtful that he's made the right call, and seemingly very remorseful for how his impulsiveness has hurt Jones (perhaps a callback of his own to his comment about humans still having trouble living up to their own standards). Leonard Nimoy, meanwhile, plays Spock very guarded and unreadable. On the one hand, the scene with the IDIC and the rest of the first act would seem to imply Spock is nothing but respectful to Jones and only wishes to honour her, but his actions with Kollos after the *Enterprise* gets lost would seem to indicate he really *is* acting in an underhanded fashion and might harbour some jealousy towards, or at the very least unwarranted distrust of, her. But the script seems to want us to unanimously turn against Jones, which leaves the whole back half feeling aimless and purposeless. It almost feels like there are two or three *jarringly* different reads or revisions of this story here that all got thrown into a blender.

It is also worth briefly talking about the IDIC. An acronym standing for "Infinite Diversity in Infinite Combinations", though that actually won't be made official until the Animated Series, it's become an iconic symbol of both the Vulcans and Star Trek to the point some Trekkers have adopted it as a life philosophy. Literally the only reason the IDIC exists at all, let alone becomes a prominent part of this episode, was because Gene Roddenberry figured he could turn Spock's pendant into a lucrative collectible piece of merchandise. William Shatner and Leonard Nimoy, along with other members of the cast and crew who I can't find by name, were absolutely livid at Roddenberry's hubris and crass commercialism they actually protested it, him and the episode to the point he had to be called to the set to negotiate a settlement before shooting could continue (and I'd like to point out that as much of a reputation as Shatner and Nimoy have for being prima donnas, it seems to me every time they've put their foot down, at least so far, they've been pretty squarely in the right). But there you have it: Just another friendly reminder about what Soda Pop Art ultimately is if you take it at face value and only consider it worthy for its extant media artefacts.

Then there's Doctor Jones herself, who's played by Diana Muldaur in her second of three marquee Star Trek appearances. And, as much as I love Muldaur and certainly won't complain anytime she appears in the franchise, of her four Trek performances I have to say this is her weakest by far. This isn't so much her fault as it is that of the people who recommended her for the role though, as I think Muldaur may have been pretty seriously miscast here. The thing about Muldaur is that she's only ever going to play one kind of character: A devastatingly competent professional who is on unarguable equal footing with her male colleagues. She can and does bring a theatrical bombast and power to her roles, but this is the kind of character she tends to gravitate towards. If Jones was indeed meant to be unsympathetic and taught a lesson about facing her inner ugliness as it were, Muldaur was absolutely the wrong person to call, because she goes out of her way to give Jones the moral high ground at every possible opportunity, and the rest of the cast are more than happy to let her have it. As a result, Muldaur ends up playing Jones a bit like Thalassa-Imperious, spiteful and vindictive with an unearthly power, and it doesn't work quite as well this time around.

Maybe the intention wasn't to give one character the ethical upper hand. Maybe it was instead to show how none of us are perfect and how we all carry inner ugliness we're continually fighting against. In that case I have two things to say: One, that's intolerably Pop Christian. It's just demons and original sin with the serial numbers filed off. Secondly, there's really nothing here to indicate the cast and crew were on board with that. Nimoy and Muldaur keep gunning for the protagonist role, Shatner's off doing something else entirely, whatever that is, and the episode clunkily changes gears midway through to become something completely different, or rather a multiplicity of different things which is in fact the actual problem. On a basic, structural level, as well as the level of production, "Is There In Truth No Beauty?" is such a shambles it should be the concluding arguments to restore "The Alternative Factor"'s classic status.

This is Star Trek at its absolute most disperse: In the past, we've seen the show at war with itself. This isn't a show at war, it's seven or eight different shows halfheartedly grasping for the same title. In a sense though, this is as prescient about the future of the franchise as the series has ever been.

79. "...suspended by a mixture of curiosity and compassion": The Empath

Science fiction aficionados of a certain age will probably remember *Starlog*. A fan magazine looking at sci-fi and other genre film and television works, often focusing on the perspective of writers, actors and the community fans built for themselves. *Starlog* actually began as essentially an unlicensed fanzine for Star Trek fan culture that broadened its scope to avoid legal troubles, which was interesting for me to read-It was always a bit curious to see Star Trek get such a focus in the magazine, although back then I just chalked it up to the massive amount of cultural capital and ubiquity the franchise had at the time I was reading it.

Starlog was really my primary entry into the world of science fiction culture. I never went to Star Trek conventions or anything like that (OK I think I did once, but it was so long ago I remember next to nothing about it), nor did I have a bunch of spin-off or reference books (well, at first I didn't at any rate). Partly because of this, I never considered myself a massive Star Trek fan, let alone a massive genre fiction fan. Star Trek had certainly captured my imagination, but a large part of the reason why it was able to do that was because at the time it was wildly popular and when I talked to people about television, it was naturally one of the things that came up.

But *Starlog* gave comprehensive coverage to a wide spectrum of film and TV projects: Articles on the latest Star Trek and sci-fi shows were mixed in with, retrospectives on the live-action Batman and Spider-Man shows, cartoons, bits on action spy fiction, cowboy westerns and interviews with the writers of *really* obscurantist stuff like *The Powers of Matthew Star*. Looking back, the magazine was probably my introduction to a lot of shows, like *Buck Rogers*, *Red Dwarf*, *Doctor Who* and *The Man from U.N.C.L.E.* (which probably directly led to my years-long belief *Doctor Who* was some kind of peculiarly and flamboyantly British version of *The Man from U.N.C.L.E.* and why Jon Pertwee remains one of my favourite Doctors). It was also my first, and for a very long time only, exposure to *Star Trek: The Animated Series:* Seeing gorgeously lush and evocative screenshots and cells from what seemed to be a Star Trek cartoon that continued the story of the Original Series was unfathomable to me at the time, and all I knew was that I needed to see a *lot* more of it and as soon as possible. But no matter how hard I looked I couldn't find anything more on it, so it remained a part of the franchise's history forever out of my grasp.

Starlog then was my window into what went into making these programmes and what allowed me to read the reflection of the people and positionalities involved in bringing them to life. I was fascinated by the stories of writers, what they were thinking, what they had hoped to convey and what they loved about the shows whose legacy they were contributing to. Reading about them was my first introduction to the people who would help to define the way I looked at not just Star Trek, but in many ways fiction in general. And of the Star Trek episodes profiled in the magazine, "The Empath" was, apart from the ones from the Animated Series, what stood out in my memory and imagination the strongest. *Starlog* peppered an interview with the episode's writer Joyce Muskat with some of the most vividly surreal images I'd ever seen associated with Star Trek: A stark black stage with nothing but an alien-looking couch in the centre, Kirk speaking with an unearthly young woman, Spock and McCoy frozen in place by a beam of rainbow energy, weird extraterrestrial beings in glitzy, sequined gowns and two guys in giant test tubes seemingly frozen in a moment of sheer horror and anguish.

Star Trek to me is as much about images as it is about characters and ideas. Actually, it's more about images.

"The Empath" is a triumph of not just atmosphere, but also minimalism and subtlety: Its setting and general look-and-feel are utterly unlike anything else in the series, possibly anything else the entire franchise. To me it's the most 1960s the show ever looked, and by that I don't mean it looks especially gaudy or psychedelic, although there are certainly parts of it that do. Nor do I mean it as a negative. Rather, what I'm trying to say is that for me, if you were to try and come up with a single piece of visual art that encompasses the totality of what the decade meant, I think it would look a lot like this episode: It's got the overt filmic contrast indicative of the black-and-white era with the theatricality of the early single-set sitcoms and dramas and there are occasional flashes of glitzy psychedelia shining through the dark to set our consciousnesses aflame. "The Empath" also at times teeters on the edge of calling to mind the bittersweetly nostalgic Neo-Expressionism of *Scooby-Doo, Where Are You!* that would define the last few years of the 60s era for me, mostly thanks to the aforementioned use of light and shadow, and before *Scooby-Doo, Where Are You!* to boot (although not before *Mysteries Five*, to be fair). "The Empath" at once evokes for me *The Twilight Zone, Rocky and Bullwinkle, The Honeymooners, Monty Python's Flying Circus*, "The Mind Robber" from *Doctor Who* and *Star Trek* itself. Watching it is like a dream of signifiers standing in for all the images from the era that captured my imagination the strongest.

While at least part of the reason the episode was filmed largely on an indoor set was surely for budget reasons, Muskat specifically requested a "bare", "theatrical" set as she not only approached writing it like a stage drama, she wanted to use a lot of visual contrast because she only had a black-and-white TV while all her friends had colour, and she was of the opinion *Star Trek* looked better in black-and-white, a sentiment I've at times shared. The cinematography is also a rare bit of genius: Muskat goes out of her way to credit director John Ermen, and says she never would have had a director other than him. For me the highlight of Ermen's work here is the use of rapid fire images, cuts and distorted, fisheye lenses. All of these techniques were utilised heavily in the last episode, "Is There In Truth No Beauty?", especially in the climactic "mind war" between Spock and Miranda Jones. But, like a lot of things in that episode, it never seemed to quite fit there and felt like a jarring intrusion into something that seemed so straightforward and simple (which could very well have been the point). In "The Empath" however, this just reinforces and builds on the episode's hauntingly psychedelic subtexts and provides a formidable visual landscape through which *Star Trek* crosses astral planes.

Curiously, "The Empath" bears a number of striking similarities with "The Cage". Both involve highly advanced aliens living in a vast underground scientific research outpost who kidnap human test subjects to test their resolve and usefulness to a larger purpose of their own. Both episodes make somewhat clunky allusions to aspects of traditional Western thought: The Platonic (read Greek) idea of the Cave Allegory in "The Cage", and a few tossed off Bible references in "The Empath". The Vians even faintly resemble the Talosians, with large, bulbous heads, flowing gowns and mastery over telepathy and emotion. But that's where the similarities end, and "The Empath" ends up about as different from "The Cage" as is possible to get.

"The Empath", rather unsurprisingly, is a story about empathy. But the empathy of whom, and for whom, is never singularly clear for more than a moment. Kirk, Spock and McCoy beam down to evacuate a group of research scientists observing the decay of a star as it starts to go nova. Scotty and Sulu want to rescue the landing party before the star's solar flares become too violent to withstand. The mysterious Vians seemingly kidnap the crew and subject the to cruel experiments on the limit of human fear and pain in order to test their reaction. And at the centre of it all is the mute Gem, the "complete empath" who can take the suffering of any person upon herself and heal it with her latent energy. Gem is embodied with an almost balletic grace by Kathryn Hays, whose vividly expressive performativity is evocative of mummers and mime artists, turning her into an uncannily sublime mirror of William Shatner. Hays-as-Gem trails the crew like a ghost, putting on the masks of every emotion Kirk, Spock and McCoy experience. She fills the palpable, physical space that opens when the landing party is split up or at odds with itself, and she cries Spock's and McCoy's tears for them when each is hurt by the other's attempt to sacrifice himself. But her masks do not work to hide or conceal anything, as she rather instead *becomes* each mask, underlining and emphasizing the emotions the show needs to express at each crucial interval.

Though initially appearing to be an extradiegetic test of the crew's empathy for one another during the Vians' brutal physiological endurance sessions, Gem is ultimately revealed to be the focus of the experiments herself. While the Vians have the technology to spare a planet from the impending supernova, they can only save one civilization, and they needed to be sure Gem's was the one to preserve. The Vians had hoped Gem would learn from Kirk, Spock and McCoy's values of loyalty and self-sacrifice and would ultimately sacrifice herself to save another person. And interestingly, as both Muskat and the characters in her script seem keenly aware, it's from McCoy, the most human and emotional of the entire main cast, whom Gem is expected to learn from. Muskat considered McCoy one of the most underutilised characters on the show and felt he was "a force to be reckoned with". DeForest Kelley responded in kind, delivering one of his most memorable turns in the entire franchise.

366

Here is where *Star Trek* strikes back and reasserts itself, but this is not the *Star Trek* we've come to expect. As McCoy and Gem lie dying, her wanting to save both his life and her own, while he steadfastly refuses to let someone else sacrifice themselves for him as he values life above all else. The Vians stand idly by on the sidelines refusing to take action despite possessing the capability to save them both because they are of the belief the only way for Gem to prove she truly has empathy and compassion is for her to die for another. Kirk and Spock suddenly break free of the emotion-powered force field the Vians are holding them back with (in the aired episode, Spock essentially meditates his way out, while in Muskat's original script Kirk would have overwhelmed the Vians with emotional overload. Both versions have their merits in my opinion), rescue Gem and McCoy and declare it is the Vians who lack compassion and empathy, having long since abandoned it in favour of pure intellect, and that Gem has more than passed their test already. The Vians finally capitulate, restoring life to McCoy and Gem, sparing her planet and returning the crew to the *Enterprise*.

Though the Vians' plan may not have originally been about *Star Trek*, it has now become about it. The series has accidentally stumbled into someone else's exploration of empathy, and instead of becoming subsumed by the story and allowing it to become a test of their own capacity for empathy as we may have expected in years past, now *Star Trek* has become the model by which *others* can be compared to. Not because the show is going around *declaring* itself to be morally superior and telling everyone else how to behave as it was in the first season and the opening half of the second: Now *Star Trek* is valued because it acts in accordance with its own beliefs, openly and respectfully dialogues with other perspectives and simply wants the freedom to remain what it is, and to hopefully make the universe a better place in the process. The role the series used to play in past stories with this kind of structure has now been passed to the Vians, who are shown to have made mistakes and are praised for admitting and making up for them. *Star Trek* has become empathetic.

(And how fiiting is it that the Vians appear as a dark mirror of one of *Star Trek*'s favourite tropes: The hyper-evolved being of pure thought.)

Joyce Muskat was not a professional writer. She was one of a handful of fans allowed to pitch stories to the Original Series, along with Jean Lisette Aroeste, who wrote last week's "Is There In Truth No Beauty?", Judy Burns, who writes next week's script, and Dave Gerrold. Without getting too far ahead, I don't think it's a coincidence that three of these four stories are among the very best Star Trek episodes ever (and also note how, with the exception of Dave Gerrold, these writers are all women). "Is There In Truth No Beauty?" might seem to be the outlier here, but Aroeste's original brief did at least seem to have one or two interesting ideas and if nothing else its first act was easily more effective than the stuff the actual staff writers were doing at this point in time. "The Empath", however, is conclusive proof Star Trek in fact both can *and should* work. No matter what intrinsic, fundamental flaws the franchise may have, it is absolutely possible to make something imaginative, provocative and positive out of it. But the people who understand this are the people who love it in spite of everything-Star Trek relies on empathy. And right now, the people running the show neither love it or empathize with it. But the fans do because they can see things in it that inspire them, and its that sense of love, loyalty, compassion and empathy that will singlehandedly keep the franchise alive for decades to come.

And at last we can perhaps see why "The Empath" seems so curiously similar to "The Cage": This is in truth the pilot for a new kind of Star Trek. In amongst all the doomsaying that makes up the 1968-1969 year, the way forward is as clear as both the inevitable cancellation and the vivid images of "The Empath" itself. The heart of Star Trek beats for itself and for anyone else who loves it.

80. All Hallows Eve: The Tholian Web

For a season so thin on actual quality, there are an intriguing number of truly iconic moments and scenes from *Star Trek*'s final year. It's difficult to forget images like the Melkotians from "Spectre of the Gun", the half-moon cookie aliens from "Let That Be Your Last Battlefield", the cloud of anger and the commandeering of the *Enterprise* in "Day of the Dove", the asteroid spaceship from (not to mention the title of) "For The World Is Hollow And I Have Touched The Sky", the Kirk/Uhura kiss in "Plato's Stepchildren", the cloud city from "The Cloud Minders", Ro-Spock from "Spock's Brain" and everything about "The Empath" (that last one may just be me, but I'll fight for it to the end).

Then there's "The Tholian Web", which is just about made of iconic moments.

Right from the start we have what amounts to a ghost starship, which is a concept so fundamentally and basically wrong the *Enterprise*'s own sensors refuse to accept it's there. Beaming aboard, Kirk, Spock, McCoy and Chekov find the entire crew dead, apparently at their own hands. While it's never explicitly stated this time, the *Defiant* bears all the symptoms of what could be called a dead starship, and when those show up it's usually the sign something very big and very serious is about to go down. Indeed, the *Defiant* takes this theme to the next level-If a starship can die, a starship can become a ghost as well, and it can also haunt. And this is very clearly what the interspatial rift is: It's a haunted region of space where weird, unexpected and incomprehensible things happen. This was even more blatant in Judy Burns' original script, which also featured cosmic spirits manifesting in space and fading in and out of existence onboard the *Enterprise*. However, as Gene Roddenberry didn't like the supernatural and had specified as much in his writer's guide for *Star Trek*, this plot point was altered somewhat in the produced episode.

But even so enough of this remains in "The Tholian Web", and the episode we get is still extremely eerie and atmospheric. What clinches it is when the *Enterprise* is attacked by Commander Loskene and the *Defiant* fades out of normal spacetime. Kirk had stayed behind when the initial landing party was forced to return as the transporter was only able to beam back three at a time, thus becoming trapped onboard the departing *Defiant*, and is declared dead by Spock. From this point onward, Kirk becomes a ghost himself, and he haunts the remainder of the episode on a number of levels. First, his absence understandably causes great strain on the crew, particularly Spock and McCoy. Without Kirk to mediate between them, their normally quasi-friendly banter becomes openly hostile, each clearly resenting the other's presence. This could be interpreted as evidence of the old reading of *Star Trek* that posits Kirk, Spock and McCoy represent the tension and interaction of the id, ego and superego, but I still disagree with that pretty vehemently. For one, that's actually not how the actors are playing these characters: DeForest Kelley shows McCoy's barely restrained distrust of Spock unleashed and free to go wild. Leonard Nimoy, by contrast, returns to the style of performance that made him famous by playing Spock as someone *trying* to be logical and collected but who is in truth plagued by self-doubt and second guessing. These are very personal moments that come expressly out of who these characters are, not some phony and tacked-on bit of pop Freudianism.

(My favourite scene in this regard is at Kirk's memorial service where Spock tells the crew that he cannot put into words what made Kirk a good man, and that each person individually must look inside themselves to figure out what Kirk meant to them personally. It's a very, very Spock thing to say and a very Nimoy moment: It's as much a confession and an apology as it is an appeal to individual positionality and experience, although Nimoy is, as usual, best at conveying this via subtle nonverbal cues).

But Kirk also acts as a *literal* ghost, as he starts appearing to various crewmembers culminating with a full manifestation on the bridge in front of Spock, McCoy and Scott. This is actually handled exceptionally well; Uhura is the first to see him, and she's at first dismissed as suffering hallucinations brought upon by the interspatial rift, which by this point has been revealed as the source of a kind of madness that causes crazed, violent outbursts and what killed the *Defiant*. And of course, they *would* distrust the only woman in the bridge crew. But, once Scotty sees Kirk too, and then the entire bridge, Uhura is vindicated, and the episode even goes out of its way to give us a scene where McCoy undoes Uhura's restraints and tells her that no, she's not crazy: The captain is very much alive.

I really like this scene because, were this just about any other show, that whole exchange would have been totally skipped, or at least briefly acknowledged with a throwaway line. We'd cut back to the action, rescue Kirk and Uhura would be back on the bridge for our "everybody laughs" denouement as if nothing had happened. I *hate* it when shows do this (and almost every show has at one point or another), leaving what really need to be important, intimate character moments to our imaginations. But *Star Trek* makes sure we get to see that, because it, at least for the moment, knows these characters are people and deserve to be treated with respect and dignity, especially as each and every one is somebody's inspiration or role model.

(And Nichelle Nichols looks positively elated, not just for her character, but to be doing this scene at all. It's little wonder she names this one of her two favourite episodes).

This peculiar otherworldly feeling is present elsewhere in "The Tholian Web" as well. There are, of course, the Tholians themselves, who have always been one of my absolute favourite alien species in all of Star Trek. Commander Loskene (who is referred to as a "he" in the episode but always came across to me as quite feminine, especially voiced by Barbara Babcock) just looks plain *weird*. In one of the best uses of the Original Series' gaudy primary colours, Loskene appears as an overly exposed glowing red geometric shape afloat in a swirling blue haze. She looks nothing like any other Star Trek alien we've ever seen before, and with just a crudely defined head and a bizarre energy web, our imaginations are racing to conceive of what these creatures might actually be like. It's yet another vividly memorable image that draws you right into both the show's world and it's mood. Indeed, one of the savviest moves *Enterprise* ever made was, when they did a pseudo-sequel to this episode and needed to show a full-bodied Tholian, depicted them pretty much exactly the way you'd expect them to look: As giant, burning, psychedelic crystalline polygon crab-spider things.

I don't use the term "otherworldly" here at all lightly: "The Tholian Web" is very much about an Otherworld in the pre-Christian heathen sense. Most obviously, there's the ghost ship *Defiant* and Kirk's passing into the region beyond the interspatial rift (itself a magickal doorway, much like the barrows, or *sídhe*, might be in Celtic-Nordic-Germanic mythology). But also there's the Tholians-Not only does Loskene not look like any alien we've seen before, she doesn't *act* like one either. She appears out of nowhere, threatens Spock and then ensnares the *Enterprise* in a perfectly geometric spider web for ultimately unknowable reasons. Although it's not made explicit, to me, the implication is that the Tholians are very clearly meant to be inhabitants of the Otherworld here, who have always been portrayed as creatures who operate by a standard of logic and morals that are completely impossible for us to fully understand. This would also explain the Tholians' aggressive territoriality: Typically visitors to the Otherworld from our plane are only welcome if they're explicitly asked to visit, and the *Enterprise* has shown up someplace it's not supposed to be without an invitation (and also note again how psychedelic Loskene looks and the reappearance of that fisheye lens, used here in the PoV shots of the crewmen under the influence of interspace) .

What's really exciting though is how Burns melds this concept with science fiction. Firstly, Spock gets this extremely telling bit of dialogue:

> "Well, picture it this way, Mister Chekov. We exist in a universe which co-exists with a multitude of others in the same physical space. At certain brief periods of time, an area of their space overlaps an area of ours. That is a time of interphase, during which we can connect with the *Defiant*'s universe."

This is *exactly* how the Otherworld is supposed to work, especially in the Celtic-Nordic-Germanic tradition. The way Spock describes the "time of interphase" is word-for-word precisely what happens during the festivals of Beltane, Mittumaarin and Samhain: The boundaries between worlds becomes permeable and can be freely crossed. With that in mind, it's also interesting that it's Shatner-as-Kirk who not only gets to spend the majority of the episode on the other end of the looking-glass, but gets to come back as well. Sure, he says the universe he wound up in was "completely empty" when we might expect it to be full of Tholians or some similar kind of space spirit, but we can also attribute this to the Nordic concept of the Nine Worlds: The Eddas describe not just one Otherworld, but eight, unified by the World-Tree Yggdrasill. Even Celtic lore occasionally makes reference to there being more then one spirit world or Land of Eternal Summer. And, of course, Spock mentions a "multitude" of other universes. So Kirk just managed to find himself in a pretty boring Otherworld then.

But the real *coup de grace*, although probably not explicitly intended by Burns, is that the Otherworld of "The Tholian Web" isn't just a Celtic-Nordic-Germanic one, though it definitely draws quite heavily on that tradition: It's also a Polynesian one. It is firstly, as

I mentioned above, overtly a Land of the Dead: The *Defiant* is most definitely dead and Kirk acts like a ghost when he's on the other side (which might even explain the puzzling rapidity with which Spock declared Kirk killed in action). The Polynesians also believed in the idea of multiple worlds, typically divided into the realms of the Sea, Earth and Sky. In some variants of Polynesian mythology, one of the places the deceased might go is the world of the sky. So now we have not only an Otherworld situated in outer space, previously only the domain of "serious" science fiction, but the vaguest hint that maybe Star Trek is *itself* some kind of Otherworld as our heroes inhabit the sky world already, even without needing to cross the interspatial rift. This actually makes perfect sense for a series moving more towards utopianism: The show embodies ideals we might not actually be capable of living up to, but it remains a powerful source of inspiration and hope. It's in many ways then an Otherworld of fiction and oral myth, perhaps even an..."ideaspace"...but now I'm getting ahead of myself.

What's really the most important about "The Tholian Web" for me is that it shows *Star Trek* on the vanguard of a major sociocultural transition that's about to take place. Star Trek began, of course, firmly in both the Golden Age and pulp science fiction traditions, but had the unenviable misfortune to come out just as both genres were beginning to wind down. The cutoff point is often put at the *Apollo 11* mission, which supposedly turned the public perception of outer space away from something that was our inevitable birthright and a place where weird, unusual and exciting adventures could happen to that of a vast, cold and most likely empty void. This, the argument goes, proved to be the death knell of Star Trek's kind of science fiction. But I don't think even the original *Star Trek* was as indebted to Golden Age Sci-fi and pulp as much as that argument needs it to be: Certainly Gene Coon and Robert Bloch at least might have some objections to voice about that.

More to the point though, both Golden Age and pulp sci-fi emerged were at their peak alongside the UFO era. Kenneth Arnold's famous "flying saucer" sighting over Mount Rainier on June 24, 1948 put the idea of hyper-advanced extraterrestrials visiting Earth in snazzy spaceships firmly into the public consciousness. Although, as Jacques Vallée points out, sightings of mysterious objects in the sky have been around for almost the entirety of recorded human history, the specific theory they are alien spacecraft is an invention of the mid-20th Century. In many ways the UFO era and sci-fi of the Golden Age and pulp variety are intertwined, and while neither UFOs nor science fiction ever go away, there is a kind of shift in the way both are read after this point. As this kind of science fiction fades away, so does the classic UFO era, to be replaced in the 1970s with what might be called a more overtly Fortean era of inexplicata that draws much more heavily on indigenous spirituality and mysticism (although Forteanism, like the UFO phenomena, has also been around as long as people the true beginnings of this particular era are really with John Keel and the pointedly bizarre happenings in Point Pleasant, West Virginia in 1966, appealingly synchronously around the same time *Star Trek* went to series).

This is ultimately more the domain of something like Scooby-Doo, especially right now, and there's in fact a truly magnificent episode of *Scooby-Doo, Where Are You!* that will air about a year from now that is the definitive statement on the death of the UFO era and first-wave science fiction. But "The Tholian Web" is about this too, with its Space Land of the Dead and overtly mystical overtones. The fact Star Trek can do an episode like this and have it not seem at all out of place is proof positive the franchise is something more than the sum of its parts, and this is yet another reason it has the ability to last forever. The *Enterprise* has learned how to travel between worlds, and it now has everything it needs to transcend itself to seek enlightenment.

Of course Judy Burns had to be a fan.

81. "But I have promises to keep/And miles to go before I sleep/And miles to go before I sleep.": For The World Is Hollow And I Have Touched The Sky

This was an episode I never saw much of. I'd seen scraps of it here and there, but it was never a story I deliberately sought out to watch, for a number of reasons. First of all, I was just never as big a fan of the Original Series as I was its two immediate sequel shows and I wasn't especially inclined to be a completionist about Star Trek. Also, from everything I'd seen of "For The World Is Hollow And I Have Touched The Sky" told me it just wasn't my kind of story. Not that it was bad, and indeed by all accounts it was a highlight of the third season, it's just this kind of weighty tragedy is not really the way I enjoy spending my leisure time, even knowing it of course had to be undone at the end of the episode. But it seemed like a very well-regarded tear-jerker of a character study awash in a dreamlike sense of poetry, as anything with a title that breathtakingly pretentious damn well *better* be.

Yeah, no, it's terrible.

"For The World Is Hollow And I Have Touched The Sky" is "The Gamesters of Triskelion" for the third season. It is so awash in *Star Trek* cliches the show itself seems tired of them. It's not even really possible to come up with a list of episodes this one cribs from, as it seems like it just stole from everything, but, off the top of my head I can maybe mention "The Return of the Archons", "The Apple", "By Any Other Name" and most obviously "The Paradise Syndrome", from which this episode takes its basic plot about a member of the *Enterprise* crew abandoning Starfleet to live a simpler life married to a high priestess, not to mention a worrying majority of its set. None of this really fills one with boundless enthusiasm.

The one innovation this episode brings to a mountain of overplayed, hackneyed *Star Trek* standbys is the idea that the reason McCoy wants to retire to Yonada is because he's suffering from a terminal illness. This isn't something Star Trek had looked at before, probably for good reason. Imagining any of the previous creative teams attempting a plot like this is a somewhat frightening prospect, and as good as writers like Gene Coon and D.C. Fontana might have been, this isn't really the sort of thing that's in either one of their wheelhouses. Of course, this logically means we should expect *this* creative team to make an absolute hash of this, as they were both stupidly confidant enough to attempt this kind of episode in the first place and blissfully ignorant of the actual extent of their grasp to the point they could tie it to a story about an intergenerational asteroid starship. We would not be wrong to expect this as the finished product is in fact embarrassingly awful, but let's briefly pause for a moment to remember that intimate character drama isn't really all that unusual a thing for *Star Trek* to attempt. The series began, after all, with an overt fusion of pulp sci-fi, Golden Age sci-fi and soap opera dynamics. Characterization *should* be a strength of the show.

And indeed it is, but doing character pieces for Star Trek is not the same as doing character pieces for other shows. It's a unique environment with its own quirky and counterintuitive rules, and failing to heed them sort of means you're not *really* doing a Star Trek story. One of the big ones, at least for the moment, is that Star Trek tends to involve going to a new place every week and the setting of the *Enterprise* has to remain somewhat constant. The show is about the interaction between two status quo: The constant of the *Enterprise* and the setting-of-the-week of the planet or starbase or whatever (and before someone says something, yes, the show you're thinking of does in fact manage to game this rule and still be Star Trek, at least at first, but that's a special case and we've got until 1993 before it becomes a major theme). The character moments need to be sparked by the plot of the episode, not the other way around. I mean this is just good writing advice in general, but it's absolutely *imperative* for Star Trek. This is a very long-winded way of saying that teasing the death of a major character really doesn't work on Star Trek (I mean it doesn't anyway, but especially not on Star Trek) unless we know for a fact the actor isn't coming back next season, which was certainly not the case here.

And furthermore "For The World Is Hollow And I Have Touched The Sky" just fails at its character moments anyway. If you're going to do a soap opera plot about how the characters might deal with a friend who has a terminal illness, it absolutely needs to be done with the utmost care and respect and more than *anything* your creative figures need to be on the same page. None of that happens in this episode. While McCoy's disease does serve as his primary motivation here, the shift between the deeply serious plot about him possibly dying and the retread space adventure is audibly clunky and, damningly, neither have very much to do with one another. The acting is also painfully poor this week, and it really, really needed not to be for this to have any chance of working: DeForest Kelley gives an astonishingly phoned in performance and doesn't at all act like anyone in that situation might. Leonard Nimoy is no better: I know Spock is supposed to be a Vulcan who hides his emotions, but Nimoy just looks he doesn't want to be here and has totally tuned out of everything. Thank goodness William Shatner makes up for them, playing Kirk as someone gently compassionate, but who's also awkwardly walking on eggshells around his dying friend because he doesn't know how he should react. Nimoy and Kelley just look utterly bored out of their skulls.

The guest cast is no better. Katherine Woodville's Natira is a neurotic, bug-eyed wild-woman who spends most of the episode mugging for the camera. She's not helped by the fact her love story with McCoy is one of the most stupendously half-assed and thrown-in romance subplots I have ever seen: It basically amounts to Natira taking a fancy to McCoy after about 30 seconds and then proposing marriage after a beat, to which McCoy's reaction is essentially "OK. Sure, why not?". This makes Kirk's studio-mandated-girls-of-the-week look intimate and meaningful. At least Shatner had the decency to play those as if he was genuinely in love. Also, while taken on its own the title "For The World Is Hollow And I Have Touched The Sky" sounds lovely and poetic, it becomes considerably less so when it turns out to be a *literal description of the major plot reveal* and is blurted out verbatim by some random crazy old guy who disturbingly creeps out from behind a curtain in Kirk, Spock and McCoy's guest quarters on Yonada before promptly dying of an acute ham seizure. This is a far cry from William Shatner's pantomime recursive artifice performance art, or even his antics in something like "The Omega Glory" or "And The Children Shall Lead". Shatner at least is never not entertaining, regardless of whether or not he's actually trying. These people are just screwing around and it's not even fun to watch.

(This non-romance also leads directly to the episode's spectacularly incoherent resolution where Natira decides McCoy has to go back to the *Enterprise* while McCoy wants to stay with her on Yonada. Natira sounds like she's explaining to McCoy why she can't go back to the ship with him...*even though that's not actually what McCoy says he wants to do.*)

It's a general rule of mine never to get hung up on production details like plot, character development as special effects, as I typically find them to be tremendously overvalued by the vast majority of people who write about visual media and to me they are largely the least important aspects of a work of fiction. With this season, however, and in particular an episode like this one, we've gotten to the point where *Star Trek*'s slapdash approach to production, which could previously be written off as pleasingly theatrical, has now actually become a major problem and is directly interfering with and detracting from the show's overall impact and ability to be read. Neither "The Empath" nor "The Tholian Web" looked especially lavish and neither were the smoothest scripts, but I didn't focus on the structure issues there because both episodes were imaginative enough they absolutely didn't matter. This one...isn't.

The problem with the Yonada sets isn't that they're "unconvincing" (very little in Star Trek actually is), it's that they're *visibly the same sets we saw five weeks ago* and *no attempt has been made to make them look the slightest bit different.* "The Empath" and "The Tholian Web" reused a bunch of props too, but you wouldn't know that because of the enchanting art design. It's possible to do wonders on a shoestring budget: I direct you once again to not just the last two episodes, but also *Raumpatrouille Orion*. Here though there's an overwhelming sense of fatigue and deflation, and it's crushingly depressing to see the asteroid-starship that was the one thing from this episode that really stuck in my imagination portrayed not just via one of the saddest, most drab and blase bits of 1960s set design, but also through stock footage from "The Paradise Syndrome", reminding me once again how cynically similar the two stories are and leading me to wonder if the whole reason this episode exists wasn't actually just to reuse all those effects shots. It all comes back to love: If you love something enough, you can make it work.

81. *"But I have promises to keep/And miles to go before I sleep/And miles to go before I sleep.": For The World Is*

Just like the loveless romance between McCoy and Natira, "For The World Is Hollow And I Have Touched The Sky" is the product of a show that's stopped loving itself.

82. "THERE WILL BE NO BATTLE HERE!": Day of the Dove

In the 1980s and 1990s Galoob produced a line of miniature models called Micro Machines. They were mostly replicas of different automobiles, but Galoob also produced tie-in sets of Micro Machines for a number of different licensed works. Merchandise is typically seen by those of a leftist persuasion as a primary symptom of crass capitalist frivolity and indulgence, and while I'm not largely inclined to disagree in the general sense, I do believe there are enough positive effects to glean out of the phenomenon to justify its existence, and ultimately it's intrinsically linked with the concept of Soda Pop Art and thus an important facet of Western culture.

But my qualified defense of merchandise will have to wait for a later date. The reason I bring it up now is that there were in fact Star Trek themed Micro Machine sets, and I happened to have a few of them. each set was patterned after a different incarnation of the franchise and typically featured three different ships, the implication being these were the most notable and important vehicles. The Original Series set featured the *Enterprise*, of course, but also a Romulan Bird-of-Prey and a Klingon D7 battle cruiser. On the back of the box there were some basic overview specs, probably taken from Mike Okuda's *Star Trek Encyclopedia*. There was also a note that indicated which episode the ship was from. Now obviously most of these ships appeared in a great deal more than one episode, so Galoob picked the episode they must have figured was the ship's most iconic appearance. For the Bird-of-Prey they understandably picked "Balance of Terror" (if for no other reason than that's the only episode unique footage of the model was shot for), but for the D7 they picked "Day of the Dove".

This is another of the most iconic episodes of the Original Series, becoming memorable enough to warrant a considerable number of sequels and references in future incarnations of Star Trek. This, combined with the generally very positive reception amongst fans makes "Day of the Dove" in many ways the definitive Klingon episode of the Original Series. It's not difficult to see why it's garnered this reputation: This is the first time we see Klingons behaving in a manner that's somewhat consistent with their later depiction, as a proud culture of warriors that values honour and courage. Kang throws out Klingon proverbs and phrases on a reliably regular basis, many of which served as the inspiration for future explorations of Klingon philosophy, and even carried through wholecloth into future series. Kang is also played with impeccable force and prowess by Michael Ansara: He's without doubt one of the most memorable antagonists the show's seen, Klingon or otherwise, or at least the one who it's the easiest to see why the fans would be drawn to him: He has a charm and charisma absent from several previous Klingons (although I still prefer William Campbell's delightfully camped-up Captain Koloth in "The Trouble with Tribbles" personally).

"Day of the Dove" is also the third outing from Jerome Bixby. Bixby previously gave us "Mirror, Mirror", which was one of the finest hours of the entire series except for the fact he didn't write it, and "By Any Other Name", which perhaps wasn't, but was still a somewhat solid outing with one or two intriguing ideas. "Day of the Dove" is closer to the former rather than the latter in theme, tone and general execution, and while it's a good showcase of Bixby's strengths as a writer, it's also a showcase for his weaknesses as well. Like "Mirror, Mirror", "Day of the Dove" seems to be a critique of imperialistic tendencies both in and out of *Star Trek*, although this one seems to be criticizing violence, conflict and negative emotions more broadly. Which brings me to my next point which is, unfortunately, like "By Any Other Name", this episode has a tendency to come across as unnecessarily heavy-handed, Pop Christian and honestly, a bit facile and morally simplistic.

At heart this episode essentially boils down to one big Cold War allegory: The Klingons and the Federation are pushed to the break of brutal, never-ending war when a(nother) non-corporal entity that feeds on anger, hatred and violence sneaks aboard the *Enterprise* and manipulates both crews to do its bidding by enhancing their inherent aggressive tendencies and confusing them with false memories, which is overtly likened to propaganda in the scene where Kirk tries to plead with Kang on the bridge: Kang is under the control of the entity and refuses to listen, while Mara, Kang's wife who Kirk had previously threatened to kill as a bluff, is confused as to why she's not being sent to a Federation death camp. Kirk informs her she's been a victim of anti-Federation propaganda. The hostilities are eventually resolved when Kirk convinces Kang that the entity is the real enemy, and they must unite to free themselves from its control. The best possible reading I could muster of this would be to say the entity represents distant politicians who send soldiers off to fight wars for their own political gain with no concern for the sanctity of life, and the worst would be that it represents what it looks like: A dangerous Other. This would make "Day of the Dove" quite paradoxically militaristic, as it would seem to be saying the only value in alliances is to forge solidarity against the *real* threats. Neither of these are particularly nuanced observations, especially taken in the context of this episode's most obvious antecedent, "Balance of Terror".

The Klingons too are not without problems. In many ways this is the best they're portrayed in the Original Series, as the episode shows them to be a unique culture unto themselves and for the first time we get to see a Klingon crew made up of more than two distinct individuals. Ansara helps a great deal too: Kang's constant speeches about death, glory and honour make the Klingons sound like warrior poets, and it's leagues better then the generically Russian or Mongol schemers they started out as. It's no surprise why this becomes the model for all of their future portrayals. But this still isn't quite enough: For "Day of the Dove" to become the "Balance of Terror" or "Enterprise Incident" for the Klingons, it would have needed to show them as absolute equals to the Starfleet officers, and it never quite gets there. For one, every Klingon character other than Kang and Mara is basically an extra and even Mara, supposedly the science officer of Kang's ship and a very intelligent person, gets an absolutely intolerable scene where she stands around dumbly in the corridor while Kirk and Spock discern the nature of the entity, contributing nothing even though she should technically be as qualified as Spock. She also blurts out to Kang that Kirk is tricking them while he's trying to make a truce *immediately after seeing the entity herself.*

Secondly, this is the most jaw-droppingly racist the Klingons have ever looked. The show isn't even trying to hide the fact all the Klingons are played by white actors (with the arguable exception of Syrian Michael Ansara) browned up and given ambiguously foreign makeup anymore, and on top of that they're still shown to be more warlike and less reasonable then the Federation. While they're not antagonists, they are aggressors and they do quickly become the last stubborn factor that keeps the plot from resolving. This isn't so much a mutual alliance where two groups of equals work together to come up with a joint solution to a problem, it's more Kirk convincing the Klingons they were wrong about the Federation, even though violent emotions exist in all of us. Even "The Enterprise Incident", neutered as it was compared to D.C. Fontana's original pitch, managed to at least hint at the Federation engaging in underhanded and unethical behaviour and gave them part of the blame for that episode's conflict.

Unfortunately, a lot of this does come down to the fact the Klingons simply aren't as interesting or effective an alien culture as the Romulans. Gene Coon did create them as generic baddies and never intended them to become reoccurring adversaries, after all. While the Romulans are our explicit parallels and represent another direction we could have gone and can be used in fascinating studies of aesthetics and sensuality through their connection to the Vulcans, the Klingons are really never going to be anything more then stoutheart warriors, and without the dense tapestry of myth, oral history and culture that tends to accompany roving bands of warriors in the real world.

And I mean for fuck's sake, the Klingons lost to *Tribbles.*

But that said there are a lot of things to like about "Day of the Dove" too. First of all, the acting is bloody spectacular, and I'll wager that's a large part of the reason this episode is as popular as it is. The entire cast is in absolute top form, every single major actor gets a scene to shine and I haven't seen this cast this energized and fired up in a very long time, if ever. Watching Nichelle Nichols just completely lose it on the bridge, portraying Uhura not crying or acting withdrawn, but pushed over the line enough to simply snap and start railing against everything, is genuinely unsettling and impossible not to relish as much as Nichols herself clearly is. DeForest Kelley looks like he's about to start foaming at the mouth and James Doohan has Scotty just have a total nervous breakdown. Ansara's great, as I mentioned, and while this in many ways feels like business as usual for William Shatner, he's an imperious, rowdy and passionate force and plays Kirk taking command without making him seem dismissive and paternalistic. What's actually more telling is that for the first time everyone in the cast seems to be following Shatner's lead now, so every character becomes a deliberately exaggerated artifice, which is actually perfect for conveying the story's artificially heightened stakes. It's truly captivating and mesmerizing.

The fight scenes are also visceral and exciting in a way they're usually not in *Star Trek*, and the fact they're actually central to the plot this time excuses the fact they take up about half the runtime. However, this also highlights another area in which "Day of the Dove" falters a bit, because the stuff that's not fighting or impassioned speechifying is kind of thin and hokey: It takes entirely too long for the two crews to figure out what the entity is doing and the *literal* "everybody laughs" ending where Kirk, McCoy, Scott and Kang crack painful "jokes" at the entity to make it go away is embarrassingly stilted and clunky. Although I suppose it's better than Bixby's original plan which would have entailed the crew *singing songs* and *holding peace marches*.

(Though as hokey as that would have been, I suppose it would have been welcome change of pace from "The City on the Edge of Forever" and "And The Children Shall Lead".)

It's at this point where it starts to become clear what the actual problems with "Day of the Dove" are. The script seems like it's trying to come down against war and violence, but its stops short before delivering anything close to a comprehensive or even-handed critique. It doesn't talk about the origins of violence or why people might be pushed towards it, or how power structures provide a climate where violence is not only allowed to exist but encouraged to (which are all things the show has said in the past, so I don't think I'm being too unreasonable in my expectations), it just says "fighting is bad" and that it strengthens the *real* enemy, which is...fighting, I guess? I suppose we could redeem this by saying "Day of the Dove" is about problematizing all parties in a fight, and that it's trying to be just as hard on the *Enterprise* crew, who are frequently tempted by their violent and bigoted impulses.

Except I don't think the episode is actually very *good* at making that argument. There's the problem of the Klingons of course, which I addressed above, but even without them I'm not sure this is the kind of story the show should be doing now. It might have actually been a better fit in the second season, maybe even the fist, coming alongside stuff like "Arena", "A Taste of Armageddon", "The Devil in the Dark" and yes, even "Errand of Mercy". Coming here, midway through the third season, *Star Trek* is now in a climate that has seen not only Bixby's own (kinda) "Mirror, Mirror", but also "The Trouble with Tribbles", "A Piece of the Action", "Patterns of Force", "Save Star Trek!", "Spectre of the Gun", "The Empath" and "The Tholian Web" (although to be fair, those last two episodes wouldn't air until after this one, though they were produced before). The ship has sailed on problematizing the show and its setting, the focus should now be on what it is that makes *Star Trek* special, important and worth preserving. We should be looking at what makes *Star Trek* *different*, in what way it's idealistic and hopeful, what we might be able to learn from it and how it can continue to grow.

Then there's the plot, which sadly kind of falls apart if you think about it too hard. There's the fundamental theme, which is already somewhat more facile then maybe might be desirable, but after a time it also starts to feel...overly familiar. One detects shades of not just "Balance of Terror" and "The Enterprise Incident", but also "Arena" (the solution is not to fight, and a external force underlines the brutality of fighting by replacing all weapons with basic implements to take the flash and glory out of it) and even Bixby's previous

381

credits (the scene between Chekov and Mara seems to be an echo of Mirror Spock's mind rape of McCoy in "Mirror, Mirror", and it's nowhere near as effective here). And, "Day of the Dove" remains Pop Christian by depicting human(oids) as inherently savage and violent and who must struggle to keep their instincts and inhibitions under control...which is also reminiscent of "The Naked Time", "The Enemy Within", "A Taste of Armageddon", "Errand of Mercy", "Wolf in the Fold", and even "Is There In Truth No Beauty?" if you're especially inclined to read that episode that way.

Jerome Bixby has one more *Star Trek* credit to his name, but I'm starting to get the sense he might not have had a tremendous range as a writer, at least on this show, and probably needed other people to give his scripts that last bit of polish necessary to make them truly shine. He was lucky enough to have sublimely good ghost-writers in D.C. Fontana and Gene Coon on "Mirror, Mirror", but he doesn't have them anymore as both have long since left their day-to-day positions on the show, and Arthur Singer doesn't seem like the kind of guy who'd gel all that well with Bixby's themes and motifs, if you catch my drift. But the writing is saved by the cast, who are absolutely on fire, and "Day of the Dove" really is a solidly enjoyable and well-done episode. It's without question the best Klingon story of the Original Series (if you don't count "The Trouble with Tribbles"), and certainly given the fact the show is churning out stuff like "The Paradise Syndrome" and "For The World Is Hollow And I Have Touched The Sky" on a frighteningly regular basis this year it's hard to get too upset at an episode that has its heart in the right place and is a spellbinding bit of television on top of it all.

But maybe the reason "Day of the Dove" is the definitive Klingon episode is because it leaves us feeling just a little bit unsatisfied and disappointed.

83. "From each as they choose, to each as they are chosen.": Plato's Stepchildren

"Plato's Stepchildren" is utterly unwatchable, critically important and incredibly easy to talk about all at the same time.

Leonard Nimoy has said the majority of the third season was "embarrassing" for him, and nowhere is that clearer than here. This is one of the most excruciatingly painful and humiliating episodes to watch of the entire franchise. It is also one of the most popular and important, and it's not at all difficult to see why. It is straightforwardly a reiteration of a number of the themes the show has been grappling with dating back to the Gene Coon era with very little new to say about them, but it's also the most concise and blunt about them the show will ever be. Actually, I'm not certain the *franchise* is ever this blatant about these ideas and concepts ever again. "Plato's Stepchildren" doesn't quite work: It almost does, but it's messy and sloppy and needed to go one little step further to really sell what I think it was attempting to drive home. Nonetheless, it had a measurably, provably positive effect on world culture, and that alone unquestionably seals its legacy.

A bit like Star Trek itself then.

Put most basically, "Plato's Stepchildren" concerns a group of extraterrestrial settlers who lived on Earth during the time of Ancient Greece and were inspired by Plato make the utopian republic he imagined a reality. When settling on a new planet, they discovered that eating the native fruit, mixed with their endocrine systems, gave them massively powerful psychokinetic abilities (OK...), through which they perfected the use of their minds and intellects...while regarding anyone else as so inferior and beneath them to be not even worthy of the most basic amount of respect and dignity. Aside from being utterly without compassion and empathy, they're also ruthlessly sadistic: Luring the *Enterprise* to their planet under false pretenses, the Platonians, as they have come to call themselves, capture the crew and turn them into human (and Vulcan) marionettes to be subject to their every capricious whim.

Obviously, "Plato's Stepchildren" is not treading any new ground here. It is once again conceptually extremely similar to many previous episodes, most notably "The Cage", "Where No Man Has Gone Before" (it even recycles the "absolute power corrupts absolutely" speech), "Who Mourns for Adonais?" and "Bread and Circuses". The difference here is in execution: As a standalone piece of television, "Plato's Stepchildren" seems to come up extremely wanting when compared to some of those episodes. It's not as poetic and doesn't feel as fresh as "Where No Man Has Gone Before" did, and it's nowhere near as boldly creative as "Bread and Circuses", at least the Gene Coon part, as that episode managed to effortlessly equate the Roman Empire, the larger Hellenistic tradition, the Gladiatorial spectacle, television and the general state of United States culture circa 1967 in a grand, sweeping condemnation of Western modernity. That said though, "Plato's Stepchildren" doesn't have Gene Roddenberry to come in and screw all that up with one of the most morally bankrupt and reprehensible denouements in TV history, and in the process drive away his show's biggest creative force.

And "Plato's Stepchildren" is leagues better than "The Cage" and "Who Mourns for Adonais?", largely by virtue of it actually being a somewhat competent production and not swimming in rape culture. And what it lacks in eloquence and craftsmanship it makes up for in volume and emphasis, because "Plato's Stepchildren" strikes right at the heart of Westernism and deals a brutal, shuddering, crippling blow. There are few thinkers more central to Western philosophy and ethics than Plato, and the secret of this episode is that it's just as strong a denouncement of Plato himself as it is of the followers who have supposedly strayed from his teachings. Central to this is the concept of the Philosopher King, who we've talked about before in the context of "Space Seed" and of which I've been more than a little critical, largely because I see little difference between "Philosopher King" and "Fascist". Parmen explicitly calls himself one, despite claiming he has "no need" of a title, and the Platonians absolutely act like they're intellectually superior to everyone else and thus are deserving of the power they wield: It's how they attempt to justify treating Alexander and the *Enterprise* crew as subhuman creatures only worthy of being playthings.

What "Plato's Stepchildren" seems to be saying is that any utopia, which the Platonians explicitly say they've created and Plato certainly thought he'd conceived of even if he didn't use the name, which values some people over others is in truth no utopia at all. Now that *Star Trek* has overtly transformed into a utopia (or is in the process of doing so), it's first test is to prove why it has a stronger claim to utopianism than others, and it makes its case on both diegetic and extradiegetic fronts. Firstly, of course, there is the character of Alexander, a little person mocked and tormented by the other Platonians because of his stature and his inability to develop their psychokinetic powers, which of course turn out to be endocrine-based. It's a self-evident and straightforward stand-in for a particularly Western form of institutionalized and hegemonic bullying that dates back to Plato himself: The other Platonians hate Alexander because they don't consider him as intelligent and sophisticated as they are, and he looks different than them to boot. Tellingly, Alexander says his bullying began at the exact same time the psychokinetic powers developed, which, given the "absolute power" speeches, can be likened with authoritarianism more generally. The very first thing the "enlightened" disciples of Plato do upon attaining power is hoard it for themselves and weaponize it to dehumanize an innocent person.

Alexander immediately trusts Kirk, Spock and McCoy because while they might look different than he does, they don't bully him and don't have the power, two concepts that had previously been inconceivable to him. This leads to his character's major turning point, and probably one of the single most important exchanges in the entire franchise. Alexander

384

asks Kirk if, "where he comes from", there are more people like him, referring both to his stature and lack of psychokinetic abilities. To which Kirk responds in a beautifully loaded quote:

> "Alexander, where I come from, size, shape or color makes no difference. And *nobody* has the power."

And with that one line, Kirk sets the stage for the entire future of Star Trek. Crucially, this advice proves vital to Alexander in the climax when he abstains from killing Parmen, even though he'd be entirely within his rights to do so. But, as Kirk later says, killing is murder, even in self-defense, and Alexander doesn't want (the) power, because he doesn't want to end up like the Platonians. He wants to be better, and he proves to himself as much as anyone else that he's capable of better. And it was Star Trek that showed him he could be better. What makes Star Trek's utopia worth holding onto is that it is, in the words of Robert Nozick, a "meta-utopia" where "...people are free to do their own thing". It is the only environment that can exist when each individual person is treated as an equal.

While catching a rerun of "Plato's Stepchildren", a boy named Dan Madsen was captivated by Alexander's story. A little person himself, he dreamed of a world where he would be "...accepted for who [he] was, not how tall [he] was or how [he] looked". But I'll stop talking now and let the founder of the first official Star Trek Fan Club and fanzine speak for himself.

Then there is of course the kiss between Kirk and Uhura, which I suppose I must talk about. It's wasn't actually the first interracial kiss on television: A year prior Nancy Sinatra and Sammy Davis, Jr. greeted each other by kissing on a music variety show, and Desilu's own Lucile Ball and Desi Arnaz had of course kissed on *I Love Lucy* long before *Star Trek*. Actually, this wasn't even the first interracial kiss in Star Trek *this season*: William Shatner shared many passionate kisses with French-Vietnamese France Nuyen in "Elaan of Troyius", though "Plato's Stepchildren" was the first of the two to air. This was, however, the kiss that the biggest spectacle was made out of, with lingering closeups of the actors both individually and together, some quite obvious shipper bait dialogue from Uhura and a cut to commercial break just as the two embrace. What's most interesting about this scene to me is firstly that despite the production team's hand-wringing there was practically no negative feedback about it whatsoever, except for one letter from a southern viewer that actually reads more like a joke, which seems sort of astonishing for 1968.

(It is worth briefly mentioning here that part of the reason the Kirk/Uhura kiss got the historical attention it did as opposed to, say, any of the Kirk/Elaan kisses or the Lucy/Desi ones was because it plays on a very United States conception of race and racism, but that's all I'll say about that.)

There also seems to be some debate about how the filming of the kiss actually went down. William Shatner seems to recall that NBC didn't want the actors' lips touching, but Nichelle Nichols says that each and every take was a real kiss. Also apparently at one point or another it was considered to have Spock kiss Uhura, but whether or not that was in the original script is a point of contention. What we do know is that Shatner apparently said of this idea "If anyone's gonna get to kiss Nichelle, it's going to be me, I mean, Captain

Kirk!", which could be seen as an example of his frequently alleged arrogance, but I can totally see this as his way of stressing how important it was that the kiss was between a Caucasian and African human via his signature tongue-in-cheek artificial and intentionally stilted bombast. Furthermore, there was originally going to be two versions of the scene filmed, one where they kissed and one where they didn't, just in case the southern affiliates objected. But Shatner and Nichols, especially Shatner, deliberately and hilariously threw every take of the "no kiss" version so they would have no choice but to go with the kissing one. Regardless of the details though, this scene alone assured that "Plato's Stepchildren" was the most talked about *Star Trek* episode of the year, possibly ever, and Nichelle Nichols recalls the show received more gushing fan mail for this one episode than they did any other. There is simply no denying its impact on pop culture history.

In spite of all this however, there are some things about "Plato's Stepchildren" that simply do not work as well as they could have or should have. There's one noticeably problematic line from Kirk and Spock wherein they denounce the Platonians for betraying Plato's desire for peace, beauty and justice. This seems to contradict the themes the episode is working with everywhere else, and without it this would have been a more then sufficient follow-up on Kirk's comments from "Is There In Truth No Beauty?" about how an appreciation for beauty is one of the last remaining unsavoury things humans in Star Trek retain of their Greek heritage. This would have been especially effective as the world of Star Trek is depicted as otherwise so pleasingly utopian in "Plato's Stepchildren". But there's also the unfortunate fact that it's hard to escape the fact that as much as it wants to critique Plato, Star Trek remains every bit as Western a utopia as the Republic it would condemn. It's hard to avoid the feeling the show is being more than a little hypocritical here.

The biggest issue with this episode though is that it really is basically unwatchable. The scenes where the crew are turned into clowns and puppets by the Platonians are absolutely excruciating. I know they were probably supposed to be, but they go on forever and the camera lingers on them way, *way* too long to the point it starts to feel as sadistic as the Platonians themselves. "Plato's Stepchildren" could have used this to make a similar attack of the voyeuristic spectacle of television that Patrick McGoohan does in *The Prisoner*, or indeed that Gene Coon did in "Bread and Circuses". But the cinematography, direction and editing simply can't pull that trick off here. *Star Trek* once again ends up feeling cheap and comes up short, which it's actually managed to largely avoid for awhile. As it stands, it takes someone of a very strong constitution to sit through this, no matter how many brilliant and landmark ideas it might have.

I don't think I'll ever watch "Plato's Stepchildren" again, but I do now respect it in a way I was never able to before. And the legacy it had on pop culture really doesn't need my approval or analysis.

84. Pearl of Beauty: Wink of an Eye

One of the things that's especially curious about the third season is that in some ways it is arguably the most thematically consistent the Original Series ever was. We've now had several stories dealing quite explicitly with the question of utopia, idealism, Star Trek's Western pedigree and what makes the show ultimately valuable and worth preserving. And then there's that odd flirtation with the mystical, something "Wink of an Eye" doubles down on to a delightful extent.

This episode sees Gene Coon back (at least I'm assuming I can attribute it to him: He didn't write the screenplay but the story is credited to Lee Cronin) and it's sort of chilling how easily he seems to have embraced the magickal head trip the series has gone on recently. What we have here is a story that can be quite easily read as being just as Otherworldly as "The Tholian Web", and takes a unique look at a number of science fiction conventions to boot. First of all we see the *Enterprise* answering a desperate distress signal from the people of a planet called Scalos, but beaming down they find the entire planet devoid of life. Spock and Uhura reason the distress call was prerecorded, but just as the landing party is about to beam back up the redshirt suddenly vanishes into thin air in front of McCoy. back on the ship, random pieces of equipment start malfunctioning and circuits start rerouting themselves. McCoy and Chapel tell Kirk the medical supply cabinet has been broken into and things have been rearranged, and people keep hearing a strange, insect-like buzzing sound. The whole first act then once again brings to mind ghosts, and this time evokes in particular stories of places haunted by poltergeist activity.

But that all changes in the second act when Kirk vanishes too. This time we get to follow things from his point of view, and it turns out that the culprits are in truth the Scalosians themselves, who beamed aboard the *Enterprise* with the landing party and have commandeered it. It turns out that the Scalosians conceive of time differently than other people, and exist in a state of perpetual hyper-accelerated existence. Kirk meets Deela, the Scalosian Queen who makes the interesting declaration that she has chosen Kirk to be her king. Deela says that long ago the Scalosian civilization was wiped out by a series of natural disasters that also sterilized the male population, and they now have to abduct men from other species and bring them into their plane to ensure the survival of their people.

As cheesy as that scenario sounds, I first have to give the show credit for inverting the stock "Mars Needs Women" scenario long before most people realised that was in fact a stock scenario that could be inverted. This perhaps isn't the episode to talk at length about this, but the kind of role reversal we see here brings up the question of the effectiveness of turnabout as a form of social criticism: "Wink of an Eye" doesn't quite manage to shed absolutely all of the disturbing sci-fi rape connotations of this kind of plot, though it's clear Deela would prefer her subjects to know and love her first, which is something of a start I suppose. It is actually possible to do a story about sci-fi reproduction from a female perspective and turn it into something resembling intelligence as there's room there to discuss certain issues regarding female sexuality and femininity, but I doubt this is the kind of thing Star Trek circa 1968 is really cut out to handle, and the fact the show clumsily skirts around the issue here is both predictable and probably ultimately for the best.

What truly salvages what is otherwise a premise that is iffy at best is Deela, who is eminently likeable. This is due largely to her actor, Kathie Browne, who is stupendously good. Browne plays Deela as someone unwaveringly confidant and self-assured, but who also experiences a wide array of human emotion. Deela is consistently both dominant and gentle in a way that makes her utterly believable and utterly sympathetic. For the first time we have a female character who is unquestionably Kirk's equal and who's not played by Diana Muldaur, and "Wink of an Eye" goes a step further: Deela's not just an equal, she's Kirk's counterpart, and commands just as much trust and respect among the Scalosians as he does amongst the crew of the *Enterprise*. One of my favourite scenes is when she coldly and imperiously shoots down the irrationally and violently jealous Rael in Kirk's quarters *both literally and figuratively*, declaring she absolutely has the right to maker her own decisions, live her own life and love whom she wishes and nobody is allowed to take that right away from her. It's a deliciously vindicating scene for the time and Browne knocks it out of the park.

If nothing else, "Wink of an Eye" and its love story is proof positive of how badly wrong "For The World Is Hollow And I Have Touched The Sky" went, because as much as Deela is ultimately another "girl of the week", her one-off romance is something we care about, whereas Natira was just a compilation of gurning scenes. Just like with Muldaur though, as likeable as Browne makes Deela this has the side effect of screwing up the ending rather spectacularly, because now we actually *root* for this romance, if not perhaps for the "Scalos Needs Men" silliness but because Kirk and Deela are so similar and seem to care about each other so deeply. Seeing her beamed down without ever learning Spock and McCoy found a cure for her accelerated state is a kick to the gut.

It's also interesting to note this episode could be argued to handle the folkloric concept of the Changeling better than the actual episode entitled "The Changeling" did. Some sources from Norway do in fact say that fairies and trolls exchange their own offspring with human children because they need new blood for their gene pools, and "Changeling" can refer to the child that was taken as well as the child that was left in its place. It's not too strangled a connection to make to see this as at least roughly comparable with what the Scalosians try to do here: Beings from another plane take someone from ours to live in theirs because of their own reproductive emergencies.

But for the Scalosians' plot to be comparable to Changeling folklore, this would of course mean the Scalosians have to be comparable to fairies, which I think they absolutely are. Starting in act 2, "Wink of an Eye" becomes an almost completely standard-issue reiteration of any number of saga stories from Celtic mythology about warrior heroes who are called upon to travel to another realm compelled by a Woman of the Otherworld. Probably the two most famous are one tale of the hero Cúchulain, who is punished for throwing rocks at seabirds when the birds reveal themselves to be the goddesses Fand and Lí Ban, who whip him and cause him to lay ill for year until he agrees to help Fand in her war against her adversaries, eventually becoming her lover. Another story concerns, perhaps even more similar, is that of Oisín, son of Fionn mac Cumhail, who is asked by the goddess Niamah from Tir na nÓg, "The Land of the Youth", to be her companion. Though he loved Niamah, Oisín grew homesick and asked to return to Ireland after what to him were three years, but what was three hundred years in the outside world. We even see that time passes differently for the Scalosians, just as it does in the Otherworld, and Deela is positively steeped in Fairy Queen imagery, in no small part owing to the fact this seems blatantly how Browne plays her. The only thing that's different is the Scalosians' fixation on reproduction and the fact Kirk is far less willing to take the journey than Cúchulain or Oisín.

Except for one small yet very explicit difference. In the traditional myths, one of the major differences between our world and the Otherworld was the sense of time. Time passed much, much more slowly within the Otherworld than it did in the land of humans: This is why Oisín can return to Ireland after what felt to him like three years, but were in fact three centuries for his compatriots. But, in "Wink of an Eye", it's the opposite: The Scalosians experience time at a much *faster* rate than others because they are *accelerated*. So what we have instead is a very obvious inversion-The hero is taken to a realm where time passes at a faster rate. Why might that be? This seems like an unusual switch to make, considering the Celtic Otherworld is meant to be the Fortunate Isles, or the Land of Eternal Youth or Summer. Doesn't that miss the whole point? Well actually, no, because the Scalosians aren't the fairies. The *Enterprise* crew are. Kirk isn't the hero who finds himself across the sea or within the barrows. Deela is.

Really, who else would they be? "Wink of an Eye" follows up not just on "The Tholian Web", but on "Plato's Stepchildren" as well. This is how you depict a utopian setting. You don't introduce petty conflict amongst the people who live within the utopia, you show how the drama emerges naturally and generatively through the interaction between the utopians and the people who are allowed to visit with them. You demonstrate what a utopian or idealistic approach to problem solving would entail. "Plato's Stepchildren" was really about Alexander: It was the story of how he was able to find his inner strength through peacefully standing up for himself and rejecting oppressive, hegemonic Westernism through being inspired by a better alternative. "Wink of an Eye" is Deela's story: It's about how she discovered a way to cross the boundary into the Otherworld because she needed the help of its people to save her own. The Otherworld has long been the residence of deified ancestors, spiritual guardians and a land of peace, life and happiness. Deela knew this and sought the spirits out for guidance, she just didn't understand that you can't bend them to your own will. That might end up being the tragedy of her character, although the ending, with her mysteriously reappearing on the *Enterprise* viewscreen, may leave enough ambiguity about her fate to posit that she might have found a way back after all.

"Wink of an Eye" isn't a perfect solution, but it's a definite step in the right direction. Other shows, including parts of some future Star Trek, will be able to handle this kind of thing with a lot more nuance and care and strike a balance between internal and external conflicts in a utopian setting. But what "Wink of an Eye" does show is that Star Trek's idealism need not be tied to teleology: This isn't a grand future Westernism is inevitably building towards, it's explicitly a magickal realm that we have to prove ourselves worthy of being allowed to visit. It's a challenge to better ourselves and an invitation for us to dialog about how best to do so.

And that to me is just about the most Star Trek message of them all.

85. "They're dead...They're all dead...": That Which Survives

"That Which Survives" opens promising to be one of the most creative and exciting episodes since "The Alternative Factor", and that it doesn't quite maintain that momentum for the whole of its fifty minutes is almost beside the point. We're still in the curious mystical territory the show's been exploring off and on since "The Tholian Web", and here Kirk even uses the phrase "ghost planet" to describe an astrogeological impossibility: A planet too young to develop life and an atmosphere, yet which clearly has both. As the landing party is about to beam down, the transport sequence is interrupted by a woman who suddenly materializes, imploring them not to go down, killing the transporter chief in the process, like you do. She's too late to stop the landing party, however, but as Kirk tries to contact the *Enterprise* Sulu informs him it's simply not there anymore and that they're stranded. Back on the ship, we learn the *Enterprise* has somehow been instantaneously flung to the other end of the galaxy.

So once again we've stumbled into a region of space where weird and inexplicable things happen. This time though, the closest analog seems not to be pagan mythology but supernatural horror movies: The mystery woman materializes every once in awhile to a specific crewmember, both on the planet and aboard the *Enterprise*. Puzzlingly declaring she is "for" them and that she knows everything about them, she gains their trust enough so she can touch them, at which point she explodes every cell in their body simultaneously. The mystery woman is a slasher villain then, and "That Which Survives" works a bit like an old haunted house movie, where travellers have to seek shelter in a dark and foreboding mansion. But it's also a survival movie, as Kirk, Sulu and McCoy are forced to search for food and water as they're now cut off from the *Enterprise* and are unsure if they'll ever be able to leave. And, in a cruel twist of fate, it seems like the planet they've found themselves on has neither.

However, this is just half the story. "That Which Survives" is split between the landing party and the *Enterprise* at the other end of the galaxy trying to return to where it was. On the *Enterprise*, the episode plays out entirely differently-While the mystery woman still hunts people down, the challenge Spock, Scotty, Uhura and M'Benga face is an entirely different one: This part of the episode is straightforwardly a thriller in the mould of "The Doomsday Machine", albeit with the inspired decision to put Spock at the centre and forcing him to react to everything. The crew soon discovers that in addition to throwing them across the galaxy, the mystery woman has somehow also sabotaged the ship's warp drive. With the warp engines locked and accelerating at a rate beyond Scotty's control and to a speed at which the *Enterprise* wasn't designed to withstand, the crew has fifteen minutes to figure out what's happened and correct it or the entire ship will blow up. Just as before, we get a tense countdown to destruction averted at literally the last second as Scotty risks his life to manually shut off the engines inches away from the reaction itself.

What's also great about this half of the episode is how it manages to build up its own unique sense of internal narrative coherence. Even without Kirk, McCoy and Sulu, the crew left behind on the *Enterprise* has great chemistry, and it almost feels like a mini-show unto itself, which hasn't really been the case on previous occasions where the main cast has been split up. One of the reasons this works is that the guest cast this week is both extremely strong and well handled: It's great to see Doctor M'Benga again, especially as "That Which Survives" is an infinitely preferable story to "A Private Little War", and the way he effortlessly fills McCoy's shoes and narrative function is both a testament to how good this script and how talented Booker Bradshaw is. Lieutenant Rahda, played by Naomi Pollack, who fills in for Sulu, is also very good: Pollack plays her as a competent professional and an equal and the rest of the bridge treats her as such. Even Watkins and D'Amato, who only show up to get killed off, are defined and likeable. The episode goes out of its way to make its one-off characters distinct and memorable, and that in turn allows each half of the episode to move along a lot smoother than they would have otherwise.

This episode then is a deft fusion of thriller, survival and slasher horror tropes all done effortlessly within the framework of an above-average contemporary *Star Trek* story. You may recognise this as suspiciously similar to the show's very first trick way back in "The Man Trap", which was also a genre fusion piece (that time it was science fiction, slasher horror and soap operas) in addition to one or two episodes from last year. This is probably because "That Which Survives" is a collaboration between *Star Trek* veterans John Meredyth Lucas and D.C. Fontana, though Fontana uses her pseudonym Michael Richards here. As one would probably expect, the result is pretty bloody excellent. This may not be either writer's absolute best work and I'm sure it was tampered with in the same way every script this season has been, but even so it's remarkable how intact this one turned out and how just genuinely enjoyable and entertaining it is. Even at this late a stage, Fontana and Lucas are cranking out some of the series' very best material. I could watch about ten more episodes just like this and be perfectly happy.

However, "That Which Survives" is not itself absolutely perfect. As is frustratingly the case with this season, it's a showcase of a lot of really good ideas brought down by really sloppy and ham-fisted production. Certainly it turned out far, far better than something like "The Enterprise Incident" or "Is There In Truth No Beauty?", both of which were episodes that had their fundamental themes torpedoed by micromanagement, but it's still very much a season three story. The biggest issue is that on a number of occasions the characterization and voice of certain crewmembers, much like the *Enterprise* itself after its molecular dissasembly and trans-galactic beaming, feels ever so slightly wrong: Kirk and Spock suffer it the worst, and they both frequently act, for lack of a better word, like assholes. William Shatner at least makes up for it by taking a lot of the edge off of Kirk's worst lines, but Leonard Nimoy is so beyond giving a shit at this point it is as calculable as the amount of light years the *Enterprise* travels. Spock is written as the most smug, obnoxious pedant imaginable and Nimoy makes no attempt to disguise this, playing him just as exasperated, snarky and sarcastic as he himself must have felt. All this is stuff that could have been avoided had, ironically enough, the episode's writers still been working for the show. As script editor, Fontana was very meticulous in preserving the characters' voices from episode to episode, a fastidiousness shared by Lucas, Gene Coon and, of course, Gene Roddenberry.

Also, it's more than a little annoying that the slasher villain is an alien femme fatale, although the episode does manage to sidestep this at the end a bit when it's revealed she's a flawed computer recreation of Losira, the last surviving member of a species wiped out by a deadly plague, created by the automated defense system of her people's last bastion (the planet, which turns out to actually be a space station...or something). Losira was very much *not* a slasher villain, heroically staying behind to maintain the base in case any other survivors happened to find it, until she herself succumbed. Nevertheless, for the majority of the episode we have someone who *looks* like a stereotypical femme fatale going around slaughtering people, which is somewhat less than satisfying.

Ultimately what's the most telling about all of this is that this is a story the show could have done in its sleep a year ago and it's struggling a bit with now. The delightfully unexpected newfound focus on mysticism is new to *Star Trek* in 1968-9, but the rest of "That Which Survives" is very much in keeping with the likes of "The Doomsday Machine" and "The Ultimate Computer". One gets the sense that, just like with those episodes, this is the kind of episode that should, in an ideal world, be an average episode of *Star Trek*. All that's really missing here is D.C. Fontana and Gene Coon's trademark polish and attention to detail. Had it been made in the second season, I'm confidant "That Which Survives" would have been remembered as the minor classic it really is, rather than being declared "camp" and thrown out with the rest of the third season. Perhaps in some parallel universe we got a tighter version of "That Which Survives" that did indeed serve as a quality standard for the third season. But in the reality we live in, it was just one more step in the Original Series' plodding march towards obsolescence.

86. "Between good sense and good taste...": Let That Be Your Last Battlefield

Personally, I've never been drawn to the idea of casually "marathoning" a television show. The idea of spending days locked inside watching every single episode of some TV show sounds to me like some heretofore unknown circle of Dante's Hell. I've never felt the need to be completionist about television because I've always understood the realities of day-to-day, 'round the clock production inevitably mean not every episode is going to be a classic, and I see no need to force myself to sit through obvious misfires in what's supposed to be my downtime.

Now for a project like this I do, of course, have to watch every episode, or at least almost every episode, because the point here is to get a relatively comprehensive understanding of the history and evolution of Star Trek. But if I were to just watch this show casually, I'd have no hesitation to skip over huge swaths of it because frankly the idea of watching "The Paradise Syndrome", "Elaan of Troyius" or "Space Seed" again is the antithesis of entertaining to me. My point being I was long under the perhaps mistaken assumption that other people might have a similar viewpoint to mine here, so whenever I've been asked by someone to introduce them to a show, I almost always give them a truncated episode list of recommendations instead of flopping a twelve-disc DVD box set on their table. I figure if a friend, who presumably shares at least some of my taste and habits, is asking my advice on *Star Trek* they're not likely to find "A Private Little War" any more enjoyable or engaging than I did. So, when several years back my sister wanted to get into the Original Series, of which she had no prior familiarity, I gave her a crash course on the show, and "Let That Be Your Last Battlefield" was the place I suggested she stop.

I hadn't seen the Original Series in quite awhile when I made that list, and were I to do it again today I would have done a number of things differently: I'd have taken one or two episodes out and put a great deal more in (mostly from this season, interestingly enough), so apologies for that if you happen to be reading. I'm not sure if I would still have put the cutoff at this episode, because I have not, as of this writing, seen the last few episodes of the third season, though I at least feel I'd be justified in calling it quits here if I were so inclined (and yes, don't worry, we'll see the old lady all the way through "Turnabout Intruder" to port, no matter how painful it might be). "Let That Be Your Last Battlefield" marks a number of endings and lasts of its own: It's the last really iconic episode of the Original Series, mostly due to Bele and Lokai, though there's something to be said about

394

the art design on "The Cloud Minders", I suppose. It's also the final episode Bob Justman worked on, walking away from the producer position he'd held since "The Cage", and Gene Coon's final story contribution to not just this show, but to all of Star Trek.

I'm going to have a lot more to say about Justman and Coon later on, in particular Coon, as Justman at least gets to come back (along with D.C. Fontana and Dave Gerrold) for the first season of *Star Trek: The Next Generation*. In the meantime, let's talk a bit about the episode at hand. "Let That Be Your Last Battlefield" concerns the interception of a stolen shuttlecraft by the *Enterprise*, in the middle of a mission to deliver a much needed cure for a devastating plague. The shuttlecraft was stolen by an alien named Lokai, who is on the run and seeking political asylum. Moments later, his pursuer, Bele, appears (through an invisible one-way starship that disintegrates as soon as it transports its crew to another location, in one of the most stunningly and painfully cheap sequences in the entire franchise), demanding Kirk turn Lokai over, alleging him to be a mass-murderer who he's been pursuing for fifty thousand years. Both claim to be from Cheron, a planet unknown to the Federation at the opposite end of the galaxy, and are products of a centuries-long programme of institutionalized segregation and oppression of Lokai's people (who are white on the right side) by Bele's people (who are black on the right side).

So a parable about racism then. This seems like a logical and straightforward thing for *Star Trek* to be doing in 1969, although the fans astonishingly seem to disagree with me: Both The A.V. Club and the normally reliable and respectable Mark A. Altman pan this episode for being "too heavy-handed" and "obvious", which just about makes me want to abandon this whole ridiculous endeavour right now and throw myself out of a third-story window. I do concede "Let That Be Your Last Battlefield" has serious problems, however-It's nowhere near as good as I remember it being, but the reasons it falls apart has nothing to do with how "heavy handed" it is. For one, the statement "apartheid and the reconstruction-era Southern United States were very, very bad" (because that's pretty much the society Bele's people built on Cheron) is *not* a claim one should be subtle and restrained about. Not in the United States, not in the late 1960s and frankly, not today. Certainly doing straight allegories of anything, not just institutionalized racism, is almost always a bad idea, because inevitably fiction writers aren't familiar enough with the historical and cultural factors that lead to such deplorable states to make an intelligent observation about them (especially if they're working on a television timetable or for genre fiction), but the larger problem here is that "Let That Be Your Last Battlefield" becomes just about the worst possible story about racism you can think of.

The fundamental problem is that there is simply no way to argue Lokai is in any way in the wrong. This is the most shining and perfect example of false equivalence and the Golden Mean fallacy this side of FOX News. Kirk spends the entire episode making bombastic speeches about how he's in charge of what happens on the *Enterprise*, how the Federation is the authority in this part of the galaxy and how pointless and self destructive hatred is, making him sound the most gratingly macho he has since the first season. In "Let That Be Your Last Battlefield", the *Enterprise* crew goes out of its way to try and stay apolitical and above things, stunned at how much hatred Bele and Lokai have for one another over irrelevant details, as if racial hatred simply springs out of a vacuum. Racism developed on Cheron the exact same way it does on Earth: By one group of people attaining power and lording it over others they personally deem inferior and easy to control. Then, the oppressed developed an altogether rational and predictable loathing of their oppressors, and, determined to take their destiny and dignity into their own hands, strike back. Despite literally everything Spock says in this episode, every single action Lokai takes is perfectly logical, but the episode doesn't want us to side with him. Instead, he's portrayed as a charismatic, populist manipulator who sends people to die in his name for a pointless cause, which is wrong on just about every level I can conceive of, and probably some others I haven't yet.

The one criticism it is possible to level at Lokai is a problematization of his violent tactics. He is a very firm believer in vigilante justice and actively calls for the death of Bele and anyone who sides with him. I, like many radical leftist anarchists, am a bit ambivalent about the concept of violent revolution. I tend to be of the belief systems of oppression come about due to structures of power and how power tempts people to make choices that privilege themselves over others. Likewise however power structures are only sustained by people choosing, ether consciously or unconsciously, to submit to them. Some might feel that this is indeed the proper natural order of things, but I'd wager the vast majority simply are brought up to believe this type of unequal arrangement is simply "the way things are". In the words of several of my estimable colleagues, this is "the banality of evil", as it were. Though there are many willfully evil people, there are also people who do evil not aware that what they're doing is evil, or without the agency to do anything else. Killing these sort of people accomplishes nothing as the underlying system remains unchanged, and Kirk is right to point this out, but "Let That Be Your Last Battlefield" doesn't go anywhere near as far as it needs to in this area: What it needed was a scene encouraging revolutionary voluntary noncompliance as a possible solution to Lokai's problem. Instead, the episode depicts the *Enterprise* crew preferring to remain disconnected and above things and to paper everything over with smug platitudes about "senseless violence".

However, it is vital to keep in mind that this accusation of "unnecessary violence" is one of the most potent and vilest weapons of the hegemony who would wish to shame the oppressed into not fighting back. It's why Malcolm X is a cautionary footnote in the master narrative of history, while Mahatma Ghandi and Martin Luther King, Jr. have been successfully assimilated, appropriated to become milquetoast whitewashed state-sponsored role models in spite of being a Nazi and the victim of quote mining, respectively. "Let That Be Your Last Battlefield" is a prime, egregious example of this phenomenon in action, and as such it's hard to read its impact as being anything other than an evil one.

In an effort to spare Gene Coon, not just because I want to fawn over him at the end of this chapter but because his actual involvement in this episode was minimal at best, this really wasn't his idea. Coon pitched the story that would eventually become this episode back in the first season and while Gene Roddenberry liked it, the network didn't. Fast forward two years, however, and *Star Trek* was nearing the end of its lifespan and out of scripts. Knowing the show was at this point just looking for anything they could dig up and throw out to fill out the last bit of the episode quota, writer Oliver Crawford found Coon's original pitch and built this script around it. Certainly the finished product simply doesn't sound like Coon: Even as recently as "Wink of an Eye" he was demonstrating a far more nuanced conception of utopia and sense of sociopolitical patterns than anything we get here. Even Crawford wasn't responsible for the half-moon cookie aliens, though: Director Jud Taylor suggested that look, and Gene Coon's original pitch mentioned a literal devil pursuing and tormenting a literal angel, which would perhaps have driven home Coon's intended political subtext a wee bit stronger.

And that's as good a segue as any into my farewell to two of Star Trek's greatest foundational figures. Bob Justman was involved with the franchise from literally the very beginning. He and Herb Solow were as important in launching Star Trek as Gene Roddenberry. While Roddenberry came up with ideas and put his name on everything and D.C. Fontana handled the parts of the production to do with scripts and story pitches (getting to a point where she would have to singlehandedly rewrite every submission that crossed her desk) it was Justman who had to bear the brunt of the day-to-day nuts-and-bolts television-making stuff. He was the one who had an eye on the budget and oversaw every single production cast change, being the guy who had to do the dirty work of hiring and firing people. And, of course, he was the only original creative figure to carry through to this season, for which took on the additional duty of co-producer from "Spectre of the Gun" to now, essentially becoming *Star Trek*'s showrunner for the majority of the third season. As I mentioned above, we're not saying goodbye to Justman forever quite yet, but it is a somber feeling knowing the show has devolved to a point where even he has to walk away from it.

We are, however, saying goodbye forever to Gene Coon, who soured on Star Trek so bitterly after "Bread and Circuses" he didn't even want to come back for *Star Trek: The Animated Series* despite D.C. Fontana personally requesting he join her writing staff, thus becoming one of the extremely few creative figures from the Original Series not to make the transition to the sequel show. Coon died not long afterward of lung cancer, which tragically meant he was unable to return for either *Star Trek: The Next Generation* or *Star Trek: Deep Space Nine*. That this, a mediocre and not especially effective pantomime of his most personal themes and ideas (the episode even has Kirk come right out and say he and his crew are the Federation's "best representatives", which couldn't misread Coon any more completely if it tried), is the note on which he has to bow out of the franchise for good has got to be one of the cruelest jokes in the history of television.

What else is there to say about Gene Coon than what I've already said? This is the man who created Starfleet, the Federation, the Klingons and the Prime Directive *and problematized each and every one of them*. This is the man who was consistently arguably the best writer in the entire Original Series, regularly turning out some of the show's most imaginative, creative, challenging and thought provoking stories. This is the man who wrote "Arena", "The Devil in the Dark", "Bread and Circuses" and "A Piece of the Action". It was Coon's tenure as producer that saw scripts from Robert Bloch, Paul Schneider, Harlan Ellison and Dave Gerrold. Coon was the one who *encouraged* Dave Gerrold to submit "The Trouble With Tribbles" and walked with him step-by-step in transforming his original submission into a story that became an instant classic. It was under his tenure that D.C. Fontana became story editor and got "Journey to Babel" made. Gene Coon was the one who got John Meredyth Lucas the job as Coon's own successor, and Lucas' tenure boasts probably the greatest run of classics episodes in the entire series.

Gene Coon is the man William Shatner and Leonard Nimoy emphatically refer to as an unsung hero. Gene Coon was the man who helped make *Star Trek* Star Trek.

Gene Coon gave Star Trek its heart and soul.

87. "All the greatest men are maniacs.": Whom Gods Destroy

"Whom Gods Destroy" is famously bad. It is also famously unapologetically repetitive, reiterating the exact same plot of the first season episode "Dagger of the Mind" down to reusing the same chair prop that was central to that episode's climax. It is also, like the vast majority of third season episodes, riddled with plot holes, logic lapses and inconsistent characterization. In terms of basic narrative structure and coherence, it's once again a mess. "Whom Gods Destroy" seems to be a particular bugbear for Leonard Nimoy, who spent the entire week writing memos and complaints about it to anyone who would listen including, but not limited to, Fred Freiberger and Douglas C. Cramer, the Paramount Studios production executive.

While the laziness and sloppiness are painfully apparent, I'm not especially inclined to tear into them here for a few reasons. One, exasperating as it is, this is not really unusual for this season, and really I'd go so far as to say it's standard operating procedure for the show at this point. Secondly, even if it hadn't been officially stated yet, it's pretty clear *Star Trek*'s time is just about up. We've had our bonus year, and the show has about two months left before it's put to bed for good. It's rather pointless to get too worked up about structural problems now. While it's possible we might get one or two late-stage minor classics along the lines of "Wink of an Eye" or "That Which Survives" in the remaining stories (I have little to no recollection of the next batch of episodes except for the really blatantly obvious ones), the show is for all practical purposes done and we're just killing time before the inevitable sits in. This run of episodes is the word death of the Original Series.

"Whom Gods Destroy" isn't even all that *bad* given the standards of the 1968-1969 year. It manages to on the whole avoid being as incensing as "Elaan of Troyius", "The Paradise Syndrome" and "What Are Little Girls Made Of?", though it does have a few ethical issues of its own. And, while it's not as much of a B-movie pleasure as "Spock's Brain", there are certainly parts that are genuinely entertaining in a way only the most gloriously trashy genre fiction can be. Indeed, though "Whom Gods Destroy" is certainly nowhere near as thought provoking as "The Tholian Web", "Plato's Stepchildren" or "Wink of an Eye", it does actually manage to occasionally drunkenly stumble into one or two genuinely captivating concepts. What we have here is probably Star Trek's first Curate's Egg: It's a disaster, but parts of this disaster are quite excellent.

Let's square away the obvious issue right away. "Whom Gods Destroy" is literally a retelling of "Dagger of the Mind", and a shitty one at that. This time the story follows the almost cartoonishly stereotypical plot of having the inmate running the asylum have a Napoleon complex, on which I'll have more to say a little later. Most catastrophically though, "Whom Gods Destroy" not only removes the single most important theme that made "Dagger of the Mind" the pinnacle of the Gene Roddenberry era, it completely botches and inverts it. The whole point of "Dagger of the Mind" was that the Neural Neutralizer was an absurdly terrible idea: Yes, Doctor Adams is a megalomaniacal crazy guy who's using it to create an army of hypno-zombies, but both Kirk and Helen Noel point out that it's leaving people with false memories and insincere personalities and there was at least an inkling of a critique of the kind of Scientistic normalizing Western society engages in with such wild abandon. Here though, the vaccine the *Enterprise* is delivering is supposed to serve the same purpose as the Neural Neutralizer, mentally reprogramming people who are considered deviant and socially unacceptable to make them "normal" and "healthy" again, and it's portrayed as an unambiguously Good Thing that the ethics of which are never once called into question. It's horrifying.

So it's probably best to avoid trying to read "Whom Gods Destroy" as a challenging and provocative critique of how mental health issues are handled in Western societies. Actually, on a brief tangent this is one of my biggest objections to the way Star Trek has traditionally been read: Each and every episode is typically seen as some highbrow and intelligent work of social commentary, which is dangerous in my view, and this episode is a good example of why. It's actually far easier to read "Whom Gods Destroy" as part of the archaic theatrical tradition of using madness as a metaphor and insane asylums as a setting for satire. It's no more progressive, of course, as it's still horrifically dehumanizing to the people involved, but it's in my opinion ironically less problematic (and significantly less likely to plunge you into hopelessness and despair) to read the story this way than it is to presume the *Star Trek* creative team circa 1969 genuinely endorsed coercive institutionalized mind-wiping for mental health patients.

In this view then while Garth of Izar remains the central character, the key scene is the dinner he throws for Kirk and Spock. Garth is a former Starfleet hero whose military exploits remain required reading at the Academy and who was a personal hero and role model for Kirk during the early part of his career. After an unspecified "accident", Garth decided that the logical cap-off to his illustrious career was launching an unprovoked attack on a peaceful planet of healers as the first front in his bid to become, I kid you not, Emperor of the Universe. As delightfully hilarious as that bit of backstory might be, it also leads to the one true moment of erudition in the entire episode. Garth's argument is that the Federation's policies of pacifism are not only irrational and illogical, but also hypocritical given the military might they wield and their idealizing of him. Garth figures the far more sensible course of action is for him to appoint himself Emperor and use Starfleet to take over the universe, and it's as he outlines his philosophy to Kirk and Spock over dinner that we catch a glimpse of the episode "Whom Gods Destroy" might have been.

What's great about this scene is how Kirk responds to Garth's arguments. Kirk states that Garth's exploits demonstrated that he was a brilliant tactician and military leader, but his is not the kind of leader the Federation needs anymore. The key moment is when Garth appeals to Kirk as a fellow soldier, and Kirk politely responds that while he was a soldier once, he's now an explorer. This is genius, because it's absolutely true: *Star Trek* started out as literally a show about the adventures of the Space Air Force or Space Navy going around dropping tactical moralizing strikes on people and Gene Roddenberry absolutely wrote Kirk (and before him, Pike) as a gruff, manly military hero. But that's not what the show became, and that's not who Kirk really is. The split between Garth and Kirk embodies the split between what Star Trek started out as and what Star Trek wants to be, or perhaps more accurately two different directions Star Trek could go. But the line that absolutely clinches it is Garth's declaration that he too is a great explorer and that he's discovered more new planets than any other captain in history.

Regardless of the truthfulness of this particular account, and I think we're supposed to take it as more of Garth's delusional ramblings, what this line also does is bring back the theme of exploration, and what the purpose and consequences of exploration actually are, that we last saw in "Return to Tomorrow". Recall back then I pointed out one of the problems Star Trek often has to fight against is the Western roots of exploration that are intrinsically linked to colonialist imperialism, in particular the notion of an objective Unknown (which in reality doesn't exist and has never existed). This is in fact built into the whole idea of a "Final Frontier": That last Great Unknown that we heroic Westerners must boldly plunge and expand into as is our inalienable right. But even here in 1969, Star Trek is actually rejecting this: Garth claims to be an explorer, but if he is one he's explicitly an explorer in the colonial sense. The only reason Garth would explore is to find new worlds to conquer and expand his reach into. Meanwhile Kirk seems to explore simply because he enjoys travelling and learning from others: Though he never comes right out and says this, by clearly placing him in opposition to Garth the episode would seem to be granting him this position by default.

Now we can maybe at least *kinda* see why "Whom Gods Destroy" casts Garth as an inmate in a mental asylum. It's trying to say that anyone who holds to the kind of megalomaniacal and imperialist beliefs Garth does must be crazy. This is not an especially effective statement, obviously, largely because the episode unnecessarily weds its anti-imperialist sentiment to a rather staggeringly awful bit of neurotypical normalization, but the basic claim is a solid one and worthy of further development. On a related note, this also adds more nuance to the scene where Garth uses his shapeshifting skills to impersonate Kirk. On the surface this seems like an eye-rolling return to a really tired cliche from the first season (the evil Kirk duplicate), especially as the rest of the episode has an aggravatingly stock pulp structure. But if Garth is supposed to be what Starfleet gone bad looks like, this suddenly becomes more interesting: Despite taking his visage, Garth really isn't in the vein of characters like the android Kirk of "What Are Little Girls Made Of?" or even the roles William Campbell played. Garth isn't a Dark Mirror of Kirk, he's actually more of a Dark Mirror of Star Trek-He embodies not only the concepts of the frontier and manifest destiny, but the dangerous egotism of any one individual (or worldview) declaring themselves absolute ruler...and an ideal to aspire to.

And further, Garth is an incredible character. Steve Ihnat is a truly charismatic and crowd-pleasing presence, delivering a memorably twisted and over-the-top performance that effortlessly (and hilariously) shifts between the character's mania and dementia while just eating everything in sight. It's a masterpiece of late-stage *Star Trek* ham-and-cheese that is consistently and laudably entertaining and is everything "For The World Is Hollow And I Have Touched The Sky" wasn't. In fact, the only thing more enjoyable than Garth is Yvonne Craig's Marta, who is amazing, and manages to actually steal the show from Ihnat. Craig, fresh off her stint as Batgirl on the Adam West *Batman* show, plays Marta as delightfully unhinged and psychotic, literally dancing around the other prisoners with a deliberately exaggerated flair. The scene where she and Garth have an overplayed shouting match of a debate over whether or not Marta actually wrote the complete works of William Shakespeare and her wonderfully medium aware declaration that since Kirk is her lover this means she is obligated to kill him are enjoyably elegant works of comic writing and actually made me laugh out loud. As a matter of fact, I'm going to come right out and say it: Marta blows Batgirl out of the water and is prime evidence that even when it's struggling Star Trek is still capable of outclassing its competition if it plays its cards right.

(Speaking of The Dark Knight, with Frank Gorshin showing up as Bele last week and Yvonne Craig here, it would seem *Star Trek* has made a name for itself a holding room for between-jobs former *Batman* actors.)

I only wish I could say all of this comprised a better episode. As entertaining as all the various elements and ideas in "Whom Gods Destroy" might be, the whole is not greater than the sum of them. The episode torpedoes itself from the beginning with is tired structure, lazy self-plagiarism and unacceptable attitudes towards mental health patients. There is a great episode you could make out of the various disparate elements here, but it's not an episode I think *Star Trek* at this stage of its life was capable of making. Even so though, there's something to be said about the arc the series has taken this year: Just last year *Star Trek* was on the whole a show that wildly swung between the extremes of retrograde garbage and oversignified progressiveness. What we've seen in the third season is a show that largely seems to have its head and heart in the right place, it's just staffed by people who have their hands tied by a number of factors in a number of different directions such that the day-to-day production is kind of spectacularly incompetent. This isn't an *amazing* position to be in (as what's going to happen in eight weeks sort of retroactively proves), but it does seem like evidence *Star Trek* has finally figured out what it wants, and needs, to be.

It's just too bad it's only happening now.

88. "Be not a cancer on the earth": The Mark of Gideon

"The Mark of Gideon" is not one of the original *Star Trek*'s finest hours. But you expected this. It has the makings of a great example of the show's newfound direction, but it ultimately ends up proving the show is just drifting at this point, painfully obviously out of steam.

It tries though, it really, truly does. For an episode very clearly produced solely so the show didn't have to build any new sets, "The Mark of Gideon" does the self-evidently correct story to make with that brief: Having a crewmember be mysteriously transported an eerily empty starship. It's a novel concept, though it would be perhaps more novel if the show hadn't pulled similar tricks in both "The Tholian Web" and "The Doomsday Machine". So novel in fact it's done again in the similarly resource-challenged second season of *Star Trek: The Next Generation* (albeit to a much more effective extent) and one of the most frequently overlooked virtues of the first two seasons of *Star Trek: Deep Space Nine* was it's ability to knock out world-class science fiction on a weekly basis while consistently only using one set.

This time though it's Kirk who, ostensibly on a diplomatic mission to a notoriously reclusive and xenophobic civilization, beams down only to find himself apparently where he started, on the transporter pad of the *Enterprise*. Only now it seems like he's the only one on the ship. To make matters worse, he has a mysterious bruise on his arm and nine minutes of his life, the period of time between when he beamed down and beamed back up again, are a blank to him. Soon though he realises he's not alone when he meets a mysterious woman named Odona who claims to have been abducted from her home planet. Although she doesn't remember much about it, she says it was extremely claustrophobic, and that thousands upon thousands of faces were constantly staring at her from every direction. Meanwhile, we keep cutting to scenes on the very much populated *Enterprise* as Spock, McCoy, Scotty and Uhura try to determine why Kirk has disappeared into thin air and trying to navigate diplomacy talks between Starfleet Command and Gideon, the latter who are clearly hiding and withholding information.

This part of the episode is actually brilliant. There is a palpable sense of mystery surrounding the proceedings, keeping us constantly wondering about whether or not Kirk has been transported to another dimension or perhaps into his ship's own past...or perhaps its future. It slowly builds tension and unease over the course of a full half-hour up until the moment Kirk and Odona look out of the portholes and suddenly see the stars transform into thousands of faces staring back at them, a scene which is genuinely unsettling. Furthermore, just like the subtle Forteanism of "The Tholian Web", the Fairy Myth overtones in "Wink of an Eye" and the supernatural horror of "That Which Survives", the first half of "The Mark of Gideon" is yet another example of Star Trek shifting its approach to science fiction from the pulp and Golden Age tradition to the more fantastic trappings that come to define the genre from here on out, and indeed that the franchise is capable of making this kind of shift at all and living on after *Apollo 11*. The concept of Kirk having a sense of missing time and a mysterious injury he can't explain is straight out of UFO abductee reports, in particular the case of Betty and Barney Hill.

On the night of September 19, 1961 Betty and Barney Hill were driving through New Hampshire on their way back from a vacation (to, funnily enough, Montreal) when they claimed to have sighted a strange object fly across the face of the Moon that seemed to be tracking them. The object, which the Hills described to be a kind of craft, suddenly came down in front of them, at which point they blacked out and swerved into a roadblock. When they woke up, they were thirty-five miles away from where they were when they crashed and two hours seemed to have passed without them retaining any memory of what happened, though their car was inexplicably damaged and Betty's dress had been torn and stained. For weeks afterward, Betty had reoccurring dreams about being led into the craft they saw land by strange beings, who proceeded to conduct medical tests on them in an effort to determine the difference between the Hills and the people in the craft. Seeking medical help and at the urging of the National Investigations Committee On Aerial Phenomena, with whom they had been having regular meetings, the Hills underwent hypnosis sessions, where they both recalled the events of Betty's dreams. A sketch Betty drew based on her memory of a starmap she saw inside the craft has been used by some UFOlogists as evidence the beings who the Hills encountered originated from the Zeta Reticuli star system.

The Hill case was one of the landmark events that helped to shift the pop perception of UFOs. Previous sightings had largely been similar to Kenneth Arnold's, where people would observe mysterious objects appear at random in the sky and then vanish after a time (indeed, this is the most common type of UFO sighting dating back to the beginnings of recorded history). With the Hill case, there was something of an unprecedented confluence of tropes and motifs that would define how the phenomenon was interpreted: There was the the contemporaneous theory that UFOs were spacecraft piloted by extraterrestrials, and now they had a physical appearance and a potential point of origin. Also new to the Hill case however was the possibility these aliens could abduct and experiment upon humans, and the Alien Abduction subgenre of UFO accounts was born.

Now, it's not an enormous stretch to see this as an extension of earlier folklore about visits to Fairy realms inhabit by strange, unpredictable and unreadable entities (in fact Jacques Vallée has made a somewhat significant second career out of historicizing these cultural comparisons), and really, UFOs have always been a somewhat mystical and Fortean mystery. It was just the 1940s and 1950s that linked them to rocket science and astrophysics. The point being *Star Trek* doing a story like this is another great example of the series, and the genre of science fiction, moving away from its roots and expanding its reach by looking a bit more closely at if not the literal supernatural (Gene Roddenberry would never approve after all), at least the roots of this kind of cultural phenomenon and what it might say about the connection between humans and their larger world, which is really the kind of story this show *should* be doing.

Except that's not the story "The Mark of Gideon" ends up actually *being*. In an unbearably maddening and frustrating twist, it's revealed not halfway through the episode that the whole thing is an elabourate psychological experiment by the Gideons to, get this, find a way to curb their out of control population problem brought upon by their virtual immortality by selectively culling random members of the populace with a deadly virus Kirk is a carrier for and that Odona was there so Kirk would fall in love with her and be compelled to stay on Gideon as a living blood bank. And it reveals all of this at about the 35 minute mark, leaving the rest of the episode to spin its wheels pointlessly as Spock, McCoy, Scotty and Uhura get caught up to the rest of us in the most tortuously slow fashion imaginable. There are a great many things wrong with this, so let's take them one at a time. First of all, that twist has got to be one of the biggest, most underwhelming letdowns ever: You don't tease us with Betty and Barney Hill in *Star Trek* and then land us with a clumsy parable about overpopulation. Yeah, the Gideons were probably always going to have to be behind everything, but to really sell this plot they needed to be a *lot* more alien and mysterious. Instead they look like a bunch of bored city councilmen in a beige meeting hall. Zeta Reticulans these guys ain't.

And furthermore, you kind of have to be *really* careful when you do an overpopulation story as so many of them tend to be cloaked in blatantly racist overtones as the argument always seems to be about how those ignorant people in Africa need to stop having so many babies and learn about condoms instead of, you know, the fact the Western world dominates the planet's natural resources and has built its entire cultural history on appropriating and exploiting them to the point they thoroughly wreck the whole ecosystem. Miraculously, "The Mark of Gideon" actually manages to not fuck this up, as the Gideons are not space Africans, but a bunch of Old White Men who go on at length about the holiness of all life, and that everyone is a full person and is sacred even from the moment of conception. The Gideons would rather encourage people to voluntarily commit suicide in the most agonizingly painful way imaginable then practice safe sex. In this regard they're more similar to the fundamentalists in Abrahamic religions who are militantly against contraception and abortion rights, and coming down on people like that is pretty laudably brazen move for 1969 (and it does come down on them hard: Kirk condemns the Gideons, in particular what they would do to Odona, who was the first volunteer, and frequently explicitly implores them to relax their hardline stance on contraception).

"The Mark of Gideon" isn't the worst episode of the year, far from it: There's actually a lot to recommend and, once again, the show seems to have its heart in the right place, and the acting and characterization of the main cast is once again where it's supposed to be. But it's also, yet again, a staggeringly incompetent bit of television. The two halves of this story might as well be two different episodes and the justification for reusing the *Enterprise* set, as good of an idea as it might have been originally, comes across as pretty flimsy in the finished product. A lot of fans complain that this episode doesn't make sense and there are a lot of logical lapses and plot holes, but I actually couldn't pick up on any more than what's sadly become the norm for the show.

No, the big problem with "The Mark of Gideon" is that it shows *Star Trek* stretched so thin it's starting to fray and crack. It's not going to be able to keep this up for much longer.

89. "You're very good-Are you a puppetmaster?": The Lights of Zetar

"The Lights of Zetar" is Ronald D. Moore's least favourite episode of *Star Trek*. Naturally, as part of my apparent mission to disagree with one of the most influential writers in the entire franchise on absolutely everything, I found it thoroughly fascinating. It's not especially *great,* and the usual season three problems submarine it, but it's one of the most enjoyable and provocative episodes, at least in theory, we've seen in awhile. Quality-wise it's at least on par with the last month of scripts.

It even opens on an enchanting note. Kirk's log entry begins

> "Captain's log : stardate 5725.3. The *Enterprise* is *en route* to Memory Alpha. It is a planetoid set up by the Federation as a central library containing the total cultural history and scientific knowledge of all planetary Federation members. With us is specialist Lieutenant Mira Romaine. She is on board to supervise the transfer of newly designed equipment directly from the *Enterprise* to Memory Alpha."

Kirk then goes on to explain how Scotty has fallen in love with Lieutenant Romaine in one of the most poetic bits of dialogue in the entire show:

> "When a man of Scotty's years falls in love, the loneliness of his life is suddenly revealed to him. His whole heart once throbbed only to the ship's engines. He could talk only to the ship. Now he can see nothing but the woman."

I'll forgive that bit about "the woman" for the moment (but don't worry, I'm not going to forget it). And naturally, William Shatner delivers a grand slam of a reading. Unfortunately, this is the most interesting Kirk is in the whole story, and this is a decent microcosm of "The Lights of Zetar"'s problems.

But before we get to that, let's talk about the episode's background a bit. For the first time since Harlan Ellison and "The City on the Edge of Forever" (and arguably Robert Bloch), we have a celebrity writer this week: Shari Lewis, famous for her television puppet shows from the 1950s, 1960s, 1970s and 1990s starring herself and her puppets, the iconic Lamb Chop, Charlie Horse and Hush Puppy. Although the episode is credited first to Jeremy Tarcher (her husband) the overwhelming majority of the episode, at least the basic story, is quite obviously Lewis', and it's her positionality that really clarifies what "The Lights of Zetar" is about. I must confess I did a bit of a double-take when I learned Lewis was behind this script: There are some things that simply cannot cross in my mind, no matter how open I may try to keep it. Lamb Chop and Star Trek are two of those things.

Although upon closer examination, they really do turn out to be a solid match for one another. Firstly, Lewis was an enormous fan of Star Trek, and it was a dream of hers to write for it. And furthermore, though her routine was ostensibly a variety act for children, Lewis always had higher aspirations: She performed for children sadly more often than not because children were the only ones who would watch her. *The Shari Lewis Show* was one of the only major network television shows of its time to star a woman who also had complete creative control and wasn't about how ditzy she was. What Lewis really wanted was to headline her own primetime variety show or sitcom, and between her stints on children's TV she bounced around in bit parts for shows like *The Man From U.N.C.L.E.* and *Car 54, Where Are You?*, desperately hoping to shed her stigmatic typecasting as a children's entertainer. And in 1969 she submitted a script for *Star Trek*.

In a less sexist world, Lewis might have been remembered alongside the likes of Jim Henson, having had all the opportunities and accolades he enjoyed. But I'm really not qualified to do adequate justice to the career and historical significance of a performer like Shari Lewis to the extent she deserves: I vaguely remember her 1990s show, and upon reflection it was pretty shockingly subversive for a PBS show (but then again this was the early 90s where that kind of postmodernism was in vogue, and the same broadcasting service would give us *Wishbone* later in the decade and blow children's television straight out of the water), but Lewis was never someone I had a lot of experience with. I will, however, link you to TV writers Mark Evanierand Ken Levine, both of whom give very heartfelt and deserved tributes to her. It is perhaps fitting then that "The Lights of Zetar" turns out to be a story bungled by network micromanagement and that Shari Lewis wasn't allowed to be as involved with the project as she would have liked.

The plot concerns a mysterious cloud the *Enterprise* encounters on its way to Memory Alpha, comprised of a multitude of shimmering lights. As it overtakes the ship, it has a palpable effect on the physical abilities of every member of the crew, though the effect is different from person to person: Kirk and Uhura are rendered unable to speak, Sulu becomes momentarily blind and Chekov is unable to use his hands. Meanwhile, Mira collapses, after which she begins experiencing wild mood swings and having visions of the future. The cloud eventually reaches Memory Alpha, wiping out the entire crew and burning out the library computer cores such that vast sections of the archive are rendered inaccessible. Eventually, Spock discovers the cloud is actually a colony of non-corporal life forms, and that Mira's brainwave patterns have become an identical match with the colony's resonance readings. In essence, Mira is being possessed. At the climax, as Kirk, Spock, McCoy and Scott work feverishly to expunge the cloud from Mira's mind, the community speaks, revealing itself to be the remnant of Zetar, a planet whose entire civilization was destroyed by natural disaster, but whose collective will and spirit simply refused to die, and they'll happily kill Mira to live the life they feel has been robbed from them.

At first I couldn't figure out where this episode was trying to go. It starts out feeling quite mystical, and the Zetarian community is definitely the sort of weird phenomena the

Enterprise crew has been running into a lot lately (which is perfectly fine by me: After all, aren't they supposed to be Seeking Out New Life And New Civilizations?), but it takes a really long time for everyone to figure out what's going on, it feels padded and the crew spend the majority of the episode fighting with the Zetarians (including blasting them with phaser beams, which also hurts Mira) instead of trying to communicate with them. Furthermore, on a number of occasions it feels uncomfortably like the show is slipping back into its Red Scare anti-groupthink propagandizing that had an annoying tendency to characterize it in the first season: Kirk condemns the Zetarians for forcing their will on Mira and not letting her be her own person.

But, once you know about Shari Lewis, "The Lights of Zetar" becomes a whole lot clearer. Sadly, its weaknesses as much as its strengths. See, the critical detail is that Lewis wanted to play Mira Romaine herself, but she wasn't allowed to. From what I understand, Arthur Singer extensively rewrote her character, which I would not put past him in the slightest, and in the finished episode she certainly comes across as a generic wistful pouty *Star Trek* yeoman archetype, instead of the formidable presence Lewis would most likely have infused her with (there are even numerous reference in the episode to Romaine's strength of character and resolve). But now the episode makes perfect sense: It's overtly about Shari Lewis' own life experiences and sense of creative frustration and marginalization. And yes, that means "The Lights of Zetar" is in fact about Lamb Chop.

The thing about Lewis' ventriloquist act is that she was so expressive and such a dynamic performer her puppets took on a life of their own, and I think more to Lewis than anyone else. I have a feeling Lewis may well have seen Lamb Chop in some sense as her own person, and someone who was both an extension of Lewis herself and someone who held her back. One of Lewis' most frequent routines was to have Lamb Chop complain about not having enough space, or that she wasn't being paid enough as her partner. When her show was canceled in 1963, Lewis apparently went back to her room and cried to Lamb Chop...in private. In the same way Lewis was a children's entertainer because she didn't have any other audience, she was soulmates with Lamb Chop even though the relationship wasn't always healthy because she didn't have anyone else. This is what "The Lights of Zetar" is about then: It's about how characters like Lamb Chop take on a will of their own (recall that the whole reason the Zetarians are still around is that they simply could not accept the fact they were dead and didn't exist anymore), and the writing, performing being has her identity subsumed by the characters she takes on. In Shari Lewis' case, it's about exploring and blurring the line between puppet and puppeteer: The Zetarians are using Mira, in essence, as a puppet.

Furthermore, the way the crew treats Mira is interesting. She finds love in Scotty, but he's also the one who persuades her not to report her visions (which turn out to be critical to understanding the Zetarians' plan) to Kirk and McCoy, dismissing them as first-mission space jitters. Lewis is saying that even people who love us (and by *us* she is most likely talking about *women*) hurt us even if they don't mean to by unfairly dismissing us. Even Chekov and Sulu aren't convinced Scotty knows Mira "has a brain". She irritates McCoy by not cooperating with his examination, which she later regrets (though that might be due to the Zetarians' influence, it's not clear). However, the idealism *Star Trek*'s lovers have previously found in the show is still present too: Spock goes out of his way to compliment Mira's abilities, intelligence and her good fortune in getting assigned to curate Memory Alpha, and while Kirk is initially annoyed by her romance with Scott, he ends up being the one who believes in her the most, demonstrating unwavering confidence that she'll survive her battle with the Zetarians in the decompression chamber even as he has Spock keep cranking up the pressure beyond what should be the limits of human endurance.

But the problem, the really big problem, is that none of this is as clear as it should be and, heart-wrenchingly, I'm not sure how much I can blame on Arthur Singer's usual antics and how much is the fault of Shari Lewis' original submission. Kirk isn't written terribly consistently scene-to-scene and he's too frequently too reminiscent of his gruff, snappy portrayal from the first season. Also, everyone except Scott keeps calling Mira "the girl" instead of by her name, even characters who really ought to know better. I know Lewis probably meant that as a commentary on how underappreciated Mira is and how everyone keeps underestimating her, but there's enough utopian content elsewhere that really wasn't necessary, or at least it didn't need to be that blatant. But the major issue is that the idea of the Zetarians being a metaphor for a writer's characters is not obvious in the slightest. There's a minor bit of dialogue during the conference scene that seems to imply Mira is uniquely susceptible to being contacted this way because her brainwaves I guess match the brainwaves of the Zetarians, but it's really not clear. *This* is the part of the episode that needed to be super overt and it isn't: The Zetarians needed to be firmly established as, if not explicitly her creations, having some kind of special bond with Mira and Mira alone and that simply never happens.

What really kills me is that had Lewis submitted this to *Star Trek* while D.C. Fontana was still story editor, I'm almost positive she would have helped her turn it into an absolute masterpiece. But Arthur Singer, like so many other people who worked with Shari Lewis, simply didn't care and wrote her off, and "The Lights of Zetar" ends up feeling not terrible, but unfinished, and that's almost worse. Furthermore, I wish Fontana had looked at this script, its author, and the potential it hinted at and had immediately snapped up Lewis for *Star Trek: The Animated Series*. She would have been a much, *much* better fit for that show than Margaret Armen. But this is all maybes and neverwheres. Fittingly, if sadly, "The Lights of Zetar" is quintessential Shari Lewis: Overlooked, criminally underrated, and nowhere near close to living up to its own potential.

90. "They live, we sleep.": The Cloud Minders

Well. This, I did not expect.

There are quite possibly no bedfellows stranger than Dave Gerrold, Oliver Crawford and Margaret Armen. Gerrold is at this point still an energetic young *Star Trek* fan and beginning writer, albeit one who, with the help of Gene Coon, penned arguably the single greatest episode of the Original Series. Crawford was an experienced Hollywood screenwriter who miraculously recovered his career after being blacklisted for refusing to disclose names of supposed communist sympathizers, but his only *Star Trek* credits have been co-writing "The Galileo Seven" with Shimon Wincelberg and somewhat misreading Gene Coon in "Let That Be Your Last Battlefield". Armen meanwhile I'm not even going to hesitate in calling the single worst writer in the entire fifty year history of Star Trek, with the two spectacular turkeys that were "The Gamesters of Triskelion" and "The Paradise Syndrome" to her name, and she only gets worse during her upcoming stint on *Star Trek: The Animated Series* and *Star Trek Phase II*: Her last two scripts probably deserve to be labeled some kind of hate crime. The prospect of a story jointly written by all three of these wildly disparate talents frankly does not compute. But hey, we got Shari Lewis and Lamb Chop last week, so stranger things have happened.

Actually, "The Lights of Zetar" is a good point of comparison because like it, "The Cloud Minders" is absolutely a flawed masterpiece, which took me completely by surprise. This one is properly excellent. I mean, it's not perfect-It has some worryingly serious flaws which, although customary for the third season, are still really annoying and keep "The Cloud Minders" from completely going the distance. But there are moments of genuine greatness in this story, and it crackles with an energy and passion the show hasn't seen since John Meredyth Lucas was running the show. This is most likely the part of the episode inherited from Gerrold, who wrote the original story pitch, entitled "Castles in the Sky". Thankfully from my perspective, Gerrold gave a quite lengthy and detailed comment about the differences between his story and the episode that made it to air in his book *The World of Star Trek*, which both gives me ample fodder for discussion and saves me having to summarise the plot:

> "It was intended as a parable between the haves and the have-nots, the haves being the elite who are removed from the realities of everyday life – they live in their floating sky cities. The have-nots were called 'Mannies' (for Manual Laborers) and were forced to live on the surface of the planet where the air was denser, pressure was high, and noxious gases made the conditions generally

411

unlivable. The Mannies torn between two leaders, one a militant, and one a Martin Luther King figure. (Mind you, this was in 1968, shortly after King was assassinated, and just before the assassination of Robert F. Kennedy.)

In my original version, Kirk, Spock, McCoy and Uhura were captured by the Mannies when their shuttlecraft was shot down by a missile. (The *Enterprise* desperately needed dilithium crystals. This planet was one of the Federation's biggest suppliers, and Kirk's concern was to restore the flow of crystals. He didn't care who worked the mines, just that the supply was not interrupted. The shuttlecraft was necessary because I felt that the crystals might be too dense for the transporter.) In the process of the story, Kirk realizes that unless living conditions for the Mannies are improved, the situation can never be stabilized.

Because Uhura has been injured in the shuttlecraft crash, McCoy starts treating her in a Mannie hospital. But he is so appalled at the condition of the other patients there, especially the children suffering from high-pressure disease, that he begins treating them as well. Meanwhile, Kirk and Spock have convinced their captors to let them go up to the sky city and try to negotiate a settlement to the local crisis.

The story focused primarily on the lack of communication between the skymen and the Mannies. Kirk's resolution of the problem was to force the two sides into negotiation. He opened the channels of communication with a phaser in his hand. 'You –sit there! You –sit there! Now, talk!' And that's all he does. He doesn't solve the problem himself, he merely provides the tools whereby the combatants can seek their own solutions, a far more moral procedure.

In the end, as the *Enterprise* breaks orbit, Kirk remarks on this, as if inaugurating the problem-solving procedure is the same as solving the problem. He pats himself on the back and says, 'We've got them talking. It's just a matter of time until they find the right direction.' And McCoy who is standing right next to him, looks at him and says, 'Yes, but how many children will die in the meantime?'

This answer was not a facile one; the viewer was meant to be left as uneasy as Kirk.

– But in the telecast version, the whole problem was caused by Zenite gas in the mines, and 'if we can just get them troglytes to all wear gas masks, then they'll be happy little darkies and they'll pick all the cotton we need...'

Somehow, I think it lost something in the translation."

Gerrold might not have liked the finished product, and he certainly has a right to as "The Cloud Minders" *is* significantly different from "Castles in the Sky" in a number of important respects. However (and acknowledging how uncomfortable it is for me to be in the position of potentially defending Margaret Armen), I think Gerrold is missing some crucial nuances of the final script that not only make it far more progressive and interesting than he grants, but in my opinion actually improves on his original story in some areas.

The first thing is that it was probably a mistake to do this overt an allegory for racism. For one thing it's doubtful to me that NBC would have allowed something this pointed through, especially this year and coming so soon after the hand-wringing over "Plato's Stepchildren" (not to mention the fact NBC had a vested interest in killing *Star Trek* off by this point). Secondly however, the thing about Gerrold is that he's not particularly known for his subtlety when it comes to hot-button political issues. It's not that Gerrold doesn't have his heart in the right place or that the issues he's interested in aren't important and worth being overtly critical about, it's just that he sometimes has trouble wrapping that all up into a functional story and, like a lot of privileged people who write about Big Important Things, he frustratingly frequently doesn't have the broad-scope understanding of sociocultural and historical factors necessary to give the issues the kind of serious overview they deserve. "The Trouble with Tribbles" started as a very overt criticism of introduced species before Coon helped mould it into the masterpiece it became, and this is eventually going to come back to bite Gerrold big time when he tries to Say Something Important about AIDS and "the plight of the gays" on *Star Trek: The Next Generation.*

(Incidentally, the other problem with the kind of brief "Castles in the Sky" was is that this isn't actually the way you go about addressing racism, or sexism or homphobia or any other kind of institutionalized oppression for that matter, in Star Trek, but that's a discussion best saved for another day. Furthermore, Gerrold's original brief commits the same sin "Let That Be Your Last Battlefield" did, by refusing to come right out and support militant activist resistance.)

So we can probably safely assume that without the necessary help (which Gerrold certainly would not have gotten six weeks before *Star Trek* got canceled), it's altogether possible "Castles in the Sky" would have ended up an ethical trainwreck, especially as in the final episode both the Stratosians and the Troglytes are depicted as mixed ethnic societies. But of all the issues "The Cloud Minders" has (and it has a number of them), the fact that it's "heavy-handed" is far from problematic. In fact, it's a virtue: The finished episode is extremely blunt and upfront about what it's saying but, and full credit to Armen or Crawford (almost certainly Crawford) here, what it largely avoids is being *carelessly* heavy-handed. The primary difference between it and Gerrold's original submission is that instead of being a parable about slavery and racial inequality, "The Cloud Minders" is a straightforwardly Marxist criticism of division of labour and the dehumanizing effects of industrial late-stage capitalism on a workforce that is so beaten down and exploited they *may as well* be slaves. And the episode is absolutely brilliant because of that.

In spite of Gerrold's complaint that adding the technobabble explanation about the gas temporarily inhibiting mental faculties removing the episode's sense of social commentary, I find "The Cloud Minders" to be quite explicitly making a very clear point about social justice: The Stratosians are absolutely Western capitalist producers profiting off of an oppressed working class, the Disrupters are absolutely a workers' revolt, and the episode absolutely wants us to side with them. Vanna is unquestionably the episode's hero, and Kirk and Spock become sympathetic to her almost immediately as soon as they learn the truth about the way Ardanan society is structured. Kirk in particular is written on the whole magnificently here: He's willing to go against the direct orders of Starfleet Command and the Stratosian government to ensure the Troglytes receive justice and vindication, as he flat-out refuses to allow the Federation to be complicit in or benefit from their exploitation. And, of course, William Shatner leaps at the opportunity, infusing Kirk with a truly magnetic sense of righteous anger.

Also, the gas plot in my opinion helps the story more than it hurts it. Rather than taking the blame away from Ardanan's exploitative society by giving it a technical explanation, I think it emphasizes how the Troglytes are victims of the social stratification industrialization naturally brings. The Stratosians force them to mine in toxic working conditions that are not only visibly harmful to their health and well-being, but that also deny them access to the education and aesthetic luxuries the ruling class enjoys, thus reinforcing their dependency on the system and keeping them from organising themselves to strike back. In this regard I am inclined to excuse Vanna and the other Troglytes not knowing about the existence of the gas and betraying Kirk in the mines-Keeping the workers uneducated, or just educated enough so they don't ask too many questions, is a key tool of the oppressors who know an ignorant workforce is a complicit workforce (although it would have helped for the Stratosians to know about the gas beforehand). Furthermore, Vanna had absolutely no reason to trust anyone who wasn't a fellow Troglyte, let alone someone like Kirk, who works for Starfleet: An organisation that explicitly enjoys material benefits from its alliance with Stratos, which, along with Ardanan more generally, is a society built on the subjugation of people like Vanna.

That said, this does lead to one of the biggest problem moments in "The Cloud Minders", during the scene where Kirk traps himself and Vanna underground by causing a cave-in, then having Spock beam Plasus to their location. Kirk forces them both to dig to prove the existence of the gas. It's unnecessarily cruel and goes against the heart and soul of the rest of the episode: Not only would it have been significantly less awkward and tone-deaf had that scene been tweaked so Kirk just abducted Plasus to make him see and experience for himself the squalor he forced Vanna and her people to live and work in, it would have made a lot more sense and been far more effective too. There was no need to humiliate Vanna further. I do, however, very much enjoy how Kirk and Plasus quickly and obviously succumb to the gas' effects and try to tear each others' throats out (and Shatner is, predictably, masterful at portraying Kirk's artificially heightened emotional state) while Vanna remains rational, level-headed and cogent.

(This is the big problem with this episode in general in my view: There are an unpleasant number of noticeably crap scenes that weigh down an otherwise terrific story: Another one is the bit earlier on in the guest room where Kirk wrestles Vanna to the bed as she tries to kidnap him, then leans over her while he says he's quite enjoying the whole situation, which is more than a little eye-rolling.)

Speaking of Vanna, she's positively stellar. She's a perfect protagonist for this story and is everything Lokai in "Let That Be Your Last Battlefield" wasn't: She's not a charismatic, populist revolutionary figurehead, she's an angry, brutal and venom-spitting oppressed worker woman who's had enough and is taking her destiny into her own hands no matter what the cost or who stands in her way. She's also a shrewd tactician and confidant, competent leader for her people and unquestionably an equal to Kirk, as the brilliant and mesmerizing Charlene Polite goes out of her way to make her so even when the script doesn't always afford her that opportunity. She's in the league of people like Daras and Diana Muldaur's characters; Simply one of the greatest female characters in the Original Series. And, perhaps most importantly, she wins: Far from what Gerrold says about how the resolution to the gas problem will mean the Troglytes will capitulate and "pick all the cotton we need", Vanna explicitly states that this "is only the beginning" of her demands, and Plasus complains about how now all the Troglytes will be just as "ungrateful" and "uncooperative" as she is, to which both Vanna and Kirk emphatically agree. And, most deliciously, it is Vanna who puts an end to the heated argument between Kirk and Plasus in the denouement, stepping in as the mediating voice of reason.

And although her relationship with Kirk is neither unproblematic (the assault scene is a bridge *way* too far, thank you so bloody much Margaret Armen) nor as overt or meaningful as some of his other dalliances, it does remain an important one. In fact, the way the cast gets divided here is quite intriguing, and it even manages to introduce some welcome minor criticism of *Star Trek*'s own ethics. Spock spends a lot of the episode interacting with Plasus' daughter Droxine, and the two seem to share an obvious mutual attraction. Droxine is very much a pampered aristocrat, and this has allowed her the freedom to pursue academic and artistic interests in a way someone like Vanna would never have had the opportunity to. This is why Droxine and Spock get on so well, as they both very much admire the other's commitment to logic and artistic expression. Spock, the character who so often tries to remain cool and distant and above petty and unhelpful human frailties like "emotion", is a natural fit for Stratos, although, importantly, he is also one of the first to condemn Stratos' oppressive treatment of the Troglytes, and it's telling Droxine does eventually turn against her father after spending time with Spock. IN spite of everything, he is still the first officer of the *Enterprise*.

Kirk, meanwhile, mostly interacts with Vanna and spends a lot of time getting literally down and dirty in the mines. Because of this, "The Cloud Minders" allows us to see a side of Kirk the show hasn't really explored since D.C. Fontana wrote it into "The Ultimate Computer": Kirk is once again the working-class spaceman here, and it's perfectly fitting that he be the one to ally himself with Vanna and take on the Troglytes' cause with her. The split between Spock and Kirk may be somewhat muted in contrast to some of the other motifs the episode works with, but it does very clearly mirror the split between Droxine and Vanna, and it's an indictment of *Star Trek*'s occasional tendency to privilege intellect and intelligence at the expense of equality and material social progress (think back on how many hyper evolved beings of pure thought we've run into, or indeed all those Roddenberry-esque logic vs. emotions debates). And, once again, it's another set of one-off romances I unabashedly champion and really wish weren't one off: Spock and Droxine and Kirk and Vanna are perfect matches for one another.

There are, of course, other problems with "The Cloud Minders", mostly structural ones: It once again feels padded at times (complete with entire dialog exchanges recycled wholesale) and the characterization is once again inconsistent scene to scene, which is really a problem when you're trying to do a story this morally and politically charged. But, sadly, this is sort of the thing you have to expect when you get Margaret Armen to write your teleplay, a writer not exactly known for her exquisite and boundless competence. But this remains the best story she'll ever be associated with by far, and the fact she and Oliver Crawford were able to take a Dave Gerrold brief and not only not totally screw it up but arguably make it a little bit better in some respects really has to be commended.

There are some quibbles to be had with the episode's resolution. While Vanna does win, her victory is less Marxist revolution of the proletariat against the bourgeoisie and more unionizing for workers comp. Which, fine, that's a worthwhile victory in and of itself, but it does little to change the underlying status quo of capitalist oppression. It's still ultimately ends up an endorsement of moderation and compromise, which is what liberalism always sells people to placate them and keep them from real organisation. But in spite of that, "The Cloud Minders" does manage to do a story about oppression without falling into quite the repugnant moral equivalency of "Let That Be Your Last Battlefield" (well, mostly-the scene in the mine is still rather distasteful). It's still the most boldly and brazenly forward-thinking *Star Trek* has been since "Mirror, Mirror" even so. Furthermore, the progressive impulses feel noticeably less restrained and the show seems far more comfortable about its stance here than it has recently, and that makes a huge difference on the overall impact it leaves. And, while it's still burdened by the usual raft of season three problems, I'm confidant enough to call it a highlight of the year, and maybe the entire show. I mean, where else are you going to get Marxism, even Marxism-lite, on primetime television?

I only wish it had come along a little sooner.

91. "...a framework for utopias": The Way to Eden

Well, it's not *quite* as youth-hating as "And The Children Shall Lead". I can at least say that much for it.

Yeah, this one was never going to be any good. You know the routine by now: The *Star Trek* team (or what remains of it) digs up an old story pitch, it gets turned into a teleplay by one or more writers who had nothing to do with the original submission, the original idea having been extensively rewritten beyond the point of recognition in the process and then this becomes the framework for the finished episode we see onscreen. Last time the show got lucky: Oliver Crawford turned Dave Gerrold's submission into something that wasn't quite his original idea, but worked almost as well, if not better in some respects (thanks, surely, in no small part due to it keeping Margaret Armen as far away from anything having to do with gender and race politics as is humanly possible). This week, well...it doesn't.

"The Way to Eden" is loosely (and I mean *extremely* loosely) based on an old D.C. Fontana pitch entitled "Joanna", which would have featured Doctor McCoy's estranged daughter, the titular Joanna, coming aboard the *Enterprise* and beginning a relationship with Kirk, thus creating tension between him and her father. Despite being one of the more famous unused story ideas for the Original Series, I wasn't able to find a lot of information on plot details or anything like that, so I'm actually going to keep Fontana out of the discussion for "The Way to Eden" for the most part (and after all, she did dislike the finished episode enough to request credit under her pseudonym). Supposedly Joanna was the character who eventually became Chekov's love interest Irina Galliulin, but if she were indeed going to be one of the Space Hippies, my guess is that it probably would have played out a lot like "Journey to Babel" where the plot is largely a basic skeleton upon which to frame a character piece (which in this case would have been about McCoy's relationship with Joanna and Kirk) and it wouldn't have gone any further than that. And anyway, unlike Gene Coon, D.C. Fontana's thankfully not going anywhere anytime soon so we'll have plenty more opportunities to talk about her. This isn't her final bow in Star Trek, this is, for at least us, the point where it becomes clear who the next showrunner is going to be.

So let's talk about Space Hippies instead. "The Way to Eden" concerns a group of free-spirited youths who have formed a movement built around peace, brotherhood and an aggressive rejection of modern technology and political structures in favour of a return to an idealized pastoral lifestyle. The youths think that they are destined to travel to the mythical planet Eden, supposedly a tranquil unspoiled paradise where they can live out their lives free of technology and on their own terms. Inconveniently for pretty much everyone, the travellers believe Eden resides in Romulan space. Furthermore, things get more complicated when their leader Doctor Sevrin is revealed to be a dangerously insane manipulator carrying a disease similar to antibiotic resistant super-bacteria: He blames modern society for infecting him, and believes those who reside on Eden will be able to cure him, and he doesn't care who he has to use to get there.

The Space Hippies are pretty much everyone's objection to "The Way to Eden" and it's really not difficult to see why. They're dressed to the nines in positively ridiculous outfits that look like parodies of Hippie clothes, spend half the episode singing intolerably bad imitation folk music and, just like in "And The Children Shall Lead", speak in strange, unfamiliar slang and have weird rituals and habits meant to unnerve decent, respectable, law-abiding grownups like us. But there's a significant difference between "The Way to Eden" and the last time *Star Trek* ham-fistedly tried to talk about "the kids these days": While the *Enterprise* crew is famously unkind to the Space Hippies at first, deriding them by calling them grown adults who act like spoiled, irresponsible children (Scotty's especially bad: I'm surprised he wasn't literally yelling at the damn kids to get off his lawn), by the end of the episode they're all, with the exception of Sevrin, portrayed as innocent (if sometimes misguided), kindhearted people who ought to be respected for making their own decisions about how they want to live their lives.

What this touches on, and with surprisingly more nuance and sophistication than I actually expected of *Star Trek* in 1969, is the oftentimes complex and troubled relationship between the Hippie movement and the larger counterculture of the 1950s and 1960s. Despite becoming the iconic and ubiquitous symbols of 1960s youth thanks to major events like Woodstock and their memorable fashion sense making them easy targets for pop culture references and pastiches, it's very important to keep in mind that the Hippies did not comprise the entire scope of the revolutionary zeitgeist of the mid-20th century. Long before them, there were the Beats, the Mods, the Situationist Marxists and psychedelic street performance artists. The Hippies were but one branch, and a particularly United States branch to boot, being in truth a movement actually based primarily on syncretism so careless is wanders into cultural appropriation: The Hippies picked and chose assorted bits and pieces from the Beats, the Mods and the Psychedelics and blended them through their own perspective with a rather populist and facile interpretation of Buddhist philosophy, crafting a unique, and uniquely United States, kind of movement.

Furthermore, the Hippies were very much middle class in a way the previous and contemporary countercultural movements really never were. The major nerve centres of the Hippie movement were big Southern Californian universities known for military industrial complex supported technoscience research, like Berkeley, Caltech and Stanford (it's worth noting here the overlap with the sources of the protests that were showcased in the news media during the Save Star Trek! campaign). Indeed, the Hippie movement is intrinsically linked to the origins of the personal computer and modern computer science, a field and industry pioneered in those selfsame institutions. Now, look at who comprises our Space Hippies in "The Way to Eden": Starfleet Academy dropouts, the son of an ambassador, a disgraced physician and several scientific specialists. In other words, all people who come from largely academic, and largely privileged, backgrounds. These are certainly not Vanna's expressly oppressed working class Disrupters from "The Cloud Minders".

Perhaps then the Space Hippies were never meant to stand in for the actual radical youth, or if they were, they were intended as a comment on the dangerous tendency for real-world Hippies to develop a somewhat blinkered worldview. This would mean Doctor Sevrin also comes across far better as an antagonist: Unlike the generically evil Other of the Friendly Angel from "And The Children Shall Lead", Sevrin is an unscrupulous person who is co-opting and using an otherwise well-meaning and harmless group of people. Just like in the real world, the good intentions of the youth can be manipulated for evil ends, such as to support a politician who outwardly courts them, but who is in truth just another establishment figure who will betray their trust as soon as his populism gets him elected. Or, for that matter, the Hippies' own deal with the devil that was the military industrial complex.

In this regard Spock is the character most worth paying attention to. He's the most sympathetic to the Space Hippies' plight (though he calls it "curiosity") as they, like him, feel like aliens in their own world. He understands their culture and language and tries to persuade them that Sevrin is delusional and doesn't really have their guiding principles in mind. Furthermore, he tries to show them how modern technology has made some developments worth holding on to and that it's pointless, counterproductive and even dangerous to reject everything simply because it's modern (actually, I think this part of the episode may resonate stronger today than it did in 1969: The behaviour of Sevrin and Adam in particular reminds me very much of the claims made by nervous and reactionary groups such as anti-vaccine advocates).

That Spock is the person to mediate in this way is actually critical, and it takes a lot of the edge off of the episode's numerous problems. It's important to remember here that, at the time, Spock was still very much seen as a countercultural figure: He was a pop culture icon respected and admired by real-life utopian idealists and was someone a lot of young people could relate to. He wasn't yet the Star Trek brand's mascot known only for the hand salute and saying "fascinating" all the time. To have Spock very overtly ally himself with the Space Hippies and stress on several occasions that while what Sevrin is doing is wrong, what his followers seek absolutely isn't is a very powerful statement, or at least an admirable attempt at one. And it's Spock, not Chekov, who gets to say the final goodbye to Irina at the end once Sevrin is defeated, delivering this gem of a line:

> "It is my sincere wish that you do not give up your search for Eden. I have no doubt but that you will find it, or make it yourselves."

This line is lovely because it has Spock come right out and state the single most important thing about utopianism, which is that a utopia really means the freedom for each individual and network of individuals to make their own utopia. The *Enterprise* might be a utopia, but it's not the utopia Irina and her friends want, and it shows great maturity on the part of both parties to accept that.

But I have to end with the inevitable and obvious. "The Way to Eden" doesn't work. It doesn't come close to working. Sevrin, for one, is still awful-Once again, he's emblematic of *Star Trek* normalizing the stigma attached to mental health issues. Furthermore, while there are definite hints at a great Star Trek story about the youth and utopianism here and while Spock's actions certainly count for a lot, most of the time the way the episode treats the Space Hippies feels like outright bullying. From their idiotic costumes and music to their incessant gullibility, it just comes across as mean-spirited. In addition, every member of the crew should have been as understanding as Spock, if not right away without question by the end, and the episode never quite gives us that resolution. Kirk sort of gets there and makes a lighthearted joke in the denouement that seems like it's meant to give the Space Hippies his approval, but it doesn't really take.

And Kirk's not the only one-Chekov's behaviour in particular is inexcusable: "The Way to Eden" paints him as almost as programmatically dogmatic as Tamara Jagellovsk from *Raumpatrouille Orion* (and any time he's onscreen together with Irina the episode becomes an excruciating showcase of the most unwatchably terrible and embarrassing fake Russian accents ever put to film). It's one more example of the character's laughably wasted potential. And finally, while there is fodder here for an intriguing and even-handed critique of the Hippie movement, the episode simply doesn't go anywhere with it. What it really needed was for a character like Vanna to come in and call them out on their self-righteous privilege.

But ultimately it's tough to get too worked up about it, because "The Way to Eden" came along far too late to do any lasting damage to the series, or to give it any help either, for that matter.

92. "If I've lived a thousand times before": Requiem for Methuselah

"Requiem for Methuselah" is an episode I feel like I should probably like a whole lot more than I did. It's got a knowingly overreaching central premise, sublimely poetic dialog, and strong, moving acting. Furthermore, it also has that signature hallmark of the very best budget-starved speculative fiction TV around: The main characters sitting around in a room debating philosophy with the guest stars. Somewhere in here is a tragic story about human frailty and the human condition: In some ways it does 1970s Gene Roddenberry better than Gene Roddenberry. It's also Jerome Bixby's final Star Trek contribution, and, judging by his later work, a story that meant a great deal to him.

And here I am trying to figure out what to say about it.

I guess a plot summary is in order. After an outbreak of lethal Rigellian flu renders the *Enterprise* a literal plague ship, Kirk, Spock and McCoy beam down to a planet on an emergency mission to acquire a sample of a rare element from which McCoy can derive an antidote. If they don't return to the ship in two hours, everyone aboard will perish. On the planet they meet a mysterious man named Flint, who claims to have fled Earth to escape it's neverending barbarism and conflict. After a "test of strength", Flint offers to have his robot servant collect the ore McCoy needs to craft the vaccine, and invites the landing party to his house, a sprawling mansion lavishly adorned with an impossible array of collectibles, including a first edition Gutenberg Bible, first drafts of William Shakespeare's plays and what appear to be brand new, authentic works by Brahms and Leonardo da Vinci. But his biggest surprise is his adopted daughter Rayna, whom Flint claims is educated in centuries of art, music and science...and who immediately captures Kirk's heart.

The first half of the episode seems to halfheartedly play with doing another critique of *Star Trek*'s claim to utopia, having Flint debate with Kirk, Spock and McCoy about how and by what standards humans consider themselves advanced, but this largely takes a backseat to the primary sci-fi mystery: Who Flint is, why he behaves so erratically and what his sudden interest in the *Enterprise* crew is. The problem is the mystery is painfully easy to guess, and this is clear to everyone except the actual characters from about ten minutes into the runtime. I'm just going to go ahead and spoil "Requiem for Methuselah"'s big trump card right now, because it's pretty much the script's only actual idea and the fact it holds it to the climax makes the whole episode feel tortuously padded: The reason Flint is able to amass such a collection and has the money for his enormous compound (and so apparently we've decided money does exist in the world of the Original Series then?) is that he literally is Brahms and da Vinci, as well as Alexander the Great, Lazarus and

421

Methuselah, as well as a whole host of other major historical figures. He was born immortal at the dawn of modern human civilization in Mesopotamia (naturally, because that's where Westerners think everything great about humanity came from) and has spent his endless life mastering every skill and amassing all the knowledge he can in an attempt to live as the ultimate human. His only failing is his endless loneliness, as he's watched all his friends and lovers die as human history inevitably moves onward without him. He created Rayna, an android, in an effort to create a perfect mate for himself who could share his immortality.

I will grant the episode this: The actors playing Flint and Rayna, James Daly and Louise Sorel, respectively, are total class acts and deliver some of the best performances of the year. Daly completely sells Flint's loneliness, detachment and crushing sadness, working wonders with Bixby's somber, piquant and elegiac dialogue. Sorel was a theatre actor and it shows, and her facial expressions alone convey the almost-humanity of the android Rayna's confusion, torn between her love for both Kirk and Flint and the slow dawning of her individual identity that her programming is ultimately unable to handle. And the final few scenes are an absolute triumph: Sorel has Rayna collapse at the conflicting emotions she feels, and Daly, along with William Shatner, Leonard Nimoy and DeForest Kelley act their hearts out mourning her loss. Shatner and Kelley in particular: Shatner absolutely sells Kirk devastated at not only the loss of his dream woman, but at how poor examples he felt he and Flint made of humanity as they were reduced to jealous violence. Kelley has McCoy pity not Kirk, but Spock, who he feels will never be able to understand what love is and what it can drive people to do. Meanwhile we know Spock understands, not just because we know Spock very well by now, but because it is he who takes the time to comfort and support the grieving Kirk.

("Forget" is a line I'm far more ambivalent about now then I was when I first wrote this, however.)

The downside of this is that this makes the script feel even thinner. Firstly, it's basically impossible to buy how Rayna is somehow different from the approximately one billion other one-off romances Kirk's had over the course of the series such that her loss elicits this distraught a reaction from him. Secondly though, Sorel is such gangbusters at portraying an android trying to comprehend what it means to be human that I would have guessed that plot twist even if I didn't already have prior familiarity with this episode and wasn't made suspicious by the title "Requiem for Methuselah" which essentially gives the whole thing away before the first act. Which would be fine had the episode been about, say, Flint challenging Kirk to prove how far humans had truly come. The *Enterprise* is now up against the literal sum-total of human history: That's a lightning-strike brief if I've ever seen one. The story should have been about Kirk and McCoy trying to convince Flint they've truly left their past excesses behind and deserve to be called a utopia as Spock mediates. But instead, "Requiem for Methuselah" fervently keeps its cards close to its chest and tries to hide from us what we already obviously know, much as Flint tries to hide his own actions from Kirk.

Also, the thing about the "immortal man who lives through history" idea is that it's just that: An idea. It's a fun science fiction concept that seems like something you could

422

get a little mileage out of, but that's pretty much *all* it is. Perhaps this gets at the difference between the kind of science fiction I tend to enjoy and the kind Bixby maybe enjoyed writing: I like sci-fi when it's being used to explore themes that, while you could perhaps do them in contemporary period drama, would be very difficult to convey genuinely effectively. A good example of this would be "The Cloud Minders", a critique of division of labour that, because it's set in the future on a faraway planet, avoids the problems typically associated with, say, historical fiction. Another good example would be, naturally, "Balance of Terror", which in my view works significantly better on *Star Trek* than it did as a World War II movie called *The Enemy Below* filmed a decade after World War II ended.

Another thing I like science fiction for, and in particular Star Trek, is its ability to talk frankly about enlightenment and borderline Fortean and spiritual concepts which are only acceptable to the majority of audiences if they're presented in this kind of context. We have in fact already seen the Original Series do this on a number of occasions just this season alone. Eventually, both *Star Trek: The Next Generation* and *Star Trek: Deep Space Nine* are going to perfect how to explore everyday human experience and show how both the mundane and gritty materialism of human social organisation and our omnipresent mystical, yet tangible, connection to the larger cosmos are equally fundamental aspects of what it means to be a living thing. An idea about an immortal man who becomes various historical figures simply because he's immortal is none of these things: It's an almost Golden Age throwback that's more interested in the tautological cleverness of the concept itself than actually doing anything with it, and Star Trek has already demonstrated that it's by-and-large rubbish at pure Golden Age science fiction.

That's not even getting into the troublingly Western-centric way Bixby handle's Flint's immortality. Although he claims to have been just about every major thinker in human history, Flint curiously only name-checks Western intellectuals and his ideal woman is almost Hellenistic (indeed, he claims to have once been Alexander). There's not a single work in Flint's mansion compound that isn't from somewhere in central Europe or the United Kingdom, and he puts the place of his birth, and that of human civilization, in Mesopotamia of all places. Flint is about as Western as is possible to get, down to him essentially being the Big Man theory of history on steroids.

For those unfamiliar with the concept, the Big Man theory is essentially the history they teach in textbooks: Every once in awhile a Unique Genius comes along and singlehandedly changes the course of history pretty much in a vacuum. The Great Man is depicted as coming up with all his historical contributions largely by willing them into existence from nothing, much like a patriarchal Godlike Creator, such as Zeus or the Abrahamic God. He doesn't have any influences, inspirations, muses, contemporaries or cultural context, he's just a Uniquely Gifted Genius who happens to come along just in time to shift the tide of human evolution. Flint is this guy (who is fictional and has never existed) taken to the extreme-Literally One Man responsible for every single notable development and breakthrough in all of history, and naturally, he's an Old White Dude.

I suppose the other thing worth mentioning is that this is Jerome Bixby's last contribution to Star Trek and apparently the story he considered his masterpiece, which I guess says more about Bixby than I could. He was working on a film script with a functionally identical premise about an immortal man who lives through all of human history off an on throughout his career, and he finally completed on his deathbed. This script eventually became the movie *The Man from Earth,* produced by his family members and released in 2007, which is famous largely for being one of the first movies to achieve the majority of its acclaim thanks to its acquiring a cult following through being shared via BitTorrent sites, increasing its notoriety more than it would have had its creators stuck to traditional methods of distribution and publicity. The biggest difference between "Requiem for Methuselah" and *The Man from Earth* is that the newer story is set in the present day, there's no Rayna and its entire runtime is devoted to the immortal man telling his story to his latest group of friends acquaintances, along with the revelation that he is also Jesus, a title he gained while trying to spread his Buddhist beliefs to the ancient middle east, which is perhaps a slightly more provocative way of exploring this concept.

So what have in essence here is a rough draft. The existence of *The Man from Earth* alone proves this idea had potential, I guess, but "Requiem for Methuselah" perhaps proves Star Trek was not the venue for Bixby to fully realise his vision. And that I guess is as fitting a farewell to Jerome Bixby as any, a talented and respected voice in science fiction who seemed more often than not to require a little help to get his ideas to work in the world of Star Trek.

Star Trek is an incredibly hard story tapestry to work with, a fact even its originators often had to come face-to-face with.

93. "History prefers legends to men.": The Savage Curtain

"The Savage Curtain" marks the return of Gene Roddenberry to Star Trek as an actual creative figure for the first time since "The Omega Glory", and it's apparent pretty much right from the start. The whole teaser is made up of unrefined methodology porn, as the bridge crew mulls over conflicting sensor reports from the planet Excalbia, which the script attempts to convey by having Kirk, Spock, Sulu and Uhura shout random bits of starship operations procedure. Almost the entire first half plays out similarly-I feel like I'm watching "The Cage" all over again. Roddenberry genuinely seems to think it's a good idea to devote lengthy chunks of his script to having his characters robotically quote regulations and jargon. This isn't even technobabble, this is Roddenberry reveling in his show's cod-military structure and pedigree. This isn't writing, this is feeding an academy cadet training manual into a paper shredder placed over a bin full of old *Star Trek* scripts. We're not even five minutes in and this is already the worst the show has been in months.

And then suddenly Flying Space Abraham Lincoln.

That's not an exaggeration. Out of nowhere, a bad transition fade appears on the viewscreen, spiraling around and around before materializing into full-on Abraham Lincoln, sitting on the Lincoln Memorial to boot like it was Wan Hu's mythical Rocket Chair, except powered by very poor 1960s visual effects. Flying Space Abraham Lincoln. And look, I'm not one to ridicule weird and quirky ideas, especially in a speculative fiction show ostensibly designed expressly for the purpose of exploring them. I'm really not. Nor am I one to make fun of outdated VFX technology, especially on a show that's been starved for funding all year. Honest. But come on. Flying Space Abraham Lincoln. You look at him and just laugh. There's no way *not* to, and even though over the course of the past five years on this show we've seen Alien Neanderthal Bigfoot, Actual Lizardmen, sentient lumps of silicon, animate balls of fluff, Poisonous Snow White Monkey Unicorns, a Giant Space Amoeba, Space Spriggans, Half Moon Cookie Aliens and a community of energy beings powered by Lamb Chop and Charlie Horse, *I'm pretty much going to have to draw my line at Flying Space Abraham Lincoln.*

Especially when he's used to tell a painfully damp squib of a story. It turns out that Flying Space Abraham Lincoln has been either resurrected or conjured up out of Kirk's thoughts (it's not clear which), along with Surak, the founder of modern Vulcan philosophy, to side with Kirk and Spock in a deathmatch against history's greatest villains, namely Genghis Khan, Kahless (the founder of Klingon society) and dictators Zora of Tiburon and Colonel Green (and yes, Genghis Khan and Kahless are made of concentrated racism. Did you

425

have to ask?). None of these other characters, it should be noted, seemed to feel the need to make their presence known to the *Enterprise* by flying through space on rocket chairs. The Excalbians, sentient piles of magma and rubble that are far and away the most sensible things in this episode, have no conception of good and evil and figure the most reasonable and effective way to learn why humans hold to such principles is to stage an all-star wrestling match the likes of which are known only in the most storied of ten-year-old boys' Trapper Keeper doodles and see who wins. The remainder of the episode after the halfway mark mostly consists of one big extended (and badly choreographed) fight scene interspersed with strangled and unnecessarily detailed exposition about why the *Enterprise* can't simply beam everyone back.

It's at this point the analysis sort of writes itself. "The Savage Curtain" is once again quintessential Gene Roddenberry, and every single of one his litany of writerly flaws is perfectly clearly on display. This episode, in fact, reads if nothing else like a fiery declaration from Roddenberry to Arthur Singer and Fred Freiberger that nobody is allowed to fail at his show harder than he does. He's naive enough to think "good versus evil" (where, I hasten to add, the participants are quite literally Objectively Good and Objectively Evil-They may as well be wearing white hats and black hats. So Roddenberry has a ten-year-old-boy's conception of morality in addition to a ten-year-old-boy's conception of storytelling structure) is a deep and profound statement and self-absorbed enough to scream about this to us at every possible opportunity and drag the episode's pacing out to such a degree it should legally be reclassified the Self-Transcendence 3100 mile. Then there's the fawning, ahistorical hero worship Kirk (and the script) exhibits towards Flying Space Abraham Lincoln, making "The Savage Curtain" almost as insufferably jingoistic as "The Omega Glory". I'm not even going to waste time going into the rest of this episode's simpering, pretentious, provincial, facile moralizing: If you want an overview of Gene Roddenberry's motifs read literally anything else I've ever written about him.

OH WAIT YES I AM. The literal black-hat, literal white-hat combatants are also *literally black and white, with the good guys all being visibly European and all the bad guys all being visibly Shiftysani.*

This episode does add one significant twist to the traditional Roddenberry formula inasmuch as it occasionally flirts openly with utopian idealism in a way he hasn't really done before now, which is fitting for a third season submission. Regardless of whether or not you think Star Trek inherits the lion's share of its utopianism from Roddenberry, and I think there's at least some room for debate on that matter, the previous scripts that were largely or entirely his work didn't actually focus on this aspect of the show all that much, perhaps excepting "Assignment: Earth". Roddenberry supposedly extensively rewrote all of the twelve scripts produced under his tenure as sole showrunner back in the first season, but none of those stories were really about the idealism of the world of Star Trek either-They were all largely one-off and incredibly simplistic morality plays. In fact the only real bit of proper utopianism I can recall from the first season at all is Kirk's comment to Stiles in "Balance of Terror" about "leaving any bigotry in your quarters" because "there's no room for it on the bridge", and in regards to Roddenberry all that hedges on whether that line was his or Paul Schneider's.

That aside, the show was only "idealistic" under Roddenberry because the primary creative figure blatantly used the main characters as mouthpieces for his own ideas and moral code, not because the show on the whole was actually demonstrating what a utopian society might look like (the other major selling point being the diverse cast, which from what I gather was at least in part NBC's idea). The setting was straightforwardly the United States Navy in Space and was only there to move the plot from one place to another: I'm not convinced even Roddenberry thought the Navy was an ideal model for progressive societies. Gene Coon and D.C. Fontana changed that, and, under them, the show started to be more about exploring the concept of idealism in a setting such as *Star Trek*'s, and after that breakthrough it seems Roddenberry started to be more open about explicitly talking about his perception of idealism, as both "Assignment: Earth", and to a lesser extent this episode, demonstrate. It's possible Roddenberry is starting to learn from his show's fans here, but it'll be a long time before he's ever capable of putting those lessons into practice, if indeed he ever does.

Regardless, the idealism on display in "The Savage Curtain" is quite revealing, *especially* Kirk's abject reverence towards Flying Space Abraham Lincoln. Roddenberry seems to think that heroic presidents are the model we should aspire to because of their strong and benevolent leadership skills. Incidentally, this is also the only way I can explain why the *Enterprise*, supposedly a *United Space Ship* from the multicultural United Federation of Planets, has actual procedures in place to welcome visiting presidents from the ancient history of a now-defunct nation-state (which, of course, we need to have explained to us in meticulous detail). And naturally, Flying Space Abraham Lincoln acts nothing like the actual multifaceted historical figure: He's a caricature who speaks entirely in inspirational soundbites.

The big problem with Flying Space Abraham Lincoln, aside from absolutely everything else about him, becomes evident in the scene on the bridge when he meets Uhura and apologises for calling her a "Negress", as he's just now starting to come to terms with how much more advanced human society is now then in his time. First of all, the real Lincoln's attitude to the Emancipation Proclamation was significantly more complicated than simply him Doing The Right Thing, and deifying him for that is a literally textbook case of the Big Man model of history that effaces the contributions of of the actual former slaves who fought an underground war to wrestle their freedom away from the southern slavemasters for years themselves instead of waiting for politicians to give them concessions, as well as the unpleasant reality the whole thing was by and large a series of calculated political machinations to make Washington look good.

Furthermore, the crew's reaction to Flying Space Abraham Lincoln's comment is abhorrent: They claim that our advanced, evolved society has learned words are meaningless and, *in Uhura's own words* "to be delighted with what we are". No, Mr. Roddenberry, actual progressive societies do *not* acknowledge that words are meaningless and that we should always "be delighted with what we are". Actually, the complete opposite of that: They recognise that words have *power* and have centuries of meaning and connotations associated with them and know that understanding this is the key to helping craft a language and discourse where nobody is made to feel silenced, alienated, dismissed or less than human. And furthermore, they realise that nobody is required "to be delighted with what [they] are" because people have the right to feel however they wish about themselves and their bodies, especially if they belong to a group or groups historically made to feel that their bodies are objects of public scrutiny and critique. *Not* doing that is how you end up with Actual Nazis on a supposedly progressive utopian science fiction show.

There's Surak too, and while his wandering philosopher archetype is very different from the patrician leadership of Flying Space Abraham Lincoln, that reveals another troubling aspect of Roddenberry's approach. For the first time in quite awhile, the Vulcans are used here to explicitly tout the superiority of pure, untainted logic as a lifestyle, and nobody once calls this into question. Surak's logic is shown to be inherently pacifistic and objectively good, and Spock's flush of emotions at seeing him on Excalbia is portrayed as a failing on his part. Leonard Nimoy and D.C. Fontana have spent over two years showing how Spock is a complex character grappling with notions of identity, faith and belonging and this feels like a giant leap backwards. Furthermore, combined with the fetishistic fixation on protocol in the first half of the episode, it comes across like Roddenberry is once again claiming we should all be some kind of idealized detached and emotionless "rational actors".

And Surak has other major problems of his own. Roddenberry associates Surak's logic with enlightened pacifism, which results in the character's behaviour not actually making a whit of sense. Surak flatly refuses to harm another person, so he goes alone to Team Evil to broker peace and a cease-fire. Naturally, he's tricked, betrayed and murdered, because Evil People are Evil and only ever do Evil Things. This has the handy side-effect of either making Surak look stupidly naive and gullible or returning to the old Roddenberry theme that violence, selfishness and an instinct to murder are all inherent aspects of the human condition and that only two-fisted diplomacy ever gets things done. Neither possibility exactly fills my heart with gladness. Annoyingly, there was the potential to do an actually legitimate criticism of pure pacifism here: Claims that, for example, purely pacifist movements are inherently more successful and more righteous than less pacifist ones do tend to overlook the history of civil rights movements in violently oppressive societies. I remain as ever ambivalent about violent revolution, but the situation is a complex and difficult one and there are a lot of variables and perspectives to take into consideration. However, Gene Roddenberry doesn't seem to be interested in engaging with any of that and just has Surak spout off some vaguely positive sounding pop philosophy and then kills him off to crank up the drama a bit.

Of course, I'm also not sure I want to ever seen Gene Fucking Roddenberry of all people attempt a nuanced and even-handed critique of pacifism on primetime television either.

One way to perhaps explain all of these confusing and contradictory statements away might be to read "The Savage Curtain" as Roddenberry attempting an early Gene Coon-style problematization of the show's ethics by way of testing Captain Kirk. Indeed, the whole idea of holding a gladiatorial contest to explore human nature is more than a little reminiscent of "Arena". But that episode was about punishing Kirk and the Gorn captain for their hotheaded aggression, and Kirk ends up proving to the Metrons he's capable of mercy after all. Here, while it's certainly possible to read the Team Good/Team Evil split as being a kind of Angel-and-Devil-on-the-shoulder temptation for Kirk (despite how stupefyingly hackneyed and juvenile that narrative device is), it's not really clear what Kirk is actually being tested on. If Surak's supposed to embody an enlightened form to aspire to he absolutely doesn't come across that way because he acts like a idiot. Maybe then Flying Space Abraham Lincoln is meant to represent Roddenberry's ideals, which would certainly fit with the rest of the episode, but he's also the one who encourages Kirk and Spock to fight dirty if they want to win against Team Evil. Even the Excalbians say the experiment was a failure because Team Good and Team Evil used the same tactics, to which Kirk responds with a truly incoherent bit of moral speechifying. And anyway, Roddenberry even has the *Enterprise* crew come out and state they're already advanced and virtuous on several occasions, so we're right back where we started.

This episode is just bad. It's Roddenberry screwing up in just about all of his signature ways and even a few new ones. It does see him moving more towards utopianism in his writing, which is going to prove critical once he comes back to Star Trek, but this isn't even a rough draft of where he eventually goes ("The Changeling" is actually the closest we've seen so far which, again, wasn't even his story): It's a half-baked series of ideas, none of which work together and that combine into an episode that's an abjectly broken mess even by third season standards. In addition, it makes me even angrier as this is actually one of the most frequently-cited episodes in all of Star Trek. Astonishingly, almost every character introduced here goes on to play a major role in one or more future incarnations of the franchise. And the only reason why that happens is because Roddenberry wrote it, and Roddenberry Can Do No Wrong, even with a script like this one. "The Savage Curtain" is self-evidently silly, impossible to take seriously by any discernible standard and yet another low for the series.

Thankfully there's not much lower to go from here.

94. "Dust to dust": All Our Yesterdays

"All Our Yesterdays" is the second, and final, submission by Jean Lisette Aroeste, whose previous credit was "Is There In Truth No Beauty?". It's also the final official fan submission in Star Trek for awhile, the last in the Original Series not to mention the second to last episode in the Original Series overall. Suffice to say, there is a distinctly funereal air about the general proceedings, which isn't at all helped by how stupendously uninspiring this episode is.

It is, however, significantly more coherent than the previous episode made out of an Aroeste script at least. While on a mission to ensure the planetary civilization of Sarpeidon evacuates in time to avoid the imminent supernova that will engulf their solar system in three hours (how exactly Starfleet was planning to evacuate an entire planet in three hours is not explained), the *Enterprise* finds the planet now entirely free of inhabited life. Beaming down, Kirk, Spock and McCoy find themselves in a gigantic library curated by an enigmatic man named Mr. Atoz, who runs the installation all by himself with the aid of his many duplicates (how the *Enterprise* failed to pick up Atoz's life signs is similarly unexplained). As the landing party peruses the discs that archive Sarpeidon's history Kirk hears a scream from outside and goes through a doorway to investigate, only to find himself on a city street in what appears to be England in the 17th Century. Spock and McCoy follow, but find themselves in a frozen arctic landscape from Sarpeidon's ice age. Spock and McCoy are rescued by a woman named Zarabeth, who confirms that the purpose of the library was to tie into a time portal, which allows people to travel back in time to any period in Sarpeidon's history, and that the planet's entire populace must have done so to avoid the supernova.

Reading this episode is enlivened by the knowledge that Aroeste was the librarian at UCLA. "All Our Yesterdays" seems quite overtly about the idea that books in a library can transport you to other places and times, especially in Aroeste's original brief, which had a lot more time travel shenanigans. Entitled "A Handful of Dust", Aroeste's original story featured Spock and McCoy trapped in a desert suffering from heat stroke before encountering a band of mutant humanoids. Kirk ended up in a period reminiscent of Barbary Coast-era San Francisco where he encounters another time traveller, who helps him return to the library and rescue Spock and McCoy. Kirk and his fellow time traveller destroy the portal and escape just in time to watch everything crumble to dust in their hands.

Once again this is an instance of an episode that was considerably monkeyed around with and for which the original submission seems considerably more interesting, so I'm going to be talking primarily about that. But first, a few major things changed between "A Handful

430

of Dust" and "All Our Yesterdays". The big thing that seems to be different is the effect of time travel on the landing party, and in particular, the fact the original brief didn't seem to specify any. However, in the aired episode, once Spock travels back to Sarpeidon's ice age he seems to devolve to the way Vulcans behaved five thousand years ago: He falls in love with Zarabeth and becomes violently jealous when he thinks McCoy is interested in her as well. This, flatly, doesn't make a damn bit of sense. Neither McCoy or Kirk are similarly affected, and, well, while I'm not one to pull continuity, this didn't happen to Spock in "Tomorrow is Yesterday","The City on the Edge of Forever" or "Assignment: Earth", so I'm not sure why it needed to happen here. Both the prosecutor Kirk associates with and Zarabeth make reference to the time machine "processing" its travellers to fit the period they travel to, which might account for some of Spock's actions were it not for the fact none of the landing party actually ever are "processed": In fact, that's what allows them to return to the present in the first place. Speaking of Zarabeth, the most notable thing about her is that she's the part of the episode a particular sort of fan might be inclined to most expect to see from a *Star Trek* fan, but neither her nor Spock's romance subplot were in Aroeste's original submission at all.

What I'm most interested in talking about here is actually the change in the time period Kirk gets sent to. In "All Our Yesterdays", he's sent someplace that looks like the UK circa the 17th Century. This is, largely, a missed opportunity. If, judging by Spock, our heroes are meant to somehow adapt to the time period, this seems like it's be a great opportunity to show off William Shatner's talent for improvised performativity: We'd expect him to turn into a drag show dandy version of Errol Flynn in *Captain Blood*, and while he does get a brief swordfighting scene soon after he leaves the portal, we've seen Kirk fence before and this doesn't seem like anything any different from what he's normally capable of. Then, there's a tantalizing moment where Kirk is able to contact Spock and McCoy through the portal, leading the villagers in his presence to immediately conclude he's a witch who communes with spirits.

This was naturally the part of the episode that got my attention, as for awhile it seemed like it was going to conclude that Kirk was some kind of shaman and the time portal was a magickal door between realms (which would neatly tie into my reading of "Wink of an Eye" that posited the world of Star Trek is a Otherworld of Eternal Youth and Summer), but ultimately Kirk just stamps his feet and screams about how "there are no such things as witches", which sort of throws a damp towel over that particular reading for me. Kirk on the whole actually utterly fails to get into a role here which, sadly, means the episode plays out as almost the opposite of "A Piece of the Action". I'm not sure whether this was just due to Shatner not caring anymore, or if he simply didn't feel the script was giving him enough material to work with. Given how haphazard the final product is though and that this is the penultimate episode of the series, I am going to lean towards the latter.

But Aroeste of course didn't have Kirk in 17th Century England originally: In "A Handful of Dust", she had him in the Barbary Coast in the Victorian United States, which is somewhat more intriguing. During the California Gold Rush, the Barbary Coast section of San Francisco became an infamous Red Light District that was also a hub for all kinds of other illicit activity, such as gambling and organised crime. Putting Kirk here when at the opposite end of the season he was playing an Old West gang leader and, a few months before that a Chicago Mob Boss, is quite interesting. Perhaps Kirk would have wound up mingling with all the lowlifes and undesirables, tacitly putting him in opposition to the ways in which Victoriana manifested itself in the United States, which had the potential to give *Star Trek* one last chance to bare the anti-authoritarian teeth we now know it was capable of, if only when the stars aligned properly. Also, I'm not sure how far Aroeste was planning to go in this direction, but it's certainly in keeping with her library theme to go to logical limit of having the landing party in some sense integrate themselves into the time periods they visit, just as a good book can sometimes be evocative enough to "draw us in" to the world it depicts.

Also, Spock and McCoy in Mad Max is an awesome brief.

But of course none of this is clear whatsoever in the episode that we can watch. "All Our Yesterdays" is positively crippled by plot holes and logic problems and commits an unforgivable sin by being possibly the most boring and uninteresting episode in the entire series. Furthermore, I found Kirk's violent treatment of Mr. Atoz in the library as he tried to rescue Spock and McCoy repugnant: Giving Kirk a gratuitous fight scene is one thing, eye-rolling as it may be, but watching him aggressively assault a helpless old man and wrestle him to the ground without once explaining himself or his motives is shockingly awful display of flat-out cruelty that goes beyond simply writing him out of character. And anyway, if the *Enterprise* was sent to check in on Sarpeidon anyway, wouldn't it have made just a *little* sense to make sure they'd been contacted beforehand? The Prime Directive isn't explicitly mentioned, but I'm assuming that's why the landing party is so reluctant to tell anyone what they're actually doing, which would have resolved the entire plot about two minutes into the teaser.

Perhaps the most important thing to take away from this episode is the idea of people using time travel to escape a coming catastrophe: The Sarpeidons retreat into their own past to live out their lives in a deliberate attempt to circumvent the supernova by, in a sense, denying it. Much the same could be said about *Star Trek* now. The end is nigh and, in a real sense, the only thing the show's fans have to hold on to for the moment are the perpetual syndicated reruns to come. Their *own* history.

95. "I became a feminist as an alternative to becoming a masochist.": Turnabout Intruder

There's a sense of poetic justice in having *Star Trek* go out on an episode that names "the *Enterprise* family" just as it threatens to destroy it because it doesn't respect women.

This was an episode I always consciously avoided. Partially because I have sort of an instinctual reticence towards big emotional finales, and while "Turnabout Intruder" certainly isn't that, it's still very much the end of an era and I have a hard time dealing with that. I guess its because I don't like the idea of my stories having to end, or being forced to say goodbye to characters I've grown so accustomed to over the course of several years. I always needed to know there were more adventures, or at least the *potential* for more adventures.

That said, the biggest reason I avoided "Turnabout Intruder" was because it looked like utter crap. This episode is famously bad, and there are certainly no more ominous signs and portents on the last bow of the Original Series than the credit "Teleplay By Arthur Singer. Story By Gene Roddenberry". So, I went into this episode absolutely dreading having to watch it. Happily, it turned out to not be nearly as bad as I expected-It's certainly nowhere near the worst effort from either of its two co-writers.

Of course, this doesn't mean it's actually any *good* either.

Answering a distress signal from an archaeological excavation on Camus II, Kirk, Spock and McCoy encounter Kirk's old lover, Doctor Janice Lester, now the head of the expedition, who is suffering from severe radiation poisoning. As Spock and McCoy go to investigate a cry for help further down the dig site, Lester and expresses resentment towards Kirk over the fact their relationship never worked out and her inability to fulfill her dream of becoming a starship captain as Starfleet prohibits women from holding command positions. So much for that egalitarian utopia thing then. Suddenly, Lester reveals her illness is a ruse and traps Kirk in an ancient consciousness transference device and transplants her life energy into his body, intending to command the *Enterprise* in his name...and then to kill him and her old body. This all happens in the teaser, mind you, and the entire remaining forty-eight minutes or so is dedicated towards watching Lester attempt to keep cover on the ship as her increasingly erratic behaviour starts alienating her from the rest of the crew, culminating in her attempting to execute the entire senior staff on mutiny charges.

"Turnabout Intruder" has, clearly, quite a number of rather significant issues. Let's tackle the really obvious one straight off, which is of course the blatantly obvious gender problems. Getting cited as the premier example of reactionary sexism in Star Trek *by the*

Star Trek fans themselves probably counts for something. This episode is typically seen as a slap in the face to feminists, and it's absolutely easy to see why it has that reputation: Lester is a megalomaniacal, murderous woman who wants to usurp a man in a position of power and, once she gets there, she slowly starts to become unhinged and cracks under the pressure, eventually culminating in a massive meltdown (that Scotty even literally describes as "hysterical"), indicating she's incapable of handling the duties and responsibilities such positions of leadership require. Considering this is the work of two of the most blatantly reactionary creative figures in the entire franchise, one is really sort of afforded that reading almost by default. And this seems especially egregious as this is going out in a time where women's struggle for civil rights was really becoming a major concern: In the context of its time, "Turnabout Intruder" seems explicitly and firmly retrograde, which only twists the knife deeper as this is *Star Trek*'s series finale.

That said, there are a surprising number of truly great moments and elements to this episode that seem to at least call into question how straightforwardly indisputable the conclusion to that above argument is. A lot of this has to do with the acting (which I'll touch on in a moment) and I'm sure my reaction is based at least in part on me wanting to close out the Original Series on a somewhat vaguely positive note. It may even be possible that Roddenberry and Singer's general incompetence has finally worked in our favour: Perhaps they actually just bungled trying to write a hateful bit of reactionary sexism. In any case, there are even bits of scripted dialog that hint at an altogether more progressive and interesting story here just beneath the surface waiting to be told. In the teaser, for example, when Lester rants at Kirk about how unfair it is that women aren't allowed to be starship captains, Kirk actually agrees: What he criticises her for is taking out her justified anger and frustration on him. This does get into stereotypically defensive reactions from men to feminism where they frequently try to make it about themselves and take criticism of patriarchy as personal attacks, which is unarguably true, but I'm not sure that's quite what's going on in this case. Lester genuinely seems like an abusive partner here, and her later behaviour certainly supports this reading of her character.

But the scene that really got me to take notice was a few moments later, after Lester steals Kirk's body. She taker her time admiring her newfound physical strength and the respect she can command in this form that she wasn't able to do before, then promptly tries to strangle Kirk to death in her old body. Lester declares that she doesn't fear killing now that she has the power to do so, and that Kirk will now understand "the indignity of being a woman" and how it's "...better to be dead than to live alone in the body of a woman". Lester doesn't sound like a cruel reactionary Right Wing feminist caricature to me: She sounds more like an evil woman who has become evil in part because of her own internalized misogyny. Lester doesn't want a Sisterhood Cabal to rise up, take over the world and crush men the way men have crushed women, nor does she even *really* want equality between men and women. Lester hates the entire concept of "woman", conceiving of it as a handicap that has held her back from achieving the greatness she feels entitled to. And now, in the body of a man, she finally has the ability to indulge every single one of her power fantasies, because self-absorbed power fantasies that oppress and marginalize others are the exclusive domain of men. It's very telling that Lester gains both the thirst for and the ability to kill upon entering a man's body.

(And it's similarly telling that Lester's power fantasies revolve around being the captain of a starship: Five years later is Gene Roddenberry finally beginning to understand how much he hurt Star Trek by infusing the captaincy with so much repugnant masculine bravado and machismo?)

Of course, the true show-stealer is the drag performance that ensues thanks to the body-swapping gimmick of the teaser. William Shatner is absolutely delightful as Janice Lester, spending forty minutes out of the runtime simply vamping around the *Enterprise* like a supervillainess from some amazingly cheesy sci-fi B-movie, which of course Star Trek is. Seriously, he reminds me of Queen Arachnea from *Space Ghost*: All he needed was to hiss at the camera during the climax screaming "Curses! Foiled again!". Thing is though, Shatner is so much fun to watch it's easy to miss the gravity and professionalism he actually brings to the part: While he does enthusiastically throw himself at the idea of an evil space queen inhabiting Kirk's body (the part on the climax where a flustered and impatient Lester, who it must be stressed is still being played by William Shatner, tries to seduce Doctor Coleman into killing Kirk must have launched a million slash fics alone), he doesn't prance around in an exaggerated caricature of femininity. Instead, Shatner puts on an extremely nuanced and multifaceted performance that goes at great lengths to emphasize the differences between Lester and Kirk.

Lester is psychopathic, cruel, vindictive, manipulative and prone to random outbursts of violence, and seeing someone who looks like Kirk behave this way tips off the rest of the crew pretty much immediately. Critically and laudably, Shatner approaches this the same way Diana Muldaur had previously approached her own two-character brief in "Return to Tomorrow": Just as Muldaur limited Thalassa's flaws to Thalassa alone, Shatner similarly goes out of his way to make clear that whatever personal failings Janice Lester might have (and it is undeniably a huge problem that so many of them embody the "emotional" and "irrational" stereotype of women), these are failings unique to her, not generalizations that should be made of all women. It's possible some of this comes from Roddenberry (starting from this point most of Roddenberry's sexism stumbles come from positive discrimination instead of misogyny) but the overwhelming majority is purely due to William Shatner. The best evidence is the last line in the episode, which doubles as the last line in the series:

"Her life could have been as rich as any woman's. If only...if only..."

But the way Shatner delivers it it sounds a lot more like "..as rich as any*one's*", which is a far more powerful statement. In the original line, it seems like Kirk is reflecting on how sad it is that institutionalized sexism still exists. Now though, it sounds like Kirk is mourning Lester specifically. Roddenberry may have meant this to be a clumsy problematiziation of *Star Trek's* utopia inasmuch as women are still not afforded all the rights men are, but Shatner wrestles the meaning away from him and reminds us that no, the purpose of Star Trek is to inspire and give hope to people, and it's up to each one individual to decide what that means for us personally, which is a much nicer note to end the Original Series on.

Really, Janice Lester ought to be remembered as one of Shatner's very best roles: She's a perfect showcase of everything he's so good at. Playing Lester attempting to play Kirk (and getting it wrong, at first slightly and later very much) is a recursive artifice as good as, if not better than, anything in "A Piece of the Action" or "The Enterprise Incident". It's an incredibly challenging, if not downright unworkable, brief Shatner works miracles with, and it's even more remarkable considering he was apparently sick with the flu all throughout filming. But Shatner's not the only one to do a drag turn. Sandra Smith too has a double-character brief, beginning and ending the episode as Janice Lester...but spending the majority of it as Captain Kirk. And it's with *her* that things get *really* interesting. As Kirk, Smith is every bit as dignified and commands every ounce of respect and admiration Shatner does. But there are subtle differences in what happens to Kirk when compared to what happens to Lester, and Smith's the one who takes this part of the episode from simply good to actually great.

See, Smith plays Kirk as being *largely unfazed* by being shunted into a woman's body. Whereas Lester is deeply uncomfortable and it is clearly costing her a lot of exertion and willpower to maintain her facade, and she's not all that great at it as is, Kirk doesn't seem bothered in the slightest and is more concerned with proving her identity to Spock and McCoy and regaining control of the *Enterprise*. In fact, delightfully, Kirk makes an *utterly convincing* woman: The scene right after waking up in sickbay and discovering what's happened where Kirk has a friendly girl chat with Nurse Chapel is simply a masterstroke-Kirk effortlessly adopts traditionally feminine mannerisms and speech patterns like it's the most natural thing in the world and Chapel is completely fooled. The contrast between this scene and Lester's bungled disguise continuously crumbling around her as more and more of the senior staff start to become suspicious is magnificent: Lester may hate being a woman, but it's a purely conscious hatred of her identity brought on by her egoistic response to oppressive social factors. She's manifestly not a transgendered person, and she has very clear problems adapting to a male role, or rather to what she conceives of a male role to be. Smith, however, has, in essence, turned Kirk into a genderfluid individual-Kirk is equally content taking on a male or a female form, and that's actually a stunningly perfect extrapolation of the character he's always been.

While the scene with Chapel is delightful, what seals it is when Spock goes to question Kirk after Lester tosses her in the brig. Kirk implores Spock to trust her, appealing to the close bond they've always shared. She even flat-out tells Spock that he is "...closer to the captain than anyone in the universe". First of all, this is the shippiest of shipper-bait dialog, but what's great about this line is that it's something Kirk would have said to Spock anyway. What Smith adds to it is her delivery: She infuses the line with a very deliberate sense of kindness and compassion that's more traditionally associated with women. There's no way a male actor would have delivered this line the way Smith does. You could read this as "straightening out" the homoerotic subtext between Kirk and Spock, but I prefer to read it as emphasizing the nature of the relationship the characters have always had by highlighting parts of it that might otherwise not be picked up on as easily. And, when Smith gets to record that marvelous Captain's Log entry and then gets to defiantly face down Shatner-as-Lester in the court martial scene, there's absolutely no questioning who she really is. Smith is so magnificent as Kirk we actually don't want to see her go back to having to channel Janice Lester.

"Turnabout Intruder"'s biggest problem isn't its messy approach to gender roles, it's actually its really terrible structure. The majority of the episode is taken up by the awful "evil twin" story and the constant scenes where Lester has nasty fights with Spock and McCoy and slowly betrays the trust of the entire crew are absolute torture. I hate, *hate* this kind of conflict: It's pretty much everything I loathe about scripted drama bound up in one episode. This would have been leagues better had Spock and McCoy figured out Lester's deception somewhere around the first or second act instead of the fourth, as happens in what made it to air. Then, we could have split our time between Spock, McCoy and Scotty colluding with Smith-as-Kirk in secret to take back the *Enterprise* while putting on elabourate ruses of their own so as not to arouse Shatner-as-Lester's suspicions. We'd get to see everyone try to outmaneuver everyone else through staged recursive artifices and *Star Trek*'s theatrical performativity get kicked into warp drive.

This would all lead up to an epic showdown where the crew perhaps has to chase Lester through the ship as Smith-as-Kirk assumes her rightful place with the senior staff monitoring the crisis from the bridge. I'd have adored a scene where Smith gets to take command of the *Enterprise* and interacts with the bridge crew as if nothing unusual was going on: That would have been one of the greatest moments in the history of the series. As Spock tells her, "the bridge is where you belong", and he never said she had to be a man to get there. But, she's kept away from the captain's chair by both diegetic and extradiegetic limiting factors: Hearing Shatner-as-Lester gloat about how Kirk is unable to take command in her current form stings, and so does the fact Smith has so few actual scenes in this episode. While I can't complain too much about the episode focusing on Shatner to the extent it does as Shatner is in fact profoundly entertaining, I can't help but wish it spent an equal amount of time on Smith. The real gender problems with this story aren't in some deliberately reactionary diatribe against feminism, it's that our female captain was never allowed to act like a captain in an episode supposedly about how unfair it was that women aren't allowed to be captains.

It is more than fitting then that *Star Trek* should end with a Curate's Egg of botched feminism and confused utopianism. Whether he meant to or not, Gene Roddenberry might just have turned in the perfect final episode of the Original Series by having the show go down mired in its inability to live up to its own promises and potential. Like the rest of the series, "Turnabout Intruder" hints at genuine greatness and leaves us with a lot of thought provoking ideas to work with, but it also makes it eminently clear that the show as it stands now is in no way capable of taking these concepts any further. Star Trek is, and always has been, capable of becoming a timeless shared myth in which we can see reflections of the best of ourselves and who we want to be. But Star Trek is also, much like Kirk in this episode, frequently shackled and restrained from being everything it could be. But now Star Trek is, for the moment, free: Ironic that the cancellation of the Original Series is the thing that seals its bid for immortality, from here on out Star Trek can be shaped and interpreted in as many ways as there are people who were inspired by it. And when next we see the Starship *Enterprise*, we'll finally get a clearer picture of what she meant to those who first journeyed with her.

Part IV.

1969-1974

96. Sensor Scan: Space Oddity

First of all, let me say I am without question the least qualified person in the world to be talking about David Bowie. I'm as familiar with him and his career as the next person I suppose, but I certainly wouldn't consider myself any kind of expert. There are people who have spent their entire lives following David Bowie and to whom his music is as formative and important as, well, Star Trek is to me I guess.

That said there's simply no getting out of writing about "Space Oddity". It's an irreducible part of the cultural zeitgeist of mid-to-late 1969 and having it released not a month after the original *Star Trek* was canceled (for real this time) is about as revealing as it's possible for an amateur scholar of media history to hope for. However, I'm also not going to pretend I have anything remotely resembling original insight to offer about something this iconic: I'll just link you to this pieceI'll just link you to this piece by Chris O'Leary out of Pushing Ahead of the Dame, which is pretty much the definitive take on "Space Oddity", and just humbly ask for your patience as I toss out some random assorted thoughts about what this all might have to do with Star Trek and the state of science fiction at the end of the 1960s.

While "Space Oddity" has been rightfully read to be about a lot of different things, one of the most reoccurring motifs I notice in the song is, essentially, Bowie eulogizing the Space Age. Far from the Golden Age archetype of the bold, heroic space explorer, Major Tom is a soft-spoken, reserved fellow and his spaceflight is a gigantic publicity spectacle. It feels like the events of the song are being broadcast on national radio, and Ground Control even straight-up asks him what brand of shirts he's wearing so they can squeeze an advertisement into the live coverage. This would of course tie into the general countercultural belief at the time that the Apollo programme (don't forget *Apollo 11* touched down that same summer) was in truth a giant PR stunt for the US government instead of an actual scientific expedition. Which, sadly, sort of turned out to be the case.

And, although I'm not keen to draw direct causal links between the Apollo missions and the change in science fiction (or Star Trek, for that matter) there was a cultural shift that this speaks to. Whatever *Apollo 11* actually was, one thing it proved pretty decisively is that when it came to outer space, science fact didn't really look like science fiction. Whether or not you think it's a problem for Star Trek that the Apollo missions proved the Moon was essentially a hunk of rock and dust (which I don't think it is: To me the Moon has always remained a beautifully stark, hauntingly evocative alien landscape: With the exception of the mushroom bit, Georges Méliès largely got it right, though Hergé was closer) the fact the space mission itself was troublingly bound up in Cold War politics, capitalist pandering and militaristic bicep flexing surely would be-It's hard to keep your sense of wonder about the

440

universe with all that going on, especially when you and your friends are being relentlessly persecuted by the very people asking you to love NASA and the astronauts.

Really though, while there are parallels to NASA merely by virtue of how central it was to the space craze of the 1950s and early 1960s, "Space Oddity" actually has the closest parallels to the British space programme. Britain maintained an active interest in rocketry and the development of space vehicles as early as 1950, but by the 1960s the programme had seen the majority of its budget slashed and numerous project cancellations. By the 1980s the entire endeavour was all but dead, though the UK continues to launch intelligence and communications satellites to this day. But the idea of "British astronauts" in the vein of Alan Shepard, John Glenn, Neil Armstrong and Buzz Aldrin has always been something of a risible one, as best described in one of Eddie Izzard's most memorable routines: Izzard plays a young child conversing with a friend and is going on about all the heroic things he wants to grow up to be, such as the president and an astronaut, to which Izzard has his other character respond "Look, you're British. Scale it back a bit". This then is what "Space Oddity" is lampooning.

This is particularly clear in the original version of the song used in Bowie's film *Love You 'til Tuesday*: Major Tom is a paragon of stereotypical British understatement and on multiple occasions describes his spacecraft as a "tin can". Meanwhile, Ground Control are a bunch of ridiculously giddy, over-eager zealots. Everything is exaggerated and played totally tongue-in-cheek and there's a sense this really isn't something Britain ought to be concerning itself with: Leave the Final Frontier to the Americans. They're still foolish and naive enough to have dreams of empire. But there's also a sadness and sense of loss to "Space Oddity" too, and this is most evident in the single version of the song. Standing in stark contrast to the jaunty *Love You 'til Tuesday* cut, the better-known single is very low-key and elegiac, and almost the only instrument is Bowie's solitary acoustic guitar. Now it seems more like something really has been lost and that the death of the Space Age might actually be a cause for some degree of mourning.

Given everything that was wrong with the Space Age, the UFO era and the Golden Age of science fiction, it can be tough to tease out what that might be. After all, isn't the damning critique of any kind of space exploration, let alone the kind that went on in the mid-20th century, that big Western governments were spending so much money to indulge their nationalistic Cold War penis envy while neglecting all the very real and tangible injustices on Earth? Well yes, but who ever said space was the exclusive domain of space agencies, or that science fiction was the exclusive domain of people like Isaac Asimov and Arthur C. Clarke? The Sky has been one of the most profound and evocative experiences in human nature since as long as there have been humans. The Fremont culture knew this when they settled in Utah's Canyonlands, whose remote isolation and exposure all but forces people to acknowledge the wind and sky. The Polynesians too revered the Sky World as one of the Three Realms, and the ancient Hawaiians believed Mauna Kea (which is, strictly speaking, the tallest mountain on the planet) was the domain of sacred ancestor spirits and the seat of the Sky Itself, one of the primal creative forces of the universe.

In early 2013, astronaut Chris Hadfield recorded his own cover of "Space Oddity" on his return from the International Space Station. It was one of the last things he did before returning to Earth and retiring from spaceflight, and he altered the song to reflect this. Now, "Space Oddity" is the story of a man saddened to return to Earth because he knows he'll never again have the opportunity to have this kind of life-changing, life-affirming experience. It's good to be home, but things will never be the same again. Coming in 2013 where the US space agency seems to be going the way of the British one (and not entirely undeservedly, I might add) this seems especially poignant: Commander Hadfield would probably say more people could stand to have their perspectives broadened by travelling to Outer Space. What Commander Hadfield understands is the same thing understood not only by his fellow astronauts, but anyone who can feel the beat of the universe: We're part of the Sky too. It was the marriage of Rangi and Papa that birthed the world, and the world is enveloped in their embrace. The failure of the Space Age is that it tried to force materialistic nationalism and imperialism into the world of the Sky, we all laughed at how ridiculous that idea was. But the failure of the eras to come in its wake was to reject the Sky entirely and turn inwards such that they could not conceive of, let alone understand, a larger reality.

Furthermore we know that Star Trek at least has the potential to tap this tradition: See again the extremely not-Golden Age "The Tholian Web" and "Wink of an Eye", which hint at uncanny mystical spaces and Otherworlds. Even "The Mark of Gideon" moved Star Trek away from its origins and marked its departure from the era of UFOs, Asimov and, yes, the Space Age. Outer Space is once more as it was: A realm that humbles us and vividly reminds us of humanity's connection to our larger universe. And this is something that astronauts know intimately, as they've witnessed firsthand the Earth and all its wonders and anxieties against the backdrop of the infinite. So, when Major Tom steps outside his capsule in "Space Oddity" and disappears forever into the void, David Bowie remains ambivalent. One the one hand he's attained his own form of Enlightenment and we are not to judge the manner in which the Enlightened achieve their apotheoses, but Major Tom has also abandoned the Earth, and Bowie knows the Earth's relationship to the cosmos is something to be treasured, not discarded. You can't have Rangi without Papa.

If the 1970s were the dawn of the Environmental Age, they were also the dawn of the contemporary Fortean age, and the countercultures, famed as they were for touting expanded and heightened states of consciousness in all forms, aren't going away either. Our worlds are about to get a whole lot weirder, and it's no longer going to be so easy to separate the world of the Stars from life on Earth and the noösphere of positionality and individual experience.

97. Flight Simulator: The Star Trek Text Video Game

In one of my other lives I moonlight as a video game journalist. Now, when I say that I mean I write largely gonzo stream-of-consciousness mytho-symbolic reactions to video games from thirty years ago, which is admittedly what you'd probably expect from me. The point being video games have been an incredibly important part of my life for a very long time. So much so that I'm far more comfortable associating with and relating to video games then I am to pretty much any other kind of creative expression with the exception of music, and this influences the approach I take to media studies and just media consumption in general.

(In the years since this was written I have dialed back my relationship with video games considerably for a number of historical, cultural and personal reasons. It's become far more fraught, but I remain fundamentally interested in them.)

It's also why I find it...not so much disquieting as ironically curious that my biggest project to date is a sprawling overview of a franchise most known for its film and television work. On the whole, I don't work well with scripted drama. I feel I've never been able to truly appreciate it the way most people do and that I keep coming at it from weird angles. In that sense my long relationship with Star Trek and the scant few other non-game or -music works I hold dear to me is really more of a fluke.

But Star Trek itself has a very important relationship with video games that goes back almost as long as video games do. The idea of a licensed video game is a difficult one: For this kind of game to be successful it has to be beholden to both the standards of good game design and fealty to its source material. It's a very thin line to walk and too far in either direction all but guarantees failure, if not commercially or critically definitely aesthetically. My own history with Star Trek is also quite bound up with my history with video games-Some of the first games I ever played were Star Trek ones, and it's been a minor life goal of mine to find that one elusive Star Trek game that both works as a game and fits with my conception of what Star Trek should be like (and given the way so many licensed games turn out and the fact not even most televised Star Trek holds to what I think Star Trek should be like, you can probably tell what a fruitless endeavour this is). But even so, there have been a number of Star Trek video games that have proved to be both historically and personally significant, and this series looks at some of them.

And so it happens that one of the earliest computer games distributed as part of a pack of games written in BASIC for early home computers happened to be based on the original *Star Trek*. What became *The Star Trek Text Video Game* was born out of an early jam session held by programmer Mike Mayfield and some of his high school friends in 1971, and was eventually ported to the HP-2000C when Hewlett-Packard asked Maynard for a version of it. David H Ahl, who worked with DEC, then found this version and included it in his list of *101 BASIC Games*. Bob Leedom then cleaned the game up, adding a new user interface and simplifying the commands for better ease of use. Ahl contacted Leedom and eventually they released this version of the game jointly as *Super Star Trek* in 1974 as part of the book *Creative Computing*. Following a reprint in 1978 just as personal computers were becoming more ubiquitous, *Super Star Trek* became the first computer game to sell over a million copies, and got a thumbs-up from Dave Gerrold himself.

The game itself has the player, in control of the *Enterprise*, hunting down enemy Klingon warships. The game world is a galaxy divided up into quadrants on an eight by eight grid, and each quadrant is a further eight by eight grid of sectors. From there, the game is simply about chasing down the different Klingon ships with short and long range sensors, engaging them in combat with phasers and photon torpedoes and occasionally refueling at Federation starbases. But there's a surprising amount of flexibility and control over different variables for a game this old: You have to manage not just the amount of fuel the *Enterprise* has, but the level of power in your shields and the range of weapons (turning and aiming are vital, and considering it's all done via coordinates this becomes pretty tiresome pretty quickly). Using the long range sensors, it's also possible scope out any remaining targets or starbases and navigate there using warp drive, which gives the game a genuine sense of scale. This is naturally very befitting of a Star Trek game set in an entire galaxy, but it's still surprising considering the first version came out in 1971: This was definitely an ambitious title for its time.

That said, *The Star Trek Text Video Game* is, as you might expect, extremely simplistic. Everything is not only controlled through text commands, it's also depicted entirely though text as well. There's no actual "gameplay" to speak of: It's more inputting a series of commands and responding to what the game prints out, which is an experience suspiciously akin to productivity on a command line interface. And here's where we start to enter into the territory of having to define what is and what isn't a video game: As of this writing, it's a somewhat contentious issue in circles frequented by people who prefer to spend their time philosophizing about the nature of the medium and how to write about video games instead of playing them (which is, I'll admit, a situation I'm not altogether unfamiliar with myself). The big debate tends to centre around whether things like the output of studios like Quantic Dream or Twine stories ought to be considered video games, or if they're better classified as something else. My own opinion on the matter in brief is "not in the slightest" and "almost, but not quite" respectively, and this is primary due to how I personally conceive of what a video game looks like.

See to me, and I'll talk about this more in a future essay in this series, a video game has to at the very least be comparable in some way with something like *Asteroids*. There has to be some baseline level of graphics and real-time action. If a work isn't meeting those minimum standards, I tend to be reluctant to call it a proper video game. *The Star Trek Text Video Game* is a really borderline case here, and I don't think I'm being too unfair in my judgment: *SpaceWar* came out three years prior to it, and *Tennis for Two* even before that, and both of those are unquestionably recognisable as what we'd now call a video game. Compared to those altogether more dynamic titles, *The Star Trek Text Video Game* comes across looking a bit behind the times even for 1971. That's not to denigrate or belittle it, as it's still very obviously an impressive achievement, it's just an indication that it might be a slightly different breed of animal than the sort of thing I tend to be more accustomed to. What I think it might actually get at is a slight schism between what we call "video games" and what might actually be better described as "computer games"

The Star Trek Text Video Game is an exercise in playing around with what personal computers can do. The fact it was eventually released as part of a bundle entitled *Creative Computing* is sort of telling: It's more a technology experiment for computer hobbyists to fuck around with alone in their bedrooms, garages, workshops whereas video games always seemed to be designed as accessible social experiences from the beginning. This also highlights, for the perhaps the first time (at least the first time since "Arena") the segment of Star Trek fandom that will ultimately become the most vocal and dominant. The only people who would be playing *The Star Trek Text Video Game*, at least at first, were people who already had access to computers. So, once again, we're looking at big universities specializing in subsidized technoscience research. Even afterwards you had to first own a PC yourself, and they didn't exactly come cheap. By definition these people are going to be somewhat affluent and privileged technologically-minded individuals, which is, if we think back to the "Save Star Trek!" business, precisely the sort of audience NBC wanted to court with *Star Trek*. Even though computer programming was not the male-dominated industry in the 1970s it is today, it's still tough to imagine the kind of person who would be writing Kirk/Spock fanfiction sitting down and loading this thing up in BASIC.

No, the people who would be playing this are affluent, white, probably socially awkward straight cis men. And that connection is going to kill the franchise one day.

Which is probably at least part of the reason Paramount gave Ahl the go-ahead to use the name "Star Trek" and why Dave Gerrold ended up advertising the game. Even then Paramount knew who their primary demographic was supposed to be and made overtures to court it. That said though, and in spite of all the officially licensed Star Trek games to come, *The Star Trek Text Video Game* is still largely a game that couldn't be made in a lot of the subsequent eras of Star Trek history. Especially when the brand became a massive cash cow in the 1990s, the idea of a purely fan made video game being initially distributed through word-of-mouth would have had sent Paramount's lawsuit instincts into overdrive (and indeed when a spiritual successor to this game based on *Star Trek: The Next Generation* emerged in 1994, Paramount clamped down on that pretty quickly). But of course by that point both the personal computer and video game industries were very different than they were in 1971.

But as for *The Star Trek Text Video Game* itself, no matter what else we can say about the climate it was coming into, it's clear it was an important part of electronics history. So much so it was eventually remade for the Atari 2600 as another classic, *Star Raiders*, which is essentially the same game except without the Star Trek license, but with actual graphics and proper real-time action. But the original game is still worth a look for its historical significance if for nothing else: If you don't mind its archaic gameplay, you can play a JavaScript recreation of the *Super Star Trek* version here.

98. Myriad Universes: James Blish and Bantam Star Trek

Nowadays, fandom-at-large tends to balk at the idea of a version of a Star Trek episode existing in another medium. It's inconceivable to many in an age of Netflix, BitTorrent and Blu-ray season box sets to think that the televised story might not be the most memorable and recognisable version of it. But, in an era when television was still just starting to shed its reputation for being disposable entertainment and before commonly available home video recording technology, the only way for fans to archive their favourite episode were from their translation and recreation into other media.

Thus, the concept of the television novelization is a particularly historical, and historically significant, aspect of media studies inexorably dated to this era, and largely this era alone: Indeed, the 1970s are essentially the last point in the history of TV where novelizations play a significant role: The first Betamax VCRs came out in 1975 with VHS coming the next year, and by 1978 both types of devices were mass-production, at which point the age of the novelization was for all intents and purposes over. Which is perhaps fitting for our purposes, as the Bantam Books series of *Star Trek* novelizations by James Blish is a strange beast even by novelization standards. Like its parent show, Blish's novelizations oftentimes felt like a leftover relic from a previous age, and their peak and subsequent decline in the early-to-mid 1970s in many way mirrors the twists and turns of Star Trek itself during this period.

The choice of James Blish to take on adapting *Star Trek* for mass-market paperback is at once curious and also somewhat telling. Blish was already an accomplished science fiction author and had been publishing stories decades before he began his association with the franchise. He was also, as you might perhaps expect, firmly and resolutely in the Golden Age tradition. Blish's background was in biology and after training at Rutgers and Columbia University, he became a medtech in the army during World War II. Afterwards, he became chief science editor for Pfizer. Before that, he was a member of the Futurians who were in fact not, as I initially suspected, the time travellers from the far future who sent a mutated King Ghidorah to fight Super Godzilla in Tokyo in 1991, but were actually a group of sci-fi fans-turned writers who got their start in the Greater New York Science Fiction Club. Outside of Star Trek, Blish is most known for his *Cities in Flight* series, which depicts a future where anti-aging drugs and antigravity devices are commonplace, and space travel has progressed to the point where entire cities can be propelled through the stars on their own volition, and his "Pantropy Trilogy" of short stories, exploring how humans might be biologically augmented to survive in extraterrestrial environments, thus removing the need for planetary terraforming.

At first glance then Blish appears to be possibly the most bog-standard Golden Age-style science fiction writer we've seen since Isaac Asimov. His biography does, in fact, seem to paint him as almost stereotypically so: If one were to come up with a list of qualities that might comprise a model Golden Age writer, well, Blish ticks pretty much all of the boxes. But, for neither the first nor the last time in Star Trek, things get a bit messier and more complicated when we dig a bit deeper. Namely, the Futurians were a profoundly weird group of science fiction fans. From what I understand, the Futurians broke away from the Greater New York Science Fiction Club because they believed it was the duty of sci-fi writers to help make the world a better place, and they had a significantly more leftist approach to doing this than was the norm in the 1940s. Quite a number of the Futurians were overtly interested in communism and Trotskyism, and actively looked to find ways to explore their political ideals through sci-fi concepts in their writing. They also, somewhat bizarrely, blended this with an *extremely* Golden Age faith in Modernist, technoscentific progress and futurism, as if things like Big Pharma or the military industrial complex were somehow *ever* going to agree to introducing full-on Trotskyism to the wartime United States.

So as an ideological movement, they were pretty much domed from the start. A lot like science fiction itself then. However, the Futurians were also a group diffuse enough that no truly solid generalizations about the group's political ideology can be safely made: Isaac Asimov was counted as a member, for one, and Blish himself has been argued on multiple occasions to have had right-wing sympathies, a case largely built on his admiration of Oswald Spengler. So really *Star Trek*, with its confused mix of both extremely left-wing and extremely right-wing concepts, was sort of a natural fit for Blish. Perhaps predictably, he makes it clear in many of his novelizations that he considered himself a serious fan and took the Bantam gig at least partially out of his love of the show rather than because he needed to job for a paycheck. And, after *Star Trek* was canceled a second time (for real), it was Blish who, in the 1970 volume of his novelizations, became one of the loudest voices for the show's renewal, calling on his readers to write NBC urging to get it brought back. Blish also penned the first officially-licensed Star Trek fiction book targeted towards adults, *Spock Must Die!*, that same year (though not, as is sometimes believed, the first officially licensed Star Trek fiction book ever: That honour goes to the 1968 book *Mission to Horatius* which, perhaps tellingly, was a children's book).

It is likewise revealing to look at how *Star Trek* morphed under James Blish. Though his novelizations tended to be as accurate as he could make them, initially he was only given very early, preliminary scripts to work from so his work from this period bears far more differences from the aired episodes then the ones made after the series was canceled, when he had access to actual filming scripts (this also means Blish's books are some of the only remaining resources through which we can piece together the production history of the Original Series, as many of these draft scripts have since been lost). Blish did take liberties with the source material on occasion as well, however. Sometimes this added more nuance to the original story: In "Arena", for example, Gene Coon was originally going to have the

Metrons destroy the ship of the victorious captain rather than the one who lost as they considered that a greater threat to peace, and Blish, obviously working from an early draft, kept that twist in. Other times though, his additions made things considerably worse-In "Who Mourns for Adonais?" Blish removes all uncertainty that Carolyn Palamas was raped by Apollo and reinstates McCoy's offensive anti-abortion joke from the denouement, which pretty much makes me hate him. Also, in "Turnabout Intruder", Blish alters Kirk's final line

"Her life could have been as rich as any woman's, if only... if only...."

by having Spock chime in with

"If only she had been able to take pride in *being* a woman."

which just messes everything up in my opinion. It's certainly not that either Gene Rodden-berry or Arthur Singer were especially progressive voices on gender fluidity, but there was enough ambiguity in the episode as aired that I was able to pull off a redemptive reading I'm actually rather proud of. Blish's take on the story though simply ends up feeling pretty gender essentialist, as if he's declaring we should all be satisfied with our lot in life and never try to change things. Blish novelized both of these episodes well after the Original Series was canceled so he definitely would have had the final scripts in these cases, and I find it tough to forgive either him or the show for that.

One thing that I find particularly interesting about the Bantam novelizations is that, regardless of how indebted Blish was to Golden Age science fiction, his Star Trek books absolutely *looked* like Golden Age science fiction. The cover art for these books is aston-ishingly beautiful: While I'm not too keen on the genre, I'm a sucker for gorgeous space art inspired by it and this is exactly the sort of thing that really turns me on. Starting in the 1990s, everything to go out under the Star Trek brand had to have a uniform and generic visual style, and it's a lot of fun to go back to a time before that to see all the varied and unique ways talented artists were inspired by the same TV show. My personal favourite covers are probably the ones for books 4, 6, 9, 11 and the alternate cover for 7: They all remind me of the jaw-droppingly lovely artwork done for Foundation that I linked to in my piece on that series, which is also incidentally the only thing about that series I genuinely enjoy.

In spite of the relative quality, or lack thereof depending on your take, of Blish's noveliza-tions, the fact remains they occupy a rather strange space in the history of the larger Star Trek franchise. The point of a novelization is, of course, to give fans the ability to hold onto a copy of their favourite episodes in the days before home video. But from the beginning, Blish's books didn't quite have the sole claim to this: Desilu and Paramount's deal with Bantam was not an exclusive one, and at the same time Blish's stories were coming out, Ballantine Press also had the rights to Star Trek (and indeed it was them who would handle adapting The Animated Series), there were "photonovels", graphic novels of episodes made of screenshots and speech bubbles and, of course, Gold Key was still regularly publishing comics. The fact that it's Blish's novelizations that get remembered over any of these others is a key sign of the revisionist history master narrative of science fiction, Star Trek and Nerd Culture that we must always keep in the back of our mind from now on. For now, reflect on what that says about gatekeeping and who Star Trek seems to be saying is allowed to be a fan of it.

But the biggest blow to the Bantam line was ironically enough its parent show itself: The last volume of Blish's novelizations didn't come out until 1977, by which point the Original Series had been in near-constant syndication for almost a decade...and VCRs were out. Indeed, the show was canceled and in perpetual reruns before the fourth book came out. This isn't like with *Doctor Who* where entire years of the show were just missing and never repeated (in which case a novelization *really was* your only chance to revisit a story): *Star Trek* was on the air all the time. If you wanted to see your favourite episode again, all you'd need to do is wait until it was rerun and, if you happened to be lucky enough to have one of those newfangled VCRs, you could tape it.

But of course, that would be something those *girls* would be more inclined to do.

Perhaps tautologically, Blosh's novelizations had a huge impact on Star Trek's later creative teams: Ronald D. Moore says *Star Trek 3* was the first book based on the show he ever read and he remarks on how important it was for him to see that other people were not just watching *Star Trek* but writing about it as well. And it's certainly true that these novelizations were the first exposure many fans had to the Original Series. What the Bantam line ultimately was then, I think, was a version of *Star Trek* by and for a certain kind of science fiction fan that reinforced their beliefs about what the show was supposed to be about. This was Star Trek by James Blish, a noted Futurian, colleague of Isaac Asimov and veteran sci-fi writer in his own right. For the upper middle class, white straight cis male technologistic subset of fandom, this would pretty much be exactly what they expected the show to be. And while this is not to say the novelizations were not bought by other types of fans as well, I'd be willing to bet the people reading these at least in part because of who James Blish was probably weren't writing Kirk/Spock fanfiction or jamming out to *Mr. Spock's Songs from Space*. What we have in the James Blish/Bantam Books then is most likely another step in the development of the type of fandom that's eventually going to come to define Star Trek, ultimately to its detriment.

99. Sensor Scan: William Shatner in the 1970s

Modern genre fiction actors are superstars. They're today's teen idols, appearing in multi-billion dollar film and television projects and have their name and face instantly splattered across the Internet the moment their franchise sees the merest inkling of popular success. Typecasting too is far less of a problem now then it used to be: Nowadays up-and-coming genre stars go out of their way to nurture a cult of personality as soon as they start to become famous, and take care to ensure each marquee role they play is a slightly different twist on their iconic public persona from the start: Benedict Cumberbatch, for example, plays a version of Khan Noonien Singh in *Star Trek Into Darkness* that can succinctly be described as "Evil Sherlock" even though he is self-evidently capable of a vast and diverse acting range. Likewise, there's not a whole lot of difference between Martin Freeman's Bilbo Baggins, his John Watson and his Arthur Dent, which was already an exaggerated and caricatured version of the character he played in *The Office*. This isn't so much a criticism as it is an observation that in contemporary genre fiction, typecasting is something that's acknowledged and accounted for from the beginning

It wasn't always like this.

It's not like the cast of *Star Trek* were ever really not famous. The series was always afforded a primetime slot in its original run: Even in the third season when it was shunted into the Friday Night Death Slot, at least it was in the primetime part of the Friday Night Death Slot. *Star Trek* was a marquee show for NBC, and all the accounts I could find dating to the 1960s indicate it was a series that was considerably recognisable and well-known. At the very least, you don't get to record novelty albums or appear on variety shows if you're not doing at least somewhat well for yourself (and certainly this also would seem to indicate there's always been some sort of teen idol appeal within genre fiction). But the flip side of this is that if you became famous for genre fiction in the 20th century...well, there was a good chance that's all you were ever going to be famous for. And, sadly, perhaps the archetypal example of this phenomenon is what happened to the *Star Trek* cast, who universally struggled to find work throughout the 1970s, forever becoming associated with the roles they played for three years on the starship *Enterprise*. No matter how rough the cancellation of the Original Series was for Trekkers, the fact is it was infinitely worse for the cast and crew. And arguably few had it as bad as William Shatner.

Shatner's bad luck started a few months before the end of *Star Trek* when his wife Gloria Rand divorced him. While things like this are of course complicated and involve many different factors and variables, Shatner himself has expressed suspicion that this might have

451

had something to do with his character bedding a different woman every week on a popular primetime science fiction show. Once *Star Trek* ended, Shatner was now responsible for supporting his estranged ex-wife in addition to his three daughters, and now he was out of a regular job and unable to find a new one as nobody wanted to hire Captain Kirk to play "real" roles (actually a case could be made this really started in 1968 when *The Transformed Man* tanked: Again, what *Star Trek* fan would believe Captain Kirk was capable of making a serious and respectable piece of avant garde performance art?). Shatner wound up losing his home as a result, and spent the early part of the 1970s living out of a flatbed truck in the San Fernando Valley.

So, all throughout the 1970s William Shatner took on any job that would hire him up to and including doing car commercials and showing up as a novelty guest at private parties. As for the actual acting gigs he landed, they could charitably be described as "subpar". Shatner spent the majority of the decade bouncing around a series of incredibly shlocky low-budget exploitation movies, most of which are regarded as the worst work he's ever done (and remember this is from a "fanbase" who already consider *The Transformed Man* to be one of the worst music albums in history). Shatner calls this phase of his career "That Period" and describes the experience as "humbling", but I can only imagine how unappreciated and unwanted he must have felt. Before *Star Trek*, this was a guy who was regularly appearing in stuff like *Oedipus the King*, *The Brothers Karamazov* and *Judgment at Nuremberg*. After *Star Trek*, he was more known for such classics such as *Big Bad Mama* and *Kingdom of the Spiders*. This is why I find it completely understandable when actors express reticence about genre fiction franchises, in spite of how upset this can make fans-Stories like Shatner's are prime examples of how being associated with genre fiction can legitimately ruin someone's career. We know now that Shatner eventually gets a happy ending, but it certainly wouldn't have seemed that way in 1971 or so.

Even in spite of being forced to appear in a string of unwatchably terrible movies, William Shatner remains as fascinating a personality in the 1970s as he did in the 1960s. Many of the films he starred in from this era, terrible as they may be, at least manage to occasionally have some interesting motifs. Like many horror movies, Shatner's 1970s output draws heavily on folklore and ancient mythology, but what's interesting from my perspective is to learn how close it actually comes to themes I've explored in this book already within the context of Star Trek. *The Horror at 37,000 Feet*, for example, concerns a Boeing 747 passenger jet coming under attack by Druidic ice elemental spirits. Naturally, Shatner's character figures out the ice spirits can be combated with fire, which puts the film roughly in the same narrative league as your average- to below-average fantasy RPG video game. However, the specific invocation of Druids, dubious historical figures widely believed to be the priest and shaman class of the Celtic and Germanic people, is kind of of fun to think about, especially given the reading we afforded "The Tholian Web".

Likewise, *The Devil's Rain* which, along with *The Horror at 37,000 Feet* is usually regarded as the absolute nadir of Shatner's filmic career (thus making them both, naturally, just as iconic and memorable as his best work), is seeped in syncrestic mashups of Satanic, Biblical and Pagan imagery. Like any Western work that tries to do this, it winds up conflating paganism with Satanism, which means its not-really-eve-all-that-Pop Christian. Most notably though, there is a strong connection between *The Devil's Rain*, through Shatner, to John Carpenter's *Halloween*: Michael Myers wears a William Shatner mask and acts in an eerily similar manner to Shatner's character in *The Devil's Rain*. The novelization of *Halloween* posits that Michael Myers was under the influence of an ancient Celtic curse, and later films attempt to tie the film's mythos into the history and symbolism of Samhain (usually spectacularly poorly, but it's nice to see them attempt it nevertheless).

So, if we were to apply our synchromystic Twilight Language skills here, we could maybe say William Shatner is a person who seems to attract mystical and occult imagery, between his movies here and the supernatural and Otherworldy aspects of later-period *Star Trek*, most evident in stories like "The Tholian Web", "Wink of an Eye" and "That Which Survives". And of course, there's his noted interest in transcendence and enlightenment that we saw in *The Transformed Man* and to which Shatner will return when Star Trek is once again firmly established as part of the mainstream. This, combined with the unfortunate dire straits he was dealing with in the 1970s, but also thanks to the way many of his characters have been written (including Kirk), we might say William Shatner is a kind of working-class mystic, or perhaps more accurately someone very good at *playing the role* of a working-class mystic.

And it's that working-class mysticism that is going to define Star Trek in the short term, at least in terms of how it comes back. *Star Trek: The Animated Series* doesn't really get a lot of respect, but one thing among many that it really absolutely must be credited for is giving its cast a job when nobody else was willing to. Although if we're being honest William Shatner was always going to be asked to come back, his co-stars were a less sure thing, and it's telling this was the only place that would take any of them. George Takei, Nichelle Nichols and Walter Koenig were originally not going to be cast on the Animated Series because Paramount partnered with Filmation and Filmation had no money and couldn't afford the full cast (not to mention this was the 1970s, a famously bleak time in animation history anyway). Leonard Nimoy refused to do the show unless they brought everybody back, partially because he knew how important *Star Trek*'s diverse cast had been, but also because he knew how poor and desperate he and his co-stars were. And even then Filmation couldn't afford Koenig (although he was able to submit a script). In addition, *Star Trek: The Animated Series* is the first Star Trek to seriously push the boundaries of what the franchise was capable of: We really are soon about to go Where No One Has Gone Before.

100. Sensor Scan: Space Ritual

There's a certain set of expectations that are put in place when you put on a record with a title like *Space Ritual*. These are further heightened when you glance at album artwork like that, which has got to be one of the most gorgeously mind-warping bits of sleeve design I've ever seen. So suffice to say I guess I expected that whatever this album was going to sound like it simply *had* to be some kind of consciousness-elevating, perspective shifting head trip. What I experienced was not *quite* what I anticipated, but an experience *Space Ritual* certainly is.

Music is one of the hardest things for me to write about, and it aggravates me no end. Probably nothing resonates with me as powerfully as music does, but it evokes such a complex tapestry of emotions, moods and imagery for me I often find myself unable to translate my feelings into anything resembling coherent language. I'm no musicologist or music critic and maybe that has something to do with it, but either way, no place do I feel the torment of Avital Ronell's ethereal phantom dictator than when I try to say something intelligent about music. I always end up feeling like the protagonist of William Shatner's "Lucy in the Sky with Diamonds", haplessly and fruitlessly trying to describe enlightenment to someone who didn't experience it firsthand. I'm also once again handicapped by the fact I'm writing about a group of artists I'm not especially familiar with and feel woefully underqualified to actually talk about.

But even so there are a fair amount of interesting things I was able to notice about Hawkwind's *Space Ritual* even given my limited experience with the band that slot the album very nicely into the cultural zeitgeist of the early 1970s. Hawkwind, firstly, are a UK-based rock outfit who combine elements of Psychedelia, acid rock and prog rock and who are usually credited as the originators of space rock, which fuses all of these disparate sounds together through an interest in science fiction motifs. While this isn't the kind of space rock I'm familiar with (which uses a lot more electronic instruments, distortion and overdubbing) it is quite an apt description of what Hawkwind sound like. With their heady themes and incredibly skilled guitar shredding, Hawkwind are also seen as the intermediate step between the Hippies of the Long 1960s and the Punks of the Long 1980s. They were also one of the most laudably workmanlike bands of their time, regularly doing one show every three days and once playing five consecutive nights for free *outside*, not *at*, the Isle of Wright Festival. *Space Ritual* itself isn't an album in the traditional sense: It's a double-disc live album chronicling a night from Hawkwind's 1972-3 tour to support their *Doremi Fasol Latido* album. However, like so many great live albums, *Space Ritual* holds together perfectly on its own to the point it more than overshadows the records it's ostensibly trying to support.

That *Space Ritual* is a recording of a concert is key to grasping its impact, as it really does feel like this kind of music is meant to be shared with a live audience. Apparently the *Space Ritual* show was a gigantic multimedia extravaganza with a full visual component that the actual performance was but one component of. This does seem to hurt the version of *Space Ritual* we can listen to today a bit, however: Without the full stage experience, the album comes across on more than one occasion feeling like a soundtrack, and a soundtrack that doesn't *quite* stand on its own. It is something of a shame there doesn't (to my knowledge) exist any video of the show to go along with the album. It feels like something's missing without it. But even without seeing the visual accompaniment, it's clear *Space Ritual* was a hell of a show, and that translates into a pretty incredible album as it.

Hawkwind refer to themselves not as musicians, but "musicnauts", and *Space Ritual* is ostensibly a rather loose narrative about travellers frozen in suspended animation and sent on a faraway journey throughout the deepest reaches of outer space set against the backdrop of an exploration of the concept of the music of the spheres, the idea that all celestial bodies have a kind of fundamental resonance and that, when taken together, the universe itself generates a kind of music. This music isn't audible as much as it is an extension of fundamental mathematical truths that organise the natural world. Tacitly, Hawkwind has these themes stated by author Robert Calvert, who recites some pieces of sci-fi poetry to introduce different sections of the performance. Calvert was one of the "New Wave" of science fiction authors who were among the first to come out of Psychedelia and attempted to blend that sort of philosophy with the tropes and ideas of science fiction and was a lifelong friend of Michael Moorcock (who even wrote the song "Sonic Attack" for this album). On *Space Ritual* however, Calvert actually winds up feeling largely extraneous, as his observations feel a bit overly futurist and facile at times.

But the heart and soul of everything is Hawkwind's instrumentation. This is certainly some of the most inventive and skilled riffing I've ever heard, creating an echoey, droning sense of space that sucks you in and propels you forever forward. This is reinforced by a neverending percussive Motorik beat all throughout *Space Ritual* that Hawkwind delightfully refer to as the heart of their starship's engines. Motorik, for those unfamiliar with it, is a term referring to a specific 4/4 beat typically associated with Krautrock meant to evoke a sense of movement. It's usually most associated with Kraftwerk's 1974 *Autobahn* album and its imitators, where the Motorik beat is literally used to represent the feeling of driving on an autobahn, although Neu!'s debut album from 1971 is probably more properly called the codifier of the style. On *Space Ritual*, Hawkwind blend their Motorik beat with their already impressive guitar work to create a soundscape that really does feel as if it's going ever onwards towards infinity.

I have somewhat mixed feelings about the music of the spheres conceit on this album. On the one hand it's a delightful concept to think about, but on the other hand it has, to me, rather troubling connections to things like "sacred geometry" that, combined with the concept's links to esoteric Christianity (not to mention Calvert's overly blunt paeans to sci-fi futurism on the album itself), tend to make *Space Ritual* feel like a very straightforwardly Western approach to mysticism. The West of course has its own long and interesting tradition of spiritual heresy that shouldn't be entirely discounted, but I personally tend to be a bit sceptical of any approach that leans too heavily on things like Platonic Ideals and the Greco-Roman conception of math and logic as some sort of fundamental Truth about the universe. The way I see it, that way lies Scientism.

There is also the problem that a lot of this album feels a bit less like an attempt to portray enlightenment and a lot more an excuse to get stoned.

But on the other hand, I'm not going to pretend I'm not rather fascinated by a philosophy that's positing music as something that links humans with a larger cosmic consciousness. Shamans have been telling us that for millennia. And that's where *Space Ritual* truly lives up to its title in my opinion: This is an album that, on the whole, works very well if you tune out of your conscious awareness: It is somewhat reminiscent of a kind of musical gathering called a drone or a trance session, where musicians come together and improvise a performance on the spot simply by becoming attuned to each other's movements and sound. Just as in a real shamanistic group trance, participants have a heightened or altered state of awareness where they're more in tune with each other and their own spirituality than external forces. That's why I would imagine this worked so well as a live performance, especially given the band's Psychedelia-tinged history: An entire arena-sized concert of people tuned into something like *Space Ritual* would have been something pretty incredible to be a part of. That's where the music of the spheres stuff really works: Hawkwind used this show as a concert-sized trance session in an attempt to attune them and their audience to the inner workings of the cosmos. Whether or not they were successful can really only be decided by the people who were there.

The other intriguingly noteworthy thing about *Space Ritual* is that Hawkwind are very much a working class kind of act: Their behaviour during their tour alone makes that clear. This is an outfit that has been quite rightly described as "the people's band". This is possibly the most important thing about this show: Hawkwind are clearly positioning themselves as working class mystics. This even explains Bob Calvert's cheesy, blustery spoken word introductions, because this means we're right back in the territory of William Shatner and *The Transformed Man*. Just as Shatner's character was ultimately unable to describe his apotheosis in an elegant manner, nor should Calvert or Hawkwind be expected to put theirs into words either. "Space Is Deep" indeed.

101. "...as eternity is to time": Beyond the Farthest Star

"*Enterprise* log, Captain James Kirk commanding. We are leaving that vast cloud of stars and planets which we call our galaxy. Behind us, Earth, Mars, Venus, even our Sun, are specks of dust. The question: What is out there in the black void beyond? Until now our mission has been that of space law regulation, contact with Earth colonies and investigation of alien life. But now, a new task: A probe out into where no man has gone before."

The canonicity, and thus ultimate legacy, of *Star Trek: The Animated Series* has been a point of contention amongst fans and creative personnel since just about the day it premiered. While I've outlined my thoughts on Star Trek "canon" previously (in brief, I think it's largely hogwash) it's important to consider the general reception works like this attain, as doing so allows us to understand the ebb and flow of the overall work that is Star Trek over time.

If anything has the right to be called Star Trek though, it's surely *Star Trek: The Animated Series*, isn't it? It served as a reunion for almost the entire creative team from the Original Series, with the exception of Gene Roddenberry, Gene Coon, Walter Koenig, John Meredyth Lucas and the Season Three team (The show couldn't afford Koenig, Coon was, well, dead, Roddenberry wasn't interested, Lucas was busy on *Insight* and I really can't say I miss Arthur Singer) and D.C Fontana herself personally spearheaded the project. Fontana stands behind the show to this day, firmly stating that her and her team always tried to make the best possible Star Trek they could under the circumstances, which I think is actually truer here than it was throughout the majority of the Original Series. In fact, Fontana considers *Star Trek: The Animated Series* the official fourth year of the *Enterprise*'s famous five-year mission, and I'm not really one to disagree with D.C. Fontana.

But in spite of her convictions, Fontana's claim has not only not gone unchallenged but it's been largely ignored. Despite the occasional in-joke or reference in future series and the more relaxed attitude of places like the Memory Alpha Wikia, Trekkers seem to have a very hard time accepting *Star Trek: The Animated Series* into their hearts. In the years and decades since it was made, there have been countless attempts to tell the story of those infamous "last two" years of the five-year mission, completely disregarding the existence of the Animated Series. There have been number of tie-in novels and comic books, not to mention the video games *Star Trek: 25th Anniversary*, *Star Trek: Judgment Rights* and the big budget fan production *Star Trek Continues* that all purport to tell the story The Animated Series has ostensibly already told.

This is highly unusual for Star Trek fans, who usually hang off of the words of creators as if they come down from On High. Dave Gerrold, who also worked on this show, reasons it has something to do with a character who we'll talk a bit more about once the 1980s roll around: The franchise's official "archivist" and "continuity advisor", who apparently hated this show. Roddenberry himself seemed ambivalent about the project in general (not that it stopped him putting his name on the show and taking a paycheck from it, of course). But, as we've established previously, Roddenberry was never all that interested in "canon" either-That's something only the fans really care about. That Star Trek fans are far more willing to take Gene Roddenberry's waffling and the words of a promoted fanboy to heart over those of someone like D.C. Fontana...Well, I'll leave you to put the pieces together there. I'd rather talk about the episode at hand, "Beyond the Farthest Star", which is, as it so happens, absolutely brilliant.

> "Captain's log, Stardate 1312.4. The impossible has happened. From directly ahead, we're picking up a recorded distress signal, the call letters of a vessel which has been missing for over two centuries. Did another Earth ship probe out of the galaxy as we intend to do? What happened to it out there? Is this some warning they've left behind?"

Now normally I do these essays in production order because I think it illuminates the creative process a bit better, but with this series I'm not largely because I messed up and didn't realise the show aired out of production order. Oh well. I can't change it now. Anyway, "Beyond the Farthest Star" is the work of Samuel A. Peeples, whose previous Star Trek contribution was nothing less than "Where No Man Has Gone Before", the second pilot for the Original Series. Not that this was any coincidence: Both Gene Roddenberry and D.C. Fontana thought it would be neat if Peeples wrote the first Animated Star Trek episode as he'd already done the first live-action one, and Peeples agreed. Perhaps understandably, "Beyond the Farthest Star" echoes and mirrors "Where No Man Has Gone Before" in its basic structure, becoming a kind of reiteration of it.

The *Enterprise* crew is beginning a bold new mission of exploration beyond the Milky Way and encounters something unexpected and dangerous at the edge of the galaxy. This time, it's a deserted starship that's been in orbit around a dead sun for 300 million years. Beaming aboard, Kirk, Spock, McCoy and Scotty discover the starship's construction resembles Terran insect colonies, and its metal seems to have been spun like it was spider silk. The landing party soon discovers the ship was abandoned because it had been infected by a hostile non-corporal life form, which proceeds to jump the transporter beam and commandeer the *Enterprise* with the intention to drive it to the centre of the galaxy with an army of similarly infected starships.

But despite its superficial similarities to "Where No Man Has Gone Before", "Beyond the Farthest Star" is unquestionably its own story and it's an unabashedly superior one on top of that. This is a stunning debut for our new kind of Star Trek. Just in terms of basic narrative form this is the best episode of Star Trek I've seen in an extremely long time, and it's a contender for the hands-down best story featuring the Original Series crew I've seen yet. I was truly impressed with how effortlessly the cast slipped back into their roles after four years: There's no discernible difference between the characters we see here and the ones from the Original Series. Actually, I take that back. There is: The characters we see in "Beyond the Farthest Stars" are far more developed, effective and memorable.

Predictably, a lot of this is thanks to the acting: The cast is energized here in a way we really haven't seen before, and it reiterates what a strong cast this actually was. Acting in live-action TV and doing voiceover work are two very different skill sets, and just being good at one doesn't mean you'll be good in the other. But everyone slips effortlessly into their roles here, even William Shatner, who is such a visual and expressive actor you'd think it might be tough for him to adapt to animation (although upon reflection, he *is* best at spoken word poetry-Perhaps we shouldn't be surprised.). In fact, some of the cast even come across *stronger* here than they did in the Original Series: Both DeForest Kelley and Nichelle Nichols almost seem like they're playing entirely new versions of their characters, and for the better.

But the real standout is James Doohan, who is absolutely phenomenal. As Scotty, he comes across as more nuanced and defined than he ever has before, and his performance is wonderfully multi-layered and charming. But it's with *Star Trek: The Animated Series* where we really get to see what a range he had: As the show was so cash-starved it couldn't afford any other actors aside from the core seven except in very special circumstances, Doohan has to play just about every male guest and incidental character in the entire show, and he's terrific at it, making each and every one feel distinct, unique and memorable. His performance as the magnetic organism in this episode is at once commanding and threatening, but also touching: We feel terribly sorry for it once Kirk is forced to shove it out of the ship and maroon it again on the dead sun. Doohan makes the creature's loneliness and desperation quite palpable.

As good as the actors are though, the primary reason they seem so excited and enthusiastic here has got to be the material they have to work with. Once again proving how badly Star Trek needed D.C. Fontana, "Beyond the Farthest Star" just sings with her in the driver's seat. It's not an especially deep or overreaching story, it's ultimately a simple little space adventure plot, but it's so perfectly put together it transcends its genre, or at the very ;east it's a damn good example of it. Given how weighed down "Where No Man Has Gone Before" was with ugly and unnecessary gender role problems, it's a revelation to see how deftly and flawlessly this one works. Though Nurse Chapel and Lieutenant M'Ress, The Animated Series' two other main female characters, don't appear in this episode, Uhura is marvelous. Nichelle Nichols is given more to work with in this one episode than I think she was in the entire three years of her tenure on the Original Series and she runs a marathon with it. Uhura is treated as every bit an equal as her colleagues and Kirk regularly turns to her expertise in communications technology and internal ship operations for advice. Given that and knowing how involved Roddenberry was in the first twelve episodes of the Original Series, not to mention how he's missing in action here...Well, I know correlation doesn't imply causation, but let's just say I'm unbelievably happy Fontana is now showrunner.

And it's not just Uhura: Every single character gets a moment to shine here: Just like the gang in *Scooby-Doo, Where Are You!*, to pick an obvious and somewhat cheeky point of comparison, each officer has an important role to play in Kirk's crew. Spock makes observations and advises in matters concerning the physical sciences and Scotty uses his knowledge of metallurgy, space drive technology and engineering to help the crew figure out how the deserted starship works and how to get the magnetic organism to leave the *Enterprise*. Along with Uhura, Sulu is firmly established as the one who runs the ship when the landing party is away and McCoy is no longer the arbiter of Bristling Unchecked Passion, he's now the person who asks questions and makes common sense conjectures, which is very much appreciated.

I was also more than impressed with the animation on "Beyond the Farthest Star". Filmation has a not undeserved reputation for looking painfully cheap and phoned-in, and the 1970s were a notoriously poor decade for animation in general. And certainly, when turning this show on the first time, it's forgivable to be taken aback by the blatant overuse of limited animation. Limited animation is the name given to the technique of drawing a handful of cels and backgrounds and just reusing them over and over again: It's most famously associated with Hanna-Barbera shows (in particular the various Scooby-Doo incarnations), but *Star Trek: The Animated Series* simply pushes limited animation to the absolute breaking point-I don't think I've ever seen so many reused action poses. It's very revealing to sit down with a Filmation show, as it drives home that no matter the reputation Hanna-Barbera has for cheapness, they always managed to avoid letting their shows drop below a certain baseline of visual quality.

But even so, "Beyond the Farthest Star" still manages to look breathtaking. It's visual style is nowhere near as creative, ambitious and evocative as *Scooby-Doo, Where Are You!*, but even so this is hands-down the best looking Filmation show I've ever seen, and it may well be the best looking cartoon I've seen from the 1970s period. The insectoid ship where the *Enterprise* crew discover the magnetic organism is one of the most unique and stunningly gorgeous images in the history of Star Trek, and it was only possible because this was a cartoon. Even the *Enterprise* herself looks achingly gorgeous: I don't think this ship has ever looked as good as it does now in acrylic. After three years of cardboard, plywood and overly-shiny botched CGI attempts at "realism", the lush and evocative hand-painted space-scapes of "Beyond the Farthest Star" and *Star Trek: The Animated Series* are like a breath of fresh air. Everything about this episode is demonstrative of a production team charged with creative energy and resolutely determined to make the best possible show they can in the environment they have to work with, and then some.

And this is perhaps why "Beyond the Farthest Star" can be read as not just an echo of "Where No Man Has Gone Before", but a remake of it, and a bettering. This episode is about beginning Star Trek anew, and endeavouring to not repeat the same mistakes a second time. The biggest threat to the *Enterprise* here is firstly being dragged into the core of the dead sun because of its hypergravitational pull, and secondly, that the magnetic organism will assume the form of the *Enterprise* to raise an army of sentient starships to choke out the galaxy. And also recall the magnetic organism wishes to travel to the centre of the galaxy, to, in essence go backward, while the *Enterprise* crew wants to depart it, to move forward.

The danger here is that Star Trek will be mired once again by its unworkably contradictory nature (the dead sun, a literal dead end) or succumb to its darker predilections and become a monster (or destroy itself, as the insectoid ship was forced to do): Spock says the magnetic organism has in essence "become" the *Enterprise*: This isn't a demonic possession like we've seen with entities like Redjack; this entity has actually manged to temporarily *supplant* and take the place of the *Enterprise*. So, the battle isn't just to regain control of the ship, it's to reclaim Star Trek's identity. But, through working together and respecting each other, the *Enterprise* crew manages to defeat the entity and avoid hampering Star Trek with another non-starter. And tellingly, once this is done, the *Enterprise* is free to continue its journey outside the galaxy towards further enlightenment.

Star Trek has finally returned. And, with "Beyond the Farthest Star", it's finally proven to itself as much as to us that it's capable of journeying forever.

> "*Enterprise* log, Captain James Kirk commanding. We are leaving that vast cloud of stars and planets which we call our galaxy. Behind us, Earth, Mars, Venus, even our Sun, are specks of dust. The question: What is out there in the black void beyond? Until now our mission has been that of space law regulation, contact with Earth colonies and investigation of alien life. But now, a new task: A probe out into where no man has gone before."

102. "...of a mingled yarn": Yesteryear

"Yesteryear" is pure D.C. Fontana.

When returning from a mission of research into Federation history through the Guardian of Forever, Kirk is stunned to find out nobody on the *Enterprise* seems to recognise Spock, and that he himself doesn't recognise the person the crew is calling the ship's first officer: The Andorian Commander Thelin. A brief scan of the ship's record banks indicates that Sarek and Amanda, Spock's parents, divorced about twenty years ago after the death of their only son, Spock. This is of course, patently untrue as Spock is sitting at the table as the computer relays this information. The computer goes on to say that Amanda was later killed herself in a shuttlecraft accident. Reasoning that history has somehow been changed by their presence in the past, Kirk and Spock return to the planet and Spock recalls that the date he is said to have died is the same day he remembers being saved by his cousin Selek from an attacking wild animal. After being pressed by Kirk, Spock recalls that actually, now that he thinks about it, Selek looked an awful lot like him.

Before we go any further, I want to talk a little about the temporal mechanics in this story, as they're fascinatingly not the norm for Star Trek time travel stories. The crucial detail is in how the Guardian of Forever works: It exists at the vortex point where every timeline in the universe converges and, as a result, endlessly broadcasts a record of every possible time stream. We can interact with it by leaping through it at the appropriate moment. What happened was that while Kirk and Spock were in the past, Vulcan's own history was being broadcast at the same time. Because Spock saved his own life and he was in a different time stream when the moment he was supposed to save himself was playing, he missed the crucial moment. But he doesn't erase himself from history, to the contrary: He turns both himself and Kirk into historical orphans by jumping each other's time streams. In other words, the Guardian of Forever works like a television set.

Although this was hinted at a bit in "The City on the Edge of Forever", it's extremely clear in "Yesteryear". The different time streams are easily comparable to television stations, and the slow, methodical cycling through them all is very much like someone sitting down and turning the dial on their set. The Guardian even looks like an old-style tube TV in this episode. This is altogether fitting in the context of the position Star Trek is now in: The Original Series is now more popular than it's ever been and is enjoying runaway cult success in perpetual, neverending syndicated reruns. Meanwhile, along comes the Animated Series attempting to make a decisive claim for what the future of the franchise should look like, and there's already a considerable amount of ambivalence about the project. Star Trek fans are, in a sense, incessantly revisiting their own past by tuning into reruns and slavishly worshiping the Original Series to the expense of other bits of Star Trek and, in doing so, they might be missing experiences that are at the very least equally worthwhile and enjoyable.

On the other hand, recall we're still in an age before home video. Spock screws up his history essentially because he missed the programme about his past, and now he has to wait for the Guardian to come 'round to it again to sort it all out. He has to wait for the rerun to catch it again, in much the same way the creative team might have felt Star Trek was cheated out of a longer success because not enough people watched it in its previous incarnation. They have the opportunity to catch up now that the Original Series is in syndication, but it remains a part of their history, distant and unreachable. But furthermore, recall television episodes used to be seen as one-time, disposable performances: Thought of this way, reruns are in a sense akin to history happening again-We're seeing the echo of a past performance. In that regard, it's fun to think of the Federation researchers dutifully cataloging tricorder readings as fans trying to take telesnaps to preserve their favourite shows, or writers attempting to transcribe a script into a mass-market novelization.

(Speaking of the Federation researchers, it's kind of nice to see a female officer wearing pants for the first time).

But "Yesteryear" is a D.C. Fontana script, and ultimately that means it's a strong character piece, and in particular a strong character piece about Spock and his family. Following up on "Journey to Babel", Fontana hinges the emotional core of the story in exploring why Spock's family dynamic evolved the way it did, showing Young Spock caught in between his father's desire to push him onto a Vulcan path of pure logic and his mother's desire for him to become more in touch with his human emotional side. After an outburst of emotional violence at the hands of neighbourhood bullies, Young Spock runs off into the desert before his scheduled maturity trial to prove to himself as much as to his father that he's capable of making it as part of Vulcan society (this actually segues into one of the things that has always puzzled me about Star Trek: Vulcan bullies make no sense to me, *especially* ones that base their torment on xenophobic attitudes).

This is also the episode that even the people who have the most diehard objections to *Star Trek: The Animated Series* have to begrudgingly admit probably should be taken as canon. Fontana delivers a veritable flood of exposition about Spock's background and Vulcan history and culture, and most of the elements introduced here (in particular Amanda's last name being Grayson, the idea of Spock being tormented as a child, the capital city of ShirKahr and the sehlats) become established parts of lore and are referenced a lot in future Star Trek. Not that future writers can be blamed, as once again this episode looks jaw-droppingly gorgeous. ShirKahr, the Vulcan desert and the L-langon mountains are at once immediately reminiscent of what little we saw of Vulcan in "Amok Time" and utterly unique and evocative alien landscapes that look like nothing else. It's a triumph of world-building mixed with exquisite art design, and I had to keep reminding myself that I was still watching a Filmation show. It's that well done. The depiction of Vulcan here clearly goes on to influence all subsequent portrayals of the planet (including, perhaps ironically, the recreated CGI effects used in the 2007 rebroadcast version of "Amok Time") and the care and attention Fontana affords Vulcan here is emphasized in what *Star Trek: Deep Space*

Nine manifestly *doesn't* do with Bajor.

The only minor quibble I might have with the conception of Vulcan here is ironically enough the acting. Leonard Nimoy is great as always and it's nice to see Mark Lenard again (and to see Filmation was actually able to afford him), though he remains a low-key presence at best, albeit a dignified one. However, Jane Wyatt was unavailable to reprise the role of Amanda Grayson (meaning Filmation probably *couldn't* afford her), so the part had to go to Majel Barrett, The Animated Series' pinch-hitter female voice actor. And, well, let's just say Barrett is no James Doohan. She plays Amanda pretty much the same way she plays the Federation historian, which is pretty much the same way she played Number One and Nurse Chapel. I mean they don't just act vaguely similar, they sound almost identical. She doesn't exactly have a terrific range as an actor, and now I see why Bob Justman and Herb Solow recommended she be dropped from the Original Series after "The Cage". But this is an *extremely* minor complaint: If Barrett's the only person Filmation could get, than she's the only person they could get. Everyone's clearly trying their absolute hardest, and I'm inclined to forgive that (although one wonders why they didn't ask Nichelle Nichols to double up on a few parts too).

(Speaking of Amanda, it's worth taking note of how Fontana has her be the one whose perspective is ignored by Sarek and Young Spock: Spock doesn't want to connect with his "human" side because he fears becoming too "emotional". Symbols and shades of more than a few things there, I should think.)

Returning to the actual plot, the episode's touching climax is, of course, when Young Spock's pet sehlat I-Chaya succumbs to fatal injuries after his battle with Godzilla (seriously, the episode straight-up jacks Godzilla's signature roar from the Toho movies for a Vulcan monster. I thought I was being clever with my *Godzilla vs. King Ghidorah* joke in the James Blish chapter), which wasn't technically supposed to happen. However, Old Spock uses the tragedy to teach Young Spock that it's OK to let people we love die with dignity, and that Vulcans can have emotion, in spite of what others think of them. The difference is that Vulcans do not let raw emotion control and consume them. It seems like a moment of revelation for both Spocks, and just like she had before, Fontana deftly and neatly resolves Star Trek's unnecessary logic/emotion schism by demonstrating that both are valuable for living a healthy and full life.

Actually, "Yesteryear" goes one step beyond "Journey to Babel": In the Original Series episode, Spock stubbornly refused to admit this and continued to take glib pot shots at irrational humans. Here though, Old Spock's defining moment is when he tells his younger self to take pride in both sides of his heritage, and his request of Sarek to try and understand his son. He even cracks a joke in the denouement that stuns McCoy, and flat-out admits to the screen that "times change". So, Spock hasn't actually restored the timeline, he's in fact created a new one and, in spite of the death of I-Chaya, arguably a better one: As much credit as the Original Series movies get for showing an older, wiser Spock who has learned to balance his Vulcan and human side (which is really code from him coming to terms with all sides of himself), it's really the Animated Series, and this episode in particular, that moved him in this direction, and it's all on D.C Fontana. And, as just an aside, this means that the Animated Series has managed to do a soft reboot of the entire Star Trek universe, which seems like a more than fitting thing for it to do. Last week we had something that was suspiciously evocative of the first televised Star Trek episode, and now we have proof: *Star Trek: The Animated Series* both is and is not a continuation of *Star Trek*. It's a new *Star Trek*, and a superior one.

103. "Whatever I see, I shall devour!": One Of Our Planets Is Missing

The title "One Of Our Planets Is Missing" sort of lets you know right from the start what kind of story you're in for. There's a giant space cloud going around literally eating planets which the *Enterprise* crew notices when, in fact, one of their planets happens to go missing. It's at once the kind of delightfully mental science fiction concept that can really only be done justice to through animation, but also a plot that's simple and straightforward enough to convey in twenty minutes.

We haven't talked much yet about the difference in runtimes between Animated Series and Original Series episodes. A necessary consequence of changing from a primetime drama to a Saturday Morning Cartoon Show is that the episodes went from being fifty minutes each in the 1960s to only being twenty minutes each on the 1970s. This is largely to Star Trek's benefit: One of the biggest problems with the pulp style of pacing and structure the Original Series had is that it's essentially built around padding. The average pulp action serial plot is nothing more than a series of tedious captures and escapes occasionally broken up with an implausible, ridiculous and unnecessarily gratuitous fight scene. And indeed, it's a model of storytelling Gene Roddenberry was quite a fan of, even judging only by "The Omega Glory" and "The Savage Curtain". What this means is that, stretched to fifty minutes, this kind of plot grows tiring and irritating extremely quickly. However, now that Star Trek is a cartoon, it doesn't have the luxury to indulge itself like that anymore: Twenty minutes is just enough time to set up the basic plot, lay out the boundaries of the conflict and than do something about it before the credits role again.

Which is exactly what we get in "One Of Our Planets Is Missing". The titular planetary misplacement occurs, we get to see some funky looking space cloud that eats things and then there's a rapid-fire bit of exposition about how it exhibits traits of unicellular organisms and grazing animals and oh, by the way, it's currently on a direct course to a planet inhabited by millions of people so we'd probably best figure out a way to stop that. Then the *Enterprise* itself gets engulfed and partially digested, so, well, shit. With that taken care of, the episode gets to focus on the actual interesting bits, which involve the *Enterprise* crew making continuous observations about the creature and debating amongst themselves what the best course of action to take is. Nobody has to get kidnapped and we don't have to introduce some left-field plot element three-quarters of the way through: It's just the distilled essence of a Star Trek space adventure. The episode doesn't quite pick up on all the intricacies afforded by its new model yet (there's a wee bit too much technobabble even for my tastes) but honestly? In the scheme of things I've complained about so far? This is nothing. Really the only concern I have now is these episodes are becoming straightforward enough and I still have to write the same amount of words on a story that's about half as long as I'm used to so I'm worried I'm going to run out of things to say.

On the surface "One Of Our Planets Is Missing" seems to borrow heavily from a number of Original Series highlights, in particular the ones called "The Doomsday Machine" and "The Immunity Syndrome". All three are taught thrillers, complete with countdown timers, all three involve giant, pan-galactic things that go around snacking on solar systems and all three also ultimately end up in some kind of ethical debate about self-sacrifice for the greater good and what precisely the *Enterprise*'s obligation to New Life is. But to say "One Of Our Planets Is Missing" is simply copying the two Original Series episodes would be misreading it a bit: It *is* most definitely similar in a great many respects, but that's because it's part of the same genre of Star Trek story, and it's a genre that the Original Series could have stood to partake in a bit more often and that the newfound leanness of the Animated Series is actually very well suited to. And furthermore, I'd go so far as to say the ethics of "One Of Our Planets Is Missing" are actually a bit more defined and more laudable here than in at least "The Immunity Syndrome".

The big difference here when compared to this story's most obvious antecedent is that the giant space creature is sentient, thus making it suitably more difficult for Kirk to just blow it up. Indeed, the scene where Kirk posits that as a possible course of action is one of the best in the episode: Even with the limited animation, it's one of those scenes that seems to call out for a record scratch as everyone on the bridge turns to Kirk in horror at what he's suggesting. Spock and Uhura rightly point out that it's the *Enterprise*'s mission to seek out and contact new forms of life, and to kill the space cloud is just about the most comprehensive betrayal of that mission possible. This is extremely cathartic for me because it's such a refutation of the paper-thin excuses the Original Series used in an attempt to waive its responsibilities in favour of Blowing Shit Up. And where "One Of Our Planets Is Missing" goes from here is really clever: Kirk says if the choice is to be his, he'll side with saving the humans over the creature (and possibly even exploding the *Enterprise* inside the creature's brain if it'll get the job done) unless Spock, McCoy and Uhura come up with a third option. Kirk was trained as a soldier first, remember.

Which they do. Spock, tying into Uhura's modified communications circuits, "projects his mind" outward in what amounts to a large-scale mind-meld (but that also suspiciously looks like astral projection, another sign that, with the Animated Series, Star Trek is embracing mysticism more seriously), showing the creature that beings live on the things it consumes, and imploring it to return to where it came from so it doesn't endanger any more lives. The creature, being both intelligent and reasonable, feels bad about the destruction its caused and doesn't want to hurt anyone, so it apologizes, releases the *Enterprise* and then goes home. The problem was the cloud was literally so vast it couldn't conceive that there were forms of life smaller than it; life-forms that would to it seem possibly beyond microscopic. In a way, this can be seen as a fitting metaphor for privilege blindness: From the cloud's vantage point, it was unable to truly know how much its actions hurt others until Spock was able to contact it, and even then only after Uhura was able to make it *hear* and *understand*

Spock's voice. Finally, through communication the cloud, the *Enterprise* crew and the planet's population have all grown a little: It's a wonderful testament to and glorification of the power and potential of discourse to make the world a better place.

However all that said, there's another consequence of Star Trek metamorphosing into a Saturday Morning Cartoon Show. It's an aftereffect that's not quite as notable yet, but will be, painfully so, in at least one future episode. That is, of course, the assumption that because it's animated its primary audience has to be children, and with that an obligation to cater *especially* towards children. There was even a little bit of this last week: D.C. Fontana has said she felt the idea of letting loved ones, in particular pets, die with dignity was an important lesson for children to learn. Never mind of course the fact that "Yesteryear" was absolutely brilliant as is and didn't at all need to be justified through or read in that light to be effective. Here though we get the other side of children's television: The irritating assumption that it has to be prescriptively educational to be worthwhile (seriously, I thought Lewis Carroll already laid that argument to rest in the 1860s).

So, in "One Of Our Planets Is Missing", we get to spend large portions of the technobabble explaining how the biological process of digestion work and what villi in the intestines are. Handled properly this would be no problem, but the show hasn't quite figured out how to do that cleanly yet: Kirk, a person who really should know better, is written as the one who prompts Spock and McCoy for all the exposition and it feels a bit off. Although all that said this doesn't really detract from the episode on the whole, certainly not to the degree ti could have. Once again, it's good enough to stand on its own and this is ultimately just demonstrative of the growing pains the series still has to go through. And, after all, a not-insignificant portion of the Original Series' fans were in fact children: There's a potential for a crossover appeal here that doesn't hurt the work itself. What "One Of Our Planets Is Missing" is really setting the stage for then is a future where Star Trek gets to be a show that can appeal to a lot of different audiences on a lot of different levels without talking down to any of them.

And on top of that this is just another great production: The cast are all once again in fine form and all used to great extent and the animation is once again gorgeous (especially the depiction of the inside of the cloud creature). James Doohan delivers another memorable performance as both Scotty and Bob Wesley (back from "The Ultimate Computer", which is nice to see as he never got any closure or resolution for that episode's conflict). In fact, Doohan is *so* good as Wesley that I initially thought the show had managed to get Barry Russo back: He sounds practically identical. Majel Barrett plays the cloud and, well, she's still not great, but I don't want to pick on Barrett's acting abilities so let's just say this is a factor we'll just have to accept and move on. I'll cut her some slack and assume Uhura channeled the cloud's voice through the *Enterprise* mainframe so it was speaking with the ship's computer's voice.

While "One Of Our Planets Is Missing" may not be *quite* as good as "Beyond the Farthest Star" and "Yesteryear" (which were admittedly almost impossibly high standards to meet) it's still excellent and without question one of the best Star Trek stories in *years*. The comparison with "The Doomsday Machine" now seems even more fitting. That was the episode I said the show needed to be shooting for as a baseline level of quality and the fact it wasn't was damning. But now it is. This is the new standard now. We've turned a corner such that the Animated Series can throw out three of the absolute best stories the franchise has done yet one after another and this is business as usual. In four years and five episodes we've gone from "The Savage Curtain" and "Turnabout Intruder" to this. Incredible.

Really, what could possibly go wrong?

104. "I may have the body of a weak and feeble woman...": The Lorelei Signal

Margaret Armen could happen, that's what!

For the fourth episode of *Star Trek: The Animated Series*, D.C. Fontana and her team brings back Original Series veteran Margaret Armen for the first of two contributions to the new show. "The Lorelei Signal" concerns a planet of women with hypnotic powers over men who, in the manner of Sirens (or really, the Rhine Maidens from Wagner's *Der Ring des Nibelungen*) lure starships to their world so they can drain the life force of their male crewmembers in order to remain eternally young and beautiful.

There is nothing in the above paragraph that evokes hope, inspiration, wonderousness or anything that embodies goodness or joy.

Margaret Armen is the single worst writer in the history of Star Trek. At least Gene Roddenberry actually made overtures to improve himself: Just of what we've seen so far, "Turnabout Intruder" marked something of a potential turnaround for him, "Assignment: Earth" wasn't *entirely* unwatchable and there were some good bits in the part of the first season he oversaw. Armen, however, is some kind of Dark Mirror of D.C. Fontana: She's the only other woman writer to contribute more than two scripts during this period, and she regularly struggles with issues of representation such that it overshadows every other aspect of her work. Both "The Gamesters of Triskelion" and "The Paradise Syndrome" are serious contenders for the title of worst Star Trek story ever, or at least worst in the Original Series just on structural terms. That's not even getting into her aforementioned terrible track record on ethnic representation: The depiction of Native Americans in the latter episode was absolutely inexcusable, and she's only going to get worse. The only thing remotely positive she's ever been associated with was "The Cloud Minders", which was already far from perfect, and she still only wrote the teleplay in that case and was working off a Dave Gerrold/Oliver Crawford joint venture.

Of all the writers to bring back, I cannot begin to fathom why Armen was anywhere near the top of the list. She's not even the second-best or second most-experienced woman writer we've seen so far, if that's what the team was going for: I can't come up with a single conceivable reason not to give Shari Lewis, Judy Burns, Joyce Muskat or even Jean Lisette Aroeste a couple more shots before bringing Margaret Fucking Armen back. Maybe you think I'm being too harsh on her. Maybe you figure that freed from the constraints of the Original Series and with D.C. Fontana's help Armen is going to be allowed to blossom here. You would be sadly mistaken-"The Lorelei Signal" is another crateringly awful disaster.

The key twist is that the women hypnotize and suck the life out of the men because they're trapped on a planet that causes rapid aging while giving women inexplicable and ill-defined powers over men. So *obviously* this was the only course of action available to them. Also, they feel their immortal lives are shallow and meaningless because while they have eternal youth they're rendered unable to bear children. If I didn't know better I'd swear this drivel was dreamed up by the the most defiantly and proudly retrograde misogynistic scumball man to ever haunt Hollywood. But no. A *woman* came up with this. I don't care what anybody says, internalized misogyny is a real thing.

Incidentally, I'm also at a loss to explain the Rhine Maiden stuff. It would have been just as easy, hell, *easier* to just flat-out call the women in this story Sirens. Although, astonishingly. this is technically more accurate, why was it necessary to evoke the Ring Cycle specifically? Just like she did in "The Gamesters of Triskelion", Armen is once insultingly oversimplifying an aspect of Germanic folklore: Wagner has as much to do with Germanic heathenism as Tinkerbell has to do with Celtic mythology, which leads me to the rather astonishing conclusion that Armen had some sort of bizarrely specific motif of badly misreading Northern European traditions and making her stories needlessly and distractingly complicated and confusing.

"The Lorelei Signal" is so deathly uninspiring that the majority of the cast practically didn't even bother to show up. William Shatner, Leonard Nimoy and DeForest Kelley deliver the most painfully phoned in and apathetic performances I have *ever* seen from them and don't even attempt to sell the rapid aging Kirk, Spock and McCoy are subjected to here. Even in "The Deadly Years", from which this episode cribs rather blatantly, those three at least managed to make the aged versions of their characters somewhat entertaining. Here they don't even try: It actually sounds like they're all on the verge of falling asleep. Majel Barrett too delivers yet another unremarkable turn here, but this time I'm less willing to forgive her because in this case it's a serious problem that gets in the way of the episode's effectiveness (I mean, such as it is). There are almost a dozen female characters in this episode, Barrett ends up voicing almost all of them and she is patently not skilled enough to pull this off. As a result, all of her characters end up sounding literally identical and none of them have identifiable personalities *including Nurse Chapel, who's supposed to have a major role in this episode.* The only time Barrett is allowed to actually emote is, of course, the scene where Chapel cries over what's happened to Spock.

There are only two people in the entire production who seem to give a damn about this story, not counting Armen herself, and even that's debatable. One is James Doohan, who is predictably good. The few non-regular male voices we get to hear are of course him, and his performances and Barrett's are an exercise in contrast. The subtle, dreamlike preoccupation Doohan affords Scotty as he starts to be entranced by the signal is masterful, and is on par with absolutely anything Leonard Nimoy ever did with Spock. The other person is Nichelle Nichols. It's here where "The Lorelei Signal" becomes a kind of Curate's Egg, because Uhura gets to carve out the meatiest role she'll ever have in the entire franchise, brazenly relieving Scotty of duty and taking command of the *Enterprise* herself. Uhura gets more material than any other character and even gets to record her own Captain's Log entries.

And Nichols just runs wild with it, delivering every bit of a commanding and inspiring performance as anyone else who has ever played a starship captain and decisively proving how disgracefully wasted she was in the Original Series. The scene in the climax where she leads an all-female SWAT team of security officers to storm the alien Rhine Maidens' temple phasers blazing demanding the release of Kirk, Spock and McCoy is poetry in motion and should be seen as one of the most iconic moments of this period of the franchise. And indeed it perhaps would have been, if it had been in an episode written by literally anyone other than Margaret Armen. And it's Uhura who gets to resolve the plot, getting the entire denouement to herself pointing out the solution that should have been screaming obvious from the start: Just move the Rhine Maidens to another planet and offer Federation assistance to relocate them.

But maddeningly, and sadly, this still isn't good enough. Despite how hard Nichols is clearly trying, the script doesn't allow Uhura and Chapel to come up with any ideas on their own after they initially figure out what's going on. They have to wait for Kirk, Spock and McCoy to advise them on what to do and don't make any decisions without their input first. Appallingly, the *Enterprise* even has gender-segregated specialty divisions now too (as Uhura makes reference to a "women's science team" and a "women's engineering") which goes completely against absolutely everything women have loved about Star Trek from the beginning and the utopian vision they saw in it. Essentially Armen is telling us that Girl Power is all well and good, but ultimately women will never be able to break out of their designated social roles and the only progress they can hope for is to cheekily play around with the hand they've been dealt. She's writing her characters in precisely the way I praised Diana Muldaur for *not* acting in "Return to Tomorrow": Armen's women are the sisters the boys begrudgingly bring along with them on their adventures because their moms told them to. They're the girls just happy the boys let them play with them for a bit, even if it means playing the neglected, subservient, vestigial support role.

If nothing else she's done to date has convinced you, this, more than anything else, should get you to join me in chorus to declare *Fuck You, Margaret Armen.*

This sort of thing really rankles me. Aside from being a flat-out betrayal of just about everything I love about Star Trek and pointedly retrograde, it's offensive to me on a *personal* level. Female role models have always been extremely important to me, to the point the vast majority of my heroes and idols *are* women. I adored Star Trek because it was one of the only places on television or books or whatever where women were unabashedly and unquestionably treated as equals. I know it isn't always like this and certainly on more than one occasion the show simply pays hollow lip service to feminist issues, but the fact remains the bits of Star Trek that *are* feminist are good enough to solidify feminism as a major and important part of the franchise's legacy. Representation issues get to me, and to see Star Trek of all things flounder around with gender issues gets to me in particular. It can do so much better. It *should* do so much better.

Really what this all does is make me feel genuinely sorry for Margaret Armen. I can't imagine the scope of the internalized misogyny issues she must have been dealing with to crank out a story this weighed down by reactionary anti-feminism, and for something like Star Trek no less. "The Lorelei Signal" is Armen's worst outing so far, though far, *far* from her worst overall, and that's saying a *lot* when we're talking about the person responsible for "The Gamesters of Triskelion" and "The Paradise Syndrome". And this was an episode Armen said she had *fun* writing. Jesus. Aside from Nichols' admittedly brilliant turn, the only positive thing to take from this episode is the knowledge that, for the first time, we can safely disregard a Margaret Armen story without fear the show's going to be permanently derailed. The first three episodes of *Star Trek: The Animated Series* were stellar enough that even the sad tale of Margaret Armen isn't enough to kill its momentum.

And next time the series gets to revisit one of Star Trek's greatest triumphs.

105. "purr purr": More Tribbles, More Troubles

Making a sequel to an Original Series episode is a self-evidently obvious thing for the Animated Series to be doing. Doubly so when the episode in question is "The Trouble with Tribbles".

I don't think there's any disputing the fact "The Trouble with Tribbles" was the moment at which Star Trek secured its immortality. It's pretty much the definition of "iconic" and an absolutely perfect bit of television. No questions asked. In fact, perhaps the most damning evidence the season three team simply didn't understand Star Trek is to be found in Fred Freiberger saying "The Trouble with Tribbles" was too silly a thing for the show to be doing. But that said there's danger in revisiting a story like this. There's a significant risk that, in doing so, the sequel will inevitably cheapen the original's impact and retroactively damage its reputation. Sequels simply are not as good as their source material, and I'm comfortable making that a firm declaration. There are rare exceptions of course and serialized, episodic stories are another matter entirely, but as a general rule that's frankly the way it is.

Things look pretty bad for "More Troubles, More Tribbles" then. However, this is no ordinary sequel: For one, Dave Gerrold is writing again (and mercifully back in what's familiar and comfortable territory for him this time) and then there's the matter of this being planned for the third season of the Original Series. "More Troubles, More Tribbles" was not meant as a cheap cash-in on the popularity and legacy of the Original Series' most beloved episode for the low-budget animated spinoff, it was a follow-up the original writer wanted to write, and for the "proper", "grown-up" show to boot. Gerrold was one of the first people D.C. Fontana called when the Animated Series was greenlit and, as the two had become friends, basically told him "and the first thing you're doing is writing that Tribble episode you wanted for the third season". And so it was.

But even so, there's an inescapable sense of...sequel-ness about "More Tribbles, More Troubles". The *Enterprise* is escorting two robot ships loaded with special quintotriticale grain (it's like quadrotriticale, except *quinto*) to Sherman's Planet (of course) and they have to be on the lookout for the Klingons (of course) who are rumoured to be testing a new super weapon. Eventually, they run into some: A Klingon battlecruiser is pursuing a Federation scout ship and relentlessly pummeling it with disruptor fire. As this is in violation of treaty, the *Enterprise* moves to intercept and Kirk demands a cease fire, which is soundly ignored. A couple more volleys of words and gunfire and the scout ship is destroyed (though not before Scotty manages to rescue the pilot and cargo) and the *Enterprise* gets whacked with the Klingon's new weapon, a projected stasis field that immobilizes all higher level energy functions on a starship, but drains a massive amount of power from the user's own ship. The pilot turns out to be Cyrano Jones (of course) carrying a cargo of Tribbles (of course) genetically engineered to not breed (of course). The Klingons hail the *Enterprise,* and it turns out the commander is Kirk's old friend Koloth (of course) who demands Kirk hand Jones over to stand trial for Eco-terrorisim.

This episode is also a good case study on precisely what Gene Coon contributed to stories he had a hand in, and indeed how much of "The Trouble with Tribbles" was in fact his. "More Tribbles, More Troubles" isn't quite as tight and smooth as its predecessor. While the writing, in particular the dialog, is still first class, it just doesn't seem to flow quite as well, and there are a few confusing logic and plot points. Jones says he was able to get off *Deep Space K-7* early because he had help from a Glommer, supposedly the Tribbles' natural predator. But later, it turns out Jones stole the Glommer from a Klingon colony, and the Glommer is an organism genetically engineered to specifically prey on Tribbles. It's never made clear at what point during his sentence Jones was able to pop off to a Klingon colony and pick one up, and indeed it's further revealed this is the whole reason the Klingons are after him in the first place. Also, the big gimmick this time is that the Tribbles don't multiply, they just grow larger (even McCoy confirms this), and this causes problems of their own. But then it turns out they *do* in fact multiply and the giant Tribbles are in truth just huge colonies of Tribbles. Things like this don't really significantly detract from this episode, but it's clear it could have used a bit more polish.

The acting too is a little bit changeable: The main cast are all terrific, in fact this might be their best outing in the Animated Series yet and light-years removed from their near-comatose performances last time. Stanley Adams is back as Cyrano Jones too and is as good as always, probably proving he was a better actor than a writer. But, because this is Filmation, we could only afford one Special Guest Star this week so that means Koloth is played by James Doohan. Not to knock Doohan, who was amazing, and he does as good a job as can be expected of him, but it's hard not to deeply miss William Campbell in that role. The banter between Kirk and Koloth just isn't the same without him there. This is more or less forgivable though, as "More Tribbles, More Troubles" was really the first episode produced for the Animated Series, so we're watching the production at a much earlier point in time this week.

But none of this to say "More Tribbles, More Troubles" is especially *bad* either. Far from it-It's perfectly delightful. There are a number of genuinely charming moments here. My favourites are Kirk repeatedly having to push the steadily-growing Tribble colony off his chair and his interactions with Jones and Koloth. This exchange in particular is just classic:

> KOLOTH [on viewscreen]: Ah, Captain Kirk. We'll take control of your ship now.
>
> KIRK: Not if I can help it.
>
> KOLOTH [on viewscreen]: I want your prisoner.
>
> KIRK: Much as I hate to admit it, Captain Koloth, Cyrano Jones is a citizen of

the Federation and entitled to Federation protection. I must, much as it pains me, refuse your request.

KOLOTH [on viewscreen]: It is not a request. Don't force me to take steps that we will both regret.

KIRK: Close channel, Lieutenant.

UHURA: With pleasure, sir.

SPOCK: Aren't you going to sit down, sir? (the captain's chair is occupied by a Tribble colony bigger than Kirk)

KIRK: I think I'll stand.

I also love what Gerrold does with the other characters: Scotty muttering under his breath as the transporter keeps acting up is terrific, and Uhura seems to have taken up the role previously occupied by Chekov as the ship's resident smartass, and its a fantastic use of her character. Just after the *Enterprise* is hit by the projected stasis field and Spock points out that literally all systems are inoperative, Uhura snarks "Well, we could always throw rocks" and you can *hear* Nichelle Nichols' eyes rolling as she delivers the line. It's delightful.

Furthermore, there's a legitimate plot reason you'd want to bring the Tribbles back aside from their marquee value, and Gerrold does seem to get this. What the Tribbles seem best suited to is the sort of story where they can hang around in the background for a bit seemingly as a cute B-story before suddenly exploding into and seizing control of the main plot as a metaphor for how the situation has spiraled out of control. Indeed, the ever-growing Tribble colonies in this story are an almost better metaphor for a "snowballing" situation than the multiplying ones in "The Trouble with Tribbles". Secondly, Tribbles are very good at diffusing conflict and pointing out its absurdity, and they gamely do both of these things here. In the first episode they showed up to put an end to the Federation and the Klingon Empire's ridiculously macho diplomatic posturing, and here they stop Kirk and Koloth from blasting each other out of the sky and starting a war, which is a fitting raising of the stakes.

(We'll ignore, I suppose, the fact Kirk resolves the crisis the exact same way Scotty did in "The Trouble with Tribbles" by transporting all the Tribbles to the Klingon engine room. At least Koloth points out that "He did it to us again!").

Ultimately though it's hard to get too worked up about this episode. It's inoffensive, more than entertaining, and at twenty minutes it doesn't take up a lot of your time. Best of all, it displays all the hallmarks of an above-average sequel: It doesn't detract from or retroactively ruin the original work and can be safely disregarded if you're so inclined. But why would you want to? "More Tribbles, More Troubles" delivers exactly what it says it's going to in its title, and it's tough to get upset about that.

106. "The Unreal McCoy": The Survivor

On the surface, there's not a whole lot interesting going on with "The Survivor". Answering a distress signal from a one-person starship, the *Enterprise* crew is thrilled to discover it's registered to Federation philanthropist and hero Carter Winston, missing and presumed dead for five years. As it happens, Winston's fiance is aboard the ship: Eager to resume the relationship she goes to meet him, only to have him break her heart by saying he's not the same person he was when he proposed. It quickly turns out that Winston is quite *literally* not the same person anymore, as he is, in fact, a shapeshifting alien Romulan operative who goes on to assume the forms of Kirk and McCoy to divert the *Enterprise* into the Neutral Zone, thus giving the Romulans a reason to justify impounding the ship so they can reverse engineer it. Similarities immediately appear between this episode, "The Enterprise Incident", "The Man Trap" and any one of the million billion other evil twin stories Star Trek has done for the past decade.

And exasperation is a not entirely unwarranted reaction, as this is definitely one of the weakest Animated Series episodes we've seen yet, with or without Margaret Armen. The evil duplicate plot is, predictably, stultifyingly boring, but thankfully the show doesn't linger on it that long and the crew figures out what's happening pretty quickly, so there's a minor plus. I'd really appreciate it if this franchise, or any show, really, never did one of these stories again, but I suppose if it must it's nice to see it somewhat self-aware and willing to address some of the inherent flaws with this kind of plot. The Romulans are, of course, wrong: Sending in spies to clandestinely violate the peace treaty with the Federation is behaviour in keeping with *Star Trek: The Next Generation*-era Romulans, but not the Romulans as we see them at this point. Of course, nobody except D.C. Fontana and Paul Schneider have ever gotten the Romulans actually right, so that's to be expected...Except for the fact one of those people is the current executive producer and therefore a person one would expect might have been in a position to catch this. Really, you could have replaced the Romulans with Klingons and the episode would have been just as effective, if not a bit more so. They're generic baddies, and indeed the Romulan ships shown here are, in fact, Klingon.

Although that said the actual Romulan Commander we get to interact with (who astonishingly *still doesn't get a name*: Seriously, say what you will about *Star Trek: The Next Generation*'s Romulans-they at least had the decency to name them) is terrific. His exchanges with Kirk are delightfully snarky and self-aware. My favourite exchange in the episode comes here, where the *Enterprise* is first surrounded by Romulan battlecruisers:

> ROMULAN COMMANDER [on viewscreen]: You appear to have a propensity for trespassing in the Neutral Zone, Captain Kirk.

KIRK: It was not deliberate, I assure you.

ROMULAN COMMANDER [on viewscreen]: It never *is*. But the rules of the treaty are clear. To contravene them would mean war. You will surrender your ship, Captain. We will release you and your crew at the nearest outpost that guards the Neutral Zone.

I just love how the show seems perfectly aware of how hackneyed and overused a dramatic crutch the Romulan Neutral Zone is. One wishes the writers of *Star Trek: The Next Generation* had paid closer attention to this particular plot point. Not that the cynicism necessarily excuses the laziness mind, but it does help. And I love the way James Doohan delivers the line, sounding tired, exasperated and *amicable*: Once again, we see the Romulans and the Federation portrayed as friendly people on opposite sides of a war forced to do what they do by their social roles. I choose to believe this Romulan Commander was unaware of what his government was plotting with the undercover shapeshifting alien spy and was being nothing less then gracious and honest.

Although that said, the space battle that takes up the back half of the episode is more than a little problematic. Much ink, digital or otherwise, has been spilled on how somewhat paradoxical it is that Star Trek, a franchise supposedly built around peaceful solutions to problems, frequently resolves its diplomatic situations through engaging in flashy ray-gun space battles. This is, frankly, mostly due to the fact Star Trek is science fiction, and science fiction as a genre is primarily based around two things: Golden Age logic puzzle plots and Pulp style action. As a result, any science fiction, especially action sci-fi (which Star Trek becomes on more than one occasion) is heavily indebted to a cinematic spectacle style of storytelling, and cinematic spectacles require big flashy setpieces. Maybe someday there will come a day when science fiction finds a way to resolve this fundamental contradiction to become something truly remarkable...But today is not that day.

(Star Trek also has the additional problem of being conceived of by Gene Roddenberry as a militaristic action show that then tries to reconcile itself with its grafted-on utopianism. And it *never* reconciles this.)

The *Enterprise* doesn't resolve tensions with the Romulans through discourse, it resolves them by blasting their engines to bits and the shapeshifting alien spy having a last minute change of heart. This is especially discouraging as this comes just one week after Dave Gerrold's "More Tribbles, More Troubles", which used the Tribbles to lampoon macho space combat. One week after giant Tribble colonies overwhelmed the gun decks of two gigantic space battleships, we have a completely unironic and straightforward skirmish played totally straight. And look I'll be honest, I like colourful laser battles and big explosions as much as the next person, but there's a time and a place for that sort of thing and this combined with Star Trek's unhealthy predilection towards militarism creates a mixture that doesn't exactly sit well with me. This is the time when Star Trek is supposed to be demonstrating it's better than this, but it looks like it still has some growing to do.

But the real story of "The Survivor", or at least what should have been the real story if it wasn't intended to be, is the relationship of the shapeshifting alien spy with Winston's fiance, security officer Anne Nored. What happened was Winston crash-landed on the home planet of the Vendorians (the aforementioned shapeshifting aliens) where he lived in their care for a time until he died. This particular Vendorian was disgraced by his people because he didn't have a meaningful role in his planets society (something considered deeply hurtful and dishonourable to a Vendorian) and fell in with the Romulans because they offered him a purpose. The Vendorian first tries to break off the relationship with Nored claiming that five years changes a person and that the people who rescued him physically "changed" him further and that he's no longer the person he was when he proposed to her. But the real reason is that he is, in fact, a Vendorian (an actually imaginative bit of creature design: A multi-limbed, many-eyed floating tentacle creature) and that he still cared for Nored and didn't think she could love a being such as he. The final twist comes when the Vendorian reveals that his people tend to adopt traits of the things they transform into, and that he's spent enough time as Carter Winston to appreciate the values he strove for and this is what causes him to pitch in and save the *Enterprise* from the Romulans at the last minute.

There's a great story here, and as little as it actually goes into it "The Survivor" is genuinely breaking new ground here. The tragic tale of the Vendorian is a very fitting analogy for precisely what he brings up early on: The fact that people really *do* change over time and things like relationships are ultimately fleeting things. People can grow apart. Indeed, the whole fact the Vendorians are shapeshifters could be seen as a metaphor for this, and it gets back at the nut of what was so genius about "The Conscience of the King": We shape ourselves into different roles and different people at different points in our lives, and this is a perfect story for Star Trek, which already inherits so much from theatre, to be telling.

But of course it's nowhere near as *clear* here as it was in "The Conscience of the King", which savvily populated its cast with members of an in-universe acting troupe. "The Survivor" would probably have been more effective if Carter Winston turned out not to be a shapeshifting alien, but some kind of cyborg augmented by a bunch of machine parts by his benefactor to keep him alive, but changing him in the process. That would have been a much more straightforward way of highlighting how people change over time. After all, the cells in our body are completely replaced every seven years. Each time that happens, we are quite literally no longer the same person. And furthermore, there was absolutely no reason for the Romulans or the sabotage plot to be here at all: This is a good enough story on its own. However it's worth pointing out this is one of the first times *since* "The Conscience of the King" that Star Trek, or any genre work really, has attempted to use science fiction concepts in this manner, so as rocky as it is "The Survivor" remains a definite and clear step forward. It's promising to see Star Trek trying to return to and update the motifs of a story like "The Conscience of the King" as opposed to a story like, say, "The Cage" or "The Omega Glory".

When watched alongside four absolute triumphs and "The Lorelei Signal", this episode certainly feels underwhelming. But really, what we have this week in the end is a filler episode, and as much as a truly effective version of "the Survivor" would have required a version of Star Trek that doesn't exist yet, this is still a very positive sign. Usually

479

when filler episodes show up it's, counterintuitively, an indication the show is on solid and comfortable ground. And the bits of this episode that do hint at a way forward are demonstrative that Star Trek is still heading in the right direction.

107. "I wanna be big!": The Infinite Vulcan

"The Infinite Vulcan" is Walter Koenig's sole contribution to the Animated Series, and if *absolutely* nothing else it's solid evidence Star Trek's cast by in large tends to have a good idea about what the franchise's virtues are, whether or not other creative figures do. Koenig was actually working on this script as early as the end of the Original Series, and it was one of those things that D.C. Fontana and Gene Roddenberry thought would be a great idea to dig up as soon as the new show took off, just like "More Tribbles, More Troubles".

The plot is one of the stranger ones we've seen so far in the Animated Series, and that's counting the one about the giant space-cloud-cow that eats solar systems that the *Enterprise* tries to give indigestion. While exploring an uncharted planet, Kirk, Spock, McCoy and Sulu discover a civilization of hyper-intelligent sentient plants called Phylosians. While they at first seem friendly, reviving Sulu after a chance encounter with local toxins, it is soon revealed they have ulterior motives as they kidnap Spock at the behest of their "Master", a fifty foot tall clone of a former Eugenics Warlord by the name of Stavos Keniclius 5. Keniclius is determined to forcibly impose peace on a what he considers a galaxy in turmoil, and in Spock's mastery of Vulcan logic and human emotion and intuition he sees the perfect model by which to base his new society, so he steals his brain and makes a fifty foot tall clone of *him* to help rebuild the Phylosians' space fleet.

A...controversial episode, to say the least, I definitely think "The Infinite Vulcan" is working through some very interesting ideas. Just like last week, the Animated Series is picking up abandoned ideas from the Original Series (and ones that it was a mistake to abandon in my opinion) and trying to take them further. However, also like last week, "The Infinite Vulcan" is held back by a lot of missteps that make it feel less then effective, and there's a general sense of "been there, done that" about the proceedings. In this case, the closest analog is naturally "Patterns of Force", which shares this episode's attitude towards liberal authority and top-down pacifism. Keniclius is depicted as being very much in the wrong for taking up the mantle of imposing peace throughout the galaxy, and the episode's best moment comes when Kirk essentially asks him why he thinks he has the right to do that. And it didn't even need to bring in Nazis. The problem is, this time the script completely fails to offer any kind of solution or alternative. The whole point of "Patterns of Force", Nazis or otherwise, was denouncing what Kirk comes right out and calls "the leader principle". Anyone who aspires to a position of power by definition thinks they know better than everyone else, and that's wrong.

But "The Infinite Vulcan" doesn't come anywhere close to following up on this. Instead,

Kirk's debate with Keniclius (and later Kaiju!Spock) flounders around a lot and doesn't seem to have any actual premise aside from "what you've done to Spock is mean and bad" and eventually ends up at "Keniclius is out of touch and doesn't realise the Federation already has peace"...which is basically the *opposite* of the point Star Trek needs to be making. When the Original Series was at its best it was able to carefully depict its setting as idealistic while showing that a Western-style Federation still had a lot of problems as a form of government. Flat-out saying attempting any sort of change (even if it's the wrong sort of change) is pointless because we already have utopia is the antithesis of promoting idealism and material social progress, it's straightforwardly Panglossian and reactionary. Yes, Keniclius is wrong for having the hubris and patriarchal egotism to think he's destined to bring peace to the universe, but *that* should have been the central conflict, not the fact he was attempting it in the wonderful and perfect Federation. On top of being well, wrong, this resolution also just feels rushed and tacked-on to me on top of it all: It kind of plays out like Kirk almost forgot he needed to give a moralizing speech so he badly improvised one at the last second.

Furthermore, Star Trek is *always* going to have this problem because of the way writers tend to interpret the franchise's utopianism: The reason it's dangerous to say the Federation is the source of Star Trek's idealism is that the Federation is a liberal democracy built on the back of military imperialism, a point this show is itself going to make in a few episodes. And "The Infinite Vulcan" itself *almost* gets there too: Keniclius' big objection to Kirk is that the ongoing tensions with the Klingon Empire and Romulan Star Empire and the Kzinti Wars (a tantalizing bit of foreshadowing) prove that the Federation is self-evidently not a peaceful utopia. And Kirk doesn't really have a response to this, seeming to just brush it off. But of course the episode ends with giving Kirk the moral high ground again, seemingly deliberately turning its back on and ignoring this potential challenge to the show's ethics. The juxtaposition of that challenge with Keniclius' faith that Spock, who remember in many ways embodies the essence of Star Trek, is the model by which to form his perfect utopia is also incredibly fascinating, but I'm not even sure the script itself is aware of the intriguing metaphors and contrasts it's brought up here.

Then there is of course the fifty foot Vulcan thing, which sounds patently ridiculous on paper but is actually probably the episode's best idea. See, in turning himself and Spock into giants, Keniclius has made them *literal* Big Men of history, which is perfectly in keeping with the way he sees himself and what he aims to do. Keniclius fancies himself a hero and thinks he can bend the will of history to suit himself and his specific ideology, thus creating a new master narrative that's ultimately more about glorifying himself then it is actual progress, and this is symbolized in the artificially giant stature he's afforded himself. That he would also do this to Spock is revealing, as it can be seen as an indictment of Star Trek's own predilection towards fancying itself morally superior to the people who watch it, and it's encouraging to see the episode cast Kirk and McCoy in staunch opposition to this idea (tellingly Spock, in the form of Kaiju!Spock who shares his brain, has to be convinced).

This all leads to the fundamental problem with "The Infinite Vulcan", which is that it has a ton of really interesting ideas that it never does anything with, that never go anywhere and never quite seem to come together. Attacking authority is good. Calling into the question the Federation's claim to utopia is good. Linking this to Spock serving as a microcosm for the franchise and fandom is smart and on point. Tying this into, through the Eugenics Wars, a criticism of Big Man theory with *literal* Big Men of history is really clever. Dropping every single thread in the resolution so we can paper everything over and go back to the status quo is a *catastrophically* bad move. When your episode ends up feeling significantly less successful and effective than the one that just barely managed to get away with Actual Evil Alien Nazis is, well, more than a little worrying. But the really frustrating thing about this episode is how little there is to actually talk about: One would sort of think a story involving a civilization of sentient pacifist plants, eugenics, cloning and Giant Monster Spock should really be more interesting and memorable than this.

But I don't want to be too harsh on this script either, because it's far from a disaster. As the first offering from an at-the-time beginning writer, this is more than promising and Walter Koenig's later career definitely proves he has talent behind the camera. Every one of the flaws here is eminently forgivable, it's perfectly inoffensive and I don't feel like I've wasted my time, which is more than I can say about a fair few of the Star Trek episodes I've seen so far already. "The Infinite Vulcan" is hitting all the right notes, it's just evidence the musician needs a bit more practice. But again, just like "The Survivor", it's indicative of a Star Trek that knows what it wants to be, and more to the point what it *should* be. It has its heart in the right place and is yet more evidence of the special crop of actors Star Trek attracts...and how it's they who frequently understand the franchise the best out of anyone.

108. "This act is the dawn of the Mythic...": The Magicks of Megas-Tu

There are very few Star Trek episodes you could point to and identify as moments where everything about the franchise simply changed, mostly because there are very few actual moments like that *anywhere*. History does not divide neatly into clean, compartmentalized bits: It's a constantly unfolding tapestry of intersecting lives and events.

"The Magicks of Megas-Tu" is one of those moments. Magick is real.

In the time of the First Ancestors, when the world was new, there was a Spark at the beginning of All Things: A barely-formed thought that dared dream. The Dream the Dreamer Dreamt was the mortal plane, the idea that things continued and shaped themselves as they would. In this Dream, divinity existed within and between each individual. And this was a very dangerous idea.

Conventional cosmological wisdom holds that the further away we can look into space, the further back in time we see. This is because the speed of light is a constant, thus the light we observe from a fixed location has taken us an equal amount of time to reach us as the distance it is away from us. Thus, the furthest, most distant objects are by definition the oldest. This is the line of thought Captain Kirk muses on as the *Enterprise* travels to the centre of the galaxy, supposedly the region of space closest to the origin point of cosmic history.

Star Trek fan lore purports that the entire franchise takes place within the boundaries of the Milky Way Galaxy, with very few excursions beyond (the events depicted in "By Any Other Name" and the two "...Have Gone Before" stories are the most frequently cited: "Beyond the Farthest Star" is typically not accounted for in this accounts). Even *Star Trek Voyager*, as removed as it is from 24th century politics, still only takes place at the other end of the galaxy, not somewhere outside it. The Star Trek universe, then this version of events holds, encompasses only the "known space" of the Milky Way Galaxy.

There is a certain line of thinking within cosmology that the universe simply could not have come into being out of nothing during the Big Bang, as the idea of something spontaneously emerging from nothing is simply incomprehensible. A more helpful thesis, this account goes, is that the Big Bang is the dividing point between two universes, and that universes exist in a constant, repeating cycle of expansion and contraction.

The *Enterprise* and her crew approach the center of the galaxy. The closer they get, the more and more the laws of physics seem to break down. All the ship's systems cease to function.

The further back in history we go, this less we can be certain, confidant and comfortable. History itself is nothing more then the narratives penned by authority and dispensed to us. At a certain point, history stops. Prehistory, the time before history, the known-yet-unquantifiable, is completely and fundamentally alien to our Modern way of thinking, and yet it's an omnipresent and irreducible part of each and every piece of matter in the universe. And when we enter into the dreamlike haze of prehistory, we are gazing into the twilight-dawn of imaginal space. In the dreamtime of consciousness, there lies magick.

At the centre of the galaxy, the *Enterprise* discovers a solitary planet. They are greeted by a being named Lucien, and he calls himself friend to humans. This planet is called Megas-Tu, and it is from where all the magick in the world came. Magick that Lucien uses to repair the *Enterprise*, and that its crew soon learn to master themselves.

This is a tale from when the world was young. The Megans wander the universe and live in harmony with it. They are a good people, and are eager to help anyone who might share their philosophy of wisdom, spirituality and inner peace. The Megans discover Earth, and make friends with many Earth people. They like living on Earth, and offer their knowledge and support to any Earth people who wish it. It is in this way the Megans come to be seen as trusted advisers. But the Earth people are jealous and distrustful and covet power for themselves. It is in this way the Megans become hated and feared and are banished from Earth forever. And this is how magick departs our world.

Lucien is the rebel of the Megans. He maintains his love for and fondness of humans long after the Megans are banished, and this puts him at frequent odds with his kin. He is a jovial fellow, with the legs and feet of a goat, the torso and head of a man distinguished only by a pair of small horns. He goes by many names. Christians of Earth seem to remember him as Lucifer the Trickster and Deceiver, though Kirk and Spock remain uncertain that this is his true identity. He is far more reminiscent, both in appearance and personality, of the one known to the Greeks as Pan and the one known to the Celts as Cernunnos.

It was a reoccurring joke in the original *Star Trek* to point out the superficial similarities between Spock and the stereotypical conception of Satan, namely the fact both have pointed ears. In "The Magicks of Megas-Tu", Spock is referred to by Lucien as an Elf.

This is a scene familiar to all of us. The entire *Enterprise* crew stands trial, accused of the crime of being representatives of a grievously savage race by the Megan Asmodeus, who takes the form of an inquisitor in a recreation of Salem, Massachusetts as it appears during the infamous Witch Trials. Asmodeus fears that the reappearance of humanity means that the sanctuary of Megas-Tu has been tainted by evil, and further declares that Lucien is to be punished for his role in cultivating it. Spock plays the role of defense attorney as he, being Vulcan, has a unique perspective on human culture. Spock calls Kirk to the witness stand, who claims that the human society he and the rest of the *Enterprise* crew represent are different from the ones known to the Megans on Earth.

Kirk posits a hypothesis unthinkable to Asmodeus: That humanity is capable of improvement and is always learning and growing and has already moved beyond the hatred and fear the Megans experienced, and invites him to peruse the ship's record banks as evidence. Asmodeus is convinced by Kirk's compelling case, but maintains Lucien must still be punished. Kirk refuses and stands firmly by Lucien's actions, even if he is Lucifer. As a display of his empathy, Kirk states that he is prepared to give his life for Lucien's. To him, Asmodeus is now no different from the humans he claims to despise and fear. A great magickal war rocks Megas-Tu. The primordial forces of the Old/New Cosmos cry out in the singular horrific moment of Knowing. It is at this moment everything dies and begins again.

The *Enterprise* lies afloat in the afterglow of the birth of the universe. Spock wonders aloud if Lucien really is Lucifer. Kirk asks him why it matters. Spock says that if he is, this is the first time Lucifer has been saved.

Ultimately, what "The Magicks of Megas-Tu" does is finally live up to the potential Star Trek has forever tantalizingly been hinting at, most notably in third season scripts like "The Tholian Web", but really dating all the way back to the introduction of sorcery to the Original Series in "Catspaw". This is no longer "telepathy" or "mental sciences" or non-corporial energy, this is literal, actual magick in the cosmic microwave background radiation of the universe. Adrift on the cosmic tide, the *Enterprise* has travelled along its own lineage back to its own Big Bang and discovered magick at the heart of the universe, and at the heart of Star Trek. Most importantly, its crew have learned how to be magicians themselves.

And it all begins once more.

And this is where our story begins. And so it continues.

109. "And when I grow up, I'll write one.": Once Upon A Planet

The three little sisters named Alice, Hedda and Tertia sat in a circle on their island. Alice was considering in her own mind (as best she could) whether the pleasure of tuning the cosmic fugue would be worth the trouble of climbing another tree to harvest more coconuts from the Earth-bones when suddenly a thought rang out.

"Please tell us another story about the spacemen," said Tertia.

"Very well," Alice replied. "Gather 'round, sisters, and I shall tell it to you."

This is a story from the days of our future ancestors.

Captain Kirk was beginning to get very tired of gallivanting around the universe's sex-birth-death. Time had been acting very peculiarly and, because he was not especially interested in associating with it until it started behaving itself again, Captain Kirk asked the Glittering Skyship to take him and his friends once more to the multiplex planar realms of invocation for a vacation (the multiplex planar realms of invocation being well known, of course as hospitable and generally agreeable places to take a holiday). The Glittering Skyship felt sorry for Captain Kirk and his friends, so she brought them to the World-Stage.

Captain Kirk thought the World-Stage would make a fine place to film a movie, so he got all his friends together and asked if they would play parts in his movie. They all thought this a grand idea, so they gathered at the World Stage and tried not to Break the World again. Now, Doctor McCoy was the first actor onstage (he really ca'n't resist it, you know, because he is thus invoked and it is his will) and he began to mime his part in earnest.

"This is where we come in, is'n't' it?" Tertia asked.

"It is indeed, as you well know" Alice replied. "This is the time Time always knows it's time for me to show up. But this is not a story about me."

Now, this particular world-stage was upset because it thought it was the best of all the world-stages and did'n't take especially kindly to a bunch of spacemen stomping around on it. So it changed the story (which was OK because we all know that story by now anyway: It re-played itself out like a gazillion times more in the reruns).

"I've heard this one before," said Hedda "At least, I think I have."

"I know," said Alice. Then she continued.

So basically the actors used the World-Stage's ambition to fashion themselves into Gods. What constitutes a God, I ask? Well, I'll tell me: A God is a ruler who perceives the Waking-Dream but not the second Dream. Captain Kirk is pretty good at defeating Gods, but it does tend to be rather a pain in the ass for him. So the first God who showed up was the First Queen (because of course it was the First Queen) who put on a right show

487

of a performance (she thought she was still in the House of False Love, you see). This took Doctor McCoy quite by surprise because he knew the First Queen was'n't in the script, and she proceeded to chase him 'round and 'round the glade in the manner of an unfortunate chicken who had chanced to cross her path in such a way that she found most displeasing.

"Mister Spock also knew this was'n't in the script," said Hedda, "But I think he had the wrong script too. He kept getting all his actors all mixed up." Alice nodded in the affirmative.

Eventually this started to irritate Captain Kirk. This was, after all, his movie, and he was'n't about to let some naughty World-Stage spoil everything for him. So Captain Kirk took his actors and fought mightily with the World-Stage's actors. Captain Kirk's companions included the following brave warriors whose valour, courage and fashion sense must be noted: Mister Spock, Doctor McCoy, Lieutenant Sulu, Mister Scott, the Other Mister Scott, Lieutenant Gabler, Lieutenant M'Ress, Lieutenant Arex and Lieutenant Sulu's God-Twin (it's a little-known fact that Lieutenant Sulu had a twin. He became a God sometime prior to this, but that's a story for another day). The World-Stage's army comprised of the First Queen (of whom we have already spoken and need not speak of ever again, because she gets far too much attention as it is and she has a terribly unbecoming habit of letting it all go to her head), several inanimate wooden signs (though they did have *rather* a lot to say), a flock of Plant-Raptors (they're purple this time), a few wayward Martians, a young Ghidorah and the Sixth-Or-Thereabouts Queen, who was, naturally, a cat (it's a well-known fact that cats can look at Kings, and also that they can be Queens).

But this World-Stage was a cunning and deceitful warrior, for it didn't just fight Captain Kirk and his actors on the ground, it tried to use their own Glittering Skyship against them. This was the ultimate insult, for the Skyship was as alive as you or I and this sort of Disillusion of Being simply isn't done. But the Skyship just laughed at this (she had her own apotheosis once and twice already by this point) and at the presumptuousness of this sad little World-Stage, thinking as it did that it could mantle her in this fashion. Oh sure, it took her by surprise a few times, but it wasn't long before she dealt the invader a crippling defeat and forced it into retreat.

So while all this was going on, Captain Kirk was busy talking to the World-Stage in hopes he could arrange some form of amicable cease-fire. Captain Kirk thought the World-Stage was being very silly, you see-This was'n't a one-act play competition after all, it was supposed to be a holiday. What Captain Kirk knew that the World-Stage didn't seem to understand was that it was actually pretty ridiculous to be fighting over a story. Stories change all the time: What manner of sense is there in getting all upset about that? But this made the World-Stage very sad, because it did'n't have a Glittering Skyship of its own, and thus could not travel and learn the way Captain Kirk and his friends could. But Captain Kirk came up with a grand solution: Though it is a well-known fact World-Stages ca'n't move, they can still travel because many people from many different places can visit in and tell many different stories upon it. And its through stories that we learn about others, because stories are what people tell when they try to speak in their own voice. The World-Stage agreed this might be a good idea, called off its actors and stopped trying to kill Captain Kirk and his friends.

"Oh look, Alice! It's Time!" Tertia exclaimed.

"So it is, dear!" Alice replied.

And it was.

After this mutually acceptable agreement was reached, Captain Kirk decided to go back to making his movie. But Doctor McCoy and Lieutenant Sulu wanted to rest for a little while, so they called lunch break and decided to have a picnic on the riverside. I was in attendance at this Time, along with Alice, the White Rabbit and Baby Ghidorah.

"Captain Kirk did'n't get to finish his movie, did he?" asked Tertia.

"Sadly no, my darling. Not this day. He was called away in the middle of filming by his chief, who wanted him and his Glittering Skyship to go yarn-spinning in Arcadia, so we never did get to see what Captain Kirk's movie looked like."

"A pity," said Hedda. "It was the best movie."

"Indeed it was," said Alice.

And it was.

110. "I love you! I hate you!": Mudd's Passion

Maybe Harry Mudd just doesn't work.

I would make the argument that when you reach the third of three appearances of a character and still come up with something that can charitably be described as a "non-starter", this might perhaps be the time to call into question whether the character and his signature plots were ever really a good idea to begin with. Except, of course, for the fact that I'm in the minority here. Harcourt Fenton Mudd is one of the most beloved characters from the original Star Trek era despite never once appearing in a halfway decent episode. If I'm tipping my hand early, it's just because "Mudd's Passion" is extremely difficult to work up any enthusiasm for. It's probably the second-weakest episode of the Animated Series I've seen yet, trailing behind "The Lorelei Signal" only because it's not a grotesque train wreck. It's simply bad in a ponderously mediocre way and is, ironically enough, utterly dispassionate.

"Mudd's Passion" begins with a dutiful recitation of Harry Mudd tropes that have already become worn and tired. The *Enterprise* is once again playing Space Cop and is sent to the Arcadian system to investigate Mudd, who is once again running a scam operation to peddle false promises of romance to horny miners. The script even tries to recycle the "he STOLE a SPACESHIP" joke from "I, Mudd" and to say it didn't work would be being kind (if for no other reason then it gives the key line to Leonard Nimoy instead of William Shatner: Spock is absolutely the wrong person to be the second half of that kind of double act). This time Mudd is selling a love potion he promises is infallible. He gives himself up to Kirk when the miners start to revolt, but once on the ship he tries to sweet talk Nurse Chapel into releasing him from the brig by bribing her with a sample of the love drug for her to use on Spock. So naturally, like an idiot, she agrees. Mudd then mugs her, steals her ID card and takes her hostage as he hijacks a shuttlecraft to escape to a binary star system the ship just discovered. And this one's by the same writer as the Original Series Mudd stories, so we can't lay the blame on someone else not understanding the source material.

At this point, the episode stops being a half-baked rip-off of "Mudd's Women"...and becomes a half-baked rip-off of "The Naked Time" instead as the love potion somehow manages to get into the *Enterprise*'s ventillation system and everyone in the crew starts falling in love with each other. We get a token "we must learn to control our emotions" speech from Kirk after he beams down with Spock to rescue Chapel right in the middle of being chased by Giant Rock Beasts (who are, again, far and away the most sensible things about this episode). This is no more captivating or less problematic than it was last time we

490

saw it, or then it will be in any other of the bafflingly at least *three more times* Star Trek attempts this story. This script is also unrepentantly heteronormative, anti-trans and a whole host of other nasty things as Mudd's love potion explicitly only works on members of the "opposite sex" and the only reason it avoids being as misogynistic as "Mudd's Women" is because M'Ress is here: Chapel is obviously the weak-willed woman tempted by the sin of her own sexuality because she endangers the ship by releasing Mudd because she wanted to get it on with Spock.

I mean there are some fun things about this one. Roger C. Carmel is back and predictably good, though not as good as he was last time and it was a serious mistake to have him interact with William Shatner as rarely as he does. The love scenes in the back half of the episode are also interesting, as brief and neutered for "children's television" as they are. The Beta Couple is, delightfully, Scotty and M'Ress, which is the sort of thing that is at once only possible through animation and also something one doesn't typically expect to see outside of fanfiction, but this episode just blatantly goes with it and it's amazing. Also speaking of fanfiction, once Kirk and Spock beam down to the planet to chase after Chapel and Mudd they start acting very emotional and talk about how close and important they are to each other, which was something that just had to have been put in to tease the shippers. This also makes the moment a few scenes later when, feeling the effects of the drug's "hangover" (which balances a few hours of intense love with a few more of intense hatred) Kirk starts to snap at Spock for being unable to keep his hands of Chapel also amusing: Do I detect a hint of jealousy there?

Back on the ship things are no less intriguing: Apart from Scotty and M'Ress, the crew seem to mostly be flirting with *each other* instead of just with "the last member of the opposite sex they touched", which was what the drug was supposed to do. Mudd has essentially turned the entire ship into a giant orgy, which is fantastic. But the person who hands down wins the episode is McCoy. In the rec room while trying to impress a young female Lieutenant, he ends up delivering what is actually one of the most memorable speeches I've heard on the show yet:

> Did I ever tell you about the time I saved Captain Kirk's life? Or Spock's? And my dear friend Scotty. And that pretty little Lieutenant Uhura. I've saved just about everybody on this here ship. If the *Enterprise* had a heart, I'd save her too. Now, let's talk about your heart, my dear.

Apart from that last eye-rolling pick up attempt, this is actually a really lovely and heartfelt moment, and DeForest Kelley sells the heck out of it. I think this is the first time we've seen any sort of exploration into McCoy's own personality and motivation, at the very least since "The Empath". In this quote, McCoy truly sees himself as a healer and lifesaver, someone whose job it is to protect and look after people who have become his close friends through many long years of service with them. He even goes so far as to suppose the *Enterprise* herself might have a heart, and if she did he'd take care of it. And he does, because he's it: He's the ship's moral conscience. It's a staggeringly good bit of dialog that stands apart from an otherwise eminently forgettable episode.

But it's not enough to save "Mudd's Passion". None of the few good (and they are genuinely good) moments are. The orgy, delightful as it is, simply isn't anywhere near as effective as it is in something like "Wolf in the Fold" because we're right back in that "emotions are bad" quagmire from the first season of the Original Series. The way some of the cast play around with gender roles and sexuality is fun and to be commended, but it doesn't work as well here as it does in even something like "Turnabout Intruder" because the rest of the episode is so ridiculously sexist. Even by the standards of Harry Mudd episodes this comes up short because while it was ultimately something of a hot mess there was a lot to recommend in "I, Mudd"'s goofball earnest Vaudeville routine, especially anytime Shatner and Carmel were onscreen together. This one doesn't even have that, the other stuff can't keep it afloat and the predictable Harry Mudd misogyny seals it.

It's exceedingly difficult to critique an episode like this because for one thing it's so short and for another pretty much everything that's bad about it is stuff Star Trek has tripped up on before. There's simply too many of these episodes with not enough unique tropes and motifs between them. "Mudd's Passion" is another example of a middling-to-poor episode redeemed by Star Trek's outstanding cast, but that's no longer enough to get a pass from me, especially given the Animated Series standard of quality and *especially* given the last two weeks. It's not enough to put the series in a dangerous position, but equally it doesn't really leave me a lot of material to sink my teeth into. It just sort of *there*, which I guess means this is another filler week for the show.

111. "Hello, little teeny-tiny people!": The Terratin Incident

The first, most immediately startling thing about "The Terratin Incident" is that it was written by Paul Schneider. The same person behind the flagrantly and angrily anti-war "Balance of Terror", "The Squire of Gothos" as well as the first draft of the equally anti-authoritarian "Patterns of Force" is now penning a story where the *Enterprise* crew gets zapped with cosmic rays and shrunk down to less than an inch tall in order to rescue a civilization of equally miniscule individuals.

This is, obviously, not at all the sort of thing we would expect from Schneider. It's also his weakest contribution by far, and as tempting (and easy) as it would be to chalk this up to good writers having bad days and leave it at that, the fact is, like so much of the Animated Series, "The Terratin Incident" isn't actually *bad*. It has a few especially egregious moments, but there's actually a few interesting things going on here. It's another example of an episode indicative of the positive direction Star Trek is heading in.

The key here is in the final shot where Kirk describes the Terratins, descendants of a colony of Earth explorers who have evolved into a new species thanks to prolonged exposure to the stature-diminishing rays (of course) of the planet their ancestors landed on, as Lilliputians. The entire episode is a version of *Gulliver's Travels* with a great deal of science fiction shenanigans thrown in for good measure. This makes sense, as Schneider and D.C. Fontana built this episode around a one-paragraph brief from Gene Roddenberry, who was well known for his admiration of Jonathan Swift's masterpiece, as well as for his cataclysmic misunderstanding of said masterpiece.

Roddenberry frequently described his ham-handedly didactic version of the original *Star Trek* as *Gulliver's Travels* in Space while Swift's original is well known as a work of political and social satire. The hook of the original novel is that Gulliver espouses a different viewpoint of the inhabitants of the land he visits in each section, which is then mirrored and exaggerated by the inhabitants of the land he visits in the next section. So, for example, while Gulliver sees the Lilliputians as inherently aggressive, the Brobdingnagians he visits in the next section (who are giants compared to Gulliver) sees humanity as equally aggressive. The joke then being, of course, any good idea or plan can go bad at some point and humans are inherently shitty at organising themselves, also evidenced by Gulliver's growing hardness and cynicism throughout the book. The hook of Gene Roddenberry's version of *Gulliver's Travels* is that the *Enterprise* goes around and runs into a bunch of civilizations based around one single gimmick and then tells them why blind adherence to that gimmick is self-destructive and unnatural and how everyone would be better off living under a Western-style

493

modern liberal representative democracy.

But while "The Terratin Incident" may be a *literal* *Gulliver's Travels* in Space, as has become the norm for the Animated Series this is considerably played around with to an intriguing degree. The crucial thing about this version of the story is that it's the Terratins, who as Kirk helpfully reminds us at the end are stand-ins for the Lilliputians, are in fact in the right here. Kirk throws a big fit about them turning their shrink ray on the *Enterprise* and beaming his crew down without permission, but as the Terratins point out, this was the only form of communication available to them and their planet was literally breaking up around them and they needed to find *some* way to call for help.

Read this way, the size difference is also another metaphor for privilege blindness: This time it's the *Enterprise* crew who are unable to hear the voices of others because of their perspective. So, while the episode is not quite a reiteration of *Gulliver's Travels* as the alternation of viewpoints is integral to conveying the book's central point, it *is* a reiteration of half of the book's core structure and, crucially, it's the half that Roddenberry spectacularly failed to pick up on (although to be fair, it's also the half most people only casually familiar with *Gulliver's Travels* fail to pick up on too). Thus, "The Terratin Incident" is another attempt by the Animated Series to fix Star Trek by re-examining its central tenets and assumptions, and a rather laudably cheeky one at that as it takes a pot-shot at the show's original pitch by inverting the structure it operated under.

That's nice and all, but the problem is "The Terratin Incident" isn't quite as good at this as "One Of Our Planets Is Missing" was, and this is largely because it saves all the interesting stuff 'till the last third of the episode. The rest of the runtime is taken up by the rapidly-shrinking *Enterprise* crew trying to figure out what's happening and how to adjust to it. This is a plot so stock I would expect it to show up on *Space Ghost* (in fact now that I think of it it might well have). Random space adventures can be fun, but sci-fi conceits this goofy do tend to strain credulity a bit, and when the story is trying to make a serious point this is distracting.

This episode also features the singular moment where Nurse Chapel finally stops being a potentially interesting character and fully transforms into the token chick she was probably always destined to be. After Sulu breaks his arm stupidly trying to fire phasers at Terratin to stop the shrink ray, Chapel eagerly volunteers to go get a microscope part that she figures will work similar to their bone-knitting device. In the process of doing so she doesn't watch where she's going (which sort of seems hard to do if you're less than an inch tall, but maybe that's just me) and trips and falls into the fish tank. Chapel apparently never learned how to swim, because she stupidly flails around for about five minutes until Kirk has to rescue her with a bit of recycled running animation, after which he basically tells her "No more independent thinking from *you*, young lady!", to which Chapel sheepishly giggles and demurely returns to her proper post. Watching this era of Star Trek really gives me new respect for Lwaxana Troi and what she did for Barrett's career and legacy.

I will grant the space adventure part of the episode a few things. For one it's not a terrible idea to have what appears to be a standard adventure plot undone at the end by a plot twist, I mean that's a fair approach to critically writing the kind of show Star Trek is at this point. And they do go out of their way to try and explain the shrinking stuff in scientific terms (or at least terms that sound plausibly scientific at first glance) with Spock's lengthy explanation of contracting DNA strands or whatever. "The Terratin Incident" really does break new ground for technobabble. I guess my issue with it, and everything about this story, really, is that I'm not sure this kind of plot really belongs here. This sounds more like something that would go near the beginning of the second season of the Original Series, not in a season that's already given us "Beyond the Farthest Star", "The Magicks of Megas-Tu" and even "Once Upon a Planet" if you're inclined to swing the same way I am on that episode. It's a problematization of Star Trek's original premise, and no matter how good and welcome that might have been at one time we're sort of beyond where it might have been appropriate to see it: "The Terratin Incident" sort of feels like it missed its moment to be relevant to me: Star Trek's clearly not going anywhere at this point and there's not a whole lot else to recommend about the episode as it exists where it exists.

Although perhaps my real objection is that this episode of a cartoon show is, well, cartoony. Which is probably revealing of a few things as well.

But "The Terratin Incident" is also where we say goodbye to Paul Schneider. Of whom, what else do you want me to say? He wrote one of my two favourite episodes of the Original Series, and one of the only two I'd call flawless. He also wrote the clever "The Squire of Gothos" and had a hand in "Patterns of Force", which at least made something of an attempt to punch above its weight. Perhaps in hindsight some of the genius of those episodes was also due to Gene Roddenberry and Gene Coon tweaking them, and "Patterns of Force" at least was technically written by John Meredyth Lucas. But that only means he needed some help to adapt his work for Star Trek, and as I've said before, Star Trek is actually unbelievably hard to write and write *properly*. Even a storied writer like Jerome Bixby needed help with Star Trek, so that's hardly something to hold against Schneider. Especially as the future will demonstrate that it's scripts like Schneider's are the ones that are the real models Star Trek aspires to in its finest moments.

112. "'We are the only path.'": The Time Trap

"Entrapment" is the key word here, on multiple levels.

While exploring a region of space known as the Delta Triangle, where starships have been reputed to go missing for eons, the *Enterprise* comes under attack by the Klingon battlecruiser *Klothos*, captained by the crew's old enemy Commander Kor. Suddenly, the *Klothos* vanishes into nothingness: Suspecting a trap, the *Enterprise* immediately warps to its last know position and follows it in before the commander of the *Klothos'* sister ship can press war crime charges. Both crews find themselves in a starless void where starships from centuries of spaceflight history aimlessly drift about. Kirk and Kor are then transported to a gigantic council chamber, where representatives of the crews from all the other ships welcome them to a world they call Elysia, a pocket universe where time does not exist that they have transformed into an ideal society where everyone relies on and respects everyone else, because there's no way to escape. The Elysians also warn Kirk and Kor that violence is strictly prohibited, and that they will be held responsible for the violent actions of any of their crewmembers by being frozen forever in a stasis field.

Elysia, naturally, is the most interesting thing on display here, though deceptively so: It's an effective and memorable concept on a number of different levels. Though writer Joyce Perry originally only came up with the idea of a Sargasso Sea-type area of space that Kirk and Kor would be forced to work together to escape from (which is in fact what ends up happening here: The *Enterprise* and the *Klothos* can only escape by combining their warp cores into a kind of Super Warp Drive), the actual final product is wonderfully oversignified. Firstly of course, Elysia is not only compared to the Sargasso Sea in the script, but to the nearby and contiguous Bermuda Triangle as well, and both very explicitly so. In Forteana, triangles, or to be more precise triangular regions of physical space, have always held special significance as areas that act as a kind of lightning rod for strange and unexplained activity. The Bermuda Triangle and its disappearing ships and aircraft is the most famous of course, though equally worthy of note, yet lesser-known, such places include my personal favourites, the Bridgewater Triangle in Southern Massachusetts and the Bennington Triangle surrounding Mount Glastenbury in Vermont, the latter of which was also chronicled in an episode of William Shatner's Discovery Channel docudrama series *Weird or What?*.

But even the famous Triangle is a bastion of a truly fascinating sort of weirdness that doesn't always show up in the stereotypical pop culture accounts of it. The Bermuda Triangle isn't just a place where ships vanish into thin air, it's a place where blatantly unnerving and otherworldly things are said to happen. Arguably the best-known (or at least one of the best-known) of the Bermuda Triangle incidents is the case of Flight 19, a bombing squadron that, while flying through the aforementioned area on a practice run, suddenly began to experience widespread instrument malfunction while its crew suffered from extreme and immediate onset confusion and disorientation. Eventually Flight 19 did what we expect to see planes do in the Bermuda Triangle and vanished without a trace, but not before its pilots were able to relay some truly chilling messages to their flight controllers, such as this one from an unidentified cremember

"We can't find west. Everything is wrong. We can't be sure of any direction. Everything looks strange, even the ocean."

And these disturbing words from flight leader Charles Carroll Taylor

"Both of my compasses are out and I am trying to find Fort Lauderdale, Florida. I am over land but it's broken."

"It looks like we are entering white water . . .We're completely lost."

Almost spookier is what allegedly happened to pilot Bruce Gernon, Jr., one of the only people who both claim to have experienced something strange in the Bermuda Triangle and returned to talk about it. Gernon and his father set off on a recreational flight in the Bahamas from Andros Island, an area they both knew instinctively, on December 4, 1970 when their aircraft was unexpectedly and immediately engulfed in a large, undulating cloud. While inside, Gernon claims to have witnessed the sky shrink in on itself and that the inside of the cloud was a dark void without any discernible meteorological phenomenon that one would expect to see inside a storm, except for a series of bright white flashes.

Like on Flight 19, all of Gernon's instruments began to wildly malfunction. Contacting Miami air control for backup support, Gernon reported that he was somewhere southeast of the Bimini islands, only to be told air control couldn't actually *find* him anywhere near that area. Suddenly, an unidentified aircraft was reported to have appeared in the skies over Miami Beach...which turned out to be Gernon's plane. Miami Beach is ninety miles away from Bimini, and Gernon had travelled that distance in what had seemed to him to be twenty seconds. Eventually landing in Palm Beach, Gernon calculated the total time of his flight: By his count, he'd made the trip from Andros Island to Palm Beach in the flat-out impossible time of forty-seven minutes.

And, just to top off an already disquieting story and make it even creepier, Gernon's eventful journey took place almost exactly twenty-five years *to the day* after the disappearance of Flight 19, with a difference of only 24 hours.

So given the tales of Flight 19 and Bruce Gernon, Jr. in the Bermuda Triangle, not to mention the numerous eyewitness accounts from the other triangles of strange beings and inexplicable phenomena, it's probably safe to say places like this have a tendency to invite and attract mystery. Speaking strictly in terms of folklore here, in many ways the stories of odd happenings in the triangles is also very reminiscent of what might be called in other time periods reports of certain faery or spirit Otherworlds: Both sorts of places are defined by the prevalence of things that go beyond the boundaries of what humans can currently comprehend. And of course, Star Trek has always been on the vanguard of this and "The Time Trap" is the next step in the development of this motif.

As we might expect, Elysia (though perhaps more accurately the Delta Triangle) is also a black, starless void where the laws of space and time break down and that causes starships' instruments to go completely haywire. But Elysia is also an Otherworld, and it's even more of one than the part of the Original Series it's arguably the most comparable to, the haunted interspatial rift full of ghost ships and Spriggans from "The Tholian Web". This time the *Enterprise* fully crosses over to the other side and finds an entire civilization that's at once extremely reminiscent of their own and strikingly different.

And Elysia very much is a sort of reflection of the Federation: Like the Federation, it's clearly a kind of vast, galactic representative democracy (the council chamber alone calls for that reading), and also like the Federation it claims to hold itself to virtues of nonviolence and peaceful coexistence. But as utopian as Elysia seems, there's a darker side, as explained by Devna, Interpreter of Laws: The council presides over Elysia with an iron fist and there is swift and extremely harsh punishment for any transgression against their unyielding and monolithic set of laws. There's arguably even a nod to the notion Otherworlds are one place the spirits of the dead might go to live on, as the Elysians are all former starship crewmembers who disappeared and were left for dead throughout history. And it's always existed, as Kirk says ships have been reported missing in the Delta Triangle since "ancient times".

What "The Time Trap" adds to this is just what it says: Elysia is an Otherworld, but it's also a trap. That worrying lack of stars is just as revealing here as it was in "The Immunity Syndrome", moreso in fact. The danger here is that the *Enterprise* will be marooned here and rendered obsolete and ineffectual. And this is very interesting, because Elysia is also very much a utopia, and at first glance the full realisation of the exact thing the Federation claims to be striving towards. Why would eternal life in a place as idyllic as Elysia be something so repugnant both Kirk and Kor would be willing to risk their ships and crew to escape from? Firstly of course there are the staunch rules: Neither the Klingon Defense Force or Starfleet have been shown to always be terribly enamoured of authority, and certainly not someone as transgressive as James Kirk. If one is trying to fashion a perfect society where everyone is respected and treated as an absolute equal, it does seem to be a rather concerning conflict of interest if the only way you can get there is by anointing yourself and demanding absolute loyalty and obedience.

There's something else about Elysia that clearly worries the *Enterprise* crew though, and in hindsight it's the same thing that that was the real threat of "The Tholian Web": It's the possibility of becoming static and unchanging. A society like Elysia's is predicated on the assumption that it has already reached perfection, and in order to maintain that perfection absolute control must be maintained. Aside from being offensively authoritarian, this is behaviour is also flatly entitled and presumptuous. Who are the Elysians to say they're the model by which everyone who chances into the Delta Triangle is obligated to aspire

112. "'We are the only path.'": The Time Trap

towards? This is absolute anathema to the *Enterprise* crew, because, as we now know from "The Magicks of Megas-Tu", it's their goal to always better themselves, to never stop learning and improving. To stay in Elysia, no matter how peaceful a life of subservience there might be, would be a betrayal of everything they believe and stand for. This marks yet another welcome honing of the Star Trek mission statement: In the Original Series, the *Enterprise* all too often took on the role of Elysian missionaries, going around and forcibly imposing their model of utopia on everyone while touting themselves representatives of an evolved and advanced Master Race. Now, however, they're overtly interested in discourse and shared ideas. To stay in Elysia would require the *Enterprise* to stop travelling, and that would mean her and her crew would have to stop growing and learning.

That's the other side of the Otherworld concept, so to speak. Certain strands of folklore and myth tend to posit that the Otherworld is still a place where people live lives and have weird cultural quirks, rituals and mores just like we do. It may be a realm of wondrous and fantastic things, but it's also *an*other world, not necessarily a better one. And it's certainly not a place you would want to end up stranded in against your will. The goal of the shaman is not just to leave one world and enter another (after all, most myths hold the dead can do that simply by being dead). No, the shaman's trick is the ability to *transgress* the boundary between worlds. The idea is to bring learning and knowledge from one world to the other while maintaining an existence in both, to be a kind of spiritual teacher. You don't want to become an Otherworld expatriot (well, necessarily: There's added nuance and complexity to these themes I'm ignoring here for the sake of argument), you want to be the ultimate traveller, journeying to planar realms as easily as you can down the street or across the ocean, and to show others how they can do the same. So, for the crew of the *Enterprise*, imposing a utopia from above and agreeing to live unquestioning under it is tantamount to bringing the natural process of intellectual and spiritual growth that is intrinsic to the human experience to a standing halt. And that's not the Star Trek way.

Somehow it seems altogether fitting now that the first-ever episode of Star Trek was about escaping a gilded cage.

113. "Well, I'll be damned. It's the gentleman guppy.": The Ambergris Element

Some episodes I have a really hard time building a chapter around. It's not that they're especially terrible, it's just there's not a lot of content there for me to really grab hold of or find new and interesting things to say about them. Thankfully, Margaret Armen wrote this one so that won't be the case here.

And I really wanted to like this one too. When I was planning this project I did a cursory scan of all the episodes I hadn't seen or didn't remember all that well, and this one looked fascinating. The *Enterprise* is conducting research on a planet that's almost entirely ocean due to persistent underground tremors causing the continents to fall into the sea. The crew hope they information they gain will be helpful in providing aid to other planets with similar geological activity. One of the things I love most about science fiction is its ability to depict wondrous and fantastic spectacles of worlds that exist far out in the deepest realms of outer space. It goes back to things like Georges Méliès, the hauntingly evocative spacescapes dreamed up by the Golden Age science fiction artists and the fist glimpses we saw of the Lunar surface from the *Apollo* missions. Few things stir my imagination quite like a well-done bit of space art. Indeed one reason, if not *the* primary reason, I don't despise Star Trek is how fantastic *Star Trek: The Next Generation* and early *Star Trek: Deep Space Nine* were at evoking this kind of imagery to me. The visual design alone was enough to get my mind racing to imagine what life in the sort of world those shows depicts must be like. And animation is a medium essentially custom-tailored for precisely this.

One of my greatest loves, obviously, given the way I've structured this project, is the ocean. When I was young one of the things I thought I might grow up to be was some kind of oceanographer or ocean explorer. I developed my love of the ocean and my love of outer space roughly at the same time, I suppose because both seemed like universes unto themselves and we knew next to nothing about either. In hindsight, this makes a lot of sense given the Polynesian belief in the intertwined world, with the realms of the Earth, Sea and Sky all interconnected. Many variations of the Polynesian creation myth even claim that the world was created out of the sea, and often that the world exists within a giant clam shell in the middle of an even larger cosmic ocean.

At another point in my life, I naively fancied myself some kind of professional astronomer and was involved in a project to detect extrasolar planets. It was my unspoken hope that at some point I'd be able to see a planet like the one described in this episode: One comprised almost entirely of ocean. I've also long had a fascination with Neptune in our own solar system: Although it's named after a Western sea god, Neptune is in fact a gas giant and even though it's thus more properly described as a planet made entirely out of sky, I still think it would be an incredible sight to visit a place like that.

But I'm not going to go too far down the road of autobiography and self-contemplation here when there's Margaret Armen to talk about. For her final Star Trek trick, Armen somehow manages to outdo herself and turn out yet another new low for the series. Astoundingly, this one is *even worse* than "The Lorelei Signal" and a contender for her worst effort to date. Only "The Paradise Syndrome" really gives it competition for the title. This episode is garbage on burnt toast.

It's always a great sign when you name your story after whale vomit. While Armen's previous efforts have showed off her well-documented problems with representation, "The Ambergris Element" returns to the other thing that was notably bad about "The Paradise Syndrome" by being constructed entirely out of narrative Swiss Cheese. There are so many serious, egregious plot holes in this story I honestly lost count. Literally nothing about this episode makes sense, and I'm not saying the script is dealing with heady concepts that are difficult to wrap your mind around, I am saying it is so shoddily put together it is actively, physically incoherent. Furthermore, Armen doesn't have anything remotely like the combined diegetic and extradiegetic narrative collapse of something like "The Alternative Factor" to bail her out here, helpfully reminding us that in addition to being a racist and an internalized misogynist she was also just a terrible, terrible writer on principle.

Two of my favourite moments from "The Ambergris Element" (and by "favourite" I mean memorably godawful) involve the civilization of merpeople Kirk and Spock find living in the planet's world-ocean (So I guess Armen really did have a thing for mermaids/sirens/Rhine maidens after all) called the Aquans (of course). See, long ago there was a dispute between the ancestors of the Aquans and a society of land-dwellers (called, presumably, Landies) who existed when the planet had continents. Eventually a massive war broke out and the Aquans became territorial and isolationist and developed a xenophobic hatred of anyone who breaths air. So, when Kirk and Spock are attacked by a giant Kraken-Lizard and flung into the sea, they infuse their blood with a special mutagen that causes them to turn into merpeople too, because when you're a xenophobic society terrified of invasion the *first* thing you do is allow your suspected enemy agents to adapt to your environment and force them to live in intimate, close proximity with your populace.

So naturally Kirk and Spock are less then thrilled about turning into Ariel's step-siblings, so they go back to the Aquans to ask their council for help in changing them back. And here's where it becomes clear how paper-thin the world building in this episode is: The Aquans are a generic race of codgy traditionalists who only act in accordance with a set of ancient dicta laid down before the grandparents of anyone who's now alive to read them were even roe. They can't reverse the mutation even though the technology exists to do so because it's not allowed and they can't go find the technology they need to make the antidote because that's not allowed either. Precisely why it's not allowed is never explained. As for why the Aquans hate the surface dwellers, that's not ever made clear either and I guess I'm not allowed to ask about that. Eventually one of the younger council members, Rila, offers to help Kirk and Spock as she believes their story about coming from another world and needing to know about their planet to help other worlds in need.

Then it gets really good, and by good I of course mean bad. At one point Kirk and Spock are captured by some particularly conservative Aquans and marooned on a rock, where they will suffocate because they have gills instead of lungs now. Scotty and McCoy come to their rescue with Rila's help, *who can of course breathe air like it ain't no thing.* Then Rila tells them they need to travel to the lost ruins of the ancient civilization to find the medical records they need to make the antidote (because all underwater cities have lost ruins of ancient civilizations, it's like a law). On their way they get attacked by another Kraken-Lizard thing, but conveniently an earthquake happens at that exact moment and crushes it under a collapsing pillar (and meanwhile Scotty, who was with them, has now mysteriously disappeared). Then it turns out the venom from Kraken-Lizards is a key ingredient in the antidote: Amazingly instead of *going back to harvest it from the one that was already killed by the earthquake*, Kirk, Spock and Rila elect *to hunt down a totally different one *with their bare hands*.* The Kraken-Lizards are, in case you couldn't guess, roughly the size of a smallish kaiju.

(It is also worth mentioning at this point that the time elapsed between the Aquans first capturing Kirk and Spock and the *Enterprise* finding them stranded and suffocating to death is supposed to be *five days.*)

"The Ambergris Element" might be the first episode I've seen, or at least the first in a while, that has absolutely nothing for me to recommend in it. The plot is a disaster and wouldn't even be terribly interesting if it wasn't, the dialog is amateurish and flat, the acting is predictably phoned in and even the beautiful ocean planet I had hoped to see is in truth the antithesis of beautiful: The whole planet looks flat and featureless to the point of feeling unfinished and the ocean itself is an unappealing pale yellow for no good reason. It looks like an ocean of stale urine. And I hate to say it, I really do, but the only positive thing I can find to say about this one is that it is in fact Margaret Armen's last Star Trek script. She submitted a pitch to *Star Trek: Phase II* called "Savage Syndrome", which she co-wrote with a writer named Alfred Harris and which we were thankfully spared by that show getting canceled in pre-production.

I wish I had something kinder to say about Armen's stint in her final aired episode, but I really don't. I'm honestly just thankful to see the back of it. As bad as Star Trek will get in the future, and trust me, it can get really bad, at the very least it never manages to get **Margaret Armen** bad again. That alone has to serve as some small comfort that there's hope for humans and self-improvement yet.

And next time everything changes. Again.

114. "We must not let it happen again." The Slaver Weapon

Like so many other stories like it, "The Slaver Weapon" is a not-actually-terribly-good episode that still manages to set in motion events that will change everything we thought we knew about the world of Star Trek and call into question the franchise's closest-held tenets and ideals.

It has an interesting pedigree though. We've heard a few hints and clues about the Kzinti and some hostilities with them before, but this is the first time we've actually seen them: An aggressive race of catlike people who have persistently attacked settlements, who make war to eat those they defeat in battle and who are so misogynistic they've literally bred intelligence out of their women. They are a frighteningly unlikable adversary for this series, and if they don't sound like typical Star Trek villains that's probably because they're not, in point of fact, from Star Trek at all. The Kzinti actually hail from the self-contained Known Universe, encompassing the collected work of noted science fiction author Larry Niven, and this episode is actually a straight translation of his short story "The Soft Weapon" for Star Trek. The reason it's here is because D.C. Fontana was a huge fan of Niven's and personally requested he contribute something for the Animated Series. The two approached Gene Roddenberry with the idea, and while it was thought many of Niven's pitches were too violent for the show, Roddenberry eventually suggested adapting "The Soft Weapon".

As a result there's not a whole lot to say about the episode as aired, because it straight-forwardly, literally *is* "The Soft Weapon", only with the names changed. An interesting consequence of this is that the episode features exclusively Sulu, Uhura and Spock in starring roles, standing in for the original story's protagonists (a human couple and a vegetarian alien scientist named Nessus), and thus none of the other regulars appear. This sadly doesn't help the episode much though, because while it's nice to see Sulu and Uhura get really meaty roles again, it's painfully clear "The Soft Weapon" had a rather blatant Pulp structure, so we get to see many riveting scenes of our heroes getting captured by Kzinti pirates, escaping said Kzinti pirates and being recaptured about ten seconds later. And of course, the female character has to be abducted and held for ransom. This is the thing about science fiction: It's so enamoured of its world-building concepts it couldn't give less of a toss about plot, which I would normally applaud as a fan of abstract film, except science fiction uses it as an excuse to just write horrid, offensive stock garbage.

There are, however, two main aspects of this episode that remain quite provocative. The first is, of course, the Kzinti: Despite being canon expatriates, the fact remains having a concept as shocking as the Kzinti here does change the game rather decisively for Star

503

Trek. Trying to weld established Star Trek mythos with Niven's Known Universe has some really bizarre consequences that, thanks to a happy accident, wind up adding a lot more nuance to our franchise. The biggest bomb comes about when you try and reconcile the supposedly pacifistic and utopian Federation with the nasty history of the Earth-Kzin Wars: The implication of this episode then becomes that at some point prior to the foundation of the modern Federation, Earth and its allies were engaged in a series of horrific and consecutive wars where they absolutely decimated the Kzinti armies.

The decisive moment comes at the Treaty of Sirius, where Earth demanded harsh concessions from the Kzinti, forcing them to completely demilitarize and give the nascent Federation total unhindered access to Kzinti space. I have little sympathy for the warlike, misogynistic Kzinti (who were, of course, always the aggressors), but the sheer scale of the repercussions Earth called for at the Treaty simply sounds vicious, and it reminds me altogether too well of, say, the quick scapegoating of Germany following World War I. In Niven's original work, he further puts this into "natural selection" terms, explaining how the instinctively confrontational Kzinti died out due to their own belligerence, thus allowing the "more evolved" humans to thrive and the more progressive Kzinti to eventually adapt. It doesn't take a whole lot to twist that into imperialistic propaganda and apologia for Social Darwinism, and this is an unthinkably serious accusation to level at the Federation. At least, that's the tack I'm going to take instead of actually arguing that Star Trek *itself* endorses Social Darwinism.

But not, in retrospect, an altogether unexpected one. We've always maintained that the Federation is far from a perfect, ideal model of government, despite the increasingly universalist rhetoric of the franchise that is slowly but surely beginning to dangerously conflate Star Trek's idealism with that of the Federation. It's not a huge leap of logic to extrapolate this back and figure the Federation probably had some kind of an imperialistic past or that a desire for empire might not in some way be built into the core of how it operates. Indeed, when next we see the Kzinti in Star Trek the Federation is put explicitly on the same level as any number of other wide-reaching galactic empires. It becomes but one massive military power among many others.

I'm also reminded of something Robert Hewitt Wolfe said in regards to the episode "Crossover" on *Star Trek: Deep Space Nine*:

> "Empires aren't usually brutal unless there's a reason. There are usually external or internal pressures that cause them to be that way."

There's more to this quote and Wolfe frames it in a way that's pretty much 100% wrong, but we'll deal with that in 1994. What I want to focus on here is the idea that empires arise out of a *need* to be brutal. The fear of the unknown, or rather of *uncertainty* and *fungibility*, a fear of the idea things can entropically change outside of your control (and a further belief that you are *entitled* to exert that control) and a panicky desire to maintain order has been a driving force of authoritarianism since time immemorial. The true horror of the Earth-Kzin wars is that it opens the possibility that this kind of fear and paranoia might actually be the defining belief upon which the entire Federation was founded.

Think about it. The Kzinti, despite how despicable they can be, are basically complete rubbish. As Beowulf Schaeffer says in Niven's story "Grendel", "The Kzinti aren't really a threat. They'll always attack before they're ready". Not to mention the fact they lost every single conflict they ever had with Earth hilariously decisively. They're not a threat, they're a joke. It's *Earth,* and by extension the proto-Federation, who commit the worst atrocities during the Kzin Wars via the Treaty of Sirius thanks to their need to assert their dominance and growing military might and influence. This becomes the new Original Sin of the Federation: Despite all its rosy utopian rhetoric, it has roots in the same old ugly empire building Westerners are so depressingly good at. Oh sure, later writers will shy away from this, try to correct it and posit other origins for the Federation, but the damage has been done. This never goes away. This is a part of the Federation and Star Trek from here on out.

This ties into the other intriguing concept Star Trek inherits from the Known Universe via "The Slaver Weapon": The titular weapon itself. In both stories, an Earth team has recovered an ancient stasis box dating from what amounts to The Old Universe, when they're abducted by the Kzinti. Apparently there once was an infinitely old race that existed billions of years ago who conquered the entire universe and enslaved every other sentient species (in Star Trek they're the Slavers, while in the Known Universe they're called the Thrint, and "Slavers" is just a colloquialism). Although no traces of their civilization still exist, they did leave behind these boxes which contain assorted artefacts preserved by a stasis field and which, through modern reverse engineering, have provided the basis for basically all technology as it exists today. The box Spock/Nessus found that he and his friends are fighting with the Kzinti over contained a weapon used by a Slaver/Thrint spy that can transform into many different forms, one of which has the power to instantaneously convert planet-sized pieces of matter into energy.

This is almost a bleaker revelation than the Kzin Wars. Literally the entire contemporary society of the Star Trek universe is modeling itself after an oppressive and genocidal race of *actual monsters* (we get to see an image that's largely assumed to be a Slaver/Thrint, and it looks like a giant saurian) not only technoscientifically but socially: The Federation and the Kzinti would go to war again over such a device-The Kzinti already proved they would be willing to kill and die to posses it, and after it predictably self-destructs at the end, Spock attempts to console Sulu, who is saddened that he won't be able to bring the device to a museum, by saying it would never have wound up in a museum anyway. This might well be the darkest ending we've seen yet on Star Trek: The *Enterprise* crew get to remain noble, but there is now overwhelming evidence that they might be the only scrupulous and upstanding people in a a universe built entirely around hatred, conflict and a desire to oppress and subjugate others. This is paradoxically the least Star Trek story we've ever seen, but, terrifyingly, *it's absolutely in keeping with the way the show works.*

Although the plot is less than compelling, the historical significance of "The Slaver Weapon" alone makes it worth a look. This is the starting point of a new approach to Star Trek: Not quite another reboot or reconceptualization, but a secondary thread that haunts the margins of the franchise popping up every now and again to remind us that we can hold to our utopian fantasies about the show as much as we like, but we'll never quite be able to distill this out of it. This is Star Trek's Dark Side, and the only way to confront your Dark Side is to accept that it exists, if not embrace it.

115. "Just think what some zoo will pay for you!": The Eye of the Beholder

"The Eye of the Beholder" concerns the *Enterprise* attempting to locate the crew of a research ship that went missing in the vicinity of Lactra VII. Beaming down to investigate, Kirk, Spock and McCoy discover three wildly different ecosystems positioned unnaturally adjacent to each other. Spock supposes that this planet might in fact be some kind of enormous zoo created by beings significantly more advanced then the Federation races, a supposition proven correct when giant telepathic slugs with trunks come, abduct the landing party and take them to a specially-crafted humanoid exhibit guarded by an unbreakable force field.

So that happened. And yet, somehow it feels like we've been here before.

This episode was written by David P. Harmon, who also wrote "The Deadly Years" and co-wrote "A Piece of the Action" with Gene Coon. However it's pretty clear now that the latter story must have been primarily Coon because this episode is much more akin to the former. In other words, it's another perfectly forgettable filler episode. And let's be honest: "The Eye of the Beholder" is totally "The Cage" all over again. It doesn't even try to distinguish itself from possibly the most famous episode of Star Trek ever, apart from having the zookeepers be the aforementioned giant telepathic slugs with trunks instead of Talosians.

Since Harmon apparently has no qualms about stooping so low as to recycle the plot wholesale from the very first episode of Star Trek I don't feel bad about reusing a lot of my commentary from "The Deadly Years". The concept of filler episodes (in the original "this-feels-like-an-off-week" sense and not the contemporary "I-have-to-wait-another-week-to-learn-more-about-my-Big-Damn-Character-Arc" sense) is a phenomenon somewhat unique to television, and United States television in particular, born as it is out of the necessity of making sure something makes it to air every week during the season. Flatly, sometimes you just need to crank something out to fill your episode quota. TV has always been one of the more visibly workmanlike of the creative mediums as a result, and this isn't necessarily a bad thing, because it gives us as viewers and critics special access to the creative process that goes into making it that the allure of the Cinematic Artifice and Singular Vision usually makes it hard for us to notice in, say, movies.

However.

As wonderful as that may all be and as criminally overvalued as I do in fact find plot and character development to be, I still tend to find that US TV engages in filler episodes alarmingly more frequently than it perhaps needs to. This is because in the US, the annual television season traditionally runs nonstop from September to May except for a hiatus in November and December and demands a quota of about 25-30 episodes as a result. There's only so many stories anyone can come up with for one setting in one sitting, and this means time, money and other resources get spread out over a huge swath of productions instead of being discreetly allocated to a small handful of them. US TV creators tend then to be ludicrously overworked and pressured, and corners get cut that inevitably bring down a show's average day-to-day potential. Eventually it can start to feel like the production team is punching a timecard and cranking out generic, formulaic stories because that's all they're physically capable of doing. This has happened to Star Trek before, and it will tragically be more the norm than the exception when next we return to mainstream television.

And anyway, even if "The Eye of the Beholder" did in fact have to be a filler episode (and given that it's the penultimate episode of The Animated Series' first season, it in all likelihood probably did) there were still ways to make it unique and entertaining without engaging in one of the most painfully obvious bits of self-plagiarism in the franchise to date. This could very easily have been a very enjoyable generic space adventure: Indeed, the first third-to-one-half of the episode is basically that-Kirk, Spock and McCoy wander first through volcanic hot springs, then a desert and finally a forest fending off giant monsters that keep popping up every now and again in search of the missing research team and bantering the whole way. The episode could have played up its already-weird and captivating setting and been about how the landing party survives in such an uncanny place.

The episode could have come up with some out-there technobabble explanation for why so many ecosystems exist in such close proximity to each other, like maybe this is an amalgam planet made up of the hunks of a lot of other planets that fused when their orbits caused them to smash into one another. Or maybe it's a planet that exists in multiple time periods or universes all at the same time and each time the landing party moves into a different ecosystem they're travelling between different realities. There would probably have to be some kind of signature Star Trek twist at the end to keep it from turning into full-on *Space Ghost*, like perhaps Kirk having to find a way to save both the lost research team and the local wildlife without endangering either of them, but that still strikes me as perfectly doable and exceedingly more interesting then defaulting back to the franchise's dead end of a pilot.

There are also a lot of little things that irk me about this one. Though they get some good lines and I enjoy how Kirk keeps imploring Spock and McCoy to stop bickering, the landing party is written in just about the most stereotypical and uninteresting way you can think of. Spock's a logic machine, McCoy is irrational, emotional and impulsive and Kirk tries to mediate between them. Furthermore, the script seems to view the rest of the crew besides Spock with some manner of disdain, because for one, hardly anyone outside the triumvirate actually appears in this episode (though Scotty and M'Ress show up near the end and play minor important roles) and secondly Spock is written to be *always right*: He has the whole plot basically figured out five minutes in, corrects everyone and just generally lectures everyone on how wrong and illogical they're being. I guess it's a return to "The Cage" in politics as well as plot, as this is a very unlikably Gene Roddenberry-esque conception of Spock (or rather the logician character, as in "The Cage" this was, of course, Number One): The character who exists to point out how fallible and naive the hopelessly emotional humans are.

The one thing that is sort of fun about "The Eye of the Beholder" is how it handles its resolution in comparison to how "The Cage" handled its. In the earlier episode, Pike broke the Talosians' thought shield by frightening them with violent imagery and physically and mentally muscled his way out. Here, Kirk and his crew make constant attempts to contact the Lactrans and convince them they're members of intelligent species who don't deserve to be imprisoned. And, in spite of Spock's gloating about the telepathic link he shares with the Lactrans it's Scotty and M'Ress who end up saving the day here: After a botched attempt to beam back to the *Enterprise*, a baby Lactran ends up getting transported up in Kirk's place and makes its way to the bridge where it confronts Scotty and M'Ress.

After a moment, Scotty beams down with the baby (who, despite being only six years old has an IQ in the thousands) and casually informs the landing party he was able to strike up a telepathic conversation with it and taught it all he knew about the Federation while M'Ress gave it access to the ship's computers to learn more. In doing so, the working-class everyman Scotty does what the highly trained mentalist Spock was unable to do and convince the Lactrans that humans and Vulcans (and Caitians) are intelligent beings: In fact, the Lactrans pay them the highest compliment by telling the landing party (as relayed by Scotty) that they remind them of the Lactrans themselves long ago, and that maybe in a few more (Lactran) centuries, the three peoples will be able to communicate as equals. It's a wonderfully Animated Series style ending that builds on the work of stories like "The Magicks of Megas-Tu" and "The Time Trap" and ends up making the whole episode worthwhile. So while it reiterates "The Cage", it also in some ways redeems it, which is I guess nice, if a bit unnecessary.

So once again this isn't a terrible episode: Like the vast majority of this series' poor stories, it's a mediocre outing that still shows Star Trek making visible progress even in its weakest moments. And that's pretty damn admirable place to be in at the end of the first season of an animated reboot of a failed Cult Sci-Fi show.

116. "Though all men be equally frail before the world...": The Jihad

This episode was written by Stephen Kandel, better known for the Harry Mudd trilogy and, the gulf between those stories and this one is chasmic."The Jihad" is properly excellent and closes out the Animated Series' first season on one of the show's high notes.

Kandell had been a regular writer on *Mission: Impossible* during the original era of Star Trek, and that's sort of what this episode feels like a little bit: A *Mission: Impossible* story. Kirk and Spock are called to a summit held by the Vedala, the oldest known spacefaring civilization. The Vedala have assembled a crack team of specialists from around the galaxy to partake in a top-secret mission to prevent an interstellar war. Aside from Kirk and Spock, there's Lara, a ranger and tracker from a planet where humans remained hunter-gatherers, Sord, a reptilian warrior, Em/3/Green, a nervous lockpicking expert who resembles a kind of insect (and voiced by Dave Gerrold no less: Gerrold has something of a habit for getting people to write him into Star Trek episodes) and Tcharr, hereditary prince of the birdlike Skorr, who is the primary reason for the team-up.

The Vedala have gathered the team together to track down The Soul of the Skorr, an ancient artefact that literally holds the soul of the Skorr's great prophet Alar, who was made immortal upon death by being bound into an energy web and whose life force keeps peace among his disciples and their descendents. The Soul has gone missing, and Tcharr fears that should word of its theft become public, the Skorr will return to their warlike roots and declare a holy war on the galaxy. Thankfully, the Vedala have traced it to the "Mad Planet", a lifeless rock constantly tearing itself to pieces due to constant earthquakes, volcanic eruptions, blizzards, tsunamis and gravity shifts. On the way, the task force will have to contend with the harsh unforgiving and ever-changing landscape of the Mad Planet while learning to trust and respect each other in order to work together as a team.

There is so much going on right from the outset here it's difficult to keep track of. "The Jihad" is simply overflowing with fascinating ideas and concepts it's hard for me to even figure out where to begin, and I couldn't be happier: This is a picture perfect example of taking the potential of science fiction television, and in particular animated science fiction television, resolutely rising to the challenge and just running with it. I've never seen a Star Trek episode quite like this one before and I'm never going to see another like it again. I suppose a good place to start would be the team itself: This is a truly creative and inspired bit of creature design. For the first time in awhile, it feels like the Animated Series team is really taking full advantage of their medium and showing us visuals they really couldn't have pulled off through live action. More to the point, each individual member has a defined and memorable personality, which is something Star Trek has been a bit changeable with in the past. It perhaps helps there's a larger voice cast than normal: Though James Doohan is predictably good and Dave Gerrold is, well, Dave Gerrold, the standout for me is Jane Webb as both the Vedala and Lara, both of which are charming and charismatic characters.

Actually, it's Lara who was the real standout for me. She's someone utterly unlike basically anyone else in the entirety of Star Trek and someone who left a massive impression on me. Even going back and revising these essays three years after I wrote them I still remember why Lara stands out so much. Lara is an indigenous hunter and tracker who eschews the technoscientific world of the Federation to live solely through her instincts and her ability to read the land. Nevertheless, her and her people have still obviously managed to develop spaceflight and Lara herself is just as cosmopolitan, knowledgeable and essential as everyone else on the team.

It helps that this is a character archetype I'm incredibly sympathetic and drawn to for personal reasons, but even so I argue Lara basically just singlehandedly solves all of Star Trek in one fell swoop: Her people are a non-Western, non-Modern hunter-gatherer society that holds women in esteem, maintain their connection to the land and the skills that allowed them to foster that connection *all the while* cherry-picking the things from more Western societies that suit their lifestyle but that don't put it at risk of extinction that's now out among the stars in equal standing with the vast, sprawling galactic empires. I mean that's just absolutely perfect. It's exactly what Star Trek needs: Proof positive there are ways for humans to live in peace and dignity in its world without becoming subsumed by the more worrisome foundational aspects of the Federation. In Lara we see Star Trek's idealistic dream of living out among the stars on a journey of self-improvement mixed with the equally idealistic, though often neglected, hope that traditional indigenous knowledge and ways of life can live on too. It's the final disconnect between Modern Neo-Imperialism and space travel story, demonstrating once and for all that Star Trek doesn't need to be Western to be utopian.

As for Lara herself, there's a wonderful little story thread between her and Kirk throughout the episode: For Lara's people, it's not customary to obfuscate one's feelings and desires, especially when it comes to romance and friendship (another thing I absolutely adore about this story and her character), and Lara makes it perfectly, blatantly clear to Kirk that she finds him attractive and that she'd like to use their brief time together to "make green memories". However Kirk gently and politely rejects her advances, saying he has too many "green memories" of his own, but they eventually grow to respect one another and become close allies nevertheless. Not only is this a clever subversion (and inversion!) of a lot of the stereotypes of Kirk from the Original Series, it's a fantastic little series of character moments and it propels Lara to the forefront of Star Trek's female characters. At basically no other point in Star Trek are you going to find someone like this, a woman who is not only an unabashed equal but who is also this blunt and forward . It's great to see, and Webb and William Shatner knock it out of the park, which is tough to do when you're not in the same recording studio as the person you're supposed to be reacting to.

Furthermore, there's yet another great scene with Lara near the climax, where it's revealed someone on the team is trying to sabotage the mission from within and kill off their teammates. For awhile I was really worried the traitor would be Lara, as she's set up to be such a bold, aggressive and determined character. But no, it's one of the other characters, and it's Lara, along with Kirk and Spock, who helps rally those who remain loyal to the Vedala to recapture the Soul of the Skorr and bring everyone back home alive. She's as much a leader as Kirk and Spock, and Margaret Armen ought to be ashamed of herself. I guess I owe Stephen Kandel an apology: Freed from Harry Mudd and Gene Roddenberry it would seem he's more than capable of writing an admirable female hero, because "The Jihad" gives us two: Lara, of course, but the Vedala star-mystic as well who summons the team and gives them guidance on their journey through her powers of foresight and telekinesis.

Speaking of which this episode is dripping with magick. It's almost as magickal as "The Magicks of Megas-Tu". The Vedala are plainly psychic and use straight-up astral projection to help discern the location of the Soul and also seem to have mastery over telepathy, teleporation and telekinesis. And, just like in "The Magicks of Megas-Tu", this is given no other explanation other than that it self-evidently exists. This isn't "mental science", it's magic plain and simple. However, this is not what we'd think of as straightforward high fantasy either, though it might appear to be this at first glance. What's really interesting about the trappings of "The Jihad" is that this is all happening against the background of what remains a science fiction setting. While the Vedala may not practice "mental science" the way Isaac Asimov might have conceived of it, what they do is demonstrate the *mundane reality* of magick within the Star Trek universe. The magick of the Vedala exists alongside all the other ways of knowing in the galaxy and is treated as just as valid a worldview as any other. Indeed perhaps it might be even *more* highly valued as the Vedala are considered the oldest and most revered civilization in the galaxy and their word carries considerable clout on the interstellar stage. The ramifications of this are cosmic, and, no matter how hard Star Trek might try, this never stops being a part of it.

Then there's the Mad Planet, which seems to operate according to a distinctly magickal logic. In particular, an animist one: The whole world feels alive, which is even more fitting considering the inclusion of Lara, as many indigenous hunter-gatherer societies also understand their connection to the land through animism. But more to the point the Mad Planet feels not just alive, but also angry and tormented: There's perhaps an environmentalist dimension to this, but not in the crass and didactic way that defines so much 1970s attempts at this. In tying into the animism theme, perhaps the planet is upset because too many people have forgotten how to speak to it. Yet another reason it's so imperative Lara be here, but also that Kirk and Spock are so respectful of her. Furthermore, the Mad Planet serves as the personification of the challenge the team must undertake to recover the Soul of Skorr, and that also gives the title "The Jihad" a secondary meaning.

See, in actual Muslim spirituality, "jihad" means "struggle" (this is, in fact, literally what the word translates out to), and the Qur'an mentions two different kinds of jihads. One is the version that's most familiar to a 21st century audience, that is, a righteous struggle against one's enemies (though crucially this is most traditionally seen as a revolutionary act done to overthrow oppressors, *not* a holy crusade against nonbelievers for death and glory). However the second, and more important, meaning is that of an inner personal struggle to overcome challenge on an everyday basis. It's a challenge to remain true to your ideals and beliefs each and every day. So not only will the Skorr launch the holy war kind of jihad if the Soul isn't brought back, but the team themselves are undergoing a kind of jihad on the Mad Planet to work together and respect one another, thus living up to their own ideals. Star Trek itself, in fact, becomes a jihad, and that's an absolutely perfect analogy.

Which brings us back to the Soul of Skorr itself, which is this message given form and, as a result, it's ultimate magick spell. On first glace it looks straightforwardly pop Christian, much like the life force receptacles from "Return to Tomorrow", but it's actually more arcane than that: Tcharr says it's the result of binding Alar's soul to the mortal plain, but there's no mention of some technobabble explanation for extracting life energies or whatever that would prompt a Cartesian reading like we were forced to afford "Return to Tomorrow". No, in practice the Soul serves a very different purpose. Alar was a beloved prophet who inspired the Skorr to leave their warlike past behind them and the Skorr made him a cultural hero and strove to follow his example ever since. Knowing this, it makes that name extremely telling. The Soul of Skorr is just that: The collective hopes, dreams and ideals of a people projected onto a sacred totem, thus giving them immortal life and power. This touches on the heart of magick, which is the appropriation and manipulation of symbols and the belief that symbols have power and agency unto themselves, because belief itself grants them. No wonder the disappearance of the Soul would put the Skorr on a retrograde path and plunge the galaxy into war, because without ideals people become cynical and, even worse, apathetic. And that's also why a multicultural team of equals culled from all ways of life and all knowledge networks is needed to get it back.

Which means "The Jihad" is, put simply, perfect Star Trek. It's a story about idealism and cultural signifiers and the role they play in our lives. It's utopian not in the didactic, authoritarian way the franchise gets a bad name for these days, but because it looks frankly at the concept of ideals, why they're important and how people challenge themselves to try and live up to them. This is not a story about the enlightened space navy going around reorganizing societies, it's a story about how all people all over the universe try to better themselves, and how magickal it is when they succeed. And on top of that, it's bloody gorgeous to look at. It's absolutely everything Star Trek is good at wrapped up in one fleeting, perfect moment.

Even across the span of decades, I think I can still hear D.C. Fontana dropping the mic.

117. Ship's Log, Supplemental: A Trekkie's Tale

Oh boy, here we go. Yes, my friends, the time has finally come.

"A Trekkie's Tale" needs no introduction. A notoriously vicious bit of satire attacking a particular trend within Star Trek fanfiction, the story is infamous for introducing the world to the hated Mary Sue. It took no more than five brief paragraphs to completely tear Star Trek fandom asunder and, as a result, "A Trekkie's Tale" has transcended fan circles to become ubiquitous in the larger pop consciousness such that it's had a truly transformative, profound, and arguably profoundly negative, effect on the way we look at genre fiction even to this day. A case could be (and has been) made that the introduction of the Mary Sue archetype is one of the largest and most sweeping acts of reactionary silencing tactics in the history of genre fandom.

And yet "A Trekkie's Tale" itself is misread and misunderstood by pretty much everyone.

First, some background for those perhaps less familiar with what this is than others. "A Trekkie's Tale" is a piece of satirical fanfiction published in 1973 and featuring a character named Lieutenant Mary Sue who is the youngest, most beautiful and most talented officer in the entirety of Starfleet. On her first day on the *Enterprise*, Lieutenant Mary Sue outperforms everyone else on the ship, causes Kirk to instantly fall in love with her at first sight, outwits Spock with logic (that is never fully explained) and singlehandedly saves the ship, the crew and the Federation at least twice before tragically and randomly dying at the end of the story to be mourned by everyone and essentially turned into a modern-day saint. Lieutenant Mary Sue, and "A Trekkie's Tale" more generally, is fairly transparently an attack on a certain kind of Star Trek fanfiction, and is most often read as a parody of (usually female) writers who create author avatar characters as wish fulfillment, thus sidelining the original cast and narrative in the process. In the years since the initial publication of "A Trekkie's Tale", the term "Mary Sue" has become a stock character archetype and nowadays gets tossed around rather carelessly, most typically as a knee-jerk reaction from insecure male fans to the concept of "strong female character I don't like and who makes me uncomfortable with my masculinity."

What's the most interesting thing about the Mary Sue archetype to me, however, is how uniquely Star Trek a concept it really is. Star Trek fandom has, in my opinion, a very peculiar fascination with an *extremely* specific sort of fantasy: It's an almost omnipresent dream amongst Star Trek fans of all ages, generations and genders to be captain of their own starship, command their own crew and, essentially, to be the star of their own Star Trek spinoff. This goes totally contrary to the stereotypical conception of the obsessive fan, which would be someone fantasizing about the characters or the actors, either in a romantic or sexual way or just a desire to meet them in person. But that's not what Lieutenant Mary Sue does (indeed, the fact Kirk, Spock, McCoy and the others are largely incidental to her story is the whole point of it) and it's not what Star Trek fans seem to want either: Instead, they want their own personal slice of the Star Trek universe to themselves and they want it to revolve around them, or at least to explore it on their terms. It's the entire point of things like the Star Trek Experience in Las Vegas or the video games *Star Trek Starship Creator*, *Star Trek Bridge Commander* and *Star Trek Online*.

So, despite how much the fans will talk up Star Trek's commitment to strong character development, it seems that when the cards are down they're ultimately going to default to projecting themselves onto the show. To me this is very interesting and unusual, if for no other reason than it doesn't match up with my own personal history of Star Trek fandom at all. This was never a fantasy that ever would have crossed my mind for a moment: What I always liked about Star Trek was its sense of wonder and exploration, the familial atmosphere the crew shared with each other and the characters themselves. I admired Jadzia Dax and Tasha Yar, saw them as role models and wanted to be like them, so a lot of my experience with Star Trek consists of looking up to people like that and trying to learn from them to better myself, and to, in a sense, take a little bit of them into me. I mean the world was fun to play in and I loved that too, but that wasn't the primary draw: For me, it was the characters, the aesthetics and the iconography. From my perspective, that's as fundamentally, purely Star Trek as it gets, but it seems like my emotions aren't shared by fandom at large in this case.

But the other thing that defines my experience with Star Trek is wanting to write my own version of it, and for that there *is* a precedent. Here's where the other half of "A Trekkie's Tale" comes into play and, for my money, it's the more interesting half. So, if we're going to get anything remotely near an understanding of what these five little paragraphs actually are and how they fit into the history of Star Trek (as opposed to merely the way people have responded and interpreted them), we need to establish some simulacrum of context. By this point in the mid-1970s, Star Trek fandom was largely clustered around a series of fan-published and distributed zines. In the 1960s, the fan culture around the show, despite how loyal and vocal it had been, was still largely a disperse mainstream phenomenon. By the 1970s with the Original Series in syndication and hardly anyone watching the Animated Series (or at least hardly anyone seemingly willing to write and talk about it), Star Trek fandom was now very definitively a niche thing, with the first proper Star Trek convention (that is, separate from larger science fiction conventions) taking place in 1972.

As such, the 1970s Star Trek fandom comprised mainly two different factions: Middle-aged women who had been general science fiction fans in the 1950s and 1960s and remembered when Star Trek first started and the scene people like Bjo Trimble belonged to (and that Gene Roddenberry overtly tried to court), and younger college-aged women who were just getting exposed to the show through syndicated reruns. Both groups were very much interested in writing their own Star Trek stories, and there was such a surplus of them the zines had trouble keeping track of them all. So a situation arose where fans would be inspired by zines and cons to write, thus necessitating the need for more zines and cons so the cycle continued to self-perpetuate in perpetuity for awhile.

Back then, there was a stronger link between science fiction fans and science fiction writers than we might think would be the case today, perhaps a holdover from the days of the Golden Age conventions where readers and writers commingled and the dividing line between was quite blurry. It was not an unheard of scenario even as late as 1973 for science fiction authors to get their start writing for zines, and the fan culture sort of acted as an unofficial pipeline to more professional gigs. The problem was, of course, there was nowhere to go if you were writing about Star Trek, because the famous live-action show had been off the air for half a decade and, once again, nobody cared about the animated reboot. So you'd frequently get a lot of writers contributing a lot of really excellent, professional grade Star Trek stories as fanfic to zines because there was nothing else to do with them. Because of this, the fans introduced a kind of loose structure of their own, with zine editors oftentimes acting as a kind of surrogate script editor. One of the most prolific and influential of these semipro writers and editors was Paula Smith who, as it so happens, wrote the story we're talking about today.

Yes, shocking as it may seem, the person responsible for giving us the insecure femme-phobic fan's favourite trump card is, in fact, a woman. It's at this point I'm probably expected to pull a Margaret Armen and take Smith to task for internalized misogyny issues, but I'm not going to because I actually don't think that's what's going on here. Like all works of satire (including *Gulliver's Travels*), "A Trekkie's Tale" has been badly, badly misinterpreted by generations of clueless readers who don't seem to get the joke. In fact, an even better point of comparison might be Upton Sinclair's *The Jungle*: Intended as a condemnation of wage slavery of migrant workers in the United States, which is helpfully and blatantly compared with the literal enslavement of Africans by that same country, history has largely proven itself to be the domain of white straight cis male middle class liberal authoritarians by comprehensively missing the point and using it as a call-to-arms against lax heath code regulations in the meat packing industry. I feel something similar happened to Paula Smith.

The key to figuring out what I think Smith is actually saying here is to keep in mind her status as a kind of D.C. Fontana for fan culture. She was responsible for vetting hundreds upon hundreds of Star Trek fanfics and giving an innumerable amount of writers tips on how to hone their craft (actually, it was from interviews *with her* that I gleaned the majority of the historical information I use in this chapter). Indeed, one of the most classic, foundational maxims of fanfic, Langsam's Law, comes largely from her. It states that (in Smith's words)

> "There is a special caveat for writing media-based fiction. Don't make an estab-
> lished character do or say something out of line with his established character,
> of if you must, give good, solid reasons why."

which is frankly just good writing advice in general as far as I'm concerned. This touches on the other side of the 1970s zine culture, which was that because *Star Trek* was off the air, and regardless as to whether or not they knew about the Animated Series, the fans sort of saw themselves as penning if not the official continuation of it, at least one semi-proper, semi-authorized version of it. So it would kind of make sense that these people would take good care to make sure their stories could plausibly have been *Star Trek* episodes themselves had the show not been canceled.

And this is the nut of what "A Trekkie's Tale" is trying to do, because what Smith is lampooning with Lieutenant Mary Sue is not women daring to write Star Trek fanfic, or introducing new female characters, or introducing female author avatar characters or even introducing new female characters who go on to be love interests for canon characters. What Smith is lampooning is bad writing in general. As many good editors often are, Smith was a prolific writer herself, penning countless fics (debatably literally so, since she used a different pseudonym practically every single time she wrote something, making her work a headache to track down today) for not just Star Trek, but also *Starsky and Hutch, Harry and Johnny, The Professionals* and *The Man from U.N.C.L.E.*. She had written enough and been around the scene enough to know what worked and what didn't, and "A Trekkie's Tale" is her way of compiling and caricaturing the most egregious and problematic trends she noticed in an attempt to show new writers "Here: This is what *not* to do".

And if we divert our attention momentarily from Mary Sue herself, who is indeed admittedly a veritable perfect storm of painful amateur writing mistakes exaggerated beyond infinity, it becomes obvious she's not the only thing we're supposed to pay attention to. The fic's dialog is stilted, repetitive and awkward, plot developments happen out of thin air, there's no sense of internal coherence or consistency, a general feeling the whole thing was banged out in a terrible rush and even the tense keeps jumping back and forth between past, present and future. Even the title "A Trekkie's Tale" itself is a dead giveaway, eschewing completely any and all pretenses that this is going to be anything remotely resembling a straightforward or recognisable Star Trek story because, their obvious boundless energy and enthusiasm notwithstanding, this is something the fictitious writer has clearly put next to no effort into (not, it must be stressed, that this is entirely their fault, however: They're clearly too young and/or inexperienced to know any better). As the saying goes, it takes talent and skill to craft something this memorably awful.

So, while Smith did hold up the Mary Sue archetype as something to be avoided, unlike successive people who have appropriated the concept, she recognised it for what it was: One type of mistake among many that beginning writers have a tendency to make but that can be expunged through experience, guidance and support. But as noble as Smith's intentions with "A Trekkie's Tale" might have been, and I do think they were noble, the question remains: Has the story actually done what it was supposed to do and had a net positive effect on fandom such that it's help blossoming writers, fanfic or otherwise, to learn and develop their skills? Of that I'm not so sure, because the Mary Sue as it exists today is a terribly problematic concept loaded up with toxic connotations and, as is well known, a favourite silencing technique of the patriarchal hegemony. Decades of reactionary appropriation have twisted and distorted the Mary Sue archetype into a misogynistic weapon.

It's an altogether too common story to hear female writers, even very famous professional ones, confess that they consciously avoid having too many female characters in their cast or writing their women too strong or too independent out of a very serious and legitimate fear they'll be scorned and attacked for writing "Mary Sue stories" and will never be respected or recognised as proper writers (or even worse, have their careers completely destroyed outright) as a result. Anybody can write a character like Lieutenant Mary Sue, and such a character can be of any gender. But the "Mary Sue" archetype has become exclusively female and *that's* a problem. That *does* retroactively harm the original work and make me wonder whether the actual satire was ever all that clear to begin with. Because of that, I'm uncertain that Smith's original five paragraphs can now be taken apart from the tangible, material and very negative effect they had on female fans and writers, as riotously funny as those five paragraphs might be (and they *are* riotously funny: Phrases like "Gee, golly, gosh, gloriosky", "Tralfamadorian Order of Good Guyhood" and "beautiful youth and youthful beauty" crack me up every single time).

But regardless of the quality of the actual story, let's make sure we don't damn the author as well. Good writers have bad days. We all do. The most important thing about Paula Smith is that she always kept trying no matter what: She wrote an incalculable number of stories, oftentimes just on a dare or as an attempt to do an experiment or proof-of-concept for just herself. Like anyone, she missed her target just as much, if not more, than she hit it. That's only called being a writer, after all. Because she was involved in zines and conventions to the extent she was and ran so much (and kept so much running), I'd call her showrunner of her own underground version of Star Trek. Hell, given the staggering scope of her fanfic resume even beyond Trek, Smith should probably be seen as someone just as seasoned as the most experienced TV writers and producers of her day. So, even if she did strike out with "A Trekkie's Tale", it's ultimately one minor bump on the very long and winding path of a career that spans literally decades and frankly puts most professional writers to shame.

Paula Smith never gave up, never stopped trying to challenge and better herself and never let anyone stop her from writing what she loved. And I think that's the lesson she'd like her readers to take with them most of all.

118. Ship's Log, Supplemental: A Fragment Out of Time

Slash fiction is a thread that's been with us for quite some time already, and it's been with Star Trek arguably since as early as "Where No Man Has Gone Before". Although certain hardcore fans might not like to admit it, it is unquestionably one of the franchise's most defining and signature motifs. Although slash has existed for pretty much as long as people have been telling stories, the current manifestation of it, the interaction it has with late-20th and early-21st century fan culture, and thus the way it is commonly conceptualized today, can be directly traced back to Star Trek.

There are any number of possible opportunities to discuss slash over the course of the franchise's history, but the one that seems to most appropriate is here, with the first documented piece of Star Trek-inspired slash fiction, Diane Marchant's "A Fragment Out of Time", dating to 1974. Marchant submitted it to one of the first (and at the time only) Star Trek zines targeted expressly towards adults, a publication somewhat wonderfully titled *Grup*. Given the zine's comparatively small audience and interviews she's given after the fact, Marchant never expected it to be the bombshell it ended up becoming.

However I think she really needn't be ashamed, because the piece itself is, perhaps contrary to what one might expect, really quite tame and laudably well-written, describing a night of passionate lovemaking between two parties of whom great care is taken to speak in vagaries (though an accompanying illustration, not to mention the fact it was published in a Star Trek zine, sort of makes it obvious who the two paramours are supposed to be). And "lovemaking" really is the proper term: Marchant is very clearly interested in the intimacy and tenderness shared by her protagonists, and the gentle, poetic tone that permeates the entire piece reflects this. Honestly, as far as slash fiction goes, or really erotica in general, you could do considerably worse for yourself than this.

Like so much fanfiction of its era, Marchant wrote "A Fragment Our of Time" largely as an experiment. However, she also always maintained that she didn't come up with the idea of shipping Kirk and Spock herself, she was merely responding to what she felt was blatant subtext in the original *Star Trek* and that everyone who watched the show recognised and acknowledged to one degree or another, regardless of whether or not they actually admitted it. Marchant was adamant that the only thing she contributed to the history of Star Trek and the broader fan culture was the first work that was bold enough to put it into words, and I'm convinced she was right.

There was, of course, (and still is, to some extent) some manner of controversy over this opinion. The popular consensus for what happened next (I mean as much as there *can*

519

be consensus about something as understudied and undervalued as fanfiction) is that "A Fragment Out of Time" caused a great schism amongst Star Trek fans and a firestorm of a debate about how proper the fic itself was and whether Marchant's argument was convincing or not. It would be altogether too easy for me to draw the line between, well, not necessarily fanboys and fangirls, but let's say patriarchal proto-nerd culture and feminist fandom, but it's not quite as simple as that. Remember the vast majority of the invested parties here are still women, including some of Marchant's staunchest critics, like one Connie Faddis, who penned an extremely negative review of "A Fragment Out of Time" and who would go on to be a pioneering figure in the Kirk/Spock scene herself.

But perhaps the most damning evidence that slash fiction didn't cause a huge rift in Star Trek fandom circa 1974 or emerge with the uncomfortable connotations it maybe has nowadays comes from our friend Paula Smith. When questioned about her views on erotic Star Trek stories (or if you prefer straight-up Star Trek pornography) at a convention, Smith gave this sparkling reply (emphasis hers):

> "I agree that ST pornography is a lousy thing – it is so *badly* written. In search for titillating themes, good or even credible characterization is ignored, and plots degenerate to the simplest push-push gimmickry. A lousy Get-Together story is worse than a lousy Mary-Sue story, because the reader doesn't *expect* a Mary-Sue necessarily to be any good. If it is uneven, juvenile, or just plain silly, that is typical, and the reader is not disappointed. But when a reader takes up a story on an adult theme, she expects an adult treatment, or ought to. A simpering, or brutal treatment of sex is evil in a most fundamental sense, because such trivializes and degrades our greatest humanity – love. But sex, and sexuality, per se are not dirty and disgusting."

Furthermore, when asked specifically about slash during her tenure as editor of the zine *S and H* when it was at its absolute peak as a debate topic, Smith responded, at once guarded, cheekily and triumphantly

> "Some folks are hobbits: they need to be aware there are wider vistas than that of Bag End. Some are wizards: they must take care not to strike and blast as forcibly as they feel like, because there is always some fuzz-footed clown out there just itching to swipe yer Ring. The most useful thing anyone can learn is when to shut up. Like now."

which I think is just hilarious, as she has documented *Starsky and Hutch* BDSM slash fanfic to her name.

So if slash is something Star Trek fandom at large circa 1974 seems on-the-whole comfortable with and the only real new ground Marchant is breaking is putting everyone's unspoken assumptions into textual form, the question then becomes, what was it about the original *Star Trek* that made it so easy for widespread and near-universal slashing to happen to the point a significant majority of fans seemingly took it for granted? We briefly talked about this back in the chapter on "And The Children Shall Lead", but, to elaborate, Star Trek in general, though particularly the original series, exists at a unique junction of events and factors that make the evolution of slash an almost predictably logical outcome in retrospect. We've discussed at length one of the primary reasons why, which is that *Star Trek* was, even amongst the notoriously puritanical climate of US television, heavily sexually repressed and confused.

Gene Roddenberry never did quite manage to get a handle on how to handle writing women and approaching gender roles, even though he does get considerably better at it come *Star Trek: The Next Generation*. Well, at least he *tries*. The closest he's gotten so far has been "Turnabout Intruder", which was still ludicrously problematic and the fact it worked to the extent it did when it did was primarily due to William Shatner and Sandra Smith. Her employing Margaret Armen aside, D.C. Fontana perhaps understandably gets it, though she prefers to demonstrate her feminism in far more subtle ways that work within the framework Star Trek already established for itself.

And yet Star Trek has proven to be wildly popular with women-So much so that literally none of the fan literature and history I've been able to dig up about this era even *mentions* the fact that men probably watched the show too, unless you count the most likely at-least-partially staged "Save Star Trek!" campaign and its strong technoscience undertones. This is self-evidently because, at least on the surface, Star Trek claims to envision a world where differences between genders no longer matter. That alone is an incredibly powerful declaration, and, in my opinion, may be the single most important thing about the entire franchise.

But even aside from its embrace of feminism (as tentative and clunky as it may often be), Star Trek has always been quite sexy and sexual, and I don't mean because the women wore miniskirts in the 1960s and 1970s and there are a lot of one-off alien ladies. Spock is simply way too easy to read this way; I mean "Amok Time" alone practically demands it. He's a very sexually repressed and conflicted character, and whether or not Roddenberry meant for his inner struggle between logic and sensuality to be a metaphor for that, it works too well to ignore (although it's also worth remembering D.C. Fontana has attempted to correct this not once, but twice: First in "Journey to Babel" and then, more blatantly and effectively, in "Yesteryear"). Either way, because of this conflict and repression, it's especially easy to see Spock as in some sense a closeted character, as the closet is all about keeping up appearances that are really a facade to disguise the way you truly view yourself.

Then there's Kirk, or perhaps I should say William Shatner. Kirk as written, at least early on, is flatly not terribly interesting. He's a generic leading man, and a generic leading man as filtered through Gene Roddenberry's positionality at that. But Shatner, being firstly an extremely talented theatre actor and secondly someone who immediately recognised how overstuffed and pretentious Roddenberry had made Star Trek, from the very beginning set about trying to knock the show down a few pegs and get it to loosen up. So Shatner deliberately overacts, playing Kirk not at all straight, but as a kind of subtly exaggerated caricature. Subtly exaggerated caricature, or in other words "playing a role and getting it ever-so-slightly-wrong", is also something that is sometimes associated with gay male culture because, as best I understand it, calling attention to one's own artifice was something that, at least at one time, could be used as a kind of secret language with which members of an underground and oppressed culture could communicate with each other (in fact, I wonder if the connection between gay male culture and theatrical performativity may even be where get "straight" a synonym for heterosexual).

Now this is not at all to suggest Shatner or Nimoy were playing their characters gay *per se* (although if I recall correctly there was a point I think in the third season of the original series where both actors have gone on record basically admitting they started to do precisely this and were stunned it took people decades to figure it out. I mean it sure is hard to read stuff like "And The Children Shall Lead", "Spock's Brain" and "Turnabout Intruder" any *other* way), it's just that the way Nimoy wound up conceiving of Spock and the way Shatner played Kirk ended up paralleling very nicely with things that were also considered part of gay male culture at one point. That aside, another reason it became so easy to ship Kirk and Spock was because, well, they were really the only characters who were allowed to express their emotions to one another.

The primary reason for this was network standards and practices. Ostensibly the leading man, Kirk wasn't allowed to actually become emotionally intimate with any women (even Janice Rand, who was originally supposed to be Kirk's closest confidant) as there could be absolutely no implication of anything untoward going on off-camera, because this was still an era where sex was still largely seen as obscene by at least the people paying the salaries of the cast and crew. This is the real reason Kirk had to be "married to the ship and the job", although some of that may have come from Roddenberry too (though I doubt too much of it, given his relationship with Majel Barrett and, well, a whole bunch of other people). This is also why so many of the female guest stars seemed disposable and interchangeable because, well, they were. This meant that if the show wanted to have any actual character moments in between the stupid fight scenes, they had to be between the supposedly very heterosexual and virile close friends. Of course, given the way Nimoy and Shatner played their characters, this was not entirely successful in dissuading assumptions about the crew getting busy with each other in their off-hours.

So we have two characters who are built out of theatrical tropes that were also associated with at least a part of gay male culture at one point and the only people they can be emotional, honest and intimate with is each other. Kirk said she was closer to Spock than anyone else in the universe in "Turnabout Intruder" for a reason, because, from a narrative standpoint, that's literally, actually the case. That's the exact logic the show works by. I mean, you do the math: How do you think fans were going to read that? Believe it or not, they tend to be a rather savvy bunch. Savvier, I daresay, then studio and network executives. But that said, there's another side to this: In spite of all the overtures we can make to gay male culture, slash fiction remains if not the exclusive domain of, at least very strongly associated with, straight women.

It is an unspoken, though widely held, belief in the pop consciousness that straight women are overwhelmingly interested in gay male erotica. That's not to say gay men don't indulge in it themselves, but so do straight women, and enthusiastically so. And the thing

522

about a lot of slash, including "A Fragment Out of Time", is that it is, counterintuitively, actually very strongly heteronormative, or at least heterosexual and heteroerotc. There was a Tumblr post making the rounds awhile back as of this writing that summarised the phenomenon quite well: The author made the point that the vast majority of the most famous and beloved slash pairings consisted of a light-haired, gregarious, outgoing "badass" character and a quieter, more reserved dark-haired character who frequently plays the support role to his partner. Most recently, you can see this manifest in Dean Winchester and Castiel in *Supernatural* and Merlin and Arthur in the 2005 BBC *Merlin*, and in fact it seems to have become so ubiquitous it seems to have been a deliberate casting choice on the part of the latter show *specifically to* encourage the slashers. Others, like Steven Moffat and Mark Gatiss' *Sherlock* and Weta's *The Hobbit* trilogy, seem to invert and play with this archetype for a variety of reasons. The author then goes on to trace this trend all the way back to what's seen as the pioneering, archetypal slash pairing: Kirk and Spock.

Now, this makes going back and re-reading "A Fragment Out of Time" interesting, because Kirk is very clearly portrayed as the dominant, "masculine" sexual partner, and Spock the submissive, "feminine" one, as it's his reactions that are depicted in the most flowery and voyeuristic detail. Even if you extrapolate this out to non-sexual slash, this pattern holds: There always tends to be an energetic "masculine" half of the pairing and a reserved, demure, supportive, "feminine" half. The whole idea of dominant and submissive power structures in sexual relationships, and the further conflation of this with "male" and "female" poles is *extremely* heteronormative. Yes, Western society is *so* patriarchal and misogynistic that even a power structure *this heteronormative* is paradoxically only acceptable if it's shown being acted out by two gay men because it conveniently cuts the bothersome woman out of the picture.

Now this is not to say that slash isn't just as much about storytelling as it is sexuality: After a point, it just starts to make strong narrative sense to ship Kirk and Spock given a lot of the textual evidence on display and the unarguably talented writing pool in the K/S scene were right to point that out in my view. Even Marchant herself recognised this. But I do think a portion of the appeal of slash, at least as far as I can tell, lies within the very traditionally and stereotypical Western heterosexual (albeit traditionally stereotypically Western heterosexual female) fantasy of one person coming in and, through doting support, rehabilitating and healing another, or at least being swept up by a powerful masculine force. It's the exact same reason *Twilight* was so wildly successful, as this is precisely the way Bella and Edward's relationship worked. Slash isn't so much GLBTQ detournement as much as it is detournement by straight cis women who are trying to find ways to be emotionally validated in an overwhelmingly patriarchal culture whose media artefacts have an unsettling tendency to pretend *even they* don't exist.

This is not, of course, to dismiss slash as necessarily retrograde. I think it serves a very important purpose and as long as Westernism continues to hold such backwards and convoluted attitudes towards gender and sexuality, and so long as Westernism continues to be the dominant intellectual framework for popular discourse, stuff like slash is bound to crop up. I'm just not entirely convinced it's quite as radically queer as I sometimes see it made out to be. It's just like what we learned in "Amok Time": Everyone has a sexual side (even if for some that sexual side is "null and void"), and trying to pretend it doesn't exist is unhealthy and counterproductive. It's going to manifest somewhere in some form. And we live in a culture where any sexuality other than that of the stereotypically virile heterosexual cis male dom is considered shocking and forced underground. Maybe it's best, and fitting, for us to learn from and share with each other and use our shared marginal positionalities to recognise this.

119. Myriad Universes: Alan Dean Foster and Ballantine Star Trek

What's the most immediately interesting about Alan Dean Foster's *Star Trek Logs* novelizations of the Animated Series for Ballantine Books from my perspective is how neatly they fit into Star Trek's own evolving and shifting position in culture during this period.

When we talked about James Blish, I mentioned that the choice of having him novelize the Original Series was indicative of Star Trek's at-the-time tentative connection to Golden Age science fiction. While his novelizations seemed marketed to the Hard SF crowd (and certainly looked the part), there was always a lingering uncertainty that this was what Star Trek really was and that these were the sort of people it should be exclusively marketed towards. This was embodied in Blish himself though his paradoxical and counterintuitive connection with the sci-fi writers' group the Futurians, who bizarrely seemed to think they could bring about a Trotskyist revolution by going through Pfizer and Boeing. Blish and the Futurians, like Star Trek itself, were compelled equally by both extremely right-wing and extremely left-wing forces.

Alan Dean Foster however, is a different breed of writer altogether. In fact, it could be argued he stands right at the precipice of the point where New Age science fiction, Forteana and fantasy meld into the blockbuster giant of a genre we're familiar with today. Foster's major sci-fi work, and probably what got him the gig in the first place, is the Humanx Collective, a constructed, self-contained universe of stories about a progressive representative democracy encompassing multiple planetary civilizations of which humanity is a member, so I wonder where we've heard that before. The primary difference between the Humanx Collective and the Federation, however, is that the former body is in many ways defined by its two founding members, humanity and the Thranx, an insectoid people, and this relationship is a symbiotic one. As a result, there's a lot more cultural diffusion in Foster's stories than in Star Trek, and this allows for a depiction of how cultures morph and grow over time as they interact with each other.

Foster's also something of a message writer, and a lot of his stories have a very strong environmentalist bent to them. Unlike someone like Gene Roddenberry though, Foster doesn't tend to have his protagonists come sailing in to tell all the Bad Polluters what they're doing wrong, but instead demonstrates how a lack of respect for nature will ultimately lead to the undoing of any people who foolishly make the mistake of selfishly exploiting their environment. Apart from just being a message I can't find any fault with, this also puts Foster very firmly into the tradition and concerns of the environmental age, which is quite fitting for 1974 and 1975. What's also great about Foster's staunch environmentalism is how it demonstrates so effortlessly that science fiction, and in particular science fiction about space travel, can remain relevant without relying on being propaganda for massive state-sponsored displays of Cold War imperialism. Foster is also a masterclass at weaving nature and natural themes effortlessly into his sci-fi-fantasy imagery, and he'll end up delivering a titanic proof-of-concept of this in Star Trek's own "In Thy Image".

But the bits of Foster's oeuvre that most interest me are the ones that actually haven't happened yet from our current vantage point, but which in my view prove far more revealing. First is his *Spellsinger* series from the 1980s and 1990s, which concern a pop musician who is also a wizard, and who discovers this when he is transported into a fantasy world where music is actual, literal magic and lyrics are spells and incantations. This is...well...Without bringing up cosmic fugues, codas, spore dreams or symphonic radial madness and going off on a gigantic tangent about stuff that really isn't related to Star Trek (but which really deserves a book all unto itself), let's just say this interests me greatly. For the moment, you can go back and read what I wrote about "The Magicks of Megas-Tu", "Once Upon A Planet" and "The Jihad" if you're tempted to try and transcend the Grey Maybe.

Secondly though, and perhaps most shockingly of all, at least for me, is the fact Foster ghost-wrote the novelization of the original *Star Wars* and is, in fact, largely responsible for the *vast* majority of what's considered canon about that universe's history, chronology, technology, cultures and planets, a fact which he has rather classily likened to being a contractor for a Frank Lloyd Wright house. We're still a ways off from discussing Star Wars in any significant way, but for our purposes right now it's worth pointing out that it suffers from an even more severe case of Singular Creator Deification DIsorder than Star Trek. It's well known now, of course, that huge swaths of what's most beloved about that franchise come not from George Lucas himself, but from a widely disparate group of writers, directors, producers, artists and designers, but it's always surprising to learn *just how much* of Star Wars is due to people who barely got any credit and recognition at all.

Star Wars is also well-known for being the first, or at least the first large-scale and well-known, fusion of science fiction and fantasy tropes and motifs. As such, it's fitting that Alan Dean Foster be the one to novelize it and flesh out its world, because Foster is the first writer we've looked at to explicitly link the two genres. Previous writers we've seen, like Robert Bloch, Joyce Muskat and Stephen Kandel, have hinted at doing something like this, but it's Foster who really breaks the doors down and embraces this shared aesthetic as an overt goal. Likewise, connecting him to Star Trek at this point in time also does well to reassure us that in spite of the pretensions of it and a specific subset of its fanbase, Star Trek is not, and never really was, purely Hard SF. It's yet more evidence that even now, when Star Trek is arguably as cult as it's ever going to be, that this is an idea that has both mutability and staying power and is going to be around for awhile to come.

As for Foster's novelizations themselves, there's one other interesting thing they do that is perhaps the most obviously prescient of anything: While the Animated Series is purely episodic, with the exception of a few sequels to Original Series stories and that mention of the Kzinti in "The Infinite Vulcan", Foster turns the show into a self-contained serial, linking his first six books together and then turning his back four into a self-contained prequel to his own original Star Trek novel. Furthermore, Foster elaborates and expands on a lot of concepts the show only touched on, such as positing that M'Ress' people, the Caitians, share a common ancestor with the Kzinti and even giving M'Ress her own extensive backstory: According to a lengthy recount in the novelization of "The Ambergris Element", M'Ress had previously served aboard the USS *Hood*, where she singlehandedly saved the ship from a Kzinti attack after the entire bridge crew was slaughtered by stalling the pirates long enough to call for help, which basically means Foster's M'Ress is the only remotely positive thing ever to be associated with "The Ambergris Element".

M'Ress is a good example of the virtues of Foster's approach to novelization. She's a likable and memorable, yet really underdefined and underdeveloped character on the show who's also somewhat let down by Majel Barrett playing a really unconvincing cat woman. But Foster has a lot more time and space, not to mention freedom, to explore these sorts of concepts so someone like M'Ress really shines under him. In fact, I'm going to posit that he's one of the primary reasons she's remained such an iconic and beloved character from this era of Star Trek, going on to appear in numerous spin-off comics and tie-in novels.

This kind of overt serialization and eye towards world-building is blatantly unheard of in genre television in the 1970s, except for maybe a few tentative experiments in that direction, but it makes a lot of sense given Foster's novelist background and what he did with *Star Wars*. Much of George Lucas' work, not to mention Steven Spielberg's as well, is heavily indebted to pulp action serials which, along with Golden Age Hard SF, is a genre that Star Trek draws on as well. And, for better or for worse, in hindsight Foster's approach did rather turn out to be a strong indication of the way science fiction eventually developed. We're thankfully a ways off from when world building and serialization completely mire Star Trek and television in general, but a little bit of this is certainly OK and, in the case of Foster's *Star Trek Logs*, quite welcome.

This is another feature that distinguishes Foster from Blish: While Blish was slavishly loyal to the original scripts (or as loyal as he could be given he was often working from early drafts), Foster is not above expanding upon and enhancing the source material in ways the TV show was unable to do, but that he was given the long-form nature of his medium. This eye towards building upon, tweaking and improvement puts him in good company with the fanfic writers we've been looking at recently, and is quite possibly one of the primary dividing lines between two different approaches to genre fandom.

The other thing I like about these books is how they're advertised: The first few books overtly play up the notion that Star Trek is *back* and that The Animated Series is the proper, official continuation of the story. Even the fact that there's a line of novelizations at all, just like the Original Series had, does a lot to legitimize the current show in my opinion. Even though the idea that The Animated Series shouldn't be treated as canon comes largely from one angry guy ranting and raving in the late 1980s, even now there is, as we saw when we looked at the fanfic writers, a kind of sense that Star Trek is a marginal, half-forgotten thing at this point. The Animated Series still gets overlooked when compared to its more illustrious predecessor. But Alan Dean Foster is making a concerted effort here to argue for the show's merit and value and that it makes equally valid contributions to the evolving franchise and should be given respect and attention. Just as D.C. Fontana is trying her hardest to redeem Star Trek and move it forward (as are people like Paula Smith, if we're honest), Alan Dean Foster is trying to redeem the Animated Series itself and demonstrate how Star Trek can build off it itself to continue to grow.

120. "...strictly neutral in this matter as you well know...": The Pirates of Orion

"The Pirates of Orion" is one of the best character pieces in the Animated Series and builds nicely on established Star Trek lore without feeling either slavish or repetitive, but most of all it fits neatly into the pattern we've been crafting for the franchise over the past few chapters.

The *Enterprise* is en route to a dedication ceremony on Deneb V while recovering from an outbreak of choriocytosis, a particularly virulent respiratory disease that prevents red blood cells from transporting oxygen. Just when the crew thinks the plague is under control, Spock suddenly collapses on the bridge. After rushing him to sickbay, McCoy informs Kirk that Vulcan physiology is similar enough to that of humans to make him susceptible, but different enough that it becomes far more serious, and that Spock will die in three days unless the crew can get their hands on some strobolin, the only known antidote. Realising the nearest source of the vaccine is four days away from the *Enterprise*'s position, Kirk calls the starship *Potemkin* and freighter *Huron* for help in forming a brigade line. However, on its way to the *Enterprise*, the *Huron* is attacked by the titular Orion pirates, acting outside the declared neutrality of their government, who hijack the ship and steal its cargo. It now falls to Kirk to track down the Orions and reclaim the cargo without provoking a diplomatic incident.

This isn't the first time we've seen the Orion Syndicate since "Journey to Babel", but it's the first time we've seen it focused on to this extent. Even so, however, "The Pirates of Orion" keeps its space opera overtones and world building somewhat in check: The Orions act in a manner totally consistent with their previous appearance, down to the mention of how any Orion ship is duty-bound to self-destruct and its crew commit suicide should their mission fail in such a way that it puts their government's neutrality at risk. Just like in "Journey to Babel" though, and decidedly *un*like some of their later appearances, infodumps about Orion society are not actually the focal point of the entire episode. Though the space adventure stuff isn't quite less important than the character drama here as they're at least about equal, so there's still an appreciable balance between the two. Furthermore, this episode firmly establishes the Orion Syndicate as one of the proper, top tier antagonists for the Federation and the *Enterprise* crew, so when they reappear a few years later in *Star Fleet Battles* and when the video game based on that universe gets named after them, it's all but expected.

Which is all good, because "The Pirates of Orion" itself is neither the most original, creative or inspiring space pirate story ever told. I was consistently hoping throughout this episode that Kirk would be forced into negotiations with the Orions to get the vaccine and that we'd eventually get to see Kirk break treaty and regulations to save Spock's life. And while that *sorta* happens, it's nowhere near as interesting as it could have been in my opinion. The Orions get a pretty stock story: They callously hijack a freighter transporting much-needed medicine, and are stubbornly unwilling to hand it over for just long enough to fill out an episode.

What I wanted to see was the *Enterprise* deliberately *seek out* the Orion Syndicate as it was the only way they could get the medicine in a pinch, and for Kirk to give some speech about how it doesn't matter who's selling it and where it's coming from if the transaction saves lives. This could even be used as a kind of minor criticism of the pharmaceutical industry, as holding life-saving treatments hostage in exchange for capitalistic profit is tantamount to piracy, and at least the Orions are honest about what they do (indeed, McCoy even gets a great little line where he's frustrated that doctors are only as good as their drugs). Instead, we get a generic space adventure with some pirates and, while that's not terrible, it's considerably less effective than what I was hoping for.

Generic space adventures are often the hardest type of episode for me to write about. I don't dislike them, and in fact I can get really into one that's especially well-done (though truth be known I do tend to prefer the ones that use their space adventure trappings to disguise something a bit more clever). But there's not often a ton to actually say about them, and they tend to succeed or fail based on how clever the premise is and what kinds of intriguing images the creative team can come up with. And "The Pirates of Orion" is pretty solid as far as these sorts of things go: The Orion ship itself is imposing and cool-looking, the exploding asteroid belt the two starships take refuge in is delightfully mental and amazingly looks like a bunch of jawbreakers floating in space and seeing a Federation starship that's not *Constitution*-Class is yet another little thing that helps make the world of Star Trek feel more alive.

(Indeed it's the *Huron* that captured my interest the easiest here: The first half of the episode splits its time evenly between them and the *Enterprise*, and we start to get to know Captain O'Shea and his bridge crew. Barring Kirk seeking out the Orion Syndicate, I was hoping we'd at least get to see some swashbuckling action scenes of O'Shea defending his ship from a boarding party, but no, the attack happens completely off-camera).

But all this doesn't take into account what a strong character piece this episode is. If not, perhaps, for the plot (Kirk and McCoy racing against time to save Spock's life as a demonstration of how close the three friends are is not a *totally* fresh concept), definitely for the dialog and acting. Kirk and McCoy get a lot of scenes together where they confess how much Spock means to them, which is nice given this kind of story and really humanizes the two in a way that Star Trek at this stage doesn't always *quite* manage to do as often as it could. If nothing else it's nice to see these three, you know, *actually being friends* instead of being racist towards each other. But William Shatner and DeForest Kelley are the real standouts here, delivering some of their best performances in the Animated Series yet. Actually, the performances they turn in here are a return to kind of gritty, matter-of-fact frankness and gravity we really haven't seen from these two since quite early on in the Original Series: It reminds me a lot of McCoy's "And in all of that, perhaps more, only one of each of us" speech in "Balance of Terror" and his "Why don't you ask Jim Kirk?" line in "The Ultimate Computer", which is very much appreciated.

And aside from Kirk and McCoy, the rest of the cast gets handled quite well too. Much like in "Beyond the Farthest Star", or perhaps even "The Jihad", each member of the crew has a dedicated role to play and they all contribute something to saving Spock and resolving the diplomatic crisis with the Orions. Kirk, McCoy, Uhura and Scotty beam over to the *Huron* once they figure out something's gone wrong, and they use their combined skillsets to piece together what happened. Scotty investigates the engine room and the hold, McCoy examines the crew and Uhura goes over the ship's logs and record tapes. Meanwhile, Arex takes over the science station on the bridge in Spock's absence, much as his predecessor Chekov used to do in the Original Series, and the *Enterprise* itself is left in Sulu's capable hands.

But as perfectly solid as "The Pirates of Orion" is, the real thing that makes it worthy of note is its writer, Howard Weinstein. Weinstein will go on to contribute a number of stories to the various and sundry Star Trek comics, but this is is first effort and when he wrote it he was only 19, making this his actual, very first published work as a writer. And it's a damn promising debut, especially given the fact he submitted it to D.C. Fontana pretty much out of the blue and got it accepted largely without incident. Even Gene Roddenberry said this was one of the best debut scripts he'd ever read. This is endlessly fascinating to me, especially against the backdrop of all this stuff about fan culture and writing we've been talking about lately: There's this huge feeling amongst the fandom that Star Trek is something dead and buried and only being kept alive through zines, and here's some random kid submitting a totally unsolicited script to what I remind you is the current, official version of the franchise and he gets it produced as a cracking season premier.

I don't really have a larger point here except to reflect on the irony of not just that story itself, but the fact this isn't anywhere near the last time something like this is going to happen.

121. "Is green, yes.": Bem

"Bem" is the final "official" contribution to Star Trek by Dave Gerrold, though his presence and influence is going to be felt on the franchise for years to come (most notably during the first third of *Star Trek: The Next Generation*'s first season, when he was on staff). From what I gather, it seems to have the reputation for being one of the better remembered and most admired episodes of The Animated Series, although Gerrold and D.C. Fontana do seem to go back and forth a bit on what their actual takeaway on it was.

So naturally I don't think it works in the slightest.

The story concerns the *Enterprise* taking on an attache by the name of Ari bn Bem, representing the planet Pandro. Bem is acting as an independent observer judging the *Enterprise* crew to determine whether or not the Federation is worthy of establishing formal diplomatic relations with his people. Though he sat out the previous six missions, Bem insists on being allowed to accompany the landing party on a dangerous reconnaissance mission to investigate uncontacted aboriginal people on Delta Theta III. Beaming down, it soon becomes apparent that Bem has ulterior motives, as he clandestinely replaces Kirk and Spock's phasers and communicators with forgeries and then runs off, getting captured by the natives in the process. Pursuing Bem, Kirk and Spock end up captured themselves, where Bem reveals to them that, as a colony organism, he could have divided into discrete parts and escaped at any time, but allowed himself to be captured to firstly study the native population from within, but also to see how Kirk and Spock would respond, disapproving of their repeated attempts to resolve the situation with force.

OK. I have quite a few issues with this setup already, and that's the briefest summary I could manage. First of all, as someone with a background in anthropology this entire premise rankles me. The ethics of "uncontacted" cultures is a sticky proposition to begin with, and the ever-present headache that is Star Trek's Prime Directive makes it worse. There's always a kind of paternalism (and, frankly, racism) present in the assumption that indigenous peoples, especially indigenous peoples who are "uncontacted", are some kind of living time capsule from humanity's prehistory. You can't tell anything objectively about human history (well, you can't really tell *anything* objectively, but that's another matter entirely), and certainly not through ethnography. All that gets you is a not-always-clear outsider's perspective of how a culture operates *in the present day*. Furthermore, it's more than a little patronizing and naive to assume that all so-called "uncontacted" people are too childlike and stupid to at least guess some kind of an outside world exists.

None of this is helped by every single person in the episode acting like a complete idiot. Kirk and Spock are in full-on colonialist mode here again, stressing the importance of this mission to "classify" the aboriginal people of Delta Theta III, like the good Lamarckists they are. Spock even throws out pointedly ridiculous descriptors like "late primitivism" as if he's some kind of imperial anthropologist from back when formal colonial empires were a thing and institutionalized racism and modernist teleology were the guiding philosophies of the day (I mean, even more than they are now). Thankfully they're both called out on this bullshit by Bem and one other character who we'll talk about later, but none of it takes, frankly, especially when Bem acts colossally stupidly himself. At no point in the history of anthropology has it been considered a standard part of participant observation to charge headlong into your contact village and let yourself get captured and thrown into a stereotypical bamboo cage straight out of old-timey pulp adventure serials. Somehow I don't recall reading that in Bronislaw Malinowski's handbook.

Actually let's talk some more about Bem. He is, in fact, named after precisely what you think he's named after. And no, he isn't one. "BEM", for the uninitiated, is a cheeky acronym for the stock science fiction concept of the Bug-Eyed Monster. Gerrold originally pitched this story as a sort of joke about how fun it might be to see an actual BEM in Star Trek...but he's also said that Bem himself was never intended to actually *be* a BEM, so I have no idea what Gerrold's point actually was. It's also worth noting that, given the way he acts in the actual episode, were Gerrold a woman, Bem would *absolutely* have been declared a Mary Sue at this point. He's a character who we've never seen before immediately made honourary commander and who, despite his deceptive machinations, goes on to lecture Kirk and Spock about their smug sense of entitlement and dangerously irresponsible reliance on technology and firepower.

So for awhile it seems like the script is making "Bem" out to be another criticism of Star Trek's authoritarian and imperialist tendencies by showing how the titular character has a better philosophy towards exploring and meeting people (even though he actually doesn't), but the problem is any story like this made in the wake of "The Magicks of Megas-Tu" that doesn't acknowledge humanity's drive towards constant self-improvement is, in my opinion, flatly outdated. Thankfully the episode does try to address this but it actually doesn't seem to be thanks to Gerrold. Gene Roddenberry took a particular interest in this episode and made a ton of edits and alterations to it and, unbelievably, *he's* the one who seemed to recognise the majority of its problems and made the biggest effort to alleviate them.

But before we can get too excited, it turns out Roddenberry doesn't really know what to do with this pitch either and his additions don't really help. Roddenberry felt that it would be a good idea if the *Enterprise* crew met God on Delta Theta III, and had Gerrold add such a character to come in and but both Kirk and Bem in their places. Starting here Roddenberry starts to develop a fascination with the concept of God or some other kind of transcendent Truth, and this will eventually culminate in his big overblown treatise on the matter in 1979. And although this never *quite* works out for him (although I do submit a portion of this might be my own hesitation about this kind of Greco-European conception of the divine and objective reality), the depiction of it in "Bem" is prototypical and ill-defined even by Roddenberry's standards.

See it turns out God, who is apparently Nichelle Nichols, is upset at the Federation and the Pandronians interfering on Delta Theta III. And here's where this episode really goes to pieces for me: Roddenberry, or perhaps Gerrold, adds in an underlying motif about testing. The *Enterprise* crew are testing the Delta Thetans to find out what taxonomical classification of people they are. Bem claims to be testing the Federation, via Starfleet, by observing how they react to certain situations and God, meanwhile, resents the hubris in either of them thinking they have the right to test and classify anything. It's at this point any possibility of this being a critique of Star Trek's narrative logic and ethics goes out the window, because Bem breaks down and says he's failed his own test by underestimating Kirk and acting foolishly by violating his orders and going against Starfleet regulation, which is obviously more enlightened then he gave it credit for. Maybe Bem then is Gerrold's criticism of the Mary Sue, which would be even more troubling as this would mean Gerrold is saying what's most valuable about Star Trek is its well-founded rigid authoritarian chain of command.

Now I don't want to totally single out Gerrold for blame here. He's a demonstrably good writer, albeit one who has a frustrating tendency to try and punch above his weight class before he's really prepared to. And a lot of the things that make Gerrold's pitches so entertaining are on display here, most notably the comic timing. Furthermore, both he and D.C. Fontana have said on occasion that this isn't a story either of them are terribly proud of. But even so, this one flatly does not work: "Bem" is Gerrold's most troubling submission yet (though unfortunately not the most troubling of his we're going to look at). The fact of the matter is Gerrold has seriously worrying bad habits as a writer that constantly threaten to undermine him if he's not careful, and "Bem" is a story where they get the better of him. But the larger issue at play here is all that testing.

Unlike previous such characters, and indeed future ones, the God in this story is very much someone we're supposed to defer to. She's a wise and benevolent God, pointing out to the now-suicidal Bem that punishment is only necessary when someone is incapable of learning. Coming from her, this is both a reinforcement and an endorsement of authority. But what really bothers me is, as Spock points out, *the God in this story is very clearly a tester too*: She's testing the Delta Thetans (to whom she refers to as children in need of guidance, thus once again invoking the racist notion that indigenous people are quaint, primitive and childlike) and using their planet as a large-scale laboratory on social evolution. She's doing the exact thing she found abhorrent when Kirk and Spock attempted it. But she has the right, because she's God and thus a legitimate higher power.

This is, of course, a very Christian, and thus Western, conception of divinity. But what marks it as such is not merely the crass authoritarianism, but also the notion that God is some kind of arch-manipulator, putting out tests to put her experimental subjects through to see if they pass muster. Avital Ronell has a great book called *The Test Drive* which equates the ubiquity of scientific-style tests in Western Modernity with Freud's Drive Theory. Westerners are thus compelled to test ourselves and each other, and this seeps into all aspects of Western thought, discourse and pop consciousness.

One of the things Ronell's book grew out of, for example, was her analysis of the rhetoric surrounding the First Gulf War, and in particular how it was promised to be "bloodless" and "safe", and how this paralleled with the then-contemporary AIDS panic. In essence, the war was the US' attempt to test itself for AIDS, and to reassure itself that its test came back negative and, implicitly, that it wasn't gay. The test then is what we use to legitimize all aspects of our lives, not just our approach to scientific research, but love, war, and, as I think Roddenberry and Gerrold show here, our own sense of self-worth. It's a powerful, if not the primary, force in both normalization and marginalization. It's how we determine what's acceptable and what isn't.

So, if the only way anything can be considered serious and worthy of consideration is if it passes a test, it's not that much of a stretch to see the entirety of existence as one great science experiment with an almighty God, or some other objective force (such as Reason, Nature or The Universe. This is another area in which Western Science and Western Religion show themselves to really be born of the same underlying mentality), as the only truly legitimate authority by which we can measure ourselves against. We are all, as Kirk and Spock say in the denouement, merely children hoping to pass muster.

A more apt comparison for this episode though would be Ronell's book *Loser Sons*, which posits a connection between belief in an omnipotent and judgmental creator God, authoritarianism and toxic masculinity. The book shows how this conception of authority passes patrilineally from "God" all the way down to "Daddy", and that this is at the root of why authority does what it does. If, the book argues, you conceive of God as an "almighty and impossible to please father figure", it's not too much of a stretch explain the actions of people like George W. Bush, Mohammed Atta and Osama bin Laden who have spent their lives trying to get "Daddy" to love them. What "Bem" does, and unforgivably so, is project this masculine conception of divine authority onto a *goddess*. According to this episode, a female god can only be divine if she acts like a judgmental Abrahamic god: She can only be divine if she is masculinized. Cultural *and* misogynistic violence then. It's one thing to be of one's culture-Everything is, even spirituality. It's quite another when you get evangelical and imperialistic about it.

Thankfully, for me at least, this Western notion of authoritarian male transcendentalism isn't the only spiritual path that exists. But that's all I'm going to say about this topic for now.

535

122. "National Tapioca Pudding Day": The Practical Joker

"The Practical Joker" was the Animated Series episode I most dreaded having to watch, even before knowing about Margaret Armen's submissions. And, while the actual episode isn't anywhere near as dreadful as I feared it was going to be, it's still concerning as it marks the point where The Animated Series treads the closest to becoming the one thing that would simply torpedo its legacy: Children's television.

Now, there's nothing inherently wrong with children's television. When it's working properly, there's an elegance to children's television that can make it fundamentally more sophisticated and effective than "adult" fiction because it doesn't shy away from being idealistic or taking a stand. Indeed, some of my very favourite television shows were, in fact, designed with children predominantly in mind or at least operated according to a logic that children would find recognisable. But this...is not the kind of children's television I'm talking about here.

Before I go any further I should probably get the plot synopsis out of the way. While taking a break from a geological survey mission, the *Enterprise* is randomly attacked by a fleet of Romulan battlecruisers. After seeking refuge in an electrically-charged space cloud, a series of strange occurrences starts to befall the crew. All the cups and silverware are replaced with trick ones, Spock's science station scanner is replaced with one that has black ink on the eyepieces and the replicators start shooting food out at anyone who tries to use them. Finally, in a woefully iconic moment, Kirk storms onto the bridge and fumes about how someone stole his uniform from the laundry chute and replaced it with one that has "Kirk is a Jerk" emblazoned on the back in bold lettering. After taking turns blaming each other, the crew soon realizes that their practical joker is the *Enterprise* computer itself, which is suffering from an electronic nervous breakdown as a result of the charged storm the ship passed through. The crew must now work against the clock to interpret and outmanoeuvre the ship's erratic behaviour before it outwits everyone by plunging them into the Neutral Zone.

So it's dumb, but inoffensively so. In fact, it's actually somewhat clever as it starts out leading us to believe it's going to be a rote and banal children's television story about a practical joker who will eventually get their comeuppance and learn a lesson about playing hurtful jokes on people before turning into a basic Star Trek techno-puzzle about a computer going out of control. In essence, the episode has played a practical joke on us through subverting expectations, but it's not really an especially good one as neither type of story is something terribly easy to get excited about. Now, the basic concept of the back half of the episode, that of the *Enterprise* gaining sentience and leaving clues for its crew to figure out, is actually pretty interesting and it's a testament to their shared skill as writers that Brannon Braga and Joe Menosky eventually do this story for *Star Trek: The Next Generation* and manage to make it something other than an unwatchably cringe-worthy disaster. But that story is not this one, and while there are significantly worse ways to kill twenty minutes, I'd be hard pressed to call "The Practical Joker" a highlight of the series. There are a few funny lines and moments, but nothing that struck me as especially memorable.

The other notable thing about this episode is that it introduces the Holodeck. It's called the rec room here, but it's self evidently what we'd now call a Holodeck: A room the crew can go to on their off hours to relax in any one of its pre-programmed virtual reality environments. Gene Roddenberry had actually wanted to introduce the Holodeck in the third season of the Original Series, but budget cuts and his own stepping back from day-to-day duties meant he didn't get to put it into an episode until the Animated Series. And, given we now have the Holodeck, we of course also now have the Holodeck malfunction: In this case the *Enterprise* plays a joke on McCoy, Sulu and Uhura by locking them in it, laying a pit trap for them and then cycling through all the different programmes until settling on a whiteout in an arctic tundra and putting them at risk for exposure. And, although the Holodeck works best when it's used to explore themes of artifice, metafiction and genre mashup and while we'll have to wait for its reappearance in *Star Trek: The Next Generation* before we get there, the first appearance of such an iconic part of the franchise is definitely worth paying attention to.

Now, having exhausted basically all the erudition I can derive from this episode, I want to focus more on the direction it seemed to be going before it pulled a bait-and-switch and why that had me worried for quite awhile. Of course, what I'm referring to is the tendency to associate animation exclusively with children's television, and not only children's television in general, but cheap, disposable and mindless children's television. At some point in its history, most typically pegged at the moment when Hanna-Barbera figured out how to make filler Saturday Morning programming cost effectively and efficiently, cartoons began to be seen as kid's stuff not worthy of serious consideration.

Soon, creators themselves began to internalize this negative reputation and started talking down to their audience, resulting in a *vast* majority of animation becoming insufferably and unwatchably patronizing, either because it was obvious throwaway work nobody put any thought into or because it was irritatingly and smugly didactic in its attempt to "teach a lesson". It eventually got to the point that James "Shamus" Culhane, a veteran animator and director who worked on the legendary Woody Woodpecker short "The Barber of Seville" (named one of the 50 Greatest Cartoons of All Time by animation historian Jerry Beck) along with numerous Disney Animated Canon movies, flat-out said nobody should make cartoons with children primarily or exclusively in mind as they will inevitably be cripplingly paternalistic. He was, of course, absolutely right: *Star Trek: The Animated Series* is far from the last work of animation we'll be looking at in this project, but it is the last where the general assumption was that cartoons exist primarily for children, *ergo* cartoons must always be prescriptive and didactic.

With the success of shows like *The Simpsons*, *South Park* and the output of Pixar in more recent years this attitude no longer seems to be quite as widely accepted as it once was, but I still see it quite a lot. Even in my own experience writing about animation this crops up quite frequently: I get the most snarky and bemused reactions and do the worst traffic numbers whenever I talk about cartoons or children's television (the exceptions being if I talk about something ubiquitous like the Disney Animated Canon or get picked up on a fluke by a huge community blog). The blog of this very project, in fact, suffered somewhat: My readership figures and comment threads tapered off significantly following the switch from the Original Series to the Animated Series. Furthermore, when I was writing Book 3 and serializing it for the blog the year after I wrote the initial version of this essay (the first half of which is almost entirely on animated science fiction), the blog did probably the worst traffic numbers of any period in its history. And, while I did expect this and can't chalk the whole thing up to me covering a cartoon show, I also find it hard to believe that's not a factor either.

And this is noticeable in the production of the Animated Series itself. There's the fact it aired on Saturday Mornings for one thing, but also look at how D.C. Fontana herself felt compelled to defend "Yesteryear" on the basis that it supposedly "taught a valuable lesson to children" and not on the basis of it being, you know, possibly the single greatest character study in the history of Star Trek to date. "The Magicks of Megas-Tu", debatably the high water mark of the entire series, was almost never made because the network was afraid it that it would cause children to believe God didn't exist (after all, we wouldn't want to make Daddy angry, would we?), and Fontana had to come up with some strangled argument about how Lucian's status as the Devil implicitly proved God existed as well to convince them to let it go through. Also look at the very obvious science lessons shoehorned into "One Of Our Planets Is Missing" and "The Terratin Incident" that in both cases jarred pretty horribly with the rest of their respective stories. While this might not be a guiding concern for those running the show, it very much seems like something that at least had to be on their minds somewhat.

And now maybe it becomes clear why an episode about a practical joker going around playing pranks on the *Enterprise* crew would make me nervous. Because there's no way in hell an episode with this kind of premise would ever have been made on one of the live action shows. And for the first time in the history of the Animated Series that's not a good thing. The sentient starship stuff, yeah: I previously mentioned Braga and Menosky and they do make it work, and they're far from the only ones to. The Holodeck stuff? I mean, come on, do I need to even say it? Of course Star Trek comes back to that. But the pranks? Absolutely not. That kind of a setup is the exclusive domain of the absolute dregs of the print-and-forget children's animation industry, and that's sobering. So, even though "The Practical Joker" isn't actually that kind of story, the fact it gets close enough so as to tease us with the possibility it might be is sincerely troubling.

It may be a joke, but I'm not laughing.

123. "Yes, I've read a poem. Try not to faint.": Albatross

In their unauthorized Star Trek episode guide *Beyond the Final Frontier*, Lance Parkin and Mark Jones said that the story for this episode would have been a great concept to explore on one of the live-action series and bemoaned the fact it was done on a cartoon show.

So naturally the first thing I'm going to do is continue to complain about how undervalued animation is as a form of creative expression. Because Parkin and Jones' argument makes zero sense to me (and I like Parkin a lot too). There is nothing about "Albatross" that could have been done better on the Original Series. The emotional core of the episode hinges on Spock and McCoy, and while both Leonard Nimoy and DeForest Kelley can be visual actors at times, especially Nimoy, visual acting skills are not expressly needed for the kind of story this is. Actually, this episode serves as a great reminder of how multitalented and versatile this cast really is: Nimoy and Kelley convey all the emotion they need to through their voices alone, evidence they're just as strong in the recording booth as they are on stage. Furthermore, neither Kelley nor Nimoy are anywhere near as visual as William Shatner, who delivers yet another memorable marquee performance here. If *William Shatner* of all people can make the transition to animation effortlessly and painlessly, really all arguments about animation as an inferior medium are invalid.

Furthermore, declaring that it's a shame an episode like this wasn't done on the Original Series does a major disservice to D.C. Fontana, the Animated Series creative team and all the good work they've done over the past two years. This is flatly a tighter, stronger and more thematically and ethically coherent show now than it was in the 1960s. In fact, far from being the mini-classic Parkin and Jones seem to think it is, I'm of the mind "Albatross" is another of this season's mediocre outings. But the fact this, a character piece about the crew's loyalty to McCoy and righteous anger at a mishandling of justice, can now be called *middling* should be seen as incredibly telling. On the Original Series, we were regularly getting fed absolute garbage like "Mudd's Women", "The Apple", "Who Mourns for Adonais?", "The Omega Glory", "Elaan of Troyius", "The Enemy Within" and "The Savage Curtain". On the Animated Series, we haven't seen anything come *remotely* close to those cratering lows with the exception of Margaret Armen's stuff, and Armen is a special case. The fact this episode even *exists* is testament alone to what the Animated Series has been able to accomplish.

I suppose it'd help if I explained a bit about what "Albatross" is about. Basically, on a diplomatic mission to the planet Dramia, the *Enterprise* crew is shocked to see Doctor McCoy arrested on charges of committing mass genocide via a plague he allegedly brought to the second planet in the system nineteen years ago. With McCoy in jail, a furious Kirk takes the *Enterprise* and the rest of the crew to Dramia II to conduct an independent investigation in search of evidence proving the CMO's innocence. That's essentially it, and that gets at the root of the problem with this episode. We're back in "Court Martial" territory, if only in general narrative structure, and while we're thankfully spared the lengthy, bombastic courtroom drama and are instead mercifully granted a minor space adventure instead, the same general problems apply. Namely, we know McCoy is innocent, and it's even more apparent here than in "Court Martial". You don't go five seasons with the same cast of characters and suddenly have one of them turn into a genocidal tyrant, unless the creative team is *completely* blitheringly incompetent. Which, I mean, I don't put a lot past some of the people who work on Star Trek, but I don't think even Star Trek could screw that up.

Now, the problem here isn't that this is some failure of the episode to build up sufficient tension, it's that this entire type of story is fundamentally unworkable. No matter how hard you try, you simply cannot build an entire episode around the possibility one of the show's major characters is secretly a killer or some other kind of awful person. Narrative logic is going to make protagonists immediately and irreversibly sympathetic simply by virtue of them being protagonists. The other option, and I mean the *only* other option, is to base your show around a straight-up villain protagonist, which requires an altogether more deft handle on storytelling craft. The best the kind of story both "Albatross" and "Court Martial" are can hope for is to make its central mystery about figuring out why our hero has wrongfully accused, that "how-is-he-going-to-get-out-of-this-one" tension, and the thing is I just don't find that interesting.

"Court Martial" tried to paper the whole thing over with a whole bunch of manly legal drama swagger and just wound up looking silly and pointless and this one has the *Enterprise* pop off to Dramia II to find the real source of the plague, which turns out to be a deadly space aurora which, while certainly unique, still isn't terribly inspiring (although this does lead towards a decent climax where Spock, the only one not afflicted, gets to break McCoy out of jail so he can cure the plague and prove his own innocence to everyone). I just really have a problem with any story that arbitrarily puts the protagonists' morality in question unless moral ambiguity is built into the premise of the show, which it's fundamentally not at this stage in Star Trek's history. Indeed, I'd go so far as to claim this kind of plot has worked precisely once in the entire history of Trek, and that success was due in part to the timing of when the episode was made and the fact it was penned by two bloody brilliant writers.

What's actually the most interesting thing about this episode to me, aside from the acting (the puckish delight Shatner imbues Kirk as he manipulates the spy the Dramian government sent after the *Enterprise* into stowing away, thus invalidating his claim to legal authority, is particularly delightful) is the aurora, and, more to the point, the idea of an aurora in space. Now, before I get yelled at by physics nerds or Richard Dawkins acolytes, I am well aware having a spaceborn aurora is scientifically inaccurate and that they're in truth caused by the interaction of charged magnetic particles in the thermospheres of planets. I also don't care.

Visually and symbolically, aurorae are phenomena of the heavens, and ancient peoples in the far north and far south have historically seen them as belonging to the domain of the sky. Inuit tradition holds that the aurorae are alternately souls of ancestors or animals, a dangerous force that would decapitate you if you whistled at it, or spirit guides for hunting and healing. While I couldn't find any Sami traditions concerning aurorae, the earliest Norse account hypothesizes that they might have something to do with sun flares, or giant fires that surround the ocean, or even the stored energy of the glaciers themselves. In Australia, amongst the Gunai and Ngarrindjeri peoples of Victoria and South Australia, respectively, the aurorae were otherworldly bushfires or the campfires of spirits, while indigenous peoples in Queensland saw them as the medium through which spirits communicated with those of us in the mortal world, somewhat similarly to the Inuit.

Irritatingly, "Albatross" doesn't seem to pick up on any of these indigenous interpretations of aurorae in the heavens. However, what the episode's conception of them does seem the most similar to is, perhaps predictably, historical Western astronomical beliefs. Tycho Brahe was said to be of the opinion aurorae cause disease by emitting sulfuric vapour, which is not altogether removed from what happens here. Although the actual mechanism by which it infects the Dramians and then the *Enterprise* crew isn't really explained, the aurora is very clearly the source of the ailment *du jour*, which would seem to put this episode somewhat in Brahe's tradition. What I find interesting about this is that it positions Star Trek in some sense into the history of astronomy, or to be more precise, the symbolism and rhetoric of historical astronomy. It's still too Western for my personal tastes, but it is intriguing to think about given the way science fiction of this period is growing increasingly invested with the idea of genre trappings and its own setting and motifs. We can now talk about the history of how people have perceived and interacted with the natural world and how that's shaped our art and philosophies, because of course it has.

But unfortunately I can't really recommend the episode at hand. This is all fascinating and gives us a lot of material to work with in the future, but the actual twenty minutes you can call up onscreen isn't the Animated Series' finest moment, though there are a few charming bits here and there. But again, the fact I can say that about an episode with no discernibly massive problems and that something this solid and effective can be called mediocre really tells the whole story here. It concisely drives home just what D.C. Fontana and her team were able to accomplish with the Animated Series, and that's something worth reminding as we approach its final curtain call.

124. "Only the beginning": How Sharper Than a Serpent's Tooth

Although there's one more episode to go according to the official episode list, "How Sharper Than a Serpent's Tooth" can in some ways be seen as the series finale of *Star Trek: The Animated Series*, and really, the first phase of the Star Trek franchise. It's a return one last time to the realm of the magickal, a conscious and deliberate claim that Star Trek is an extension of indigenous spirituality (or at least should be), and, somewhat incredibly, is "Who Mourns for Adonais?" done properly, written as a tribute to and eulogy of Gene Coon. It's also the solitary Emmy Award win of the entire Star Trek franchise.

After a mysterious probe visited the founding homeworlds of the Federation and attempted to contact them before randomly exploding, the *Enterprise* is following its trail back to what it hopes will be its source, where it discovers a gigantic starship that suddenly, before everyone's eyes adopts the visage of a ferocious-looking feathered lizard. Helmsman Dawson Walking Bear, a student of indigenous cultures, in particular Native American and Mesoamerican, immediately recognises the creature before them as Kukulkan: An ancient Mayan deity associated with the Vision Serpent, the symbolic embodiment of the gateway to the spirit world, and the intermediary between mortals and their ancestors and gods (serpents being very important in Mayan spirituality anyway, oftentimes seen as the vessels the moon and stars use to travel across the heavens). Kukulkan is saddened that humanity seems to have forgotten him, but, because Walking Bear remembered, he wonders if the *Enterprise* crew can do what he claims their ancestors failed to, and transports him, Kirk, McCoy and Scotty to his ship.

The crewmembers materialize in a large, empty room that morphs into a gigantic city modeled off of Maya, Aztec and aspects of ancient Chinese design. Walking Bear points out that Kukulkan is said to have asked his followers to build him a city and that, once they had, he would return (a trait which, according to my cursory research, is actually more similar to the tales of the K'iche Mayan feathered serpent Q'uq'umatz). Kirk figures the city must be a kind of signal, that Kukulkan must have appeared to many different peoples, and, since each culture only focused on one piece of the iconography, none of them built the city exactly right. However, they might be able to figure it out now together. Naturally, they succeed and Kukulkan appears before the landing party. Kukulkan claims that he's upset by the ceaseless violence of human history and fears all the work he's done to to help humanity has been for naught. It now falls to Kirk, McCoy, Scotty and Walking Bear to convince the serpent god that humanity's capacity for self-improvement demonstrate that his faith was not ill-placed, but also that the time has come for humans to learn their own lessons by themselves, because a parent cannot keep a child forever.

My enthusiasm belies the fact that this one is obviously *really* good and it comes so, so close to being just about everything I want out of Star Trek. The concept is just about perfect, and a masterstroke as is. The iconography and animation? "How Sharper Than a Serpent's Tooth" has been one of those episodes that's haunted me for decades. Finally being able to see it was breathtaking. And, just as Kukulkan's faith in humanity was restored by the crew of the *Enterprise*, so was my faith in Star Trek reaffirmed by learning about the backstory for this episode. The episode's writer, Russell Bates, happened to be a Native American himself, a Kiowa, and D.C. Fontana immediately sought him out because she explicitly wanted a science fiction story from a Native American perspective.

Bates was paired with Robert Wise, an animator who would go on to write for a number of shows from the Renaissance Age of Animation, such as *Jem, Chip 'n' Dale Rescue Rangers* and *Batman: The Animated Series*. And, although it's not well-known, Wise also was a major architect for the original *Teenage Mutant Ninja Turtles* TV series, and is largely responsible for giving the four turtles the distinctive and iconic personalities now strongly associated with them. Fontana hoped that together the two creators would bounce ideas off of each other and come up with something vivid and memorable that really took advantage of animation as a medium. And, while the end result is most certainly that, here's also where things start to go a bit downhill for this episode. Maddeningly, as brilliant as it is, there are one or two conceptual things about "How Sharper Than a Serpent's Tooth" that don't sit quite right with me.

Firstly, while the story was supposed to be about Native American mythology, the primary character is Kukulkan, who is quite blatantly a Mesoamerican deity and that's not *exactly* the same thing. According to Wise, Kukulkan's role was originally supposed to be filled by a Thunderbird, which *is* part of Native American mythology, but the decision was made to change it to the feathered serpent because Mayan culture would be more colourful to depict and, well, more recognisable to a Western audience. I'm not sure how I feel about this: Considering the whole point was to do a Native American science fiction story, shifting the focus to the Mayans feels like cheating, although Bates *does* say his people share some ancestry with the Mayans (I'm finding that hard to corroborate, but I'm not about to presume I know more about Bates' people and heritage than he does).

Then there's the other big problem. This is quite clearly a von Däniken-inspired story again, with all the requisite racist, colonialist baggage that goes along with him, and this time he's specifically name-checked by Wise so there can be no mistake. Wise said he and Bates decided to do a story built around *Chariots of the Gods?* because it was about science fiction and ancient people and the book was popular at the time. Which, you know, I can't fault their business sense, but that's the banality of evil, isn't it? Isn't that how hegemony reasserts itself? Little things people do because it's expected, or "that's just the way things are" or...because it sells well? Come on. I expect a *little* better of Star Trek by now. Though, to their credit, Bates and Wise, in particular Bates, do try to pull a formidable reconstruction effort on von Däniken and end up sidestepping a sizable portion, but not all, of his more problematic connotations. Of the von Däniken-esque structure,

Bates says (emphasis his)

> "I always had been outraged that Europeans said the vast cities in Central and South America could not have been built by the 'savages'. They had to have had help: the Egyptians, or the Chinese, or the Phoenicians, or even the Atlanteans came, taught the poor Indians how to build their civilization, and that's how it all happened. Horse breath! So, the story about Kukulkan became that Kukulkan visited ALL races of mankind, taught them his knowledge, and then departed. Now the story said that NOBODY on Earth invented a damned thing! They all got their knowledge from somebody else!"

and while that is an admirable way of approaching this kind of brief, *it still doesn't quite work*. For one thing, Bates and Wise only mention the Maya, the Aztecs, the Chinese and, briefly, the Egyptians: The script never mentions any Western cultures. This could be read a couple different ways, but none of them are totally unproblematic.

On the one hand this is bad because you could read it as implying that the West is the only human culture that didn't need outside help and sprung up of its own volition. There is a fun way you can spin this though, and it's a take I wouldn't put past someone like Bates: Kukulkan here stands in for the divine more generally, and there are a lot of secret histories that talk about the gods and spirits having a hand in the development of art and culture. Maybe then the West is the only culture who have *lost* their connection to the divine, which actually leads into Kukulkan's frustration at the end of the episode really nicely. This is still a *tad* bit reductive and trends a bit too close to White Goddess territory for my liking, but it's way, *way* better than *Chariots of the Gods?*.

Another thing worth mentioning about this is that in having each culture fixate on one specific aspect of the city, the episode positions itself firmly within an extremely Platonic conception of external transcendent Truth. This is the "blind-men-feeling-about-an-elephant" motif, where everyone understands a piece of the grand, discrete, complete Truth, but never the entirety of it. Being Platonic, and thus Western, this is also a model I'm not especially enamoured of and is also not necessarily the conception of metaphysics the ancient Maya had. I tend to be drawn more to the idea of "truths" rather than "Truth": Lower-case-t truths do exist, but they come into being due to the interaction of many different human and nonhuman factors. I feel assuming there's a monolithic, objective "Truth" that is only revealed to us a little at a time presumes a Greco-European and pop Christian view of things I'm trying to exorcise from at least my personal vernacular and rhetoric.

In the comments under the post on "Who Mourns for Adonais?", on which this episode is explicitly and heavily based, friend of the project Adam Riggio said that, if you can look past the horrific rape apologia (which I can't) the way to go about redeeming that episode would be to read it as Star Trek's Hail Mary grab for mythic cultural relevance. In destroying the Golden Apollonian Male ideal central to Western myth and Western mysticism, Star Trek has not only slain its gods but supplanted them, a reading endorsed by the status the franchise has in pop culture now. I think this argument, with a few tweaks, is actually far more applicable to "How Sharper Than a Serpent's Tooth": This time though, the *Enterprise* isn't killing its gods, because it recognises Kukulkan is a kindly and helpful spirit, albeit one who's a bit overbearing and overprotective. We once again get the metaphor of humanity as children so beloved by Gene Roddenberry, which will continue to be a major theme that will see us out of the 1970s. This is still a problem be because it still has that whiff of patrician authority about it, though there are other ways you could potentially interpret the humans-are-children-of-the-divine analogy.

In fact, we could even go so far as to read this episode as declaring that the *Enterprise* crew is on the way to becoming gods themselves: They speak to Kukulkan as equals, while they spoke to Apollo as enemy combatants. We're no longer petulantly declaring we have no need of gods, instead we now understand that gods and spirits have many things to teach us. However, any good teacher knows that they don't know everything and there will always be more to learn, and this is what the *Enterprise* crew now know themselves, and what they remind Kukulkan of. The ideal teacher-student relationship is a symbiotic one: Teachers should learn as much from their students as the students do from their teachers, and indeed, the gods and spirits have as much to learn from us as we do from them. This is the true shaman's trick, much as we saw in "The Time Trap". And this is what we would all do well to remember, as McCoy and Kirk helpfully point out by reciting the *King Lear* quote from which this episode takes its title:

"How sharper than a serpent's tooth it is to have a thankless child."

After all that, maybe it's fitting that we go out on a wildly ambitious and terribly exciting, if somewhat flawed, episode. "How Sharper Than a Serpent's Tooth" may not be the perfect, definitive episode of Star Trek and it may not even be as conceptually tight as something like "The Jihad", "The Magicks of Megas-Tu" or "Beyond the Farthest Star". But it doesn't have to be. This is a story all about how Star Trek is continually striving to better itself, and how much of a strength it can be when humanity does so too. It's proof the show is now firmly on the right track and is committed to always trying to be better than it used to be. D.C. Fontana and her team have left Star Trek in a much better, much stronger and much healthier place then her predecessors on the Original Series did.

The weird, ropey show that was chronically behind its time and never seemed to know what it wanted to be finally has a purpose and a legacy and, at this rate, might just turn into something that lasts the ages.

125. "Forget": The Counter-Clock Incident

Perhaps Western fiction is obsessed with time travel because modernity is fixated on glorifying the past. We are discouraged from living in the moment and told to plan for the future, a future that we are also told to be afraid of.

From the beginning, Westerners are taught, some only subconsciously, that our lives are by definition imperfect. Heaven does not exist on our material plane; it is something we must suffer for to earn in the afterlife. Faced with a present that promises only depression, hopelessness, fear and nihilistic complacency, Western storytellers see three options: Glorify the sinful present through the pornography of grief, conflict and tragedy, look forward to an imagined future where life might one day be bearable or turn back to an imagined Golden Age in the past where it was, but that we have fallen from due to humanity's depravity and corruption. A Garden of Eden that we were banished from because of our natural sin...And yet that taboo of sin is so sexy and exciting we can't help but get off on how naughty we are. Celebrate our depravity, misery and grief because, in the end, that's all we have to hold on to.

But Golden Ages never existed, and the future can only ever be the present and the decisions we make in these moments. The history of the human species is a mixture of progress and regress, and we can see evidence of this is any historical period we choose to explore. In my experience, time as we know it does not exist. It is not what we think it is. I think we only exist in the present because consciousness only exists in the present moment. The present is all we have, and we should always make the most of every moment in the unfolding steam of experience. But there are things we forget. Some things we forget when they fall away into the mists of experience, and others we forget because we are *told* to forget them by someone in authority.

Sometimes we want to rekindle a connection with those things we have forgotten. Some people, I think, conceptualize this through a genuine desire to return to the mental and emotional states they experienced in previous moments. I can understand that. If your life in this present moment is filled with stress and suffering and you remember a prior version of you feeling happy, it is in many ways natural to want to return to those feelings and that state of being. But I think we can learn from our lives in the unfolding present. Should you commit yourself to it, I think it's very easy, and indeed natural, to ensure subsequent iterations of your being are better people then previous ones. Yet still, reflection and re-evaluation are important to our developing being. We forget a great many things, and some things we forget are worth remembering.

History is only what is written down, and writing history transmutes lived experience into a master narrative. That which is not history is forgotten, ignored and consigned to the realm of hearsay. There are worlds in prehistory and the counter-factual that history will never know, but they can be visited and interacted with. Like our own past lives, these realities exist in our memory, and sometimes they leave artefacts behind to jog it. I think there may be some things that we all have an instinctive recollection of, perhaps due to the actions of a collective consciousness. For all that we don't, art and oral history exists to remind us. The creation of art is the first act of performative artifice; the dawn of the analogous age that begins where language, history and science end. The Old Art has power because it was imbued with it-The Old Art was meant to convey and transmute it.

By re-evaluating our memories we transform ourselves and our identities, because so much of what we attribute to the self is bound up in the collection of memories of experiences. The entire process of a critical retrospective is to re-evaluate memory and identity through artefacts. But Star Trek, as it exists in the 1960s and 1970s, was not part of my experiential memory, and thus only a marginal part of my identity. By all accounts I should be at the centre of any book I write, but I won't enter the narrative prominently until 1984. I've tried then to take on the role of cultural anthropologist and comparative mythologist, to a point, and ask the question: Can Star Trek help us remember the things we have forgotten about ourselves and our world?

We who were raised in modernity do not have the oral traditions and wisdom that other peoples do. As Americans (and I mean America as in the *Americas*; the Western Hemisphere), we all came to this part of the world from somewhere else. We had hoped to form new identities here, giving birth to ourselves anew, but we found once we got here we found we weren't entitled to lay claim to anything (those of whom thought they did were inexcusably wrong, unless they got here before everyone else), and unless we managed preserved the traditions of our ancestors we were left with nothing. And that's harder than to sounds, what with the countless cultures and traditions that have been exterminated around the world. And even if we did to some degree manage to, and even if we somehow evaded the worst of the imperialists' fascism, traditions and stories inevitably change, and the truth of our gods with them. Cultural diffusion is an inescapable fact of life, and cultural diffusion begets syncretism. Syncretsism need not be negative I feel because everything must adapt and change to better themselves, even the spirits, but the reality of change is constant.

Change the history, change the narrative, change reality.

So we as moderns turned to pop culture. The only thing we have that's ubiquitous enough to reach the level of shared cultural experience the old stories used to. These are the stories we are told from childhood: We see ourselves in their heroes, understand ourselves through the reading and the telling and try to live our lives in emulation of the lessons we gleaned from them. Just as people did with the old stories. But our stories of pop culture are different then the art of old, because pop culture is art by, for and about capitalists. There's the material reality of copyright. Gods and mythological heroes are not under copyright. But in a more esoteric and insidious sense, pop culture *normalizes* life under late-capitalist modernity,.

Pop culture is cultural imperialism. It travels the world, absorbing, assimilating, conquering and converting all those in its wake. The modern West gets to set the discourse for the rest of the world, and this has consequences on ideaspace that need to be considered. It's not hard to see how this could happen: If pop culture is our earliest and only window into what the world looks like, it can be hard not to read those culturally-specific themes as being universal, and then we can't imagine life any other way. And there *has* to be a better kind of life than life under late-capitalist modernity: I know there is and there was. Even Star Trek eventually boldly declares that there is-It takes it awhile and it's inelegant about it, but it does. We as moderns have just forgotten.

So the question remains. The question that has hung over this project from the outset. Can the art of modernity remind us of the best of how things once were and could be again? Can it give us hope and provide examples of a life that is at once healthier and more fulfilling than what we have now but is also attainable within our lifetimes? Can it give us a glimpse into the world of more cosmic and eternal things through its artistry? Or, because it's a product of late-capitalist modernity, is all this kind of art capable of doing is reinforcing the hegemony and status quo and keeping us mired and complacent in our suffering and tragedy porn?

Well, consider Star Trek. Here was a series that overtly, albeit entirely unintentionally, gave voice to legions of voiceless people all over the world. In this ropey B-grade science fiction show with terrible politics, they still saw a potential future for themselves at a time when it seemed like there wasn't going to be a future for anybody. It's a lesson we could stand to revisit today. This alone seals Star Trek's legacy as a force for positive material social change in the world. Even I am walking proof of this: I would never have ended up on the path I travel had I not been exposed to Star Trek at a young age. It had a profound and positive effect on me, just as it did on many other people. On the other hand...Star Trek doesn't hold up. Star Trek is also unarguably complicit in the violent factionalization of white straight cis male Nerd Culture that has spanned Actual Terrorist Organisations that have made the world provably worse. Both things are inescapably part of the story of Star Trek, neither can be safely ignored and, perhaps most damning of all, you can't have one without the other.

Star Trek may have slain its own gods and doesn't think it has need for them anymore, but it's so far been unable to prove that it's capable of filling their roles. And that's as true in 2016 as it was in 2013, 2009, 2005, 1994, 1987, 1974, 1969, 1966 or 1964. And, so long as the world as created by late capitalist modernity and its master narratives continue to exist, it will always be true. Star Trek, and all Soda Pop Art, does not deserve to be counted amongst the ranks of the great myths and oral narratives of past cycles. And as moderns, we are so much the worse for it, trapped in a spirituality-starved gilded cage of our own design. Perhaps somewhere, in some other reality, Star Trek really has been sublimated to that level, but such a thing is impossible in our world so long as certain accepted truths remain standing.

Perhaps it *could* be, but, as has been the case time and time again, the power, and the choice, lies with us.

Made in the USA
Lexington, KY
15 December 2016